City of Fallen Souls

- Underverse -

Book 3

2nd Edition

Jez Cajiao

Published through MAH Publishings Ltd

Audio production was handled by Chris and Jessica of Actors Everywhere in collaboration with Podium Publishing

Editing by Jack Cameron of CringeWorthyStudios

Editing by Jenny Thomas

Editing by M Evan MacGregor

Cover by Marko Drazic

Typography by May Dawney Designs

Formatting by Emily Godhand

This is a work of fiction, all characters, places, spells, realities and secrets of the Upper and Lower Realms are entirely my own work, and if they offend you, it's not intentional. Probably.

TABLE OF CONTENTS

UNDERVERSE SYNOPSIS

BOOK ONE:

Jax is working a dead end job, in a semi-stable relationship, and searching for his missing brother, while plagued by dreams of the UnderVerse. This terrible alternate reality is where he, and his brother Tommy, are pulled against their will on occasion. When in the dream they inhabit artificial bodies and fight to protect abandoned villages and more, standing between the inhabitants of the Old Empire and the creatures of the night.

They awaken back on earth once the threat has passed, or they've been killed, with their injuries following them. While they heal at a tremendously accelerated rate, it still requires days to recover, and in that time, they hide their injuries, lest they be locked away for self-mutilation.

After one such session, Jax decides to come clean to his GF and explain everything. Badly injured and bleeding heavily, he arrives at her home, only to find her in bed with another man. He loses control, half beating the man to death, and having his skull shattered in turn by her, using the baseball bat he'd bought her for self-defense.

Jax comes to in the hospital, chained to the bed, and is interviewed by the police and warned he faces a significant jail term. While alone and contemplating this, an unknown doctor slips in and assures him it has all been taken care of, before drugging him.

When Jax wakes up this time, it's to find himself restrained, again, but on an airplane heading to meet 'the Baron Sanguis'. A lawyer assures him that should he carry out the reasonable requests of his new employer, then not only will all legal concerns be a thing of the past, but he will find his brother as well. Jax accepts, warned that refusal means death, and meets the Baron, an inhuman monster who admits to being an interplanar traveler, and a member of the original nobility of the UnderVerse, the Realm that Jax and his brother dream of.

To be free and to find his brother Jax must travel to that shattered Realm, and open a stable portal back to this Realm, as the mana here is simply too low in concentration for the portal to be held open for more than bare seconds. Alternatively, a portal from that side, to here, would be secure and enable the nobility to return with servants and forces intact, ready to reconquer their home.

Over the next several months, as Jax is trained for the 'little task', he discovers more about the past of that Realm, including that the voice of madness that occasionally speaks to him, and that he'd written off as himself being mad to some degree, is actually the voice of the Eternal Emperor Amon, a fragment of His soul being all that's left, clinging to the genetic line.

Amon was murdered, by the Baron, His son, and others of the nobility, with the aid of the God of Death, Nimon. In the process, and as his price for this, the followers of the other nine greater gods were purged and their temples cast down. Leaving the God of Death, who dragged one of the moons down to impact the Realm, with a powerful enough surge of His 'aspect' (death) that He managed to banish the other Greater Gods.

Jax grows to hate the Baron, but has nothing left in his life beyond his missing brother, and so takes the opportunity, training heavily, before facing eleven other nobles' choices in the arena to 'earn' the right to go to the UnderVerse. He wins, barely, and trades the remains of his opponents and their personal items to their sponsors, in exchange for several magical artifacts, before passing through the great portal.

Once on the other side, and having made a deal with an opposing noble 'house' for access, he finds himself in a ruined tower. The Great Towers were bastions of the old Empire, powerfully magical, self-sustaining and intended as entire self-contained cities. At half a mile wide at the base, two to three miles high, and sustained by their own mana collectors they acted as garrisons and secure imperial bastions in places of danger.

The Tower that Jax finds himself in, however, was never inhabited fully. It was finished, intended as a research and security station, but had only a skeleton crew when it was assaulted by a SporeMother. The SporeMother, a multi-limbed monstrosity of legend, flooded the defenders with undead and possessed creatures, birthing DarkSpore creatures, parasitical clouds that could puppet flesh, turning the unprepared defenders into attackers, claiming the Tower. The few remaining survivors, beleaguered on all sides, ordered the Tower's controller Wisps to shut the entire structure down, sealing the Wisps themselves away, and preventing the creature from being able to feed on the mana of the Tower to grow stronger, expecting that the Tower would be assaulted and retaken shortly by the Imperial Legion.

Then, before reinforcements could take the Tower back, the Cataclysm came. Seas and mountains rose, islands vanished and the creatures of the deep and of nightmare were set loose to roam. When Jax arrives at the Tower he finds it dark and silent, populated by the ancient dead, with only occasional more recently killed adventurers scattered here and there. He also encounters Sporelings, immature SporeMothers, hidden in the portal chamber, fighting them and locking himself away in a side room.

Jax uses one of the spells he gained, resurrecting one of the Sporelings he killed to form a companion to fight alongside him. Using his new companion, Bob, and his weapon of choice, a bastardized naginata, Jax proceeds to clear the Tower partially, discovering the 'Hall of Memories' and its sleeping Wisp, Oracle. He is gravely injured, and alone, Bob having perished in the fight to enter the room, and when he awakens the Wisp takes the chance it unthinkingly offers, to use some of the stored knowledge of the Hall of Memories, in the form of spellbooks, to enable him to defeat the undead outside the room.

Unfortunately, all magic he has accessed so far has been through books such as this, impressing outside knowledge across his brain and damaging it each time. This final spellbook is one too many, and results in scarring, internal bleeding and more. Jax is dying and Oracle, the newly awakened Wisp, bonds herself to him in an attempt to save him, gaining access to his manapool and enabling herself to cast the needed healing spells to save his life.

Over time Jax recovers, and with Oracle's guidance, reawakens and names Seneschal, the Wisp that controlled the tower, reactivating the mana collectors and beginning the basic repairs the Tower requires, as well as awakening the Goddess of Fire, Jenae. This awakens the SporeMother, now ancient and decrepit, but still powerful. In the fight that follows between Jax, Oracle, the newly reformed Bob and the SporeMother and her minions, the Eternal Emperor Amon makes contact with Jax, guiding him to use an artifact recovered in the Tower earlier. This Silverbright potion (Dragon's blood) transforms his weapon from a standard construction into a basic magical, but evolving, weapon. Jax kills the SporeMother, but is gravely wounded. Over the next day, as he is healed, the companions clear the remaining sections of the Tower, and find the creature's nest underground, along with the remains of the Golem Construction Cradles or Genesis Chambers.

They also find the Wisp responsible for the golems, name him Hephaestus, and take the time to reclaim the single working Genesis Chamber. This begins the construction of the most basic of stone golems to protect and rebuild the Tower. In the process, HeartStones are uncovered, a magical way to send a memory, as a method of communication. Most are long drained of mana, but the fragments that remain make it clear that Barabarattas, lord of one of the two nearby cities, has been trading slaves to the SporeMother in exchange for Sporelings, hoping to raise a captive army of SporeMothers.

The Wisps sense an intrusion higher in the tower and Jax explores, finding a group of slavers, heavily armed, using their slaves to loot an old armory. Jax attacks when seeing a child beaten, killing the slavers, with Oracle's help, and driving off the two airships that had been docked on the balcony. One is damaged and crashes in the courtyard below, while the other escapes to land at a nearby lake to effect repairs.

The freed slaves pledge allegiance to Jax, and while they rest, he takes one of their number, Oren, the captain of the crashed ship, down to the courtyard. He discovers that they were pressed into service, and had no desire to work with the slavers. The remaining surviving crew swear as well, and inform Jax that there is a third ship. This is the warship that was enforcing the City Lord's will, and it was still incoming, having stopped to raid a village along the way. Jax and the slaves use the weapons they have, the remains of the damaged ship and subterfuge to lure the warship in to land, while Oracle disables their engines.

Jax and Bob, aided by some of the former slaves, fight and kill the soldiers aboard the warship, capturing the crew, freeing a group of slaves taken from the villages and locking the crew in those same cages. Jax formally claims the Tower as his, and through the right of blood, having found that he is an illegitimate son of the Baron Sanguis, and therefore noble in his own right, he begins the right of Imperial Succession.

Barabarratas, like all nobles remaining in the Empire, with no Imperial House to swear to, had been unable to lay claim formally to the Imperial Throne, but once the succession has begun, sees a way to claim the throne. He threatens war against Jax, unless he surrenders. Jax, being short of patience and self-control, as well as occasionally being an asshole, in turn declares war on Barabarratas and his city of Himnel, taunting him before leading his people in a wake. The end of the book comes to Thomas, Jax's brother, languishing and injured in a jail, before being sold as fodder, the lowest caste of soldier, to the Dark Legion of Nimon.

BOOK TWO:

Thomas fights his abusive jailor and draws the eye of a Paladin of Nimon, who grants him a chance to prove himself. Thomas is happy to take that chance and prove his worth in battle to escape the rank of fodder.

Jax awakens with a hangover, the wake having gone well, and proceeds to set about trying to repair the Tower. Two of the new recruits, now citizens of the Great Tower, Oren the Dwarf airship captain, and Cai, a Panthera humanoid with a skill for organization, assist him. Teams are formed for hunting and defense, with a personal squad geared around Jax. This is formed from ex slaves who are determined to never be cowed again. Lydia leads them (mace and shield, heavy armor), with Jian (dual wielding swords), Arrin (mage), Cam (Axeman), Miren (archer), Stephanos (archer) and Bob. Jax and his new team go to try and capture or recruit the escaped second airship, but upon arrival at the lake, find the ship deserted.

They are attacked as they search by small four-armed amphibious creatures known as the 'Mer'. In the course of the fight, Jax realizes they are young, ranging from a young adult, to a child, and they were attacked by goblins prior to Jax's arrival, attacking him in pre-emptive self-defense. The young ones are joined by older, more experienced warriors, who agree to a truce at first, and then request help to deal with the nearby goblin horde.

Jax agrees, and three of the Mer join them, assaulting the goblin camp. In the course of the fight, Jax saves the life of one of the Mer, the oldest of the younglings, and upon clearing the ruin, and rescuing the surviving crew of the airship from them, claims the land as part of the Empire. In the process, the goblin cave is revealed as a buried outpost, complete with basic golems, which are claimed and returned to the Tower.

The Mer village remains neutral, but several of their people join Jax, including the youngling, Bane. The leader of the Mer that join the Tower is Flux, an accomplished adventurer, and he supports Bane's desire to be Jax's bodyguard. Several of the older Mer decide to join the Tower, many of whom are skilled, but crippled. Jax heals them, magic being increasingly rare in the UnderVerse since the fall of the Empire, and his abilities and the knowledge stored at the Tower are revealed as being incredibly valuable. The rescued crew join Jax, bringing their ship and joining the resurgent Empire.

The older banished Gods are awakened, and Jax has a disagreement with one, Tamat, the Lady of Assassins. Using a draconic legacy from Amon, Jax manages to beat Her in Her weakened state, before being forced back by Jenae, who begins the process of spreading the worship of the original Gods again. The Gods are weak, but They have abilities They can grant, and information from the past that is relevant. Nimon is unaware They are back.

Jenae, after an earlier disagreement with Jax, helps him to find that his brother was recently in the city of Himnel. Oren and the others implore Jax to free their families, to bring them to the Tower from Himnel. He agrees, pausing only long enough, to have his body inked with tattoos, guided by Jenae, Ame, a Mer runesmith, and a tattooist named Renna.

While attempting to find a hidden entrance to the city, used by smugglers, Oracle, who has fallen in love with Jax, and he with her, is captured and taken deep underground by the Drow, a race of Dark Elves that are scouting the city for an unknown reason. Jax catches some of them, and in a bout of frantic insanity, imbues his body with sufficient mana that he gains a new ability 'Mana-Overdrive' speeding his movements and strength up, but it is short lived, and results in a 'crash' afterward. Jax uses this ability to kill two of the Drow, and then, driven mad by Oracle's capture, pain and fear allows his darker side to come out as he tortures the Drow for information.

Bane calms him down, hides the body from the others, and guides Jax back to himself. Jax's group, now including Barret, a former soldier and a member of Oren's ship's crew, dives underground, hunting the Drow. Over the underground trip, they meet Ashrag, an ancient Cave Spider, who remembers the Empire, and despite her monstrous appearance, was once an Imperial Citizen. Jax resurrects ancient Oaths, claiming them as his own at Amon's direction, and passes out from the mana drain. This convinces Ashrag and, after fighting a group of her brood, she swears allegiance. She agrees, on the condition that Jax free the tunnels of the Drow who view her kind, and their bodies, as a great delicacy.

Jax eventually leads his team through the various dark places, and finds Oracle, captured by the Drow leader, a Drider. The half woman-half spider, has several smugglers held captive and fights the group. Jax is triumphant, but Cam dies at the hands of the Drow. Oracle is freed and the smugglers are mainly compliant, save their leader, who ends up making a comment that Jax disagrees with pointedly, and dies.

The last few Drow fight a retreat, until they are killed by a new threat coming the other way along the tunnel. The three newcomers slaughter the Drow, then, after a tense standoff, are revealed to be Imperial Legionnaires. The Imperial Legion has been dismissed and derided since the Cataclysm, slowly dwindling in numbers and through several bad apples in leadership, have become outsiders in their own homes. They are disliked and disrespected by the locals, even as they march out to fight the creatures that nobody else can.

The Legion is falling apart, its members lost and despairing, until Jax resurrects the Oaths, and finally a chance at a future is given back to them.

The three scouts, Yen, Tang and Amaat swear to Jax, and reveal that they are even now, below the City of Himnel.

JAX

PROLOGUE

The ground shook and pebbles danced as Mattin dug frantically, clearing the last of the totem stones. He worked claws across the surface quickly, sweeping the dirt and debris free. Then he shoved the last fallen stones back, exposing the flickering rune seconds before the flickering shield would have been extinguished.

"Mattin!" a fearful voice shouted. He turned as quickly as he could, panting in fear, his job done, and scuttled back, diving into the burrow.

He landed hard, his breath whistling as he tried to calm his racing hearts. Moving closer to the middle of the tiny space, he tried to catch a glimpse of Tern through the drifting dust and darkness.

"I'm over here," she snapped, waddling closer, her short legs and missing front pincer forcing her to walk upright with the use of a cane. "I swear, Mattin, one more mistake, and we'll all be dead! This is no time to have your head in a den of beetles!"

"I know," Mattin chittered apologetically, scrubbing at his long, pointed nose and trying to calm down.

"What were you doing?" she asked him, softening her tone and reaching out to stroke his tufted fur.

"I was inspecting the secondary shield, trying to figure out why it stopped cleaning the air…"

"That's Jaken's job now, and you know it," Tern said sadly. "If you get caught meddling again, they'll pull you from the line; then what will you do for food? If you'd been watching the way you should, the soil would never have covered that glyph totem to begin with!"

"I know, Tern. Believe me, I know, but I think I've figured it out. I just need a few hours—"

"No. I'm sorry, Mattin, but I can't watch your section and mine, not since the ground awoke. Maybe at the end of the shift, you could go to Jaken and tell him what you think."

"No! He'd only tell the elders it was his idea! That grub-licker would do anything to get higher up in the city."

"If it brought the second shield up again, would that be so bad?" Tern asked Mattin sadly. He regarded her, burdened by her filthy fur and cracked carapace that had once shone so brightly, her glorious claws that had gleamed like the darkest onyx, now split and dull. "At least we'd be able to return to the city walls."

"And he'd be inside, while we had to fix the mistakes he made all over again!" Mattin snapped, his voice rising.

"Shhhh!" Tern said frantically as others turned and glared at them both before returning their gazes to the swirling dust clouds and darkness of the deep places of the realm.

"I'm sorry, Tern, but—" Mattin started to say crossly before a scream in the distance made them all freeze.

"Shhhh!" Tern repeated.

"Idiot! Shut it, before they hear us!" another of the clan snapped, fear and anger clear in his voice as the shield pulsed above them. Thankfully, their manasight made up for their species' poor vision, degraded after centuries in the dark places.

The shield wall had been composed of dozens of layers once, designed to protect its inhabitants from all that meant it harm. It had been faithfully maintained around the Prax, known to some as a war-city, by the Xon'dike since the day it was launched to soar like an eagle.

The glory of the shielded Prax, named "Marauder" in the human tongue, had given hope to the lesser creatures that had seen the mighty structure flying past. Now, centuries after the Cataclysm that had forced it into the ground and had killed ninety-nine percent of its population in the crash, the last pitiful remnants of the crew struggled to survive.

Only three of the shields remained after the crash. One hadn't lasted a full century before it failed altogether. When a second had also failed a little over a week ago, the load had proven to be too much for the last one. It became weak, holes appearing and re-sealing sporadically as the heavily damaged Prax desperately tried to hold itself together.

Mattin, Tern, and the rest of the Sect of Endurance had been sent to maintain the final outer shield, while Jaken, whose mate was the local official of the Artificer's Sect, had been given the damaged Shield Totem that they'd found in the second shield. He'd been puzzling over it for days now, eating their food and pretending he was making progress.

Mattin had suggested shortening the line somehow to cover a smaller section of the city, which would allow the rest to be consumed by the creatures of the deep, but the Artificers had been horrified by the notion.

"Our great ancestors constructed the shield wall this way for a reason!" they had said, refusing to even countenance sacrificing some of the city, despite the hundreds of unused, abandoned buildings and lost rooms that made up more than ninety percent of it.

He's been thrown out of the Artificer's Sect office, reduced two ranks in the Sect of Endurance, and warned that if he spoke his "heretical beliefs" anywhere within earshot again, his carapace would be cracked, and he would be left for the S'barrr.

He'd kept his mouth shut in fear after that. It'd been four days since that terrible day, though, four days without sleep, the sect abandoned to the outer ring, trapped outside the walls, racing from failing totem to totem, hiding from the S'barrr as they roamed endlessly.

Now, with the shield wall barely active as the S'barrr tunneled and battered at it, and the boundary's mana slowly seeping into the darkness through dozens of fractures in the crystals, he'd reached rock bottom.

"It's our only chance!" Mattin whimpered, anger and frustration tingeing his natural cowardice and forcing him to speak. "The only way we survive today is if the Secondary Shield comes back on. Already, the air grows thick enough to choke on. Without it cleaning the air, we'll all die long before the S'barrr can eat us!"

"Not if you let them know we're here first!" another clan member hissed, swiping at Mattin with his claws extended to leave three scratches across his fur in a clear, final warning.

Mattin hissed in pain, then pushed up to stand on his rear feet, blowing his chest out and raising his crest in warning. The others hastily backed away from the clearly visible acid glands he pushed into view.

"Enough!" Tern snarled. "Both of you, leave it! Mattin, you're an idiot, but you've got a point. We'll cover your section, between us all, but you've got two hours. If you can't make it work by then, you'll give all your notes to Jaken, and you'll get back on the line. Accept that, or we won't help you."

Two members of the clan started to snarl in protest before she hissed at them, her venom glands spraying the air where they crouched, a clear warning that she was tired of their shit.

"Fine!" the clan member who'd scratched Mattin snarled after a few seconds. "But he leaves his food here. If we have to do his work, we get his food!"

"Fine!" Mattin snapped back at the miserable excuse for a weasel. "And when I fix the shield, I'll tell the elders how much you 'helped'." He bared his teeth, shifting to the edge of the small burrow they were all hidden in.

He stared out, the pulsing of the shield indicating when the S'barrr brushed against it in their eternal hunt for food. Mattin sniffed then spat. The taste of the air was growing fouler by the second as too many creatures' exhalations built up inside and poisoned what had once been their greatest strength, the magically purified air of the Lost City of Marauder.

"I can do this…I can…" he whispered to himself, peering over the lip of the burrow and waiting until the nearest S'barrr moved away. Wasting no time, he dug his claws into the dirt, pulling himself forward as fast as he could. Sniffing the air and searching as he went, he drew the symbols he'd memorized over and over in his head as he waddled across the open space to the edge of the shield.

"Okay, I can do this. It's not like I'm really doing anything heretical; I was just studying the patterns of the shield wall. The elders will understand. If it works," he muttered, pulling a sheet of imbenim steel free of his pouch, which he'd secreted away for just this chance, days ago. "They won't kill me, not if I manage it…probably." he whimpered as he laid it flat next to the port he'd uncovered.

The ports were everywhere around the outer ledge of the city. He'd always assumed they were just another part of the city, like the light globes and the wall tiles. They were simply things that were just there in the background, until a few days ago. He'd seen the fractured plate that had been taken to Jaken, glowing and spitting, until it was removed from the port, fading to black and dying.

He thought he knew what it meant now, that it was a focal point for the shield. He'd examined the others he could find for the second ring and found that they were all identical. That meant— he was sure— that if he could replicate it, he could fix the shield!

He'd stolen the imbenim steel plate from the Sanctified Stores, despite the knowledge that they'd kill him if they caught him, and now he was ready…just about.

He sat there on his haunches, rocking back and forward as he tried to build up the courage, his claw extended and his acid glands ready. He tried not to imagine what the elders would do to him if he failed and they found out about it.

Minutes passed as he sat, frozen in fear, until the rumble of the ground warned him of the approach of another S'barrr. He turned slowly, hoping the creature wouldn't notice him, and began to shake.

His fear grew into bowel-loosening terror as the S'barrr stopped its endless wandering and pressed up against the shield, lighting the darkness with an aurora of blues and whites. The energy crackled, resisting the creature's attempts to pass through…for now.

The shield wouldn't hold. The horrible creatures still got in from time to time, stubbornly pressing their way through and melting their own skin off in the attempt. Entry left them vulnerable to the Sect of War, who protected the Holy Lost City, but never without Xon'dike losses. And there were no warriors here…

The S'barrr hissed in pleasure at scenting him and pushed harder, its chitinous exterior sliding back to expose the jagged teeth of its maw in its frenzy. Its rear legs skittered and gouged lines in the stone of the cavern as it worked.

"Mattin!" Tern hissed.

He blinked, shaking himself free of the instinctive reaction to look over at her, her beautiful eyes staring out over the lip of an old burrow nearby.

"What…what are you—" he started to ask, terrified of the S'barrr so close and horrified that she'd seen his loss of control, the cause of the stench filling the air around him.

"Do it!" she snarled, her head poking over the rim again to glare at him. "I gave you this chance, Mattin, and by the Holy Waters, if you don't use it, I'll never mate with you, I swear!"

"You'd mate…with me?" he whimpered.

She growled. "Not if you don't fix that shield, I won't!"

He swallowed hard, turning back to the steel plate. Blanking the skittering and hissing noises of the S'barrr out, he lightly touched one shaking claw tip to the smooth metal surface, drew in a steadying breath, and began to draw.

He etched the outline first, inscribing the lines slowly and ensuring they were all correct before letting acid drip from his claw tips to sear deeper into the plate and create the paths. It seemed to take forever, but after a measure of time he would never be able to remember later, it was done, and he took out the final component.

A gasp came from Tern as he slowly, oh so slowly, poured the crystallized mana concoction out. The glowing fluid, currently filling in the carved channels, was a rare and valuable commodity. He'd intended the concoction to be his gift to Tern's father, if he ever got up the courage to ask her to accept him as mate.

Once the mana had filled the channels, it began to harden, slowly at first, but then like cooling wax, the surface solidified, and it glowed gently, reacting to the ambient mana leakage beneath.

"I did it…" Mattin whispered in shock, staring down at the plate in his claws in awe.

"Mattin!" Tern hissed.

He turned to her, waving it frantically. "I did it!" he cried, then immediately froze as his voice echoed back from the vast emptiness all around him. In the deep places of the realm, silence was life, as noise…

A roar sounded from his left, and Mattin spun to gawk up at the S'barrr that had wrestled almost a third of its body through the shield wall. He forced his gaze away and chittered in horror upon seeing the telltale shimmers of others closing the distance, running to join in the feast of whatever had been foolish enough to make noise in their territory.

"Run!" Tern squealed, matching her advice to action as she scrabbled out of the burrow and scuttled across the ring to head for the wall, shouting to the others to retreat inside.

Mattin scanned the area with his manasight. The familiar bronze bumps revealed the mana flow of the Holy Prax of Marauder, even as the deadness of the S'barrr started to break through the final shield.

He felt the need to fix it, as his father and his greatfather had said he would. The knowledge of a turning point in his life awoke, and in feeling those around him, he knew.

For the first time in his life, he wasn't too scared, too small, too hungry, or too weak to do what was right. He stood straighter, racing across the short distance to the nearest space, then he crouched and pushed the plate into the port on the floor. Feeling the click as the hidden springs depressed underneath it, he slid it in along the runners, grit and the dust of ages making it catch for a harrowing moment before releasing.

A thin line of metal curled up where it had caught against a burr on one edge, and he gibbered in fear. Terrified that he'd just ruined everything, on he went still, pushing it into place until it clicked, and the air changed.

All around him, the atmosphere suddenly felt subtly wrong, his fur standing on end as tiny crackles and faint lights flickered across his form, jumping from hair to hair. Mattin backed away, slowly at first, then rapidly gaining speed until he was bounding along. His limbs worked with a coordination he'd never known he possessed, making the ground fly away beneath him as he raced for the wall, even as a new light flared in the darkness behind him.

The first S'barrr was almost entirely through by now, only its hooked stinger left outside as it roared and pulled, trying to break free. Three more were shoving at the shield nearby, their preternaturally sharp senses having spotted the fleeing Xon'dike inside, and their tiny brains sensing a change in the shield that protected their quarry.

More monsters slowly pushed through, and cries of alarm rose from the walls of the city. Bells rang out, summoning the Warrior Sect to fight as Mattin ran closer. Panic filled his chest, his hearts pounding in fear as the gates slammed shut, barely a dozen feet ahead of him, the others vanishing inside just in time.

He skidded to a halt, digging his claws into the metal of the outer ring deck, and he let out an unconscious moan of fear, the acrid stench of urine filling the air around him.

He ran forward the last few feet, shoving at the doors, pounding on them and pleading to be let in, but it was no use. The bolts had slammed home as he'd come to a halt. The great doors couldn't be opened now, not without hours of grueling work to haul the stone blocks free again. He knew this, but it didn't stop him from pleading, promising anything to the guards as he scrabbled on the doors. A tiny, disconnected part of his brain noted the chips and scratches left in the past by others in the same situation.

"What's that?" a voice from the ramparts cried out in shock. He turned, gibbering in fear as the S'barrr that had first attacked the shield wall tore itself free at last, roaring in triumph.

"It's coming for me," Mattin whispered, dread filling him, until he saw what they had been talking about.

It wasn't the S'barrr they'd meant; it was the light. The faint blue light that was glowing, growing steadily stronger and filling the cavern, rising from hundreds of symbols on imbenim steel plates that ringed the outer deck of the Holy Lost Prax…it was lighting up, like it used to, but with so much more power!

The luminous streams flickered, the S'barrr snorting and biting at a mote of glowing blue light that floated upwards from its feet. Then they solidified, a wall of bright blue light arcing upwards to meet in a dome above the city, high overhead.

In the light particles' race to rejoin, to complete the shield wall, they tore through everything in their path, including shredding the dozens of S'barrr that had been attempting to pass through the space the freshly activated shield now took up.

Mattin screamed along with all the others as his sensitive, darkness-adjusted eyes were almost burned out by the light, tears running free as he panted in fear at his sudden blindness.

Minutes passed, and still nothing moved, before a great voice called out above him, and he sighed in relief.

"Who activated the Second Shield Wall?" the voice asked, its strange timbre echoing as the First Warrior himself spoke.

Mattin broke down. He wanted to cling to the knowledge that he was safe again, but being this close to the First Warrior was too much for his addled, panicked brain. He passed out, the most wonderful words being spoken somewhere above him…

"My mate did!" Tern declared proudly. "My Mattin fixed the Second Shield Wall!"

"Then cheer for Mattin! Cheer for the Herald of the Second Age of the Holy Lost Prax!" the First Warrior boomed. Mattin sank into darkness as his name was chanted, the echoes reverberating from the walls and hanging in the suddenly clear and rapidly purifying air.

CHAPTER ONE

I stared down at the three legionnaires who knelt before me and shook my head in confusion.

"What the hell just happened?" I asked as the threads that ran through my soul to theirs suddenly ceased to vibrate. I could feel them, similar to the way I could feel my bond with Oracle, though this was far weaker.

"You just took the Eternal Emperor, Amon's, Oaths as your own, including his claim over the legion," Oracle whispered to me, silence filling the cavern as everyone gaped in shock.

I closed my eyes and looked inwards, forcing myself to breathe deep and slow, and I sensed him then—*Amon*— in the back of my mind.

His mind was, and would always be, fractured and filled with moments of madness. One minute, he was offering sage advice. The next, he was giggling uncontrollably or screaming in rage, but worst of all was the grief.

He regularly descended into his own personal hell of recrimination, punishing himself with every suspected death of innocents, imagining the terrible fates that could have been inflicted on the billions that had died since his time. He blamed himself for every single one, and he flayed himself with them, his broken mind shattering anew every day.

The times when he could perceive the world were rare, but thankfully, they were growing more frequent. He'd never taken over before, though, and the knowledge of how easily he'd managed to do so in order to activate the Oath freaked me the fuck out. What if he took over permanently? Or lashed out when he was in one of his moods?

Worse yet, I sensed that he was now aware that he could as well. I shivered and swallowed hard, forcing myself to dismiss that thought for the moment.

"So…you three have sworn to me now?" I asked, feeling the threads of power joining us.

"Yes, my lord," they replied as one, looking up at me from the floor.

"Well, you can fucking stop that, for a start," I said, shaking my head. "The whole speaking at the same time is freaky…and call me Jax. I don't see any reason to be 'lord' this or 'lord' that, unless there's a good reason, okay?" I gestured for them to stand. "Look, get up and relax. I've got no idea who you are, beyond your names, so how about you introduce yourselves and explain how the hell you found me?" I asked them plaintively, ignoring the urgent flashing of my notifications.

All three climbed to their feet, the bird-dude, Amaat, shaking his wings out as he stood.

"Well, as I said, L— Jax," Yen said, smiling as she took a seat again, "We are part of the Speculatores Praetoria, and form the scout wing of the surviving members of the Legion of Dravith. Your companion clearly knows who we are, but I will explain it. The Praetoria was once a unit with wide-ranging requirements.

"I believe we started as a scout formation then grew into everything from investigators to advisors to the legion. It granted those among us who rose to the Praetoria further authority, becoming councilors, monster hunters, and justicars, amongst other roles. We traveled the lands, bringing law and order, seeking out corruption and killing the creatures of the night." Yen shook her head, delving into her memories to provide the history of her order.

"Our primary purpose was to give advice to the Great Houses who ruled the land," Tang said, taking up the tale. "We were also tasked to report on the corruption that was growing in the empire. We would deal with it ourselves in situations where it was low enough and report it to the Cohortes Praetoria Prefects when it was beyond us.

"When the Cataclysm struck, most of the legion was ordered to return home to the capital. They allowed less than one in a hundred legionnaires to remain to assist the populace, but they ordered our division to stay behind, and our role grew. The higher ranks of the Great Houses were all in the capital, leaving only the minor sons and daughters to look after things in their lord's absences. They were the members of the family least viewed as being worthy of power. When they took their parents' places, it went…badly."

"It was a clusterfuck," I said, nodding.

"A…clusterfuck…yes, I like that," Yen agreed. "In essence, the realm was torn apart with the loss of the emperor and the Great Houses, the moon Ishtic fell from the sky, and the legions vanished into abruptly violent seas. Waves, miles high, washed over the land.

"Monsters, which had been thought long extinct, emerged from the dark places. Creatures that had been captured and used to train the legions broke loose. The dead walked the land, and all the nightmares of the prophecies came to pass. Less than five percent of the population survived. The world ended, and those that remained were left to pick up the pieces."

"The Legion of Dravith worked with the survivors to rebuild. We pulled in, abandoning the majority of the continent in favor of saving what areas we realistically could. For the next several hundred years, we simply tried to survive while the creatures of the night came for us.

"The legion was reviled for abandoning the people, and each year, we garnered fewer recruits while losing increasing numbers of our experienced fighters. The council played games and used every trick in the book to appropriate our budget as the nobility grew in power, while we lessened. Of late, the legion's funding has been cut even further, as the ruling house of Himnel, Lord Barabarattas, hates any who stand against him. We have been fighting the rise of the slave trade, and as such, we are paying the price now," Tang said bitterly.

"You're against the slave trade?" I asked carefully, and Yen met my eyes gravely.

"We enforce the old laws of the empire inside our enclave, but in the city proper, slavery is growing in popularity. We are few in number and strength now, but we heard the clarion call of your arrival. We saw your declaration of war and your assumption of power.

"When Barabarattas ordered us to declare our support publicly for him and deny your claim, we refused. The Legion General was immediately cut down in the street by 'unknown criminals' in response, and we pulled our families in to shelter within the enclave. We are under guard, the remnants of the great Legion of Dravith, Himnel Division, reduced to fewer than three hundred in total.

"We remain barely over a hundred soldiers, with our families, non-combative staff, and loyal supporters, all surrounded by our enemies. Now, after all this time, you come forth and claim your place as a Scion of the imperial Line? At our weakest point, you come, and we have failed you already."

"Bollocks," I scoffed. The three of them stared at me, clearly shocked, and I shrugged. "Look, how old are you, Yen? I know it's generally considered bad taste to ask, but fuck it."

"I…I'm seventy-six, this past spring," Yen admitted, struggling to keep her face smooth.

"Okay, and you two?" I asked the others.

"Forty-seven," said Tang.

"Thirty," Amaat supplied.

"Okay, well I'd love it if you had brought me a fucking army. Really, I would. The thing I need, though, and I really mean *need*…is you. I need experience, I need help, and I need a way through the politics and shit that I'm no good at. I can kick someone's arse all day. I can't sit down with lords and ladies and convince them to not do shit."

I shrugged, sweeping my arm around to indicate the wreckage throughout the room. "You see all this? The damage and the death? This is me. I'm a blunt fucking instrument. Amon had people to help him, to curb his temper, to guide him through the sneaky and the nice ways around things, because he was a hammer, when all that was needed was a fucking teaspoon. You must have studied him, Yen. Tell me I'm wrong."

"You're not," she said, leaning back and crossing her legs with a smile. "The Eternal Emperor hated details. He despised dealing with 'fiddly bits'…he just gave the orders and expected us to make things happen. It worked because the legion and the senate all knew if they let things get out of hand…*he* would deal with things personally. Such as with the island nation of Vellum."

"The archipelago of Vellum you mean?" asked one of the smugglers, listing in nearby and Yen snorted.

"No, the archipelago is all that's left. They decided piracy was a better choice than paying their taxes and tried plundering their neighbors. The emperor disagreed, and now a collection of tiny islands is the only surviving evidence of one of the most prosperous islands in the western realms. That is only one example of why people behaved when the emperor told them to. They sent his emissary back to the capital, minus his head, so he rode a greater dragon and personally sank their ships, killed their armies, and destroyed their island."

“The man really was batshit,” I said, seeing his memories for a second. The rush of wind pulled our beard back as Shustic’Amon dove down through the high, thin clouds into brilliant sunshine, the green trees of the island growing before us as we gathered the spell. Our heart hammered with an odd mix of fury, regret, and relief as we prepared to kill tens of thousands for the crimes of their leaders.

“He regretted that day,” I said musingly, still lost in memories. “He knew it would save more lives in the long run, though, and that was always key. If one death today would save a thousand tomorrow, He’d not hesitate.”

“How…how do you know this, Lord Jax? And the voice we heard, was that truly him?” Yen asked in a low whisper, eyes wide as she watched my face.

“He’s my ancestor; something about his assassination and the things they did to kill him, combined with the gifts he had from the gods, meant that his soul survived. He’s always been with me and occasionally my brother. No idea how or why, beyond that; might as well ask why water’s wet or why rum always makes shit better.”

“Rum, eh?” Tang asked, grinning, clearly seeing something he could use to make me less terrifying and more mortal.

“Aye, and I’d kill for a decent drink right now, I tell you,” I muttered, forcing a smile. “And please, seriously, call me Jax.”

“So, these are your people?” Yen asked.

I shook my head. “No, these four are smugglers the drow had captured.” I said gesturing to the four of them. “The others are my people, and the rest are—”

Yen held up a hand, and I stopped, frowning at her questioningly.

“These four are known smugglers, criminals…and they’ve sworn no Oath to you?” she asked.

I grimaced, glancing over at them. “No, no Oaths, and I’ve no control over them.”

“Then I think we need to consider them as criminals that are overhearing important state secrets, Jax. We need to silence them by steel or by Oath.”

“They can’t swear an Oath, as they’ve already sworn one to the Smugglers Guild,” I replied.

“Really?” she said, snorting at the now-scowling grey-haired man before turning back to me. “You can take as many Oaths as you like, provided you don’t swear to any with terms at odds with each other. Considering he’s already lied to you, he’s clearly untrustworthy.”

“Hey, now, I’m not untrustworthy!” the grey-haired older man said, stepping forward.

“Really? You’re the world’s first honest smuggler, are you? No wonder you’re naked!” Tang snorted in disgust. “I recommend we kill them, my lord. They’re admitted smugglers, which is a crime punishable by either thirty years hard labor, or death.”

“We’ll swear!” said one of the others in the group, stepping forward and ignoring their leader.

“I’ll swear an Oath, too!” shouted another, when the lead man sighed and raised his hands, gesturing for everyone to calm down.

“Look, it’s not that easy, okay? The Smugglers’ Guild makes us swear a very specific Oath, and I can’t repeat it, but it includes a section that we cannot hold back information that could be vital to the guild.

"I can't swear an Oath to you because I'd then have to tell the guild about it, and all the details of that Oath, if they asked me. This," he said, gesturing all around the cavern, including the bodies and then finishing with me, "…and you, are exactly the kind of information I *have* to give the guild.

"I can't swear to you, because I've already sworn that the guild will be my only true master, and that the guild's needs come first. I have to report all of this to the guild leadership; who you are, what's been going on down here, all of it, okay? I'm not playing games. I can't take a second Oath, because the Smugglers Oath is so specific.

"You saved my granddaughter. Believe me, if I can, I'll help you, Oath or no Oath. But all I can do right now is warn you, and these idiots are willing to take the Oath because they think they can get away with it. I've seen what happens when Oaths fight for dominance; they haven't."

"Is that possible?" I asked Yen, and she nodded slowly.

"It is, but it's unusual. Are there levels of Oath?" she asked him, and he nodded.

"Yeah; you take the basic Oaths when you accept the contracts, then more as you move up the ranks. Theirs will force them to return to the guild and tell all they've seen…mine will kill me the moment I try to speak secrets only known to the caravanners."

"So what do we do?" I asked. "I'd rather not kill them, not after I've just saved them."

"We can try to get into the enclave? The prefect was rousing the legion when we left, preparing to fight our way out if need be. Barabarattas's forces are well dug-in, though, and under the guise of 'protecting' us while he investigates the Legion General's death. He has declared we are to remain inside, and his forces are ready to enforce that, but they're only regular soldiers, and we are the legion," Tang said proudly.

"We're also on the wrong side of the enclave's walls," retorted Yen, shaking her head. "We would have to fight our way through to the enclave, and who knows who we might lose. Add to that, Barabarattas would know and would use it as an excuse to storm the enclave. He'd be justified by the declaration of war, as well. He'd kill us all."

"Then we go out fighting!" snapped Amaat, shaking his wings out fully and glaring at Yen. "Better to die an eagle than a sparrow…we are willing to die for the empire!" he stated, his fervent gaze focused on me.

"Or, better idea, we make the *other* guys die for the empire, and we all fucking live," I replied. "Better us than them, right?"

"Well, yes…but…" Amaat said, his wings drooping slightly.

"But you liked the sound of it and just went for it?" I asked.

He nodded, looking crestfallen.

"Okay…so maybe you don't get to talk for a bit." I dropped into the chair I'd abandoned when accepting their Oath, putting my head in my hands and taking a deep breath. "God, I miss it being just us and Bob," I muttered to Oracle.

She snickered, turning to the legionnaires. "We have a minion called Bob; he's a really big skeleton that Jax rebuilds and makes better after each fight."

Yen frowned at her. “Very well. But I must ask, Wisp, why have you assumed this form?” Yen gestured to Oracle, and my companion drew in a deep breath before using a chunk of my mana to grow to full size.

“Because Jax loves it! I mean, I looked in his mind, okay? He let me see what he liked, and I saw all these pictures…and memories, and he just loooooved these girls. They had really big boobs like these.” She cupped her chest, making them bounce for the entire room. “And really long legs, and he loves my ass, too! I—”

“That’s enough!” I gabbled quickly, cutting her off and getting to my feet quickly before Oracle could show off any more of her body or her excitement and pride in the details she’d collected.

She’d literally gone through my mind like a hoover, stripping out every sexual thought I’d ever had, and patterned herself on a mix of them, because she’d heard that sex was “fun,” and it’d looked interesting when she was an asexual wisp dedicated to the tower’s library.

The combination of adopting these forms and her already happy-go-lucky nature, added to the bond she’d created between us, had given her a personality that was one minute sunny and sensible and the next, nympho on crack.

She bounced across the spectrum constantly. Her natural cheerfulness was supercharged by my own borderline manic-depressive tendencies and my stereotypical male libido to create a supercharged sex kitten who had absolutely no sense of modesty.

I loved her for it; well, I loved her for who she was. When she’d been kidnapped, I’d well and truly lost my mind entirely. I’d admitted to myself that I loved her, and, yeah…pretty soon, she was going to be getting to experience things as she’d always wanted. I admitted that to myself as well, as she was literally my kryptonite, sexually. I couldn’t resist her much longer.

The one thing that held me back— besides the obvious fact that we were effectively behind enemy lines, and I didn’t have so much as a bedroom door between me and the rest of the group— was that, once I crossed that line, it would change everything.

I’d been alone for years, ever since Tommy was taken from me. I’d met girls; hell, I’d dated a few dozen over the years, but the only one that I’d trusted, the one that I’d actually been falling in love with, and I’d been planning on settling down with?

I’d gone to her in my hour of need…and found her in bed with her “friend,” Martin.

Oracle wouldn’t do that—I *knew* she wouldn’t—but I was damaged goods, and I just couldn’t bring myself to take that final step. We’d talked about most of it, and we’d admitted our feelings, more or less. Now it was just a case of me getting over my internal hang-ups and well…going for it.

Which I definitely freaking wanted to do.

She was wearing a sports outfit of sprayed-on yoga pants and a tiny, bright red sports top that could never contain her…assets…in reality; it would explode under the pressure if the material was real. Her long hair hung around her waist in ringlets and curls, her smile was bright enough to blind, and her ruby-red lips were perfect.

All in all, she’d make the most beautiful of the reality stars run weeping over how unattractive they were, and she only had eyes for me.

Aaaaand right now, she was bouncing up and down in the middle of the room, with everyone staring at her.

"Okay…look, there are a few rules in my lands. The biggest and most important is simple: 'Don't be a dick.' That's all there is to it, and I think it's an easy one to follow, okay? As an example, asking me about the images of naked women in my mind that Oracle used to pattern herself after would be firmly in the 'dickish move' category."

There was silence around the cavern as the new people tried to figure this out, broken only by the snickering of those who had been with me a while.

"I can feel that laugh, Bane!" I snapped, pointing a finger at him, and he held up his hands.

"Sorry, Jax, but—"

"Ah! No!" I said, cutting him off. "Look, we need a plan here, and that would be really convenient to move onto, as I don't want to talk about the naked ladies!"

"I don't mind the naked ladies," muttered Tang.

"Don't worry, I'll tell you all about what we've figured out once he's asleep!" Barrett promised, grinning at Tang.

"Really, dude?" I said, shooting him a glare. "You had to go there? I *can* fucking hear you; you know."

Barrett shrugged and grinned back at me unrepentantly as Yen spoke up.

"Very…well, Lord Jax, perhaps we should concentrate on the next steps. Before we speak of any further plans, we must come up with a solution for the issue with the smugglers."

"Yeah, okay," I said, still glaring at Barrett before turning to face them. "Right, then. I'd rather not kill you fuckers, especially right after I've saved your lives, but we need to sort this out. What kind of an Oath could you give me?" I asked, addressing the smugglers.

"I couldn't give an Oath, my lord," their leader said, stepping forward. "I can give advice, and I can offer to help you, but I will need to report everything that happened here to one of the Smugglers Guildmasters. It's not a choice…I…"

"Is there a Guildmaster named Mal?" I asked cautiously, and he blinked in surprise.

"Yes…? He's one of the three; he's taken over the arena, though."

"Okay, could you report to him, and only him? Tell him what happened and that I'm claiming all of this as my spoils of the battle. If he wants to make a deal, he needs to come talk to me. Tell him I know Oren and that we've got an offer for him."

"I can, but I'm not leaving my people—"

"Yes, you are," I said, cutting him off. "Your people stay with me until you return, and if you return with a fucking army from Himnel behind you, they'll be the first to face them." I met his astonished eyes coldly. "Let me make this clear: you're a career criminal, and you've refused to give me the only thing that would enable me to trust you, an Oath. Maybe you can't; maybe you're a lying sack of shit. I don't know. What I do know is this: knowledge of me is valuable at this stage, and I. Don't. Fucking. Trust. You. Your people stay with me until you return. Oh, and for fuck's sake, find some pants at least, dude. I don't need to see that waving around."

"I won't leave her!" he snarled, grabbing his granddaughter's arm.

"You'll be staying here, then," I replied. "That can be as a prisoner while we come up with another plan or as cold meat for whatever monster moves into this place when I leave. Up to you."

"Grandfather, stop being an idiot! You have to go. You know this is a good deal. What do you always tell me?" his granddaughter said, poking him in the chest with one finger.

"'Look at the deal you have, not the one you want,'" he muttered, and she nodded emphatically.

"Then look at what you're being offered. We were being killed by the drow, one-by-one, but now we're all alive! We're being offered our freedom, and all they're asking is that we keep quiet on who they are because they're at war with the city lord! I know your Oath means you have to report it, but even there, you can help them.

"Look at the deal as a trade for him freeing us. All you have to do is go to Arena Master Mal, tell him what's happened, and pass a message on; that's it. When you come back, we can go free, right?" She directed this last bit at me.

I nodded, looking over to Lydia. "Any idea what happened to their clothes?" I asked. As much as the view of the girl was great and all, I didn't need the distraction, and the rest of the group were nowhere near so nice to look at.

"Find them some clothes," Lydia said to Jian and Miren, keeping Stephanos on lookout close to the entrance to the tunnels.

"Oh…I…uh," the girl said, reaching out hesitantly. I turned to look at her, and she shrugged, shame clear on her face. "About before, when I slapped you. I understand now. I was just in a lot of pain, and you…well, you sounded like you didn't actually care to help…" She faltered, staring at her hands.

"Shit," I said succinctly. "Seriously, it wasn't that. I was trying to do the best for everyone at the time. I needed to make sure we all survived; that's all. Still, I am sorry. I'd have just given it to you, happily, if the situation had been different." I shrugged and turned to her grandfather after she nodded in acceptance. "So, is this sorted now?" I asked, gesturing to the smuggler, who glared at me. "Look, I don't need you to like me, I just need you to get this done, then you and your group can fuck off into the sunset, for all I care."

"You've a real gift for people, haven't you?" Tang murmured, his lips curling into a sardonic smile.

"We saved that dick, losing one of our own in the process, and haven't gotten so much as a thank you from them yet, just complaints and demands." I regarded him seriously. "How would you feel towards them?"

"Fair enough," Tang admitted as he made his way to join Yen.

"If everyone's stuck inside your enclave under house arrest…how did you three get to me?" I asked them, leading them off to the other side of the cave where the smugglers couldn't hear, and they both grinned.

"We're scouts, L—"

"Please, just Jax, okay?"

"Okay…Jax…but we're scouts; we're sent out to hunt monsters and find enemy armies. A bunch of townie guards have no chance."

"Fair enough. Think you could get back in?"

"Probably, but why?"

"To send word to the legion to prepare and tell them who I am. I came here to free people, to recruit for the tower, and to get supplies. I'm thinking the legion can help with that tenfold."

"I can fly in and out of the enclave," Amaat said proudly, displaying his golden wings. "All I need to do is escape the tunnels."

"Don't they have ships on guard?" I asked and got another doglike shake of his head in response.

"They had a single airship that floated above; it was easy to avoid when we left, and I doubt it's gotten smarter."

"Good. Will the legion follow me?" I asked Yen, who seemed to be their leader.

"Yes…" she said hesitantly, drawing the word out.

"But?" I prompted, and she grimaced.

"The legion will follow you, but they'll need to meet you. You'll need to convince the legion prefect."

"So I can't just send them orders to get ready, despite all this?" I asked, exasperated.

"Amaat will tell the prefect that we have formally recognized you as a Scion of the Empire and that you hold legal authority over Dravith. This will help, but you need to do whatever you did before and reach out with the Oath. We felt it become active, like the old stories said it used to be, but only those of us nearby could feel it. There are hundreds of legionnaires in the enclave, and they will swear to you when you swear to them."

"Yeah, minor issue there; each single person I pull in costs me a fuckton of mana. I passed out and had to be put into a coma when I connected to the eleven imperial citizens that were within range, including you three. Hundreds of people will probably kill me…unless I can figure out a way to get a bunch of mana potions ready."

"The tower, Jax!" Oracle said excitedly. "You can use its mana to do it!"

"Can I? I thought I'd have to be at the tower." I sighed, feeling relief wash over me, before…

"Oh, yeah…sorry, my bad." She casually shrugged one shoulder.

"Seriously?" I shook my head. "Oracle, you can't tease a solution like that to me and then just toss it off! With a 'my bad'…fuck's sake." I groaned, rubbing my hands through my hair.

"You do," she said, looking at me askance.

"Yeah, well…okay, look, that's not important!" I snapped, trying to ignore the dozens of times I'd done exactly that, plenty springing to mind in seconds. "Gods…just give me a minute, okay?" I growled, walking over to lean against the back wall for a few minutes, far back from the torchlight, and closed my eyes.

I thought back over the last few days, how everything had been a mad scramble. Hell, the last six or seven months had been nonstop. Ever since that prick Daphne had kidnapped me, I'd hardly had a damn day off or five minutes to myself to just…stop and think.

I stayed there for a few minutes, recalling a technique used by one of the chefs I'd worked with ages ago when a day was going to shit.

No matter what was happening, when it was all balls to the wall, he'd shout "Stop!" Just stop, that was all. Then he'd flick a switch on a little ancient egg timer he had just for that purpose.

The entire kitchen, even me as the pot washer, had to stop for the full sixty seconds. You could look about, but your hands stayed where they were.

It was weird, now that I thought about it, and it'd sound even weirder to try to explain it to someone I knew, but that sixty seconds was all you needed. You stood and planned your next move, you figured out where you were and what you could do better, then *ding*, the timer would go off, and the kitchen would explode into movement as we all ran like we were batshit crazy, getting things sorted.

It sounded mental, but inside of five minutes, the kitchen would be running smoothly again. It shifted from chaos to organized chaos, and that was a massive step up.

I used that same trick now. I thought about my goals: where I needed to go, what I knew, and what I didn't, where my weakest points were. I went over it all, and then I took a deep breath and turned around. Walking back to the group, I felt in control, more or less.

I had a plan, anyway, and fortunately for everyone, it wasn't "stab them and run away with Oracle."

CHAPTER TWO

“Okay, people, gather ‘round,” I said, a cold calm filling my voice as I scanned the cavern, my gaze lingering on Cam’s body where it lay at the back of the cave.

When everyone had moved closer, including the prisoners, who’d finally been clothed, I smiled and laid out the plan.

“Right, there’s been a change of plans.” I made eye contact with each of them individually, feeling better now that my thoughts were somewhat organized. “The arena Mal runs, where is it in relation to the exit from these tunnels? And how far is the enclave from there?”

The smuggler spoke up. “The arena is about a mile south across the city from the exit, and the enclave is about two miles from there, hard up against the western wall. Why?”

“Anything in your Oath about not being allowed to take us directly to Mal yourself? Without telling anyone else about what happened?”

“Well, no…”

“Good. Amaat, you’ll travel with us until we reach the arena, then you’ll break off and head straight to the legion enclave. You tell the prefect where we are and what’s happened so far, and you get him ready. Then you sneak out and come back to us at the arena. Anything happens to us, you bring the entire fucking legion in and cut us free, understood?”

“Yes, my lord,” Amaat said. The characteristic harshness of his voice made it hard to be sure, but I thought I detected approval from him.

“Good. Yen, any of you have any bags of holding?” I asked.

“We’ve each got a small bag; makes it a lot easier to carry supplies. Can I ask why?”

“I need to loot as much of this as possible,” I said, gesturing around the room.

“Ah…the smugglers would have been using bags to transport what they could. The bigger things are items that couldn’t fit in bags.”

“Yeah, that’s what I figured, so we need to strip the cavern of everything we can. The least-valuable shit gets left behind, and the rest, we take. How much farther is it to the city? I’ve been assuming you killed the drow and anything else that was along the path from here?” I asked Yen.

“It’s about half an hour’s traveling from here to the exit, and we killed everything that moved, just in case. We’re directly under the city right now.”

“I like it,” I said, nodding approval. “And the size of the tunnels?”

“Fairly large, certainly none smaller than this one.” She gestured to the tunnels behind her, which led back to the city.

“Fan-friggin-tastic,” I said, grinning. “Bane! Looks like we’re going back to the stables. We’re bringing the horse here, along with anything else that looks useful.”

“Can we bring the cat?” Barrett asked.

I chuckled, remembering how well he and the giant tiger had gotten on. "Yeah, fuck it. Barrett, you're with us; Yen, one of your group as well, please. The rest of you, stay here and strip the cavern. I want items piled and sorted by size, value, and usefulness."

"What's the difference between useful and valuable?" asked one of the smugglers.

"'Useful' is stuff that can be sold or used, while 'valuable' might be like those strips of wood there." I pointed to a load of lustrously glowing planks that had been stacked against one wall. "They're clearly magical, but if we can't lift them or sell them, they get left. Valuable to only a few people means low-priority, as opposed to things that are useful to us or can be easily sold; you understand?"

He nodded, and Lydia raised an eyebrow to me in question. I gestured her over and spoke to the group clearly.

"This is Lydia. She's my squad leader and is in charge when Barrett and I are gone. Do as she says, or she'll fuck you up. She doesn't need me to threaten to punish you; she can do it all on her own. This is your only warning," I said, making my point by looking directly at the leader of the smugglers.

"Thanks," he said sourly, scowling at me.

"Anytime," I replied, smiling coldly in return. "Okay, all of you, I want this entire cavern searched. Strip it and pile it, and we'll sort it all out when I get back, but plan for whatever we can carry or strap to the horse, okay?"

I got a series of nods, and I took a final deep breath. I was determined to be the bigger man, and I was aware that, in all of this, I wasn't the only one who'd been stressed. "Look, I'm sorry I couldn't just give you the potion for your granddaughter, okay?" I paused and looked at the caravan leader. "What's your name?"

"Gar," he muttered, taking a breath and straightening his shoulders. "My name is Gar…my lord," he repeated, clearly making his own effort to not be an ass.

"I'm pleased to meet you, Gar. I'm Lord Jax. Who's with you?"

"My granddaughter, Ellen. Durrm is the big lad at the back, and Frank is the skinny one," he said grudgingly.

I nodded to each of them. "Good to meet you all, and I'm glad you survived. We've all been a bit stressed so far, so let's try to start from scratch, okay?"

I got a round of nods and affirmative sounds from them. Satisfied, I began heading toward the tunnels with Bane, Barrett, and Yen.

We set off at a quick jog, following behind Bane, who ghosted ahead. His worldsense was the best safeguard at keeping us out of trouble.

It took maybe twenty minutes, if that, to reach the branching path down to the lower level, and a few minutes more to get to the larger cavern the Drow had been using as both a stable and a slave pit for the kobolds.

When we arrived, we found it had been stripped bare, with dozens of kobold footprints indicating who'd done it. Even the corpse of the big raptor-looking motherfucker had been stripped down to bones. They'd clearly gutted it and taken all the meat they could carry.

"Should have thought of that myself," I muttered, considering the corpse. "Could have sold the bits."

"What was it?" Yen asked, and Barrett filled her in on the fight that had taken place, while I moved to the motionless Fenris Heavy Automaton.

"Okay, how does this work?" I muttered to myself, looking the construct over and scouring my memories for the commands. I knew it'd had a fuck-ton of commands available, but…

"Fuck it," I muttered. I didn't have time to dick about, not with Tommy possibly close by. "Wake up." I knocked on its nose with one hand, and predictably, nothing happened. "Okay, start?" I said, shaking my head. "Activate…awaken…s—"

The Fenris shifted to look at me when I said "awaken." I froze, the memory of fighting the damn thing still fresh in my mind. "Okay, so 'awaken' works. How about 'follow'?" I tried, and it shifted its weight. "Great, okay."

"I take it you don't know what to do with that?" Yen asked, and I grimaced.

"Nope, not a fucking clue," I responded, and she nodded, grinning.

"They tend to have simple commands that are common to all these creations, things like 'follow,' 'come', 'stop,' or things like to open its storage, or empty it, to…"

"Storage?" I asked, perking up.

"It's gnomish built, right?" she asked, and I nodded. "Then there should be a manual, but…"

"Nope, manual didn't work," I said, unwilling to discuss the details of my fucked-up brain yet again.

"Okay, well, they usually have limited internal storage, like a bag of holding, but bigger. This is a warhorse, so I'd imagine it'd be designed to carry a full field kit, tents, gear, weapons, armor, and so on. I haven't seen this model before, but the civilian models are generally designed for speed, and they have some storage, so why wouldn't this one?"

"Any idea of the commands?" I asked hopefully.

"The people I've seen with these don't share the details with the likes of the legion," Yen admitted with a little laugh. "The noble houses hate us, and nobody lower than a noble is going to have something like this…"

"Great. Just one more thing to have to hide, then," I muttered, shrugging. I grinned as Oracle slowly buzzed around the Fenris. She'd been quiet on our run here, just staying close, but she finally seemed interested in something besides staying as close as possible to me.

"What's his name?" she asked, landing on its nose and staring into a glowing red eye.

"Name? No clue. You can name him if you want?" I told her. "He's a 'Fenris' model apparently, but…"

"So, he does have a name!" she slowly stroked the automaton's nose. "Hi, Fenris! We're gonna be such good friends!" she cooed, trying to give it a hug.

"I'm not sure it can hear you, Oracle, but…" I shrugged again and looked into the horse's glowing eyes and spoke slowly and clearly to it. "Your designation is now 'Fenris,' and you are to take orders from Oracle"—I gestured to her—"as well as myself. Nod if you understand." Fenris nodded once, its head moving smoothly up and down with a faint whirr of servos.

I grinned at Oracle. "Now you can try to figure out the commands!"

"Wait. Did I just get a pet horse or a job?" she asked, confused.

"Yes!" I agreed with a smile, walking off in the direction which Barrett had gone. The tiger was lying at the back of the cave again, out of sight of the main area, and was contentedly sleeping off a huge meal…of one of the two giant lizard things I'd been planning on using to transport the bulky stuff from the main cavern.

"Well, shit," I muttered, hands on my hips as I looked down at the tiger. It slowly opened one eye and locked onto me, immediately dismissing me as unimportant, like every goddamn cat I'd ever known.

Barrett stepped closer to it, and it let out a warning growl, rolling to its feet as Oracle shot between us to reach it, screaming "Kitty!" It swiped a huge paw at her, and she dodged it easily, laughing and giving off a bright light.

Instantly, the cat was up, batting at her as we backed away. It was an odd experience, watching a tiger the size of a shire horse acting like a kitten with a laser pointer. Oracle giggled, spinning and dancing through the air, while it purred and chased her, occasionally hunkering down, butt stuck in the air and wiggling as it planned an attack.

We let the pair of them play for a few minutes before I put a stop to it. I felt bad, but we needed to move on.

"Oracle, let Barrett try to talk to…Kitty…please," I said, trying not to smile as he glared at me.

"Seriously?" he asked me, frowning. "Kitty?" I just grinned at him. He sighed and moved over to crouch closer to the tiger, speaking in a low, calm voice. "Hi, you remember me. I…"

We left him to it, easing away to remove any additional distractions. He'd told us on the way back that he had a vague idea of how to form an animal bond, and he wanted to try it out. He said he'd done the first bits already when the tiger was injured and they were waiting for me to wake up.

I thought he was fucking mental, as it was a giant cat. Everyone knew cats were evil sociopaths in furry coats, but hey. It was his life, no matter how short it might be.

I returned to Fenris and looked it over briefly, then let Oracle take over to do her thing. She immediately started talking to it as Yen and I chatted, getting a bit more familiar with each other's backgrounds. She'd grown up in the legion. Her father had been a legionnaire and had raised her to work towards the Praetoria, the elite force of the legion. She'd never known anything but legion life, as had most of her friends. I asked her a few more questions as we waited and found that life in Himnel was pretty much split into three groups: the nobility, the legion, and the citizens.

Joining the legion was a twenty-year service, but it was also one almost nobody left. You were either in the legion or you weren't, with whole families that were based around it. The city treated them as second-class citizens, for some reason. The legion suspected the attitude was being forced along by the nobles, but there was nothing they could do about it, so they turned their backs on it.

The legion enclave was a town inside a city, as self-sufficient as it was possible to be, with everything from greenhouses to blacksmiths, fletchers to leatherworkers. They were experts in providing for themselves but incapable of creativity after such a long history of making the same things.

I'd asked about clothes, about food, and about life in general, and from the sounds of it, it was literally an army camp. The armorers were experts at producing the legion armor, and due to regulations stating that this was the armor they made, they never made anything else. Food was made in the commissary and was paid for with chits. Clothes were made from the same patterns for everyone; a formal uniform, training clothes, and off-duty clothing. Everyone had a set of the former and two of the others.

I listened without interruption as she detailed what the legion provided: stability and training, safety in numbers, and a life, and she seemed totally unaware of what the legion cost them.

Their crafters were all novices, bar a couple of journeymen, as they never made anything new. Each year, the legion shrank as fewer joined than died. The legion wasn't stable; it was fucking stagnant, and worse, it was insular. The "us and them" mentality, which was all she'd known, should have been kicked on its ass long since.

In the city as it was? It probably cost them as many recruits as the nobility shitting on them from on high did.

There was always a difference between serving and ex-personnel, and an even bigger one compared to civilians, but the legion didn't even have that in common with the army or the guard. It was all I could do to not scream in frustration.

I'd allowed myself a few minutes of fantasizing about the difference the legion would bring to my tower. Skilled crafters, dedicated warriors, and an entire military group that would understand discipline and dedication could change our very culture. I'd have people I could pass a load of the shitty leadership details to, and I would just have to say "make it so" like fucking Picard did.

I was sure it was going to be the opposite after hearing more about them. I'd take them if they'd come—hell yes, I would—but the problems people so rigidly traditional would cause?

Fuck.

Yen had realized I was pissed and had trailed off, leaving me to stew as she took up a guard stance by the door. Oracle landed on my shoulder. She reached down, and I took her diminutive hand in mine and sighed.

"What's wrong?" she whispered, and I shook my head slowly.

"The legion. The Praetoria were the best in my world. The legionnaires were respected as amazing fighters and disciplined soldiers, even thousands of years after the last of them died. The fact that here, where they still exist, they're so dismissed? It's crap. Add to that, they're so…insular. It sounds like they've turned their back on the world they were created to protect, and now they just…exist. I hoped for better, I guess," I said sadly.

"Well, they lost everything. They lost the rest of the empire; they lost their leaders and their heart with the death of the emperor. They have nothing left, now that the city has turned its back on them. Are you really surprised?"

"No. I don't blame them," I said, shaking my head. "I blame that fucking dickhead, Sanguis. He did this with his insane demands for power." I suddenly realized that I wasn't sad…I was fucking *furious*.

"These people, the people who form the legion right now? They're people who came out of the woodwork, despite all this shit. Despite knowing that, if you take up the standard, you'll be looked down on and despised, probably dying young, fighting some goddamn monster. Yet they still do it.

"These people should be fucking worshipped as heroes! Instead, they just bumble along, ignored. Well, I'll tell you something, Oracle…I'm not fucking having this shit!" That last bit came out as a shout, and I stormed over to Yen, who stared at me in shock and a little fear.

"You're better than this! Do you hear me? You are *not* a second-class citizen. You're the fucking best of them! You signed up to protect them, to stand up for those fucking idiots when the night comes calling. Even when they treat you like shit, you still do what's right, because it is. Not for rewards or for glory! You fucking stand there on the line between the day and the night, and you fucking well say 'No. Not one more person!'"

I paused, trying to find the words, trying to put the frustration and the goddamn pride I was feeling into words. "You fight for them; you and your friends dove into a fucking cave system that you knew was full of monsters and fuck knows what else to come to me, because you knew I needed you.

"You are not a failure; the *legion* is not a failure! I am the only failure here, because I haven't made a place where all of you can be safe yet. A place you can live, not just fucking exist! Well, that stops right fucking now, okay? We're going to get my people out, we're going back to the tower, and we're going to sort out this fucking goddamn monster-infested continent and make it safe for people to live in.

"We're going to make it so you can have kids and not fucking worry about what's waiting out there! WE ARE GOING TO MAKE THE NIGHT GODDAMN FEAR US!" I roared at her.

I could feel him. Amon. I could feel him there with me, almost like a physical being, his hand millimeters from resting on my shoulder, the furnace fire of his approval roaring through me. I could feel the fire of his convictions filling me.

I would do this.

I would bring back safety and respect to these people.

I would raise up the oppressed. I would heal the sick, and I would crush the evil under my bootheel. I would return the empire to its rightful place, and I would ensure that its people knew what was right from fucking wrong, even if I had to carve it into each and every one of their foreheads with my goddamn naginata personally!

I spun, feeling Amon slip back into the netherworld where he now existed, Barrett and Bane watching me. I turned my attention to Yen, unshed tears in her eyes, and I nodded to all of them, once.

"Get your gear. We're going up top. We've a goddamn city full of sinners and some heroes to save." I tried to smooth my voice out, but still it came out rough and full of emotion.

"Yes, my lord!" Yen responded fervently, a second later echoed by Bane and Barrett, and I met Barrett's gaze.

"Is your friend joining us?" I asked shortly.

"Yes, Lord Jax. Artur has accepted my bond."

"A good name," I said, and I forced a smile at him, thinking inwardly about the insanity of naming a giant snow-white tiger Artur, when names like Deathmachine or Tiddles were available.

"Oh! I wanted to call him Mr. Snuggles," complained Oracle.

I blinked. *Actually, Artur is a great name…*

"Right, let's go. Fenris…follow," I commanded awkwardly, but it seemed to work, as the horse set off smoothly powering along behind us.

The ceilings were too low for riding, so we all ran, but even on foot, it didn't take long for us to arrive back at the main cavern. The squad had made excellent time in our absence. As I emerged from the tunnel, the last of the boxes were broken into, and bolts of cloth examined. There were distinct piles of equipment in three separate areas, as I'd asked. Small, easily stored items filled one area, valuable but larger items composed another, and the bulky shit had been placed at the farthest end of the cavern.

Before I could deal with that, though, there was something important that I'd been putting off, with everything that had happened so far. I couldn't ignore it any longer, not without disrespecting him, so I nodded to the others and moved across the room to the space where Cam lay, carefully wrapped in a bundle of fabric.

I knelt next to him, drawing back the silk that covered his face, and I smiled sadly. They'd put him in one of the silken drow bedrolls, an item that must be worth a fortune. While it was the best we could have given him, it still wasn't good enough, in my eyes.

"I'm sorry, Cam," I said, reaching out to lay a hand on one cold, stiff shoulder. His skin was pale now, rather than the deep tan he'd always had, his color almost grey after bleeding out. I squeezed gently, noting the slow stiffening of rigor mortis, and I gritted my teeth against the tears that rose involuntarily to my eyes.

"I'm sorry that I wasn't faster, that I wasn't stronger. I needed you, my friend, so you came with me. You gave your life to protect me and the rest of the team. You're a hero, Cam. You lived and died a hero, and I'll make sure you're remembered. I don't know what I can do, now that you're gone, but I'll find a way to honor you the way you deserve. Sleep well, my friend."

I didn't know what else to say, so I settled for giving him one last squeeze then covering him back over before standing up.

"What do we have that's flammable?" I asked the room in general, and Miren pointed to the softly glowing enchanted wood.

We laid him on a plank, carrying him into the remains of the demolished building and piling more wood all around him.

"We'll set light to him once we're ready to leave," I said quietly, and I turned my back on him, walking over to Fenris, which stood calm and patient. I frowned at it, running possible commands through my head, when Gar interrupted me.

"Look, sentiment is all well and good, right? But that wood is worth a fortune! It's literally enchanted wood! You could make a dozen staffs from the amount you've piled on him. We're talking hundreds and hundreds in gold! We can pile some old clothes on him and burn them or some."

I moved without thinking about it, my boosted Agility coming to play as I struck with the speed of a cobra. My right fist closed around his throat as I lifted him almost effortlessly from the ground. His feet were dangling a good six inches from the dusty floor of the cavern as I glared into his greedy little piggy eyes.

"Never…ever try to tell me my people aren't worth that," I whispered, my words carrying across the suddenly silent cavern. "I'd pay that, and a thousand times more. That man died to free you, you sackless piece of shit. The least you could do is show some respect for him."

I threw him backwards, and he fell to the ground, his hands grasped protectively over his throat as he glared up at me.

I tried to calm the simmering lake of my anger, knowing I needed him in order to reach this "Mal," or that he'd at least make it easier…until he spoke up.

"Fuck you and your little band of assholes! Just you wait, I'll make sure— urk!"

I was standing over him, glaring furiously down into his eyes as he struggled to draw a breath. It must have been a lot more difficult than he was expecting, considering my naginata's tip was buried a good two inches into the stone floor of the cavern that lay under him. I'd moved without thought, skewering Gar through the sternum and out of his back, the force of my strike powering the blade cleanly through him.

I stared into his eyes as he reached up frantically, his fingers scrabbling on the razor-sharp blade and being sliced to ribbons as he tried to free himself.

The light left his eyes, and I straightened up slowly. Fury bubbled under the surface as I spoke, my voice full of a cold danger.

"If *any* of you wants to make a comment about how little the lives of my people are worth, now's the time." I pinned the remaining three smugglers with cold, dead eyes. "If you make me deal with you again later, after I've already given you chance after chance, I won't be as calm. I'll make sure the next one of you fucking *suffers!*"

Silence filled the room, and I stepped back. Channeling a touch of fire into the naginata so that it glowed white-hot to all but me, I put a boot on Gar's shoulder, holding his corpse in place while I pulled the blade free.

I turned and walked away from them to stand alone. I drew in deep breaths, concentrating on my heart rate and putting my anger back into the box.

I slowly sank to my knees, then folded my legs beneath me, drawing a deep breath in and setting it free. I repeated my breathing exercises and started at the top of my head, locating each individual muscle I could. Slowly forcing them to relax, one at a time, I moved on, continuing until I reached my toes.

When I opened my eyes again, the cavern remained silent, and I slowly rose to my feet, returning to the group.

I looked around at my squad, Barrett, Bane, and the three scouts from the legion. "We need to get as much of this gear packed away as possible, then we're moving," I said simply, turning to the three smugglers. All three had concerned looks on their faces, but strangely, none of them showed any anger toward me.

"I've given you all chance after chance. I've freed you and asked little in return. For the last time, will one of you lead us to Mal, or do you want us to give you a torch and set you free? I've got no interest in playing games with you. I'll either take an Oath from you, and you can go free, or you can come with me, or I'll leave you to bleed out here. I have no more time to waste on you."

"I'll lead you to Mal," said Ellen, the caravan master's granddaughter. Her eyes were red-rimmed, but she only looked sad, not angry.

"I'm sorry I killed him," I said into the silence that followed.

A flash of grief twisted her expression before she tamped it firmly down. "It was always going to happen. Grandfather Gar was a good man, but he…he always had a foul temper and had to push. We all warned him, but he hated nobles, and he never could just do as he was told, never mind the deal."

"Well, I'm still sorry…for your sake," I repeated. Taking my leave with a respectful nod, I made my way back to the group and approached Fenris.

"Open storage" I said. Unsurprisingly, nothing happened, so I tried again. "Awaken…open storage. Open. Ah, crap…inventory?" I asked on a whim, and I was rewarded with a new notification that flashed in my list. I sighed and pulled up the notifications, knowing I'd put it off for too long.

You have been acknowledged as a Scion of the Imperial House, confirmed by Emperor Amon before legionnaires of the Cohortes Praetoria.

This act will send ripples across the realm!

**As the only acknowledged Scion of the Imperial Line,
you have been granted full authority to act in the Emperor's stead
in the territory of: Dravith.**

Do you wish to declare your Primacy at this time?

Yes/No

Probably better not to, just yet, I decided, and I slid it to the side, moving onto the next one.

Congratulations!

You have cleared The Smugglers Path and have the prerequisite authority and abilities to claim this hidden location, adding it to your territory as an occupied base. As this location holds less than 10% of sentients that are actively hostile to your rule, it can be claimed.

Do you wish to annex this territory now?

Yes/No

Again, probably not a good idea. I might as well announce my presence in the city with a marching band. I slid it aside as well.

**You have accepted three Praetoria of the Dravith Legion
into your personal retinue….**

Fair enough; that was clearly a personal thing. Moving on…

Do you wish to access the Inventory for the Fenris Model 017 Heavy Automaton?

Yes/No

I nodded to myself, but continued on, determined to finish the prompts, now that I'd started them. I read through each of the notifications before reaching the ones I'd probably been looking forward to the most.

Congratulations!

You have raised your spell Firebolt to its first evolution.

You must now pick a path to follow:

Will you choose to spread the damage with FIREBALL, or increase it with FLAMESPEAR?

Choose carefully, as this choice cannot be undone.

FIREBALL:
The many times you have changed this spell to incorporate AOE (Area of Effect) damage has had a permanent effect on it. Now you can choose to create everyone's favorite AOE spell: FIREBALL!

Remember, while a Firebolt might have someone's name on it, a Fireball is addressed "to whom it will concern." Concussive effect is tripled within the first five feet of the impact site, dropping by 25% per two feet of distance while radiating outwards. Chance to inflict secondary fire damage is increased to 20%.

FLAMESPEAR:
You've thrown Firebolts with such force and aggression that you have a chance to imbue them with additional piercing damage. For every 5 points of mana injected past the general cost of 25 points, you will gain 1 point of damage and a 1% chance to pierce your target's armor. Pound that meat!

I read them both, and fuck, I wanted them combined into one! I loved the detonation effect that I got from overcharging my Firebolt, but to add piercing damage? Hell, if I sank another fifty points into it, I'd have a one-in-ten chance to blast through fucking armor with it! I had a vision of idiots in full plate armor getting skewered with a casually tossed Flamespear…then I considered what a Fireball would do to a charge of knights on horseback, or to an entire regiment of soldiers….

I wanted Flamespear—damn, did I not—but gaining the AOE without pouring all my mana into it? Hell yes.

You have chosen Fireball as your spell's evolution.

For a cost of 25 mana, you can throw a ball of superheated flame at your target, covering a distance up to one hundred meters. The Fireball will explode on impact, doing between 50-250 damage to anything inside the first radius of impact. The secondary radius, starting at five feet out from impact, will inflict 5-50 damage, depending on distance. Secondary status effects of Fire and Stun are possible but will lower depending on distance from impact.

This spell will increase or decrease in damage depending on mana input.

I nodded to myself, already second-guessing my choice, but it was done now. I brought up the next prompt and grinned again.

Congratulations!

You have raised your weapons skill Staffs to its first specialization.

You must now pick a path to follow:

**Will you choose the path of DEFENSE,
or concentrate on OFFENSE on the battlefield?**

Choose carefully, as this choice cannot be undone.

DEFENSE:
Your many battles have taught you that a defensive fighter lasts longer than a damage dealer. Perhaps a shield would help? Selecting this path will enable the use of a shield in your offhand, with only a 10% damage reduction penalty on attack.

Ability Learned: Taunt!
Once per fight, you can force stamina into an AOE ability, Taunt, pulling all attackers in a ten-meter radius to attack you directly for 30 seconds.

OFFENSE:
Surviving the fights that you have has taught you one thing: if you want to win…ATTACK! This path will increase damage dealt to your target by 5-25 points, depending on force, vulnerabilities, and speed used.

Ability Learned: Gore!
Once per five minutes, you can force double the stamina of a normal strike into twisting your blade inside your enemy. This creates a much larger wound and has the chance to add a Heavy Bleeding debuff.

"Hell yes," I thought to myself. Comparing the options, it was pretty clear what was being offered. I could either go tank or go DPS. DPS was the term we'd always used for a damage dealer, which is what I normally fought as, but tanking? I glanced over to the tightly wrapped body of Cam, laid atop the pile of softly glowing wood, and I knew what I had to do.

I didn't particularly want to. I'd deliberately created Bob so that he could perform the role. When I'd realized he wouldn't be any use to me while sneaking around in a city, and I'd had to leave him behind, I'd then given Lydia the tools she needed to become the tank…

But Cam had still died.

Others would, as well. More of my people would die in the future, I knew it. This ability, this Taunt, was the bread and butter of the tank skill set. It let you control the fight. While I could think of countless uses for Gore, especially considering the monsters in this realm, not to mention the assholes I seemed to find under every rock…I chose Defense. I couldn't live with myself if I didn't try to save every person that I could.

You have chosen DEFENSE as your first battle specialization, selecting the path of the mighty Tank.

Your muscles will change, enabling higher-impact handling, faster twitch reactions in your muscle fibers and powerful boosts of speed to help you get where you need to go. Shields are your friends!
You are the bulwark that lesser creatures hide behind, the wall that protects, the bastion that shelters the innocent!

*

You have learned the Ability: Taunt!

This Ability will enable you to control the battlefield, pulling attention from your allies and directing your enemy's hatred directly at you. Better armor is a must with this skill!

"Well, fuck-a-doodle-doo," I muttered, realizing what I'd just done. I was the tank…*That's fine. I'm a big boy; I can live with that choice…*The problem was, as the last notification said, I needed better armor. Shit, I even had a shield specialization, and no fucking shield!

I sighed and pulled up the next notification, grinning as I did so.

Congratulations!

Through hard work and perseverance, you have increased your Constitution by one point.

Continue to train and learn to increase this further.

*

You have been assigned a new Class!

*

Your Patron has assigned you the Class Champion of Jenae!

As a Champion of one of the Elder Gods, you will gain two additional stat points per level to assign, and you can now select an ability:

Seeker of Knowledge:
As the Champion of the Goddess of Hidden Knowledge, once per 24 hours, you can activate the ability Seek That Which is Hidden. The Goddess Jenae will provide a hint that can lead you to knowledge that has long been thought to be lost or is yet undiscovered by any mortal. Beware: just as the Gods see your reality differently, so the hint may be different than you may expect.

The Soul of Fire:
As Jenae's Champion, you have a fraction of a fraction of her power. It fills your soul, infuses your blood, and burns along your nerves. Selecting this ability will grant you a one-point increase to all stats....

Choose now, Champion of Jenae.

"Well, fuck," I groaned to myself, skimming through the prompts and comparing the changes. "So, I could accept the one-off ten-point increase, bumping all my stats by one, or I could get a really nebulous ability."

"Think carefully, my champion. I did not enforce the class change lightly. Consider your needs and choose well." Jenae's voice whispered to me in the silence of my mind, the sense of her presence passing through in a second, leaving me thoughtful.

If it had been ten points to put wherever I wanted, I'd have taken them in an instant, or one point per stat per level—of course, I'd be mad not to—but a one-off boost? Clearly, Jenae wanted me to choose now for a reason, and I couldn't see how one point in each stat would be that big of a benefit.

"Fuck it, a man can take a hint." I sighed, choosing Seeker of Knowledge.

You have gained the Ability Seeker of Knowledge.

Once per 24 hours, you can choose to search the surrounding area for hidden knowledge.

I nodded to myself, looking around the room and wondering whether I should use it in this cavern. Was that what she was hinting at? Or did she want me to have the ability to use later in the day? I decided to save it, for now. That done, I pulled up my character sheet again, checking the changes reflected.

Name: Jax				
Titles: Strategos: 5% boost to damage resistance, Fortifier: 5% boost to defensive structure integrity, Champion of Jenae: One search for hidden knowledge every 24 hours				
Class: Spellsword > Justicar > Champion of Jenae			**Renown**: Imperial Scion, Lord of Dravith	
Level: 14			**Progress**: 131,393/140,000	
Patron: Jenae, Goddess of Fire and Exploration			**Points to Distribute:** 0 **Meridian Points to Invest**: 0	
Stat	**Current points**	**Description**	**Effect**	**Progress to next level**
Agility	42	Governs dodge and movement	+320% maximum movement speed and reflexes, (+10% movement in darkness, -20% movement in daylight)	87/100
Charisma	20	Governs likely success to charm, seduce, or threaten	+100% success in interactions with other beings	31/100
Constitution	37	Governs health and health regeneration	720 health, regen 44.6 points per 600 seconds, (+10% regen due to soul bond, -20 health due to soul bond, each point invested now worth 20 health)	17/100
Dexterity	28	Governs ability with weapons and crafting success	+180% to weapon proficiency, +18% to the chances of crafting success	97/100
Endurance	25	Governs stamina and stamina regeneration	250 stamina, regen 15 points per 30 seconds	99/100
Intelligence	29	Governs base mana and number of spells able to be learned	270 mana, spell capacity: 17 (15 + 2 from items), (-20 mana due to soul bond)	81/100
Luck	20	Governs overall chance of bonuses	+10% chance of a favorable outcome	53/100
Perception	25	Governs ranged damage and chance to spot traps or hidden items	+150% ranged damage, +15% chance to spot traps or hidden items	22/100
Strength	26	Governs damage with melee weapons and carrying capacity	+16 damage with melee weapons, +160% maximum carrying capacity	41/100
Wisdom	35 (30)	Governs mana regeneration and memory	+250% mana recovery, 1.75 points per minute, 250% more likely to remember things, -50% mana regeneration until mana manipulation reaches level 10	22/100

CHAPTER THREE

I dismissed the notifications and walked back over to the rest of the group. As I came face-to-face with Fenris, I grimaced and began sorting through the prompts for the one I'd seen relating to its inventory. I selected yes, and a ten-by-ten grid appeared before me. It was empty, of course; as much as I'd have loved to find a set of magical fucking armor and a goddamn shield in there, nothing was that easy.

I concentrated, and Fenris reacted smoothly, making me sigh with relief as it trotted to the piles of gear and lowered its head. The mouth split apart to reveal the familiar dimensional rift of a bag of holding. Or, in this case, a *horse* of holding…Seconds later, each item disappeared into its storage easily. As Fenris worked, I took the time to examine the loot, discovering that the sets of drow armor, weapons, and personal effects were easily the best of the gear.

Gloom Spidersilk Tunic		**Further Description** *Yes/No*	
Details:		This spidersilk tunic is woven from the strands of the Gloom Spider, a species bred by the Drow for specialized material properties. This tunic grants a +5 to armor, is resistant to cuts and tearing, and has additional padding sewn into the shoulders and chest.	
Rarity:	**Magical:**	**Durability:**	**Charge:**
Very Rare	No	96/100	N/A

Gloom Spidersilk Pants		**Further Description** *Yes/No*	
Details:		These spidersilk pants are woven from the strands of the Gloom Spider, a species bred by the Drow for specialized material properties. These pants grant a +5 to armor, are resistant to cuts and tearing, and have additional padding sewn into the upper thighs, groin, and shins.	
Rarity:	**Magical:**	**Durability:**	**Charge:**
Very Rare	No	97/100	N/A

Gloom Scalemail		**Further Description** *Yes/No*	
Details:		This scalemail is of Drow manufacture, built to the slim specifications of an elven warrior, with exquisite craftsmanship. Each set is painstakingly customized to the wearer's figure and is attached to a Gloom spidersilk undergarment. It has a minimum armor value of thirty, with a maximum of fifty in heavy impact areas, such as the chest, forearms, and thighs.	
Rarity:	**Magical:**	**Durability:**	**Charge:**
Very Rare	No	87/100	N/A

Gloom Armor Plating		**Further Description** *Yes/No*	
Details:		This set of Gloom armor is designed to be worn in conjunction with a spidersilk tunic and pants. It consists of thickened, blackened, overlapping plates, which cover the chest, neck, shoulders, upper arms, and upper thighs, with close-combat blades attached to the outside of the elbows.	
Rarity:	**Magical:**	**Durability:**	**Charge:**
Very Rare	No	76/100	N/A

Drow Shortsword		**Further Description** *Yes/No*	
Damage:		18-28	
Details:		This shortsword is of Drow manufacture and is both lighter and stronger than a similar weapon made of regular steel.	
Rarity:	**Magical:**	**Durability:**	**Charge:**
Rare	No	82/100	N/A

Drow Scythe		**Further Description** *Yes/No*	
Damage:		13-26 + 2-11	
Details:		This scythe is of Drow manufacture and is both lighter and stronger than a similar weapon made of regular steel. The rear edge of the blade is covered in serrated scallops which are designed to tear and inflict bleeding damage.	
Rarity:	**Magical:**	**Durability:**	**Charge:**
Rare	No	91/100	N/A

Drow Bow		**Further Description** *Yes/No*	
Damage:		20-45	
Details:		This bow is of Drow design, with a recurve construction, and has a full quiver of 36 arrows. Drow bows are famed for their +5 bonuses to accuracy and power, and their durability. As well as regular hunting arrows, this quiver contains arrows designed to inflict bleeding and additional piercing damage.	
Rarity:	**Magical:**	**Durability:**	**Charge:**
Rare	No	96/100	N/A

Drow Throwing Star		**Further Description** *Yes/No*	
Damage:		5 - 25	
Details:		This throwing star is of Drow manufacture and is shaped into a six-sided star. The blades can be coated in poison for extra effects.	
Rarity:	**Magical:**	**Durability:**	**Charge:**
Very Rare	No	87/100	N/A

Ring of Destruction		**Further Description** *Yes/No*	
Details:		This ring gives an additional boost of 5% to any destructive magic cast by the wearer but inflicts a -10% modifier to healing spells used.	
Rarity:	**Magical:**	**Durability:**	**Charge:**
Rare	Yes	72/100	N/A

Ring of Defense		**Further Description** *Yes/No*	
Details:		This ring gives an additional boost of 10% to the wearer's armor as long as it has charges remaining.	
Rarity:	**Magical:**	**Durability:**	**Charge:**
Uncommon	Yes	56/100	7/25

Necklace of Vampirism		**Further Description** *Yes/No*	
Details:		This necklace grants the ability Vampiric Drain. Vampiric Drain can be channeled through a weapon and will siphon health and mana from a target as long as the weapon remains in contact with them.	
Rarity:	**Magical:**	**Durability:**	**Charge:**
Very Rare	Yes	72/100	36/100

I also checked through the gear and the general loot that the smugglers had been carrying. Most of the smugglers' gear was primarily a collection of powders that I assumed to be drugs, booze, and some metals that were likely more valuable in the city than in smaller towns, judging from the common quality of them.

There were also a handful of manastones, which we'd be keeping. Six large skins, which looked great, but were a bit weird, were revealed by my Examine spell as rare and that they were Jumna skins, whatever that meant.

There were crates of meat, which the Drow had been eating—apparently, while they were happy to feed the prisoners their own kind, the Drow had better taste—as well as three smaller crates crafted of the enchanted wood. All of it went into Fenris, except for a small, ludicrously ornately carved box that contained worms, of all things.

I shrugged and was about to toss that in as well when Bane stopped me.

"The storage in bags of holding cannot store living tissue, or so I have heard," he said quietly, and I paused.

"Okay, but are these things valuable at all? I mean…"

"Extremely," said Yen, glaring at the remaining smugglers, who all looked stunned.

"What am I missing?" I asked the room, as everyone clustered in around to look at the weird little worms.

"They're silkworms, Jax," Yen said, reaching out one hand to gently stroke one. She carefully pulled her finger back as it curled up, and a small strand of glistening thread pushed out of its end.

"Right…that's nice," I said.

She shook her head, grinning. "Silkworms cost an absolute fortune, because if you can breed them, you've got a steady supply of free silk. All it costs you are leaves, which are cheap as all hell."

"So, they're controlled, then?" I guessed.

She nodded. "The noble houses all got to be filthy rich because they control the commodities everyone else needs. The Mori family has an iron grip on all of the silkworms in the city, and as far as I knew, the continent. Wherever these came from, they're worth a fortune!"

"Sweet." Nodding my thanks to Bane for not letting me chuck them into storage, I passed them to Miren and asked her to keep them safe, figuring she was the least likely to be in a close-quarters fight.

The final pile in the room was composed of money and jewels, coming to a total of ninety-six gold, three hundred and eleven silver, and forty copper, as well as sixteen emeralds and nine amethysts.

I had been planning on sorting it all out later but decided not to risk it and passed out the drow gear to my team. All in all, we had five swords, four of which went into Fenris, unclaimed.

The drow bow, I gave to Miren, and she grinned as she sorted through the quiver that came with it and put her old bow into Fenris. There were five tunics in total, six pairs of pants, and two full sets of scalemail and Gloom plates.

I gave the team the choice of the gear, having taken a set of Gloom plate for myself already. Quickly changing out of my normal gear, as badly damaged as it was, I dressed in Gloom spidersilk pants and tunic, equipping the set of Gloom plates over that. I felt almost as though I had less protection than I'd had previously, as this gear was far less restrictive, but I knew that was all in my mind.

As I jumped up and down and stretched to get a feel for the gear, I noted that it was both lighter and stronger than the Night's Embrace set I'd been wearing previously. My stealth was lowered considerably, but it was compensated by the fact I could move much easier and faster in the drow gear. I kept my old Boots of Night's Embrace for the passive sound reduction they gave to my footsteps, not to mention the fact that the drow had shitty-looking boots that reeked.

I gave Bane the nine throwing stars, Arrin the Ring of Destruction, Lydia the Ring of Defense, and took the Necklace of Vampirism for myself. Arrin accepted a mana potion, while I took the other that we'd found. The remaining three potions of healing were handed out to Lydia, Bane, and Barrett.

I skimmed the room, now much clearer than when we arrived, and nodded to myself, when a sparkle coming from under the rubble caught my peripheral vision.

"What's that?" I asked, making my way to the shattered remains of the building. All that remained were cracked and shattered slabs of thick stone. Whatever magical means the drow had used to construct the building in the first place had seemingly given up when the drider and I had smashed down through the roof.

I couldn't initially see whatever had gotten my attention, but after shifting a few of the larger rocks, I found it. The boulder that I'd used to smash the drider into paste had also ruined the creature's whip. The weapon had basically exploded among its scraps of clothing, so we'd just left them. However, off to one side of the crushed corpse, a small orb glowed, pressed up against the remains of a statue. I reached out to pick it up, and Yen grabbed my wrist, shaking her head in warning.

"It's an altar of Illoth. There are stories about the consequences for anyone but drow that touch them…"

"So, take the hint and leave it the fuck alone?" I asked, and she grinned ruefully and nodded.

"And the orb?" I asked.

"Looks like the essence core for the drider…what?" she asked when I started in shock at her knowledge of it.

"You know what a core is?" I asked cautiously.

"Yeah, it's a trophy some monsters leave behind. There are a few shops in the city that deal in them; why?"

"Seriously? A trophy? And there are shops that stock them…oh fucking yes!" I chuckled, using a rock to roll the core back from the altar and picked it up, dropping it into my pocket with a grin.

"They're not worth much, unless you find the right buyer," she said, shrugging.

"To me, they're fucking priceless, believe me," I whispered, shifting the rocks away from Illoth's altar. "Give me a minute, okay?" I braced myself on the edge of the uncovered section, closing my eyes and summoning my mana. I reached out, the process far faster and easier with my new class, and I sent a mental call to the Goddess Jenae.

"Jenae!"

There were several seconds of silence before I felt her presence surrounding me, and I relaxed, hearing her voice in my mind.

"Eternal, it is good to hear from you."

"It's good to speak to you too, Jenae. Look, I've found an altar to Illoth, and..."

"That dark abomination?!" Jenae's mental voice was suddenly filled with loathing, and she spoke quickly. ***"Don't touch it! She traps her altars, and where you find one, there's usually a Drider close by. Have you dealt with it?"***

"Oh, yeah, don't worry; that bitch is toast! Well...more like marmalade, actually. She kinda...splattered."

"Well done! I saw that you had completed the quest, but I'd not realized that it involved a Drider. Else I would have warned you, as they can be fearsome foes...So, if it's dead, and you know not to touch the altar, why have you reached out to me? I'm sorry, I don't have the strength to cast another tracking spell yet, but soon I will. Provided it's a short range one, I hope. A day; two, at most."

"I appreciate that, and thank you, Jenae. No, I was wanting to know what you want me to do about any altars I find. You said that your altars being destroyed injured you and stripped you of some of your power?"

"Yes, very well, Jax. I'll give you a quest, if you're willing? Destroy the altars of the dark minor gods Illoth, Asmodeus, Baphomet, and Ardat. It's too soon for us to start actively destroying Nimon's altars, but if you get the chance, I'll reward you well. Be warned, though—you'll be making powerful enemies."

Congratulations!

You have received a quest: My God is Better Than Your God (2)

> For each altar or sanctified place of worship dedicated to Ardat, Asmodeus, Baphomet, or Illoth that you destroy, you will receive a Mark of Favor and a random blueprint for your crafters from the Goddess Jenae.

"Sweet!" I said, lifting the nearest, largest rock I could find. I grunted as I lifted it high over my head, then slammed it down as hard as I could.

A screech of rage filled the air, and everyone crouched reflexively, looking around.

Silence spread as the screech died away, and I straightened up, meeting the shocked gazes of those around me.

Beware!

You have attracted the attention of: Illoth, Spider Queen of the Pantheon of the Dark, Goddess of the Drow! The Lady of the Deeps knows the flavor of your soul and will send her minions to punish you for desecrating her altar!

"Anyone else get a notification there?" I asked casually, and everyone nodded. "And?" I asked.

"You've made a new friend of Illoth," Bane said flatly.

"But you're all okay, right? She's not after you?" I asked, wanting to be sure.

"No, but she did offer me a quest to kill you," he said, caressing a dagger. Instantly, the three legion scouts moved, putting themselves between me and Bane. The smugglers backed the hell up, and the rest of my squad either shrugged or started laughing.

The scouts looked confused but still stood their ground until I spoke up. I had to admit that I was pleased by the demonstration of their loyalty.

"It's all right. Bane is my bodyguard," I said, a little sourly. I still didn't like the idea of needing one. "He's just got a shitty sense of humor, that's all. You can all relax, okay?" I said, gesturing for them to move away. I checked my final new notification and dismissed it, as it was just confirmation of a new Mark of Favor. I could tell that Jenae had left my mind, going back to whatever she was doing.

"Didn't even say goodbye…" I muttered to myself as I moved the rock aside, looking down at the shattered altar.

All that remained was a pile of broken black and purple rock fragments with what looked like the remains of a tiny spider inside. I crouched down and peered closer, using my dagger to shift it, just in case, when it moved.

I jumped back upright, shoving both hands down and letting loose with my Firebolt spell in reflex.

Unfortunately, I'd forgotten two things. First, the pile of rubble was unstable, and my people were all watching me make an absolute tit of myself. Secondly, and much more importantly, I'd just upgraded my Firebolt…to Fire*ball…*

I was blown backwards by the concussion, staggering and falling on my ass as everyone else dived aside, rolling and trying to escape the flying rock shrapnel thrown off by my ill-advised pyrotechnical display.

In the silence that followed, broken only by the ringing in my ears, I let out a little "owww," and Bane whispered loudly enough that Ashrag could probably hear him in her fucking nest.

"He doesn't like spiders…"

"You're such a dick, Bane," I groaned, lifting one slightly blackened and mildly toasted hand to give him the finger.

I lay there for a few minutes as everyone else got up, brushing rock dust and debris from their clothes and checking on things, finally sighing in relief as Oracle hit me with a healing spell and washed away the aftereffects of being so close to that explosion.

I slowly rose to my feet, brushing dust away as I looked around the cavern a bit sheepishly.

"Okay, sorry, guys. It moved, and I kinda overreacted. My bad."

"I thought you said you couldn't just use that phrase like that?" Oracle huffed.

"Meh." I shot her a grin. "Let's get ready to move out."

Everyone started getting their gear sorted and staged by the exit to the cavern.

Once everyone was ready, we took the last few minutes in silent reflection and remembrance, standing over Cam's body. Each of us from the tower took a minute to talk about him. I told everyone how he'd refused to wear armor, saying only that he "didn't like it," and how taciturn he'd been with everyone at first, only to do things like make sure there was a hot drink ready for whoever took over from him on guard duty. The way he'd hammered out the dents in my chest armor, and the way he'd always given people a hand without being asked.

We talked for easily half an hour, longer than I'd expected to, but by the end, we all felt a little lighter, a little less depressed, and we all had a chance to say our goodbyes.

Yen surprised me by stepping forward at the end and calling for a salute from the legion scouts as she thanked him for his service.

"You weren't a legionnaire in the 'Rolls of Service,' but you were in your heart. You served the empire as you served Lord Jax and helped to protect him as a member of his personal guard. You will be remembered, Legionnaire-Aspirant Cam." She bowed her head and stepped back, the other two legionnaires moving with her.

The smugglers stepped up next, Ellen leading Durrm and Frank to give their thanks. They only said a few words, Frank just literally saying "thank you," and Durrm mumbling "I'm sorry yer got dead, mate," but Ellen spoke a little longer.

"Thank you, Cam. I didn't know you in life; none of us did, but I spent more than a week in that cage. My friends were killed, skinned alive, and eaten, and all I could hope for was a quick death. You came out of the darkness and stood up for me.

"You and your friends answered every prayer I ever dared to make. You saved us, and I'll never forget you for that. I'll make sure you're remembered." She had tears in her eyes as she stepped back, and I took a second to grip her shoulder in thanks before stepping up again at the front.

"Cam, you were a good soldier, a great man, and a terrible fucking cook when it was your turn to make the meals, but I'll miss you, mate. Rest now, sleep away the ages until you're reborn, and know that you did well. You were loved. Always know that." With that, I lifted both hands and channeled as Oracle and I had discussed, weaving together fire and air to send a flowing, curling stream of flames to lick across his body. The wood charred slightly before catching with an audible *wumph.*

I cut the spell, stepping back and watching as the bedroll caught, the flames crackling as a thin smoke lifted from his body. I cleared my throat roughly.

"Okay, people," I said, my voice hoarse with unshed tears. "It's time." I led the group over to our gear, and we set off, the tunnel to the surface beckoning.

CHAPTER FOUR

The passageway was empty and silent for another few minutes, going up and down, following some faultline, until we found the bodies of the drow that Yen and her team had intercepted.

"They give you any trouble?" I asked her, noting the twisted, blackened corpses.

She shook her head. "I have a spell that I like to use for creatures like the drow; Flamespear, it's called. It creates up to a dozen spears of fire that can track your target, but if they are compressed into a single spear, it tends to get…messy. I had been wondering what would happen if I used it in an enclosed area while we traveled, so…poof." She gestured towards the drow.

"Glad we didn't get into a fight accidentally, then," I said, looking closely at the bodies. They'd clearly not gotten a single attack off, and judging by the half-melted remains of their armor, they'd died almost instantaneously.

We moved on quickly. The scent of burnt meat lingered from the dead, and the thin tendrils of smoke from Cam's pyre wafted down the tunnel, encouraging us not to linger as we moved towards the surface.

The last section of the smuggler's path took forty minutes to cover in the end, mainly because it climbed so steadily. But finally, after what felt like weeks in the darkness, we came to the end of the cave system.

The end of the tunnel was sealed by a set of doors, reinforced and old. But the doors opened surprisingly easily, speaking of regular maintenance, and led us into the basement of a seemingly abandoned building.

We crept out cautiously. The creaking of the hinges had probably been enough to wake anyone, but as we paused in anticipation of a confrontation, we quickly realized there was no reaction.

No sounds filtered down, except the distant shouts and clattering of a city, somewhere far outside. I glanced at Bane, and he nodded, slipping past a surprised Yen as she was about to climb the stairs.

"There was nobody here when we entered, Jax, and I can hear nobody close. But I'm a scout; my team should lead the way," she whispered.

I frowned. "Yeah, believe me, Bane is a stealthy motherfucker, but about that…you're the legion. How come you knew about a smuggler's path out of the city, but you didn't stop it or report it?"

"In earlier times, we would have, but now? We've known about this path for years; we just didn't need to use it before. The city doesn't want anything to do with us, so we don't see any reason to help them." She shrugged dismissively.

"See, that's just fucked up. Don't get me wrong; I love the fact that you could reach me because of all this, but man…what a shitty situation," I muttered.

Yen nodded in agreement.

A few minutes later, Bane returned and spoke quietly.

"We're in the basement of what appears to be an old weaver's shop. It's been completely abandoned on the other floors, and this section of the building is hidden behind a false wall. I'd guess that's why there are no guards nearby. They trusted that the building would remain empty due to being uninteresting rather than being secured."

"No," Ellen interjected, and we turned to her as one, my eyebrow raised questioningly. "The weaver's shop was a good cover, but when we lost the first few caravans, some creatures came out of the path, some big spiders. Our people killed them and abandoned the building after the smugglers sent in to clear the tunnels went missing."

"Spiders? Big ones?" I asked, then held my hands apart, indicating the size of a pit bull. "Were there any this big? Red and black markings?"

"I think so, yeah! Guildmaster Mal has its head on the wall above his desk! It's horrible…" Ellen replied.

"Great," I said, shaking my head.

"What's up?" Yen asked, and I gestured her over to one side with her fellows so the smugglers wouldn't be able to hear.

"Do you remember any tales of giant cave spiders from before the empire fell? Specifically, a species that were peaceful and sworn to the empire? That could talk?"

"Hmmm, I don't think so. It was a long time ago, and the records are spotty, but spiders are widely known to be evil," Yen replied, rubbing her neck and frowning.

"Why do you say that? Specifically, why spiders?" I asked.

"Really? You used a Fireball on one just—"

I cut her off with a shake of my head.

"No, that was one that escaped from Illoth's altar, so it was definitely fucking evil. Yeah, spiders kinda freak me out, but I'm working on it. You don't have any known records about spiders from back around the Cataclysm, then?"

"Just that some of them attacked from within the city when the other monsters all rose up. The legion has always taught that spiders are creatures of the night, monsters like all the rest, I guess. Why?" Yen said.

"Fuck," I hissed, shaking my head. "I hoped they would either have records about it, or they'd have forgotten about that." I paused, scratching my neck and cursing the feeling of my beard growing on my lower neck. The damn thing always itched like mad. It was fine on my face, but my neck? It made me want to scrape my goddamn skin off!

"Okay, look…History 101. Back before the Cataclysm, there weren't just asshole spiders. There were also sentient ones, more or less; an entire clan of giant cave spiders had sworn to serve the empire. They walked the streets of this city, sold their silk, traded for various meats, and so on. They even helped the legion, from what I heard."

I watched the scouts, seeing disbelief on their faces. "Look, it seems weird to me, too, but I *know* it's true, okay? Amon confirmed it when we met their queen down there, deep underground. She's old, and I mean *old*. She remembers the Cataclysm." Yen exchanged glances with Amaat and Tang.

A memory from my training surfaced, and I realized that Ashrag would have to be nearly seven hundred years old. I couldn't really blame them for their disbelief, but I pressed on. "She remembers her sister being sent for the legion to beg for help, for the Oaths they all swore to uphold. The legion kicked her aside as a monster, leaving her to die in the gutter as they fled to the ships to return to the capital.

"Her sister and her escort were slaughtered, their corpses stripped for their alchemical properties. The queen helped to punish those who were responsible, but she ended up being hunted for it, when she was villainized as a monster attacking the citizens. She was betrayed by those she had faith in, then attacked when she tried to get justice. The legion and the empire failed her, and she went into hiding."

"My lord, are you sure?" Tang asked me.

"I've spoken with Amon. He confirmed that she was a citizen, and her Oath transferred to me at the same time yours did. The only difference was that she set me a quest before she agreed to become a full citizen and follower of mine.

"She asked me to kill the drow. With your help, we did just that, and now, she and her nest will be preparing to support me. Knowing that the head of one of her daughters is mounted in a smuggler's den…isn't going to be helpful, if she ever finds out about it."

"Then let's not tell her," Tang said, shivering. "A spider the size of a dog is disturbing enough, but I have heard tell of larger, and I personally saw one the size of a small horse once. Don't need to see that again!"

"Ha, well…let's just say that Ashrag is even bigger, okay?" I shook my head. "Arrin, how big would you say she was?" I asked, calling across the room and getting confused looks from the smugglers.

"Oh, I once stayed in an inn that was a bit bigger, but not by much!" he said cheerfully, and those who were fresh to joining us looked sick.

"So, yeah…not someone you want upset with you," I said quietly to them.

"Definitely," Yen agreed. "So, with regard to the city above…"

With Bane's help, she drew a rough map of the building we were in, marking the hidden wall to the basement where we were currently sheltering. She slowly sketched a general layout of the city before showing me where we hid.

The City of Himnel was shaped like a giant C angled slightly upwards, the harbor filling the mouth of the city to the east, and high walls surrounding it on the other three sides.

The city lord, Barabarattas, occupied a large keep that stood alone on a promontory to the west, on its own small hill attached to the city. The area immediately around the keep was filled with the homes of the nobility, while the area to the south of the noble quarter encompassed the slums and the legion enclave. To the north and east of the noble quarter was the Cloudring, and that included the underground arena. Past the arena sat the airship shipyards and, finally, the industrial area filled the remaining end and ran all the way down to the harbor.

The industrial sector's border ran along the harbor shore until it changed from industrial docks into commercial docks halfway. The merchant quarter ran adjacent to the commercial ports and filled the center of the map. Adjacent to the southernmost border of the slums and the enclave, the remaining bottom third of the map was broken into standard housing, with the army and guard-training facilities around the wall on the southeast, with further training areas constructed outside the city along the coast.

The smuggler's path exited into the basement of the disused weaver's shop in the northern sector of the industrial zone.

"Okay," I said, frowning. "We're here, and the arena is here..." I touched the map. "And the legion is all the way over here?" I got a firm nod from Yen and the others. Joy, the damn legion enclave was on the far side of the city from where we stood, but..."What was that?" I asked as a loud explosion sounded somewhere in the distance.

"I don't know," Yen said, looking upwards. "We need to go. The legion—"

"Lead the way to the roof," I said, gesturing. "We should be able to see something from there, right?" I asked.

Bane nodded, darting away.

"You three stay here," I instructed the smugglers. "Jian, keep an eye on them." With that, the rest of us set off running, chasing after Bane.

The basement stairs ran up along the wall, exiting onto the main floor and into a small room that held the mechanism for the hidden wall. Slid back as it was, it looked bloody obvious. But as we barreled past, I had to concede that it was well-made, composed of a series of gears and chains that looked well-maintained.

The next room appeared to be a stockroom, with a loading bay attached for wagons. We ran past the large doors that led out that way and found a small stairway at the back that took us up to the next floor. Bane guided us up through floor after floor, passing through disused corridors until we came across a set of iron ladders attached to the wall.

"This is the only way I can feel to get up there," Bane said. I gestured for him to lead the way.

The rungs were rust-covered, flaking, and shaking ominously as we climbed. But still Barrett, Bane, Yen, Lydia, Tang, Amaat, and I went up, exiting into the open air of the city of Himnel.

A city with fire and noise, smoke and clanking metal contraptions, shouts and screams and raucous laughter, all filling the air. I ran to the edge of the nearest wall, looking out, enthralled with the view.

Behind me towered the city wall, easily twenty meters higher than the building I stood on, which had to be at least another thirty meters from the ground to the roof where I stood gaping. Buildings all around me belched smoke and unidentified chemical fog into the sky. Hammers hit metal, and waves of heat lifted from what looked like a foundry next door, and the air tasted of steel.

The wind sent the rising smoke from hundreds of chimneys spiraling around to disappear into the night sky, and sparkling, flaring motes of ash rose along with them.

Before me sprawled a city in the full grip of an industrial revolution, the smoke and fire of heavy industry mixed with flaring multicolored light from mana engines. I turned slowly, working from left to right, inspecting the Industrial Zone first, then the shipyards, then the Cloudring district. Mansions in the distance climbed up the side of a hill, and the enormous keep dominated the skyline, lit by fires. The thing that got my attention and held it, though, was the ship.

The hulk of a large ship was just visible in the distance where it remained docked in the airship shipyards, scaffolding surrounding it as it grew. I noted its long, wide frame disappearing from view behind another building, and I turned to look at Barrett, shaking my head in amazement as he nodded to me in confirmation.

That was the battleship that Himnel was building, and the fucker was huge.

The warship we had, Oren's baby, *Agamemnon's Wrath*, would be tiny compared to that thing. It was like looking at a pleasure yacht next to a super-carrier. I'd seen the *Intrepid* at dock in New York on the discovery channel, and the *Growler* submarine alongside it; that was easily equivalent to the kind of disparity in size we were looking at here.

It was insane that people thought they could get something that big to fly!

I was still staring at it when Yen grabbed my arm and pointed to a mass of torches progressing down a street in the distance. People were shouting something; one man was screaming it, and they shouted it back to him. My stomach dropped.

Whatever was going on, it wasn't good. That was the sight of a mob being whipped into a frenzy, and not only were they between us and the Cloudring, but they were all headed in that direction.

"Amaat, think you can give us some information?" I asked.

He nodded once, stretching his huge wings and jumping from the edge of the roof. He flapped hard, lifting quickly and disappearing into the dusk while I watched the mob.

Amaat was gone for more than an hour before he returned. We'd spent the time discussing different paths we could take, but as more and more people marched in that direction, we became increasingly concerned.

When he finally returned, swooping in for a running landing, his wings beating hard to arrest his momentum, he looked haggard and worried.

Something dark that stank was slowly dripping from one wing, and his eye was blackened. When he landed, he limped and almost collapsed as his left leg went out from under him.

"What happened?" I asked him, aghast, and he clapped a fist to his chest in salute before responding.

"My lord; scout leader…" he said, nodding respectfully first to me, then Yen, before going on. "The mobs are filling the outer Cloudring and the surrounding area. The guards on the border of the noble district have closed the gates, cutting it off. The merchant district guards won't let them cross the bridges. It's like…"

"Like they're being funneled into the slums and the legion enclave," Yen finished, getting an exhausted nod from Amaat. "Now, what the hell happened to you, legionnaire?" she asked with a growl. "Who dared to attack you? And I better be hearing that they look worse than you do!"

"Sorry, scout leader," he said, shaking his head. "I flew in to see what was happening, and a bunch of harpies got the drop on me. When I turned to teach them a lesson, there were people ready in the buildings on either side, and they started throwing things."

"Hell, are the legion really that hated?" I asked in shock.

"No…but…" Yen shook her head in confusion.

"They were shouting at me," Amaat interrupted. "They said, 'This is for the children,' and they looked…furious."

"The children?" Tang asked, coming closer and grabbing Amaat's shoulder. "They said it was for the children; are you sure?" When Amaat nodded, Tang and Yen exchanged long, dark looks. "Bastards! They know it's not us…wait, how the hell did they know you were legion as well?"

"What the hell am I missing here?" I asked, crossing my arms and starting to get annoyed.

"There's been a series of grisly murders in the slums lately…" Yen replied slowly. "I don't know most of the details, beyond that the children were being drained and left in public places, often in bits." She straightened and looked out across the city, gazing at the smoke and flames belching into the air from industrial processes, and more to the point, far fewer of them than she was used to. "The city guard was investigating when the Legion General was murdered and his body taken for 'examination' by the guard, just like the children's bodies."

"Right…" I paused, taking a deep breath and letting it out in a long sigh. "And let me guess: no other adults were murdered, and their bodies taken? Just the Legion General?"

"Not that we know of," said Tang, and I nodded to him.

"I don't suppose there's actually a realistic chance that it was him that was killing the children? Or that it's just a coincidence that his body is taken and the entire enclave is put under house arrest 'for your safety'?"

"Not likely," replied Yen.

I shot her a glare. "What the hell did you all do to make yourselves a target like this? Who wins if the legion is wiped out?"

"Too many people," Yen replied with a sigh. "Look, let's get inside so we can't be seen, just in case the harpies come looking for Amaat, and I'll explain it, okay?" she asked.

I nodded, gesturing toward the trapdoor that led back into the building. "Okay, lead the way; and what are harpies doing in the city? I thought they were evil creatures?" I said, reaching down and helping Amaat to his feet, before taking his arm over my shoulder and helping him walk along. Tang and Yen exchanged a look as I supported Amaat, and after a pause, Amaat spoke up.

"The harpies aren't real harpies as you might know them. The real thing would be hunted down and killed, but these are just as much of a threat, if not more so. They're a gang of fliers; some alkyon, some djinn, a smattering of imps, a few prometheans…they're a gang, specifically criminals the city hasn't been able to purge entirely because their territory is so big, and they're good at hiding, as well as buying off guard commanders." That last bit was added bitterly, and I grunted in hearing that corruption was universal.

"I don't even know what those races are," I said.

He laughed. "I'm an alkyon. We've branched out into a few different subspecies, much as humans or dwarves do. The djinn are powerful creatures when they reach maturity, a form of air elemental with powerful magics, but as children, they are weaker than most. The harpies like to recruit them, hoping they might stick around once they reach maturity and grow in strength. They generally don't live long enough. The prometheans are evil bastards. They…" Amaat grunted, folding his wing in close and shook his head at the pain as he prepared to climb down the ladder.

"Okay, wait up a minute, guys," I said and looked to Oracle, who nodded, knowing me well enough to understand what I wanted without my saying it. She lifted higher into the air and began to fly a fast circuit, watching for anyone coming closer.

"Okay, let's see if this helps," I muttered under my breath, weaving the spell then pouring more and more power into it as it reached out, the glowing arcs of magic connecting me to Amaat then sweeping through his avian body.

I felt strains and popped muscles, old, half-healed broken bones, twists and tears on muscles where the natural healing that had happened over the years had gone wrong. I felt them all, and I grunted in amazement at the amount there was.

Amaat had clearly spent most of his life in one fight or another, either recovering from or about to receive an injury. I found entire sections of scarred and almost dead skin where it felt like there should be more, like a scar running through an otherwise healthy patch of hair.

I focused, starting with his head, then chest, aiming at the most important areas, his heart and more, chasing off a section of dense fibrous tissues at the base of a lung…

I forced myself to stop at half my mana pool, but I damn well knew I could have used double it and more on him. Even that amount had made a noticeable difference as he stood straighter, drawing in a deep breath.

He shifted on his feet, rolling his shoulders and flexing his wings, stunned at the changes. He ran his claw-tipped fingers through the freshly regrown feathers and plumage on his chest and sides, then reached up hesitantly to touch the crest that bloomed from the top of his head.

His coloring had changed from the dull grey and worn-out yellow he'd been in the caves to a brilliant, golden hue. The feathers that poked out around his breastplate and ran through his crest were now a bright and vibrant red, and he tilted his head back and screeched in pleasure at the changes.

"Dammit, Amaat!" Tang cursed, covering his ears as the loud, exultant cry echoed off nearby buildings. "I told you to cut that shit out!"

Amaat closed his beak with a loud clack, then grabbed my shoulders and nutted me. I staggered slightly, then reacted by growling and nutting him back, which sent the smaller bird man reeling, much to Tang and Yen's laughter.

I had tensed, ready to defend myself, until I heard their laughter and saw the way that Amaat was shaking his head, rubbing the top of his crest where I'd planted my forehead.

As my conscious mind caught up to my reflexive one, I realized that perhaps headbutting a creature with a beak clearly hard enough to break bones wasn't my most intelligent action…but fuck it.

Amaat straightened up and clapped his fist to his chest in salute.

"Thank you, my lord! You don't know what this means. I have my plumage back!" he babbled, preening again.

"I'm more interested in why you head-butted me, to be fair," I muttered, frowning and feeling at my head, where a bump was starting to rise already.

"It's an alkyon thing, my lord," Yen said with a smile. "When they're happy, they tend to do…well…that. It's a mixture of thanking their higher caste members and declaring their strength. Most other races don't take too well to it, but it's kind of ingrained in their species, much like loving the water is with the Mer…"

"Fair enough. Did I do right in returning the nut?" I asked.

"The 'nut'?"

"The headbutt."

"Ah, yes! Although I'd suggest being a bit more careful in the future; it's commonly the beginning of a ritualistic battle for hierarchy with his species. It's not an issue here; he's a member of the legion and already submitted to you after all, but if we meet unaffiliated alkyon…"

"We've got some fliers heading our way!" Oracle called, and the conversation broke off.

"Shit, okay, everyone outta sight!" I called, gesturing to the black square of the trapdoor.

"No!" Amaat said, straightening up and flexing. "Let me show these harpies what it means to cross the legion!" I looked into his eyes and saw a gleam that hadn't been there before.

"Oracle, how many?" I called up, and she shouted back down quickly.

"Too many! At least twenty."

"Down the hole," I ordered Amaat. Tang moved and jumped down through the trapdoor first, then Yen stepped up and grabbed Amaat's beak, yanking him around to look into her eyes.

"That's an order, legionnaire!" she snapped.

He glared back at her for a split second before blinking and closing his eyes, nostrils flaring in apparent submission.

Yen seemed satisfied by that, and she gestured for me to drop through the trapdoor.

"After you, my lord," she said. I peered down, confirming that nobody was in the way, and jumped in. I'd seen Tang do it and figured it mustn't be that far, despite the ladder we'd climbed up…and being the idiot that I was, I even went for a superhero landing.

I slammed into the floor two stories below and swallowed a scream as my knee cracked, the sound audible to the entire room as it echoed.

I gritted my teeth and looked up at Tang, who offered a hand to help me up, a wince clear on his face.

"Damn, that stings…" I whimpered, straightening up and limping to one side to allow Amaat to climb down the ladder into my freshly vacated place.

"Yeah, well, I'm an elf. Humans shouldn't try to keep up," Tang said with a wince, looking down at the spreading dampness of fresh blood coming from my pulverized kneecap.

"Well, I'll be sure to pass along the warning when I next meet one," I offered, forcing a smile and getting a frown from him as he looked me over.

"You mean you're not a—"

Yen interrupted him as she slammed into the ground next to us, barely seeming to stagger as she landed, with Oracle zooming down beside her. The trapdoor slammed shut with a clang, and I realized Yen must have pulled it as she jumped.

"What did you do this time?" Oracle asked me, buzzing down to look at my knee, then rising to eye level to shake a tiny perfect finger at me. "I've a good mind to not heal this! You need to learn to look before you jump!" she scolded me.

"Oracle," I started to whisper, and she nodded, breaking off as she sensed and saw the pain on my face, even as she started healing me.

"It wasn't the jump; it was the landing," called Bane.

"Really, dude?" I asked, turning to stare daggers at him as the pain started to recede. A popping and clicking sound echoed from my knee as it was rebuilt in seconds. It felt horrible, like crunching rice crackers. But instead of breaking, they were reforming, hardening, and…and his laughter vibrated through the air.

"No…not another '*superhero'* landing?" Oracle whispered, facepalming.

"I should never have told you about that," I grumbled, shaking my head. "Look, there's more important shit to discuss here, okay?" She started muttering about "idiot men" as I turned back to the scouts.

"Okay, we were talking about the mob out there and you being ambushed. Explain what you think is going on and why, please," I said. The three of them looked at each other, clearly uncomfortable, but it was Tang who spoke up.

"There's a bit of…uh…discussion about what's been going around of late. Not the murders, so much, but the legion and the city."

"Gossip, you mean." I sighed. He colored but nodded. "Does it make sense?" I asked

He nodded again. "It does, if you think the nobility—pardon me, my lord—are out to look after themselves, and nothing else matters."

"Yeah, that sounds like them," I said, nodding. "Go on; tell me what you all think."

"Well, the legion enclave is pretty big, and by imperial law, the legion receives ten percent of all taxes taken in the city for the empire."

"Right? So why the hell are you losing people? Ten percent is—"

"Not what we get," Yen interrupted, and I raised an eyebrow.

"There was a legion general a few years back who thought he should be kept in a 'manner befitting his station' and spent most of the gold stockpiled to 'improve' the enclave. Most of it was spent on his quarters and those of his cronies; even more was spent on the arena and on gambling. In the end, it got so out of hand, there was a rebellion within the legion. Articles were cited, and the Legion General was…removed," she said, looking ashamed.

"Okay, a dickhead officer took the piss, and you got rid of him for it, so…" I shrugged.

"So, the noble houses used it as an example of legion corruption. We were ordered to leave the enclave and set up a new base outside the city walls. The legion general who took over refused; he said that the legion was bigger than one man who'd crossed a line, and he instilled an ethos of conservatism.

"The taxes were cut, or at least the portion that we received was. We went from ten percent to one, while the news of the 'legion tax' was spread about the city. We told them that we received one percent, but the nobles claimed it was twenty, and that if we ceased to exist, then the taxes would be lower. The nobles keep insisting that the other nine percent is being held back to cover 'additional expenses' in the area.

"By law, they can do it, but it's getting to the point that their Oaths will compel them to hand it over soon. People hate the legion now, because they think we live a life of luxury. When a legionnaire dies, *protecting them*, they think it's the least we can do to make up for milking them of their money."

"And why do the nobles want to be rid of the legion?" I asked.

"The enclave is on the edge of the noble quarter and is almost a quarter of its size. We think the nobles want to use it for themselves, but who knows. Add to that the fact that the legion general had a seat on the council.

"He opposed the war with Narkolt, and most of the excesses that the nobles seem to love. He pushed for the old laws, and a good chunk of the people housed in the enclave are escaped slaves, as slavery is illegal in the empire. They escape and come to us, and once they step inside, they're free. The nobles hate that.

"Plus…well, the nobles keep pushing on the council to clear out the slums and force all those who live there to relocate outside the city walls. On the other side of the slums are some old docks. Word is, the nobles want to clear out the enclave and the slums to make them into a larger private dock for their posh ships, and so on."

"And the murders?" I asked.

"They've been going on for a few months. The city guard wasn't that interested until a few of the merchant's sons and daughters were taken; then guards started patrolling the merchant quarter and the surrounding homes. The slums…well…nobody cares what happens there."

"Okay, so you've got a city of nobles who want the land that the enclave is using, plus they wouldn't have to give you the taxes if they got rid of you; they've got a murderer in the city that they're probably blaming the legion general for; and they've whipped up the population against you. Is that about, right?"

"Yeah, that about sums it up," Tang said gloomily.

"Well, that's just fucking brilliant," I muttered. "This has become a real shit sandwich, you know that?" I grimaced, shaking my head.

"A shit sandwich?" Tang asked, a grin quirking his lips.

"Yeah, good-bad-good," I said, catching the confused expressions on their faces, and I elaborated. "You tell me, 'Hey, you've got the legion here to help,' and that's good. Then you say, 'But we're under house arrest and are probably going to be attacked soon, which will end in either being booted out of the city, or every legionnaire killed…' That's the bad."

"And the last good bit?" Amaat asked.

I grinned. "You've just given me a way to get my people out of the city, but it's gonna be fucking difficult."

CHAPTER FIVE

"What are our chances of making it to the Cloudring from here, and to the arena?" I asked, and Yen shrugged.

"The streets were fairly busy, and the mob was spilling out into the side streets, but we chose gear that wasn't too obvious. What worries me is the fact that, despite none of it being legion standard, Amaat was still targeted. He should have looked like just another armed alkyon flying in for a look. If the gang was waiting for him and tried to bring him down, that means either they're out to get anyone they can, or they knew he was legion."

"Are they still up there, Oracle?" I asked, and she zipped out of the top of a broken window. She was shrunk down to her smallest size, but it still made my butt pucker when she was out of arm's reach, ever since the drow had captured her.

It didn't take long for her to return, and she landed on my shoulder again, reaching out to stroke the back of my neck as she quietly updated us on the streets around the building.

"The harpies are circling nearby; they clearly don't know where we are, but they know Amaat went this way."

"I could try to draw them off?" Amaat said, drawing a deep breath. "Or I could fight them, see how many I can take down?"

"No," I said firmly as I moved to the window, looking up at the night sky between the buildings. I could make out a patch of darkness, filled with smoke and floating ash. A flash of movement caught my eye, followed quickly by two more.

"Tell me about the harpies," I murmured, still watching the sky.

"They're a street gang," Yen replied. "One of the strongest of a dozen that fill the city; thugs and criminals, essentially, but they dominate the sky. There's around a hundred of them, or so we guess. Nobody really knows."

"And what do the guard do about them?" I asked, still staring up and watching as another one passed by.

"Nothing," Yen said.

I turned to look at her in question.

"The guard isn't interested in the gangs, so long as they keep their business confined to the slums and the normal folk. Once in a while, they cross the line and hit a merchant who screams loud enough, pays enough, or has important friends, then the guard goes out and hits the gangs. Then they all back off, things go quiet for a bit, and people wait for the next time."

"So, the city guard are corrupt as well? The whole guard, I mean, not just the upper ranks?" I asked and got a nod in return. "Okay, what about the merchants? You said there are guards on the bridges to stop the mob from going that way; explain that for me," I said to Amaat.

"There's a river that runs through the center of the city. It splits the industrial docks in the north from the commercial docks in the south and runs up to the slums. There are three bridges across the river, with the majority of the merchant's quarter on the far side of the river from us. The guards are lined up around the merchant houses and the bridges, keeping the mobs back from crossing into the area."

"And what are the chances that there were enough guards just hanging around to be able to do that and to cut off the Noble Quarter as well?" I asked.

"None. They had to have been in place before this. It would require a huge force to do both; easily all the guards in the city plus some of the army. Hell, there's probably some of the Dark Legion fucking around as well, and that's all we need," Yen said gloomily.

"Hold up, who the fuck is the 'Dark Legion'?" I asked.

"They're the legion of Nimon, the God of Death." Tang glowered out of the window. "They were set up by the church, copied most of the legion's training methods and gear, then were given a fortune to spend to improve it.

"Everything the legion used to be, respected, strong, backed by the people, and fully supplied? That's the Dark Legion now. They took the legion and twisted it. Now they use our skills, our training, and our knowledge to kill and to spread the Law of Nimon, the Dark God of Death."

"Well, that's just fucking peachy," I snarled. "Is there anything else you want to tell me about? Any other minor details you forgot to mention?"

"Well, no," Yen said, swallowing hard and straightening. "I apologize, Lord Jax. We didn't know that you were unaware of the Dark Legion, or the realities of—"

"The realities of fucking life." I cut her off. "Yeah, okay, sorry. I shouldn't have snapped at you, but this shit sandwich just got a lot shittier, okay? Give me a few minutes," I said, shaking my head.

I sat watching up through the filthy, cracked glass, trying to spot different members of the harpies, but gave it up as pointless after a few minutes. The smugglers sat despondently at the back of the group, and I frowned as I studied them. They were just normal people, or so they seemed…

"Yen," I said, and she straightened to attention. "Think you could make it to the arena with one of the smugglers? Just the two of you?"

She turned and looked them over, settling on Ellen, the dead caravan master's granddaughter.

"We could; two women would draw less attention."

"Three would be better," Lydia added, stepping forward.

I nodded to her in thanks and looked over at Ellen.

"You up for this?" I asked her.

She shrugged. "If it means I get to go home and get some clean clothes and a bath? Yeah, I'll do it," she said, sniffing her clothes and grimacing.

"Okay, then, you three head for the arena, find this 'Mal' guy, and get him back here."

Ellen looked like she was going to say something, and I quirked an eyebrow at her in question, but she shook her head, instead turning to tell the other smugglers to wait with me.

I frowned and drew Yen and Lydia off to one side.

"Yen, I know you've just met Lydia, but let me be clear on this, she's got my complete confidence. If she says something, I need you to listen to her as though it's come from me, got it? It might not be right; fuck knows I don't ask the right questions, like, ever, but listen to her," I said.

Lydia straightened, giving me a quick, pleased nod.

"Of course." Yen nodded to Lydia.

"I trust you both. Keep an eye on Ellen, but most of all, keep yourselves alive. I don't trust her. There's something not right there. If you get separated, retreat back here. Do you need anything?"

"No, sir. We're just a group of girls heading out to see a friend," Yen said.

"Well, have fun…and I know that, to Lydia, 'having fun' means kicking some poor bastard's head in, so at least try to behave, okay?"

"Well, I'll try," Lydia said, looking dubious. "Don't know what I'll enjoy if I can't do that, though…"

"A girl after my own heart!" Yen laughed.

"Will you all be okay in your armor, I mean—" I started to say, only to be cut off by Yen.

"There's a lot of female mercenaries in the city, don't worry," she assured me. I sighed and nodded, not liking it, but sure as hell not about to tell them to strip off first. They both headed over to the door to take station on either side of Ellen.

"Get out there, and be careful, okay?" I said, forcing a smile at them all.

"Yes, sir!" came the response from both Lydia and Yen, followed a second later by Ellen. I shook my head and watched as they pushed the large wooden door open a few feet with a loud, resounding creak, creeping out cautiously before hurrying out into the night.

I watched them from the window as they neared the mouth of the alley, each of them crouching to gather some dirt from the road and rub it into their clothes and hair. Ellen adjusted her top as Lydia attempted to hide her mace with her cloak.

As soon as they disappeared, Amaat was by my side.

"Do you want me to follow them? Watch over them?" he asked, and I shook my head.

"No, I think you'd put them more at risk. Best to stay here and trust in them," I said, already feeling worried about them myself.

Oracle shifted on my shoulder, opening her mouth, and I shook my head.

"Not a chance," I whispered to her.

"I could sneak along. The drow caught me unprepared, that's all…"

"Not a chance!" I repeated more forcefully. "I'm never letting you out of my sight again."

"I'm a wisp, you know. I can look after myself."

"You're my companion, and—" I cut off abruptly, moving back as someone flew down into the alleyway.

"This way!" a high-pitched voice called as three more silhouettes dived down.

"What is it?" the second one said, landing on a box outside the window and rubbing at it to try to move some dirt. He looked in, but clearly couldn't see anything, and started making his way along the windows, peering in each one.

We all moved quickly, pushing ourselves up against walls and behind abandoned, dust-covered equipment, trying any means necessary to get out of sight.

"Those women, they came from this way," the third voice said, and my stomach clenched in fear for them.

"So?"

"So, there's nothing over here! Nothing but the old weaver's…so there's something going on, isn't there!"

"Because there's nothing here, there's something going on?" the second voice said, clearly confused.

"Yeah!" said another voice as the door shifted.

"Open the door!" a fourth voice shrilled, indicating that there were at least two on the near side.

"That's an alkyon," Amaat said to me quietly, glaring at the door as it shifted back and forth.

I gestured to Bane, and he crept over, taking up position next to the door, while Stephanos and Miren nocked arrows on their bows, one aiming at the door, the other at the one who was staring in the windows.

Arrin moved over to crouch next to the window closest to the first voice, and Barrett just grinned at me as he hefted his greatsword and strode into the middle of the room. I nodded to him and gestured for Tang to join him.

"Bane!" I hissed, and he met my gaze. "Take one alive."

He nodded.

I grinned, shifting my naginata around to point it right at the wall between me and what I assumed was the fourth member of their team.

I could hear movement on the other side of the wall, the crumbling masonry and cracked windows making it easy to see their movement. I looked to Amaat and gestured up towards the ceiling and the trapdoor. He nodded, launching himself upward with a powerful beat of his wings.

"Hey!" came the second voice. "Wese's think there's something in there…" This time it came from a small creature, maybe two feet tall, bright blue, with tribal tattoos covering his skin. He drew a small knife from his belt, his bat-like wings beating quickly to keep him in the air as he grinned malevolently at the window. His left hand came up, and a flicker of flame flashed to life in his palm. "Come out, come out…whatever you are," he crooned into the darkness, throwing the tiny Firebolt forwards to shatter the glass. It impacted into Tang's shield and burst, barely rocking the enormous elf, who just looked over the shield at the imp and grinned evilly.

"Attack!" I roared, slamming my naginata through the brickwork next to me and sinking it into the figure skulking there.

The blade punched through something that was noticeably softer than the bricks, resulting in a scream that cut off abruptly. I twisted it then yanked my weapon back.

The sounds of battle erupted all around me. Bane had jerked the door open and grabbed an imp that was on the other side, yanking it forward and punching it into unconsciousness. Stephanos and Miren had both released arrows through the window into the second imp, one taking him in the face and terminally ruining his day.

Amaat had blasted through the trapdoor and out into the empty air, diving down at tremendous speed towards the alkyon, who'd jumped back when the door opened, then leapt into the air and was now frantically trying to reach the open air over the alleyway.

I moved across to the window closest to me and looked out into the alley, finding another small, blue imp trying to drag itself away as it bled out, my naginata having punched straight through it.

The battle was over for the rest of us before it began, the only one still in the fight being the alkyon. Judging from the screams and the falling feathers, that wasn't going well for it.

A few seconds later, it slammed into the cobblestoned alleyway with a crunch of breaking bones and a squawk of pain that cut off abruptly.

I walked out, looking around to make sure nobody else was coming as Tang retrieved the bodies of the imps, including the bleeding crawler, tossing them through the broken window. Bane and Barrett grabbed the alkyon and dragged it inside, dumping it alongside the pile of imps.

We closed up quickly, shutting the door and dragging some planks across the shattered windows. I asked Oracle to go keep watch through a cracked window that had a view of the length of the alleyway.

Amaat landed with a thump through the still-open trapdoor, his clawed talons gripping the wooden floor as he lifted his arms and threw back his head…and Tang grabbed his beak, shutting it before his triumphant screech could get out.

Tang growled something at him, and he seemed to recover himself. The massive elf gestured to the trapdoor and growled at him again.

Amaat took off, looking a bit sheepish, while Tang crossed the room to speak quietly to me.

"Sorry about that. Alkyon are great aerial scouts, but their instincts…"

"Got it," I said, shaking my head.

Tang nodded, muttering low enough that I'd hear it but nobody else would. "Damn bird brains."

I snorted and walked over to the two live harpies, noting the pool of blood spreading out from beneath the alkyon. It was in bad shape.

It had landed on a wing, shattering the bones and ripping them through skin and membranes alike, and was clearly bleeding out. Added to that, great gashes in its wings from where Amaat had torn it from the sky made it obvious that, unless we stepped in, it wasn't going to live long, let alone ever be capable of flight again.

I stared at it for long seconds as its lifeblood pumped out, considering. It had attacked us, and I was low on mana now, thanks to healing the injuries on Amaat that this dickhead and its friends had inflicted. Plus, we already had a prisoner…and it wasn't like it was going to be let go once it told us what we needed to know.

A dark part of my soul had been set free when Oracle had been taken from me, and it had taken root after all that had happened in the drow tunnels. I looked at these creatures, and I found that I didn't care if they lived or died. They were only alive because it was convenient to me; they could give me answers, or one could, at least…

I started to turn away from the Alkyon, and she was there.

Oracle had abandoned her post, hovering before me and staring into my eyes as I froze. I gritted my teeth and held firm, staring back at her, expecting condemnation. Instead, I found…sadness.

She looked into my eyes, and for what seemed like the first time in forever, she and I felt different things. I'd expected her to be furious that I wasn't going to save it, but instead, I found sadness and regret.

"I'm sorry, Jax…this is my fault. If I hadn't been taken—" she started.

I cut her off gruffly, swallowing the lump in my throat.

"No!" I said, then tried again, a little calmer. "No, it wasn't your fault. It was those fucking Drow—"

"No," she said, cutting me off in turn. Shaking her perfect head, she set her hair swaying. "It was my fault, because I was overconfident. I thought nothing could touch me, and I got taken, and then this part of you got free."

I froze at the mention of the darkness inside myself, my heart seeming to stop as a sudden fear filled me. Did she want to break our bond? Was I too much, too broken…was she going to leave me like the others? I searched her eyes frantically, my heart hammering in my chest as she held my gaze.

"It's okay," she said, moving closer and reaching out, her tiny hands on my cheeks holding me in place as she gazed into my eyes. "I'll never leave you," she whispered. I blinked away hot tears that I hadn't realized were there. "I'll *never* leave you," she repeated.

"But you need to ask yourself if you're truly who you want to be right now. Jax, the man I first met, would have saved her. He'd have been angry, but he'd have done it." She gestured down at the unconscious Alkyon who was bleeding out on the floor.

"I…"

"The man I first met would have saved her. The man you became when you freed Amon into your soul might not, but you need to decide who you want to be. You need to pick if you're going to be who you were or who you are, or if you are going to continue to try to be more."

I replayed the things I'd done since coming to this realm through my mind at speed, comparing them to who I'd been before. I saw the change, the darkness and the fury. It had been set free when Oracle had enhanced our emotions accidentally, but it hadn't been created by her.

It was me.

It had always been me. I'd always struggled with my temper, with the need to give someone just one more punch, one more kick. To leave them an injury that would last, to remind them of their place.

I'd killed in dreams, and gods knew I'd left enough people in the hospital back on Earth that I'd never bothered to check on. But my guiding ethos had always been that Tommy and I were making the world a better place.

We'd fed a dealer a pound of his own badly cut shit after he'd fucked up a friend of ours with it, but that was because he was scum and needed to learn about customer care. We'd fucked up people who started trouble in bars and who'd tried to steal cars.

We'd beaten a guy half to death for mugging a little old lady, then we'd sat there feeling really awkward and desperately wanting to get away when we'd taken her purse back to her. She'd made us come into her house to have cake that was stale as cardboard and drink tea that had no flavor, because she had nothing. But she'd still wanted to show how thankful she was to "such nice boys."

We'd hated the belief we'd seen in her eyes that we were a pair of "nice boys," hated that it made us want to be what she thought we were, for her, even though it was for just a minute. We'd gone out and we'd made it clear to people that she was to be fucking well looked after.

We'd taken her milk and sugar, dropped off cakes, and made sure people cut her grass and fixed her door.

We'd done it because it was the *right* thing to do. Not because it was easy, but because it was needed, no matter how uncomfortable. We listened to her stories, ignored it when she called us by different names. We forgave her when she didn't know who we were, or when she was afraid of us, because her mind was going. We told her that her grandsons had asked us to drop the food off, and those days when she invited us in, we sat there, in chairs too small, while her half-blind smelly old cat rubbed against us or clawed the shit out of our hands. We were there when nobody else was.

We did it because it was right.

I did it because it was right.

I took a deep breath and turned back to the alkyon sprawled on the floor, and I knelt. The knee of my shiny, new, and probably insanely expensive Gloom spidersilk pants rested in their blood as I started to channel.

I used almost all of my mana, with Amaat silently straightening the wings and limbs as I went. The hollow popping sounds, as bones realigned and healed, echoed around the room as we worked.

When it was done, I slowly stood up, exhaustion filling me along with a mana migraine pounding behind my eyes. Shame in what I'd almost done was warring with the fury and belief that they'd started it and deserved to die. I sought out Bane, finding him across from the now-stirring alkyon and the imp's body. I growled out an order, marching away to sit in the corner, separate from the others.

"Question them."

CHAPTER SIX

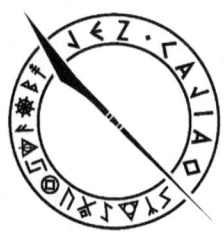

I sat in the darkness of the abandoned weaver's building, barely registering the occasional scream ringing out from the imp as Bane questioned him. I heard nothing from the alkyon, but I didn't care. I'd done what I had to, and now Bane was doing what I needed him to do.

"It's a bit wrong," I whispered to Oracle as she sat on my knee, looking up at me.

"What is?" she asked. I shrugged, gesturing to the other room where Bane worked.

"I saved its life, now he's going to torture it for information."

"Her life," she corrected me.

"Really?" I frowned, and she nodded. "Weird; no tits makes it a lot harder to tell, you know?" I said. She laughed at me, shifting to show hers off better.

"Well, trust me, she's a she. And as to what Bane's doing…well. If they tell him the truth, then they'll be okay. You didn't tell him to kill them after he finished. That would have been a bit…yeah." She shrugged. "But you healed her up when you could have let her die. Now she's going to have a choice, to speak the truth or not, but that's her decision to make. You made the right one for your situation."

"Well, it still feels fucking weird," I muttered, leaning my head back against the brickwork and closing my eyes. I drew in a deep breath and shifted, feeling Oracle take flight and relocate to my shoulder instead, as she understood what I needed to do.

I tried to meditate again, despite being crap at it. I needed the increased mana regeneration that Xiao had promised me I'd get from it, so I tried.

It took nearly an hour, but thanks to the increased mana regeneration, I was finally back to a respectable amount of mana when Bane came to me.

"We've got a problem," he said.

My eyes shot open, staring up at him as I unfolded my legs and came to my feet with a fluid grace that I'd never been capable of in my old life.

"What's happened?" I asked.

"The legionnaires say that the arena is maybe half an hour away, usually. With the city as busy as it is, an hour at most. If we're lucky, the three of them made it, but the imp just talked. They were on the lookout for the three legionnaires; Venta confirmed it as well."

"Venta?" I asked. He let loose a subsonic *thrummm* of amusement.

"The alkyon; she said her name is Venta, and it's hilarious watching her and Amaat dance around each other. Turns out, they establish hierarchy and find mates by fighting it out. As far as she's concerned, she's his mate now, since he smashed her from the sky, and he's not sure if he's loving the situation or terrified by it."

"She's talking?" I glanced in her direction in surprise, and he nodded.

"Amaat ordered her to tell us what we wanted to know, and she did. Anything we ask, she's happy to share."

"Well, that's something, I guess," I said, leading the way through back into the center room, with Oracle remaining perched on my shoulder. When I entered the occupied area of the room, Miren and Stephanos stood on watch at either end of the windows, and Barrett by the doors, with the rest spread out around the room. Venta was crouched next to Amaat, who jumped to his feet when I entered. The solitary surviving imp lay next to the far wall…a bloody mess.

As I started walking forward, Amaat headed to me, with Venta following along behind.

"Lord Jax!" Amaat said, ducking his head and clapping his fist to chest in salute. I nodded to him, returning the salute, and he straightened up, locking eyes with me. "I ask permission to accept Venta T'Ashar Clear-Sky as a mate, and that you accept her into your followers."

I looked from him to Venta, who stood behind him. When my gaze met hers, she crouched down, dropping to one knee and flaring her wings out behind her. I studied her, surprised that she looked more like a hawk than an eagle, like Amaat, but beyond that…

"Can she swear the Oath?" I asked him, and he nodded once, jerkily.

"Then she can swear the Oath of the tower, and I'll accept her, as long as you vouch for her. Understand that I'll be watching you, Venta," I said, directing the last bit at her. "You attacked us, and I don't trust you, not yet."

"I know, my lord," she said, her voice harsher on the ears that Amaat's.

"Oracle," I prompted, and my companion lifted a strand of mana from my chest somehow making it visible as she touched it to Venta.

"Read the words you see there, Venta, and join us in a better life," Barrett called from the door, nodding to her. She looked at him, then nodded in return, straightening and standing as tall and proud as she could.

I blinked as I realized the size difference between her and Amaat. It had not been clear when she'd been stooping before, but she was considerably shorter than he was, maybe only four feet tall, and scrawny to boot. A pair of daggers were her only weapons, and they were held in Amaat's hands.

She took a deep breath and began to recite the words of the Oath that had become the standard for my people.

"I swear to obey Lord Jax and those he places over me; I will serve to the best of my ability, speak no lie to him when commanded otherwise, and treat all other citizens as family.

"I will work for the greater good, being a shield to those who need it, a sword for those who deserve it, and a warden to the night."

"I will stand with my family, helping one another to reach the light, until the hour of my death or my lord releases me from my Oath.

"Lastly, I will not be a dick!"

I always grinned at the last part, unable to help myself. I stepped forward, Amaat shifting aside, and I put my hand on Venta's shoulder, giving her a momentary squeeze.

"Welcome to the family, Venta," I said, nodding when Amaat lifted her daggers questioningly. He passed them back to her, and I picked my way over to the imp's corpse. I crouched down and looked at it, examining the tiny face frozen in death, the pointed teeth and horns that made it a creature of legend, and I sighed deeply, reaching out to close its staring eyes.

I suddenly felt that I was guilty of the one thing I'd always hated the most back in my old life.

I'd decided this creature should die because of its looks, and even now, I didn't regret it.

Back home, it had been the color of someone's skin; a fucking stupid denominator, in my opinion, when compared with the opportunities there were. Entire sections of the population were marginalized by governments and others in positions of power, who then told us all not to do it.

Newspapers claimed that all of X crimes were committed by Y group, and the idiots out there believed it. I'd met people I fucking hated who had the same skin as me and great friends who were totally different. I didn't give a shit what color a person was; I just hated everyone until they proved they weren't assholes.

I wondered now if I'd held an unfounded prejudice against this creature. In the past, we'd apparently all decided that if they looked like this, they were evil. Yet here I was, recruiting and giving a bird-wo— person a chance.

I grimaced and straightened up, banishing the concerns from my mind; I had more pressing things to worry about right now.

"Venta!" I said, turning back to her, and she jumped as I glared at her.

"Yes…my lord?" she said hesitantly.

"Bane said you were on the lookout for the legion scouts…Why? And who told you?" I asked.

"I…Skyking said we were to watch out for them, that they were up to something, and that they had to be stopped. Said the legion was the one killing the kids, said they were ruled by vampyres and monsters in the enclave."

"Skyking?" I asked, and she nodded jerkily, making me realize just how many bird-like mannerisms she and Amaat had. Her head was constantly on the move, focusing on me with one eye, then the other, then both, then scouting the room out.

"He's the ruler of the harpies," she said quickly, "He's our…their king."

"And he sent you all out to look for the legion. Any members of the legion, or just those three?"

"Both! His officers described the three, but said we were to report any sightings of the legion to them…There were more of my group up above. You know that, don't you?" she asked suddenly. The entire room seemed to stiffen.

"Explain," I commanded her, and she pointed upward with one black claw.

"There were two on overwatch; there always are. One followed the three women, but the other would have been up there. She will have seen my group disappearing around here, even if she didn't see the fight…"

"Fuck!" I snapped out, looking around the room. "Okay, we need to be ready, people! We can't leave here, not yet, but it sounds like we're going to get company unless we take them down quick! Barrett, get them ready," I ordered, nodding to Lydia's squad as I gestured to Tang, Amaat, and Venta, while Barrett started organizing our remaining people.

"Tang, I know you're a scout; how good are you at stealth?" I asked him outright.

"Want me to steal your teeth?" He grinned at me.

"Ha, no…I want a lookout set up on the building across from us. Have you got any spells?" I asked. He shook his head. "Well, fuck."

He reached into a small bag of holding and pulled out a vial, which he held up, grinning. "I do have a smoke vial, though."

I glanced at it, realizing that it was actually two vials melded into one, one side filled with bright yellow, and the other with a noxious green tint.

"What does it do?" I asked.

"When I break it, it makes a cloud of smoke and stuns most who breathe it in for a few seconds."

"Right. Get up there, into that building. I want you to watch over us, and if they come to attack, smoke bomb them, then flank them." I pointed out of the window to a nearby taller building, and he nodded, turning and slipping out of the door.

"Venta, I guess it's time to roll the dice," I said, shaking my head. "Get up there and eliminate the harpies' overwatch, Amaat. Chase her, make it look like she's escaping, then the pair of you kill anyone up there who's watching us. If you get into trouble, lead them back down here, and we'll be waiting with spells and arrows." They both nodded, breaking away to speak quickly and confirm what they'd do between them.

As they took off, flying up to the trapdoor and getting ready, I pulled Barrett to the side, and we talked quickly. I outlined the orders I'd given, and he sent Miren, Arrin, and Stephanos up onto the walkway that led to the trapdoor. All three were ready to either head up or give cover down here, as needed.

"Bane." I said, and a second later, he was by my side. "I need you up there." I gestured to the roof. "I need you on watch, ready to protect the archers. I need you to have our back."

"Always," he said, vanishing as quickly as he had shown up.

My eyes found their way to Barrett and Jian, just as the others were getting into position, and I couldn't help but grin.

I fucking loved this shit. My heart was pounding, and I had no idea if we were about to be attacked, or if I was just being paranoid, but the three of us stood in the middle of the room, ready for whatever was coming.

Venta and Amaat flew out of the trap door suddenly, and I squashed my second thoughts about whether I could trust her or not. *It was time to toss the dice…*

I thought back to the character in my favorite books who'd loved to say that, and I grinned as I admired my chosen weapon. I'd tried the naginata with him in mind, and damn, it'd been like I'd spent my life waiting for it. It just *fit* me: the reach, the power, the utter batshit insanity of a giant murderstick with a fucking sword on the end…

I fucking loved it.

I looked at Barrett and Jian again, catching the same mix of emotions in each other's faces. Jian gestured to the door. He walked over to it, sheathing one of his scythes, and slowly pulled it open, looking back to me. I nodded, and he peered out, staring up into the sky for long seconds before he froze.

He moved quickly, stepping outside into the alley and looking up into the rain that had begun to fall over the last few minutes. Covering his eyes and staring, it didn't take long before he was ducking back in.

"They're coming, and they're bringing friends," he said, and Barrett called out immediately.

"Get ready!"

Jian moved back into the alleyway, staring upwards and counting quickly before ducking back inside.

"Amaat is leading at least a dozen back here. I couldn't see Venta."

"Get ready to give Amaat some support!" I shouted up. Arrin, Stephanos, and Miren all ran to the ladder, quickly climbing it as Bane shouted down to the rest of us.

"There are at least two dozen. Amaat is leading them around to get them all in a line...looks like he's headed back to us now!" He got out of the way, and I shouted back up to them.

"Take out who you can but be ready to get back down here. It'll make it a lot harder for the fliers if they have to fight down here!"

They shouted assent, and I walked into the middle of the room, giving myself plenty of space to use my naginata. Barrett chose himself some space near the center, as well. Jian stood out in the rain still, a scythe in either hand as he stared up into the dark, weeping sky.

There came a sound of the air being cut by a fast-moving body, then the reverberation of bowstrings being released. Almost instantly, the *thwack* of arrows hitting their targets followed. As two bodies fell from the sky, a scream of "Oh yeah!" from above told me that Arrin was also in the fight, just as two more bowstrings sang.

A handful of arrows released with a whirr, then a sound like hailstones hitting the roof and grunts of pain. Arrin, Stephanos, and Miren retreated back inside, pulling the trapdoor shut.

I ignored the fact that Bane was up there still; he was either biding his time, or I couldn't help him.

A rush of wings indicated more bodies flying past at speed, and a second later, Jian ran back inside to take up position near the door, scythes drawn back.

Amaat flew in, landing hard and skidding to a halt in a crash of wooden boxes. My mana dipped as Oracle instantly flew over to heal him.

Less than three heartbeats later, the first of the harpies followed him into the room, a small green imp who noticed Jian lying in wait by the door too late. Jian's twin scythes flashed out, the first missing its mark, but the second beheading the small creature as he stepped back into concealment.

The body hit the floor, wings still flapping spasmodically as death throes ripped through it.

Barrett kicked the head aside and drew his greatsword back like a baseball bat. I backed a little further apart, then channeled a thread of mana into my naginata, bringing it glowing to life.

We didn't have to wait long. No sooner had Jian moved back than the second harpy flashed past him, the third and fourth following straight after, while a hard swing from his scythes connected with the fifth. His twin blades were ripped from his hands as they buried themselves deep in the alkyon. A second of panic tore through my veins as I thought it was Venta. But it wasn't, and the others that had burst into the room were imps. Barrett had hit the second hard enough it didn't seem cut by the sword, so much as exploded by an internal bomb.

I stabbed out, skewering the third, and the fourth barely managed to avoid impaling itself right after its friend, only to crash straight out of a window with a shriek. The cry was cut off abruptly when an arrow flashed out after it and dropped its moaning, concussed form from slumping against the far wall of the alley to slowly cooling in the gutter.

After that, it became a free-for-all. Easily thirty more fliers flew down, and the minutes passed in frantic stabbing, kicking, and punching before a sharp whistle broke through the grunts and screams.

As the fliers fell back, fleeing the room, I slumped against my braced naginata, getting my breath back while I glanced around the room. Ten more corpses littered the floor. I knew I'd punted at least one into the middle of next week, as it had landed before me while my blade was deep in its friend's gut.

I'd lashed out, catching the diminutive, red-skinned figure in the crotch and firing it across the room, reaching out and grabbing another by its horns as it flew past and slamming it into a wall.

Its bones had snapped, and I quickly counted the eliminated harpies as I waited for whatever was coming next.

Seventeen down, that I could see, and by contrast, all we had sustained were a collection of bruises and aches, thanks to Oracle. I had forty mana left, and I glared out at the heavy rain of the alleyway as lightning illuminated it.

More harpies were landing out there by the second, glaring in at us and scrabbling claws on the trapdoor above us indicated that they were opening it.

"Everyone okay?" I asked, getting a grin from Barrett, who looked like he'd been bathing in blood. Jian, on the other hand, looked spotless, but I could have sworn his arms looked even bigger; the crazy fucker had been assigning points during the fight.

"You been upping your Strength again?" I scoffed, and he grinned and flexed his biceps at me. "Mad bastard," I muttered, thinking of every goddamn fight I'd had.

The one thing I always, and I mean *always,* decided mid-fight was that next time, I was going to be investing in Endurance. I almost never did, but fuck me, I needed to start.

"How many mana potions you got?" I called up to Arrin. He lifted his middle finger, making me grin. Either he was telling me to get fucked, or he had one, but either way, his sense of humor was intact.

Everyone, bar Stephanos, looked to be okay. That poor bastard was getting an arrow pulled out of his arm by Miren, who gave him a healing potion straight after. I was about to say something else when a new figure entered the alley.

He slammed down onto the cobbles hard, his enormous wings batting smaller members of the gang aside effortlessly as he straightened and glared at me.

He stood easily seven feet tall, bearing a massive sword and triangular shield in his hands. He looked human, except for grey-blue skin, enormous wings, and the twin glossy black horns erupting from his temples. They curved like a bull's, coming to wicked points that gleamed in the rain.

Promethean Sky Warder
The prometheans are a proud and hardy race. They once ruled much of the realm, before the coming of the empire, and they yearn for the glory of their past. Prometheans are cruel and sadistic to those they view as lesser than themselves and will not hesitate to attack at a sign of weakness.

Promises made by a promethean are said to only be genuine if they fear those they swear to.

Weaknesses: Unknown
Resistances: Unknown
Level: Unknown
Health: Unknown
Mana: Unknown

I glanced over the details as I used Examine, but I cut off the spell rather than plow more into it. I couldn't afford the distraction or the waste of mana.

"Stand down and surrender," it ordered.

I waited.

After a handful of seconds, it bellowed in fury and stepped forward out of the rain, filling the doorway. Overhead, the trapdoor was yanked up, torn off its hinges when the second promethean couldn't get the lock open.

"I ordered you to surrender!" the first one bellowed again. I decided my best chance was to make him mad so he couldn't think tactically…or so I'd die sooner.

I stabbed the metal-clad base of the naginata into the ground and faced him, knowing everyone was watching and praying that both Bane and Tang were ready to help out.

Venta landed behind the promethean and gave me a sharp nod, surrounded by her old gang and acting for all the world like one of them.

I grinned at him and extended my left fist upright, palm toward my chest, fingers clenched, and reached up with my right hand. I pretended to wind an invisible crank attached to my hand, to the vast confusion of the group, until my left middle finger was fully extended…then I blew the promethean a kiss.

There was a second of stunned silence before Arrin broke it by laughing and sending a Firebolt skyward to take the promethean over the trapdoor in the face. Two arrows followed a second after, before a scream and a spray of blood from the promethean told me that Bane had joined the fight.

I grinned at the promethean standing before me. He howled in rage and rushed at me, his sword flashing down as I stepped back, whipping my naginata around and readying myself. His gang rushed in around him, and Miren started firing arrow after arrow at them, taking them down easily.

Amaat took off in the confusion, two more alkyon following in hot pursuit. Barrett was swinging for all he was worth, smashing the smaller imps out of the sky as they tried to surround him, and Jian moved like he was dancing, spinning and thrusting, taking down fliers with his twin swords, while his scythes lay embedded in a corpse nearby.

I twisted my weapon sideways, deflecting the strike off to the side. As I pulled the blade back, I struck out with the base of the naginata instead, smashing it into my opponent's ankle before he could get his shield down.

I stepped back, dodging a thrust of the sword, and took the shield bash on the braced haft of my weapon. Feeling my feet slide a couple of inches across the ground, I grunted. However, while this fucker was strong, he wasn't as fast as the drow or as overpoweringly huge as the SporeMother had been.

His little gang was nothing in numbers compared to the goblins, and that damn drider had him beat on sheer freakiness.

I grinned at him, watching his fury rise as he limped, and I refused to be intimidated by him.

A scream came from above as the promethean died on the rooftop, and arrows flashed out to take down more of the swarm of fliers. A Firebolt shot past me to rock my opponent back on his feet, and Venta spun, suddenly whirling with her daggers, taking down former allies in seconds as they panicked.

All of this happened in a blink, and the promethean's eyes widened in shock as his gang members were slaughtered. Venta took off from the gaggle of fliers beyond him, and a heartbeat later, a crash signified Tang getting involved. A thick, grey cloud of smoke erupted, cutting off visibility for the remaining fliers in the alleyway, while arrows continued to hammer out into the coughing, frantically moving shapes that briefly materialized through the smoke.

I grinned at my enemy, and he roared in fury, activating some kind of ability. His sword and shield began to glow, as did his slim silver necklace. His eyes filled with blood, and veins all over his body stood out proud and rigid.

His attacks suddenly sped up, and I stepped back, ducking a sword swing and lashing out with a stab. My strike was battered aside, deflected by his shield, sending me staggering. He stabbed forward, forcing me to jump back again before spinning and almost taking Barrett's head off as he tried to take the creature from behind. Bellowing furiously, he spun back in time to raise his shield and block a second Firebolt from Arrin, the flames licking across the metal.

"Leave him, he's mine!" I shouted out to the others, glaring at him.

"You think to face me?! One of the Chosen?!" he screamed at me, froth appearing at the corners of his mouth.

"Oh yeah, I'm gonna fuck you like your daddy!" I growled at him, spinning my naginata around, end-over-end. Switching it from hand to hand, I smiled as the whistle of its passage filled the air, a touch of mana blazing the haft to life. I couldn't use much, not with Oracle providing heals to the group, which meant I definitely couldn't use my new Mana Overdrive ability.

I didn't need it. I could do this.

I stepped forward, edging closer to him as he stabbed out, testing my speed. He could test all he wanted, I decided. I didn't have the time to fuck about. I went on the offensive, all out. I lashed the heel of my weapon down hard, smashing it into his sword blade and knocking it aside.

Spinning around and loosening my grip with my right hand, I used it solely to control my aim as my left hand provided the power. I pushed the haft forward through my loose grip, then yanked it back. As I cleared the edge of his shield at the top left, the blade punched deeply into one unarmored shoulder.

A twist and pull opened the wound wider. I stabbed forward again, going for the right thigh, just below the stupid-looking kilt he wore. The blade sank into the thick muscle of his leg, severing entire bands of it before I pulled back and went for his face.

The pained look of shock broke from the berserker fury he'd been reveling in before, then disintegrated into fear as the tip of my blade cut a neat flap from under his right eye. He somehow managed to shake himself into action and leaped backwards, beating his giant chicken wings as I dropped down low.

His attempt at a counterstrike flashed over my head, and with his shield arm useless, he was left exposed. I shoved my naginata forward with all my force, the tip punching up through his sternum and into the space where his heart would have been in a human. I didn't know if that was enough to kill him on its own, but the damage added by imbuing my weapon with fire probably helped. The tip erupted from his back, emerging between his wings.

I yanked it back out, rising smoothly to my feet as he sagged to his knees. I Sparta-kicked him in the face, sending him sliding across the floor in a heap of feathers and blood.

As I straightened back up, I took one look at the remaining few harpies in the room and shouted over the noise:

"Surrender or die!"

There was a lull in the fighting for a second as everyone paused, and an alkyon on the other side decided to try for a leadership position and pointed at me, shouting, "Kill him!"

Then…he screamed in pain as four daggers punched through him in different places from behind. The blades were rapidly jerked sideways, eviscerating him and leaving behind a screeching, dying lump on the floor.

"Anyone else?" Bane asked almost conversationally, spinning his blades and sending blood flying to spatter across the nearest few survivors.

There was no hesitation this time, as weapons were dropped by those too close to escape. Those further back on the roof beat their wings frantically, lifting into the air as Miren, Stephanos, and Arrin took them down. Only three made it out of range in time.

CHAPTER SEVEN

"Get their weapons and make sure they're no threat," I growled to Barrett as I turned to look them over. I couldn't see anyone who'd tried to give any orders now. They'd all died fast, so I called outside instead.

"Venta!" A few seconds later, she landed in the alleyway, bloody and injured, blood dripping from both her daggers and her taloned feet. Amaat landed behind her a second later and stomped in after her. Clear pride showed in the way he moved, shaking blood from his feathers and weapons.

"Yes, my lord?" Venta asked me, and I acknowledged her salute with a nod of my own.

"Who's the most likely to know about the others here? Whether my people made it or were captured?" I clarified, realizing she'd never actually met Lydia, Yen, and Ellen.

I turned and looked over to the corner where the smugglers had been hiding, noting that they both had claimed shortswords from somewhere. They were bloody as well, but both nodded in respect to me.

"Oracle, heal them as well please." I'd totally forgotten about them in the chaos, and I felt a little guilty as I realized it.

"I will, if you ever get around to drinking that mana potion," she said.

I grimaced. I only had the one left, and it was one of the insanely powerful ones we'd looted from the Drider. I couldn't waste that when a little meditation would be fine instead.

"Bane, Barrett," I called, and they both appeared, heading over to me. Barrett walked with a limp, and Bane had three long, thin cuts across one shoulder, but they were otherwise okay. "I need you to question these dicks and see if you can find any potions or useful gear. If you do, spread them out to those who need them. We can't stay here much longer, not after that fight, so you've got five minutes to do what you need to. I'm going to meditate to get some mana back; interrupt me if you find any mana potions."

They both nodded, and I turned, making my way over to a corner that was mostly clear of corpses and blood. Sighing wearily, I sat down and closed my eyes.

I drew in a deep breath, my heartbeat still hammering in my ears from the adrenaline, and I forced myself to focus in on my breathing. I really, really needed to get better at this, I reflected…then I banished that thought along with all the others, visualizing a clear lake before me.

I focused, seeing everything and nothing, then created a collection of stones, big, rounded fuckers, imagining them slowly stacking themselves atop each other, moving in time with my breathing, slow…steady…

The lake rippled, and I banished it, returning the surface to a glass-like mirror of the world above…Fog swirling across it…gods, I was shit at this…

When the five minutes were up, Oracle landed on my shoulder and whispered in my ear that it was time. I opened my eyes, scanning the room. I stood slowly, my notifications pulsing like crazy again. I ignored them, as usual.

There were dozens of bodies stacked on the far side of the room, with eleven prisoners crouched in a line by the wall next to the corpses, looking terrified.

Bane was walking slowly toward me, wiping blood off his dagger. A reasonable pile of gear had been stacked in the middle of the room. Scattered throughout the heap were over a dozen healing potions, food, a load of small coin purses, a couple of bows, some shortswords, and a few bits of armor. Of particular interest to me were the sword and shield, along with the necklace from the promethean I'd fought.

Lastly, there were two dull blue mana potions, and I looked at Oracle questioningly.

"I told them not to interrupt you for that," she said. "They're barely better than water, and we managed to heal everyone with the use of the health potions. It was better to let you get your mana as high as possible."

"Fair enough," I said, passing one of them to Arrin and drinking the second myself, agreeing when I saw it that the miniscule boost to regeneration from such a weak potion hadn't been worth interrupting me for.

"Okay, guys, what did you find out?" I asked Bane and Barrett as they came to a stop beside me, with Bane gesturing to the two bodies of the prometheans. I found it interesting that the other didn't have the same coloring as the promethean I'd fought, but I supposed that races like theirs didn't come in standard features any more than humans did.

"Those two are lieutenants in the harpies' gang. 'The Boss' and his personal guard are much stronger, but he keeps himself hidden away, somewhere that only the fliers can get to. I couldn't get much more than that on their hierarchy, and nobody knows what the Skyking actually is.

"They were told to watch out for the legion scouts, but nobody associated our group of three with them, or at least none who lived to talk about it. They dismissed any groups that weren't made up of two elves and an alkyon. It looks like they basically saw the ladies heading out from here and either thought there might be loot to be had or that it was weird that workers were leaving this section of the city at this time. Who knows, but the women probably made it through. As to the reason they were looking, again, all they know is that they were told to do so."

"Okay, so now what do we do with them?" I asked half to myself, looking them over.

"It's up to you. I'd say kill them all; safest way," Barrett said loudly, winking at me where they couldn't see.

A chorus of pleading voices arose from the group. Venta stepped forward to stand between them and me, bowing her head in submission.

"My lord, you chose to give me a chance, demanding an Oath of obedience. I swore that I'd serve you, then you set me free. You trusted me. Can you not give them the same chance?"

I considered the group: three imps, four alkyon, and four djinn. The imps and djinn especially looked pathetic, as small as they were. The djinn were twelve-to-sixteen-inch-tall variations of short, gangly teens from the waist up, their skin a multitude of colors.

At the waist, they vanished into mist that condensed into a wispy tail. The imps were generally closer in features to the imps of my world's fables: short, muscular creatures that looked like flying demons, complete with bat-like wings, pointy teeth, and horns. They were each covered in tattoos, and as I looked them over, I caught all the imps shaking their head in resignation.

"Why not?" I asked one. It looked up at me, flicking its forked tongue over its teeth nervously.

"We's can't," it whispered, and I gestured for it to go on. "We's owned, body and soul, by Skyking. We's can't swear to another, not without it letting us go free."

"It?" I asked, and the imp went rigid, twitching and moaning. After a full minute of watching the creature convulse, I asked Oracle to heal it, but still it shuddered. Nearly five minutes passed before it was able to speak again, and when the painful effect had finally worn off, the little creature began to weep piteously. Its health was barely ten percent, and we'd been about to heal it again.

"Was that a punishment?" I asked.

"We's not allowed to talk about the master…" it muttered, covered in sweat and panting.

"Are you allowed to talk about the deal you made?" I asked. It cowered fearfully, shaking its head. "Would you swear to me if I got you free of the Skyking?" I asked the imp, and it stared at me in fear for a long series of heartbeats, before finally nodding once, sharply. It tensed up, but after a few seconds without any change, it opened one eye cautiously before relaxing.

"Okay, what about the rest of you?" I asked, and Amaat stepped forward, croaking something at the alkyon. Two of them responded, one glared at the floor, and the final one shrieked something back at him. He gestured from me to himself, then to them. I shrugged, letting him take the lead. While he communicated with them in their language, I ordered Bane up to stake out the alleys neighboring the building, joining Stephanos and Miren on the roof.

Amaat shot forward, grabbing the one who'd shrieked back at him and yanking it upright. He struck its restraints off and threw it at the nearest wall. It slammed into the crumbling brick, falling to the floor. As it scrambled to stand, Amaat pulled off his own armor, revealing his vibrant red plumage and larger muscles.

He made the other birdlike creature look like a pathetic example of the species in comparison, and he drew in a single deep breath, letting out an ear-piercing shriek of his own. The challenger staggered with the force of it, momentarily stunned.

Amaat covered the distance, grabbing it by the throat and hurling it against the wall again. This time, when it fell to the floor, he was there, a taloned foot pinning it to the ground easily.

It let out a weak cry and arched its head back, exposing its neck in submission.

Amaat let loose another almighty shriek, echoed meekly by Venta, the alkyon he had just pinned, and the three who were still tied up. When the last notes disappeared, he turned to me and nodded in satisfaction.

"They'll swear the Oath to you now, my lord. They accept me as their master, and you as mine."

"I'm…you know what? Forget it. That's fine. We can sort all this shit out later, okay?" I said, shaking my head and resolving to set them free when we escaped the city and had time to sort this "master" crap out.

"How about you?" I asked the djinn. They turned to look at each other, carrying out a low-volume conversation while I waited. "Look, I've not got the time to fuck about with this right now, so what's it gonna be?" I pressed after a couple of minutes.

"We will agree to swear, on the condition that you free our mother," one said. He lifted his arms, and the ropes used to bind them fell through to land on the floor as his body became momentarily transparent.

"Nice trick," I said. "Air elemental, right?"

He nodded in reply and flowed slowly forward, lifting into the air so that his body floated a few feet from me. He hovered at eye-level, and he made sure to keep his arms to the sides to show his peaceful intent.

"Yes…we can become insubstantial for a few seconds, but it costs us a lot of mana. It's also the only reason we were captured rather than killed. Your people are fast and vicious."

"Hey, you attacked us, bub," I said, shaking my head. "You don't get to complain because we didn't roll over and die."

"Well…"

"Tell me about your mother." I folded my arms and focused on him.

"She is our Clan Mother, and the Skyking holds her hostage, forcing us to obey," he said simply.

"And where does it hold her?"

"We don't know. We only know that she is held still, and is alive, or we'd feel the bond break."

"Aaaaand you've no idea where? Absolutely no fucking clue?" I asked skeptically.

"We don't. We cannot be compelled by the Skyking to give an Oath, so instead we are forced into servitude by our Clan Mother's captivity. If we knew where she was, we'd already have freed or killed her."

"Killed her?" I asked.

"She is held somewhere and blinded by the power of another. She weeps in the darkness for her freedom, and for her children who thieve, murder, and die. She wishes to be free but would rather accept death than her prison."

"I can't just let you go free until I manage to find a djinn Clan Mother, who might not even exist, for all I know. You know this…right?"

"We know. We accept the risk. You have taken alkyon into your service. We will swear as well, giving our Oath willingly, but only if you give an Oath in return, that you will try your best to free the Clan Mother, or failing that, to kill her."

Congratulations!

You have received a Quest from Xerix: Free Our Mother

You have been asked to free or kill Hellenica, Clan Mother of the Gueric Clan. If you agree to do your best and not to ask the djinn to leave the city without securing her freedom, they will swear a Conditional Oath to you. If you free her, she and her children will swear to obey you for ten years….

Free Hellenica: 0/1

Kill the Skyking: 0/1 – (Optional. If you succeed in this secondary objective, the Djinn will swear for your lifetime instead.)

Reward: Allegiance of the djinn of the Gueric Clan, 62,500xp, Unknown

Accept? Yes/No

I studied him for a long minute before finally nodding. It was another "free the slaves" mission; I just fucking knew it. *Why the hell couldn't I get something nice and simple, like "kill the fucking rats in the bakery cellar" or something?* I wondered inanely.

"It's worth it," I heard Barrett whisper directly behind me. I frowned at him and lifted my chin in question. "The djinn might not look like much, but it's because they get hunted and harvested for magical components so aggressively in the cities, and they usually get eaten in the wild. Those who survive to maturity become damn powerful. If you could gain their allegiance, it could be a huge bonus. They don't expect to survive either way, or they'd not offer so much so easily."

"You think that was easy? Next time, you get to fight the damn promethean," I muttered.

He snorted. "Ah, no, I'm all right, thanks. I'll leave the scary big guys to you."

"Chicken," I muttered.

"Rather be a live chicken than a dead fool!" he retorted, grinning and stepping back.

I regarded the djinn, the imps, and the alkyon, shifting my gaze around to take in the piled bodies and wishing there'd been a way to avoid all this slaughter.

"Okay, Xerix, you've got a deal. You all swear to me, and I'll swear to do my best to free your Clan Mother."

Oracle lifted off my shoulder again, reaching out and directing my mana as the djinn began to speak among themselves, reading the prompt from me.

"We need to change this," Xerix said after a hurried discussion. "It makes no mention of saving our mother or killing the Skyking."

"It's the Oath; you all need to give it," I said flatly, then drew in a deep breath and bottomed my mana out again.

"I, Lord Jax of the Empire, Lord of the Great Tower of Dravith, give Oath to free Xerix and his clan of djinn from the Oath of allegiance they offer me if I do not honestly try my best to free, or failing that, kill Clan Mother Hellenica of the Gueric Clan."

There was a minute or more of silence before the djinn huddled in again, discussing the details of what I'd said. I started to get annoyed, but Barrett gestured to get my attention then held his hands up in a "calm down, just wait" gesture. I gritted my teeth...but waited. Eventually, Xerix floated forward again and bowed his head.

"There are loopholes in the Oath you offered, but we are satisfied that you give it in good faith, and we agree, provided that you swear that you will follow the spirit of the agreement, not just the letter?" he asked tentatively. Barrett covered his eyes and stifled a laugh.

"Very well," I said around gritted teeth, and the djinn waited while I used the dregs of my mana to bind myself further.

"I, Lord Jax of the Empire, Lord of the Great Tower, swear to follow the spirit of the agreement between myself and the Gueric Clan, not just the letter, provided the Gueric Clan and all djinn present swear to me do the same."

A few more seconds of discussion followed, before the group all spoke their Oaths, binding them to the tower and to me.

"I swear to obey Lord Jax and those he places over me; I will serve to the best of my ability, speak no lie to him when commanded otherwise, and treat all other citizens as family.

"I will work for the greater good, being a shield to those who need it, a sword to those who deserve it, and a warden to the night.

"I will stand with my family, helping one another to reach the light, until the hour of my death or my lord releases me from my Oath.

"Lastly, I will not be a dick!"

It didn't take long, and once it was done, I gestured to the djinn and the alkyon that they were free to move around, and I turned my attention back to the imps last of all.

"Now, what do we do with you?" I asked, half to myself, rubbing my chin.

"Jax!" came Bane's voice as he appeared in the trapdoor. I looked up at him and nodded, and he went on. "There's a group headed this way through the streets. A couple dozen of them, no uniforms."

"Watch them and be ready to move if I shout," I called up. Dismissing him, I looked to Amaat and Ven. "Looks like you two are up, so get out there and check it out. Find out if they're gang reinforcements, or if Lydia and the others are returning."

They nodded and took off, flying out of the door and disappearing upwards sharply out of sight, while I turned back to the trio of forlorn-looking imps.

"We's can't swear...we's don't want to die...We go? You lets us go free?" the one who'd spoken before asked hopefully, gazing up at me. Its jet-black eyes remained locked on my own.

"I can't do that," I said slowly, shaking my head. "If I do, you'll tell the Skyking what happened. Then it'll know who I am and what's happened here...so far, all it'll know is that its gang got their asses handed to them."

"We's gonna die, then," the imp said sadly. It tried to struggle with the ropes, but gave it up after a few seconds, slumping down, its friends doing much the same.

"You were constrained by an Oath, but the others weren't. Can you tell me why?" I asked the imp, and it shrugged.

"We's serve the Skyking direct, serves the promos, too, and the dogs. We's be seeing too much."

"You know where the Clan Mother is?" I asked it quickly, and it shrugged again, slowly, as if unsure.

"We's think so. Me no see her though. Only promos go in there."

"Promos?" I asked and then I caught myself. "Promos…the Prometheans?"

"Yup. Promos be assholes. Always shits on poor imps. Hateses us."

"Are the 'promos' always with the Skyking?" I asked, and it nodded. "Okay, and have you ever seen the promos anywhere else?"

"Lotsa times. They leads us sometimes, makes us do things."

"Okay…have you ever seen the promos somewhere when you've not been led by them? Do they all stay with the Skyking unless there's a need for them to go elsewhere?"

"Not know. Sometimes see them with Skyking, then alone, then with Skyking. Not know."

"He doesn't mean 'no'…I think, anyway. He just doesn't understand," Barrett interjected hastily.

"Okay, do you think the promos all live with the Skyking?" I asked the imp. It frowned, then went pale, screeching as pain ripped through it. "Dammit!" I cursed, hunting around. "Quick, give me a healing potion!" Barrett pulled one out and grabbed the imp's arms, pinning him down as I bit the cork off the top and poured it into its mouth.

We ended up giving it a second potion a few minutes later, once the first had elapsed. Thankfully, it was worth it, as the imp lay there, panting and terrified, but alive.

"It's okay," I reassured it. "I'm sorry your Oath hurt you, and I'm not going to ask you any more questions for now. You just rest and recover, and we'll try and come up with a solution that doesn't involve killing you, okay?"

The little creature nodded frantically, and as we released it, it scuttled back to huddle with its friends.

I straightened and looked solemnly at Barrett, just as Amaat and Venta dropped in.

"Lord Jax, the group coming…our people are with them, all of them. I showed myself to Yen, and she signaled it was okay, but to use caution. She's signaled she's not under active threat, but she does not trust the men with her."

"And there's an overwatch flying high above us, too high for just the two of us to reach before they can flee," Venta added, and I growled to myself as I considered it.

"Okay, then, looks like we've got Mal's attention with the group. Ignore the overwatch for now; nothing we can do about it until we know what's happening with the smugglers. How far out are they?" I asked, and Amaat answered.

"Maybe ten minutes. There are a lot of them. A few scouts are running ahead, so they'll be with us sooner, maybe three or four minutes. No other fliers."

"Listen up, everyone!" I said, standing straight and addressing the entire room. "In a few minutes, we're either going to be leaving here to make a deal or fighting again. Either way, we've made enough noise that we can't stay here long before the guard comes to investigate. Gather up anything you don't want to leave behind. Oracle," I said quietly, turning my head to look at her where she sat on my shoulder. "I want you to go as small as you can and hide in my gear. Stay close and stay hidden!"

"I could fit in your pocket," she said, glancing down at the openings at the sides of my pant legs.

I snorted. "Fine, but no playing with anything! There'll be time for that later."

"Promises, promises!" she whispered, shrinking even further and slipping down to hide in the fold of my outer pocket. I couldn't help but wonder at a race of creatures that had pockets built into their armor that led diagonally across to their crotch with an opening over it, and yet apparently were categorically unable to get "it" up without chemical aids…My skin suddenly threatened to crawl off my skeleton at the curiosity of what the previous drow owner of these pants had been doing in them. I resolved to have them washed ASAP. Preferably in bleach. Or acid.

Banishing the thought from my mind, I walked over to the piles of gear that had been sorted from the dead. I didn't have the mana or the time to Examine everything, so I decided to "risk it for a biscuit" and only checked the shield, chucking the rest into the Fenris's storage. Despite being a horse of holding, the cargo space was becoming full enough that I started to worry about it being able to move.

Promethean Heater Shield		**Further Description** *Yes/No*	
Defense		50-60	
Details:		This shield is of promethean design, constructed of multiple thin layers of metal fused over wood, and has a reinforced outer rim. This shield has been enchanted to reduce its overall weight and increase its durability.	
Rarity:	**Magical:**	**Durability:**	**Charge:**
Unusual	Yes	87/100	64/100

I strapped the shield onto my arm and hefted my naginata, finding the combination a bit unwieldy but doable. I guessed I had a few minutes before the main group arrived, so I pulled up my notifications and grinned as I saw one of my favorites.

Congratulations!

Through hard work and perseverance, you have increased your Endurance by one point. Continue to train and learn to increase this further.

I nodded to myself, glad that the pain had been worth it, and moved on, reading and discarding most of them quickly.

Congratulations!

You have killed the following:

- 1x Promethean, level 23 for a total of 5,000xp
- 7x Imps of various levels for a total of 2,800xp
- 2x Alkyon of various levels for a total of 740xp
- 3x Djinn of various levels for a total of 1,125xp

A party under your command killed the following:

- 1x Promethean, level 16 for a total of 8,000xp
- 11x Imps of various levels for a total of 6,600xp
- 14x Alkyon of various levels for a total of 11,500xp
- 13x Djinn of various levels for a total of 9,750xp

Total party experience earned: 35,850xp

As party leader, you gain 25% of all experience earned

Progress to level 15 stands at 150,020/140,000

*

Congratulations!

You have reached level 15!

You have 7 unspent Attribute points and 1 unspent Meridian point available.

Progress to level 16 stands 10,020/165,000

Seeing my new level gain, I cheered internally. It had been a while since the last one, and the fact that I was getting seven points per level, rather than five was more than helpful. The new meridian point was also amazing, and I brought up the options for it while I had a minute spare still.

PRIMARY

Brain: 1/10 Spell Cost Reduction: -5% (Primary Bonus: 1 spell slot per point)
Head: Primary Node: Additional points invested will reduce mana cost by 5%.

SECONDARY

Eyes: 1/10 Vision Improvement (Secondary Bonus: +10% chance to notice important visual details)
Eyes: Important details will glow to your vision. This will level with the relevant skill.

Ears: 0/10 Hearing Improvement
Ears: Important sounds will become clearer with concentration. High levels will aid in translation.

Mouth: 0/10 Vocal Improvement
Mouth: Your voice will become 10% more likely to have a desired effect on a target, soothing, seducing, persuading as required.

Nose: 0/10 Tracking and Detection Improvement
Nose: Scents will be stronger, aiding in tracking.

Heart: 1/10 Health Increase
Heart: You will gain an additional ten points of health for each point invested in your Constitution.

Lungs: 0/10 Stamina Increase
Lungs: You will gain an additional ten points of stamina for each point invested in Endurance.

Stomach: 0/10 Sustenance Improvement
Stomach: You will gain the abilities to resist poisons by 5% and to gain sustenance from more sources.

Legs: 0/10 Speed Increase
Legs: You will gain a boost of 10% to your speed, as well as better stability over various terrain.

Arms: 0/10 Strength Increase
Arms: You will receive a boost of 25% to your carrying capacity and your damage output with melee weapons.

Hands: 0/10 Dexterity Increase
Hands: You will develop crafting abilities at a 10% increased rate, along with a greater chance to succeed in crafting complicated items.

There were several good options for my meridian point, some of which would help in the coming fight, and some of which were more long term, but I'd been complaining about my lack of stamina in fights for weeks which only left one real choice.

With a quick warning to everyone around me, I dumped four of my attribute points into Intelligence, and, hating every second of it but knowing the necessity, placed three in Charisma. That done, I chose Lungs for my meridian point, and accepted all the changes.

After half a minute of pain ripping through my body, I relaxed again, opening the next notification waiting for me.

Congratulations!

You have practiced enough to raise your Meditation skill to level 2. Continue to practice and learn to increase this skill further. Skilled meditation will increase your mana, health, and stamina regeneration levels to realms you cannot imagine.

+2% increase in Regeneration speed per minute spent in meditation.

Once this skill reaches level 10, you may choose its first evolution.

"Jax." At Bane's low call, I dismissed the notification, looking up to find him and ignoring a final prompt regarding the tower's population growing. It was a minor issue for now, considering only the alkyon were new, really; the djinn might not be staying yet. "They're here," he said simply, climbing down and quickly moving out of sight to melt into the shadows.

Stephanos and Miren clambered down as well, closing the trapdoor as best they could, due to the damage from being ripped off its hinges.

We gathered around, making sure we were all as ready as we could be. Weapons drawn and ready for an attack, our archers and Arrin crouched out of sight as much as possible on the walkway overhead. Barrett stood beside me, Amaat and his alkyon team armed again and ready to fly. Bane was out of sight again, no doubt skulking around, and Jian quickly came to stand close by me. As the djinn spread out and took up positions around the room, I gave out a handful of last-minute commands.

Silence reigned for another minute, until forms started moving into the alleyways around the building.

I watched them walking along, casually surrounding the building. A few began heading for the entrance, while easily a dozen stood back, watching the structure with that special brand of arrogance and thuggery that private guards and poorly trained bouncers always displayed.

I stood there, waiting, as they moved aside to allow a much more coordinated group to approach the entrance. There were seven of them, four men and three women. All but their leader appeared human, and the bastard grinned at us as he came close enough to see us inside. He gestured with both arms held wide, and Lydia, Yen, and Ellen were ushered into sight, but not allowed to join us.

He smiled even wider as he motioned for us to come out, the unnerving expression never leaving his face as he indicated the alleyway.

I strode forward, keeping my eyes locked on him and ignoring movement in the shadows nearby, knowing that Bane was watching over me.

I came to a halt five feet from him, staring up into his eyes. The irises were a weird shade of yellow, almost luminous, and the fucker had to be eight feet tall, at least. I'd grown, with all the changes to my body, but this fucker? He towered over normal people. Barrett especially gritted his teeth looking up, considering he was short enough to be declared an honorary dwarf.

"You ask for us, yes?" The big fucker beamed, making my every instinct scream that he wasn't to be trusted.

In addition to his height, he was muscled so heavily that it looked as though a professional rugby player had had kids with The Rock. The only reason he couldn't be called barrel-chested was because it was unfair to barrels.

His skin was a dull red, his teeth sharp and pointed, and he was entirely bald. A ring of small horns around the top of his head made it seem like he'd forgotten which order to put his crown and skin on and had picked wrong.

"Your friends, they ask for you. They say you wish to meet the arena master, yes?" he asked, still smiling like he was mental.

"Yeah…" I said slowly. "I need to speak to Mal. Call me crazy, but I don't think you're him."

"You're crazy," he said, nodding.

"Are you Mal?" I asked, confused, and he shook his head.

"No, but you ask me to—"

"Forget it." I sighed, interrupting him. "Where's Mal?" I asked, and I gestured to the ladies to move inside.

"Ah, no," the creature said, shaking its head and holding its hand out to the side, making some of the group step forward to keep the ladies back from us. "Forgive, but the arena master, he says you come to the arena. Says you will have fun. Your people, they come as well, yes?"

"No," I said flatly.

"Yessss," he repeated. At his gesture, six more people stepped out of the crowd, holding up hands that suddenly filled with fire or lightning. "Arena master, he says 'Tell them come here, and no take no for an answer.' So, I bring enough to make sure you come to the arena, speak to the arena master, and maybe he says you can leave, yes? Maybe he makes deals with you, maybe not. Not my concern.

"Hektor is told 'Go get people,' and Hektor does this. You come with us now, and we lets you keep weapons, keep goods. Fight? Maybe you all dies. Then Hektor takes shiny stick." He nodded to indicate my naginata.

"Maybe you try it, Hektor, and I feed you your horns through your asshole," I said, smiling right back at him as icy anger filled me.

He looked at me quizzically for several seconds as I turned to call out to the others.

"Okay, people, looks like it's plan B. You know what to do." Amaat and his four alkyon burst into flight, hammering up through the trapdoor and out into the slowly lightening sky. Half of the djinn followed them, ready to act as distractions, while the rest moved up to surround me.

"Wheres do they go?" Hektor hissed at me, gesturing to the sky.

"They're keeping watch over us, you fugly bastard," I said, winking at him as I stepped closer. "They see anything they don't like, and they make sure that your asshole and the arena end up looking the same…bloody and badly fucked up. Now, I'm going to tell you what's going to happen here, you dumb shit…I'm coming with you, and so are my people, but that's because I want to meet with Mal.

"Don't be stupid enough to think it's because of your pathetic little gang of animal fuckers. If you try to separate us or try to take our weapons and gear…I'll slaughter each and every one of you." I reached up, and before he could stop me, I grabbed his ear and pulled him down 'til his face was level with mine.

"Believe me, you ugly bastard," I whispered, glaring into his eyes. "I didn't gut that fucking SporeMother, slaughter the drow, or kick the shit out of this gang of harpies just to have you try to screw me over. Give me one fucking reason, and I'll rip your head off and shit down your neck. The deal I'm bringing to Mal, he's not going to give a damn if I gut you on the way, so behave yourself…understood?"

I let go of his ear and turned to the assholes between Lydia, Yen, and Ellen and me, and I slammed the base of my naginata into the ground, sending a flare of magic into it and making everyone step back. "Now, are you gonna get the fuck away from my people, or do I have to slaughter each and every one of you?" I asked, almost conversationally.

Hektor growled something at them, and they backed up as he glared at me, rubbing his ear. He was either smart enough or had been given specific enough orders that he backed off, and I let out a little sigh of relief as I gathered the group.

I ordered that the imps should not be harmed, but they still had to be tied up. We bundled them on Fenris's back, and before long, we were all ready to go. We prepared to leave, but before we could set off, I held up one hand, gesturing into the air…and a few seconds later, we were joined by two more of the alkyon, who brought the remains of the overwatch from the harpies with them. Evidently, they had been able to get the imp before it could get away from their expanded group.

Satisfied at last that the group was no longer being blatantly watched, I nodded to Hektor, and he snarled the orders to get going.

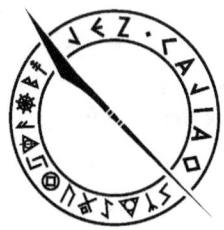

CHAPTER EIGHT

It took about half an hour to cover the distance across the city to the Cloudring district, and it wasn't fun.

The first ten minutes or so, all we got were glares from people who were forced to move by the guards, and with it being either very late at night or very early in the morning, the majority of innocent people were gone from the streets. That left only criminals, rioters, and nightshift workers, who were by their nature a bit batshit. I hoped they'd gone to bed, or work, rather than gone to join the mob, but the closer we got, the more obvious it became that they hadn't.

Soon we came across smashed windows and crap in the street. I mean literal crap; we actually walked past a guy curling one out in an alleyway, and the fucker just stared at us as we went. It took all of my self-control not to lightning bolt the dirty fucker on general principle.

We crossed alleys that were choked with rubbish and less identifiable…waste… and walked along roads that were clearly filled with small businesses, many of which had been ransacked by the mob in passing or damaged by "accident."

We passed buildings that gave off horrific smells and jets of steam, buildings that belched smoke into the skies, and, occasionally, buildings that poured stinking chemicals literally into the gutters and the river that others were drinking from.

We eventually passed a single large building on the edge of the district that was visibly protected by armed guards, including a trio of wolves that looked of similar design to my Fenris automaton. Aside from the glares the guards gave us, nobody else showed us any interest. Clearly, as much as certain members of the mob all around us would like to try something, they weren't going to attempt it with so many of our weapons openly on display.

It wasn't until we crossed a wide street and moved into the next district that things changed for the worse.

The buildings along the path we followed all had their own guards outside, and the closer we grew to the "Cloud District," the more these guards wore masks. They sported long, pointed beaks, wide, wolfish grins, and horned visages that stared at us as we passed. They weren't scary, not at first, but the farther we went, the more cloying the smoke around us became.

I eventually opened my mouth and deliberately drew it in, tasting it, and got a notification almost immediately.

You have been infected with: Weak Hallucinogenic Stamina Poison!

You feel lethargic, confused, agreeable, and relaxed. You will continue to lose one point of stamina per second for the duration of this effect.

Warning!

This effect stacks.
As your exposure to this compound grows, so will your stamina drain.

Time remaining: 7 seconds…6 seconds…8 seconds…7 seconds…

I spat the taste out and glared around at the group that surrounded us. I caught them grinning at each other…but making no aggressive moves.

"There's a poison in the air," I growled, my naginata flaring to life and the rest of my core group moving closer, hands on their weapons. Noticeably, neither the legion nor the locals seemed upset; they just looked at me, confused.

"It not poison," Hektor drawled, rolling his eyes as he continued to stomp on through the smoke. "It Cloudring, what you expect?" He shook his head, muttering about "idiot outsiders" and went on.

"Jax, it's okay. It's just the way it is here…I should have warned you. Sorry," Yen said, moving to my side.

"What the hell is it?" I growled, but I started walking again, with my people following closely around me. Oracle shifted in my pocket, and I swallowed hard, well aware of the slit in that pocket that allowed easy access to Mr. Happy…and I sent her a quick mental communication.

"Behave!"

"Would you?"

"I…well…at least don't play those games now! I need to concentrate!"

"Then concentrate."

I swallowed hard and forced myself to ignore Oracle's movements, sighing in mixed relief and disappointment when she settled back down and relaxed.

"I can read your mind a bit, remember…?"

"BEHAVE!"

Thankfully, she just sent the mental equivalent of a chuckle, while I tried to think calming thoughts and to concentrate on anything but the tiny, sexually curious woman hiding in my pants.

I shook myself and listened to Yen's explanation of the Cloudring.

"It's a drug that they pump into the air here to make people happier, more relaxed, and more willing to spend their coin. The nobles like it because it means more taxes for them, and the Cloudring makes a fortune, as their own workers build up immunity before they're allowed to interact with people. Everyone knows they do it, but nobody cares. The mob went through the south side of the district, and the clouds were turned off there, keeping them angry and aggressive."

"So whoever controls the Cloudring is involved in the rioting as well," I muttered.

She shrugged. "Maybe, maybe not. If they were offered money to shut off the clouds in a single area for a few hours, the local shop owners and bosses wouldn't hesitate."

"Is it just me, or is every fucker corrupt here?" I muttered, shaking my head.

"When everyone else is taking a backhander, and you don't, it only makes you poor," she replied philosophically. "It's one of the reasons we never relax unless we're in the enclave. Our Oaths mean most of it can't happen with us, anyway. However, after we all got 'tarred and feathered' due to the legion general's corruption years back, nobody wants to risk it now. We live in a city that hates us. Who else can we trust, if not each other? Everyone needs somewhere safe."

"Yeah, well, I'm gonna have to see if there's anything I can do about this," I said, leaving her clearly confused.

"Oracle, stop thinking about my dick and concentrate."

"I am concentrating!"

"Yeah...on my dick.... Anyway, I need your help. This smoke, the drug they're putting in the air, it's going to leave us at a hell of a disadvantage in here."

"I know; I'm thinking about it. Problem is, our mana is just too low. Even if we were at full, we could only do something for so long."

"I know, but how about we come up with a spell first, then we can worry about the cost?"

"What do you want it to do?"

"Well, we need two spells, really.... One that's a simple one to clear away the smoke and give everyone a light heal, maybe? Then I've been thinking we need a more powerful one to heal our people in a fight, like the way that Cleansing Fire heals me and damages others. Maybe an AOE healing spell, but one that just targets our people?"

"That's going to be insanely difficult, you know. Think about it. We need a spell that checks on people and decides if they are with or against you? That alone is a pain to create, and we couldn't do it with just the spell knowledge you have. We'd need more; we'd definitely need a specialist healer to help us create something like that!"

"Well, okay...how about the smoke? How about a spell to clear that away and heal its effects on us for now? Maybe tie it to a position? Make it spread out like five meters from a fixed point?"

"Easier if we tie it to you, make you the focal point...maybe ignore the smoke itself. Pushing it out would cost more mana. Just have a localized heal on everyone? Say...five-meter range, with a weak healing effect. It'd cost a lot still, but you could activate it when you need to for a bit...Hmmmm..."

"We could take the secondary weave from the Battlefield Triage spell. You know, the one that sweeps the body for infection? The weak one?"

"Yeah! Hmmm, that'd be useful, actually. It clears away anything that's affecting the body, so if someone's using a potion to boost their abilities, or a buffing spell, it'd affect that. Maybe make it run out faster."

"That could work; maybe we could—"

"Lord Jax?" Lydia said again.

I blinked, having lost myself in the conversation with Oracle. We'd emerged into a square in the middle of the Cloudring district, ringed by manicured gardens and streetlights that gave off a mystical glow. Small creatures flitted about, leaving glowing trails that gently faded. I shook my head in confusion, turning to look behind our group as we began following a new path. This one, like the others, was segmented by vents every few feet, releasing the fragrant, thick smoke to cloud the mind.

We'd just come through a large gate, entering a secure, inner section of the district, people outside the gates peering in, hoping to catch a glimpse of the private areas.

"Where are we?" I asked Yen.

"We're in the Inner Ring of the Cloud District, Lord Jax. This area is generally reserved for those with money or influence or both."

"And the Outer Ring?" I asked.

"Anyone can be in that section, but the real business of the Cloudring is done in here, or so I've been told. It's an invite-only area."

"If your name's not on the list, you don't get in, eh?" I muttered, snorting.

"Essentially. A few other of my fellow scouts and I have had a wander around, but none of us are ever invited into the more…*select* areas."

"Fair enough. Thanks for the info." I gestured to Lydia to move over closer. Yen moved back to give me some space, and I shook my head, pulling her back in close.

"So, what happened when you left us?" I asked.

"Well, it took a little while ta get through the crowds, but we were ignored once we were on the way. We saw a few o' the 'arpies swoop down to look, but they're either better actors than we thought, or they didn't see anythin' in us to interest 'em. When we reached the Cloudring, though, it got a bit different. Ellen said she knew someone that'd be in the south section, so we followed along with the crowd for a bit, blendin' in.

"When we got to the right area, she seemed surprised the smoke was gone, but she took us to a plain little buildin'. She 'ad a quiet word with 'er friends, an' they let us through. Nobody seemed to care about anythin' besides the fact she was alive, and we 'eaded into this inner district. Not long after we got in, we got pulled aside by a group who wanted to know where the other smugglers and the cargo were, but she said she could only tell the Arena Master, an' they let us go. They weren't 'appy, though."

At Lydia's dismissive shrug, Yen picked up the tale. "Once we were inside, we got told to wait, and Ellen was taken off on her own. There wasn't a good way to stop it without making her our prisoner. She was gone about fifteen minutes, when we were summoned to a courtyard. She was waiting for us, and the rest of this group was assembling. Few minutes after that, we were on our way to you. There's not much more to tell."

"Yeah, the big guy, Hektor, kept tryin' to question us about you. He acted all nice and everythin', but 'e wanted to know about our team's skills, and specifically, your fightin' style."

"What did you tell him?" I asked Lydia.

She grinned proudly. "That you were 'ell to face, an' that you killed anythin' an' everythin' that annoyed you. I refused to tell 'im anythin' else. Yen played the star-struck follower routine, said you were just wonderful an' so brave an' all that crap."

"Hey!" I complained, pretending to be hurt. Yen went white and started to explain, while Lydia just snorted and hit Yen's arm.

"Don't believe 'im; 'e likes to wind people up."

“Damn, you’re getting to know me too well,” I said, grinning at her as we turned another corner. A large building came into view at the end of the path.

With the clouds of smoke wafting about, it was hard to see far, but as the building gradually emerged, it became clear that it wasn’t a house, or even a series of small businesses.

The building was made of a yellow stone and formed into a stepped pyramid. Each floor held bordering gardens with flowering plants climbing the walls and dangling from balconies to reach for the floor below.

Torches stood at regular intervals along each level of the construction, and a few people staggered about or passed out on benches, where guards watched over them and glared at the group passing by. The smoke that seemed omnipresent and pervasive over the district was even heavier here. But after a second, I realized that wasn’t true. The smoke here wasn’t heavier than the surrounding areas; it was *stronger*.

Whatever they were using, this was clearly the good shit.

We were led off to the right, passing under a series of arches and through a large pair of double doors that opened out onto a courtyard at the back of the building, hidden away from prying eyes. I felt my hackles rise as soon as we walked in.

The courtyard seemed almost empty. A solitary pair of people stood before us, waiting. One was a huge hulk of a man, covered in a mix of heavy armor and spiked plates. On a lesser man, it would have looked ridiculous. On him, it looked as natural as stripes on a tiger. He stood glaring at us as we filed in, and I noted the way we were funneled into the middle of the courtyard to face him, while our “escort” ringed the outside.

The second figure was a woman, humanoid and tall, dressed mainly in leather. A pair of small crossbows on either hip emitted a glow of mana, indicating that they were either enchanted, or mana-powered devices, like Fenris. She had dark skin, curly black hair that fell to her shoulders, and bright yellow eyes, with the pupils slitted like a cat. While the larger man had gotten my attention on arrival, she was both the real threat and the authority.

I came to a stop before the pair of them and tried not to flinch when the double doors slammed shut behind me. The sound of bolts being driven home echoed around the courtyard, as did a series of sniggers.

I looked up, my gaze attracted by movement, as another dozen men and women of various species stepped out of concealment on the balconies that ringed the courtyard, all with bows drawn and arrows pointed squarely at me.

“So, you killed our people and want to sell us back our own shit, do ya?” the woman asked, one eyebrow quirked, her voice and demeanor cold.

I stepped closer to the pair, and a growl rose from the man. He was covered in weapons, but the steel-backed gloves he wore seemed to be his weapon of choice. He was flexing his fingers and curling them into fists, ready to attack.

I looked around the courtyard a second time, noting that while the archers had their arrows nocked and drawn, their party that had accompanied us were still packed in too closely for them to fire cleanly.

The last detail I caught was that I could see open doors into the pyramid behind them on the ground floor. Nobody would leave a way out that easily accessed if it was a real ambush.

If I ordered a charge now, at least half of us could make it out of the sight of the archers and into the building, but I'd have to be willing to take that loss…

I glanced back, finding the smugglers at the back of the party. Ellen looked scared, but not terrified, and she was still in our midst, not vanished into the surrounding group. It was all enough for me to draw a conclusion that was either right, and we'd move on, or wrong, and we'd end up cutting our way through and losing people. God, I hoped it was right.

"I did kill one of your people; a feckless arsehole called Gar, who tried to tell me my friend's death, *while saving him*, wasn't worth some goddamn wood to burn his body. He chose the wrong time to push me…want to see if this is *your* moment?" I asked, glaring at her and ignoring the big man.

He growled and stepped forward, only to freeze as the tip of my suddenly glowing naginata pricked the skin of his Adam's apple. I looked from him to her, finding that, in the second I'd taken my eyes off her, she'd drawn both crossbows and leveled them at my face. The quarrels rested against quivering, lightly glowing strings as the weapons gave off a faint whirr of mechanical movement.

"Maybe you'd all better calm down." A voice floated down to the courtyard from the second floor, where a man leaned against the wall, a pair of crossbows the same as the woman's pointed down at my people.

"Maybe you'd better tell your people to go fuck themselves…Mal," I called back, guessing that he was the person I'd come to see, if Oren's description of him was remotely accurate.

"Now, now, ain't no need to be like that," he said, still pointing his weapons at us. "Put down your weapons, and we'll do the same."

"Put yours down first," I growled. "We came here to meet you in good faith, and your dickheads started this."

"Ain't gonna happen," he called back warningly. "Drop your weapons, and we'll talk. Best offer you're gonna get."

"Put yours down, and maybe I'll not kill this piece of shit for being so fugly," I replied, pointing my chin at the big guy.

The woman before me snorted and lifted both her crossbows from my face, flicking something on the outside of the weapon. The humming, whirring sound died, the arms of the bow relaxing and folding in.

"He's got a point, Mal. Jay is fucking ugly," she called up, stepping back. "How about you relax now, hmmm?"

"Hey!" the big guy—Jay, I assumed—complained. "Ah'm not ugly! Mah momma told me so!"

"Believe me, she lied," the woman said, shaking her head with amusement before looking from him to me. "Well…?" she asked.

I forced my anger down, feeling Oracle ready to burst out and fight. The mental image of her ripping through my pants to attack the woman made me grin ruefully. Maybe my pocket hadn't been the best place for her.

I looked up at Mal, seeing that he had lifted his crossbows vertically but hadn't put them away. I nodded to him, then stepped back, lifting the tip of my naginata away from Jay's throat. A single bright drop of ruby-red blood welled to the surface to mark the occasion.

"Stand down," I said, and I felt as much as heard the group relaxing. Mal mimicked the woman's movement, retracting the arms of his crossbow-pistol thingies.

"That's it! Show's over, folks! Go get some rest or whatever, but if you're still here in five minutes, I'll be giving you all cleaning jobs, you hear?" The woman gestured to the surrounding force, who started grumbling and moving away, which allowed my people to relax a lot more. "So, how about we go have a chat, and you can explain what happened to Gar. Ellen told us about his death, and while she ain't all choked up over it, he was still one of us, and you ain't."

"Fair enough," I admitted grudgingly. "What about my people?"

"We'll sort them somewhere to relax for now," she responded calmly, flagging down a man who stood close by. He nodded and moved over to open another set of doors that led into the pyramid, and I could smell hot food wafting out from somewhere deeper inside.

"Lydia, go with them and get everyone sorted. You're in charge. Barrett, Yen, you're with me," I said, making no mention of Tang or Bane, both of whom would be hiding nearby. I also neglected to bring up Amaat and his fliers, who I damn well hoped were still on overwatch. "Look after the imps; make sure they're fed and unharmed…for now."

"Yes, m'lord," Lydia said, nodding and gesturing to the others to follow the man into the building.

"Artur, go with her," Barrett said, stroking the goddamn giant white tiger. The beast chuffed at him, then moved to follow her, knocking him with his shoulder as he passed and practically sending Barrett to the floor. "Goddamn cat," he muttered, and the tension relaxed a bit.

Until I locked eyes with the big guy, Jay.

He was glaring at me, breathing heavily and flexing his hands even more, shaking the fingers out, slowly clenching them back into fists and squeezing hard, then repeating, clearly on the edge of control.

"You want something, buttercup?" I asked him.

He blew out a breath and stepped even closer, staring into my eyes. We were about the same size, both just under seven feet, but he had maybe an inch or so on me. Where I'd hammered my Agility and had gone with an all-around build, he'd clearly gone brawler. Heavy slabs of muscle covered every inch of him, and his armor shook with repressed rage and a need to lash out.

"Jay…" the woman said warningly, and he glared at me.

"You an' me…we're gonna have this out. Ain't nobody calls me ugly," he growled.

I raised an eyebrow. "Really? I'd expect you to be used to it by now…buttercup." I gathered myself and met his gaze full-on, wondering if he would back down or attack.

"JAY!" the woman shouted, smacking his shoulder. He glanced at her, then back at me, and slowly stepped back, glaring at me.

I could tell it was the hardest point for him, backing up like that, so I did the sensible thing.

I blew him a kiss.

His face went white with rage, and he lunged, only to be shoulder-charged by the woman into a pillar. I slammed my naginata into the ground, driving the base deep enough that it would stand upright on its own.

I grinned at him, and he shoved the woman aside, her skill being beaten by his bulk, and he charged at me.

He lashed out at my face, a straight jab, followed by a left hook and a few more jabs, making me duck and weave as I backed up. I'd stepped away from my weapon, giving myself room, and I slapped his punches aside, watching him. With him so covered by armor, I couldn't see the muscles bunching, giving away his attacks, but his eyes, red-ringed and enormous, told me plenty, his nostrils flaring as he snorted with each attempt to strike.

I grinned at him, backhanding his latest punch and twisting to slide behind him. I kicked the back of his right knee, grunting and backing away as his backward elbow strike caught me in the chest. My own armor deflected most of the blow, but it was still powerful.

We started circling each other, our moves settling into probing attacks and fast counters, kicks and punches flashing out until I made the mistake of kicking too high, and he grabbed my leg before I could pull back.

He yanked me from my feet, twisting around and lifting me into the air. He spun once to gain momentum, making me feel like a shot put as he released me to fly across the room. My body slammed into a pillar with a crunch.

I fell, landing heavily on my side. Before I could get to my feet, the person I'd most wanted to keep secret was out. Oracle flashed from my pants to hover between us, her hands glowing as she screamed at him in fury.

Lightning crackled from her palms, arcing between them in streamers of liquid light that left afterimages. She slammed her hands together and blasted him from his feet, sending him across the courtyard to clatter into the far wall.

Silence fell, broken only by Oracle's enraged panting, the occasional sizzle and crackle of the spell's remnants grounding out, then the laughter that floated down from above us. I forced myself upright, looking up at Mal, who shook his head, looking down at Oracle, Jay, and me.

"Well, thanks for that, Oracle," I muttered, shaking myself and twisting to pop an ache in my back from my embrace with the pillar.

"He attacked you!" she growled.

I snorted, shaking my head. "I provoked him," I said.

"What?" Her tiny brow furrowed.

"I needed to establish that I wasn't easy meat," I said to her in the silence of our bond.

"Right…"

"And instead, you jumped out and zapped the bugger," I finished.

She went pink, her anger dying away. ***"I ruined it, didn't I?"***

"Not entirely, but next time, I'll warn you first. They know about you now."

"Sorry…"

"It's okay." I stepped forward and pulled my naginata free of the ground. Oracle flitted to my shoulder, and I walked over to where Jay was sitting upright, glaring.

"You used magic," he muttered.

"I'm a filthy cheater," I admitted, offering a hand to help him up.

"Damn right you are," he grumbled, but he took my hand and hauled himself up, nodding to me and walking away into the building.

"Good to see you don't take that kind of thing too seriously," mused the woman, stepping forward and offering her hand. I reached out, and we clasped wrists, shaking once and letting go.

"Where I come from, it's not that big a thing. Glad to see it isn't here, either. You can kick someone's ass, and as long as it doesn't go too far, you can have a beer after," I said, thinking of the Bigg Market in Newcastle, an area notorious for its violence and terrible beer, yet always packed.

I realized I missed it. It might have been full of assholes and watered-down cheap beers and lagers—the brand-name bottles of rum were always filled with as much paint stripper and bootleg knockoffs as real stuff—but it had been home.

"God, I'd kill for a dirty burger and a pint right now," I muttered, shaking my head.

"What's that?" she asked, and I shook my head again.

"It's not important." I banished the thought and looked around the courtyard. Barrett and Yen continued watching me like I was a lunatic as we were led inside and guided to a stairwell leading upwards.

"I'm Soween, Mal's right hand," she offered as we walked.

"I'm Jax, and this is Barrett and Yen," I replied.

After a short ascent, we came out onto the next floor, passing a long bar and heading toward a pair of doors at the back of the room. I nearly grabbed a bottle from the bar as I went but decided against it at the last minute.

"I think I'm going to need that clear-headed spell soon," I sent to Oracle, realizing that the drugged mist had to be at least partially responsible for my willingness to step up and fight Jay, viewing it as no big thing when it could have buggered everything up.

"Ready when you are. It'll take a few seconds to prepare, but I think I've got it worked out," Oracle responded.

We passed through the doors into a small room with a dozen seats spread around it, which took up most of the space. The man I assumed was Mal had taken a seat on the far side, a table next to him. On the table sat a brown, unmarked bottle with condensation running down its sides, and I locked onto it like a homing missile.

The bastard had cold beer.

CHAPTER NINE

"So, seems we've got somethin' to talk about," Mal said, gesturing to the seats across from him. Soween crossed to sit on a seat close to him, but not too close, I noted. She was spaced about ninety degrees from both me and him, but on his side of the room, and she drew both crossbows, nonchalantly setting them on the couch on either side of her.

I sat in the middle of the room, Yen taking up a seat on my left, across from Soween. Barrett plonked himself down on my right, groaning as he pulled his greatsword free to sit comfortably.

"Now, please, Oracle," I said, and she lifted off my shoulder into the air, spreading her hands to either side and glowing with an internal light. She floated in midair, her tiny wings buzzing as the knowledge seeped through our connection into my mind.

The cobbled-together spell was simple and range-specific, I realized by the outline. The basic framework had been torn from my Cleansing Fire spell, as I'd suggested, but instead of laying down a hard barrier that would be patrolled by semi-sentient flames, it simply washed out a breath of air that carried a gentle healing spell. It was weak and would take ages to heal a real injury, but that same weakness meant it could be channeled for significantly longer amounts of time.

I opened my eyes, a faint blue glow in the air as Oracle finished the chant. She settled back down next to me, growing to twelve inches in height as she looked around the room coolly.

"What the hell was that!" Mal growled at us, his crossbows back in his hands. His partner, Soween, rested her hands on her own, glaring at us.

The door behind him burst open, and a blond man erupted into the room, causing us all to go for our weapons in response.

"I felt magic…" he started, then froze as he saw the weapons leveled at him.

"Dammit, Josh!" Soween jumped to her feet and strode to the middle of the room with her arms held out to both sides. "I told you to knock!"

"Okay, this is gettin' outta hand," Mal snarled, and I snorted in response. "Josh, sit down and shut up. Soween, lock the doors, so nobody else decides to join in and start a fight. And you! You don't cast spells without warnin' a body! What did you just do?!"

"We just set up a little healing for everyone. Check your notifications; see if there's anything bad in it at all," I said, noting the way he'd ignored Oracle as a person, presumably viewing her as an extension of me.

"Well, stop it. We don't need healing," he growled.

I smiled, spreading my hands evenly.

"Of course, just as soon as you shut off the smoke. We don't need 'relaxing,' either."

Mal glared at me for a few seconds, then gestured to Soween, who walked to the back wall, sliding a picture aside and pressing a blue gem set in the hidden space. A gentle hum filled the air, and the smoke cleared away.

The sudden combination of the smoke being gone and the effects of our healing spell brought my brain back to full clarity. I straightened, blinking, then cut off the spell. I felt Oracle's annoyance that she'd gone to so much effort to create the spell, only for a few seconds of use, but it had been worth it to me. Mal would have never given up his advantage if he had not been convinced it was worthless.

"So, last time offered. Tell me what the hell is goin' on here, what happened to my people, and why you wanted to speak to me, or get out," Mal growled.

"Sounds fair enough, but it's complicated ...It'd be better told with a beer," I said, sitting forward hopefully.

He paused, eyeing me for a long second, then grunted, leaning to one side behind another chair and pulling a handful out from somewhere. He threw one to each of us, and I popped the cork cap off, taking a swig, ignoring the risk of poisoning or being drugged as I enjoyed my first cold beer in what felt like forever.

I let out a sigh of pleasure, the cold, crisp taste reminding me of a Corona. It was missing only the lime to make it heavenly.

"Right," I said, nodding my thanks to him as I settled back. "This is going to be a bit complicated, but you and I have a few mutual friends. Oren, for one," I said, catching the slight narrowing of his eyes as I mentioned his name. "Oren was captaining a ship that came for me and my people at the Great Tower," I began, filling in most of the pertinent facts. Leaving out only details of our forces, I attempted to make it sound like we were far stronger than we were.

"...so that's how we ended up taking the Great Tower," I finished.

"You're this 'Lord Jax' we've all been hearin' about, eh?" Mal said, sitting back and taking a swig. "What's to stop us from just turnin' you over to the guard? Seems there'd be a right nice bounty paid on your head and all."

"Well, first because you're not a native of the city, as Oren described it. He seemed to think things would end badly for you if you did. Second, there are a lot more reasons why we came to you besides simply finding the entrance to the tunnels...and last of all, because if I can kill a SporeMother one-on-one, do you really think it'll end well for you if you try?" I asked him evenly.

"Tell me what's in it for me and mine," he said after a few moments of quiet reflection.

"First, tell me why Oren never mentioned you being the arena master. He said you were a smuggler," I replied.

"Probably because he's not been involved with us that much of late. I took over the arena about a month back, around the time when he'd lost the runs to the villages. He probably just didn't hear about it. I saw a chance, and I took it: a game of five star with the old arena master. He was down on his luck and put the arena in as collateral."

"You won it gambling?" I asked him. I couldn't help but grin as he nodded and fingered a pocket unconsciously.

"Perhaps there'll be time for a friendly game later, depending on how all this turns out," he said casually.

I realized I had just found a way to level my Luck stat, provided I wasn't too stupid with it. Then I considered that gambling with this man would be fucking insane, as every instinct screamed that he'd have two dozen ways to cheat me if we were both stripped naked and playing underwater, let alone over a beer in a "friendly game."

"I'm aware that the lower-level members of the Smugglers' Guild are required to report anything and everything to a higher authority. As long as they tell you, does that qualify?" I asked, and he nodded. "Good. Then in that case, besides your enforcers—who really know jack shit, I assume—nobody knows that the Smugglers Path is back open for business, right?" He nodded again.

I grinned. "I've not claimed it, even though I have the right to, as I realize it'll be like ringing the bell that I'm in the city. What I'm willing to offer is transferring ownership to you, or to another you designate, once I've got my price."

"What price?" he asked, nodding along as though mildly interested.

"I need to get a few people out of the city and do a little raid while I'm here. Get a few supplies and such," I said casually.

"How many people?" he asked.

"Oren and his crew's families, plus a list of people that Barrett here got from the engineers, from Decin's crew, and from the crew of the *Agamemnon's Wrath*," I said as Barrett pulled a rolled-up list out of his pocket, unfurling it to show dozens of names…most of which had a marker of "and family" next to them.

Mal choked on his beer, spraying it across the room as he calculated the number of people, then sat bolt upright, wiping his chin free of foam.

"Are you insane? How the hell do you think you'll get that many people out of the city!" He choked, and I grinned at him. "Wait, what kinda supplies?" He frowned, reconsidering my request.

"Oh, you know, manastones, food, a variety of metals and building supplies, a forge, smelter, looms, and the kind of equipment we need to start a small settlement," I said nonchalantly.

"How many manastones…" he growled.

My grin widened. "Well, you'll like this, as I hear you and yours hate Barabarattas as much as I do," I said evilly. "I'm thinking, oh, say…all of them? I want to raid his stockpile and rob him blind."

"You're fucking insane," Mal said, and Soween looked at him, clear concern in her eyes, while Josh sat staring at me with his eyes wide.

"Josh, what are our chances?" Mal asked him.

Josh shook his head. "None. I mean *literally* none. Robbing the city lord? Sneaking a couple of hundred people, people that are skilled and important to him, out of the city? And stealing the most important war resource he has? There's no chance!"

"Well…you heard the man. Ain't happenin'," Mal said, shaking his head. I leaned forward, looking at him.

"Really?" I asked. "Because I'm doing this, with or without you, and I'll be taking the legion with me as well. This is going to happen, Mal. Look into my eyes and tell me I won't manage it, because I can promise you right now that I will. The only difference is that you will either be helping me and profiting from it, or you'll be sitting here afterwards wishing you had."

"You're insane," he said, shaking his head but avoiding my eyes.

"Look at me, Mal," I ordered. He frowned, looking at me properly. "You're from Narkolt, right?" I asked him, getting a nod in return.

"The way I hear it, Narkolt was attacked by Barabarattas, not the other way around. Once his battleship is finished, he's going to be unstoppable. The war's a stalemate at the minute, but that won't last much longer. Your home, your friends, are all going to be conquered by that asshole, and seeing what he's done with this city, you take a minute and imagine what he'll do to those people, his enemies, if he does this to his own."

"I don't got no friends there," Mal said stubbornly.

"Bullshit. You might say that, but I don't believe it. But okay, let's pretend for a minute that's true…you don't have any friends there. You have friends *here*. People you've been trying to help. The way I hear it, you've spent a fortune from your smuggling profits by helping to keep the smaller villages going. You've been helping slaves to escape, according to Oren.

"Last of all, you're a smuggler…think your business will do well once the war is over and Barabarattas cracks down on everyone? When his army doesn't have to be on watch, and they can be put to better use by making sure he and his cronies are getting their gold?" I watched his eyes as I spoke, seeing a telltale flicker. "Go on, look me in the eye and tell me you've not been considering exactly that."

"Maybe I have; doesn't mean I need to throw my life away helping you, though, does it?" he said, watching me. "I've not heard what me and mine get out of helping you, just a lot about why I should be damn careful not to draw any more attention."

"What do you want, Mal?" I asked him. "Gold?…A ship and a safe harbor?…Magic? I can provide them all, and more besides. I'm a Scion of the Empire, Mal. The law is what I damn well say it is. Think the legion is following me because I've got a pretty ass? I'm the rightful ruler of this fucking continent.

"I'm going to smash Barabarattas into paste and bring back the empire as it was, not this pathetic remnant you have now. I'll be banning slavery entirely, paying a fair wage for a fair job done, and making sure people can sleep at night without worrying some fucking creature of the night is going to smash the door in and eat their kids. Magic will be available to learn, and people will have some goddamn respect for each other!" I snapped, getting to my feet.

"Look out there, Mal!" I said, gesturing to a doorway that led out to a balcony garden. I strode out, and grumbling, Mal and the others followed me.

"Look at the city; actually look at it!" I gestured out into the early morning as smoke rose from fires in the distance, the haze of the Cloudring preventing any visual accuracy. "They're all at each other's throats…all the people in the city are desperate, stabbing each other in the back, stealing a crust of bread because it's them or their victims. None of them have anything, except for those bastards."

I gestured to the other side of the Cloudring, where the palaces of the nobility rose up the hill, and Barabarattas's keep loomed behind them. "The nobility have plundered the people until they've got nothing to lose, then they've set them against the legion, all so those shits can have a nice place to moor their fucking yachts."

I pointed out a ship that flew on a constant circuit around the city, soldiers visible on its decks and cannons pointed downward.

“Even there, the soldiers aren’t *‘protecting the city’*; they’re protecting the nobility *from* the city! Look at all of this, Mal. Look at it, and tell me this is something you’re proud to be part of. My people are free. They swear an Oath to me and to the tower, and it’s not fucking complicated. There’s no sneaky shit in it…here, see for yourself.” I concentrated, pushing an offer to join the tower to him. I knew he wouldn’t take it, but if I could just make him *see*…

“I don’t expect you to join me, Mal, not yet. Just read it, think about it. See the potential of what your life could be, if you weren’t getting fucked over every time you turned around, if you didn’t have to constantly worry about who’s coming after you.”

“Who’s comin’ after me? Damn few of ’em right now, but if I joined your fight? A hell of a lot more would be! If I help you, I’d be burnin’ my bridges. I’d lose my home, my business; hell, my people would be hunted, all for helpin’ you! Seems to me, we don’t need you half as much as you need us.”

“I do need you. I need you all. I need my brother, who disappeared near here a month ago. I need soldiers, I need merchants, I need smugglers, and I need farmers. I need *people,* Mal!” I gestured to him, Soween, and Josh. “I need you all, and I’m willing to pay for your help. Just think about it. That’s all I ask.”

“We’ll talk about it, but don’t go gettin’ yourself excited just ’cause I didn’t say no straight away. I might lead ’em, but my people have a say, and I don’t see much they’d be likin’ in all this.”

“Just consider it, all right?” I said, deflating slightly with the sudden awareness of how much I’d been talking, raving almost. I was shit at speeches, I knew I was, so why the hell did I have to convince people of shit all the time? Why couldn’t I just drink and fuck and fight? Those, I understood.

“We will…and we’ll sort rooms for you and your people for the day. We can talk tonight,” Soween spoke up suddenly.

I caught the look Mal gave her. He was surprised.

“Thank you,” I said, nodding. “I’d kill for some sleep right now, then I’ve got some goods I need to sell. You interested, or shall I go to the merchants?”

“What kind of goods?” Mal asked sharply.

I grinned at him. There was still something in the smuggler’s cargo that he wanted, at least.

“Mostly shit I looted along the way. We’ll keep the stuff I looted from the drow for now, just in case you want to make a deal later. The rest, the weapons and such, I’ll need to trade, as I need to get some gear while I’m in the city.”

“What of the smuggler’s goods, which are the rightful property of the guild?” Mal snapped, looking at me suspiciously.

“I’ve got most of that, but you’d have lost all of it to the drow if not for me. Since I am already offering you rightful ownership of the Smugglers Path, I think we can come to some sort of agreement?” I said, grateful for the fact that no one could get any of it out of Fenris without my knowledge or consent.

“Hmmm. Well, Josh will show you to the guest quarters. Me and Soween got to have a chat now, see if there’s any part of this we want in on.”

“Sounds good. Thanks, Mal, for the conversation, and the beer,” I said, standing and reaching over. He gripped my wrist, and I felt him squeeze hard. I squeezed right back. We held the grasp wordlessly for a few seconds, both of us squeezing harder, until I said in a tired voice, "Seriously, dude, if it's dick measuring you're going for here, I'd better warn you. My nickname's Tripod, and it's not because I'm surprisingly fucking stable, okay?"

Mal snorted and let go of my arm, shaking his head. I grinned at him and followed Josh out of the door, Yen and Barrett following along silently.

We passed down a flight of stairs, across a few corridors, then down another flight, descending deeper underground. A few minutes later, I was led out into a small corridor with rooms on either side, the first two of which housed Lydia and Jian.

"I'll leave you here, then. There's, uh, water in the jugs and…you know," Josh said, looking a bit uncertain when Lydia and Jian appeared, still fully armed and armored. I had noticed that he couldn't keep his eyes off Oracle as we walked. He'd barely said anything, just stared at her, until we'd reached the guest rooms.

"That's great. Thanks, Josh," I said, waving him off as I walked forward.

"How was it?" Lydia asked once Josh had left and we'd checked out the little suite of rooms, comprised of a large common area surrounded by numerous doors, each of which led to bedrooms.

Most of them held either two or four beds. The largest, at the farthest end, also contained a small private garden, which the others had generously set aside for me. I let out a grateful sigh as I relaxed into a chair in the sitting area, Lydia checking to ensure the doors and windows were all sealed tightly.

"It went about as well as we could expect," I said, giving a little shrug. "I need some sleep, then we can start going out into the city. Maybe do it in two groups, so it's safer?"

Lydia nodded. "Jian and I are on watch now. We'll be wakin' the next watch in a few hours. Get some sleep, an' don' worry about the details. You've been fightin' and runnin' fer the last couple o' days straight."

I closed my eyes, taking a deep breath, and felt myself sway slightly. The fact that, as soon as we'd left Mal's office, we'd been breathing the smoke in again, didn't help the exhausted feeling. I nodded to her, forcing my eyes open and standing up.

"So have you, Lydia…but thank you," I said, reaching out and putting a hand on Lydia and Yen's shoulders and squeezing, looking at Barrett to make sure he knew I was including him. "Thank you all. I couldn't have done this without you. Get some rest as soon as you can.

"Once people are starting to feel a little more like themselves again, split the group into two. Let people go out and find their relatives, if they can be quiet and subtle. No fucking parties. Stay hidden. If they can't do that, keep them on lockdown for now. Get some rest, though. I get the feeling this will be our only chance for a while."

The others nodded and filed out. Lydia closed the door behind her as Oracle flew down from my shoulder. My companion gracefully sat on the edge of the bed to watch me pull my armor off. Walking into the bathroom, it was a damn pleasant surprise to find an actual toilet, as well as a sunken bath, and I made full use of the facilities while Oracle gave me a few minutes of privacy.

When I checked the bath, it was cold, but even that wasn't going to stop me. Not when it was my first chance at a proper bath in what seemed like forever.

Oracle flew inside, and I smiled at her tiredly, then stripped off, dumping my clothes and gear on the floor and wading into the water.

The bath had steps on one side that I walked down, shivering when my undercarriage met the cold water, but I wasn't stopping. Not when I had the chance to be clean again, rather than making do with a goddamn sponge.

I settled onto the bottom, gritting my teeth as the water washed up to my neck. I swore I felt my asshole pucker—the water was that cold—and I gasped when Oracle threw something into the water in front of me, splashing my face.

When it bobbed to the surface, I let out a sigh of relief at the sight of a grey lump that started to foam slightly. I climbed out and sat on the side of the bath, scrubbing myself from head to toe, suddenly wide awake and shivering as I tried to rid my skin of the grime of battles, blood, and sweat. It was both gratifying and disturbing to watch the water turning cloudy with filth.

Eventually, I let out a contented sigh. I felt thoroughly clean, if damn cold, for the first time in forever. I turned to find Oracle sitting there, watching me, as she had done throughout my entire bath.

"I'm surprised that you behaved yourself," I said to her, half joking, half complaining.

"I thought you needed that." She shrugged, rising to her feet and taking advantage of my now fully regenerated mana bar to shift and blur into full human size. She stood before me, clothed in a simple white chemise, her wings gone, and she lifted a hand out to me. I rose to my feet, pulling her into my arms, leaning down and kissing her soft lips.

She smelled of vanilla and coconuts today, and her skin was softer than silk. The feel of her firm muscles as I picked her up in my arms and carried her to the bed, made me very conscious that, in any right and sensible reality, she'd be miles out of my league.

We kissed again, and the cool, whisper-thin satin of her clothing vanished.

I opened my eyes, gazing into hers, and smiled into the perfect sky-blue irises staring back at me. I reached up and brushed her hair back from her face, and I kissed her yet again, drinking in the vision of her.

She was quite simply the most stunningly beautiful woman I'd ever seen, but the reasons I had fallen for her weren't her figure, her looks, or the fact that she could shift to become whatever fantasy I'd settled on that day.

It was her soul. Her mind, and who she was, in every way. Her personality, the kind and sweet side of her that wanted to love and protect the realm from all possible ills. The way she loved to ride around on Bob's head, the way she grew enraged to the point of insanity at cruelty, and would gut those who hurt the innocent, but would also be distracted by something shiny.

The paradoxical mix of fury and softness, rampant sex kitten determined to play and sensible schoolteacher discussing magic, all made up who she was. I'd never met anyone like her, and I had accepted now that I loved her. I loved her fiercely.

I opened my mouth to tell her so, when shouting erupted down the hallway. We froze, staring into each other's eyes and praying that it was a mistake, that…

"Lord Jax! We need you!"

"Goddamn motherfucking ass…"

The fact that Oracle could swear like a fucking sailor also helped, I reflected. As I got up, she shifted to her smaller flying form, wings erupting into existence as she continued to curse, heading towards the door.

CHAPTER TEN

"What the hell's going on?" I growled, stomping out of my room while cinching the belt tight on my pants. I was still naked beyond that, and my hair and beard were obviously soaking wet.

"I'm sorry, milord! This man says he's come from Mal, and that we have to go with him right now," Lydia said, still in full armor but bleary-eyed, like she'd just woken up.

I looked past her, trying to block out the sight of Jian in his tighty-whiteys as he stood alongside Stephanos and Yen, who were evidently taking their turn on guard duty.

Beyond my people stood Jay, the enormous melee fighter I'd brawled with earlier, and he looked *pissed.*

"You! Mal says yer gotta come with me right now an' sort this out. Says the Skyking and the harpies are comin' fer yer!"

I waved at him. "Yeah, okay, give me a few minutes to get dressed, and we can sort this shit out."

"No, Mal said—" he started, and I cut him off.

"I doubt he wants me half-naked, and it'll take a few minutes to get to him either way, so you can damn well wait two more while I grab some clothes," I said, returning to my room and gathering up my gear as quickly as I could.

I pulled my clothes out of my bag of holding, sorting out the three pairs of pants and two tunics that fit the drow armor. I reluctantly sniffed them to find the least dirty and damaged. My skin crawled at the thought of putting filthy clothes on over a clean body, but I didn't have much choice.

By the time I'd found some reasonably clean undercrackers to wear under my pants, put the pants back on, and started getting dressed properly, the voices in the hallway were getting out of hand.

I stuck my head out and saw Jay shouting at Barrett, whose head barely reached past his sternum. Barrett had equipped his two-handed greatsword, though, and it looked like things were going to get out of hand, until I spotted Oracle's furious face. She'd obviously had plans for our time alone, and I could see the tell-tale signs of lightning crackling across her fingertips even at this distance.

"Jay! Stop being a dick. Oracle! If I have to come back out here again, I'm gonna be pissed off, so I expect to find someone twitching and pissing themselves from a fuckload of lightning if I do. Understood?"

"Happily!" she said. Jay spun to look at her, eyeing the buildup of power cracking across her hands and swallowing hard.

"Good! Now, two minutes, then I'll be ready. Lydia, Yen, you're with me. Barrett, get everyone back on watch or rest." With that, I slammed my door, feeling my anger mounting now that I knew we weren't under attack.

I checked my markings, seeing they were healing nicely and grunted, finishing dressing quickly.

I was sooo close! We'd crossed *that* line, and we were finally going to do it, when some fucker interrupted, and my sexy time was taken away. The more I thought about it, the more furious I became.

By the time I walked back out into the hall, my naginata was glowing with a crackling blue-white light, and streamers of power lifted from it with every step I took. I locked eyes on Jay, who swallowed, then stepped back, gesturing to the corridor behind him.

"Mal's this way," he said, his voice much less aggressive and demanding, setting off, and we followed.

It took until I was nearly across the building before I managed to dampen down my anger. It took the sight of Oracle, furiously glowing and flashing with the same power, to make me realize our bonded emotions were feeding off each other. I forcibly tamped it down to manageable levels, and Oracle landed on my shoulder again, drawing in deep breaths and trying to master her own anger. The sight of her bouncing chest at eye level did wonders to distract me.

By the time we entered Mal's office, I was able to think again, and managed to not stab the man on sight.

"What the hell did you do!" he roared at me, poking a finger at my chest. I slapped it aside and glared into his eyes, which filled with a mix of fury and fear.

"I had a fucking bath!" I growled at him, and the room went silent as everyone considered the apparent non-sequitur.

Jay glowered at me from the corner where he leaned against one wall. Josh, looking concerned and chewing on a fingernail, sat next to a stoic Soween. I eyed Mal's own disheveled state, who looked like he'd also dressed in a hurry.

I turned and sat down, running my hands through my hair and beard, trying to get them into some semblance of order as I took a deep breath.

"Okay, Mal, let's take it from the top, shall we? I left you in a calm, collected mood, and I went and had a fucking bath. You clearly found something out since then, and you're suddenly furious with me, so how about you tell me what it was?" I said, trying to be reasonable.

"I got a message from the damn Skyking! That's what happened…here!" he snarled, throwing a piece of parchment at me. As I caught it, I noticed something I'd missed earlier in all the excitement. Under a chair on the far side of the room, the corpse of an imp lay on its back, three crossbow bolts protruding from its chest.

I looked from the corpse back to Mal and saw the fury in his eyes. That hint of fear remained, and I nodded to him then looked down at the note.

Arena whelp,

You give succor to my enemy. I send my creatures to collect them. You put them on roof tonight, with all gold and smoke-herb, and I let you live.

Skyking

"Well, isn't he fucking articulate," I muttered, looking up at Mal and the others. I stood up and shook my head. "Look, once we arrived in the city, I sent one of my men to scout the area, and he was attacked by the harpies. We sent the ladies to you, and while we waited, we were attacked by a fuckton of the little bastards. We killed most of them, captured a few to question, then your glamorous assistant Hektor arrived, and we came here. That's it. We didn't find out why the harpies were hunting my people, just that they were told to find any legionnaires out of the enclave."

"It's the legion? Not the rest of you, just your legionnaires they want?" he asked me, turning to glare at Yen.

"I can leave, my lord," Yen said to me. "I can try to make it to the enclave…"

"No," I said flatly.

Mal glared at me. "You don't get to make that choice," he growled.

I stepped up close to him, glaring right back. "If you want one of my people, you go through me first," I whispered to him, heat rising through my body as it prepared subconsciously for the fight.

"You can't win against the Skyking!" he snapped. "Right now, we can give her up, and maybe it'll leave us alone. Ain't nowhere safe from that thing in the entire city. Those damn prometheans will come tonight, and if she ain't sat up there, ready for them, they'll tear the arena apart to find her. I'm not riskin' my people for her."

"You're not risking anything for her," I said coldly. "You're risking it for me and for your freedom. I don't care what they offer. You don't get to give one of my crew up. No chance."

"I never said I'd join you!" Mal snarled.

I lifted my eyebrow at him in question. "Really? Seems the Skyking thinks you have, and it wants all your gold and drugs to just leave you alone now. Tell me, Mal…what happens after you feed that thing all it wants? What's gonna stop it from coming down here after you, from taking the arena for itself? What, you think it'll just leave you alone?

"Or if one of the gangs is after me and my people, that the others won't be?" I snorted, shaking my head, and stared into his eyes. "You know the mob was whipped up to hurt the legion, and it won't stop there. Whoever is out for them will keep going until they're all dead. Now someone's told them you're on my side. Word's going to spread, and you know it."

"You think you can trap me? You think I'll just go along with it? Boy, you know how frequent I'm chased and hunted? I spend my whole damn life on the edge of the wheel!" he snarled, fingers stroking the butt of one crossbow as he watched me.

"Fancy trying it on the inside some day?" I asked him.

"Like your path's any easier?" He snorted. "You, who's pickin' fights with the damn city? You think I don't know you've got no fighters? What kinda lord comes into his enemy's city, thinkin' he can win with a few raggedy men?"

"A desperate one. One who could do with your help, Mal," I said.

"I still don't see what's in it for me, boy. Me an' mine need this like a hole in the head! You brought the goddamn Skyking down on us!"

"You killed its messenger," I said.

"It said something I didn't like."

"Have I said anything you didn't like?"

"Repeatedly."

"Why haven't you shot me yet, then?"

"You want to be shot?"

"Not particularly."

"Then why the hell are we still talkin' about this?" Mal threw his arms up and stalked away to throw himself into a chair.

"You started it," I said, sitting down.

"Soween, tell him," Mal said as he pulled a beer out, cracking its top and taking a swig.

"We're interested, but there are conditions."

"Go on…"

"First, we get paid regardless. If it goes wrong, and you die, we still get our gold. Second, we get magic. Josh needs a lot of it, so we're wantin' five spells. Last, we want a ship."

"A ship?"

"An airship. You said you've got some. We've got some people who can fly, and the rest we'll figure it out. We want an airship: fully loaded, cannons, all of it, and we get repairs done for free," Mal said, cutting in.

"You expecting to get damaged?" I asked.

"I wasn't expectin' to wake up today. Make it up as we go along, some days."

"How much gold?" I asked.

"Ten thousand."

"Ha! No. Try again," I said, sitting back and shaking my head. "And pass me a damn beer."

Mal pulled one out and threw it over, pulling two more out for Yen and Lydia as well. Yen declined, but Lydia popped the top off hers and guzzled it down in one go.

"Damn, girl, take the time to taste it!" Mal said, shaking his head and chucking her the second one, which she caught and relished.

"Okay, five thousand gold," Soween said.

I shook my head. "You've got gold here, or you'd not give a damn about the Skyking threatening you. I'll give you a ship, I'll let you choose two spellbooks from, say…ten different spells, and I'll give you a single memory crystal. It'll be of my choice, but I guarantee it will be useful to you, not fucking astrology or something like that."

"Stars do be interestin'…" Mal muttered, rubbing his chin. "Okay, let's say we agree to that. It'll take a few days to get everything sorted, and I need time to plan, time to get people in place. Skyking won't give us that time, not unless we give it a reason to do so…how good are you with that thing?" he asked, nodding to my naginata.

"Pretty good, why?"

"Need to be more than 'pretty good,' if you're going to survive the arena."

"What fucking arena?"

"The one we're sittin' on, of course!" Mal said.

"What the hell would I need to fight in the arena for?"

"Well, let's just say there's a painless way for me to get the time I need to sort all this out…"

"Painless?"

"Well, yeah…for me."

"I'm going to be fighting in the arena, aren't I?" I asked.

"If you're as good as you say, then there's no issue. You killed a SporeMother, right?"

"With help."

"You didn't say that before."

"You didn't fucking ask."

"Well, maybe you can have some help in there, depending on what they put forward for you to fight. There are some gladiators and people booked in already. We start off a bit tournament, say four nights of fights, and that'll give me the time I need.

"We tell the Skyking it can put in some fighters; maybe contact the other gangs, say we caught you, and they can put in one each to try to kill you. They pay a fee, we make some gold. Everyone wins."

"Except me, the guy who has to do the fighting."

"You don't win, you don't got nothin' to worry about. I'd call that a damn relief, personally."

"There are times I'd agree with you, got to admit," I said, shrugging. "What do I get out of the whole 'fighting for my life in the arena' deal?"

"Well, I'll put some bets on for you, less a little 'handler's fee,' and you'll get to live long enough for me to pull this shitty plan together."

"I could go hide somewhere the harpies can't find me," I suggested.

"Only place you could hide would be the enclave, and they already want to smash it. Think you being there will help or hinder them?"

"Fuck."

"Yup."

"Jax, seriously, you can't be thinkin' o' agreein' to this?" Lydia interrupted.

"Why not?" I asked. "He's got a point that makes sense."

"Then let me do it. We don't even know if it's us or the legion team that the 'arpies are after!"

"Doesn't matter," I said, sitting forward and stretching to crack my back.

"It doesn't matter?" she asked, staring at me.

"Nope. They swore fealty, same as you did. That makes them my people, and anyone who's out to get you goes through me first."

"That's not how it's supposed to be!" Yen said, speaking up and shaking her head. "We're the legion and your guards. They have to get through us to get to you, not through you to us! You don't protect us—"

"No," I interrupted her flatly, looking at both of them. "This is exactly how it's supposed to be. My life for yours. I live to protect you all. I might have to let you lay down your life at some point, in order to save others. But the empire exists to protect the innocent, and as the heart of the empire, I exist to protect you. All of you, even that fugly piece of shit, Jay."

"Hey!" Jay complained.

I grinned, as did the rest of the room at seeing how pissed he was.

"Oh, and no magic," Mal said calmly.

"What do you mean 'no magic'?" I asked warily.

"I mean, no goddamn magic in the arena, not until the last night, if then. Most legionnaires don't have access to it. Just the scouts and a very rare few others. If you're gonna pretend to be a legionnaire, you dress like 'em, and you fight like they do. None of the magic shit; that way, we all get to play the part of your captors, and we can rack up a sweet pot in bets on the fights."

"Well, that's just fucking peachy," I muttered, but I understood where he was coming from. "I need a few extra things from you, if this is going to work," I said to Mal.

"Like what?"

"I need to visit a couple of shops, and I need to find a healer, specifically one who chose the Path of the Reconstructor. I also need to get to the legion enclave; I have some details to hash out with them. I need you to bring some people here to meet with me in secret and take Barrett to meet up with others. These people don't know we exist, so they must be given the choice to come with us, to join their families in the tower. Lastly, we need to check out the slave traders."

"Why do you want those scumbags?" Josh asked, frowning.

"Because we're going to rob the fuckers blind," I said with a smile. "Make no mistake, what we do over the next few days won't be easy, but when we pull it off? We're going to cripple the city of Himnel. They'll have no choice but to sue for peace, especially since the best way to get the gear out of here is to steal a few airships. We'll raid the shipyards and draw attention that way, while the people escape down the Smugglers Path."

"I'll see what I can do," said Mal, and he nodded to the balcony. I took the hint and stepped out, realizing that I was seeing the city for the first time in proper daylight. Mal followed me out, the others staying inside.

"Now, tell me the truth; what's in this for you? You aimin' to be the next emperor?" he asked me, his voice low and cold as he stared at me. "Tell me the truth, son. I need to know."

"What do I want?" I echoed and shrugged, shaking my head. "Truthfully, Mal, I was kidnapped and offered the choice to come here to open a portal for the ancient nobles to come back or die. I found out that my brother was kicked through to this realm five years ago, and I want to find him.

"I want to have a good life, drink some beer, have some sex, chill the fuck out and relax, but I can't do that. I can't just sit back when people are getting hurt, not if I can stop it."

I sighed, shifting around and leaning against the railing as I thought about his question and the best way to answer it.

"I can make a goddamn difference here, Mal. I've got kids back at the tower who were slaves. They run around, and they laugh and play now. They have a chance to grow up and be free, to be better than we are. I couldn't live with myself if I just looked out for myself. I don't want to be in charge, but considering the other options? I'm not going to step down. I'm not going to let dickheads like Barabarattas just do whatever they want."

"That's real pretty, but it don't answer my question."

"Then, no, I don't want to be the emperor," I said, and I felt Amon wake inside my mind, shaking and grumbling. "But…for better or worse, I'm going to rule my lands. I'm going to enforce the empire's rules and raise the legion back to what it was. I'm going to ban slavery, and I'm going to have a goddamn safe land where people can go to bed and have a reasonable expectation that tomorrow won't be worse than today.

"I don't want to be the emperor. Hell, I don't even want to be a lord, but I'll do whatever I have to, and if that means I *have* to be the next emperor, then I will. Just don't expect me to like it."

"Seems to me you don't want much," Mal grunted.

"Hey, you asked," I said with a nonchalant shrug. "Now, I was honest with you, so it's your turn. Why are you considering helping me?"

He shrugged as casually as I had. "Maybe I'm sick of the way things are, and I just wanna be out there again. Maybe I liked drivin' a caravan and doin' deals. Maybe I'm sick of the slavin' and the murder that goes on, or maybe I just wanna make some gold, take a ship, and fuck off, and this is the best chance I see for that."

"Fair enough. It's a shitty world, Mal."

"Always has been, son."

"Meh," I muttered, too tired to argue over how the empire used to be. "Look, I'm going back to my room, and I'm going to get some sleep. Think you can find me that healer?" I asked.

"I'll have Jay come wake you when it's done. Maybe take a couple hours. Woman I think might be able to fit what you're lookin' for don't see new clients often. She's a bit…eccentric."

"Great…just what I need. Another nutjob in my life," I grumbled. I turned and started to walk back inside, when a sudden thought stopped me. "Oh, quick question: I heard you had a spider's head in here?"

"Yeah, one of the rare ones popped up a while ago, all black and red. One of the boys killed it and made me a gift of its head. Hung it in my office. Why?"

"Get rid of it. Fast," I told him shortly. "Make sure there's no trace of it on you or any of your people you like. Use chemicals to get rid of the smell, all of it."

"Why?" he asked suspiciously.

"Because I made a deal with their queen, and she gets pissed about anyone killing her sentient daughters…and she's about the size of that building." I nodded toward a structure that was just visible through the smoke and fog of the city.

"Seriously?" he asked, then shook his head. "I don't wanna know about the deal; just tell me it doesn't involve feedin' me and mine to it."

"It doesn't, and so long as you get rid of any evidence of her, they won't have a reason to ask for it, either."

"Deal," Mal said, and I gestured to my crew as I reentered the main room. "Okay, let's try this again. Bedtime, people." I started to lead them to the door. "Oh, and Mal?" I said, looking back at him. He quirked an eyebrow. "You have anyone that does washing and repairs? I think we all need some clean clothes."

"Yeah, we've got a guy here who does it. Josh, send him to their rooms," Mal said distractedly, waving us off and already talking to Soween in hushed tones before we left the room. This time, nobody followed or led us back down, but we found our own way, as it wasn't far.

A few minutes later, a small, fastidiously dressed man turned up in our common area. We loaded him down with our stinking clothes, and he scuttled off, looking sick but promising that the clean gear would be back by tonight.

I closed the door to my room, and Oracle flew from my shoulder to sit on the edge of the bed, smiling at me hopefully.

"Look, Oracle, I desperately want to, believe me, I really do, but not now. I can barely keep my eyes open…okay?" I entreated her blearily.

"Okay…but next time?" she said, a little cross at the delay, but clearly understanding.

"Next time," I promised her, stripping off and climbing into the bed. I felt her brushing my hair back from my eyes and stroking my beard as the world went dark, and I slipped into a deep and dreamless sleep.

CHAPTER ELEVEN

I woke again in the early afternoon, the sun slanting across my face, and I rolled over, groaning.

"Jax, you need to wake up," Oracle said, and I pulled the pillow over my head.

"Nope. Not gonna do it," I mumbled, loving the feeling of an actual, honest-to-goodness, goddamn pillow. It'd been so long!

"Mal sent word ten minutes ago; the healer has agreed to see you in an hour. I let you sleep as long as I could."

I pulled the pillow back from my face and squinted up at her. She had changed again, back to full size. Her hair was long and black with a hint of purple, curls and waves of it running down her back, and her eyes were a deep brown. Her face was…perfect, and as I looked down from her ruby-red lips, I couldn't help but wake up a lot more.

She was naked and poised on the edge of the bed, right within reach.

I rolled over to face her fully, reached up, and wrapped my arms around her. Pulling her down, she slid across my body like silk. Her skin was warm, and her breath sweet as her lips met mine, the feel of her body firm and glorious where I cupped it, and we both felt me rise to the occasion.

"Ah, ah!" Oracle said, putting one finger on my forehead and pushing my head back as she gently but firmly disengaged herself from me and my wandering hands. She rolled aside and jumped out of the bed before I could grab her, moving back to lean against the wall. Letting me drink in the full view of her, she grinned at me.

I pulled the blanket aside, allowing her to see me fully in return as I stood up. I moved to her with one thought firmly in mind, a thought she could see very well, I damn well knew.

She lifted both hands up, wrists crossed, and held them against the wall over her head. I took them in my left hand, pinning her there as we kissed, and I stroked her hair back with my right hand.

I moved from her lips, to her cheek, to her ear, and down to her neck, lightly trailing kisses as I went. I staggered when she suddenly became incorporeal, making me fall forward as she *shifted* back to her usual twelve-inch self and flew around me.

"What the…?" I grunted, shocked, as my blood-starved brain tried to come to terms with what had just happened.

"We've got less than an hour now to get you to that healer," Oracle said huskily, shaking her head as she backed away from me. "And you doing *that* isn't going to get us there any faster!"

"But I thought…I mean, you wanted to," I mumbled, trying to make sense of the horrible concern that I had made a mistake. Had I misread her, or didn't she want me now…or?

"Oh, no," Oracle said, flitting up to hover before me, still naked. "I want to, and you can't imagine how hard that was to stop," she said, then made a point of looking down delicately. "Okay, maybe you can understand how *hard*, but still…I love you, Jax. I have to do what's best for you, and getting you healed now, before anything else happens, rather than screwing your brains out, is what's best."

"Whoof," I muttered, shaking my head and trying to get my brain engaged. "Okay, but…"

"Later." She nodded vigorously. "Believe me, *definitely* later."

"Now I need another cold bath," I muttered, shaking my head as I walked into the bathroom to relieve myself.

I glanced at the sunken bath and shuddered at the color of the water. I decided I really didn't need it that much. There's nothing like a scum of blood, sweat, and dirt floating across a bath you'd been considering dipping into to kill the mood.

I dressed quickly, wearing the same filthy, stained clothes as I had the day before, hoping the rest of the clothes would come back soon. I made sure everything was packed away in my bags, just in case, and headed out.

Lydia and Yen were waiting in the corridor, as was Stephanos. The rest were out in the city already, either visiting family or having some "downtime," albeit after a very stern talking-to by Barrett.

"You all ready?" I asked them, receiving a variety of nods in reply. "Glad to see it. Right, let's check in with Mal on the way out, see where this healer is." I started toward the door, and Lydia and Yen followed along. Stephanos brought up the rear, holding his bow tight to his chest.

"You know you're not gonna be able to use that in the streets, right?" I asked him.

"If I need to I can. If not, it's just a big stick if I take the bowstring off. It'll still hurt when I use it on people."

"Fair point."

"You know you're gonna have more trouble with that thing?" Yen asked me, nodding to my naginata.

I frowned. "Why?"

"Why?" she repeated, looking confused. "Besides the fact that it's a huge sword blade on a stick, out in the open, where people brush against each other all the time on these streets? You'll end up chopping someone's arm off!"

"Well, I sure as shit ain't leaving it behind," I said, glaring at her.

"You can't carry it out there in the daytime. Seriously, Jax. I'm sorry, but the first thing the guard will do is claim that it's dangerous and take it for 'safe-keeping.' And they'd be right, even if they weren't a bunch of thieving scumbags. Once they get their hands on it, it'll be sold to the highest bidder, or you'll have to kill them all. Do you want that?"

"I can't just leave it here," I said, conflicted.

"You'll have to leave it with Mal, or one of us can stay with it," she offered.

"I don't know," I muttered.

She shook her head. "You'll trust him with your plans for the city and everything else, but not with a weapon?"

"An evolving weapon," Oracle said quietly. The others froze.

"Seriously?" asked Yen after a minute, and I caught Lydia staring at it in awe, while Stephanos looked it over, slowly stroking his bow. I assumed he was thinking about having an evolving bow, or at least, I hoped that was why he was stroking his "wood," anyway…

"Yeah, seriously," I said, and she rubbed her mouth slowly, still staring at it.

"Okay, then. Yeah, that makes sense, I suppose. Maybe we can disguise it?" She suggested, shaking her head. "Normally I'd say just dump it in your bag, it's a bag of holding after all, but an evolving weapon is powerful magic, and to put it in what's a really basic bag? Probably not a good idea."

"Point with the bag, but disguise it as what?" I asked. "Do we just claim we're off to play the world's weirdest and most fucked up game of cricket?"

"What's cricket?"

"It's…it's not important, is what it is, okay?" I muttered, leading them up the stairs toward Mal's rooms. A handful of minutes later, we were escorted in to find Mal and Soween sitting and talking. A dozen lists had been strewn across the tables in the office, and two new people I didn't know were also in the room.

"Jax!" Mal said, nodding as he saw me. "Good, 'bout time you got here. Look, we're gonna need you to free those imps. If they carry the right message to the Skyking, we can get it to come on board with the arena fight, but nobody but them knew where it lives."

"We can't free the imps," I said, shaking my head. "They know too much about who I am, and they're constrained by Oaths to return to the Skyking and serve it. They want to be free as much as any of the others."

"What others?" he asked absently.

"The rest of the harpies that I made swear fealty to me," I said, waiting. When he blinked and looked at me, I winked at him, then moved out onto the balcony. The others followed me out as I turned slowly, scanning around and *feeling* the bond.

It took me less than a minute to pick him out, crouched on the top of a building in the distance. A slight flutter of his feathers in the wind was the only movement he made. I waved to him, pointing with one arm first, then waving both arms out to make sure he saw me, then waving him in. He'd clearly been waiting for us to make contact, and he ran forward, diving off the side of the building. His wings flared to catch him and lift him from his dive.

In less than a minute, Amaat was swooping in for a landing, his mace held lightly in one hand as he glared at those he didn't know.

"Amaat. Good to see you, buddy; sorry that took so long. How's it going out there?"

He looked at me, then cocked his head to the side as he regarded the rest of the group before answering cautiously.

"All is well," he said, watching the others.

"Amaat, this is Mal and Soween. They're with us. The other two, not a fucking clue," I said, arching an eyebrow at Mal, who gestured at the new pair. He continued rubbing his chin consideringly, watching Amaat.

"Ah, uh…I'm Muskin. I arrange the fights at the arena, and I'm pleased to meet you, sir?" One of the men introduced himself, bowing jerkily and straightening back up, while the second stepped forward, watching us all carefully.

"And I am Gaion. I help Mal…procure…things." The second man was dressed like he'd just wandered in off the street: plain trousers and tunic, no rings or anything, a simple, heavy-bladed dagger belted at his waist. He wore plain workman-style boots and had a little grime on him, dust on his clothes, a ragged tear here and there. His sandy blond hair was a little shaggy and needed a trim, but not badly. Literally everything about him screamed "forget me, I'm ordinary…"—until I looked into his eyes.

He had that weird genetic trait that caused a person to have two different-colored irises, one blue and one brown. One look at them totally destroyed his illusion. He'd clearly gone to great lengths to look as dull and ordinary as possible, even wearing his hair over his left eye, but the intelligence and cunning shining out of them was unmistakable.

I'd barely noticed him on entry into the room, but now, that fucker needed watching!

"Hi, Muskin and Gaion," I said, greeting them both.

"I'm not a demon," Gaion said coldly.

I frowned, meeting his gaze. "Of course you're not, just like I'm not a fucking horse. What's your point?"

"Most people think I'm a demon when they see my eyes," he said, relaxing a bit and acting intrigued by my response.

"Well, they're clearly fucking idiots, then," I said. "It's a mutation of a gene in your eyes, not because you're a fucking demon. That's mental."

"I'm no mutant," he growled.

"Not like that." I shook my head. "Look, I haven't got time to explain this, but where I come from, this kinda thing is well understood. You ever see a ginger kid with parents that have black and blonde hair?"

He nodded.

"How do you think that happens? It's a mutation. When the bairn was born, the genes for black hair and blonde both mixed together, so you get a ginger. Doesn't mean the kid's any more of a mutant than any other ginger is, though, right?

"Well, your eyes are the same. One color from one parent, one from the other. No magical supernatural shit, just who you are," I said, tossing it off easily from what I remembered about biology classes. Then I froze, realizing that I was in the goddamn UnderVerse, and the fucker could actually be a damn demon, for all I knew.

"Interesting. I'd like to hear more of this, when you've time?" Gaion asked me slowly.

"Yeah, no worries. We need to sort something out, then I'll need a guide to the healer, okay?" I said, looking to Mal.

He gave the clock on the stand a quick glance, then grunted. "You don't want to be late for her; she'll chew yer ear off," he said but settled back down.

"So, first of all, this is Amaat. He's a legion scout and commands my little team of sworn djinn and alkyon. One of them could probably arrange to get the message back to the Skyking."

"Okay, sounds good. We've got a few hours yet before we need to send out the invites, so I'll get them knocked up. We're going to say we've caught a few 'legion scum' and they're going to get what's coming to them in the arena. Let each of the four gangs pick a fighter to face you in the arena, one at a time. That sound good to you?"

"Yeah, that's fine," I said, a little worried about the kind of people who would choose to go into the arena, but not overly so. They chose this path, so fuck them.

"Okay, so what's the problem?" Mal asked.

I grinned, hefting my naginata. "I need a cover or something for this, so I don't end up chopping bits off people in the streets."

"Hmmm, could put a sheath around it, I suppose…" Mal said, rubbing his chin, then shrugging noncommittally. "Or just leave it here; I'll lend you a sword."

"I've got swords, but this is my main weapon. It stays with me," I said, shaking my head.

"It doesn't tonight." He met my eyes. "Legionnaires use swords, shields, spears, maces, and axes, not fucking sword-staffs. You'd never be able to use that in a shield wall, so you'll have to use something else, or nobody will believe you're legion."

"Fuck," I muttered. "Fine. I'll use my sword tonight, then, but for now, it stays with me."

"Whatever. Muskin, sort it out, will you?" He dismissed it as unimportant, and Muskin darted out of the room. The furtive man returned a few minutes later with a soft leather sheet that he quickly wound around the blade, drawing it tight and cinching it with leather straps, while the rest of us talked quietly.

"Is everything okay out there?" I asked Amaat.

He nodded, gesturing upward. "It's been fine, but the Skyking sent some more minions to watch over the Cloudring, since we killed the rest. Now that I've broken cover, I'll be hunted again."

"Shit, sorry, man," I said, shaking my head. "I should have thought about that, but unfortunately we needed you down here." I leaned in, pitching my voice low enough that nobody else could hear but him. "Do you know where Bane and Tang are?"

"They're close by. Bane is in the courtyard outside, and Tang is back on the roof I just left."

"Good to know. I need you here to help Mal sort things out, maybe pick one of the ex-harpies to deliver the invite to the fights, while I find this healer. I'll not be long, hopefully, then you can at least get some rest in our rooms."

"I'd rather return to the enclave, if you don't mind? The legion prefect sent us to help you, or at least to find out what you were…our brothers and sisters deserve to know that there's some hope."

"After the healer, I'm heading to a few shops, then onto the enclave myself. I'd do it the other way around, but I get the feeling that I won't have any chance for sightseeing on the way back."

"Then I need to prepare the enclave for you. Please, my lord?" he said, fixing me with a glare. I sighed. Those damn eagle eyes turned even a simple request into a demand. He had a good point, though.

"Do you think you'll be able to get back out?" I asked.

"Alone, I probably couldn't, but with my wing? With their help, I will, and I can bring more from the legion."

I paused for a minute, then realized his "wing" must be his new flying buddies.

"Okay, Amaat. Get an ex-harpy down here and ready to deliver the message; then you can watch over us as we head to the healer. Once we're there safely, you head straight for the enclave and bring the legion up to date. Tell them I'll be there later today."

"That's madness," Mal called from where he was sitting back in a chair and watching me, tinkering with his crossbow.

"What is?" I asked.

"You tryin' to get into the legion enclave. Ain't no way you're comin' back if you *do* manage it. Better to send him. He's a flyer; he can get in easy enough. Gettin' out will be a mite harder, sure, but he's flyin'. You think you're just gonna walk through the gangs and the mob? Think the guards keepin' everyone inside the enclave'll just not notice you?" He shook his head. "Kinda dumb to think they'll just ignore ya."

"You got a better idea?" I asked him.

"Yeah. Don't go," he shot back.

"And you think the legion will just pack up and be ready to go without me meeting them? Without me proving myself to them?"

"Probably not," he said, shrugging.

"Well, then?"

"Send your scouts. Their whole job is gettin' in and out. Tell 'em what you want done, and give the legion the orders. Might work yet," Mal said.

"No chance," I replied, shaking my head.

"He's right," said Yen, and I looked over at her, raising an eyebrow. "Mal, I mean," she clarified.

"Oh, thanks very much."

"Do you want me to tell you why I agree with him, or just keep my opinions to myself if they're not what you want to hear in future?" Yen asked.

I glared at her, before realizing what I was doing and rubbing my eyes.

"Okay, I'm sorry," I said. "What do you think? And yes, I always want to hear your opinions and advice. I might ignore them, but I'll listen."

"The legion is run on orders, always has been. You're the highest-ranking official in the empire now, so you just have to issue the order. The legion wants to see you; they want to meet you and know you, but to do that, you have to survive long enough to reach them. Send the orders through Amaat. I'll give him phrases to use to prove to the prefect that you're who you say you are. The next few days, we get you a ton of mana potions, and you do…whatever you did before…I guess. Turn all the Oaths active for the legion. That'll help convince them. Then, on the last day in the arena, that's when you go to the enclave. When they already believe, you go and you lead them out of the enclave, all of them."

"You think they'll just pack up their lives on my order?" I asked, shaking my head. "I don't see it happening, Yen. I'd be happier if they would, but I can't expect them to do all that just on my say-so, not without even meeting me first."

"They won't be. They're acting on the lawful orders of the Lord of the Great Tower of Dravith, Scion of the Empire, duly confirmed by members of the Praetoria. Yeah, in normal times, a lot more convincing would be needed, but right now? The Legion General was murdered in the streets, mobs are howling daily for the legion to be disbanded and probably murdered.

"We were already considering having to leave the city and strike out, set up a new settlement somewhere. Maybe take over one of the old ruins or something. The only thing that was stopping us all was our Oath to protect the citizens of the empire, even when they're being dicks, I guess. Now?" She snorted.

"The legion is sick of being treated like second-class citizens, and you're offering an 'out' that's both honorable and hopeful. We get to be what we all signed up to be, but without the hatred that we currently have to put up with every day? Where do we sign?"

"You honestly believe that?" I asked her, and she nodded. "Then I'll trust you to know your people better than I do. Write up a message confirming who I am. I'll write the orders when I get back, and Amaat can take them back to the enclave today. I need to get to this healer and sort this out." I straightened up and nodded to her and Amaat.

"About time you started thinkin'," Mal muttered.

I shot him a look that could've melted steel. "Really, dude, do you just have to run your mouth constantly?"

"Wouldn't know what to do with myself if I didn't," he replied, smiling smugly.

"Asshole," I muttered.

"Takes one to know one, 'tats."

"What?" I asked, frowning.

"Tattoos." Mal repeated. "You got some interesting ones there, boy. Think I hadn't noticed?"

I grunted, tugging the bandages over and recovering them as I changed the subject.

"Can I get a guide to the healer before the fighting starts tonight?" I asked.

Mal shrugged, accepting that I wasn't talking about them and hopefully assuming it was irrelevant.

"If you're late to that appointment with the healer, fightin' might start a mite earlier than yer expectin'…"

"So give me a goddamn guide, then!" I growled at him, trying to decide if I was pissed or pleased to be working with Mal. I liked the guy, but damn, he made my fists itch.

"Gaion, take them where they need to go, will ya?" Mal said, and Gaion nodded.

"See, that wasn't so hard," I said.

"That's what she said," he muttered under his breath with a grin.

I froze. "Say, Mal…where was it exactly you came from?"

"Narkolt. You forgotten that already?" he asked, cocking an eyebrow at me.

"Riiiight…" I nodded slowly, suddenly less at ease with the man.

"I'll draft a set of the orders as well, if you want?" Yen asked, frowning at the sudden change in the atmosphere.

"Yeah, you do that," I said, shaking my head and forcing a smile. "Think you can give her what she needs so she can do it while I'm with the healer?" I asked Mal, who looked to Soween.

"I'll sort it," Soween said, sighing as she stood up and left the room.

"I'll fly overwatch for you," Amaat offered. I nodded to him in thanks as he clambered up onto the ledge that ran around the balcony of Mal's room.

He crouched and jumped off, thrusting down hard with his powerful wings, and we were all buffeted with the wind as he soared upward.

"God, I'd love to fly," I muttered, looking to Oracle, who remained perched on my shoulder. She'd been quiet since we had arrived, and I could tell, after the drow incident, that she just wasn't comfortable around others right now.

"It's nice," she whispered, stroking the back of my neck with one small hand. I smiled at her in reassurance, patting her legs where they dangled against my chest and upper arm.

"There's everything you need inside," Soween said less than a minute later when she returned with a leather folio, which she passed to Yen, then threw her a bag as well. "Might be a good idea to change your gear again, after they made you last time, if you know what I mean?" she said.

Yen colored, darting into the antechamber to swap her plain legion scouting attire and cloak for a more common design.

"Thank you," Yen said when she returned. I nodded my thanks to Soween and Mal as well, leaving the room behind Gaion as we all hurried outside.

"How long will it take to reach the healer?" I asked Gaion.

"Normally, fifteen or twenty minutes, depending on the time of day. She's only a few streets away, on this side of the river in the Merchant Quarter. Now, though? Depends on anything. Could be quick, could be slow, but Mal asked me to get you there, so I will, and I'll make sure it's safe."

We moved quickly through the corridors, passing through a few rooms and across a bar area that was empty save for a bored-looking lizard man who was mopping in preparation for the night's festivities.

Once we left the shade of the building, I glanced around. The courtyard appeared empty, besides the Fenris, which still stood where I'd left it.

"That thing yours?" a voice called, and I spotted a man dressed in ale-spotted leathers, dragging a wheelbarrow of dung out of a stable on the other side of the open space.

"Yeah, why?" I asked.

"Why, he asks…because the damn thing won't move! I've got deliveries in and out all day, and that damn thing won't budge! Just attacks anyone who touches its bridle. Why have a bridle if you can't use it, eh? I ask ya," he said, setting the wheelbarrow down.

"Crap," I muttered. "Okay, good point. where do you need him moved to?" I asked, and he gestured to the stables. "Fenris, go and stand in the stables where this man…" I looked to him and raised an eyebrow questioningly.

"Bart."

"Go into the stables and wait where Bart asks you to. Don't go anywhere else," I added at the end, just in case.

"About time," Bart muttered, gesturing to the stables. "Get in there, last stall on the right. Don't break nuthin'." Fenris shifted and strode across the courtyard calmly.

Lydia, Yen, Stephanos, Oracle, and I set out into the streets. Following Gaion, we crossed the manicured gardens of the private, richer areas of the Cloudring, and passed through the outer gates into the city proper.

Here, the smoke was heavier, the cloying taste of the herbs in the air stronger, yet with less of an effect, thankfully, my head clearing as we walked through the streets.

Gaion picked up the pace again, and we all started jogging along, until he spun suddenly, knives whipping out, and he shouted out a warning to the rest of us.

"Assassin!"

We reacted instantly, Yen and Lydia taking up station on either side of me, Oracle lifting into the air from my pocket, and Stephanos grunting as he hefted his bow, nocking an arrow. I could feel the presence of Amaat, swooping nearby, and…

"Bane!" I said, relaxing. "Tang!" The boxes nearby shifted as Tang moved out into the open, grinning at me and the rest of the group.

"You know him?" Gaion asked, a pair of long daggers braced in his hands as he looked to me. I nodded, gesturing to him to calm down.

"I do. He's sworn to me, as is…" I searched around, and a swirl of smoke drew my attention to Bane, who stood only a few feet away.

"About time you spotted me," he said, letting loose with a sub-sonic *thrummm* of amusement.

"Yeah, well, you're a stealthy fucker," I retorted, grinning at him. He'd not been with me long, but damn, I felt better knowing Bane was close by.

"Where are we going?" he asked.

"This is Gaion." I gestured. "The deal's done with Mal, that's all I can say here, but he's taking us to an appointment with a healer."

"Then we'll follow and watch over you," Bane said, stepping back into the smoke. His form became hazy almost instantly, and a few seconds later, he was gone, while Gaion stared around in annoyance.

"Anyone else I should know about?" he asked gruffly, his daggers still in his hands, and I shook my head.

"Not that you need to worry about. Lead on, mate," I said. Tang moved into the group, taking up the left rear position, clearly intending on staying close to Yen from now on. Oracle rolled her eyes at Gaion, slipping back into my pocket and giving me a subtle nudge to remind me of where she was hiding, and the view this morning when I'd woken up.

Gaion nodded to me and sheathed his daggers, clearly on edge, but he soon set off jogging again. A few minutes later, we were out of the smoke, emerging into a faint ray of sunlight.

I drew a deep breath, closing my eyes for a second and enjoying the sun on my face, until a passing airship moved across the sky and blotted the pleasantly warm rays out.

Glaring up at it, I jogged along with Gaion and the others, crossing a few more streets and passing down a third to emerge into a slightly nicer area.

The buildings were still built up against one another, but here in the Industrial Quarter, they looked grimy and dull, coated with who-knew-what, and the gutters were coated with a residue of unidentifiable chemicals and crap. The first thing I smelled that wasn't offensive was a stand offering baked goods.

I passed it, still following Gaion, who'd slowed to a walk now, while my nose searched for scents I could identify.

I suddenly realized it'd been forever since I'd had a pizza, and with that thought, I couldn't help but imagine a thick layer of cheese, ham, pineapple, and pepperoni topping a slice. Some people hated pineapple on pizza, but hey, some people believed that gingers had souls, and that was just crazy talk.

I swallowed my drool and went on, passing dozens of shops with stands outside. Ribbons and swords stood next to armor that glinted in the sunlight filtering down through the clouds, smoke, and Airships that hovered over the city.

We passed a striped pole, and through the open door, I caught a glimpse of a barber trimming someone's hair. I nodded to myself. I needed that, and damn soon. We passed tailors, apothecaries, shops selling bags, and occasional stands selling fruit and food. I passed a building I swore was full of minotaurs, all arguing over leather harnesses and nose rings.

I shook my head, following Gaion and trying not to be a complete tourist as I gawked at the city around me.

My toe suddenly caught on a raised cobble, and I almost fell. Lydia caught my arm, and I grinned ruefully at her as she smiled back.

"Sorry," I muttered, shaking my head. "This city, it's just so different from those I grew up in."

"Really?" she asked, seeming far less impressed than I was, and I frowned as I looked a little closer.

At first, it looked the same as I'd seen already, a steampunk reimagining of a Victorian era, with added magic and beastmen, everywhere I looked I saw something new, and something wonderful…or terrible.

I looked past the food carts, watching the vendors hawking their goods to passersby but ignoring the thousand-yard stare of the woman half-sprawled against the wall nearby, the infant clutched to her breast staring around hollow-eyed. Her hopeless gaze pierced the air as the child snuffled, the man leaning against the mouth of the alley nearby shooting predatory looks in her direction.

Laughter floated on the breeze as a pair of women, dressed like they'd stepped out of Victorian times, chatted gaily about where they'd have afternoon tea, while a child no older than seven or eight stumbled along carrying a case, a gold collar and chain leading from his neck to one of the women's belt.

A female slave followed another pair of women who were chattering animatedly about the ribbons and bows on a table. The stoic look on her face seemed a permanent expression as she stood silently, loaded up with the bags of her "betters." The collar around her neck glowed malevolently, and a matching ring entwined one of the women's fingers. A person turned into a possession, with a pretty badge of ownership around her neck that would punish her if her owner so desired.

I saw the starving and the destitute, the pretty and the poised. Thugs lurked in the alleys, and city guards walked past a small child that sobbed, desperately looking for a parent and ignored by everyone except the flesh peddler stalking forward, forcing a smile onto his florid face.

"No," I snarled, coming to a halt, my people swirling around me in confusion as they tried to see what had attracted my attention and my ire.

"Lydia, that child," I said, gesturing to the sobbing little girl. "Yen. The woman." I nodded toward the woman slumped against the wall.

Lydia didn't hesitate, knowing me too well. She was off, stalking forward, dressed in a mix of full armor and drow gear. Her shield covered her left arm, and she clutched her mace tightly in her right fist as she covered the distance in record time, stepping between the flesh peddler and his planned victim.

His face went white, and he smiled fearfully at her, spreading his hands in apology and backing away quickly. The little girl never even noticed the exchange.

Yen looked from me to the woman, pausing, then realized what I wanted and moved forward. She slipped through the crowds; her legion attire had thankfully been left back at the arena, as Tang began to draw suspicious glares. People had begun spotting his unmarked, but still distinct legion-style gear. Adding to that the haircut and the rigid stance, and he just screamed legion.

Yen moved to the woman, crouching and speaking softly to her before helping her to stand and leading her to join our group.

Lydia was crouched next to the girl, helm pushed back, as she spoke in quiet, calm tones. "What are you doing?" Gaion hissed at me. "We're drawing attention!"

"I'm helping people. The damn healer can wait if she has to!" I glared at him, stalking forward to kneel next to the small girl. She was young, a toddler, really. A short, scuffed dress covered her to her knees, which were as skinned and scabbed as her dress was frayed. Her face was filthy, with lines cut through the grime by rivulets of tears.

"Where are your parents?" I asked her quietly, ignoring the hustle and bustle of the market and the shops around us.

"Momma's gone!" she bawled. I looked to Lydia questioningly.

"She said her mother went to sleep and didn't wake up. Now she's on the streets, looking for somewhere to stay."

"Well, fuck," I muttered, holding out a hand to the little girl. "I'm Jax. What's your name, little one?"

She shied back, uncertain of me. I snorted, feeling the sad smile that came to my face. It was ironic, considering the mass of steel that covered Lydia, yet I was the one the girl was afraid of, with my cleaner, better-made armor and rings on my fingers in plain sight. I furrowed my brow at Lydia.

"Is there anywhere we can take her where she'll be safe?" I asked her, and Lydia shook her head.

"There's the orphanages, but she'll be sold from there to the slavers if there's an offer made. Safest place for 'er is probably with the gangs, and that's sayin' somethin'. They'll pimp 'er out, but they'll protect 'er, as she'd be an asset." Lydia spat in disgust.

"Then she comes with us," I said, nodding to Lydia, who turned to the girl.

"Would you like to come with us, sweetie?" she asked, getting a scared look from the girl. "I'll make sure you get food and somewhere safe to sleep. You'll be okay, I promise."

The girl looked at her, clearly scared, but the offer of safety and food from an adult was clearly enough, and she took Lydia's hand when it was offered to her.

I found Yen leading the other woman and her baby towards our group, and saw the blatant glares Tang was getting, the way more and more black looks were being thrown our way. I growled to myself. This was horrific; the weak being fed upon and ignored, the honorable being despised, all so that the rich could feed on their misery.

"I think you'd be better off if I was leaving you now," Tang said to me, looking ashamed and swallowing hard. I shook my head.

"No chance, Tang," I said firmly. "You're one of us. If you get shit, we all do. I'm not leaving you to be attacked by this scum."

"Scum?" said a nearby man, who'd overheard, and he spat on the ground. "Yer with a legion thief an' yer call us scum?"

"I do," I growled, straightening and turning to face him fully, my anger rising.

"Who'd yer think yer are, sonny? Callin' me scum!" he snarled back at me. Several of his friends began slinking out of the growing crowd to back him up, while others started to move to surround us. Grumblings turned swiftly to swearing and catcalls.

"Look! They're trying to kidnap a girl!" the blatant predator who Lydia had scared off before cried, pointing to the little girl whose hand she held.

"I've had about enough of this," I snarled, stepping forward as a trio of guards came running into the crowd, pushing people out of the way and lashing out with cudgels at those who didn't move fast enough for their liking.

"What's going on here?" the lead guard shouted, scanning the crowd, then focusing on us.

I glared right back at him, and he curled his lip up as he saw Tang trying to hide the legion markings on his chest plate.

"I should have known. Another legion thief!" the guard said loudly, sweeping his gaze across the group until it came to rest on me. "And what're you lookin' at?" he said, stepping forward self-importantly. "Come on then, papers! Who're you, eh? Another legion tick feedin' on the city?" He thrust his hand out.

I smiled coldly and stepped forward instead, coming to a halt a few feet from him, clear of my own group and standing in an open space between the two groups.

"Who am I?" I asked slowly, as though unsure what the question meant. "Who am I?" I repeated, feeling my anger rising, but far from it feeling wrong, or shameful, it felt…honest, and right.

"I'm your fucking worst nightmare, you self-obsessed, arrogant little shit!"

I snarled, rolling my shoulders and cracking my neck. Amon's simmering rage as he saw things I'd missed, bled through the thin barrier between us.

"I should be asking who *you* are!" I snapped, slamming the butt of my naginata down hard on the cobbles. A thick weave of mana flashed into it, making it flare into incandescent white fire, the leather wrap that coated it catching fire and floating free, crumbling to ash on the wind.

"I should be asking who any of you are!" I roared. "You stand there, dressed as a guardsman, pretending to uphold the *law*, while fucking *creatures* like that"—I pointed at the predator who gasped as I leveled my glowing blade at him—"…try to abduct little girls from the street in broad daylight! You did nothing to help her, not one of you!" I roared, spittle flying as I swept the glowing blade around, in some cases barely missing eviscerating some of the crowd.

"You would let a mother starve, right there!" I growled, pointing at the wall where Yen had helped the woman to stand. "You were content to let her waste away, her baby with her!" I swept the blade around to aim at the well-dressed women, who screamed and tried to push themselves backwards through the wall behind them.

"You laugh and fucking frolic around with a goddamn slave carrying your baggage!" I snarled, stepping forward and slamming the base of my naginata down hard before them as I reached out, lightning-fast with my left hand, my fingers curling around the collar the slave girl wore. A shiver passed over me, running from my heart outwards across my body, as I *squeezed*.

I glowed with an unearthly light as Amon's rage grew to new heights. I felt him acting through me, infusing the spells I knew, my magic with his knowledge. He fed magic through my skin, miniscule tendrils of magic flaring into being. They sank into the collar, flying through it, mapping out crystal matrices, then flooding them with power.

The collar crumbled like baked clay, falling apart in my hands as the corresponding ring on the rich girl's finger exploded. The spell feedback sent her screaming as she clutched at her bloody hand.

"Who am I?" I roared into the shocked stillness, hearing my voice echoing off the surrounding buildings. "Who am I?!" I repeated, the magic that hissed and crackled in the silence of my soul rippling out, my eyes shifting from the dark brown I'd been born with to a luminous blue as lightning crackled and popped across my skin.

"I AM YOUR LORD," I said, magic filling my voice and making my words reverberate with power, echoing back and forth from the buildings that rose on either side of the street, windows quivering with the force of my magic. "The LAW of the EMPIRE is clear. *SLAVERS* are to be given the death penalty," I growled.

My feet lifted from the cobbles. As I floated, an unearthly blue nimbus shone from me. Gasps rose around me, and people started to try to run, frantically shoving each other aside.

"All slaves in the bounds of the empire are declared *free*, imprisoned without right nor warrant! Against all slavers I declare an imperial anathema!" I roared as Oracle arose from hiding, hovering next to me as the words came to me from Amon.

Her head thrown back in an ecstasy of power, she began glowing like a tiny sun as a second burst of power emanated from me. A wave of magic rippled out, a glowing ring made of light, life, and fury, cracking lightning and hot thunder. Pressure of the storm combined with the life-giving rains.

It passed through bodies, walls, and gear. It sank into the floor and rose into the air. Before it dissipated, every slave it touched, almost a hundred meters out from me, screamed in joy at their bonds breaking. Collars crumbled, and keys exploded in pockets, controlling devices killing dozens of slave owners and adding to the pandemonium.

"I AM JAX!" I roared into the air, my voice carrying fury, joy, and triumph in equal measure.

"I AM YOUR LORD!" I howled, the air shaking with my radiated power.

"I FIND YOU *WANTING*!" I screamed, the cobbles around me rippling, flowing outwards as if a creature beneath them had awoken. The roiling earth threw people aside, hurling them through windows and into walls and overturned carts. The blast made walls crumble and statues fall. Terrible screams rose into the air, but the slaves stood on firm ground. My people didn't feel so much as a shudder as this strange power stilled the earth they stood upon.

"Jax!" Lydia shouted, and I spun violently, my fury in full flow. I could feel Oracle slowly turning, her gaze like the tracking laser for a hellfire missile.

"We have to go!" she screamed at me. I glared at her, feeling Amon's fury at being interrupted as we dealt out punishment. "Please!" she called up, and I saw the one she held in her arms.

The little girl she'd rescued. Lydia held the tiny figure pressed to her chest, her shield strapped to her arm and covering the child as she sobbed in terror, her face buried in Lydia's neck.

She was terrified of me.

She'd grown up in the city, a city that fed on the weak and the innocent, and she'd just lost her mother, but still, the most terrifying sight she'd seen…was me.

Her savior.

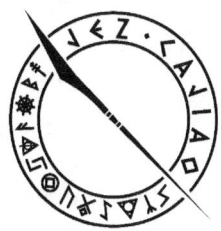

CHAPTER TWELVE

I froze. The realization of what I was doing, what I had done, tore through me. I forcibly choked back my anger, my rage, that strange power leaving me as I fell to the ground. My feet slammed into the cobbles with enough force that I staggered, having been carried aloft on the wave of power flooding through me.

I swallowed hard. In the silence left behind, the faint echoes of my shouted words still sounded in the distance until the cries and moans of pain began to fill the air.

I turned back, seeing the devastation that I'd wrought. Buildings had been torn apart, and the streets were shattered. People lay everywhere, some injured, some unconscious, and some dead.

Legs poked out of rubble, broken bones and torn flesh with blood seeping out…Cries for help rang out, the sobbing rising in volume, but as I scanned the carnage, stunned by what I'd done, I also saw hope.

Men, women, and children; human, elves, and creatures I didn't know, easily a dozen or more, clutched at their necks where skin that hadn't seen sunlight for years was suddenly exposed. Scales, bent and grown around bonds, were suddenly free. Fur that had rubbed raw for years was suddenly exposed to the healing winds and gentle sunshine.

I gazed up, seeing that the clouds above me were slowly rolling back in. The sunlight, which shone down through the forcibly pushed back smog and contaminants, slowly dimmed as the smoke rose to cloud it again, but most of all, I felt *HIM*.

Amon was there, stronger than I'd ever known him, his mind more focused. I felt his madness, the centuries of punishment his soul had endured roiling though him and into me, his fears and the mental whips he'd used to flay his soul for his failures.

I felt them all, and I felt him reaching out, determined to take hold of the real world, to walk again, to feel the light of the sun and the cool breeze against his flesh, even if that flesh had to be taken from me first.

I felt his sadness and regret at what he believed he had to do, but I also saw what he intended. He would rain fire upon this city, and every other city of the empire. He would scourge them all, the guilty and the innocent, to give the innocent of the future the chance at life.

He had decided that a cleansing was necessary.

He would cleanse the realm and raise the races up again, bring them to the light…by force, if necessary. They were as children to him, and clearly, they'd proven they couldn't be trusted to make things right.

No, they had to burn so that their sins would be forgiven.

I shuddered as his phantom claws reached out. I could feel mana running through me, filling my mana channels, shifting in preparation for his call. I could feel him there, standing by my side, then his soul staring out through my eyes at the world around us, and I clamped down, hard.

Pain ripped through me as he fought to push through the thin barriers I erected in my mind. I fell, shouts coming from those around me, I felt hands lifting me, and movement as I was carried, even as my mind collapsed inwards, creating a safe bastion from which to face the Eternal Emperor.

The world around me changed, and suddenly I stood alone in the darkness, looking up. There, before me…was a portal out, and I knew it was my vision; it was what my eyes were seeing now, but I was separate from it.

I stood in a circular room of rough-hewn stone, as though in a cave, and to my left, bisecting the space neatly, was a shimmering barrier of rippling power.

I turned to face it. The curtain ran into the distance somehow in both directions, as though it was the surface of the sea, and I hovered above it.

It was the Veil, I knew…somehow…

The Veil between life and death, between Amon's reality and my own.

He'd never gone deeper, to his rest. Instead, he'd been tethered to it, bound to the Veil itself, forced to peer through it to see everything he'd ever believed in despoiled by his greedy, squabbling children.

He'd seen billions die, seen their souls pass through the Veil, sinking deeper into those peaceful waters. Those blessed spirits went on to the rest they deserved, lifted in some cases, by higher beings. He'd seen and felt the miasma left by the passing of liches and other dark creatures who transcended the Veil.

He'd felt the dead's rest invaded as stinking, disease-ridden claws sank through to tear souls out, stealing them to be used in sick games as they wept with pain.

He'd felt the good, the sweet, and the innocent lifting on their own and passing through the Veil, traveling back the warmth and the light, being reborn.

Some of those same souls passed him time and time again, returning because they knew they were needed. That the realms needed them.

He'd seen some of those same souls broken, tortured into insanity, sinking eventually into the darkest deeps.

He'd wept and screamed. He'd railed against the realities, screaming for the lost gods to awaken and grant him justice, to save those souls he was responsible for or to give him the power to do it himself.

Now that he had it, he could feel the Veil was at its very weakest since he'd passed through. He wasn't dead, not fully, not while one of his descendants still drew breath. He could never die, and now he knew how to pass back through, how to right the wrongs, and how to save the souls he felt being tortured, even now.

He just had to abandon all he stood for in life to do it.

I felt him, I saw him as he floated up, coming to a rest before me, staring into my eyes.

He was a tall man, or had been in life. Solidly muscled, with brown hair that floated around his face, he had a strong jaw and deep, sapphire-blue eyes. He stared at me, a frown of anger furrowing his brow as he regarded the last step to his return to the land of the living.

He made me feel like a local bully, turning the corner to find a child crying, holding Dwayne Johnson's hand, and pointing at me. I felt like I'd just been judged, that all I'd done, all the achievements I'd managed were as nothing compared to this mountain of a man, the actual Eternal Emperor, who was watching me through the Veil of death.

I couldn't stand before him. I couldn't compare, not to *that*...He was the emperor, and I was nothing. I was...

I was *Jax*, that was all. I didn't know what I was doing, not really. I was making it up as I went along. I didn't know how to rule the tower, how to fix the problems. I didn't even know where to begin! I'd spent most of my time in the tower, after gaining control, just running back and forth. I was always chasing the problems, trying to find a solution. This man—no, the emperor—wouldn't be doing that...

He'd...

He'd be raining fire down on the realm...

He'd be killing the innocent and guilty alike, so that the dead could finally rest in peace.

He'd be preventing the possibility of all the good that could come, stilling the laughter of children with their tears, because all he could see now was the cost of it, not the gain.

He'd be sacrificing love and honor to end the pain that filled the world for so many.

He was going to "cure" all the pain and sadness that existed by destroying all the hope, all the love, and all the happiness.

I stared into his eyes, seeing the death there. Not just the effect of his dying, but the centuries of pain that had deadened his soul as well.

"No," I said, my voice echoing around in the silence of the cavern in my mind.

He would kill that little girl we had just rescued, in order to stop her pain. But I would bring her life; I would bring her joy.

I saw the woman that Yen had helped to her feet, and she was, even now, being dragged along by my people, being forced into life, because life was pain. Life was hardship, and it was never giving up. Never giving in, because to do so was to rob yourself of the sweetness of love, passion, friendship, and hope.

I could save her. I might not be able to save her for long; I might not be able to give her the happy life she deserved, not long-term, too much was unknown, but for now? For today, and tomorrow? For all the days yet to come, that I could?

I'd be there. I'd reach out, and I'd take her hand. I'd help her to stand, and I'd lift that child up to stand on my shoulders, to see the sun shining through the clouds.

I'd make sure that she got that chance.

I looked into Amon's eyes, seeing the film of death, the cold greyness as they stared back at me. In that instant, I had a choice. I could allow Amon through; I could let him become me, and I'd share in his power, share in his knowledge.

He would spare those I loved, Oracle and a few others, until the end. I could enjoy days or weeks with them as he destroyed the realm, taking turns to breathe the air, and feel the sun on our skin. He would accept that, give me that chance, then when they and all around us were dead, he would use his magic to gain more power.

He would raid the secret places of darkness, destroying the liches and creatures of the night, collecting their artifacts and items of power to himself. Once he had power enough, he would sit upon the throne of life, judging the souls of the dead.

He would choose who were to be given the chance at rebirth, and he would allow them to pass back through, creating bodies of magic for them.

He would watch over the realm and ensure that they were good. That they lived in harmony with one another, and he would rip free the soul of any who disobeyed.

It would be a world of glorious order and peace…and fear and tyranny.

The Eternal Emperor would have broken everything, becoming a far worse evil than the SporeMother, or Nimon, or any other being, all because he was *doing good…*

"No," I repeated, and his brow furrowed further.

"You cannot stop me, child of my line," he said, his voice ethereal, yet filled with resolve.

"Yes, I can," I replied, staring into his dead eyes. "All I have to do is not let you through."

"You cannot stop me. Even now, I grow in power, in awareness."

"I know, but I also know that you're a soul. You are centuries dead, and you can't come back through fully without a willing vessel," I said, not knowing how I knew it; I just did. "You can't transfer to another being, as you're tied to me. You're bound to my soul and my body, somehow…but this fucking body's full, pal," I growled, tapping my chest with one finger. "It's my body, and I'm fucking using it!"

"It is just a sleeve of flesh, a home for the soul. A vessel that would allow me to bring peace to the realm."

"Yeah, fucking eternal peace," I snapped.

He nodded slowly, his hair floating as though moved by the tide.

"Of course. Why would you wish otherwise? The peace and solitude of the grave is the best the living can hope for. I have seen them, the souls of the good and the wicked alike, sinking through the veil. The relief when they accept the end, sinking into the comforting darkness…"

"You didn't," I said.

"I cannot." He frowned. "I was prevented from my rest; my soul has never known peace."

"So you don't actually know if it is peaceful, or if it's just numbing? Or so terrifying that it shuts down its victims?" I asked, sensing a thread I could pull on.

"I feel their peace—"

"You feel their somnolence, their exhaustion, not their peace. Just because I'm tired doesn't mean I don't want to live!" I snapped, and I remembered something else. "You gave your life to the empire you created, so that people could have peace and love and happiness."

"And they suffered more for it!" he snarled, emotion bleeding through in his voice.

"Yes! They suffered in the end, because a fucking dickhead of a god dropped a moon on the empire! Because some of your asshole children wanted to rule in your place! Not because the empire was wrong, not because peace is impossible, but because greedy fucktards screwed it up. *We* can bring it back. How many hundreds of thousands—hell, how many *millions*—lived good, safe lives because of the empire, while it lasted?"

"Tens of millions lived in the empire at its height, with hundreds more in the lands of our allies," he whispered sadly.

I jumped on that detail. "Yes! Millions and millions lived in peace and prosperity. They were happy, and they were sad, but they lived and they loved. Now you think it's okay to wipe away the last remnants of that, without trying to salvage it? What would you have done, in those days, if a dead soul decided to wipe all life from the realm to 'bring peace'?"

"I would have burned that soul from existence."

"Exactly. You wouldn't have given in." A thought occurred to me, and I spoke quickly, sensing the certainty of Amon wavering. "And what about Shustic? What about Tuthic'Amon? *What about their children?* You swore they would be safe, that you would make sure they lived."

"That Oath fractured my soul!" he howled at me, waves of darkness suddenly emanating from him, and the peaceful ripples of the Veil became choppy storm waters.

"And now you want to break it further!" I roared back at him. "Tuthic still lives, his children live…and you want to kill them!"

"Never!" he screamed. Tendrils of black, necrotic energy hit the surface of the Veil, spreading across it as they fought to pierce through. They coated the Veil, hiding him behind a blackness that made the heart of a dying star look peaceful.

"You want to kill them all!" I screamed back at him, his fury and his madness lashing out.

The room I was in, a cavern in my own mind, shook. The walls of darkness crumbled, and light started to shine in; not a pleasant light, but the light of destruction.

Crackling, spitting whips of fire dug through the walls of my mind, reaching for me. I spun back to the Veil, the now-black surface roiling with riptides and shaking with pressure as twin glowing eyes moved closer.

He stopped on his side of the Veil, less than an inch from the surface. Even there, he was barely visible, and I saw the conflict. I felt it in him.

Centuries of pain and horror had split his mind. He wanted to protect the innocent, but he wanted to kill them all to do it. He wanted them to be safe, to do all he could to protect them from anything that could harm them, but he wanted to destroy everything to fulfill that goal. He couldn't see the catastrophic flaw in his plan.

He was well and truly broken.

"I…" I started to say, when a memory came to me, a memory of anger, of Amon standing by me as I faced Jenae in the realm of the gods, and I remembered what Tuthic'Amon had given me…

"Aegis!" I gasped, and I felt it activate.

Power spread out from the center of my chest, rippling out across my skin. It flowed up and down, spreading to cover every inch of me in glowing white light that lasted barely a second, before it changed.

What had been a glowing covering of white light suddenly became solidified silver, condensing into full-body armor made up of overlapping tiny scales that fit me like a second skin. Larger plates protected my chest, back forearms, upper thighs, shins, and head. I reached up and found that I could feel through it, a cool sensation of perfectly wrought metal under my fingers.

I admired the silvery claws that overlaid my hand, each finger tipped with a short, jet-black talon. As I considered the obsidian points, they grew. and I grinned, running my tongue over newly sharpened teeth.

I met Amon's glowing eyes, and I caught his hesitation. The energy, the rage he'd been so filled with a mere second before, left him…

I frowned, glancing at my HUD and realizing that my health, mana, and stamina bars were all steadily dropping. I remembered that Tuthic'Amon's gift had a cost: to make me essentially invulnerable to outside influences. To shield my mind to this degree would cost me my life as long as it was active.

I glared at Amon, watching him weaken more and more. The blackness that had spread out from him to darken the waters of the Veil was dissipating, and…

I looked around the cavern; the crackling power that had been eating through the stone, ready to tear me apart, had vanished. My head spun as I looked back to Amon, who was slowly sinking backwards. His eyes were fixed on me, but the power that had filled them was gone, and I knew what it meant in that instant.

The powers he'd been using weren't his! He'd been using my own power to fuel his rage! In his maddened state, he'd been lashing out at me with it, and I'd been letting him!

I concentrated, flexing mental muscles and cutting Aegis off. As I felt the drain cease on my health, mana, and stamina, I saw the glow in his eyes begin to grow again.

This time, I didn't wait; I didn't watch or try to understand…

I reached down within myself and grabbed onto my power. I tore it from him, sealing it deeper inside my soul as I glared at him, at what he'd tried to do.

I felt something resist me. I felt…pain…a deep pain in my chest, and spiraling along my spine, a sensation of something that had integrated itself with my spinal column and had spread up into my brain. Thousands of tiny filaments had taken root within me, similar to the way the Pearl had bonded with my body, but this felt deeper and far more sinister.

It had been there since before I was born, a parasite that fed on me to sustain itself. It was a vestige of the UnderVerse, something that had been with me my entire life. It was a seed that had grown, once I began to level, and the injuries that Jenae had sensed, that Oracle had sensed, the drain on my experience that had been holding me back, it was connected to this.

I didn't know how it had come to be, or how it had infected me, but I knew it for what it was now. I only had seconds to act before it recovered and used my own magic to shield itself again.

Reaching out, I ignored the surrounding cavern. Holding my hand up before myself, I concentrated, activating Aegis again, but forcing it to not form the full shield it was designed to be.

The power pulled in to coalesce around my right hand, and before I could think better of it, I drove it into my stomach.

My claws burrowed deeper into my body, digging through the layers of my flesh and my psyche at the same time.

Then I pushed harder, sudden resistance flaring as something pushed back, and I grabbed it. Pain tore through me as it writhed in agony, digging its pseudopods deeper into my nervous system.

I screamed, white-hot torture lancing through my nerves as I felt it digging in deeper, frantic to hold onto life. Gritting my teeth, and knowing it would likely kill me, I pulled on it, hard, and tore the thing from me, separating first along my spine, then higher.

Each section that came loose released massive gouts of blood and viscera, as well as ripping fragments of my soul away. Nerves tore, my spinal column snapping, and the messages from my brain cut off as the parasite tried to stop me. I focused everything I had on the Aegis.

I flexed the power inside me, using it on my arm, forcing the muscles to contract. I maintained my shielded hand's grip on the creature, and I pushed and pulled, forcing the muscles that were now beyond my nerve control to continue their bloody work.

Heat bloomed in my head as connections ripped, as bleeding began inside my brain. My physical body, distant and heavy, was jostled and bounced as it was carried by frantically shouting people, and I felt the damage to it as I tore out this invader.

I lost the sight in my left eye as bloody chunks of my brain were torn apart, the last hooked tips of the parasite coming free in a shower as it was yanked down and out of my stomach.

I held it up before me. The thing coiled furiously, twitching and spasming, a hideous black mess of tendrils and hooks, suckers, and mouths. This creature had been tearing the life from me, slowly draining me of everything I was. I roared in triumph at Amon, who floated helplessly on the other side of the Veil, and I saw the confusion on his face, then the recognition and the horror that filled him.

"No…not the Valspar," he whispered, and a flash of memory, one that he had shared with me during the battle against the SporeMother, came to mind with his words.

I didn't remember it clearly, but whatever had killed Shustic'Amon had been the Valspar, I thought? I shook my head. It didn't matter. The only thing that mattered was that I had won.

I scowled at it with my single functioning eye, at the pseudopods that wrapped themselves around my armored forearm, frantically reaching further, trying to connect with my flesh, to re-enter me…

I growled and pulled on my mana. Somehow using it inside my mind, with Amon's help, I conjured a flame. A flame that would evaporate steel and cause the oceans to boil.

Dragonfire flared to life. Without a spell or any clue as to how, beyond deepest instinct, I drew in a deep breath and roared out flames, my mouth blackening and charring, my teeth exploding in the heat. My arm withered and crumbled, even as it held the remains of the creature aloft.

As the last fragments of the Valspar turned to soot, blowing away from me, I collapsed, and Aegis with me. My body was ruined, my soul charred black by the power I'd unleashed. My mind had been flayed, and I saw him reach out, a single hand pushing through the Veil to touch me. I would have screamed in agony, if I'd had anything left to scream with.

"You were right" was all he said, but the power that flowed down into me brought terrible pain, even as it began to reconstruct my soul.

The building blocks of myself snapped back into place as fragments were yanked back into existence. I felt…bits…of myself pulled back into my soul, my body being reconstructed, and a white-hot flame poured into me from outside.

"You are stronger than you know, Jax…use that strength…I will not seek to supplant you again, worthy Scion," Amon said.

I stared warily at him as his hand slowly retreated through the Veil.

"One year, I will serve you; a single year from today. Then, once again, we will meet, we will face each other, and we will decide the future. If you have succeeded in your attempts at bringing peace and life, then perhaps I will be able, at last, to sleep. To rest. If not, we will again test each other, but this time, without the Valspar twisting our minds and souls."

Fresh pain tore through me as my mind suddenly slammed back into my body. I screamed in agony as the cave we'd been in vanished, and I was back in the real world. The Veil swirled around me, a shadow's depth away, and I felt Amon sinking deeper as I returned to the realm of the living.

The confused welter of memories and madness that I'd had with me all of my life, the voice of utter *insanity* was only a part of Amon. It was a phantasm, a fragment of a fragment. The being I'd met there, in that space between worlds, was the true Amon, his soul. What I'd had, and what I'd been using to survive this long, was a shadow of the real man. In using it, I'd almost allowed the Eternal Emperor, driven mad by grief and hatred, to live again. Had he gained control, he would have destroyed reality as I knew it.

I bit down on my scream, forcing the pain down, suddenly able to manage it. In comparison to what I'd just endured, it was truly a weak thing, even as I suddenly felt…it was Tommy, for just a split second. His presence reached out, and I remembered stitching each other's wounds and cleaning away tears…the love of my brother and the knowledge that he was there for me…

Then it was gone, washed away in another surge of pain, forgotten in the madness and blood.

I found myself lying in a small room. The sallow sunlight shone in through dirty windows, and I was surrounded. Oracle was there, sobbing as she held onto me. Full-sized, she knelt by the table I was laid across, her arms wrapped around my neck as she wept into my hair.

Lydia and Yen held my left arm and leg, Bane and Tang my right. a middle-aged woman I didn't recognize glared at me as I glared back. My armor had been torn free, and I had been eviscerated, my insides on display for all the world to see. I saw others: Gaion, the woman and her baby, the little girl, and dozens more.

They crowded the room, staring at me in a mix of horror, awe, and elation. They stared at me as though unsure if I was going to murder them all or save them. More were crowded outside, guarding the door. Three djinn were present, each of them holding a glowing ball of energy that poured light directly into the spell being woven by the woman who was glaring at me.

"Hold him still!" she snapped, and my friends redoubled their efforts, clamping down as a fresh wave of pain tore through me. I could move, but spasmodically. The world looked wrong as I attempted to shift my gaze around. The damage I'd done to my brain was growing worse as the bleeding tore open more sections. I felt the world spinning, and I tasted colors…

"Put that in his mouth before he bites his own tongue off!" the strange woman snapped. Oracle jammed a wooden block between my teeth. She frantically wiped my face, her hand coming away bloody as tears flowed down her cheeks, and she looked into my eyes.

"It'll be okay. You just have to hold on," she whispered, forcing a smile. "You'll do that, right? For me?"

I couldn't move. She shifted, grabbing a leather strap I'd missed before. As she drew it across my forehead, snapping it into place to stop any movement, she maintained her smile for me.

"I need more mana!" the woman cried out, and Oracle reached out her hand. I felt the draw from our pool increase, and I suddenly understood that, in using Aegis as long as I had, I'd drained too much of myself.

I focused on the spellform constructed above me, sections reaching out, locking onto my body. White light seared into me, and I heard her as she spoke to me.

"You will not die, my champion! Not without my permission!"

"Jenae…" I mumbled around the block, feeling the others shudder at her presence, and the pure white light was suddenly tinged with the red of flames, flames that grew in strength, shifting green and blue, then white again. The woman gasped in shock, shaking violently at the infusion of divine mana, before frantically regaining control of her spell, just before it could tear free and kill her.

I roared as the spell ripped through me, scanning and locating the issues, tearing some sections wider to make room for regrowth within the deepest, most damaged sections.

It seemed to take forever as cells were rebuilt and weaknesses purged. I felt impurities burned out of me, and I knew that what was left behind was stronger.

I endured what seemed like hours of agony as blood sprayed and was replaced, my body completely remade, but eventually, the spell finished. With nothing left to repair, it vanished, breaking apart like hoarfrost before the sun.

I sagged in my restraints, my people collapsing around me. The woman fell, unconscious, as Jenae released her, their collective exhaustion reaching me in mine. Shouting arose outside, but when I tried to turn my head, I found that it was too tightly restrained. I settled for just shifting my eyes, and I saw the form of soldiers approaching from outside. More shouting ensued as the door was smashed in.

I swallowed hard. My health showed that I was healed; it was full, after all. However, my stamina and mana were completely drained, though I still tried to pull up the energy to react, sagging back in relief as Jenae spoke into my mind. Her voice was filled with exhaustion as Oracle removed the block from my mouth.

"It is the legion. Do not be afraid, my champion. Amaat brought those he could to you in your time of need."

"Thank you, Jenae," I croaked out, feeling as though every drop of water I'd ever drunk had been torn from me.

"I must rest. Good luck, Jax. I'm sorry; I cannot use the tracking spell to find Thomas now, not for some time, possibly weeks," she said, sadness and regret clear in her voice.

"I…I understand," I whispered aloud into the still air. "Thank you, Jenae. I owe you."

She faded from my mind, and I felt Oracle, shifted back to her small form, clutching my head and sobbing.

"I'm okay, Oracle," I whispered.

"I know, but that…that thing, that creature," she moaned, pushing back from me. Planting her feet on my chest to stand over me, she stared down into my eyes. "What was that, Jax?!" she cried out and shook a finger at me accusingly. "Why couldn't I see it with my magic? How the hell did that thing even get inside you?!"

"Valspar…" I croaked and coughed, trying unsuccessfully to get up, as I was still strapped to the table.

"Here," whispered Lydia, pulling the strap free on my left arm. I smiled appreciatively into her red-rimmed eyes. I felt others releasing straps, and I reached up, unlatching the one that held my head down. I slowly sat up, exhausted beyond belief, scanning the dozens of men and women packed into the room around me. Most of them I'd never seen before. A few, I recognized from the market square, but the majority…

Amaat pushed into the room, coming to a stop in front of me. He clapped his fist to his chest in salute, then stepped back, revealing a bear of a man outfitted in the steel of the legion. I met the man's gaze, forcing myself to fight through the exhaustion in order to stay somewhat upright as he pulled off his helmet. A stray part of my mind idly noted that the horsehair plume was doing an amazing job of clearing the cobwebs from the ceiling.

He bowed his head, clapping his fist to his chest in salute, making the steel breastplate ring as his gauntlet hit it.

"Lord Jax, I am Centurion Primus Augustus, second Maniple of the Legion of Himnel enclave. I was dispatched to see to your safety by the legion prefect. I have a full squad outside, but I cannot guarantee your safety here. With respect, my lord, we need to move," he said firmly, straightening up.

I let out a sigh, and cracked my back, forcing myself upright. The others were all still recovering, save the woman who'd been casting the spells. The healer had clearly been broken by what had happened and was still unconscious on the floor.

"My lord," Augustus started.

I shook my head, forcing out the words. "I heard…ya, Centurion…Primus Augustus? Was it?" I asked weakly.

He nodded as angry words rose outside. His gaze darted towards the door before locking back on me, and I swallowed, attempting to stand.

"We need to take these people with us," I managed to get out as the room started to spin. I fell forward, only to have him catch me and set me back on the table.

"Yes, my lord," he said simply, turning to Yen and Tang, who straightened and clapped their fists to their chests in salute to him. "Scouts!" he snapped at them. "Get out there and screen our path back to the enclave. Second Squad, you're leading. First Squad! Close protection detail. Third Squad…"

He started barking out orders, and I coughed, forcing air into my lungs to speak.

"No…no, Augustus, I need to go back to the arena…the Cloudring," I choked out, slumping as Bane caught me.

"Lord, the safest place in the city—"

"Is…of no use to me. I'll…only make it…more dangerous for the legion…than it already is. No. The arena, Centurion Primus," I ordered. Hesitation reigned on his face, as I had clearly given him contradictory orders to those he'd received from the prefect. It only lasted a second, though, before he saluted.

"Yes, my lord." He spun around and began shouting new orders, dispatching two fliers, both alkyon, back to the enclave. A handful of seconds later, a pair of stretchers had been made ready, and the healer and I were being loaded onto them before being hustled out of the nondescript building where she had saved my life.

THOMAS

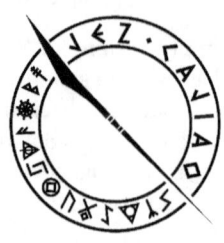

“What the hell was that!” Barked Coran, hoisting an ashen-faced Thomas upright as the Dark Legion spread out, assessing the destruction.

“I…I don’t know…” Thomas whispered, eyes wide. “For a minute, I thought…I felt…”

“If it wasn’t the fucking God of Death’s personal touch, then you better shut it, Thomas!” Coran hissed, eyeing the others that were nearby. "I mean it, shit man, do you know what I had to trade to Barishka to get put on the collection detail with your unit? To actually get to see the city without a brand and a chain holding us together?”

“I know…” Thomas growled, thinking about the surprise when he’d heard Coran was being sent from Sergeant Belladonna’s squad as well. He straightened up, swallowing hard, and pushed down the memory of Jack, the sudden feeling of phantom pain and of closeness.

As soon as he’d realized what it was, as soon as he’d recognized it from all the times it’d happened in the past, he’d reached out, and found…nothing.

The connection between them was long gone.

He was stuck here, in the fucking UnderVerse, a million, billion miles away, on the arse end of the cosmos, surrounded by monsters and magic.

Jack would tell the baron to get fucked. One look at that monster, and he’d go for him, try to stab the old bastard, then the guards would shoot him…hell.

If there really was a connection between the realms? That was probably what he’d just felt…Jack getting shot or stabbed, then boom. When he just wasn’t there anymore?

He was probably dead.

Thomas nodded to Coran, noting the concern in his squad mate’s eye, and straightened as Sergeant Nix stalked over, snapping out orders.

They’d been on a trip to one of the Dark Legion’s sanctioned armorers to collect more weapons for the new recruits, and while they’d been a decent distance away, hell, they’d almost been out of the city entirely, a section of the market just exploded with magic, killing dozens. Of course, they wanted the Dark Legion, not the guard.

They’d been the closest unit, just heading down the road, sat in the back of the wagon and watching the passersby. Thomas had been amazed at the difference from the last time he was in a wagon passing through the city.

That time, he’d been pelted with stones and shit, occasionally kicked by the others in the wagon who felt the need to lash out at one they should have pitied.

This time? He’d been in Aspirant’s armor, polished, gleaming plate, well-fed and healed, and the looks he’d gotten? Who needed the street of negotiable affection!

Hell, if those looks were anything to go by, he could probably charge *them*! Then the whistles had been blown, and the Iron Bell, standing tall and proud in the Cathedral had begun to ring, summoning the Dark Legion.

They'd known where to go. The Quest they'd all received from the priest to find the criminal had specified the street, after all. Ten minutes later, Thomas and his team were coming to a halt in the market, stunned by the devastation.

"It'll be a rogue mage…mark my words." Nix growled to them all. "We'll get directions soon enough, trackers are on their way, and they'll find them. We get to go slaughter the fucker when they know the address. For now, though? Its shit detail, my lads and lasses, digging the bodies out from under the ruins of the street!"

He slapped his hands together, probably thinking it was a sound like the crack of doom. In reality, it was a pathetic clank.

Nix was a third-rate Sergeant, if that, promoted more because he had friends in high places that he owed money to, rather than any real skill.

"Thomas!" Coran hissed.

Thomas jumped, darting after his friend.

"What the hell are you doing!" Coran asked

He shook his head. "Nothing mate, I just…"

"You just what? By the Dark One's balls, Thomas, we're aspirants! You want to spend the next year cleaning the latrines? Get working, man!"

"You two!" Nix bellowed. "Check for survivors in there!" He gestured to a shop to their left, then started ordering the guard that had been entering to move elsewhere.

"Yessir!" Thomas barked, following his friend over to the collapsed side of a shop. He winced internally at the rolls of expensive fabrics—probably meant for some posh boudoir—that were now covered in dust and blood.

Then he shook his head. Sticking out from under one of the rolls was a lone foot, the ankle broken and the flesh already white with blood loss.

"There." Thomas said to Coran, pointing and getting a grunt.

"Leave it." Coran said standing next to him and peering in through the shattered window. "That next one, under the table…give me a hand." He stepped to the window to pull himself in, the door buried under a mound of rubble.

"Why?" Thomas asked.

Coran grunted, gesturing at the first. "The blood; if they've lost that much, even if they're alive, they'll not live long. That one, though, not much blood. We save them, might get a reward out of it."

"What about healers?"

"What about them?" Coran asked, confused.

"Will the healers not come to help?"

"You ever seen a healer do anything for free?"

"Well, no…but…" Thomas broke off, looking around, gesturing vaguely.

The street was a scene of devastation, the fronts of buildings had collapsed, sections of the cobbled street had been thrown into the air, rippled upwards like it had become liquid, and a stone flung into the depths of the city from on high, then solidified again.

There were bloody bodies everywhere, some charred beyond recognition, others…

Two young women, well-dressed, clearly on an afternoon jaunt, were laid side-by-side. One's hand looked to have been hit with something, an explosive firebolt variant maybe, judging from the destruction and the way she'd bled out. The other, dressed similarly, was laid by her side on a section of cleared path.

She looked fine, apart from a few bloody splatters on her dress, fine that is, until you looked up and saw her head.

A section of wall, a lintel or something equally large, easily two feet long, had fallen from the building above, and when it'd hit…

The only way the father kneeling between them and screaming about his beloved daughters' deaths could have recognized her was the clothing; because, from the neck up, she just plain didn't exist anymore.

There were dozens, if not hundreds of them like that. Some still smoldering, filling the air with the sickly sweet smell of barbecued flesh, others were buried or covered in dust.

Some were just a random limb.

"What the fuck kind of an asshole does something like this?" Thomas muttered.

"Someone we hopefully get to kill later, now come on, man!" Coran barked, smacking Thomas on the shoulder.

"Right." Thomas agreed, turning away from the street and clambering in through the shattered window after Coran. As he'd recommended, Coran literally stepped over the first body, ignoring it and moving to the second, slowly lifting the edge of the table.

"How bad?" Thomas asked, shifting the cloth to look down at the first body and quickly moving it back to cover the corpse when the cold eyes stared up at him.

"Dead."

"You sure?"

"Oh yeah." Coran said, rubbing his chin thoughtfully. "Keep an eye out, give me a minute."

That was all he said, but Thomas trusted him, turning around and moving back towards the shattered remains of the window. He stared out at the figures moving around, filling the street along with the screams of the injured.

"What you doing?" Thomas asked in a low voice after a few seconds. Coran was doing something, and he hated himself as he covered for the man, but wasn't willing to risk losing the only friend he had.

"Checking for loot. They're dead; they don't need it."

"Don't." Thomas ordered quickly, turning back around and shaking his head. "Fucks sake, Coran! We're aspirants; you want to be busted back to a slave?"

"You think the others won't be doing it?" Coran snapped back, pulling a coin purse free and hefting it in his hand with a grin. "Hell, there'll be more stolen in the next ten minutes than the pickpockets and thieves manage in a year, and…"

"And we're aspirants!" Thomas repeated. "They fucking search us when we return to the camp remember!"

"Yeah, but…" Coran started to say, gesturing to Sergeant Nix who wasn't even trying to be subtle as he pocketed a golden chain from a dead body on the far side of the street as he was 'checking for signs of life.'

“They’ll search us, and they’ll make an example of us for the others! You know they will. Hell, Nix probably sent us in here planning to search us later and pocket whatever we’ve grabbed! We can’t spend it, not ‘til we’re full Legionnaires and get let out, so don’t be an idiot!”

“You think he…?”

“Yeah, that fucker’s setting us up.” Thomas said with certainty filling him. The shop they’d been sent to was a posh one, all silks and fabrics for the nobility, and nobody to watch over them?

He turned back to the window, seeing Nix straighten up from the body and glancing around, before eying the shop he’d sent them into.

The glass was filthy with dust and splattered blood, not to mention being shattered. Thomas was fairly sure the Sergeant couldn’t see him, but just in case…

“Come on!” He growled to Coran. “Get a move on, search the rest of the room, then we’re out of here.”

“Man, this sucks.” Coran muttered, hefting the pouch then dropping it on the floor.

“You don’t have to trust me.” Thomas pointed out.

“I do. It’s exactly what that dick would do.” Coran shook his head. “Too lazy to loot himself, so he’d have us do it.”

“Exactly.” Thomas agreed, ducking under a shattered support beam, looking around in the back room.

“Nothing here,” he reported after a few seconds, turning back and seeing Coran looking at him in the doorway. “What?”

“Thanks.”

“It’s fine.”

“No, seriously. It makes sense, and yeah, I’ll be pissed if we don’t get searched, but…”

“We’re mates.” Thomas grunted, shrugging as if it was no big thing.

“Yeah. Well, it’s good knowing I’ve got a brother watching out for me.”

The words hit Thomas like a sledgehammer coming so soon after that feeling of Jack’s closeness. He swallowed hard, a lump rising in his throat.

“Anytime,” he whispered, imagining he could feel that phantom connection again and knowing it was all in his head.

Jack wasn’t here.

He’d never be here now, if the connection was real, and not just something they’d imagined as kids? Then he’d just felt the severing of it. He’d just felt Jack dying, and considering the time since he left Earth? It was probably around the right time for Jack to have been beginning training, to fight in the arena, if the Baron had found him.

Hell, it might be a year earlier, or three longer, or more.

He could only guess.

The only way his brother would live now was in his memory. It was time to let Jack go. If, somehow, they did meet again? It’d be a pleasant surprise, rather than the way he felt now, hollow and alone.

“Bye bro…I love ya.” Thomas whispered, imagining the connection between them, if it ever truly existed, was now dead. He was glad of the helm he wore, as tears tracked down his cheeks.

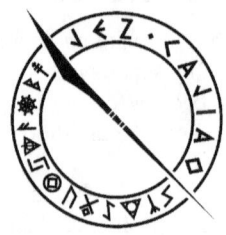

CHAPTER THIRTEEN

The next half hour passed in a blur. Buildings sped past me, abuse was shouted at our backs, and more than once, the clash of steel and screams of pain trailed in our wake.

I lay there, carried on a stretcher by four legionnaires as they sprinted along. Their full armor jingled and clashed with every step, and always, Augustus was there, watching over me.

Oracle sat by my head on the bouncing stretcher, glaring at the world around us as she flexed her fingers. My slowly refilling mana danced across her hands as she fumed, determined to kill anything she saw as a threat.

The minutes seemed to melt into each other as I tried to focus. The addition of the Cloudring's pervasive smoke was not helping, growing thicker as we neared the stepped pyramid of the arena. The shouting and fights faded away as the outer doors of the Cloudring closed, sealing off the "common people" from the wealthier inner district.

Voices raised in argument, then Gaion was giving orders, and we were off again. The guards looked angry but allowed us to proceed.

Finally, a handful of minutes later, we were inside the pyramid again, and Bane helped me from the stretcher into a chair, only to be accosted by Mal.

"What the hell did you do, son? The city's been goin' crazy! You wanted to see a healer, do a little shoppin', you said. Barely over two hours, and you're back; meanwhile, half of Horseshoe Street is demolished, dozens dead. The legion is cuttin' people down in the street, and you brought 'em here! You…"

"Blood and bloody ashes!" came a groan from the doorway, and the healer forced her way into the room, rubbing her head as she looked around, confused.

"…and you've kidnapped Mistress Nerin. Oh, that's just *wonderful!*" He bolted to his feet and crossed the room. "You remember the plan? The one that gave us a few days to do a month's worth of work? The one where we had to try to meet all your stupid wants?" he shouted at me. A growl rumbled from Augustus, who stepped forward, his hand on the hilt of his gladius.

"You'll watch your tongue when you speak to the High Lord of Dravith!" he snarled, and the room changed as Soween went from lounging against the wall to both crossbows drawn, glittering with magic. Jay moved across the room in an instant, grinning as he prepared to square off with the enormous Centurion Primus, and Josh jumped to his feet, shouting in panic.

"What the hell do you all think you're doing? I didn't heal the boy just so you could all fight each other over here!" Nerin pushed further into the room, furiously shoving people out of her way.

"Now, what the hell just happened, and why, by all that's holy, am I *here*?"

Everyone paused, looking at each other. I forced myself to sit upright from where I'd slouched bonelessly into the chair, and I waved at her.

"That'd be my fault, I think," I whispered, exhaustion filling my voice and getting a glare from more than half the room for my troubles. "Look, everyone calm the fuck down, and we'll talk this out, okay?" I rubbed my face. "I don't have the energy for a fight right now."

"Lord Jax—" Augustus started.

"Shut it!" I forced myself to take a deep breath and straighten up again. "Sorry, Augustus. Loving your help so far, I really am, but right now, I need every fucker to shut the hell up while we try to sort this thing out. I'll start…The last thing I remember, before finding myself gutted like a goddamn fish on your table," I said, nodding to Nerin, "was losing my temper a touch in the market. So, how about we all get the whole story laid out first, then we can come up with a plan to fix things."

"Fix things…we *had* a plan! We had a goddamn way out of the city, a way to make some real money and—" Mal wailed, cut off by Nerin turning around and smacking him across the back of the head. "What the hell?"

"Shut it, boy!" she snapped at him absently. "I want to hear what brought that fool to my shop, and what the hell that thing was that he tore out of himself!"

"We had a plan," muttered Mal, rubbing the back of his head.

"Yeah…this is gonna take some explaining, but that in itself is an issue, considering the situation. Until I've got a more concrete handle on people, some parts of this story aren't going to be easy to explain.

"Other bits…well yeah, they're going to be harder to accept without telling you the whole story, I suppose. Can we agree to an Oath here? What gets said in this room doesn't get repeated to anyone else, by word, deed, or omission, for a week from today? That gives everyone time to get over things and for our plans to be put in action."

"Not gonna happen," Mal said at the exact same time that Soween spoke up.

"That sounds reasonable," she said, then sent Mal a calm shrug. "It's the only way we're going to salvage any of the plan."

I grinned at him as Josh nodded, agreeing with her.

"I don't like it. Can't trust the legion," said Jay.

Augustus stiffened, his fingers reaching for the hilt of his gladius.

"Jay, you were born an idiot, and you've only gotten stupider as you aged. Shut up while the adults are speaking," Nerin snapped. "So, you want an Oath, we all agree to it, and you'll explain what that thing was?"

"Yes and no," I replied tiredly. "I'll explain as much as I can, but certain things, I'm not going to discuss with anyone who isn't sworn to me. Even then, there are few I'll discuss those kinds of details with."

"Sworn to you?" Nerin asked. Then her eyes shimmered with an internal light as she stared at me fixedly for a few seconds.

I grabbed Augustus's wrist as he started forward, determined to place himself between me and danger, and I shook my head when he looked at me.

"Augustus, I know you see your job as protecting me right now, but please, chill the fuck out," I said, shaking my head carefully. My exhaustion and his "help" were making things far harder than they needed to be. "I'm too goddamn tired for this right now. You relax, and you'll get to hear the story, or you can go wait in the corridor, okay?"

He swallowed hard, then nodded, stepping back and moving to stand behind my chair.

"I accept," Nerin said.

I gaped at her, as did most of the room.

"What? Are you people all crazy? I ain't swearin' no Oath," Mal said, but Nerin spoke over him.

"He's a Scion of the Empire, confirmed by the Eternal Emperor, as well as the Champion of the Goddess Jenae. Those are two titles I can't imagine are possible to fake, so you'll shut your mouth and leave the room, or you'll swear the Oath, boy.

"I've got things to do tonight, not least of which is to sort out my damn shop from the mess I'd bet you all left it in! Did anyone think to lock the door when you carted me off like a sack of potatoes?" she asked.

The tension in the room changed to embarrassment.

"Great! Wonderful…so now I've probably been robbed blind, as well." She gestured irritably at a pile of maps on a chair, which Gaion quickly moved. "So this Oath, let's get it done. I'll use a modified Confidence spell I know. Not the kind that makes you feel good about yourself, before you say anything either, Jay. It's confidence like 'in confidence.' I occasionally have to cast this for certain…neutral parties…so that they can meet. It examines your words for truth as you believe it and increases the level of pain and injury felt, depending on intent, as that's the safest way. If you say something in here, accidentally in the heat of the moment, it will warn you with pain, and we will all know about the lie. Speak it elsewhere, to others…you'll not survive, understood?

"Now…'I swear by my power and by my life that I will not repeat, discuss, or share by intent, word, or omission, any information shared in this room with anyone not present at this time, for the period of seven days, following today. I further swear that all words I say will be honest to the best of my knowledge,'" she intoned, lifting her right hand, palm up. A small circle appeared floating above her palm, and a dozen lines of blue-white light flashed out, reaching to hover before everyone in the room.

I started, surprised at the casual display of power, but I reached out, touching the thread of magic with my right forefinger and repeating the words. Once I'd finished, the thread sank back to the circle, causing the ring to pulse slowly.

With my example, the others followed suit; Bane, Lydia, Soween, and Josh, everyone reached out. Even Jay complied, despite then rubbing his finger on his leg, as though trying to get something off it.

I tried not to laugh as I realized everyone was doing it exactly as I had, touching the hovering line with their right forefinger.

When Mal finally was the only one left, he started to swear, grumbling under his breath as he reached out to touch the line as well.

"Not that finger!" I shouted, causing him to jump and pull back. Staring around in panic, he caught me trying to hide a laugh. He swore at me and prodded the line, repeating the words faithfully while staring daggers at anyone who sniggered…which was half the room.

"Sorry, Mal," I said, still trying to contain my laughter at his reaction, then grunted as my throat constricted and made me cough hoarsely.

"Are you?" he demanded. I forced a grin.

"No, not at all," I admitted. I wrestled myself to an upright position again and drew in a deep breath before beginning my story. "I think I need to go back to the beginning, more or less. I'm Jax, Lord of the Great Tower, and of Dravith. I am an acknowledged Scion of the Imperial Family, and I was named so by Eternal Emperor Amon. I'm in command of the tower now, but when I arrived…"

I spoke for nearly an hour, occasionally interrupted with requests for more detail, but by the end, I'd covered my arrival in the world, the SporeMother, the Great Tower, Jenae, our arrival in the city, and the plan to free the people. Finally, I reached the incident in the market.

"Once we were in the market, I saw things I couldn't ignore," I said, struggling to shift myself upright yet again. "I…uh, Nerin? Why am I still so exhausted? Surely I should have recovered by now?" I asked, and she shook her head.

"The magic that I used to reconstruct your body and fix the extensive damage was complicated and immensely powerful. It's not the kind of spell I use regularly, and it'll have side effects for the next few days, maybe a week. Also, I've yet to be paid for my part in all this, not to mention the damage that bringing the legion to my door will have done to my reputation!"

"That's not gonna work for me." I frowned anxiously. "I have a fight tonight in the arena."

"Not if you want to live, you don't," Nerin replied, shaking her head.

"I do want to live…thank you." I fought to keep the exasperation from my voice, and I was conscious of the need to be careful with everything I said, thanks to the spell. "I also need to be in that damn arena; it's central to our plans!"

"You've just had over a third of the most complicated sections of your body rebuilt from a cellular level. Entire sections of your brain and nervous system were shredded by that thing and had to be completely regrown. I'd be surprised if you can walk unaided tonight. You've got no chance at fighting," she said calmly as I slumped back. "Even now, while you've been talking, you've had to depend on your companion to hold you upright."

"I…" Something froze the words in my mouth, and I stopped, realizing the truth. I'd kept having to sit upright, but I hadn't noticed myself moving. I must have been sliding down as I was talking. *Great. Bet that looked fantastic…*

"Okay, so I'm a bit worn out, that's all. How can we fix it?" I asked.

"Food, rest, and sleep," she said. "You could use potions to stimulate your body, stamina, mana, and healing concoctions to keep you on your feet, but the bill will come due, and when you least expect it, you will collapse. Also, using true stimulants, like 'Bull's Heart Potion' would leave you unconscious as soon as it ran out. There is no substitute for food and rest, not when you've taken such severe injuries."

"I've never needed to before," I said, but I felt a worrying niggle as I spoke.

"You just skirted close to a lie there, boy," Nerin said disapprovingly, and Oracle spoke up for me.

"No, he said what he believed to be true. He just didn't realize it wasn't, until this conversation."

"What do you mean?" I asked, confused.

"When you're healed by magic, it takes its toll on your physical body," Nerin said, slipping into lecturing mode. "The magic rebuilds the body, but it does so by utilizing the body itself. It doesn't just create bits out of thin air. While that level of repair is possible, that magic is far beyond a simple healing spell. No, a healing spell usually just provides the power to increase the speed of the body's natural healing capacity. You've had a significant portion of highly specialized parts rebuilt, and judging from your tale, this has happened many times?"

"Yeah, and I was always…" I paused considering my previous brushes with death.

In the tower, I'd passed out after many fights, always when I'd had to heal myself heavily. I'd been exhausted afterwards, and I'd basically crawled into the nearest hole I could, in order to sleep like the dead.

"Okay…yeah. Now that I think about it, I guess that makes sense," I said.

"The plan is well and truly fucked, then!" Mal cursed, throwing his arms up and scowling.

"What's the problem?" Augustus asked, and Mal glared at him.

"We were supposed to be puttin' the first phase of the plan into action tonight: gettin' the local gangs to put in fighters to face 'Legionnaire' Jax in the arena. Now what are we supposed to do?!"

"Submit another legionnaire," Augustus replied, shrugging. "I'll do it."

"No. You don't know what they're going to put in to fight," I said weakly.

Augustus just grinned at me.

"Believe me, Jax," Yen interjected, and I looked at her in question. "You don't make it to Centurion Primus in the legion without being able to fight. No offense, but he's probably far deadlier than you are."

"I don't like it, I—" I started to protest, when Mal cut me off.

"Yes! That's it! August can fight in the arena! Then…"

"Augustus," the dark-haired, massively muscled Centurion Primus snapped, glaring at Mal.

"That's what I said," Mal replied dismissively, waving him off. "So, now that's sorted, how about you explain what the hell happened in the damn market?!"

"I'm not happy about this," I muttered, but in looking the massive legionnaire over, I had to agree that he was probably more suited to the fight, especially dressed in his segmented steel armor over black leather. A huge shield rested against the wall where he'd placed it on entering, and he wore a short gladius on his left hip.

A wicked-looking, single-handed axe with a thick-bearded head hung on his back, the handle protruding over his right shoulder, and a pair of sheathed daggers had been strapped to his chest, the handles pointed down for easy access.

Thick, overlapping plates protected his shoulders, upper chest, upper arms, and forearms, with knee guards, upper thighs, and greaves all fashioned similarly, and chain mail covered the rest. I'd noticed that the armor was the same that the rest of his legionnaires wore. It appeared far heavier than I'd have expected, but that explained why they were so damn big. The entire group looked like they'd be able to steal Schwarzenegger's lunch money.

"The story, Jax," Oracle said, and I craned my neck to look up at her. "Tell them what happened, then we can get you to bed. Look at it this way: if you feel up to it later, you can fight in the arena, provided you can convince Bane, Lydia, and me that you're fit enough."

"Yeah, I'll believe that…At any rate, long story short, I saw a little girl in the market. She was crying her eyes out, looking for help, and this guy was blatantly up to no good. I saw him going for her, right after seeing slaves all over the place, and a woman…I saw a woman who'd given up.

"I saw a woman who was broken by life, and a tiny fucking baby that was going to have no chance. I saw all of that, and the goddamn rich shits that were wandering around, laughing and living their fucking best life, okay?!" I snarled, the memories coming back to me. "I don't just get mystical messages from Amon; I've got the mental bastard riding in my soul. He saw it, the same as I did, and I felt his rage. We were both so fucking angry that…that…"

"That you lost control and destroyed the market?" Soween asked, shock in her voice.

"Yes! Okay? It was probably wrong, it's probably buggered all our chances, and yes…I'd fucking well do it again in a heartbeat!" I growled, sitting forward and clenching my hands into fists. "It might have been wrong. It might have cost lives that we could have saved. I should have kept control, I *know* I should have, but I can't. I won't just stand by and let that shit happen! I spent my entire life being called here to fucking save people.

"I've died hundreds of times, and I fucking well won't stop! I will *not* let them die, not when I can save them, not fucking one of them! Amon, that dick, he'd have burned an innocent to death in an instant to save a hundred more. I know it might make sense; I understand fucking numbers, okay? I just can't do that! I can't let them die, not if I can stop it!" I bit down on my last words, nostrils flaring as I tried to bring my frantically beating heart under control.

"Truth," Nerin said quietly, and everyone gaped at her.

"What?" Josh asked, looking from her to me and back again.

"Every word he just spoke was truth," she said slowly, clearly considering my explanation. "He said things exactly as he believes them, without even a slight tremor. This is literally the truth of his soul, the most basic tenets of his mind and personality." She lifted the ring of slowly spinning mana for all to see. "I used a section that would allow me to detect any hedging or attempts to disguise the truth as part of that spell. There was absolutely none in anything that he said."

"Well, that's just fuckin' peachy," Mal griped, rubbing his hand through his hair. "So you're sayin' every time he sees someone in trouble, he's gonna jump right in? You know where you are, right?" Mal asked me sarcastically. "This is the fuckin' arena; we don't do pillow fights downstairs!"

"And I'll kill any fucker who faces me by choice," I snapped back at him. "I just won't kill an innocent."

"This is Himnel! There are no fuckin' innocents here!" he snapped back at me, then coughed, grabbing at his throat as the Oath punished his use of hyperbole.

"I won't fight slaves, then; I won't fight those who've got no choice in the fight! There are innocents out there. That's why all this happened, because I won't let them suffer!"

"Then you're an idiot!" Mal shouted, getting to his feet and waving his hands around. "You'll let hundreds die, all our plans fuckin' fail, just because you want to be the hero! You think you're the only one? You think we don't all want to be that guy, standin' up there and savin' the kids? *It doesn't work, Jax*…You can't save 'em all, and when you try, you just get your friends killed!"

Silence filled the room as the echoes of his shouted words faded away, and I noticed the looks people were giving him.

The spell, or Oath, or whatever Nerin had used, had forced us to only speak what we believed to be the truth…so Mal really believed that, and I wondered what had happened to him to make him feel that way.

"Look, I know you want to help 'em," Mal said hoarsely, rubbing at his throat. "I understand that, okay? But to throw everythin' away because you can't walk away from one person is just stupid. The plan was hard enough already; now, it's even worse. You could lose the chance to help hundreds to save just one. I know what you're sayin', but those numbers don't add up…they just don't." He slowly shook his head.

"I know that, Mal," I said, equally quiet in the silent room. "I understand it in my head…but in my heart, I can't accept that. Logically, it makes sense, but I can't live by logic, not with something like that."

"Then we've got no chance," Mal said bleakly.

"Of course you have!" Mistress Nerin pushed herself to her feet. "What, you think because you idiots can't see a way forward, it can't be done? Fwah!" She blew her lips out in exasperation. "Men always think in straight lines. Can't see it, it can't be done! What do you think has happened here, boy?" she said, looking at Mal.

"You think just because he can't fight tonight or tomorrow, it's over? You've already got a legionnaire who's volunteered to fight in his place. As to getting out there and bringing in the people on this list…that just got easier."

"How? Now the damn gangs will be watchin'. Hell, the guards will be in an uproar trying to figure out what happened! There'll be investigators everywhere, tryin' to trace the magic used!"

"True," Nerin said, smiling. "But that just means *he*"—she pointed at me—"…can't go outside again. That means he won't have another chance to get into trouble, either. Instead, we send his newly devoted friends."

"Who?" I asked, confused, and she smiled.

"The slaves you freed. You literally tore the market to shreds in a display of power I cannot imagine, while leaving a ring of safety around each and every slave. Men, women, and children who had believed their lives were gone. They had no hope of ever being free, yet saw their tormentors punished by—…and I quote from what was being said while I was working on you—'…the light made flesh.' You think they won't happily go carry a few messages for you, if you ask?"

"I…" I grimaced. I didn't like the idea of people looking at me like that, given that a few months ago, I had been working in a bar, but…

"What about the gangs, though? He's already crossed the harpies and the Skyking," Mal asked Nerin.

"You said you were going to pull them here with an offer to let them submit fighters to punish him. You told them that you'd captured him and were going to use him in a series of fights, along with his friends.

"Do that still. Say that he's a legionnaire and say that he came to you to try to bribe you for safety. Tell the gang leaders they have to pay a fee, or they go last in the fight. That way you get gold, and it matches your reputation as a greedy son of a bitch, as well as giving you a reason to spread the fights out over a few days."

"I already told them it was going to last a few days."

"Well, say you captured more of them, then. Or not. I don't care! I just want this dealt with, so I can go back to my shop before the damn nails in the walls have been stripped out!" she snapped at Mal. Still fuming, she turned her unspent ire on me. "And I've still not been paid, lordling! Two hundred gold, and the truth of what that…thing…was!"

"I'll pay that happily…if you'll consider joining us?" I asked her

"I've already helped you, boy. If word gets out, it'll be my head on a pike alongside yours. Nobles don't care if I helped by choice or not."

"I mean in the Great Tower," I clarified. "We need a real healer. I've got two novices who are helping as they can, but you? You're gifted, and you know what you're doing."

"I'm also old enough to know just how much work that would be! I have a shop and a good thing going here. Nobody in the city messes with a healer, and most of the nobles don't know I exist. I want it to stay that way, so make sure you don't get caught." She let out a tired sigh. "Ten years ago, I'd have jumped at the chance. Now, all I own is tied up in that shop. I can't leave it. Not even for you, lordling."

She shook her head regretfully.

"At least consider it, okay?" I asked her. "And for the next few days, help us out here, heal our injuries, and I'll make it worth your while."

"I'll think about it! Now, that creature…gimme!" she said, gesturing impatiently.

"I don't know much beyond a name and a few scattered memories," I admitted, forcing myself to sit upright again. "They were called the Valspar, and Emperor Amon hated them with a passion. They're a form of parasite that was supposed to be wiped out.

"They exist in the space between the living and the dead, and they're a bastard to kill. Somehow, one got into me, and they're powerful enough or sneaky enough that they completely hid from me, from Oracle, and hell, even from Jenae."

"This is true." Jenae's voice echoed around the room, causing everyone to flinch. ***"The Valspar are an ancient race, evil beyond what you can imagine. They hid from me when I examined Jax, but they would not have been able to hide, had I used a more…specialized examination. There are spells that can detect and eliminate them, though they were thought long lost from the world. I will not have these creatures return, and as such, will aid you in the retrieval of the needed spellbooks, Jax."***

"Thank you, Jenae," I said, bowing my head and smiling. "I know you helped Nerin to heal me, so thanks for that, too."

"You're welcome...although that was the boon that I promised you. I don't care that you didn't ask me to use it; you needed it."

I froze in the act of opening my mouth to complain, and instead shrugged. *Easy come, easy go...*

"Well...thank you again." I scanned the room, mildly amused at the expressions of shock and awe that filled every face. "Oh, and yes, people, that's the voice of the Goddess Jenae, Mistress of Fire and Hidden Knowledge."

"Goddess," Nerin whispered, sliding to her knees and bowing her head.

"Yes, child, I am here, and yes, I aided you in healing him. The strain was too much for you, as Life-aligned as you are, so you succumbed to shock. I apologize for that."

"I...he...he's truly your champion? Does this mean...are the gods returning to us?" Nerin whispered.

I lifted an eyebrow at the ceiling, waiting for Jenae's response.

"Yes, child, we are awakening again, and we will be here to help the realm. However...we have been weakened by our long sleep, and we must build our strength before we show ourselves fully. Circumstances overrode this, but I will have each and every one of you swear on your soul, to me, that you will not speak of our return except to aid us."

I grinned as I caught the confusion and caution on everyone's faces.

"Look, people, it's like this," I said. "The Goddess Jenae isn't the only goddess out there, and she and her siblings need our help. We need to spread word of their return, but not yet, as it'll start a war between the gods. We need to help them recover their strength first. You can choose which god or goddess to follow, based on your own choices and tastes, but you cannot spread the word of them, not yet." I forced myself to stand and looked around the room. "For now, you can follow any god or goddess, or none, but you cannot tell others who are not sworn to me."

"You mean, we have to swear to you?" Soween asked, irritation clouding her voice.

"No," I replied, shaking my head. "You don't have to. You can help me just as you've sworn to, and then you can go on your way. You only have to swear to me if you want access to the Great Tower and the altars of the gods. You only have to swear to me if you want my help to spread the word of those gods, and if you want to help in what's coming."

"What is coming?" Mal asked me, cocking his head to the side in question and drumming his fingers on the stock of one of his magical crossbows. "Besides us robbing Himnel blind?"

"A war," I said simply. "A war between the gods. Believe me, you can be with us or against us, but you won't want to be on the sidelines."

"Why not?"

"Because, Mal, if you want to survive it, you'll need to pick a side...and our side cares if you live or die. The God of Death doesn't."

"Good point," Mal muttered.

"Exactly, mate. Now, I think the goddess asked for an Oath, and it's one directly to her, not to me, so let's do this one together," I said, closing my eyes, sinking to one knee, and speaking slowly and clearly as the room watched on.

"I, Jax, swear upon my soul that I will not speak of the return of the gods, save to aid them, until given permission by the Goddess Jenae." I felt a burning sensation pass through me. It only lasted a second, but the aftermath was weirdly cooling, and I let out a sigh of relief as I slowly straightened up again. I smiled to myself as the others started to make their own Oaths.

"Jax, I can't help you much in the days to come, not with as much as that spell cost me, but call to me if you need me, and I'll provide you with quests when I can," Jenae said, and I found a prompt opening before my eyes.

Congratulations!

You have been given a Quest by the Goddess Jenae: Bring Home the Bacon.

The Goddess Jenae has commanded you to retrieve all you can from those that skulk and raid the corpse of the empire. Take your rightful place as their lord and bring back that which you need to repair the seat of your Power, the Great Tower.

Recover Magical Artifacts and Technologies: 0/?

Retrieve Manastones: 0/100

Recruit Additional Citizens: 0/100

Recruit Skilled Crafters: 0/100

Recruit a Tower Healer: 0/1

Bonuses will be given for exceeding these numbers.

Reward: Basic functionality of the Great Tower, Unknown, 250,000xp

"I'll reach out to you soon with a location for the spellbooks you'll need, Jax, as well as other powerful artifacts."

"Thank you, Jenae," I said, nodding my head, the shift in pressure letting me know she'd gone.

Silence filled the room for a few seconds as I sat back down.

"So, everyone happy that the plan goes ahead?" I asked, my exhaustion insistently clawing at the inside of my brain. I looked around the room, getting hesitant and firm nods, depending on the person, until I finally came to Mal and Nerin.

Mal was staring into the distance, refusing to make eye contact, and Nerin was watching me.

"Has Ashante, Goddess of Life, joined this fight?" she asked me, and I managed a smile.

"As far as I know, they're all awakening. Jenae has filled me in on some of the past, so they won't be joining the other side, if that's what you're worried about. The gods are all with Jenae."

"Hmmm, I'll consider it," she said, standing up. "Now, I need to leave. I'll come back tonight and see what happens in the arena; maybe I'll even help this big lug out." She gestured offhandedly at Augustus before heading to the door.

Others soon started to drift away, so I forced myself to my feet. Oracle shifted to her full form and helped to take my weight as Bane moved in close, offering me a shoulder.

"Mal?" I asked, and he looked back at me, his mind seeming to return from miles away.

"What?" he asked, his tone short.

"Are you still with us?" I replied bluntly, hoping the remnants of the spell would make sure he gave me an honest answer.

"Yeah," he said, after a moment's hesitation. "But unless there's a good reason, you're staying in here. We'll have people brought to you."

"Until the last night," I pressed, fixing him with a glare. "I promised to deal with the Skyking. Three days, I'll wait, and I'll fight in the arena as soon as I'm able, but on the fourth night, our last night, I'm taking him down."

"If we can find it, you can. If not, you damn well leave with your head held high. This is going to be the biggest theft ever. My name's going to go down in history, son, and I'll not jeopardize that!" he said, a faint grin coming to his face. I grinned back at him weakly, relieved that I still had my team.

"Come on," Oracle whispered to me, hugging me as much as helping me to stay upright. "Let's get you back to our rooms."

"Yeah, baby, yeah," I whispered back to her weakly and got a snort in response.

"Like you've got the energy now," she replied quietly. "Next time, I won't miss the chance!"

I grinned at her, forcing myself to walk. My knees nearly buckled with each step, until at last, I returned to my room and collapsed on the bed.

The last thing I heard was Oracle speaking in hushed tones to Augustus and his men, filling them in on what had happened. Augustus gave Amaat orders to return to the enclave and fill in the legion. The last thing I saw, though, was the flickering shadows surrounding Bane as he took up station in my room, watching over me, as the world fell into blackness.

CHAPTER FOURTEEN

I woke up slowly, lying exhausted in my bed. Each individual muscle and joint ached as I forced my arms and legs to stretch out. I extended each one slowly, and both felt and heard my back pop and crack.

I opened my eyes, barely able to focus as an enormous yawn cracked my jaws. It didn't take long to find out what had awoken me: an extremely urgent need to use the toilet.

I shuffled myself across the bed, slowly heaving myself upright and yawning again. My entire body felt weak and sore as I staggered into the adjoining room and relieved myself. I noted absently that the sunken bath had been scrubbed clean again.

I yawned yet again, pouring some water from the jug on a shelf into the stone basin and washed my face and hands, trying to force some life back into my fuzzy brain. I skimmed the room absently as I shuffled back to the bed, finding my clothes stacked neatly, cleaned—thank god—and repaired. I started pulling different items on, when my brain seemed to finally kick into full gear.

I blinked, straightening up and scowled at the small balcony garden outside of my room. More specifically, I scowled at the darkness that filled it, when the noise that had been at the edge of my hearing since I awoke finally resolved.

Past the nearby sounds of low voices talking, I could hear the cheers and chants of a crowd, and the call of an announcer as they broadcast a name…

I couldn't make it out, but I knew what it meant as the last of the sleep was banished from my tired brain.

The arena.

The fight had begun.

I swore viciously and began grabbing my gear, dressing quickly. I paused briefly as a calm voice spoke in the darkness of my room.

"On your left…"

I froze at the sound, then realized who it was.

"Bane?" I asked, and he stepped forward from a patch of shadow, nodding in greeting while reaching out and pulling the cinch strap tight, on my left, as he'd pointed out. I shrugged inside my armor for a second, feeling it settling more comfortably as I nodded my thanks to him.

"What happened?" I asked, and he cocked his head to one side.

"With what?"

"Everything!" I snapped, getting a low *thrummm* of amusement back from him.

"Well, some trees grew a little taller, some animals were eaten, others were born, and—"

"You know what I mean, you prick," I cut him off, trying not to grin at him.

"Oh, you mean what happened with the rest of us while the 'Mighty Lord Jax' had a nap?" he asked sarcastically, his tone letting me know he was taking the opportunity to mock me.

"Yes, you git," I said, half-frustrated, half-relieved. If he was joking, it couldn't be that bad.

"Well, your champion Augustus seems to be doing well. The first round of fights were easy enough; only two of the gangs sent fighters, and he killed them both easily. He actually cut one almost in half with the man's own battleaxe, so, yes, he's fast becoming a favorite with the crowds," Bane said, more seriously. "The second round is going well, from what I can hear. They've chanted his name three times so far, so I can only guess the night's fights are nearly over now."

"Wait, the first round? The second? How long was I out?" I asked, confused.

"Over a full day. You slept straight through the fights last night, all of today, and now it's the early hours of…well…tomorrow now, I guess?" He shrugged.

"I've lost two nights?!" I gaped at him, stunned. "What the hell—"

"Mistress Nerin returned and checked on you. She said that you were recovering well, and she wanted to see you as soon as you woke up. Oracle is with her in the arena now, talking to a group of engineers from the shipyards."

"I…I need to get there," I said, dismayed at how much time I'd lost, and at least in part, a little bemused by how little anyone seemed to care. My notifications were flashing insistently, and I quickly pulled them up, grimacing as I read the first.

Congratulations!

You have killed the following:

- 11x Shoppers of various levels for a total of 2,785xp
- 1x Felar Trader, level 16 for a total of 1,390xp
- 2x Imps of various levels for a total of 300xp
- 6x Refugees of various levels for a total of 1,200xp
- 4x Horses of various levels for a total of 90xp
- 411x Common Sewer Rats of various levels for a total of 411xp
- 27x Greater Sewer Rats of various levels for a total of 108xp
- 2x Skaven, level 23 for a total of 845xp

Progress to level 16 stands at 17,149 /165,000

I dismissed it instantly, feeling sick as I was forced to read the list of deaths I'd caused with my little temper tantrum, yet it was nothing considering the deaths I'd nearly caused by releasing the maddened shade of Amon on the realm.

The second prompt dealt with increases in my skills, and I closed it without looking. I couldn't deal with that shit right now.

"Jax?" Bane asked, and I met his gaze, swallowing hard.

"Yeah?" I mumbled weakly.

"Are you okay?" He reached out as if to steady me.

"No. No, I'm really not, mate. I just saw how many died in that incident in the market, and I..."

"Did you get any other prompts?" he asked intently, and I shrugged.

"I closed them; I can't deal with that shit right now."

"Did you receive any new followers?" he asked.

I frowned at him, confused. "No, why..."

"Then I suggest you pull them up and look again, my friend. It's not all as bleak as you fear. You killed people, yes, and regrettably, some died who should not have, but there are many who lived, and now live free, because of that 'incident.'"

I took a deep breath and pulled the notifications back up, dismissing the skill gains again in order to read the third and final prompt.

Congratulations!

Your companion, Oracle, has administered the Oath of Allegiance in your stead, Master of the Great Tower.

The following citizens have taken the Oath and joined your ranks.

- 11x Elves
- 4x Dwarves
- 14x Hybrids of Various Species
- 3x Halflings
- 3x Panthera
- 2x Saurians
- 7x Humans

Furthermore, 22 children of various races have been granted sanctuary after being informed that they are too young to swear the Oaths.

"Where the hell did they come from?" I asked Bane in surprise.

"They're the slaves you freed in the market, and some who joined us as we returned to the arena, believing that we were their best chance at freedom or a second chance at life," he replied calmly.

"But...Mal's gonna go apeshit," I muttered, facepalming. "There's no way we can keep this quiet."

"He already did," Bane said, watching me carefully. "Yesterday, remember?"

"I didn't realize there were so many," I said.

"Well, we all accepted that you were a bit...dazed...yesterday, but your speech was enough. Mal and the others are still with us, and of the fresh volunteers, most have been used to spread the word, bringing in people to meet with Oracle and Barrett. Lydia has had her squad training with the legionnaires."

"How's that going?" I asked, wincing.

"Surprisingly well," Bane replied sanguinely. "The legion were careful with them at first, as it seems these legionnaires are some of their best; they're the quick-reaction force that gets used for monster sightings, mainly. They started out being a bit…unimpressed with the squad, or so I hear. Tang said they changed their minds and adopted them when they realized they were your personal squad. They seem determined to 'beat them into shape,' as Augustus put it."

"Augustus…" I said, shaking my head. "Okay, get me to the arena and Oracle. I need to see what's going on."

Bane moved to the door ahead of me, cracking it and glancing outside before opening it wider and leading the way. All talk ceased in the corridor as Miren and Lydia got to their feet, along with four legionnaires.

As I stepped out into the corridor, all four immediately clapped their fists to their chest plates in unison, dropping to one knee. I froze, thoroughly freaked out by the formal salute, and glanced at Lydia, who shrugged.

I swallowed, returning the salute, then gestured for them to get up.

"Thank you," I said to the legionnaires as they started to stand. "But please, I don't want that kind of response normally. I'm…pretty informal."

"Yes, my lord," one of the legionnaires replied, straightening. "We will strive to be less…formal. Now, what can we do for you?"

The other legionnaires turned back out with crisp movements, watching the corridor and the doors leading from it with barely concealed ferocity.

"I need to get to the arena, find our people, and find out what the hell is going on," I said, and the legionnaire nodded to me.

"Yes, my lord. I'm Centurion Grizz. We know the way. I'd ask that you allow us to take the lead and the rear, with you and your party in the middle. Is this acceptable?" he asked. I nodded, gesturing to him to carry on. "Thank you, sir."

I swallowed my instinctual desire to tell him to knock it off with the "lord" and "sir" shit, figuring I needed to allow at least some of it, since it was an authority thing for the tower.

Grizz and another legionnaire moved to the front of the group, leading us, and I fell in behind him, with Bane at my side. Miren and Lydia fell into step behind us and the remaining two legionnaires brought up the rear.

We set off down the hall, passing two more cross-connecting corridors before going deeper underground. Three flights of stairs and a couple of hurried conversations in back corridors, and a flustered serving girl led us out onto a private interior balcony that looked down into a sand-filled arena.

The first thing that hit me as we entered the private booth was the wall of sound. I'd been hearing the noise grow as we descended, but down here, hemmed in by stone and lifted by the crowd's love of blood and gore, it was a hundred times louder.

I could barely hear myself think as I moved forward, finding Mal and Soween watching the fighters below. There were three men in the arena; one, in full legion plate and looking like a bear that had been shaved and squeezed into it, was Augustus. The other two were smaller men, one with a trident and net, the other wielding twin daggers. Both were dressed in tight leather, with their faces covered by what I could only describe as gimp masks.

I felt my lips pull back from my teeth in discomfort as they circled Augustus, and I just hoped they only wanted to fight him…

"Welcome to the arena!" Mal shouted at me, and I turned to regard him, surprised by how calm he seemed. He picked up on my concern and shook his head. "Don't worry. He's in no danger from them."

I nodded uncertainly and looked back down in time to see the trident flash out towards Augustus, who bore a massive shield on his left arm and a short spear in his right hand.

He deflected the trident easily, sweeping it aside with his shield and turning to keep the dagger wielder in sight, then stabbed out, catching the first guy in the lower leg. sinking the leaf-bladed tip in and yanking it back out in one smooth, fluid motion.

The man screamed, backing away, and he followed, slamming his spear into the ground, point-first, deep enough that it stuck and trapped the trailing edge of the net that the man had been carrying.

The Centurion Primus spun, leaving the limping, heavily bleeding first fighter and ran at the second, driving him back with his shield.

The second man tried a few quick stabs at the shield, all of which glanced off. Augustus lashed out with his gladius, the blade darting forward in three fast strikes to open up the inside of his opponent's left wrist, slice the top of his thigh, then to sink into his throat.

A quick, efficient twist of the blade finished the man off, and he turned, jogging with a jingling trot back to the injured first fighter as the second collapsed behind him.

The first man tried to put up a fight, but it was over in seconds. Augustus calmly left the arena as people shouted and cheered.

I turned to gape at Mal, stunned by the casual skill shown, and he grinned at me, gesturing for me to follow him as he led us out of the room, down the corridor, and into another room located on the far side of the corridor from the arena.

The space was decorated in deep reds and gold trim, furnished with a private bar and several couches. Expensive-looking bottles glittered on the shelves, while a dozen bottles of beer lay chilling in a bucket of ice.

I gazed around, sinking gratefully into a chair. I was still surprised at just how tired and aching I was.

"What's this, then? Your personal bar?" I asked Mal. He grinned, pulling a bottle of beer free to throw to me. I caught it and popped the top, taking a swig as he offered beers to the legionnaires and the rest of the group.

The legionnaires refused, two taking up station outside the door, and two inside, while Mal rolled his eyes at me.

"You can have a beer, guys," I said to them, and I noticed the look that passed between them. "I won't tell Augustus, if you don't," I said, grinning, and saw the edges of their mouths quirking.

"We'll take turns on watch outside, sir, and thank you," Grizz accepted. He slipped out, sending in one of the men to get a beer and drink it first, clearly planning on being able to enjoy his own, rather than rushing it.

I grinned as I noticed Miren having her beer taken away by Lydia and being handed a fruit drink instead.

"I'm old enough!" Miren complained in a whisper that carried across the room, making her go red as Lydia growled that she wasn't getting beers after "last time" until she could learn to control herself.

"You've finally woken up, then," Mal said, taking a swig from his bottle and looking at me.

"Yeah, sorry I was out so long," I replied, feeling guilty as all hell. I'd literally rocked up, turned his world upside down, then had a nap, leaving him to fix things…

"Nerin explained it. Whatever that Valspar was, it sounds like it was pretty evil shit." He nodded to me, his expression uneasy.

"Yeah, it wasn't nice," I agreed, shrugging.

"You really rammed your hand into yourself up to the elbow and tore it out, though?" he asked incredulously. "I didn't think that kind of thing was even physically possible."

"It probably isn't; I used magic at the same time," I said, feeling uncomfortable at the looks the legionnaires were giving me.

"Yeah, I heard your hand was glowing," Mal muttered, still staring at me.

"Guess so. I don't remember much of it, okay? So…what have I missed?" I asked, only to have my mind almost blown out of my ears by Oracle's excited shout.

"JAX!" she screamed in my head, ***"YOU'RE AWAKE!"***

"And deaf, too!" I responded to her, a note of sarcasm in my projection. She paused, then went on at a much lower volume.

"Well, it's about time! I'll bring the engineers up to meet you now; are you in the red room?"

"The red room?" I asked aloud, unsure. Mal snorted as Soween laughed.

"You're talking to Oracle, aren't you?" Soween said, and I nodded. "She loves this room, for some reason. She was having most of her meetings in it, until we told her about the view from the ground for the fights. She's a bloodthirsty one, that girl."

"Yeah, the red room," I replied, getting a sense of happiness mixed with a feeling of impatience before she cut off the connection.

"Ah, Oracle and some people are coming up here, I guess," I explained bemusedly.

"We'll watch out for her, sir," said one of the legionnaires standing inside. He finished his beer and elbowed his companion, who did the same. They efficiently swapped over with Grizz and the other legionnaire outside, filling them in as they passed. Grizz took a beer, passing the other to his companion, and they took up station on either side of the door again.

"So, what have you missed…" Mal drawled, shifting to get himself more comfortable on his seat. "Well, we've had meetings with some of the families of the crew, or Barrett has, anyway. He also ran into Joya, who's apparently his ex…. She was a caravan guard for me, currently workin' as a bouncer here, so that was fuckin' hilarious.

"She's over six foot, and he's about an inch off being declared a dwarf, rather than a human. Must have carried a stepladder around with him everywhere, is my guess," Mal said, rubbing his head and taking a long draw on his beer.

"Your Oracle has been meetin' people from the shipyards and their families, and she's been workin' with Mistress Nerin to heal them. Seems there's a lot of 'em think she's one step from a goddess now, and it's a damn small step…These are people who've been crippled, spendin' their lives beggin', as they couldn't afford healers, then *boom*. She strolls in, asks them to swear to you, and heals them. Nerin has been doin' the ones Oracle couldn't and rackin' up quite the bill."

"Bill?" I asked.

"Seems her shop was ransacked pretty thoroughly when it was left open, so she's been runnin' a constant total for the work she's been doin' for you. Hope your pockets are deep."

"Ah…" I muttered, swallowing hard then taking a swig from my beer as he considered me shrewdly.

"Yeah, I guessed you'd been bluffin' about the gold." He shrugged. "That's why I wanted the fights. I've been bettin' pretty heavily on them, and that's bringin' in a nice little extra. Not enough to make me forget the rest of what you owe me, but enough that I'll survive if things go sideways."

"And the plans for the raid?" I asked.

His grin widened. "That's comin' together nicely, even if only because there's not a thief in the city that hasn't fantasized over doin' it themselves one day. I've got the plans that show the layout of the Stockpile, and I've found a worker who knows where everything is. He's happy to tell us, for a price…"

"And the price is?" I asked.

"He wants to come with us. Says he's got some score to settle with the noble who runs the guard."

"Do you believe him?" I pressed, and Mal snorted.

"Son, I'd not believe *you* if I hadn't been there when Nerin made us all swear that Oath. I don't trust him at all."

"So…"

"So I've told him I'm puttin' together a plan to rob the next shipment out of there. It's arriving in a week, and it will go from there to the shipyards to power up the engines for the test flight of the battleship. Makin' him think it's in a week, rather than two damn days, makes it a bit harder as he's in no rush, but better than lettin' him know the truth."

"That battleship's going to be ready in a week?" I asked, surprised.

"No, just the engines and frame, apparently. Nothin' else. It's a test flight, make sure everythin' is integrated. If it is, then great; if not, they've got time to figure out the problems before they start puttin' in all the big bits, like armor and cannons, on her."

The conversation was interrupted by a loud knock, followed by the door opening and Oracle strolling in.

She was full-sized, unsurprisingly, as she was meeting with people. She had gotten rid of her wings. Instead, she wore a silver-white dress that reached halfway to her knees. A belt of interwoven black and red leaves wrapped her slim waist, and silvery mid-calf boots clung to her shapely legs. Her hair was black as midnight and arranged to fall loosely down her back in a mass of curls that bounced as she walked.

Her lips were a deep, ruby red, and her perfect teeth shone white as she smiled at me, her eyes a dark mixture of chestnut and charcoal. She was dressed far more demurely than I usually saw her, her impressive bust hidden, rather than the way she usually showed it off, but damn. I wanted her.

"Hi, honey," she whispered, kissing my cheek and taking a seat next to me as I looked her over, smiling. I turned to the three who'd entered with her, having had eyes only for her until now, and I forced a smile for them as well.

The small group was composed of two dwarves, both women, and a tall elven man, all dressed in scruffy, grease-smudged overalls.

"This is Elise, Viktoria, and Finbar. They're the shift managers on the *Ragnarök*." Oracle pointed out Finbar and one of the dwarves, and nodded to the second. "Elise is a shift manager on the structural team for the battleship, which hasn't been named yet."

"Good to meet you all," I said.

"Aye, well ye might say tha'…but I dinna ken why we be here, laddie?" the dwarf introduced as Viktoria said, crossing her arms across her chest and tapping a foot on the floor.

"Perhaps a drink, while we talk?" Mal offered innocently, gesturing to the glittery bottles on the bar. The dwarf's eyes lit up.

"Well, aye! I could no' be accused o' bein' rude by sayin' no, now could I!" she said, stomping over to the bar to pour herself a drink and crooning over the glittery bottles and shiny glasses. She knocked it back and groaned as it went down, bringing over the bottle and two glasses for her friends. She passed them out and poured quickly, as though concerned she might be told to go steady with it.

"So, you've had the chance to talk to my companion now?" I asked them. Oracle picked up the conversation, as though we'd planned it all along.

"…And you seem to have no loyalty to the city, after all they've done to you," she said, sitting back and intertwining our fingers, giving them a quick squeeze. "So, I ask you, friends…what would it take?"

"Ta get me an' mine ta come with ye an' swear to ye fer a ten-year contract?" Viktoria asked, and I nodded, hearing a time limit placed on the deal for the first time. "Well, as we'd be leavin' the city, an' all, we'd need a good payment, upfront, naturally," she said slowly, gauging our reactions. "Say…a hundred gold per engineer, per month, half upfront, with the guarantee that we be no expected ta fight fer ye, we be free ta leave iffin things look bad, an' we work four days outta seven, the remainin' three bein' for ourselves…an' we get ta sell what we make on 'em fer full price, wherever we want."

Oracle squeezed my hand hard at that, and I felt her anger spike, despite her placid face.

"Thanks for the offer," I said, smiling sharply as I sat forward. "But let's be realistic. I've had my people healing yours, with nothing asked in return so far. How many have you helped, Oracle?" My companion pretended to consider it.

"Sixteen so far," she said, and I nodded.

"Then that's enough," I declared, and Elise stiffened slightly. "We healed your people as a gesture. We were demonstrating the benefits of being with us, instead of against. From now on, though, only those who swear to me will get healed."

"But…" Elise started to say, glancing at Viktoria, who looked back at her, then to me, firming her jaw.

"But nothing," I said shortly. "You see, I know the going rate for an engineer is nowhere near that, and I'm not even going to mention the working hours, because that's just fucking offensive. You clearly thought you'd try and milk me for all you could, not act in good faith, not the way you just tried to deal."

"Especially considerin' that, as dwarves and elves, you're never goin' to get any higher than your current rank, and you'll always be paid half of what a human is here," Mal muttered, just loud enough to hear.

"So, you've tried to milk me for what?"

"Eight times the going rate…for a human engineer, sixteen times what they're getting currently," Mal slipped in.

"You've come here, had a night at the arena for free, drank our booze, and eaten our food, then decided that rather than dealing honestly, as you could have, you'd fuck me over? What, you think we've not already made offers to others in your situation?" I asked, shaking my head and bluffing for all I was worth.

"Aye, well…it's a startin' point fer negotiations, isn't it!" Viktoria said hastily. "I did no' expect anythin' like that, yer understand, I just wanted ta see whut ye'd say…"

"So how about you show a bit of common sense and ask for what you actually want, and I'll consider it," I said. She looked at her friends and back at me, confused.

"But tha' no be how it's done…Look, I dinna ken whut it be like where ye come from, but here, we haggle."

"And we do where I come from as well, but when we have time, and we start at a point that's reasonable. It's a demonstration of honorable intent to make a realistic offer, and dishonorable to go the other way," I countered, making it up as I went along.

"So, I be showin' meself ta be dishonorable in yer eyes?" Viktoria snarled, puffing herself up and clearly getting ready for a fight, when Finbar cut her off with a sigh, reaching over and patting her hand. They made eye contact for a minute, and some silent communication between friends passed before she deflated and slumped back, grabbing the bottle and pouring herself another one as she grumbled under her breath.

"What my friend has said is true, for here," he said, and he smiled gently as he looked at me. "I don't know where you're from, but clearly it's not too far away, if you're here recruiting as carefully as you have been.

"You want us to stick our necks out, to leave the city where we're under contract, and go with you. We would literally be gutting the city's war effort if we convince our people, as your companion seems to want. We can accept that asking for the realm and a side of sprinkles is a bit much, but we also need to be convinced that siding with you and abandoning our home is worth it for us."

"Okay, what are you currently paid, truthfully?" I asked him.

"A very sensible question." He smiled. "I, as a shift manager, earn twelve gold pieces a month, which includes my bonus if we hit the target. Nine, if not."

"Okay, and what about your family?" I asked, and he blinked in surprise.

"I have a son; he earns four gold as an experienced baker."

"Okay, then here's what I think is a fair deal. Engineers get eight, shift managers get twelve, and all craftsmen get six. These wages are separate from your cost of living, which I'll cover for a year, all food, rooms, and basic needs. You work six days a week currently?"

"Seven, actually."

"Well, unless there's a good reason, you work six with us. Whatever you produce in your own time, you can sell to any other citizen. But we won't be allowing outside trade at first, as I also have a little something to sweeten the pot, as the saying goes." I reached into the bag, pulling out one of the extra books Oracle had brought when I'd asked her to select the skillbooks for everyone.

"This, as you can see, is a skillbook," I said, making damn sure I had their attention. "I have more of these, and I give them out to my most skilled and valuable workers. The engineers who recommended that you be recruited have already earned some of these, I swear by my soul." I injected enough mana into my words to make it clear that I was making an Oath.

I'd hoped to earn a bit more bargaining power through the display, but what I got stunned me, as all three jumped to their feet, speaking at once.

"I'll swear!"

"What books?"

"I'll take it!"

"Whoa, whoa, stop!" I said, waving them back and noting that not one of them let their eyes slip from the book. "I'll be honest here, people: I'm not promising *you'll* get these books, as I only give them to the people who impress me most of all. To get one, you'll have to earn it."

"Ye think I can't earn it?" Viktoria growled at me, still watching the book.

"I think you'll all need to work your arses off to do it," I said firmly, grinning at them. "Although, I will make you a little deal, if you're willing to swear allegiance first? After all, I don't want you to spread the word of our plans."

"Ye swear by yer soul that ye will treat us fair? No favoritism ta humans or other species, all treated the same? Ye'll pay us eight gold per skilled engineer, twelve for shift managers or leaders, and six for crafters, and look after us?"

"I do," I said, drawing in a deep breath as I concentrated. "I swear these things, and more. I swear that as I grow in strength, and the tower does, I will help you all to rise with me. I swear to never waste a life if I can help it, and to do my best to heal, or have healed, any injuries you suffer in your time as a citizen of the Great Tower and the empire."

As I spoke, I could feel Oracle twisting our magic around, making a bond with each of them, and tying them to me. As I finished, they each started to speak, reading from the Oath of the Great Tower, as others had before them.

"I swear to obey Lord Jax and those he places over me; I will serve to the best of my ability, speak no lie to him when commanded otherwise, and treat all other citizens as family.

"I will work for the greater good, being a shield to those who need it, a sword for those who deserve it, and a warden to the night.

"I will stand with my family, helping one another to reach the light, until ten years have passed, the hour of my death, or my lord releases me from my Oath.

"Lastly, I will not be a dick!"

"Thank you." I nodded to each of them, then drew out a second book and set it down on the table before them, turning it around so that I could be sure they could read the cover.

"Mana Engine Integration and Magical Device Creation are two books I'd imagine you'd each find a use for, considering they're journeyman-ranked," I said, watching their eyes bugging out. "So, here's the deal. Get your ships ready to fly in two days, by midnight. Anyone you plan to bring will need to be aboard, and I'll give you these books. Two of you get the reward when we're in the air. The third gets to pick when we get back to the Great Tower."

"Ah, Lord Jax," Viktoria said apologetically. "We're…Finbar an' me, I mean, we're on tha *Ragnarök*. She's in tha middle of a refit, but I think we can make it, iffin we work hard. But tha battleship? It be a shell, tha' be all."

"It can't be done," Elise said angrily. "We've only just started installin' the engines. They need test firin', the entire structure be needin' fixin' and powerin' before we can fly, an' we won't be given all the parts we need until next week!"

"The way I hear it, she's got the basic systems, right? Just none of the trimmings?" I asked.

"Aye, iffin ye call decks an' cannons, walls an' cabins trimmin's!" she said, shaking her head in disbelief.

"But she could fly, if you had the manastones?" I pressed.

"Well, aye, but she'd be a bitch to guide. She'd no have a helm, nor half her decks. She's literally just got tha structure in place, and tha mana channels laid down. Tha engines will only be fired to test iffin w' need te add more!" she said, frustration clear in her voice. "An' even iffin we could get her launched, then what? They'd send ships after us! We'd have no cannons, no decks, no hull to absorb hits. We'd just have ta turn around an' land, an' then we'd all be sent ta prison!"

"But if I could get you cover, you could fly it, with hundreds of people aboard, as well as equipment and supplies?" I asked firmly.

"Well, aye, but we'd no get far—"

"Then do it; do whatever you need to. You'll have friends turning up each night to help you. Tell your people that they're there to work off a debt or that the nobles want the ship done. Tell them anything you want, but get the ship ready!"

"You're changing the plan…" Mal groaned, rubbing his temples.

"I'm fixing it. Taking hundreds of people out by the Smugglers Path was never going to be a good option, and we'd always planned on stealing a few ships to carry everything." I smiled. "Good to meet you three, though I think you all need to go now, and get to work…oh, and one last point. The deal is only on if you all make it. Three books, or none," I said, smiling evilly as they started to protest.

"Ah, ah! Now go on, get to work. I'll make sure you get some help tonight!" With that, I waved them to the door, which Grizz opened for them, grinning at their attempts to change the deal. He closed it firmly in their faces as Mal started swearing at me.

"You crazy bastard! The ships were going to be the small ones, ones we could run fast out to sea and swing around with. Now these? We can't do this!"

"We can…if we take more ships," I said, smiling.

"Oh god, no." Mal swore, rubbing his eyes. "Look—"

Mal's tirade cut off before it got properly started as a loud knock on the door interrupted us. It opened to reveal both Mistress Nerin and Augustus.

"You!" she snapped, pointing at me. "It's about time! I've a bone to pick with you, boy, and it's not one you'll like!"

"Mistress Nerin," I said, attempting a smile at the platinum-haired woman. "It's great to see you—"

"Don't give me that, boy! You cost me my shop! It was looted to the damn wood by the time I got back from helping you!" she said, striding in and poking me in the forehead.

"Ow!" I rocked back, noting that the legionnaires' protectiveness that had previously kept her back had evaporated at some point, and now they were all grinning.

"Well? What have you got to say for yourself?" she snapped.

I grinned up at her mischievously. "That I'd like to offer you a job as the official healer at the Great Tower?"

"You already asked me to join you, boy. Have you forgotten?" She crossed her arms, her stare boring through my skull, and I shook my head.

"No, but I know that you've lost the only reason to stay here now, so how about you reconsider and come with us? I'll introduce you to Ashante? Maybe chuck in a new healing spellbook or skillbook?"

"And a hell of a lot of gold!" she fumed. "I've been healing people ever since I met you, and not one has paid up yet, so you better be good for it!"

"So, we're agreed, then?" I pressed. "I'll give you a spellbook, and a healing-oriented skillbook, and some gold, and you'll be a member of the Great Tower, taking over the role of official healer?"

"Not 'some gold,' boy! A lot!" she corrected.

I quirked an eyebrow at her. "What's a lot to you?" I asked.

"A thousand gold!" she barked.

"Done!" I said, grinning.

Nerin blinked as she unfocused her eyes, reading the notification, even as I felt my mana dropping as Oracle cast the spell.

"I swear to obey Lord Jax and those he places over me; I will serve to the best of my ability, speak no lie to him when commanded otherwise, and treat all other citizens as family.

"I will work for the greater good, being a shield to those who need it, a sword for those who deserve it, and a warden to the night.

"I will stand with my family, helping one another to reach the light, until the hour of my death or my lord releases me from my Oath.

"Lastly, I will not be a dick!"

"I, Lord Jax, do swear to protect and lead you, to be the shield that protects you and yours from the darkness and the sword that avenges that which cannot be saved. As the tower grows in strength, so shall you," I said, grinning.

"I…I…"

"Welcome to the family, Nerin!" I said.

"You tricked me!" she huffed.

"Nope, I gave you exactly what you wanted."

She stomped off, sitting down hard in the chair to my left and continuing to glare furiously at me.

"So, anyone else I need to speak to?" I asked the room winningly, smiling around and pretending not to notice the angry stares I was getting.

CHAPTER FIFTEEN

"I think it's probably best to quit while you're ahead, Lord Jax," Augustus said calmly, striding forward to take up station where he could watch over the entire room.

"Bollocks," I said succinctly. "Honestly, Augustus, I've spent all my time trying to damn well survive so far. I count being alive as a win these days, so let's just keep on fucking trucking."

I grinned at him. "Besides, I have to thank you. I caught the end of the fight with the two men in leather masks…that was pretty fast work."

"I'm a Centurion Primus in the legion, Lord Jax. If they'd managed to land a hit on me, I'd have died…of shame."

"Well, still, it was impressive." I smiled, glad that he was on my side.

"It was. A bit *too* impressive, unfortunately," said Soween as she was sorting through some papers.

"How bad?" Mal asked, and she grimaced.

"Two to one, if he fought again, and that was the best odds. The gangs also didn't like that they had to submit to a random number draw for their place in the fight. They all wanted to go first."

"Thank the gods we already moved to the next round, then. Handicap," Mal said, grinning, and Soween winced.

"What's this?" I asked, and got an even bigger grin from Mal.

"Bettin', son. It's where the big boys make their money. Now that they're pissed off, we've offered a handicap, and they've demanded a level limit. We said we'd consider it."

"While making it clear we can be bribed," Soween interjected.

"Exactly!" Mal said, pointing at her.

"What?" I asked.

"We offered a handicap, such as limitin' the fight to the lowest-leveled member of the legion…that'd be you," Mal said, nodding at me. "Then we let the gangs know we can be bribed, so they're payin' us a fuckload of extra gold to put more lethal creatures in with you."

"Okay…" I said, looking from one of them to the other. "And how does this help me?"

"You said you'd be the one fightin' in the arena." Mal chuckled. "So, when we had to substitute this absolute unit for you, we let 'em know this would be the option after round two. The gangs all have their blood up now, and they have to pay more to put someone forward each round. But if they win, they get the entire purse of fees that has been put in so far. They think it'll all work out in the end, because they've all got their 'ace' killers…"

"What?" I asked suddenly.

"Their top fighters, like the prometheans that are basically muscle for the Skyking. The ones you see on the street are low-level, but there are a couple of really high-powered enforcers out there! I'm betting they send Altair; he's insane!" Soween said, grinning maniacally.

"Yeah! Let's hope they send him. Man, the odds we'd be able to get for that fight…" Mal stared off into the distance dreamily.

"Uh, guys…?" I asked, looking from one of them to the other. "What level are we talking here?"

"For Altair?" Soween asked, tapping her chin. "Oh, I don't know…thirty, thirty-five, maybe?"

"What?!" I said, although it may have come out as a squeak.

"You killed an ancient SporeMother, right? This isn't gonna be an issue for you?" Mal asked, shooting me a hard look. "Because it better not be. I've already placed all their fees on you to win the next round!"

"Ah…I love the confidence and all, but maybe this would have been better discussed with me?" I shot back, glaring at them. "The SporeMother was fucking old, and I was damn lucky!"

"You were there while we were plannin' this!" Mal snapped, pointing a finger at me.

"When did we say this bit?" I asked him suspiciously.

"When we were plannin' it out! When you were…oh."

"When I was…"

"Destroying Horseshoe Street," Mal said, rubbing his chin. "And then we put the finishin' details on it yesterday, before the fight started…"

"So you planned it without me, basically?" I asked him.

He grimaced. "Well, maybe some of us didn't have the luxury of lyin' around! Some of us had to make the best of a shitty situation to make the plan work!"

"I was unconscious!" I snapped. "I wasn't having a Sunday fucking lie-in!"

"Details!" Mal snapped back, waving his hands dismissively.

"Look, you cock," I said, sitting forward and pointing at him. "I gave you the outline of the plan, and you swore you could make it work…I don't know the damn city, or I'd have done it myself! I just found a way around the worst part: trying to get loads of people out of the city through that fucking tiny passageway! We were always going to steal a pair of warships; now we're just going to steal more, that's all!"

"They don't just leave 'em fuckin' runnin' and ready to go!" Mal snarled. "They're heavily guarded…the engineers shut the engines down when they're on the ground. They take ages to restart!"

"Then that's even better!" I said, grinning. "All we have to do is steal the fucking manastones from the ships we're not going to be taking, then they can't chase us."

"No, but the ones up there can!" Mal snarled, pointing at the ceiling, and I grinned at him. "What? Why are you smiling?"

"Remember I said we needed to take out the Skyking?" I asked him.

His frown grew with his slow nod.

"That's because I'm going to take his place and free those he's enslaved. I'm betting the chance to be free trumps fucking with us for the imps, when we kill their captors for them. The djinn already offered me a contract if I free them, as well. Add into the mix the legion fliers?"

"Damn…" Mal said after a few seconds of thought. "Augustus, will they do it?" he asked. "Will the legion follow him? Will they steal the ships?"

"No," Augustus said flatly. "The legionnaires are not thieves; we won't steal anything." He clipped the words harshly, then let the silence linger before rubbing his chin in thought. "Buuuut…as the rightful Lord of Dravith has declared war on the city, he would have the right to order any spoils of battle to be used for the empire…"

"You fucker," I said, shaking my head. "I nearly redecorated my trousers there."

"Well, it was probably worth it," he said, winking.

"Probably," I agreed. "I'll still get you back, though." I winked in return.

"Right. Let's stop everything, right now," Soween said, holding her hands up and becoming the center of attention immediately. "These plans keep changing, because we're all doing things, making little changes"—she glared at me—"and others are making damn big changes. So, let's just lay it all out here and now, make sure we all agree, then that's it. We don't have time to change anything else, not if we're going to make our deadline."

I nodded, the others doing the same, and Soween started to pace the room, the focus of all our eyes.

"So, tomorrow night, instead of Augustus, Jax will fight. He'll face the creatures and higher-leveled gang members, one-by-one. The point of this is threefold: it keeps them from attacking the arena to get at the legionnaires who are sheltering here by making them think we've captured them; it provides money and experience; and it lets us bleed the gangs without going to war with them."

I nodded, thinking about the fights to come. I wasn't happy about the changes, nor about the fact that they'd be sending their top killers after me, but alternatively, they were gangs. They weren't monsters out there, just existing; these were scum that preyed on the innocent of the city. It'd be hard, but I had confidence I could do it…somehow.

"While Jax is fighting, we continue bringing in the people from the list. Some, we hide in the Cloudring, while others go back to work and keep quiet. Maybe a few more, we can assist to get jobs with the shipyards to 'help out' on the battleship. Either way, we continue recruiting and preparing, as well as scouting out the Stockpile in preparation to raid it."

"About that…" I said, and immediately, half the room glared at me. "Whoa, whoa, guys, relax!" I held my hands up defensively.

"That…*that* right there, is why we're doing this," Soween said, rubbing her forehead. "Okay, go on. How are you going to make my life harder now?"

"Uh, I just wanted to ask about the raiding side of things…I know we're going to get the manastones from the Stockpile, but we need food and building materials as well, sooo…"

"All kept there," Mal said brusquely. "And it'll be considerably less-well-guarded than the stones."

"Okay. Can we add in another location to be raided?" I asked hopefully, wincing as more people glared at me.

"Why?" Soween voiced warily for the group.

"Because I'm thinking that there has to be a location with skillbooks or spellbooks here, right?"

"No," Mal said firmly, raising a hand to forestall any objections. "You're talkin' about raidin' the *Emporium*. It's not gonna happen. We'd lose people by the dozen. It can't be done, not without weeks of preparation. At least at the Stockpile, we'll only have guards to deal with. There, they have golems and magical shit. Not gonna happen."

"Golems?" I perked up, an evil smile coming to my lips.

"Yeah, great big stone fuckers. They've got six of 'em, from what I heard, and I only know of one time that someone got the better of one golem. The second golem turned him into a smear on the floor. So no, we're not gonna just stop off and rob the place on the way past. *And why the hell are you smilin' like that?!"*

"Oracle?" I asked, and she nodded slowly.

"They could be, if the Emporium is built on a location which they were ordered to protect, and someone found out how to charge them…"

"Where is the Emporium?" I asked Mal, and his scowl deepened.

"Nowhere you're going fuckin' near. You agreed, you don't leave the arena!"

"I'm just curious…"

"I could go, check it out," Oracle said hesitantly. I frowned at her, shaking my head.

"No! Definitely not. Not after the drow."

"Mal, you could take me, right? With some guards?" Oracle said, and I turned to glare daggers at him as he looked from me to her.

"If one of you *has* to go, it's not gonna be you, son," he said flatly. "I can take a coach through the city. It's not cheap, a couple of gold, but it'll make sure she's there and back safe, and I'd be with her."

"I don't like it," I argued, shaking my head. "There's too much that could go wrong…"

"That's how we feel about you goin' anywhere now," Mal said. "And I already told you, we can't raid the Emporium."

"Which is more valuable, in terms of goods," I asked, looking at Oracle. "The Emporium or the Stockpile?"

"Stockpile," Soween and Mal answered immediately in unison.

"So why are the golems at the Emporium instead of the Stockpile?"

"Because they don't go anywhere else. They just patrol the Emporium. From what I heard, they don't listen to anyone except the owner, some old wizard, and he's always complainin' about how hard they are to control. Now tell me why."

"Because if they are golems, especially proper ones from the empire, then I can probably take control of them," I mused.

"Only if you take control of the control crystal," Oracle said warningly.

"But if they're active, will they accept my authority?" I asked, and she shrugged.

"I don't know, they might…but it'd depend if the control crystal was able to identify you. If not, you'd have to capture it. That could cause more issues than it'd solve."

"What do you mean, you can control 'em?" Mal asked hesitantly.

"I captured the Great Tower, and the golems that we've built there obey me. That was understandable, but we found some at a waystation we reclaimed, and as soon as we charged them, they just started up and took orders straight away."

"That might be because they were linked to the waystation, though," Oracle warned me.

"Yeah, but if we go look at these golems, we can try to take control of them. If it doesn't work, then we just leave."

"You're not goin'," Mal said. When I turned to look at him, he shook his head adamantly. "I mean it, son. If you go, the deal's off. You jeopardized everythin' when you were out last time, and we lost nearly two days. We can't afford that again. I'll take her, and she can have a look; maybe you can buy what you want, but I'm tellin' you now, you can't afford much."

"Mal's right," Nerin said suddenly, interrupting. "I've been in the Emporium before. I've bought spells there. It cost me over six hundred gold for one, and he didn't have many. As to skillbooks, except for the common skills, such as carpentry and leatherworking, he only had a few. The one I wanted was inside a special case attached to the wall, and covered magical gardening…" She sighed, shaking her head as she recalled it. "The things I could learn from that book."

"Gardening?" I asked, disappointed.

"Magical gardening, boy!" she snapped. "The growing of ingredients and herbs in such a way that they complement each other and increase the potency of the plants!"

"Oh, right," I said, trying to make myself sound excited. "I suppose that could be useful. I do know some alchemy, after all." I shrugged. "There *are* spellbooks, though, right?" I asked for confirmation, grinning.

"No, Jax! You know…" Oracle started, then paused.

"Yup," I said, grinning evilly. "I'm all cured now."

"Oh dear." Oracle began rubbing the bridge of her nose.

"Oh yeah!" I said, grinning even wider.

"What am I missin'?" Mal asked, and Oracle just held up one slim hand to stop him.

"We can talk about this later. I'll go with you, Mal. We can check to see if the golems are imperial first; if they're not, then it's not important. If they are, then we can try to come up with a plan. Soween, you were saying," Oracle said, gesturing impatiently.

"Thanks, Oracle," Soween said, folding her hands. "So, we gather up as many people as we can without drawing attention to ourselves, and we start collecting any necessary gear that we can get easily. We hire wagons and stash them in Old Buswisk's yards near the Stockpile. While we're doing this, Jax communicates with the enclave through the legion fliers, gets them ready to break out. They make a run straight for the battleship?" she asked, and I turned to look at Augustus.

"Provided you can convince the prefect of your identity, he will follow you. He won't be happy about breaking the laws, but as I say, this is officially a city we are now at war with, making it a valid target.

"We can dispatch squads to board and capture ships, provided they are in the shipyards. Our fliers can probably capture a single vessel in the air, but we only have eight in the entire legion, so if it's a larger ship, then there's a good chance they will suffer losses."

"Right, then. On the fourth night, two nights from now, when they get the signal, they break out and go straight for the shipyard, capture what ships they can, while we raid the Stockpile. We use the wagons to get the stores to any ships the legion captures. We can send a few thieves to raid the ships we aren't going to steal, get them to steal the manastones from those engines so they can't follow us. That should restrict the number of ships that could cause any problems." She made a few notes as she spoke. "We'll need some of the engineers who swear to you to train the thieves, maybe an engine to practice on as well…maybe a mock control system."

"Oh!" I said suddenly, a thought coming to mind. "Oren told me about a prick who took his contracts for visiting the villages, said he was happy to do slave runs…"

"The *Star's Glory*; she's owned by a wanker called Bateman, why?"

"I want that ship," I said firmly.

"It's a shitpot." Mal snorted. "Bateman uses it for runs to the villages, all right. Almost always brings back slaves, and he spends nothin' on the ship besides the bare minimum, as near as I can tell. It's one of the reasons I didn't offer him a deal, even before he started slavin'. Now, it reeks."

"Well, is it in dock?" I asked.

"No idea, not somethin' I care about normally," Mal said, shrugging.

"It's due in any day," Soween said, looking over a piece of parchment. "She's out doing a tax run now, visiting some of the smaller villages to the west, on the border of Himnel and Narkolt."

"If it comes back and is docked while we're here, I want it taken," I insisted. "That fucker is a slaver, so stopping him dead is a requirement of the empire."

"I'll see to it, sir," Augustus said.

"Good man. Anything else?" I asked Soween.

She grimaced. "Look, this plan relies heavily on 'if' and 'maybe'…you need to lock the legion down, make sure they'll do what you say, and then we can do this. We've already hired some extra mercenaries to help with the raid. They're good men, so they'll do what we need them to on the last night."

"Good men?" I asked, raising an eyebrow in suspicion.

"Well, no. They're scum, actually," Mal interjected. "But they like gold, so fuck it."

"Oh god," I whispered, running a hand over my face. "Okay, to change the subject back to one of the main reasons we're here: any word on Tommy?"

"No, unfortunately," Soween said, shaking her head. "In a city this big, finding a single person is difficult, but even with the descriptions you've given us, I haven't found anyone yet who'll admit to seeing him. I've got someone out looking; for now, that's all we can do. I'm sorry."

"Well, is there anything I can do to help?" I asked, "Maybe if I—"

"No!" most of the room snapped.

I sat back, glowering.

"Is there anything else we need to add to this plan?" Soween asked, staring at me. I scanned the room and realized how many people were doing the same.

"What?" I asked.

"It's always you who changes shit," Mal said. "Consider this the last chance."

"Slaves," I said slowly. "Are there slaves at the Stockpile?"

"Dozens," Mal said coldly, then nodded in understanding. "We'll grab any we can, take them with us. This battleship better be as big as it's supposed to be."

"How many ships are going to be available?" I asked Soween, and she started running the numbers.

"Looks like there should be six on the quick launch routine, with maybe two or three in the air that night. The others will be having work done, out of the city on patrol, or possibly raiding. Ships usually take between an hour and three to get aloft from a shutdown, so the others, we won't have to worry about for a while.

"There'll also be maybe four ships in the private docks. Those will be shut down if they're landed, as their owners won't want to run the cost up."

"So, how many can we take?" I asked the room, and Augustus frowned, rubbing his chin.

"If you and the prefect confirm orders, we can probably take three, maybe four of them. In addition to the battleship, depending on your choices," he speculated. "Working on an average of ten legionnaires to the fast-attack scouts, and twenty to the heavy scouts, with forty to the cruiser class, and maybe thirty to the battleship, as it's not going to be crewed?

"I believe we have a hundred and ten legionnaires in the city. We need to split off some to guard our non-combatants, and to take out guards on the gates and other protected areas of the shipyards.... Hmmm." He pulled his helmet off and scratched at his short-cropped black hair. "If we take thirty of the legion to screen our people and secure the gates once we punch through, that will leave eighty ready to capture the ships and secure them. What will be in dock, then?" he asked Soween, and she flipped through the papers.

"Unsure," she said. "I don't have access to the deployment orders. Most likely, depending on the way things go, there'll be either a cruiser, four fast-attack scouts and a heavy scout, or possibly six heavy scouts...I just don't know; all I can go off is the current staffing we got from an informant."

"If it's the first, then have the thieves take the manastones from all of the scouts. Take the cruiser and battleship at all costs, and we've got enough for a crack at the *Star's Glory*, leaving us with a reserve of ten men.

"I'd rather have more ships than fewer, but the battleship is the priority, since we need the capacity," I said decisively. "If it's the second, well, we take all the scouts and do the best we can; just make sure the ships we're not taking are grounded."

"And you're happy with this? No more changes?" Soween asked again.

I snorted, shaking my head.

"Of course, I'm not *happy*! We're surrounded by everything we need to make the tower into a fully functioning city and bastion. There are going to be thousands who die because I abandon them here. Fuck knows what's going on out there right now, when I could be helping them. But I have to draw the line somewhere, I know. Final condition is that if we do decide the Emporium is a valid target, we add that in."

"Damn right," Mal said. "Now, once the legion is takin' the shipyard, and my people are raidin' the Stockpile, you and I are gonna be here, drawin' the gangs' attention, as well as the nobles'…We'll leak the news of the fights; that should get the place packed, and we just have to hope our people can find the Skyking's lair. If not, we're gonna have a much harder time takin' off in those ships."

"Find the lair, and I'll raid it while you get the powerful representatives of the gangs drunk here. You party hard with them, make your gold, and be ready, because as soon as we hit the Skyking, I bet his people will know about it and go batshit."

"You'll need to finish the fight here first; if you don't show up, they'll know something's up," Mal pointed out.

"I know, but I can't be in two places at once."

"We can handle it." Lydia spoke up, and everyone turned to her. "My squad, I mean. If Jax is taking down their major fighters in the arena, we can mop up what's left in the lair."

"Could you?" Soween asked, tapping her lip with one finger. "Don't forget that the Skyking won't be alone, not entirely. A creature that keeps itself this hidden—especially one that's so paranoid, it doesn't let anyone even know where its lair is without a binding Oath of allegiance—won't be unguarded. Add to that, anything that's strong enough to command prometheans won't be easy to take down. No offense, Lydia, but I don't see it."

"We're not just guards or backups for Lord Jax," Lydia snapped. "We can fight! We got 'im 'ere through the fucking drow, didn't we?"

"True, but the drow didn't even show themselves to the city, let alone face the Skyking. I'm not being cruel here, Lydia. I'm sorry, but I don't see you and your team winning that fight."

"No, I'll be with you, Lydia," I reassured her. "As soon as we can get out of the arena, Augustus, you and your team of legionnaires will come with us. We hit it hard and fast; we'll be heading straight for the Skyking.

"Once we've eliminated the bastard, we head for the shipyards and the *Star's Glory*. We'll be launching the attack right after the final fight of the night. Whoever is left at the arena will be summoned back, if the Skyking has that ability. If it doesn't, then that's good, too. We keep a few people back to escort me, I hit the Emporium, then up to the Skyking? No, that's not gonna work, is it…?"

"No. Timing-wise, never mind the rest, it won't," Mal confirmed. "Instead, if you're damn determined to do the Emporium, we hit it after the fight tomorrow night, if, and only fucking well *if*, you can take the golems out. We strip it bare, bring back whatever we can, and hide it here. I'm betting there'll be some magical shit we can use the night after."

"Well, how the hell do we fit it all in, then?" I growled.

"We stagger the fights," Soween said suddenly. "We tell the Skyking it's got the final slot of the night and that we'll be holding a load of minor fights before the main event. To sweeten the pot even further, we want it to submit someone that you can't beat, someone powerful.

"Then, after the third fight, we make our move. While the minor fights are happening, we spirit you away to attack the Skyking and kill the fucker, backed up by your current legionnaires and your squad. Once it begins, I'll bet the

Skyking has some way of magically communicating with its creatures. Whoever is waiting to fight you will leave, we call it cowardice, and we still take the win."

"Fuck the win. If that goes wrong, the strongest fighter the Skyking has will attack us from behind," I said, frowning.

"Well, you got a better plan? A better way to fit everything in?" Mal grinned.

"No, but—"

"But nothing! The attack on the Skyking starts the whole thing off at, say, midnight. The attack on the Stockpile can get underway, and we make sure word gets to the guards outside the enclave. As soon as we're finished there, they go runnin' to protect the Stockpile; maybe have a helpful urchin who points 'em in the wrong direction.

"While they're lookin' the other way, the legion breaks out. They hit the shipyards while the guards are distracted. You kill the Skyking and send the legion fliers and any harpies you can recruit straight at the airships above the city, and we get the ships in the air!"

"Head out to sea, pretend we're heading south, maybe?" Soween interrupted, clearly thinking aloud.

"No, then we'll have the Narkolt fleet coming to intercept us…Can't go straight for the tower, either, so maybe…"

"Why not?" I asked.

"'Why not,' what?" Mal asked, clearly distracted.

"Why not make straight for the tower?"

"Because they'll send the armies after us, obviously. You got a strong enough force to take down the entire army? Because if you do, what the hell are we trying to do here?" Mal snapped.

"No, but by the time we've done this, we could have the *Agamemnon's Wrath* and the *Libertas* both heading to us. Combining them and the ships we are able to steal, we might be able to take out any attackers."

"Might," Mal said, shaking his head. "That's not good enough, Jax. I've been on the wrong side of battles before. Better not to risk it, iff'n you see reason?"

"Okay, but…"

"But what we do is head out to sea, head east by southeast, straight for the Sunken City. It's about ninety miles out, but pretty much the only thing out there until you hit the shippin' lanes to Mathai and the Pirate Isles. I heard that the traders who were in the city a few weeks back were tryin' to buy the secrets to makin' an airship, and the locals nearly sunk 'em to teach 'em a lesson.

"The nobles and Barabarattas'll hopefully all think it was them, tryin' to steal the ships. Once we're a few days out, maybe four or so, we swing around and head northeast for another two days. Then we swing back inland, come in low, and we should be able to reach your tower in another six, maybe seven days, with nobody sure where we went. Add to that, if we've got all the stockpiles of manastones, they won't be able to risk following us out to sea, since they'd crash when they ran out."

I regarded Mal for a long minute, and he stared back.

"That's a long time to be on the ships…especially the battleship, considering it's barely a skeleton frame."

"Then we add a day on. Stop at the Sunken City and pile all the engineers onto the battleship, put some barriers up to protect people as best we can from the weather. Tell me it's not the best way to do this. Until now, we were plannin' on gettin' 'em out via the forests and hundreds of miles' slog. It'd have taken weeks to get to the tower that way. Only difference is they'd be fightin' creatures along the way. This way, they get to ride."

"Shit," I said, shaking my head. "I know it's the best plan we've got. It just it feels so…"

Soween let out a huff. "Off the cuff? All of his plans do, sir. Scares the shit outta me. Somehow, they work…usually."

"I really don't like the extra time away from the tower, either," I admitted.

"Then take off once we're at sea. Take the fastest ship and head back, and we'll bring the rest of the ships the long route," Mal offered.

"Not a cat's chance in hell." I snorted. "We're in this together, Mal. We either all make it, or we die trying."

"Then you need to send those orders to the legion, son. Get 'em written up and give 'em to one of your fliers, with orders to eat the papers if they get captured."

"I will," I said, already planning out the letter, and just hoping that they'd agree.

"Then it's settled?" he asked, and I nodded. "Then you're stayin' here until tomorrow night if Oracle confirms the Emporium is a valid target, and the night after, if not. So fuck off while I try to get the final details sorted here. I need to sort out what I'm takin' and what I'm leavin'."

"We'll need a shit ton of potions as well: mana, health, stamina, all of them. Oh, and make sure you get some of the expensive bottles as well; the dwarves loved that shit." I nodded toward the gold-leaf covered bottles, and he started to laugh.

"That? It may be gold leaf on the bottle, but it's filled with the cheapest shit I could find! I tell people it's the good stuff, they take one look at the bottles, and boom, they believe me! Once you pay the bottles off, it's all profit. My beers cost me more than that rotgut."

"Sneaky fucker!" I said, grinning.

"Damn right, son. Make 'em look at the right hand and take their purse with the left. Now go on, fuck off."

"Love you too, mate!" I said, grinning and levering myself to my feet. "Come on, then, guys. Let's get back to our rooms and get some shut-eye. First thing tomorrow, I'm gonna need a favor from you, Augustus."

"Of course, Lord Jax. What do you need?" Augustus asked, straightening to attention.

"Training, mate. If I'm going to look the part of the legion and not embarrass you all completely, I need to be taught to fight with a sword and shield."

Augustus blinked and looked taken aback. "You mean, you can't fight with them already?"

"I've had some training, but I usually rely on my naginata and my stubbornness. Oh, and my magic…"

"Well…damn."

"Well said, Centurion Primus, well said." I clapped him on the shoulder as he took up position in front of me, leading the way back to our rooms for a sleep I was sure was going to be far too short.

CHAPTER SIXTEEN

I was shaken awake six hours later, bleary-eyed and confused. When I'd fallen asleep, Oracle had been refusing to get into bed with me, insisting that I needed to rest. Now, standing exactly where that vision of loveliness had been, was Augustus.

And the fucker was stripped down to his pants.

I jerked back, scrabbling away and smacking the back of my head off the wall behind the bed.

"Owww, goddammit!" I muttered, rubbing my head and scowling at Augustus. "Okay, dude, what the hell are you doing here, and where are your clothes?"

"Ha! Your companion asked me to awaken you, as she has gone to examine the Emporium with the arena master. As to my clothes, all the clothing you need for training is your skin! Gives you a reason to avoid blows even more!"

"Depends on the blow," I muttered, dragging myself across the bed and getting up. Augustus moved back to the door and opened it, speaking over his shoulder as he headed out into the corridor.

"Dress in whatever you feel appropriate, my lord, but if you want me to make a legionnaire of you before the fight tonight, I need as much time as possible. I'll meet you in the arena."

With that, he let go of the door and walked out of sight, just as I realized two things. First, I was naked, having attempted to entice a laughing Oracle into bed last night with a willycopter…and second, Yen was leaning against the wall opposite my room, talking with another legionnaire. Meaning I'd literally just flashed her my third leg.

Dammit.

I just knew I was bright goddamn red as I searched my gear for some pants that were close enough to what Augustus was wearing, swearing about the big bastard.

Not only was he massively muscled, he must have been one of those fuckers who got waxed or something. I looked like a bear that someone had speckled with paint and then played "join the dots" with all my scars. He looked more like a cross between Dwayne bloody Johnson and a friggin' underwear model.

I hated him already.

I hurried to get dressed, then picked up my naginata and headed out of the room. Meeting Yen in the corridor and seeing her beetroot-colored cheeks made me grin, at least, as I nodded to her and pretended to have no idea why she was red.

I was led through the quiet halls by our rooms and out into the building proper, where I got my second surprise of the day. It was full of people. Everywhere I looked, someone was either crashed out on the floor or sleeping on a hastily erected cot. As Yen directed me through the space, people began to stir, and here and there, I recognized a face.

They were slaves I'd freed in the market or the djinn. Some looked at me as though confused who I was, while others stared at me worshipfully, as if I were the creator made flesh.

Worst of the two was the second look, as they'd invariably drop their eyes down to gawk at my practically naked body. I hurried through the corridors, until we finally reached the stairwell that Yen assured me led to the arena. I practically fled down the stairs, spotting Augustus waiting in the middle of the sandy arena floor while examining a wooden gladius.

"Dude, seriously?" I said as I walked through a preparation room, then emerged into the arena through a metal gate. "You could have warned me that the damn corridors were full of people; they've all now seen me in my tighty-whiteys!"

"Are you ashamed of your body, Lord Jax?" Augustus asked me, frowning. "I'm surprised, from the number of scars you bear, that anything so minor should bother you."

"I…well, no, I'm not ashamed, not at all. It's just that where I come from, you kinda keep it covered a bit more, you know? And my scars are…oh fuck it, this'll take a while to explain. Maybe later, okay?" I said awkwardly.

"Very well. So, my lord…"

"Just Jax, please, and tell the others. Unless there's a reason like a formal order or outsiders being present, just call me Jax. No need for more."

"Very well; thank you for that. So, Jax…you want to learn to be a legionnaire. I can't teach you all of it in a year, much less in a day, but I can teach you a little. I have to ask, though: do you really think you need a bodyguard here?"

"Bane! Do me a favor, and fuck off and relax, will you?" I called without even looking. A second later, I heard him muttering as he left the arena. "Sorry about that," I said. "He's protective of me."

"As he should be. We can talk as we warm up, then we will do some basic forms to prepare, and we can have a quick fight to see where we need to concentrate. Sound good?" He pointed out the areas we'd be using for each stage, and I nodded. "Excellent. First of all, we will do a light jog around the arena, then one lap at full sprint, then a lap at a jog. We will do this thirty times, followed by a hundred pushups, sit-ups, and jumps."

"Burpees," I muttered. "Even in a fucking different reality, those bastards follow me."

"And your gear is here," Augustus added, smiling and pointing to a backpack resting on the sand by a heavy spear.

"What's that?" I asked.

"A weighted backpack. It will aid your training."

"Why's there only one?"

"Because I don't need to prove myself to myself." He smiled. "The first time you fail, we will add an additional weight to your wrists. The next time, it'll be to your ankles, then your backpack, waist, and thighs. Last of all, if you stop without permission, you get the pilum."

"What the hell, dude?" I gasped.

He chuckled. "It will make sense later, but this is the quickest way to make you stronger that I know of."

"And the pilum?" I asked.

"Here," he said, sweeping an iron javelin up from its resting place against a cross bar in the arena cage and throwing it to me. "Hold it above your head, and we will do a few laps, as an example."

With that, he set off at a "light jog," and I had to run to catch up. He nodded approvingly to me and jogged silently as I kept up with him.

The first minute was all right, but after that, the pilum began to dip. Not intentionally, but the longer I held it aloft, the more my arms drained of blood, and the harder my heart had to pump to keep them up. At the end of the third lap, we stopped, and I dropped the pilum to rest against the wall. I let my arms sag, feeling relieved. Considering a lap of the arena was less than a minute, it seemed ridiculous, but still…

"Now, strap on the backpack, and we can get started," Augustus said, pointing to it. I walked over and picked it up, grunting with the effort. The fucker was heavier than it looked, and as I swung it onto my back, pulling the straps tight to keep it from chafing, I just fucking knew it was going to suck.

We set off at a fairly fast jog as soon as it was in place, and for the next hour and a half, we ran, talking constantly as he asked me inane questions. I started to explain about the scars, telling him stories about the various fights I remembered. He laughed at the right times and told me about some of his own fights, and the time passed fairly quickly. When we finally came to a halt, he told me we were ready to "start."

I groaned, hating the way all trainers did that: kicked your ass and then said it'd only just begun. Thanks to the boost I'd gained since coming to the UnderVerse, the first sets weren't as hard as they would have been on a normal Earth human. My boosted Strength, Endurance, and Agility helped massively, until he told me to keep up, and we set off running, not jogging.

We did a full lap of the arena. Its deep sand flooring was a pain, as it was far harder to run on sand than solid ground. At the end of each lap, he demanded ten pushups, then the burpees, and we were off again…

We kept it up for another hour solid, by which point I was trailing him massively and staggering as I tried to keep up, and he finally called a break.

"Well, your fitness is poor, but your heart is strong. I can work with that. A lesser man would have given up before now," he said heartily, gesturing to the pair of wooden gladii. I grabbed one, huffing as I tried to get my breathing back under control.

"First, you catch your breath, then we fight." He regarded me seriously. "I want to see how you do with it; then I can set you some forms and teach you to follow them."

I nodded gratefully, shaking my arms out and wiping sweat from my forehead to clear my vision before lifting the gladius to show I was ready.

"Already? Good!" Augustus said, and he attacked. Covering the distance between us with his sword low, he stabbed toward my stomach. I'd barely deflected it when his left hook hit my chin, and I was sent sprawling on the sand.

I rolled over, spitting blood from a busted lip onto the floor and glaring at him as he stood waiting, a grin on his face.

"Lesson one!" he said cheerfully. "The enemy doesn't care how they win, just that you don't!"

I growled and lunged forward, stabbing at his left thigh. He casually smacked the wooden sword aside with his left forearm in a blow that sent my sword wide, bringing my charge up short as the tip of his sword pressed my throat inwards uncomfortably.

"Lesson two. Anger is not your friend," he said, watching me carefully.

I backed up and started to swing the sword from side to side in a figure of eight, advancing on him again.

He stepped forward, bringing his sword around to catch mine by the guard, deflecting it aside as he moved inside my reach. He blocked my punch and wrapped his arm around mine, locking me in place as he headbutted me, releasing me as I fell backwards onto the sand yet again.

This time, when I hit the floor, I didn't stop. Instead, I kicked out, sweeping his legs out from under him and rolling over onto him.

I dropped my sword, grabbing his right wrist and punching him hard in the upper left arm, right where the deltoid met the bicep. The strike caused the limb to spasm and weaken momentarily, but when I tried to pin his arm with my knee, he twisted, throwing me off, dropping his sword and going for the grapple.

We rolled, coming to a stop with him up on top, and I twisted, managing to get his right arm and head between my legs. I locked my ankles together behind his head, grabbing the back of his neck and pulling his head down. He grunted, punching me in the thigh and trying to get free.

I grabbed his right arm, locking both upper limbs around his. By twisting my hips and chest and pushing his arm out and pulling it down, I was able to lock it so he couldn't use it. I leaned back, heaving with all my strength and squeezing his neck as hard as I could.

I grinned down at him as he struggled, his face turning purple. Then he forced a grin back at me. My guts went cold as he levered himself to his feet, ignoring the pain of my lock.

He maneuvered himself upright, lifting me into the air, and slammed me to the ground full force, his weight crashing down atop me. Bones gave way with a series of cracks…from both of our bodies.

I grunted, releasing him and coughing blood as a shard of rib punctured my lung. The centurion roared as his collarbone snapped, but that didn't stop him from punching me in the face and turning the world black…

A bucket of water across my face brought me back to consciousness, spluttering and swearing as I spat water away, my hands coming up reflexively to touch my…completely healed chest.

I blinked in shock, searching around, and observed Nerin stepping back, a satisfied look on her face and an empty bucket of water in her hands.

Augustus stood behind her, grinning at me as he stepped around her and offered a hand to help me up.

I took it, and was pulled to my feet, shaking my head as Nerin walked off, looking satisfied.

"Well done, Jax," Augustus said, nodding to me approvingly. "Your grappling technique is different, but effective. You'll have to show it to me again at some point, but you let your guard down." He met my eyes, his tone serious.

"Never let your guard down, not even when sparring. If I'd wanted to kill you, that's when I'd have done it."

"You're just full of fucking sunshine, aren't you?" I muttered, and he grinned.

"Well, let's get all the bad out of the way, then. Your sword skills are shit, but you're good at fighting, so let's work on those first."

We got a drink each, and he started to show me some basic forms. Some of them, I recognized from my first round of training back on Earth; others were similar to ones I'd seen on TV. The major difference from what I'd seen elsewhere was that these were so dedicated to my feet and legs.

Augustus slowly circled me, occasionally stopping me and making me change my stance. Other times, he would kick my thighs or lean in and shove me in the chest. If I was standing correctly, he'd brace against me, or I'd shrug it off, depending on the force. If I was standing wrong, though, I'd hit the floor and have a hell of a bruise to show for it.

I'd noticed people wandering in and sitting in the "common" seats around the arena as we trained, and by late afternoon, as we finished a hasty meal before returning to do some forms, I noticed the area was full.

Easily over a hundred people surrounded us, and I looked at Augustus questioningly. "Ignore them," he advised. "You'll have people watching your fights tonight, so this will help you get used to it."

The hours sped by until early evening, when he told me that we'd done enough, and finally, that he wouldn't be completely embarrassed by my fighting as a legionnaire now. We'd done hours of shield and sword drills, but by far the most common was the close-quarter fighting.

He'd taught me dozens of dirty tricks, from kicking sand in their eyes to bleeding them with a million cuts to targeting muscle groups that would weaken an enemy, and more. Breaking bones with my shield and gouging eyes with stiffened fingers was practically second-nature now.

With Nerin there, we'd done it all, to a certain point. He'd stopped, as had I, once the hit was confirmed beyond doubt to work. A blow to the eyes didn't need to drive deep, not when it was on target, so we'd cut off the force then, judging similarly with other attacks. It still left me tired and worn out when I finally staggered off to rest, finding Oracle in our room already.

"Where've you been?" I asked, having missed her. I'd been able to feel that she was okay, but still…

"Mal took me to the Emporium, then we visited a few other older locations around the city." she said, smiling. "I knew you'd be back soon, so I made a few changes next door." She gestured to the bathroom, and I stumbled through to find it lit by dozens of candles, with the water in the sunken bath steaming merrily.

"Oh baby…" I muttered, gazing at the water hungrily.

"Go on, get in." She smiled, and I didn't need to be asked twice. I stripped off the filthy, sweat-stained shorts and waded down the steps cut into the side of the bath.

The center was the lowest part, with deep steps on either side to sit or rest on. I took a deep breath, folding my legs under me and plunging to the bottom of the small pool.

I sat there for long seconds, holding my breath and feeling the odd pressure of the water around me. I relished the feeling of my aching muscles slowly going silent, and I opened my eyes, blinking as they adjusted to the water on them.

I looked up through the dimly lit water to the candles flickering above, and I saw a slender leg sink into the water nearby. I enjoyed the view as Oracle slipped into the water, slowly sliding her perfect figure down to sit across from me, equally naked as I was.

Her hair had changed, shifting from the long black curls she'd worn yesterday. Silken strands of a rich, deep golden red floated up, moving with the swirl and dip of the water. She smiled at me, her skin pale, and her eyes almost glowing in the dimly lit liquid.

I slowly stood up, blinking as the water cascaded down, running out of my hair and beard as I shook my head and sat back on one of the steps, holding my hand out to her.

Oracle rose up through the water, tossing her hair back over one shoulder and smiling at me. She slid the few steps through the water to come to rest in my arms. I wrapped them around her waist, and she sat on my knee, sliding one arm around my shoulders as we kissed.

The room was silent apart from the occasional crackle and pop of the fat in the candles, the faint conversations outside muted down to a faint buzz that barely registered as I slid my hot hands up, exploring her body. She laughed huskily while I nuzzled her neck.

Her skin was pleasantly cool, soft as silk over firm muscles, and my god, she tasted amazing.

She laughed again as I bit gently on her neck, but when she felt Mr. Happy rising to the occasion, she gently, but firmly, disengaged me from her embrace, pushing back in the water to sit across from me.

"Ah…no!" she said, smiling sadly. "I've been speaking to Augustus and the others already; apparently 'women weaken legs'?"

I growled, in no mood to be teased again, when what I wanted so badly was within reach.

"I don't care," I muttered, standing and moving forward, only to have her slip out of the water. The view of her long, red hair and perfect ass dripping with water only made me surge forward faster.

"I do!" she said, pushing me back into the bath, before standing at the edge of the pool and considering me as I lay back to float in the water. I got my own fun out of watching her, my flagpole saluting her as I reclined. It was impossible not to grin at the look of hunger on her face.

"You sure about that?" I teased, flexing and "waving" at her.

"Yes…" she said, sounding unsure before swallowing hard and forcing herself to look me in the eyes. "Two days, Jax; that's it. You fight tonight, and tomorrow, then we're out of here, flying away on the ships for days, where we won't have to fight, where we won't have to worry about being interrupted. You survive these two days, you win, and your prize," she said, reaching up and cupping her chest suggestively, "…is to do anything you want with me."

"I want…" I growled, coming back to my feet and staring up at her hungrily. She smiled, letting my eyes travel all over her body as she slowly turned to display every enticing curve.

"I do, too," she whispered.

With an apologetic glance, she stepped back, and clothes sprang into existence. A white dress, demure by her standards, but still figure-hugging, covered her as she shook her head.

"…But if what they say is true, even a slight advantage could be all your enemies need." She gestured to a table I had not noticed when I'd entered the room. "Climb onto that, lie face-down, and I'll massage you."

I groaned.

"Don't you want that?" she asked.

"Yeah, I do, but do you think that I'll be able to relax with your hands sliding all over my naked body? Seriously?" I explained.

"Okay, fair point." She bit her lip as her shoulders slumped. "Well, in that case, there's some food by the bed, and I can leave you alone, if you want?"

"I don't want you to leave. I really don't. But if you're serious about not coming to play, then I think you need to tell me about your day instead of rubbing my body…unfortunately. God, I want you right now," I muttered, looking her over hungrily and twitching at the memory of her in my arms. "You do know that teasing me like that is only making things worse, right?"

"I do," she admitted. "But it's also payback for all the times we had the chance, and you weren't ready."

"You're evil."

"Thanks!" She grinned and walked out of the room.

"Two can play at that," I muttered, lifting myself out of the water and toweling dry. Ignoring the clean shorts that had been set out, I opted to walk through naked to sit across from her.

I helped myself to the food and reclined back in the chair to eat, watching her eyes as she tried not to look down.

"So, what did you find?" I asked her, and she jerked her eyes back up, gritting her teeth at the realization of what I was doing.

"I've got good news," she said, shifting in the chair and blurring away her clothes to sit equally naked, "…and better news."

I choked on a mouthful of dried fruit as she shifted to get more comfortable, then almost swallowed my tongue as she started to bounce lightly in her seat, leaning forward for maximum effect.

"Okay! Okay, you win! Please, for the love of God, either put your clothes back on or get over here!" I begged, holding my hands up in surrender as she laughed. She shifted again, now fully dressed, and I sat on the bed, pulling the blanket over to hide my nakedness as I continued to eat.

"So," she said, smiling. "The good news is that the Emporium is an imperial structure. It was an old security station, I think, and its golems are running on an automatic routine. They watch anyone who enters and guard against theft, obeying the orders of whoever is wearing the rank insignia of the commander. That's how the current owner keeps them under control; the control crystal isn't active, as near as I can tell."

"Will they obey me if I declare myself?" I asked, popping a mouthful of cheese in and chewing thoughtfully.

"They probably won't, and even if they did, your orders could be countermanded by the insignia-wearer. I suggest we raid them. I can assume control over them one at a time, while you find and activate the control crystal. With that, we can order them to ignore the insignia," she said, grinning. "All we need to do is make sure the owner isn't there, so Mal has invited him to the arena tonight. If he shows up, Mal is going to get him drunk and keep him busy while we rob him."

"Okay, and what's the better news?" I asked.

"There are more than six! The owner probably doesn't know, but I could feel the mana in the building, and there are definitely more fully charged cores in that building; I'd guess at least a dozen."

"Golems or cores?" I asked excitedly.

"Both, I'd think; if there are more cores under there, then there must be a genesis chamber somewhere close by. The cores wouldn't last if they were stored too far from it, after all!"

Congratulations!

You have received a Quest from the Goddess Jenae: Reclaimer.

You have been offered a Quest to reclaim the lost imperial artifacts from the location known as the Emporium. For each golem reclaimed, you will receive 5,000xp. For each functioning facility brought under your control, you will receive 10,000xp, and for each magical artifact retrieved, you will receive 100xp.

Claim the Emporium: 0/1

Reclaim the Golems: 0/13

Reclaim and Activate Facility: 0/1

Reclaim Magical Artifacts: 0/60

Reward: Experience, Unknown, Unknown

Accept: *Yes/No*

"Fuck yes," I muttered. For the first time since returning to my room, my mind was entirely sidetracked from boinking Oracle. "What was the Emporium like?" I asked.

"It's a shiny shop, with a dozen or two genuine magical artifacts on display, I'd say, so there must be a lot more hidden away. Most of what they have, they've no idea about. I saw a harness for an aspiring dragon rider; it was designed to train the dragons, get them used to carrying someone, and they're trying to sell it for training horses!

"They've also got a shield rune on display. They've half-covered it, so you can't just copy it. But Mal got him to admit that it's useless, as nobody could provide enough mana to power it for more than a few seconds. It's part of a set of plates that generate a shield around something like a Prax, the old war-cities that had them designed. They think it's a teaching aid!"

"It could be," I said, rubbing my chin. "If we got that, and Ame could figure out what to do with it..."

"Then you could generate a shield for the entire tower, like we used to have!" Oracle said, nodding.

"Or put them on our ships. Imagine the battleship with shields..." I stared into the distance, lost in thought.

"Exactly!" She was fairly humming with excitement. "They've got books there as well. Not many, not compared to those we have, and certainly no memory stones, but still!"

"So, we're raiding them tonight, then, after the fight," I said, grinning at her.

"Provided you win, yes!" she confirmed. "Now, the letter?" She nodded to a stack of parchment by the side of the bed.

I picked it up reluctantly and looked it over. Finding that the majority of it had already been filled out, I sighed in relief. I remembered Yen and Augustus offering to put down the details, and I scanned them quickly, adding in a few extra bits at the beginning and the end, as carefully as I could, then passing them to Oracle.

"Can you get them to rewrite it with these bits in? I know my writing is terrible," I asked her. She agreed, rising to her feet and grabbing the empty plate from the table next to me. I blinked, having not realized I'd finished it, and she smiled at me, leaning forward to kiss me gently.

"Get some sleep, okay? I need you to be in top form tonight. The gangs are going to bring something evil; I just know it." With that, she slipped out into the corridor, closing the door gently behind her.

I checked the clock on the wall. Seeing that it was just past six, and the first fight was at ten, I could sleep for three and a half hours, if I was lucky. I lay back, letting out an involuntary moan as I settled onto the pillow. And I swore, come what may, even if I had to fight a dragon or another goddamn SporeMother on acid, I was taking the damn pillow with me when I returned to the tower.

CHAPTER SEVENTEEN

I was brought slowly to consciousness by a heavenly aroma, and I raised my groggy head to inspect the room, before blinking to make sure I was actually seeing what I thought I was.

I sat bolt upright, throwing the blankets aside and heaving myself up to sit on the edge of the bed. Before I realized what I was doing, I'd grabbed one triangular cut, thick wedge of bread, filled with bacon and topped with as close a match to brie as it was probably possible to get.

I bit down hard and moaned through a mouthful of pure heaven. Bringing up my other hand, I sniffed the steam rising from the cup and sighed in contentment.

"Coffee…" I sighed contentedly, my eyes closed still as I savored the first sip and found it rich, the flavors subtly layered with a hint of smokiness. "Oh, thank you god," I whispered, opening my eyes to find Oracle perched across from me, her face split by a huge smile.

"Is it right? I tried to explain it to the arena cooks," she said, and I smiled ecstatically around another huge bite.

I hated people who spoke with their mouth full, so I didn't answer verbally. I just nodded emphatically as I powered my way through the sandwich, barely coming up for air until I was licking the melted cheese and butter from my fingertips.

"Soooo good," I mumbled, then took a sip of my coffee while settling back against the wall and radiating contentment like a nuclear reactor radiated weird-looking kids.

"I don't know what I did to deserve that, Oracle, but fuck me…thank you," I said eventually, beaming at her.

"You deserve it and more!" she insisted. "The orders are there."

She nodded to a fresh stack of papers. I read them quickly, nodding approvingly at the sections that had been added, and I scrawled my signature at the bottom before rolling them up and sliding them into the case that Oracle handed me.

"I'll give them to the fliers and make sure they get to the legion before the fights are over tonight," Oracle said determinedly.

"I don't know what I'd do without you, to be honest," I admitted with an appreciative smile.

She returned my contentment with a smile of her own. "Now, you've got an hour before the first fight. Augustus said you'd need time to digest your food and time to wake up properly, so this was as long as we could let you sleep…oh, and he's got some armor for you outside."

"Armor?" I asked confusedly.

"Yes, lad, armor!" he cried, opening the door and barging in with a legion breastplate in one hand. He was fully dressed, his armor's silvery steel set atop a layer of black leather. He dropped the breastplate onto the table next to me, and other legionnaires followed him in.

"Oracle, if you wouldn't mind, milady, we will dress him." He bowed his head respectfully to her, and she looked at me, then back at them, confused.

"I've been able to dress myself for a long time now," I said, a sardonic smile twisting my lips as I glanced at the centurion.

"Not like this," Augustus said, a half-smile curving his own lips. "It's traditional. A new legionnaire is dressed by his brothers and sisters the first time he goes to war, so that he…and they…know he won't have to worry about that, at least."

He threw me a pair of shorts from the table, and I pulled them on, standing as he and the others came to surround me. "Tonight, High Lord Jax of Dravith, you are a legionnaire of the empire, going out to his first battle as a member of the legion," he said, pulling a leather undershirt over my head and tugging it down into place, while another legionnaire took the straps at the sides and pulled them tight.

"We can't be with you, out on the sand of the arena, but we're with you always," he continued, gripping my shoulder tight enough to nearly bruise the bone. "Remember this, as you face the worst the gangs have to offer. You're no longer a man alone. Now, and forever more, you're a legionnaire of the empire," he finished, stepping back as I stepped into the pants another held for me.

It was strange…it was always going to be a bit weird, being dressed by men and women I didn't really know; that was a given. But the care and respect they showed in the process…it wasn't the way that some of them had looked at me until now, like a god made flesh or like they weren't sure of me and thought they might be making a mistake. Now they looked different. Proud.

They pulled my arm guards on, cinching them tight, and I immediately missed the hidden daggers that my bracers held. The belt was thick, black leather, with my sheathed gladius attached to it, instead of the one I'd brought with me from Earth, which held the razor wire surprise that had helped me so often.

I felt them pulling the toggles tight on the hips of my pants and attaching armored greaves and chainmail to hooks embedded in the leather underclothes. Plates of metal were strapped in place next, as they built me from the ground up.

My breastplate was one of the last bits to attach, once the cuirass had been cinched around my chest by leather straps. They topped off the entire outfit with an articulated shoulder and upper chest section that was lowered over my head before being locked down with clasps.

I felt like a steel armadillo at first; then I started to move as they asked, and they shifted clips and straps, loosening some and tightening others.

Soon, we were warned by Lydia, shouting in from the hall, that we had fifteen minutes, and then ten, and five. Finally, with a minute to spare, Augustus stepped forward, grinning, as I ran through the stretches they ordered. My armor now felt comfortable and right, instead of restrictive and rigid, the way it had at first.

It was designed to allow a full range of movement, far more than I'd expected, and I realized that the modern legionnaire wasn't the holdover of some pre-Cataclysm ancient time that I'd first thought. The legion armorers couldn't advance their skills, not the way a normal armorer would, by creating a thousand different styles and pieces, since they could only create armor for the legion.

However, in doing so for so long, they'd managed to refine it fantastically. A hinge here, a spring there, and I had a range of movement I couldn't have imagined in such full-coverage gear. Add to that, the lower sections were designed to redistribute part of the weight higher, and the way the entire thing hung on me, and it wasn't heavy like the armor I'd fought in while training on Earth.

It was magnificent.

"Now, High Lord Jax, now you look like a real legionnaire!" Augustus said, clapping me on the shoulders and looking into my eyes. "Lastly, we came to you because we know who you are. We obey you because of that. We've brought you these."

He gestured, and another legionnaire set six large mana potions down on the desk nearby. "Oracle explained what you'd need in order to activate the Oath. We want to swear to you; we will serve you in death as we do in life. Lord Jax, Scion of the Empire...will you have us?" he asked, meeting my eyes seriously, and I swallowed hard.

"Yes, legionnaire," I said, knowing somehow that he didn't need a title beyond that right then. "I will take your Oath; I will take all your Oaths."

I stepped forward, moving to the table as he gestured to a legionnaire by the door, who opened it and glared at Lydia as she tried to warn me that we were going to be late for the arena.

They didn't care. He barked an order at the pair of legionnaires in the hallway, and they crowded in, making my small room even more cramped than it was before.

All the legionnaires knelt as one, right fist clenched to their chests, heads up, watching me, and I popped the top off each of the mana potions.

I found Oracle, feeling her presence, and she smiled at me from where she stood by the door. I smiled back at her and took a deep breath, confident that she was ready and able to help me.

"I am Jax, Lord of Dravith!" I declared, loudly and clearly. "I am Amon, the Eternal Emperor's descendant, and I claim his Oaths as my own!"

With that simple phrase, my mana reserve flashed and dropped at an almost unbelievable rate. As Oracle wove the strands of an ancient form of magic for me, I grabbed the bottles, downing them one after the other.

My mana bar would jump, then drop, then jump, as I knocked each of them back. I saw a warning flash up that I'd already pushed my mana regeneration past the maximum as I lifted the sixth bottle, and I paused. My rate of regeneration was at nearly three hundred points per second now, and still, it was being pulled out faster than it was replaced.

I downed the bottle for the immediate boost anyway and gritted my teeth as my health began to drain, along with my stamina.

Ten seconds, it lasted, with my body feeling like it was being torn apart as magic streamed out of me. The weaves reached out as Oracle manipulated them, guiding them. They touched each of the legionnaires, one-by-one, locking onto them and holding tight as new awareness bloomed inside me. Each and every individual took up a space in my soul that I'd never known was empty.

I clenched my jaw tighter and stood there, forcing myself to stay upright and feeling the power surging through me.

"How the hell did you do this with hundreds of thousands?!" I threw at Amon, not expecting an answer, and I started when he responded.

"I did it with tens of millions, but I had Oath-Keepers, and the Great Towers were linked to the Capitol. I never had to do it with mana of my own…Stand strong, Scion. Know that the emperor believes in you."

"Thank you," I sent after a few frozen seconds, then I felt the draw cut off. My mana suddenly jumped like crazy as the final seconds of enhanced regeneration were used to fill my reserves, rather than being pulled away in an instant. I drew in a deep, shuddering breath as Oracle hit me with a healing spell. She glided through the kneeling legionnaires to hand me a stamina potion before turning and starting to heal the legionnaires around me.

They were all in fantastic physical condition, fit and healthy, but they were the survivors of hundreds of battles. Like Amaat, they had more than their fair share of permanent damage.

Or what without magic, would have been permanent. Mis-healed bones, clicking elbows, missing digits, damaged lungs and knees, all of them, Oracle swept away, glorying in the insane levels of mana regeneration I was experiencing.

I downed it, letting out a relieved sigh as my health, mana and stamina all reached full. Then I froze as she kissed my cheek and stepped aside, the voices around me rising into the still air.

"I am Augustus. The name of my birth was Augustus Vertais Asen, and I chose Augustus as my common name. I am a Centurion Primus in the Dravith Cohortes Praetoria, and I serve the empire. I acknowledge my Oath and its validity."

Each and every legionnaire in the room echoed those words, and I felt them as each of them swore their lives to me. I saw their faces, these scarred and grizzled veterans, men and women who'd battled since long before I was born, who now gazed at me with reverence, with belief, and with trust.

I stared down at my legionnaires, familiar fury filling me at how they'd been treated.

The way they'd been spat on by society for holding true to their Oaths and their honor.

I saw in my mind's eye the battles they'd fought, the way their numbers had dwindled. The way they'd gone out and saved villages, fought the creatures of the night, and on their return, they'd been met with price hikes when they went to buy food, because they were "legion scum."

I heard the growl in my throat as I regarded them, and I spoke without thinking about it.

“No more!” Thunder filled my voice. “No more will you give your lives for those who treat you like dirt. You are now *my* legionnaires, and you will never have your lives thrown away. You will protect and defend the empire. You will grow and become all that your ancestors did, and more besides. You are the LEGION, and those fuckers will rue the day they threw you aside! I will lead you.

"I accept your Oaths, and I swear I shall be worthy of them. We will rebuild the empire, we will shatter those who plunder its corpse, and we will protect the innocent! We will rise; we will be all that we should be, all that you have dreamt you could be, and we will fix this broken realm!” I roared, my words answered with a ringing, silvery sound as each and every legionnaire drew their swords, holding them aloft.

“All hail Jax! All hail the High Lord of Dravith!” they chanted as one, and I drew in a deep breath, forcing down my anger at all they’d had to endure, as they rose to their feet.

You have accepted 274 legionnaires and supporters of the Dravith legion into your personal retinue….

“My lord, we have an appointment, I believe,” Augustus said, grinning at me. I nodded sharply at him. He turned, barking an order.

“Centurion Grizz! Lead the section!”

“Yes, Centurion Primus!” Grizz roared back, his voice echoing off the walls as he about-faced and started forward. Half the legion fell in ahead and half brought up the rear behind me. We marched down the corridor, Lydia and the others grinning as they joined the procession.

Oracle winked at me as she shrank to fly alongside me as we descended into the bowels of the building. We passed doors and hallways that practically rocked with the shouting from the crowd, and seconds later, we erupted onto the ground floor. Two doors stood ahead, and Mal waited by one of them, freezing as he saw us coming.

He’d clearly been about to complain about us being late, but when he saw my escort, he swallowed back the words and nodded once. Oracle flashed to her full size again and landed, taking my hand and kissing my knuckles once before whispering into my ear, “For luck.”

Then she took Mal’s proffered arm and was escorted up a flight of stairs towards his private booth.

We passed through the doors, entering a private suite next to the arena, where I could rest and recover between bouts, and I found Mistress Nerin waiting. As the legionnaires split off, some taking up stations by the doors, others examining the room, she pulled me aside to bring me up to speed on my opponents.

“The first fight is against the harpies’ choice; a promethean by the name of Golmar. He’s an arrogant shit who owes me thirty gold pieces from a healing he refused to pay for. I’d appreciate it if you’d remind him of that,” she said, her sharp eyes boring into me.

“Consider him dead as an apology,” I growled.

“It’ll do, as a start. Now go on, get out there. He’s been calling the legion cowards, since you’re late.”

“Get him,” Grizz said, raising a fist.

I bumped it, grinning at the notion of fist bumps being universal. The other legionnaires gave me approving nods while Yen grinned at me from across the room and called out:

"Teach him to fear the legion, my lord. Teach him respect!"

"Yeah!"

"Damn right!" came more calls, as the others agreed. I looked at my squad; Barrett, Lydia, Jian, Stephanos, Miren, and Arrin were all there, smiling proudly at me. I felt something behind me, and I grinned, turning to check the corner of the room.

"You can stay in here as well, Bane," I said.

He straightened, dropping his stealth cloak as he cocked his head. "You might need a hand…"

"I'll be fine, but thank you, my friend. Besides, we can't risk being accused of cheating. If I can't take Oracle or use magic, I certainly can't have a bodyguard in a one-on-one match."

I grasped his shoulder and gave it a grateful squeeze. He tensed, then stepped back, silently acknowledging the arena's terms and my need to follow them. I turned from him and looked around the room once more.

"Thank you all. Now, someone get me a cold beer and keep it waiting while I teach this shithead not to insult the legion!"

"Hoo-ah!" Augustus roared, and the others echoed him. Lydia pulled the door open that led out into the arena.

"Good luck, Jax," she said as I passed her. "Yer can do it!"

I grinned at her beneath my helmet. A stray thought caused me to chuckle over the fact that it appeared more Spartan than Roman legionnaire, but she heard it and grinned back.

I took the last steps out and felt my feet sink slightly into the sand of the arena as the metal door clanged shut behind me, sealing me in.

The roar of the crowd was almost a physical pressure as I moved forward. I surveyed the space, seeing the arena differently from my practice earlier today. Then, it had been a training field, somewhere I could focus and improve; now, it was more. Now, it was a place of death and glory. Blood had been spilled already in the warmup fights, and sand had been kicked over it, but the stains were still obvious.

The walls were made of bars twisted together, and hundreds of spectators clung to them, obscuring the seats, and all of them howling for blood. The upper third of the arena had been set aside for the private booths, and I felt a moment of nostalgia as I remembered the arena that I'd fought in to come to the UnderVerse.

God, I'd have loved to see their faces, if I'd been the man I was now when I fought there. I'd have torn the damn place down around their ears.

I locked eyes on Oracle and Mal, nodded once, then banished everything from my mind besides the pale-skinned fuck who stood on the other side of the arena, facing me.

Golmar was taller than me, nearly nine feet, I guessed, with long, blond hair and huge mustachios that curled upwards. He was heavily muscled, but I suspected he'd be fast for all of that, and his wings were huge. The white-blond feathers jutting from his back invoked memories of artistic depictions of the classical angels in holy scripture. The similarity ended there, though, as he swore at me, his pointed teeth and malevolent glare making it clear he wasn't one of the "good guys."

I couldn't decide whether those teeth made him uglier than the grey-blue fucker I'd fought in the weaver's shop. His armor consisted of golden bracers and shin guards with a waist wrap in the style of the ancient pharaohs. Surprisingly, he was naked from the waist up.

He held a single huge sword in his right hand, clenching and unclenching his left fist as he growled at me in clear hatred. I grinned at him, stepping forward again. I shrugged, reveling in the feel of my armor following my movements perfectly.

I drew my gladius from its sheath, slapping the blade against the front of my shield three times, making the arena echo with the metallic clangs.

"You dare to make me wait, mortal?" he screamed at me, slamming his wings down and hurtling across the arena even before the announcer could speak. He swung his huge sword down with a blow that would have cut me in half...had it landed.

I grinned inside my helmet, rolling to the left and coming up under his powerful swing. I flicked my blade out and drew a line of blood from his back, managing to catch the bottom of his right wing before he hit me with the flat of his blade and sent me flying.

I hit the ground, rolled again, and sprang back up, noting pain from the blow, but nowhere near as much as I expected. I grinned again, loving the feeling of such well-fitted armor.

"You think this is funny?" Golmar screeched, spinning his blade around and glaring at me. "The Skyking has decreed your death, fool, and I have been sent to make that order a reality!"

"That's nice," I called out. "And did the Skyking send you some help?"

"I need no assistance!" he bellowed, slamming his wings down again and covering the distance between us. This time, I didn't dodge. I angled my shield like Augustus had shown me, and I grunted under the strain as I deflected the sword to the side, causing the heavy blade to sink into the sand. I took advantage of my opponent's temporary immobility and stabbed out, the tip of my gladius sinking deep into Golmar's upper right arm and cutting the bicep free.

He screamed, pain and fury echoing around the space, and he grabbed me by my upper right arm with his massive left land, yanking me from my feet.

"Die, mortal!" he snarled, opening his jaws impossibly wide. A forked tongue flickered over his pointed, foul-looking teeth. I dropped my sword and shield, grunting at the pain of his crushing grip even through my armor.

I struck out, my left hand stiffened into a solid bar of bone, reinforced by the gauntlets, and I sank two of my fingers in good and deep on either side of his nose. I wasn't aiming for his mouth; hell, no.

I drove my rigid fingers into his eyes, using the momentum of his pull and all the force I could bring to bear to gouge out both of his eyes.

He screamed in a mixture of horror and agony and dropped me, his hand going to his face as I landed hard. I rolled and swept up both my sword and shield, then snorted at his screams.

"This is from Nerin," I growled as I lashed out, hamstringing his left leg. The blinded promethean spun around, staggering and disoriented.

"This is from me," I shouted, hacking through his right wing, and sending his screaming, mangled form to the floor.

"And this is from the LEGION!" I roared as I sliced horizontally, beheading him in one swift move.

The crowd went silent as the massive promethean's body fell to the floor, blood fountaining from his severed arteries. I turned, looking up at them.

"You all came here for blood!" I roared, my anger clear. "You came to see the legion humbled, hurt, and killed! You won't! Not now, not ever!"

I slammed my blade against my shield again, hard, making the clash of metal ring out across the frozen arena.

"LEGION!" I bellowed and smashed my blade against my shield again, shouting louder. "LEGION!" I repeated, catching the legionnaires grinning and watching me through the bars of the door to my "rest room."

"Fuck it if they can't take a joke," I muttered, then I threw my head back and shouted out to all those watching. "Who's next?" Silence filled the air as the spectators gaped at me, stunned. "Come on, then! I SAID, WHO'S NEXT!"

I spun to face the other private booths, finding men and women of all species staring down at me with hate-filled eyes.

"WHAT'S WRONG?" I roared. "YOU TOO SCARED TO FIGHT ME NOW?"

The crowd began to chant again, now split between cries of 'Death, death, death!" and a hardier few who were chanting "LEEEGION, LEEEGION!"

The announcer stepped forward in Mal's booth, clearly having been prodded by the arena master, and he called out in a magically enhanced voice that carried over the slowly rising chants.

"Honored guests…the challenger has turned down his rest cycle and has demanded a new competitor immediately. I believe the next in line is Nigret, the Demon of the Sands?"

"Come on, then, Nigret!" I shouted, clanging my sword and shield again. "I'm fucking waaaaaaiting!"

I glanced back at the legionnaires in my room, watching me through the bars of the door, and I saw them cheering me on. I saw the looks on their faces, the desperate hope and pride, of men and women who'd been forced to take shit for far too long, forced to not rock the boat. Now they had a new leader, one who wanted to burn the boat down and piss on the ashes, and they loved it!

The door behind me clanged as the bolts holding it shut were released, and a huge, white-furred felinoid stalked into the arena. He was taller than me, but only by a few inches this time. He wore a heavy metal chestplate with a bright red ruby set into the very center of his chest.

Beyond that, he was armored much as I was, with heavy plates attached over leather and chainmail, and he bore a pair of scimitars. Their heavy curved blades and his plate armor made me nod in grudging respect. He was a tank and looked as though he knew what he was doing, unlike the dick who was slowly cooling behind me now.

I started forward, my blood up, and I ignored the announcer calling out the fight. I held my shield in place, slowly swinging my sword from side to side.

"You are a brave opponent, but foolish," the cat man called out, and I nodded, accepting the facts as he said them.

“You should have rested, prepared for our fight. Perhaps you would have lived longer, yes?” He shifted closer, then started to circle me at a distance of about two meters.

“Maybe you should have found some standards, instead of coming to face the legion,” I retorted and he scoffed.

“These fools might believe you are a prisoner, captured and forced to fight, but Nigret knows different…no prisoner walks like you do, taunts the crowd, or wants more fights. A prisoner would have taken the time, gone back to his room and rested, yes?” he said, flicking his scimitars out to lightly touch my shield, testing me.

“Maybe you should reconsider your life…while you still can,” I said to him, blocking and deflecting his second strike, then taking his next hit to the shield as I stepped forward.

We exchanged a series of blows, each testing the other. Our training had clearly been similar, displayed in our mutual method of watching our opponent’s eyes as much as the blades. Then we backed away again.

“You seem strange, cub,” Nigret said. “Unsure of your claws, yet confident of the fight. Why is this?” he asked, almost conversationally, before stepping in and sending a blinding flurry of blows into my shield and sword, trying to break through my guard.

“Truth be told, I usually use a different weapon,” I said, grinning as I came up with a plan. “I don’t suppose I could convince you to throw the match, surrender, and come work for me, could I?” I asked hopefully.

“Alas, no. I think that Nigret and the legion’s views on property would not match. Also murder, and…”

I lunged forward, my shield angled upwards, along with my sword, forming two-thirds of a triangle. As both of Nigret’s scimitars smashed down, his eyes widened as he realized this wasn’t another test. He tried to frantically back away, even as I chased him, my sword flashing out to bounce off his upper thigh. The strike made him grunt as I managed to cut through a few of the chainmail links, sending blood trickling down his leg.

I knew I had to keep going, and I did, rushing him as he tried to retreat, blocking his scimitars as they swung again and again.

He shifted styles, jumping and kicking my shield hard enough to stagger me. Suddenly, I was the one retreating as his scimitars flashed faster and faster.

I backtracked across the ground I’d just gained, and more, blocking and deflecting more than counterattacking until I noticed a particular cadence to his attacks. He’d use a stab, then a pair of thrusts, then a kick, then start a separate pattern clearly designed to keep me moving.

I reacted to the suspicion as soon as it clarified in my mind; if I was right, then his next attack would be a kick, so…

I dug my back foot into the sand and put my weight behind my shield, becoming as immovable as I could. I paused a second, then stabbed my sword over the rim, aimed upwards and thrust!

It worked! He’d fallen into a pattern, and as he kicked, I met him with a suddenly immovable shield, rather than one that was constantly shifting. He staggered, giving me the chance to cut him across the face. The tip of my blade sliced from his left cheek, across his face, to rip a large, hooped earring from his tufted ear.

He snarled in pain, backing up, and I ran at him, taking a flurry of blows on my shield and sword as I closed the distance again. I deflected his left sword wide and struck him in the face with the pommel of my gladius on the return.

"Tricky little mouse!" he hissed, backing up and spitting blood out onto the sand.

"Should have worn a helmet, mate!" I called out, catching my breath as we started to circle again.

"For my kind, they must be custom built, and are often uncomfortable," he said dismissively, then crouched, stabbing out with both scimitars angled to strike my right ankle, I managed to block the right one with my shield, but the left bounced off my greaves and staggered me as he sprang up, leaping into the air.

I tried to bring my shield up in time, but his speed was too much, combined with its weight. He landed on it at an awkward angle, pushing me back and forcing me to drop the shield or be pinned beneath it.

He rolled off it, coming to his feet and grinning at me, clearly thinking he had the advantage now. I grinned back at him.

I almost cast a spell, but then I stopped myself, knowing that once I did, the secret was out. Most legionnaires wouldn't have access to spells, and for all they knew, I didn't either…I had to keep them hidden as long as possible for emergencies, which meant…

Thought and action were becoming simultaneous by now, and I sprinted forward, catching him by surprise. I lashed out, deflecting his left sword with my own, while catching his right sword on the metal plates on my forearm. My block stopped the blade enough to only cause a shallow cut to my upper arm.

I barreled into him, jumping into the air and taking him to the ground. As the pair of us rolled, we both released our weapons and resorted to fists.

I grinned, thinking I'd have the advantage now with my metal gauntlets, until I saw his triumphant grin and felt pain tear through my right leg. I punched him in the face and looked down. Observing the three-inch claws extended from his fingertips, I swore internally.

He released my leg, grabbing my wrist. I grabbed his opposite wrist, turning the fight into a wrestle while blood ran from both of us.

"Not so wise…to get in close…with a Trigara…no?" he growled, a strange chuffing sound coming from him as he strained. I felt blood streaming from my leg, where his claws had punched through the links of my chainmail, and I glared at him.

"That was my second favorite leg, you dick!" I growled in return. Both of us strained to our feet, pushing with our legs as I felt the weakness in mine…

I grinned and shifted to pulling instead of pushing, and we fell again. I swiftly brought my feet up as high as I could, then kicked out, catching him in the stomach and flipping him over me to crash on his back with a yowl of surprise.

I rolled, then jumped at him as he flexed, flipping himself to his feet, and I took us both down again.

This time, I twisted around faster, locking his left arm and head between my legs and gripping his arm in both of mine. I hauled back as hard as I could, arching my back and squeezing for all I was worth with my legs as I locked my ankles together into a chokehold.

We rolled as he choked, his right hand unsheathing claws that flashed in the torchlight of the arena. He drove them into my left leg over and over, frantically trying to sever an artery or a muscle group. I felt my leg weakening, and I let out a snarl of fury, reaching out with one hand and locking it on my ankles, pulling harder and making damn sure that he couldn't escape.

"That's…my third…favorite…LEG!" I shouted, and I popped my hips to the right as hard as I could. The force of the movement was finally enough, and his eyes rolled back in his head as he ran out of air and started to black out.

I saw a flash of silver to my left, and I grinned, releasing my grip on his arm. I grabbed out, cutting my fingers on the blade of one of his scimitars as I hauled it in. Swapping it over to my right hand in order to grip it properly, I unlocked my legs, letting him get some air in.

I leaned back and kicked him in the face, hurling him away from me and making sure he was too stunned to resume the fight. Then I dragged myself over to him and put the tip of the blade to his throat, waiting.

After a few seconds, he came around enough to understand his predicament, first stiffening, then slumping in defeat.

"Why wait, legion? Finish us; set our soul free to the ether to join our ancestors," he demanded quietly.

"That what you want?" I asked, huffing as I got my breath back. "Because I'll be honest, that was a hell of a fight, and I'd rather recruit you."

"Ha! This one would make a poor legionnaire…"

"What about a hunter, or a scout?" I whispered. "I need both."

"Why? Why do you offer this?" he asked, after a long pause in which we both heard the crowd chanting for his death.

"Because you fought well," I said, shrugging. "I'm not fucking stupid, though…You renounce all Oaths right here and now and swear to obey me for the next ten years, or I'll give a little push," I said, lightly pressing the tip of the blade against his throat.

"I have no Oaths, but many gambling debts. This one likes the shiny gold. They will come for me."

"Swear fealty to me, and that becomes my problem, not yours."

There was a long break where he seemed to consider things. Then he slowly reached a hand up to dip his fingers in the blood of his still-weeping cheek. He lifted the bloody tips of his fingers into the air and said slowly and clearly, if only loud enough for me to hear…

"I, Nigret, hunter of the Trigara, second son of Tzuulli the Wise, forswear all Oaths, and swear to the one who holds his blade against my neck. For ten years, I will serve, no more and no less, but if Nigret is asked to dishonor his ancestors, this Oath is broken," he said warningly.

I grinned, leaning back and dropping his sword by my side.

"I've taken Nigret as a bondsman!" I called out, my voice echoing around the arena. "He is mine now, and any who take issue with this can suck my fucking balls."

There was a sudden pause, then the air erupted in a mix of approval and screams for death. I didn't give a damn about their opinions, though, and drew a deep breath, wincing at the pain that radiated from…everywhere.

I tried to rise to my feet, staggering as my leg went out from under me. Then he was there, one hand rubbing his neck as he grinned down at me. It was far more gruesome than he likely intended, since half his face was hanging open from my thrust earlier.

"Nigret offers help, but this day is strange, as Nigret is a bondsman, but he doesn't know to whom!" the Trigara said, tilting his head in question.

I reached out and let him pull me to my feet.

"I'll explain in a few minutes. Let's get these wounds tended to, and get the proper Oath sworn."

"Proper Oath?" he asked, confused.

"Trust me; you think your day was going weird before? I should warn you, it's only gonna get weirder," I muttered as the door manned by the legion opened. Two of my men came out to help us back into the rest area, while others came out and grabbed our weapons and stripped all valuables from the body of the promethean Golmar, leaving the cooling corpse in the sand.

CHAPTER EIGHTEEN

We staggered into the preparation room, slumping down into chairs, and I grinned at the legionnaires around me, pleased with the nods I was getting. Augustus stepped forward, pushing Nerin aside as she tried to go to us.

"Wait please, Mistress Nerin," he said firmly, then he pointed at Nigret. "Can you explain, please…Jax?"

He stroked his sword hilt.

"It's okay. I gave him a choice, and he forswore all Oaths and gave one to me instead. Oracle is on her way, and as soon as she's here, we can—"

I was cut off as the door to the corridor outside slammed back and Oracle ran in, with Mal and Soween close behind her. I also noticed a patch of darkness just behind Nigret, and I grinned, knowing that was Bane, the sneaky fucker.

"That was amazing!" Oracle gushed, sprinting to me and jumping onto my lap.

I grunted in pain, but she shifted, becoming lighter. I relaxed, though I still had to grit my teeth against the pain.

"Sorry!" she yelped, jumping up and weaving her hands before her to send the healing weaves of our Battlefield Triage spell into me. Nerin did the same for Nigret after a nod from Augustus.

I groaned as the spell poured through me, healing and rebuilding shredded muscles, bringing me back to fighting trim.

After a handful of seconds, I sagged back, though the final twitches of magical repairs made me sit up straighter.

"So…" Mal started, glaring at Nigret. I took a quick look around the room and was surprised to realize that the entire room was doing the same. Now that Nigret was unarmed, he started to look scared, a panicked smile on his face as he hunted for a way to escape.

"You'll get used to it, Mal," Oracle said, smiling. "Our lord likes to take in strays."

"Nigret is no stray," Nigret muttered darkly at the same time as Mal corrected her quickly.

"He's not *my* lord."

"'Lord'?" Nigret perked up at that and squinted at me, confused.

"Yeah." I grinned. "Oracle, can you extend the Oath to him, please?" I asked, winking at him.

Nigret stiffened suddenly as the Oath arrived in his notifications, and he started to growl low in his throat as he read through it.

"I see no limits on this Oath…*LORD JAX*," he rumbled angrily. "Nigret agreed to serve you for ten years, and to do nothing dishonorable. This Oath has no such limits!"

"I, High Lord Jax of Dravith, Scion of the Empire, swear that after ten years of *faithful* service by Nigret, I will release him from his Oath to me, should he wish it. I will never intentionally order him to do something dishonorable, and I will raise him in my service as he deserves and earns, should he do well," I said, smiling reassuringly at him before the mana drain of the Oath made me grit my teeth and take a deep breath. I kept eye contact with him and nodded. "Now it's your turn, mate. You know you'll be free in the agreed term now."

"And if I refuse? I never agreed to support you in your war," he snapped.

"Then you're an Oathbreaker, as far as I'm concerned. I hear the consequences for that aren't pleasant."

"Nigret is no Oathbreaker!" the Trigara snarled. He paused, bringing himself under control, closing his eyes and swallowing hard as something clearly affected him. He groaned in pain, then glared at me and started to speak.

"I swear to obey Lord Jax and those he places over me; I will serve to the best of my ability, speak no lie to him when commanded otherwise, and treat all other citizens as family.

"I will work for the greater good, being a shield to those who need it, a sword to those who deserve it, and a warden to the night.

"I will stand with my family, helping one another to reach the light, until the hour of my death or my lord releases me from my Oath.

"Lastly, I will not be a dick!"

As the final words left his lips, I felt the Oath becoming active, and I sighed in relief. I met his furious eyes as I intoned the words I'd used for others who had joined me.

"I, Lord Jax, do swear to protect and lead you, to be the shield that protects you and yours from the darkness, and the sword that avenges that which cannot be saved. As the tower grows in strength, so shall you."

Once the last word had left my lips, my people started to relax. "I'm sorry to have to do this, Nigret, and I know this isn't going to leave a good impression on you, but please understand, a handful of minutes ago, you were trying to kill me, so you'll have to trust that this is as much for your safety as it is mine." I took a deep breath, speaking firmly.

"Nigret, I order you to speak the truth to me now, for the rest of this conversation. Are you planning to break faith with me or any of my people?" I watched the phrasing of the Oath take hold, making him hiss in fury as he tried to stop himself from speaking, but couldn't.

"Nigret had no intention of breaking faith with you or your people until this Oath was used. Now, Nigret wants to be free!" he spat, his eyes blazing with anger.

"Then I am truly sorry, Nigret, that I had to use it. Rest now and relax. I needed to be sure, since you're going to hear a lot of things in the next day or two that cannot be betrayed. If you want to be free after all this is done, I'll honor that, despite the ten years you promised," I offered sadly. It had felt cruel to compel him to tell me the truth like that, but it had to be done. The other option was to kill him.

I shook my head to clear it and gazed around the room. I was met by the approving nods of the legion, and the mixture of looks the others gave me. Clearly, nobody liked seeing the compulsion magic behind the Oath, but it'd been needed.

"So…that's two fights down now." Mal switched topics suddenly. "You ain't plannin' on another stupid trick like that for the next ones, are you?"

"What, recruiting my opponent?" I asked, flashing a smile.

"No, movin' straight into the next fight! I missed bein' able to place the bets; I lost a goddamn fortune!" he fumed, and I snorted in laughter.

"Bets," Grizz muttered, clicking his fingers. "Can we put some coin down, Lord Jax?"

I shrugged dismissively.

"You're welcome to, mate, though I think you'll have a job getting Mal to hand over your winnings…"

"I'll take the bets," Soween said, waving her hand to a round of relieved sighs and nods.

"Hey! What, none of you trust me with your coin, but you'll trust me to plan all this mess out?" Mal asked, looking hurt.

"Would you give the gold over without taking a cut?" I challenged him. He froze. "…And that's why they trust Soween more than you, mate!" I said, grinning.

"You're all friends here?" Nigret said suddenly. "We…the gangs, that is…were told you were prisoners. Nigret thought he saw hints that it was fake, but this…how did you convince the legion to play along? This is setup, you're bleeding the gangs of their gold!"

He gaped from me to the legionnaires to Mal.

"Oh, you're in for a treat, son," Mal said, shaking his head at Nigret. "If you think this is the main event…we ain't even started the real game yet."

Nigret blinked at the sea of grins that surrounded him.

Oracle started checking over my armor, and that spurred the legion into motion. I was pulled to my feet as they examined my armor minutely, and Mal and Oracle were pulled out of the way while they got to work.

They started to strip off sections while another legionnaire who was close to my size began removing some sections of his armor to replace my damaged ones, grinning enthusiastically at me as I thanked him.

"Are you crazy, Lord Jax? I'm the one who needs to thank you! You're wearing my armor as you step out there, teaching those assholes to fear the legion!" he said proudly.

"We're headin' back up there. We'll put the bets in, then I'll invite our victim to my booth for the final fight. Make it a good one, and I'll keep him at the bar as long as possible." Mal tossed me a wink as he headed to the door, Soween and Oracle joining him. Oracle spun back to blow me a kiss as she left.

I winked at her, and while they fixed my armor, I pulled up my notifications from earlier in the day, since I'd been too worked up to look at them earlier.

Congratulations!

**Through hard work and perseverance,
you have increased your stats by the following:**

Agility +1

Constitution +1

Dexterity +2

Endurance +3

Strength +2

Continue to train and learn to increase this further…

*

Congratulations!

You have killed the following:

- 1x Promethean Warrior Golmar, level 18 for a total of 11,000xp

Progress to level 16 stands at 28,149/165,000

I grinned, thrilled with the jump in the experience that I'd gained from the fight with the promethean. It was a bit of a sickener that I got nothing from the harder fight with Nigret, but I shrugged. I'd still earned more than I would have otherwise.

I was far more pleased with the first notification. I'd increased my stats by nine damn points due to letting Augustus kick my ass for a day. The noticeable boosts prompted me to check my skill notifications, as I'd disabled them long ago, except for the big ones. After a few seconds of searching, I found it…my shields skill had jumped to level four and my swordsman to eight!

A few more fights, and I should be able to get my sword skill up high enough to evolve it, and I just knew that would fucking help.

"That's you ready, Jax," Augustus said, slapping me on the shoulder. I jumped, returning to the world as I blinked my eyes clear.

"Sorry, checking notifications."

"I guessed." He snorted. "You can always see it in someone's eyes when they're reading those damn things."

"You don't like them?" I asked.

"I just think a man doesn't need to be told if he's improved or not; he should know."

"Where I come from, people would disagree, mate," I replied, thinking back to Earth. "With nothing to track growth, people ignore it. I've gained more in the last few months here than in my entire life back there. Millions would jump at the chance to be here, even with all the mental monsters everywhere."

"Mental monsters?" he asked, confused. "Like the Drachim?"

"Ah, no. Sorry, mate, no idea what that is. I meant 'mad' or 'crazy.' Just a carryover from my world's speech, that's all."

"Well—" Augustus was cut off as a gong sounded outside, and two skinny men ran out of opposite doors in the arena. They sprinted at each other, screaming and swinging their weapons, and we all crowded forward to watch.

It was over in seconds, one of them tripping and sprawling full-length in the sand. His opponent leaped up and brought his sword down, stabbing it through the fallen man's back with a sickening crunch. The blade smashed bones as it pierced all the way through to hold him impaled, screaming, while the victor tried to yank it free. It lasted a mere handful of seconds before the fallen man died from massive blood loss and shock. The legionnaires all grunted in disapproval over the sloppy attacks.

"Is it normally like that?" I asked the room at large.

"No. The poor are given the chance to fight for money if they wish, but only the weakest take it. Generally, those with no hope. It is a sad and shameful thing," Nigret said, his voice low and grim.

"So, it's pretty much either professional gladiators or poor fools, is that it?" I asked, and I got a snort from my left.

"They also allow monster matches," Grizz said. "Fools go out and capture wild beasts, often losing people to do it, then they sell them to the arena. Teams of fighters are made up, and they go in to face whatever creature's been caught. Sometimes it's a bear or a fellbeast; other times, it'll be a damn vampyr or a chimera, and the teams all die until a group of professional gladiators is brought in."

"Sounds fun," I said.

He shook his head. "I've not heard any rules against using a monster in these fights with you, sir, so watch yourself."

"Well, fuck." A couple of people dragged the corpse out of the arena while the winner frantically collected the handful of coins that had been thrown in for him as a reward.

"Exactly," Augustus agreed. "They will probably hold them back until their last chance to win, as they're expensive to capture and keep, and they can earn a fortune in the arena normally. The arena master should know if they're moving monsters in, though, and there have been none so far. Two fights to go, Jax, then we move onto phase two of your plan, so don't make any mistakes here, okay?" he said, and I nodded.

"I'll be careful."

"Good man. Also, remember the fighting order is officially drawn by lots, so they could be in any order. Don't be deceived if your opponent looks weaker or stronger than you expect. Face them all as deadly, and you'll survive."

"Officially, yeah," I retorted, remembering the conversation last night. Mal was going to let them bribe him to get more gold, the sneaky fucker.

The gong sounded again, triggering the doors to slam shut and lock tight around the arena. I took in a deep breath, shifting my shoulders and resettling my armor again as Augustus passed me my sword, and Lydia stepped forward with my shield. I grinned when I saw that she'd attached a dagger in a sheath to the back of the shield, and she grinned back.

"Just in case," she said, and I looked closer at the dagger, grinning wider as I recognized my Dagger of Ripping.

I nodded to acknowledge my readiness, and they opened the door, stepping back to let me pass. Mutters of "good luck" and "kick their ass" rose around me as I walked out onto the sand again, feeling it shift under my feet as I went.

I moved halfway into the center of the arena and stopped, waiting for my opponent to come out…and I waited…and waited.

After a handful of minutes, another man was pushed out, wearing a mismatched collection of black and brown leather, topped with a hood that almost hid his face. He had evidently been equipped with only a whip in one hand, and a dirk in the other. The man staggered forward briefly before turning in an attempt to go back through the door, which promptly slammed shut and locked in his face.

A chorus of boos arose as he scrabbled desperately, pleading with whoever was on the other side to let him out. I straightened, letting my shield drop as I watched him. My anger built at the gangs for throwing someone in that obviously didn't belong here.

"Jax! Mal said it's a trick!" Oracle's voice suddenly came to me, and I froze, just as the man spun around, his whip flicking out and wrapping around my exposed throat.

I grunted, trying to bring my hands up, but they were full of my shield and sword. Before I could think to drop one or both of them, my opponent yanked back, hard.

I staggered forward, finally dropping both my sword and shield to grab the whip. Yanking hard with my right hand to gain some space, I tried to unravel it with my left. My fingers scrabbled at the ring around my throat, and I stiffened my neck as much as I could, gasping down a lungful of air before he started dragging me forward over the sand.

Each time I got enough of a grip to start to search for the end, hoping to unravel it, he'd yank me again, making me gasp and fight for every breath as I was jerked around the arena.

I fought against the panic of not being able to breathe and the increasing pain. The rising anger that filled me over being tricked, amplified by Oracle's panic, was not helping my chances at all, and I forced myself to remain calm.

I kicked out with a foot, spinning, then digging both feet into the sand, forcing myself to use the pressure against the whip to jump to my feet. I landed hard, staggering, as he frantically tried to wind the whip in. Refusing to give him the chance to tighten it further, I rushed forward, feeling lightheaded as I started to black out…a dozen feet…seven…three…I leaped into the air and shoulder-charged him back against the door that stood behind him, causing him to bounce off it. I took the opportunity to drop myself atop him as he fell, and I pinned him, my fingers grabbing at the whip around my throat and searching…

After another few seconds, long enough that I nearly passed out, I found it! I yanked at the end, feeling it resist for a second before coming free, and I frantically unraveled it, gasping in huge lungfuls of air as I threw the whip aside. Heaving, I glared down at the man trapped below me as he stared up with angry, hate-filled eyes.

The fucker was slightly built, wiry, but slim, while I was huge and wearing a metric fuck ton of armor. He managed to get his left hand free and stabbed out, his dirk bouncing off my armor without doing any damage.

His eyes widened, and I punched him in the face with my right fist, pinning his left arm and yanking the dirk free of his hand.

"I surrender!" he snarled, his eyes still full of hatred, although fear was strongly evident as well now. I snorted, frowning down at him in disgust. He'd obviously seen the last fight and thought I was some "white knight" who'd rather take prisoners.

I flipped the dirk in the air, then caught it in my right hand. Pressing down on his forehead, I pinned him back and exposed his throat, as I lifted the dirk.

"What are you doing!" he snarled, fear and anger staining his voice. "I surrendered!"

"And I don't give a shit," I said, driving the dirk up under his chin to punch clean through the roof of his mouth and into his brain.

I stood up, bracing my foot on his forehead and yanking the blade free of the bone with a crunch. I shook it, flicking the blood off it as I scanned the crowds that watched in stunned silence.

"You think the legion is stupid? You think that if our positions were reversed, he'd have taken me as a prisoner? Nigret was an honorable fighter. He deserved a chance." I turned and spat on the corpse, then set off across the arena to retrieve my sword and shield. "That scumbag got what he deserved!"

Grizz opened the door for me as I walked from the arena, and I nodded my thanks as I passed him, throwing myself into a chair when the door slammed shut.

"Are you okay?" Augustus asked me, his words stark in the suddenly quiet room.

"Not really," I admitted. "That guy was a snake; I saw it in his eyes. If I let him swear to me, he'd have spent all his time trying to fuck me over. He'd have been a threat, every fucking second of the day, but still…"

"But you executed him, and now you regret it?" he asked.

After a moment's thought, I shook my head. "No, no…I don't regret it. I could see it in his eyes; there was nothing but malice and hatred there. He deserved to die, but…"

"But you didn't hesitate, and that's what bothers you," Augustus surmised, and I nodded.

"You are our lord," he said firmly, taking a seat across from me. "You are now also the sole source of law on the continent of Dravith, Jax. If you had decided you were killing him because you didn't like his dress sense, we would accept it, but you didn't. You killed him because he was a criminal who openly opposed you. It doesn't matter that he didn't know who he was facing; he didn't care. Saying a few words and expecting to be given a chance to escape or betray you is ludicrous."

"I know." I scrubbed my hands over my face, feeling weary. "It just doesn't mix with what I was taught as a kid, you know? I grew up knowing the hero always gives the benefit of the doubt, and all that."

"Sounds a bit daft," Grizz interjected, frowning. "How often does the hero get stabbed in the back in those tales?"

"All the damn time," I admitted gloomily.

"Well, in that case, it's obvious, isn't it?" Augustus said, straightening up.

"What's that?" I asked.

"Whoever told you the stories was a villain. They were trying to make sure they'd always be given a chance to escape."

"I…I don't think so, but damn, that makes a scary amount of sense."

"Well, regardless, look on the bright side."

"What's that?" I asked.

"Only one fight to go, and this is a damn nice whip." Augustus hefted the whip, which one of the legionnaires had passed to him.

"Ha!" I said, smiling. "You have fun with it, mate. Take it home for the missus!"

"I'm serious, Jax. Take a closer look," he said, offering it to me. Curious, I took it and used my Examine spell.

Corseiga Whip		**Further Description** *Yes/No*	
Damage:		15-45 DPS	
Details:		This is a whip made from the metal cobalt, treated and layered according to a method known only to the Corseiga people of the Southern Isles. It is both flexible and extremely strong. The whip is tipped with a clip that, when closed correctly, forms a tight seal with pressure, preventing the whip's release by those who are unfamiliar with its secrets….	
Rarity:	**Magical:**	**Durability:**	**Charge:**
Highly Rare	Yes	87/100	N/A

"Damn…" I muttered, twisting the whip around until I could see the end of it. The entire length was made of extremely thin wires that fed into rings, connected in some way that allowed flexibility, yet kept short enough to enable the entire length to remain strong. I tilted and flexed it between my fingers as I tested it for suppleness. "It's like rope or leather, but the damn thing's made out of metal," I muttered; then my eyes found what I'd been looking for.

The tip of the whip was formed like the front of a stingray, displaying a raised projection on either side of the outside and a scalloped edge inside. When I pressed the projections firmly against the "body" of the whip, they clicked and locked tightly to the nearest ring. It took a few minutes of poking and prodding, but eventually I figured out how to open it again, making me suspect it had either not clasped fully when it'd been around my neck, that or I'd been insanely lucky.

"That's amazing," I said, nodding, and I passed the whip to Grizz, who'd been looking on with clear interest.

"Careful, Lord Jax. That bugger *will* try to take it home for the wife!" one of the other centurions laughed, and Grizz grinned in response.

"Or someone else's wife, anyway," I chimed in.

"Hey, as long as we're all having fun?" he said with a suggestive wink.

"Then take it with my blessing, mate!" I said with a laugh. "Just remember, you still need to be able to fight the next morning!"

"Good point!" He nodded seriously, then glanced around and said in an overly casual tone, "So, this deal about having a healer in the tower; I heard something about us not having to pay her…?" Laughter rose around the room, and Mistress Nerin threw a cup at Grizz's head, making him duck, but everyone could see the smile quirking the edges of her mouth.

"You come to me scarred by your sex life and expecting to be set right before your day, and you'll pay for it all right, boy!" she called, still trying to hide the smile. I met Augustus's gaze and saw him grinning back at me.

"The legion's always been the same," he explained to me. "We're formal and reserved with outsiders, as nobody else can understand who and what we are, but once you get to know us—once you're one of the legion—you've always got brothers and sisters."

"Ones who'll kick your ass and pull you apart for a laugh!" someone said.

"But you love it!" another chimed in.

I sat back, relaxing unconsciously. The feeling of the room wasn't the same as my old army unit, but damn, it felt good as well. My squad, or more accurately, Lydia's squad, was mixed in around the room. Some looked stiff and unsure, like Jian, who was blatantly the center of attention between two female legionnaires, and getting glared at by Miren, while others loved it.

Miren was the youngest of the group, still in her late teens, but I could see some of the legionnaires eyeing her up. I frowned, feeling protective of her, until I saw the way Lydia was watching them while rubbing the head of her mace warningly.

I couldn't keep the grin from my face. This room felt like home. I just hoped we could find some trace of Tommy soon, as it'd be ten times harder, once we'd raided the city, to come back and search again.

"Come on, Tommy," I muttered, my good mood dipping as I worried over him. "Where the hell are you, you shitbag?"

"What was that, Jax?" Augustus asked, me and I shrugged.

"Just thinking aloud. Wondering where that idiot of a brother of mine is," I said, looking at him.

"I understand," he said. "A brother or sister is a constant worry. Tell me about him?"

I snorted.

"I wouldn't know where to start. He's my twin, non-identical though," I said, beginning to smile. "He's the ugly one, born six minutes after me, and I've always enjoyed winding my 'younger' brother up. He's a fighter; damn, that lad can fight, but he's not good on self-control, you know. Constantly chasing something…women, booze, fast cars…not that we had the money for any of them."

I sighed heavily, momentarily distracted as a lizardman and a pair of halflings entered the arena at the gong, and the crowd started to yell in excitement.

We moved over to huddle around the grate, watching as the halflings kicked the crap out of the lizardman, while I told Augustus and the rest of the room about Tommy and our early lives. I avoided things they'd not understand as much as possible, including the money rackets, the drug dealers, and the gaming, but I told stories that made people laugh, and for a while, we all relaxed…

…until one of the halflings hit the lizardman in the balls with his mace. The entire arena winced and crouched in sympathy as a high-pitched whimper rose. At the sight of a woman who topped out at three feet hammering him there repeatedly, the sound of bones breaking with each impact…we all moved away from the grate, leaving the sadistic little sod to her work.

Finally, the announcer declared the match over and the halflings left the arena, while their opponent's mangled corpse was dragged out, and the final gong sounded.

My last fight of the day, in the arena at least, was about to begin.

CHAPTER NINETEEN

I took my shield and sword again, nodding gratefully at the flurry of words of comfort and encouragement, and I slowly walked out onto the sand again.

I lifted my gaze to skim around the stands. The arena was utterly packed now; the lower tiers revealed people clinging to the bars everywhere, shoving each other aside and staring in, raising a wild cacophony of noise. Some of them shouted encouragement, while others screamed about how they'd see me dead.

I shrugged and moved on, sparing a single glance up to the booths that wreathed the upper section of the arena. I quickly found Oracle, as stunning as ever, sitting with a glass of wine watching me as some lecherous old fuck tried to look down the front of her dress.

I guessed he was the Emporium owner, and I suppressed my flare of anger as best I could. That fucker was going to pay for his view tonight, in more ways than one.

The gate on the far side of the arena clanged loudly as the locking bolt was pulled back, and a figure stepped through, crouching to fit.

Once it was free of the doorway, it stood up, and up…the thing rose about the same height as the promethean, around nine feet tall, but this bastard was at least twice as wide! He—and his clothing made it very, even overly, clear it was a he—was covered in thick, grey skin, outfitted with what could only be described as "accents" of leather and fur armor, and carrying a massive war axe that must have weighed nearly as much as I did.

"Mal's furious, says he wasn't supposed to be in there with you…you're supposed to be fighting a human!" Oracle sent to me, and I nodded absently, dismissing her words. It wasn't like I could shout that I didn't want to play now, or that they'd broken the rules. There weren't supposed to be any.

"Tell him to use this to get a lock on whatever I'm facing tomorrow, then," I sent to her, cutting the connection as I watched it move. I surreptitiously triggered Examine, sub-vocalizing the spell, as my fingers moved, hidden behind my shield.

> **Gromesh, Orc Warrior of the Khaatoon Clan**
> Gromesh was a leading warrior of the Khaatoon clan, until he made the mistake of catching the eye of the chieftain's daughter. When he refused her advances, he was declared "Untai" and banished from the clan's ancestral lands. Since making his way to the city of Himnel, he has risen high in the Copper Ghost Gang and made a name for himself as a vicious and amoral fighter.
>
> *Gromesh delights in creating a brutal spectacle of those who cross him.*

Weaknesses: Unknown
Resistances: -25% to Piercing Damage, -10% to Bludgeoning Damage
Level: 21
Health: 1,125/1,125
Mana: 100/100

I dismissed the screen quickly after skimming the details. I'd ignored the majority, retaining only the important ones: he had a fuckton of health, took reduced damage from piercing and bludgeoning attacks, and was clearly going to be a bastard to beat.

"Arrrrroooooga!" Gromesh bellowed into the air, lifting his axe high and turning in a circle to view the crowd. His lower jaw jutted forward, his massive underbite made even more obvious by the twin yellowed tusks that curved up, while fangs protruded out as much as down from his upper jaw.

He turned around and glared down at me, his eyes a weird coloration of grey irises with white pupils that just looked *wrong*.

"Legion," he growled at me. "I hate the legion."

"I bet there are a lot of things you hate," I taunted him, "starting with fucking mirrors. Man, you're fugly…"

He huffed for a second, then drew in a deep breath and roared, arcing his back and throwing his arms out. His entire body shook as the noise erupted from him.

Anger—no, *fury*—came over me, driving me forwards. I screamed with rage, ignoring the notification that began to frantically flash in the corner of my vision.

I covered the dozen feet to my target at a sprint, seeing him for what he was. Gromesh was the reason for all of this, for all of the things in my life that had ever gone wrong…everything! He'd been working with the Baron to kidnap me and Tommy, I just knew it! He'd been there, whispering in Louise's ear, convincing her to fuck Martin; he'd been the reason that…

My mind was full of every possible reason to hate the orc, and I flew at him, my feet scrabbling across the sand. The weight of my shield drove me further into a fury…it was keeping me from him, slowing me down!

I tried to throw it aside, catching my hand on the dagger underneath in my desperation to free myself, when it dipped into the sand.

The drag of the spiked twin blades on the bottom of the shield, as they dug into the soft ground, was enough to pull me off-balance. My frenzied rush was suddenly twisted off to one side. I fell, sliding, losing my grip on my shield, and the world suddenly came into focus as Gromesh finished his scream, his axe flashing through the air just above the plume of my helmet.

What the hell was I doing? I could feel the unholy rage as it receded like the tide at the beach. As he pulled his axe back, I saw my own insane charge, and the screams around me slammed back into focus. They were petering out, dying in confusion as the orc's Taunt or Enrage talent wore off.

He'd managed to send the entire crowd into a fury, desperate to reach him, but the bars had held them all back. I saw the axe coming back around, aimed squarely at my chest…

I felt it then, the fury rising.

The fury of the imperial line. The fury of the emperor. The fury of Jax, Lord of the Great Tower of Dravith, and the thing that Gromesh had instilled in me was shamed in comparison.

I clenched my jaw, almost shaking with rage as I lifted my legs up quickly, then slammed them down, feet flat against the floor. Kicking upwards and twisting my body as hard as I could, I flipped myself over to land on one hand, pushing up. With my momentum, and massive Agility, I defied the weight of my armor to land on my feet, facing Gromesh as his axe slammed into the sand where I'd been a split second before.

He looked up, stunned, his own fighting anger clear in his eyes as he growled. He started to yank the blade upward to free it of the suck of the sand.

He didn't do it fast enough.

I leaped forwards. The first slash of my borrowed sword sliced across the inside of his right wrist. I rolled my wrist in turn, slashing across the upper left arm on the backswing. My gladius sliced deeply into the furs and leather pieces he wore. The blade dragged a spray of blood free as I reached out, grabbing the front of his armor with my left hand.

I moved in fast, yanking down with my left as I planted my right foot on his left knee, and kicked off.

I climbed up his torso faster than he could dodge my feet, and, using my grip on him, I flipped my sword over and drove it down into his chest, deep between the trapezius muscle and the clavicle. The white fur that surrounded his neck was stained red with a sudden eruption of fountaining blood.

Then I hauled back as hard as I could. Using my feet on his knees, my grip on his armor, and my sword, I stabbed into him for leverage then headbutted him as hard as I could.

I felt the pain, the stunning force of headbutting something that hard, but I ignored it. This was no longer a fight, nor was it a battle; it was a brawl, a no-holds-barred street fight, and that, at least, I was good at.

This cocksucker of an orc had woken the rage in me. He'd messed with my mind, and I rode him backward as he staggered. His arms, weakened by my cuts, reached for me, and I headbutted him again.

I saw a bright flash of light as I stunned myself by hitting him that hard. A second later, I was flying through the air. He'd managed to smash me from my perch with a heavy punch.

I hit the sand and rolled, shaking my head in an effort to clear my vision. He'd managed to duck enough that my second Glaswegian kiss had landed badly, and my helm was restricting my vision.

I yanked it off, feeling it scrape my skin as I hurled it aside, and I glared up at him just in time to see his foot swinging at me.

I crossed my arms in front of me, taking the blow, and flew backwards. I tucked inward, landing and rolling into an upright position and spitting blood from my busted lip onto the sandy floor.

The crowd was going nuts, screaming for more blood, chanting for my death or Gromesh's. I didn't care.

All I cared about was the need that filled me, and the rising tide of anger and hunger. I grinned, saw his momentary surprise, then I was moving again, sprinting across the sand to jump and slide under a punch, grabbing my shield and yanking it back onto my arm.

I sprang to my feet as he yanked my sword out of his chest, a gout of blood spurting upward as he roared in fury. Fully enraged, he ran at me, clearly intent on killing me with my own sword.

I'd done a number on his left arm. It was hanging limply, and he was bleeding profusely from the cut on the inside of his right wrist…I guessed that was why he wasn't using his axe, but I didn't care. Not really.

I grinned up at him, pulling the cinches tight on the back of my shield, tying it to my arm and bracing it.

"Come on, then, pretty boy," I called to him. "Come play with me." I made a "come here" gesture with my fingers.

He bellowed and sprinted forward, lashing down with my sword, and I took it on my shield, allowing the strike to push me back. He whipped the sword up and brought it down again and again. He hammered my shield with terrific force, and I crouched under it, taking the beating.

Three more times, he struck, all the while screaming at me, then I fought back.

As his last hit landed, I twisted the shield aside and rose from under it, swinging the shield around to point the twin spikes at the base forward. I slammed it down, punching the metal protrusions through his right foot. and pinning him to the ground. He roared in pained fury as I yanked the Dagger of Ripping free of the sheath on the back of the shield.

I'd poured a tiny amount of mana into my Mana Overdrive skill when he'd been hammering down into my shield, boosting my strength just enough to hold him off. Now, I moved so fast that I almost blurred, diving through his legs and rolling to my feet.

I slashed left and right, hamstringing him, then grabbed his belt from behind, using the leverage to haul myself up his back. I scrambled higher, reaching over his shoulder and slamming the blade deep into his chest, stabbing it into the weak point under his right armpit then ripping it free.

He grunted, a wet, tearing sound, and sagged sideways as his legs gave out.

I held onto my skill, trying to minimize its visible effects as I grabbed his chin with my left hand from behind, pulling his head back.

I plunged my dagger into his neck and sawed it back out.

Muscles and tendons, gristle, and various tubings that composed the orc's neck snapped and twanged as I hacked through them, before I yanked his head hard to the side. With a final burst of Mana Overdrive, my furious wrenching motion ruptured the last sections of skin as I jerked his head free, his corpse falling to the side.

I lifted the massive cranium by the hair with my right hand, turning in a slow circle to ensure that everyone saw it, stopping to meet the eyes of an arena spectator who'd been particularly vehement about calling for my death.

I pointed at him, then dropped the head and punted it as hard as I could, sending it hurtling across the intervening distance. It hit him in the face, making it through the narrow space by some godly intervention, I had to guess. The impact of the gory mass knocked him free of his perch to fall out of sight, covered in blood and knocked senseless.

I spat on the floor then grabbed my helmet, my sword, which was sadly pretty damaged now, and my shield. I yanked it free of the big bastard's foot before stalking from the arena to the rising cheers of the legion and dozens of new supporters, who were clinging to the cage.

I marched out of the arena, my head held high and my helm under my arm. As I walked into the rest room, the gongs went off behind me, signifying the end of the evening's fights.

I looked around the room as Grizz slammed the door shut behind me. The ringing of the viewing grate closing echoed a second after. I nodded to Augustus, who stood nearest to me. He clapped his fist to his chest in salute, and the rest of the room followed, the legionnaires and Lydia's squad almost in unison. Even Nigret and Mistress Nerin saluted a second or two after, looking unsure.

"Impressive move, my lord," Augustus said, and a chorus of agreement rose around him, making me laugh.

"Damn right it was!" Grizz agreed, clapping me on the shoulder, "You tore his fucking head off! Literally!" he crowed as I tried to shake some of Gromesh's blood off.

I scanned the faces of the legionnaires, then held my borrowed sword aloft.

"Whose is this?" I asked, and Augustus coughed, staring regretfully at the blade. "Sorry, mate." I winced, handing it to him.

"It served me well…Ten years, I've borne this blade, and it barely lasted you, what, three hours?" he said, shaking his head ruefully.

"I'll make it up to you; don't worry," I promised, hefting the shield next. It was scarred and battered, but still serviceable, as was the helmet, despite a clear dent in the front.

"Don't worry," said a particularly thick-armed legionnaire. "I can get those scratches out." He winked.

"I appreciate that." I grinned at him. "Right, then; guess it's time to get back to our rooms and get ready for the fun bit," I said, and Nigret raised a hand cautiously.

"What's up?" I asked him, and he cleared his throat.

"Nigret is curious…What is the 'fun bit,' if the arena was not?" He looked confused as I snorted.

"Sorry, mate; you're a bit too new to the group to take part in that side of things yet. Tomorrow, you'll get to join us. For tonight, I'm sure someone will give you a beer and show you somewhere to relax."

"Ah, Nigret understands," he said sadly, leaning back in his seat as the door banged open and Oracle blasted across the room to throw herself into my arms, heedless of my gory state.

"You did it!" she cried, smothering me in kisses.

"I did!" I laughed, kissing her back and hugging her tight, before regarding our audience. "Ah, Oracle? Down, girl," I cautioned, laughing even more at the quirked eyebrow and dirty grin she gave me.

"Well, looks like this is a strange group," Soween remarked dryly from the door, wandering in and closing it firmly behind her. "Pretty sure you should be in private for that," she said to Oracle and me, "and pretty sure you should all be looking elsewhere. This isn't the Street of Negotiable Affection."

Instantly, the room erupted in coughs and uncomfortable expressions as the various legionnaires suddenly found the walls and ceiling absolutely fascinating and pretended not to understand what she was talking about.

"Okay…?" I said uncertainly, then my mind caught up, and I grinned at the awkward glances the legionnaires were giving each other. Out of nowhere, Miren piped up.

"The what? There's a street you can go to for affection? Can I go? It sounds amazing; I bet I'd love it!" she squealed.

This time, even Lydia winced.

"Maybe next time, okay?" Lydia attempted to placate her, glaring around at the sniggers and low conversations that Miren's suggestion had prompted.

"Okay! Moving on," I said firmly. "Is that wanker from the Emporium doing okay upstairs?" I asked.

Soween grinned mischievously. "He thinks Mal's trying to do a big deal with him, so he's drinking for free, and he loves it! He's a filthy swine, though," Oracle grumbled at her statement, and I frowned at her.

"What's up?" I asked, and she huffed.

"He's a lecherous old pig. I told him I was with someone, and that I wasn't interested, and he just kept trying to grab my ass or look down my top." She scowled.

I felt a sudden desperate need to rush upstairs and punch his teeth down into his colon. Trying to calm myself, I drew in a deep breath then smirked sideways at her.

"I bet he's gonna have a nasty surprise when he gets home, then!" I said.

She grinned back. "Can we go?" she chirped excitedly, and I nodded, seeking out Augustus.

"Augustus, I want six of your best with me. Lydia," I said, waving her over. "You can bring two; sorry it's uneven, but let's face it. Not many of our people have the skills needed here."

"I know, Jax. I'll bring Stephanos and Arrin. They're both idiots, but they'll be useful if it goes badly."

"Sounds good," I agreed, as Augustus barked orders, unsurprisingly choosing to lead his team himself. We headed back up to our quarters, and I quickly stripped off. I opted for my usual gear, pulling it on in a few minutes and sweeping up my naginata.

"Bane?" I asked, and he slipped out of stealth, leaning against the wall next to the door. "You know, one of these days, I'm gonna forget to ask if you're there, and you're gonna see a sight you'll never be able to forget…no matter how much you drink, right?" I said to him, grinning.

"I know, and the fear haunts my dreams," he retorted with a *thrummm* of laughter.

"I didn't mention you in the plan for tonight, but I assume you want to come?"

"Of course."

"Coolio." I nodded, then paused. "Oh, and what do you think of Tang? He seems to be a sneaky fucker that might be useful in your little group?"

"I think he's crouching behind your spare chair right now, but that he'll probably do. We've already been alternating shifts watching over you, after all," Bane said. I spun around, staring at the chair as Tang stood up, grinning from ear to ear.

"Fucking hell, man, is there anyone else in here?" I asked in exasperation. A giggle rose from Oracle, who'd been sitting on the other seat, watching me dress. "That's it!" I said, throwing my hands up. "Unless I'm boinking you, you stay out of my bedroom. You can search it, but then you leave, okay? And to be very, even *exceedingly*, fucking clear on this, the offer of a decidedly good weinering isn't open to either of you fuckers," I said, pointing at Bane and Tang.

"Glad to hear it; not sure what a 'decidedly good weinering' is, but I don't think I want one," Tang muttered as he strolled out of the room.

I shivered at the thought. Nope, I just didn't swing that way, and even if I did…man, he was a stealthy fucker. I'd never know if he was hiding and watching me with someone else…

"Hey, Bane, Oracle?" I asked suddenly as a thought came to me. "I've got the perception boost from my meridians, yet I never seem to spot things, or at least almost never. What gives?"

"Practice," Oracle piped up before Bane could answer, and he nodded instead, shutting his mouth with a *click*. "It means you've got a better chance to see things, and when you search, it'll even outline important details, but if you're not practicing or consciously looking, it won't do anything."

"Damn, now I need to work on that, as well," I muttered. "When do you get to just stop trying to learn new shit?" I asked rhetorically.

"When you die," Bane said, completely straight-faced. I considered explaining rhetorical questions when I realized the fucker probably knew better than I did and didn't give a shit.

"Fuck it." I gestured to the door, Bane leading the way out as Oracle and I followed.

In the corridor beyond were the chosen few, all ready for our trip, and I couldn't help but grin. They looked absolutely batshit.

The legionnaires had stripped their easily identified gear off and had donned gear that Mal had found for them, mismatched mercenary clothes with a variety of colors, styles, and weapons.

Augustus even wore a fucking hat that was adorned with what had to be an entire peacock's plumage. I didn't know much about UnderVerse fashion, but I was certain I hadn't seen anything like it before.

"Seriously?" I asked, and Soween glanced at me before looking back at him, clearly trying to hold back laughter.

"What? Mal suggested it. Says as the legion lads don't get to wear 'normal' clothes usually, they should make the most of it."

"Oh, I bet he did," I muttered, trying to hide my smile.

"What?" Augustus repeated, trying to look up at his hat. "Does it really look that bad?" he asked anxiously.

"Oh no, not at all," I said, biting down on my laughter as hard as I could. "It's perfect!"

"Perfect?" he asked, scowling suspiciously.

"Oh yes, definitely," I assured him. "After all, nobody's going to look at you and think, 'That guy's a Legion Centurion Primus."

"Oh, okay then." Placated, he turned away. With all the bustling noise in the corridor as people prepared to move out, he entirely missed my muttered comment.

"They'll think he's lost from an Aussie Pride festival, maybe, but a legionnaire? Noo…"

We moved through the corridors quickly, the rest of our people saluting us and grinning as we went. We started to slip out, a few at a time, blending into the crowds milling around.

I passed people dressed in all sorts of outfits, from the stylish, to the slutty, to the bloody stupid, but nobody, and I mean nobody, had a hat like Augustus'.

People turned in the crowds to watch him go by, and I overheard Grizz whispering for him to "Own it."

It made the entire day worth it.

I absolutely fucking loved the walk through the crowd, looking around and watching the other legionnaires trying to hide their laughter. One man, a guy who I swore must have been born through a dalliance one winter with a particularly large grizzly bear, was trying so hard to suppress his laughter that he was shaking, tears streaming down his cheeks and mouth constricted into a rictus of amusement.

It took us about ten minutes to pass through the crowds and gather together outside. Looking like we were off to a particularly fucking weird New Year's Eve party, we split into two parties and casually made our way through the VIP gardens.

Not long after, we emerged outside, mingling with the crowds in the main areas of the Cloudring, and our scouts led both groups forward.

We passed out of the smoke and into the dimly lit streets of the industrial sector. I secretly reveled in the misty rain that gave the cobblestones a gentle sheen, reflecting the torches that lined the streets. We moved at a faster walk now, passing equal numbers of inebriated people staggering and shouting and nightshift workers trudging to their shifts. Occasionally, carriages thundered past. Shouts from the drivers, the crack of whips, and the echoing hooves were the only warning we got.

"This way…" hissed a voice, and I turned my head to see Gaion, dressed in sooty worker's clothes, gesturing to me. I changed direction, and our other group noticed the change and followed suit.

He led us down an alley, across another dimly lit street, then paused at the foot of a set of narrow stone stairs leading up to the bridge above us.

"There's another mob being whipped into a frenzy in the slums," Gaion said quietly. "Whoever's behind it already started closing down the other bridges across the river to the merchant's quarter, so you'd better move fast before they get this one, too. Once you're on the other side, you won't get back this way easily, so be careful. If you need to, give me a signal of some kind, and I'll set up a diversion to help you cross back."

"Fireball good enough as a signal?" I asked him, and he scowled at me.

"If you want the entire city to know, yeah; otherwise, how about you try a little subtlety? I swear, fucking mages and Fireball…!" he muttered quietly, shaking his head.

"How about a bird whistle?" Oracle suggested. "There are loads of birds, and nobody ever pays them any attention."

"Really?" Gaion asked crossly. "First off, there's no fucking birds here. It's the city, it's night, and the imps fucking eat them. Maybe in the countryside, there are, but here? Some bird goes whistling a merry fucking tune, and it becomes breakfast, supper, or a handbag. That's it. Secondly, if there were loads of birds around, how the hell would I know which one was you?! Seriously, people, just think a little. The bridge is too far to see in the dark, so I need something I can identify as you!"

"Look," I said, getting annoyed. "I'll do this, okay?" I conjured a small Fireball, waving it in a circle, then reabsorbing it.

"Fine, but don't blame me if you're seen," Gaion muttered, heading back into the night.

"Well, he's a cheerful guy," Oracle said grumpily, landing back on my shoulder in her tiny form and crossing her arms in a huff.

"It's the nature of the work we're doing tonight, little lady," Grizz said quietly. "Some people get angry, others get stressed. I usually get excited. Everyone's different."

"Why is he not cheerful, then? If you've got to be something, why not choose to be happy?" She frowned.

"It's not that easy, unfortunately. Some people just don't handle stress well."

"He's a spy, though. Surely, he should be good at it?" I asked.

"You spotted that too, huh?" Grizz grinned at me.

I nodded. "He's the most instantly forgettable person I've ever met. I bet even his height and weight are the exact average. He screams 'spy' so much, I want to nail a bell to his forehead," I admitted.

"Okay, let's go!" Augustus said, cutting off the conversation and leading the way up the narrow switchback stairs. I slipped twice on something I preferred not to think about, but judging from the smell, either the city was full of dogs with severe intestinal issues, or it had another source…and I'd seen a grand total of three dogs so far.

We moved carefully, climbing the last dozen steps up to the bridge. I breathed a sigh of relief as I emerged into the open air, shaking my head at whoever decided there was no need for things like handrails or light on that death trap of a staircase.

Augustus strolled along in the lead. His group surrounded him as he marched down across the bridge, feathers flapping in the breeze. I couldn't help but grin, and Grizz did the same next to me.

"Seems like an amazing coincidence that every time I turn around, you're there, mate," I whispered to him.

"Centurion Primus Augustus told me yesterday to keep close to you. I'm to keep you safe, no matter what happens," he said calmly.

"Really, dude? How does that order square with me fighting in the arena, then?" I smirked.

"Yeah, that's a bit of a kick in the balls, considering my entire job right now is to watch over you, but hey. It is what it is," Grizz said philosophically, looking uncomfortable.

"Talk to Bane," I suggested, shrugging. "He's my bodyguard, and he spends half his time having to watch me fighting from the sidelines. I think he's getting used to it, though."

"Not even close," Bane muttered from my right. I grinned in his direction as we walked, but I couldn't see him.

We left the bridge and made our way through the alleys and down streets. The current path was much nicer than the one we'd passed a few days earlier and considerably more intact than the market I'd last visited, I guessed.

We passed shuttered shops, many with the glow of candles shining from the rooms upstairs. Several of the more richly appointed ones even had small huts by the door, with the occasional guard wrapped up tight against the cold drizzle and glaring at us as we wandered past.

Every so often, one of the groups would comment loudly on the fights or something similar, as if to make us look more authentic. To me, it just made me worry that we'd be more memorable.

We took a final left, then crossed to walk down a wider cobbled street with actual sidewalks. Here stood two guards in sight, one at either end of the street, and lit by a pair of magelights on either side of the door, slap bang in the middle of the street was our target: The Magical Emporium.

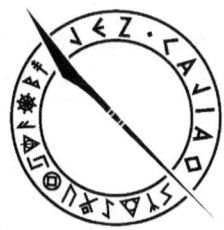

CHAPTER TWENTY

I made eye contact with Augustus and gestured to the guards with my chin, getting a nod of confirmation in return. Two men slipped away towards either end of the street, and I looked up at the entrance to the Emporium. The doorway was flanked by an impressive pair of columns on either side. A single magelight, glowing steadily, jutted from a recess on each, casting a subdued glow as if in warning, the pull of magic coming from inside.

I peered up the street, my legionnaires positioned in the guard huts, and I drew in a deep breath. They'd have almost certainly killed them, and my stomach knotted up at the thought of casually killing innocent guards, until I made myself consider the slaving, the bribery, blackmail, and worse they indulged in. Grizz had told me about the kind of strings that would have to be pulled, according to rumor, to get a guard to literally watch over an empty street, while the mobs were being held back on the outside of the district.

I didn't know if I believed it, but I did know I needed this, and they were, technically at least, my enemies. I forced the thoughts of the guards from my mind and concentrated on the Emporium, walking up the steps to inspect the door. Oracle flitted forward from my shoulder, and we examined it together.

"It's a big lock, and it's chained shut," I pointed out, and she nodded. "But it seems a bit…clumsy?"

"It's not magical, or at least, I don't think so," she said, slowly circling it.

"Maybe he thinks the golems are all he needs, then?" I asked. She shrugged, evidently reaching the same conclusion. "Joy. Well, let's go find out, then, eh?"

I took a deep breath and closed my eyes. This was the riskiest part of the entire night, including the arena fights. If I couldn't get control of the golems before they attacked, we'd have to run for it.

"Be careful," Yen whispered up to me. "It's probably trapped. Do you want me to look at it?" she offered.

I shook my head. "Maybe, if I can't, but I need the practice…"

I reached out, feeding my mana into the lock, forming a flexible "finger" of mana to fill it. It seemed like ages since I'd used my spell Manatouch, and it expanded out to lift the little bars and levers that composed the lock, pushing the tumblers until they clicked, one by one, and then turning it, ever so slowly.

There was an audible *clunk*, and a needle suddenly appeared, jutting out from the lock, right where my hand would have been. I would have been unable to avoid it if I had used a standard lockpick instead of one created by magic.

I let out a grunt of surprise, examining the needle and seeing the glistening tip, coated with something I didn't want to think about. Not wanting any other surprises, I slowly, and oh so carefully, undid the chains and set the lock on the floor.

The door opened slowly to my touch, a gentle creak emanating from the hinges as magelights around the room sprang to life. I stepped inside, feeling the air for magic as much as looking, and I grinned at the display before me.

It looked more like a high-class jeweler than the other merchants' shops that we'd passed during our last trip to the merchant sector. The floors were marble, gold inlay climbed the walls, and every surface shone. The entrance led onto a small balcony jutting into an atrium, with steps to the left leading down, and steps to the right leading up.

The visible floors appeared to be circular, with display recesses every few feet and occasional aisles of items between. The main floor, one level above me, was huge with windows that rose twenty feet high and ornate chandeliers suspended above the bookshelves.

Looking around, I found a second flight of stairs that led upwards from the next floor up, marked "private." A large, glass-enclosed bookcase stood behind a desk at the far end of the floor below and had been secured with a huge padlock.

Oracle and I sent each other quick looks, the fear and excitement in her eyes matching mine.

"Augustus, Grizz, Bane, keep everyone back here until I say otherwise," I said, waiting for confirmation before passing my naginata to Bane with a nod and slowly easing forward, scanning the room. I hated leaving my weapon, but if it came to me fighting the golems, I'd already lost. I needed to be fast, stealthy if I could, but beyond all else, I needed to be fucking lucky. I had to reach the control crystal before they could catch me.

"Where the hell are they, Oracle?" I asked, and she shook her head.

"There were two when we were here, both on the next floor up, but they were in sight when we came in."

"Fuck. So either they're hiding, or…"

"Or they're gone? Or…" Oracle said, then squeaked as she pointed at the far wall on the upper floor, where an alcove was suddenly eclipsed from view by a shimmering blur. "Or someone cast a camouflage spell on them!" she hissed as something moved to my right on the stairs.

"Shit!" I cried, diving forward on instinct as something huge hit the floor where I'd stood a second before. A crunch of metal and stone echoed through the vaulted chamber as the spell hiding the golem failed.

It was huge, easily ten feet tall, with a humanoid shape. Shoulders that were at least four feet across had been outfitted in stylized plate armor. I had the sudden thought that, considering it was made of goddamn stone, the last thing it needed was more friggin' armor, but that thought was banished from my brain as I caught the sparkle of the gemstone embedded in its chest.

I rolled to my feet and jumped up onto the balcony railing, turning and running along it. I wobbled precariously from side to side as I went, while Oracle dove for the gemstone, her right hand sinking into it up to the wrist.

"I've got it!" she shouted to me. "I can force it, but I can't do more than one at a time! Find the control crystal!" I ran for it as the golem she'd latched onto slowly ground to a halt, straightening and freezing as she overrode its commands.

I staggered, running up the banister and frantically looking around for anything I could identify. The room blurred past me as I ran, when I saw something coming from my right, too close for me to change direction.

A second blur, closing fast. I threw myself off the banister, hoping to slide past it, only to have a massive stone foot come down on my little finger as I passed.

I felt heat more than pain for all of a second as the bones in the bottom of my right hand were reduced to fragments and bloody flesh.

The gauntlet was crushed, the steel plate snagging me and pinning me under the golem. I screamed in agony as my entire body pivoted around. My momentum came to a halt as the flesh and bits of gristle connecting the healthy parts of my hand to the pancaked bit tore.

The camouflage spell fell away as the golem tilted its head to look down at me, spinning its spear around and lining it up to thrust into my chest.

I gritted my teeth and pulled, my flesh tearing as I howled through lips white with the force.

The gauntlet resisted, and I frantically yanked harder, pulling and panicking until a link gave way, and I finally came free. The spear slammed down point-first into the marble, carving a narrow furrow in the floor as I fell back, blood spurting from my ruined hand.

I rolled frantically and forced myself to my feet. I was panicking, desperate to find somewhere to hide away from the golem, running as my eyes helpfully linked up the sight of the furrow on the floor with multiple similar markings that had been inexpertly patched or smoothed over. My Perception bonus kicked in, and suddenly, half the floor was glowing.

Lines crisscrossed the floor in all directions, and I started jinking from side to side, running down aisles of bookshelves and paintings, skidding past decorative pieces and armor that glowed golden. *Golden armor? Seriously, what fucking use would that shit be?!* My brain screamed at me, latching onto the mundane in an effort to gain control again.

I came to a stop by the end of one aisle, now thoroughly confused, clutching my bloody hand and trying to work out where the hell I was. I desperately tried to predict where the golem would be, which made me flinch as I realized I had not seen this area from the door.

I'd only seen a few bookshelves and the one locked case that was behind the desk downstairs, so either there was an illusion from the door, or…

I felt the tremor in the floor and sprinted forward in the same instant, as the golem suddenly emerged from the middle of a goddamn shelf. The fucking room had illusions in place to confuse me! I must have triggered them somehow, and the golems either knew they weren't real or didn't care.

I raced between various shelves and items, reaching out and getting a jolt of electricity in warning as I touched a sword on a stand. I'd been testing to see if it was an illusion. Nope! Guessed wrong there!

"Fuck!" I swore, using a healing spell and frantically hoping it would be strong enough to heal my mangled hand. The flesh and bone regrew and closed slowly, but I realized how much mana Oracle was using as well. I panicked, knowing she needed it to save my ass with the golems.

I scanned the surroundings quickly, finding a rack of potions on one far wall and sprinting toward them. The thundering steps of the golem followed behind me, spurring me forward. I had nearly made it when Bane tackled me from the side, sending me sprawling just as a huge, spiked mace flew through the air where I'd been a second before. I hit the ground and rolled, shoving myself upright as Bane shimmied up a shelving unit and leaped away, vanishing again.

"Bane!" I growled, ducking under an enormous stone fist and sprinting off again, trying not to get cornered. "I told you to stay outside!"

"Let's argue about that later, okay?" he called down. "There are two more to the left. They're standing by the end of the desks!"

I swore, turning and sprinting down another aisle.

"Find the control room!" I barked, jumping as a massive spear flew through the air and slammed into a bookshelf with a crunch, then fell to the floor as books rained down around it.

I changed direction again, diving down another aisle, frightfully aware that some of these aisles were fake and others real. I was being funneled around the room, taking my one advantage in speed away from me.

I couldn't keep this up.

"Jax, it's done!" Oracle shouted.

"Order it to protect us and get to the next one!" I shouted back.

"Got it!" She launched herself across the room to land on another golem as it started to pick its spear up from the floor. It slowed, grinding to a halt as she sank her hand into the gemstone on its chest, slowly taking over its commands and instilling loyalty to me instead.

"They're following an old set of orders!" she called out after a second.

"What orders?" I screamed, jumping up, planting one foot on a display cabinet and using it to leap higher to grab ahold of the bottom of the balcony on the next level. I pulled myself up, grunting with the effort as my still-healing little finger screamed with pain. Bracing myself, I jumped again, landing on top of a bookshelf nearby.

Thankfully, it was real, and the axe-wielding golem took a chunk out of the balcony where I'd been a second before as I took off again.

"Two golems down," I muttered to myself as I ran, jumping from the top of the case I was on, and falling straight through the illusory one ahead. I screamed briefly, landing hard on the marble floor and frantically throwing myself into a roll.

I came to my feet, wincing as my right ankle screamed at me, and I hobbled forward, frantically casting another healing spell. The throbbing had just started to go down when Bane shouted out.

"To your right!" His voice carried across the room. "Look out!"

I set off again, trying to run, my spell fizzling out as I lost concentration, and I groaned as the backlash tore through me.

"He's not going to make it. LEGION!" I heard Bane call, and a second later, a trio of huge legionnaires passed me, sprinting at full speed. I turned, forcing my eyes open to look through pain-constricted eyelids at them.

All three, Augustus and two others I didn't know, hit the golem at once. They took it head on, no weapons drawn, leaping and piling onto it, driving the tons of magical construct to the floor through sheer determination and aggression.

"No!" I managed to get out, horrified as a huge hand reached down, grabbing an arm of one of the men I didn't know. It crushed the bones almost effortlessly. Then Grizz and Lydia were there, adding their weight, followed a second later by Stephanos and two more legionnaires, who hurled themselves onto a second golem that had just emerged from a nearby recess in the wall.

The legionnaire who'd been grabbed screamed in pain, then grabbed the arm holding him and tried to pin it down.

"Go!" Augustus roared, and Arrin flew past me, jumping onto the second golem's head, pulling back and slamming it in the face with a spell.

"Fuck!" I screamed, my brain rattled by pain and my friends being in danger. I turned, glaring around, when my eyes snapped back to the alcove the last golem had just abandoned. It was empty, and far too shallow for the construct to have been hiding in; in fact, why would it hide? It…

Just then, I remembered Jenae's gift, and I frantically activated the ability Seek That Which is Hidden. A number of places in the room flared to life. Some held hidden objects, like a painting on one wall with something glowing behind it. But the one that stood out to me most of all was the suddenly obvious false wall at the back of the alcove that the golem had exited.

I was moving before my sluggish brain had made sense of my thoughts, sliding to a halt in the alcove and hunting around. I focused, frantically searching through it as more screams rose behind me, until I saw it: a ledge outlined in blue, matching the rest of the decorative patterning, except for a worn edge, as though it had been touched again and again over the centuries.

I grabbed the ledge, fingers questing desperately for the catch at the back. There! Pushing it frantically, I gaped as the ledge shifted and sank, a soft *clunk* sound coming from the back wall as it slid back.

I strained to see into the darkness as I rushed forward, the pained shouts of my companions spurring me on as my DarkVision activated.

The space beyond was totally different from the outer floors; all grey, worn stone, dust and cobwebs, with a flight of wide, shallow steps that descended into the underbelly of the building. I hurried down the stairs, passing another exit that I assumed led out onto the lower public floor before the stairs came to the hidden lowest floor.

Four additional golems waited, three on one side and one on the other. The gigantic constructs stood at attention, their eyes closed and the gemstones on their chests glimmering. As soon as my foot touched the ground, their eyes opened, and they started to move. I caught sight of something glittering on a desk at the far end of the room and I sprinted to reach it, activating Mana Overdrive and powering myself forwards.

I hadn't used it yet, reserving it in case Oracle needed the mana, but if I failed here, it was all for nothing.

The golems were moving, slowly at first as they pushed free of the wall. Their weapons rose as eyes like a warship's searchlight tracked me. I saw the spear coming, the first golem stabbing out, and I twisted, feeling it scratch my shoulder as I passed it.

I continued sprinting forward. A fist flashed out, and I dove under it, rolling and springing to my feet, just in time to take a kick to the side of my chest. The blow snapped ribs and bent my armor, flinging me across the room to smash into the opposite wall.

I grunted, unable to breathe; the pain was that bad. I reached up, feeling the crushed-in side of my armor. It was bent inwards, and my right lung was being squashed by it. I opened my mouth, desperately trying to breathe, but my diaphragm quivered in shock, the injury overcoming my need to breathe as I tried and failed to pull in air.

I frantically tried to force air in, tried to make myself breathe, when I saw them, glittering on the desk. A golden wreath of what looked to be laurel leaves, laid casually on a velvet cloth alongside books and a dagger, a spyglass, and a handful of gems.

I reached out, triggering Manatouch and floating the glittering symbol through the air to me, even as I shoved off the wall, half-falling, half-running the last few steps until I was close enough.

I grabbed the wreath from the air, and not knowing what to do, waved it frantically at the golems, who came to a slow halt, facing me.

"Re-relea-se the people upstairs," I managed to get out, my chest shaking as I forced out the little air I could get in, to order the golems to stop.

I heard relieved shouts from upstairs and a scream of panic from Oracle as she tried to find a way in to help me.

"Jax!" she shouted. "Where are you?!"

"Obey her," I gasped, sinking to my knees then collapsing onto my back. Coughing up blood as I scrabbled in my pocket, I pulled out a powerful healing potion I'd been given by Augustus and forced it down my throat, mentally ordering the nearest golem to help me. It reached forward, long flexible fingers sliding into place beneath my armor and effortlessly bending it back out. I gasped again, a small amount of air filling my lungs. The potion helped with the pain, but my ribs were still crushed out of place.

I heard a crash upstairs, and a second later, the light of Oracle's fury and panic filled the room as she flew to me. She landed quickly, skidding as she examined my wounds. Wasting no time, she hit me with a supercharged Battlefield Triage spell.

An involuntary groan escaped my lips as bones rearranged, fractured sections sliding around and reforming. I coughed up blood and curled up as the pain of the healing spell ran through me, finally coming to a shuddering halt as it finished, and I could draw in a full breath again.

"Jax!" Oracle wept, throwing her tiny arms around my neck and hugging me. I let my head fall to the floor and I stroked her back, my fingers gently caressing the skin between her wings as I caught my breath. "I almost lost you, you idiot!" she raged, wiping her tears away.

"Yeah, I know, felt that one," I whispered, gingerly rubbing my side.

"Two of the legionnaires died," she whispered. I closed my eyes against the lump that filled my throat.

"Help me up," I said quietly, reaching out a hand and feeling the flexible and insanely strong fingers of the nearest golem pull me to my feet with delicate precision.

I looked up at it, recognizing the same three-faced, four-armed, and three-legged servitor class that I'd found at Waystation Four. The damn thing looked like it had been transported here and hidden, identical in every way.

I looked at the other three golems, which were all war golems; both a relief and a shame, I knew at once.

"Can that prick still countermand my orders?" I asked Oracle, and she nodded.

"You've got one of the commander's insignia. If he's wearing the other, which he was when I last saw him, his authority is the same as yours now. You say go, and he says stop, and they'll listen to whoever speaks."

"Right. Go help our people, Oracle. We can't afford to waste this, not after the cost we've paid." I turned and began inspecting the room. "Send Bane to me, though, please."

"I will. You be careful, okay?" She sniffed, wiping her cheeks before flying back upstairs.

"You called?" Bane said a minute or so later. He was limping but appeared okay otherwise.

"Are you okay?" I asked.

He shrugged dismissively. "Nothing a large drink and a good night's sleep won't help. I'm okay."

"As soon as Oracle's done healing people, I'll—wait," I said as a thought occurred to me. I turned to face the servitor and spoke to it clearly. "Where is the control room?" It lifted one arm and pointed at the back wall, which seemed solid.

"Hidden room again, gotcha. Go get me a couple of mana potions, okay?" I requested.

It flowed away, heading down the corridor. The weirdness of the three heads and the fact that it didn't need to turn around to move away made me pause before gesturing to Bane.

"Come on then, mate, Let's find the room." It took a few minutes, but as the golem returned, two mana potions held carefully in each of its four hands, eight in all, Bane and I found the release. It was hidden in a pattern in the wall again, this time in a frieze of a battle. Both of us reached for the gemstone bas-relief on the chest of a giant golem at the same time.

I grinned at him as we both paused, seeing the other had spotted it at the same time. Bane moved back slightly, politely gesturing for me to go ahead, and I reached out, pressing it inward.

At first, it resisted, the buildup of hundreds of years of dust clogging the mechanism, but as I increased the pressure, it slowly sank into the wall, a grating suddenly giving way with a solid *clank*, followed by the wall shifting slightly as dust and debris rained down.

I grinned at him, ordering the servitor to put the mana potions on the desk and to come open the door.

I sorted through the potions, finding that the golem had chosen two weak, two average, two potent, and finally two grand potions, obviously unsure as to which I wanted. I nodded as I looked them over, glad it had brought them at all, and chugged the two weak ones first, followed by an average. The boost in my mana and subsequent drop let me know Oracle still needed more, so I downed the last average one and summoned a fountain of water for Bane, holding it long enough for him to refresh himself as I entered the control room.

It was a small room, maybe four meters on a side, square, and dominated by the control chair and table. The large panel was similar in design to the one I'd found at Waystation Four, and it had clearly never been found by the residents, judging by the skeleton that was slumped in the chair. Rotten armor, disintegrating clothes, and rusted gear were scattered around it, having fallen with their owner in death.

I looked the corpse over quickly, not wanting to be disrespectful, but I needed to find out what the hell I was dealing with. Thankfully, this guy had been dead long enough that it went from grave robbing to archeology.

I bowed my head to him in respect, recognizing that he'd died at his post while doing what he could to protect the building. Judging from his gear, he'd been a legionnaire, but I still had to move him, lifting his desiccated corpse and depositing it on the floor before sitting in the seat and reaching out to the control center.

Unlike the other times I'd interacted with these artifacts, this one was active and fully powered. A display appeared, opening in my mind in the same way the notifications usually did.

I skimmed the page, noting the options it offered, and I couldn't help but grin.

Congratulations, High Lord Jax of Dravith!

You have accessed the section control center for Himnel Golem Maintenance Facility Three. Do you wish to assume direct control of this facility?

Yes/No

I paused for a second, thinking about the possible alerts that would spread, but it was too late to leave it now. I'd lost two legionnaires to capture the facility so that we could raid it for supplies, artifacts, and golems. We couldn't turn around now.

I chose yes and swallowed hard as the next notification appeared.

Congratulations, High Lord Jax of Dravith!

You now have full control over Himnel Golem Maintenance Facility Three.

This facility has the following capabilities:

Golem Production: Disabled. Golem production system has been damaged and must be repaired before production can commence.

Mining Capacity: 1,000/1,000, Full. 3x Mining Golems have been placed into inactive mode.

Golem Recharging and Maintenance Capacity: 10/10, Maintenance facility is intact and maintained at 100%, contains 2x Complex Servitor-Class Golems, 6x Simple War Golems, 2x Complex War Golems.

Mana Storage Facility: 10,000/10,000

I read the notifications twice, nodding in satisfaction.

"Oracle, how's it going? Is everyone okay?" I asked, and a second later, I got a response.

"They're okay. Lots of injuries, but I've fixed most of them now.

"Well done! Okay, can we get them all down here for now? I've got a plan."

"Why do I always feel scared when you say that? And I thought we'd agreed with Mal, no more changes!"

"Just get everyone down here and tell them not to worry about the golems. They're under our control now."

"Oh gods..."

I felt her break the connection, and I concentrated, sending orders to the golems through the control crystal embedded in the table before me. I wiped the authority of the commander's insignia from the golems. Instead, I instilled a specified user authority for myself, Oracle, Augustus, Barrett, Lydia, or Bane, attaching a mental image to the orders to identify us all.

"Okay, let's see how to do this," I said to myself. I closed my eyes and concentrated, pulling up the details for the facility. Reaching out to the table, I tried to remember how I'd gotten the creation table at the Great Tower to show the map. It took a few tries, but eventually, I felt a response from the control center, and an image blossomed in my mind.

The building appeared as it had looked originally, in greyscale, with red outlines of additional structures that had been added more recently.

It rose four floors above ground, counting the mana collectors that surrounded the building like a huge onyx crown. The next floor down was clearly the living quarters for the current owner, then the two floors of the Emporium. Next, below ground level, was the first floor of the real facility, composed of the maintenance and charging cradles for the golems and the control room at the end of the corridor.

The real shock came when I found the next floor down, accessible through the false wall at the far end of the control center. The stairs led down to the genesis chamber, storerooms, and mining facilities, followed by tunnels sinking down into the ground that appeared to have long since collapsed.

I read the details over for a minute as the legionnaires came down, along with Lydia, Arrin, and Stephanos. I immediately left the control center and walked down the corridor to join the group, who were gathered around the two dead bodies. The first one, the nameless legionnaire who had tackled the second golem, had his arm and skull crushed, and the second, well...it looked like she'd died from a single punch; her breastplate had been completely caved in.

I stopped before the cluster of soldiers, the legionnaires making room for me. As I looked down at the mutilated bodies, then around at the group, I swallowed hard against the hot tears that rose unbidden to my eyes and the shame that filled my heart.

These people had died because I had insisted on raiding this place. They'd died helping me to rob a shop, after they'd spent their lives devoted to upholding the law.

"I'm sorry." I spoke softly, meeting the gazes of those who filled the room. "I'm sorry that these brave legionnaires lost their lives, and even more sorry that they lost their lives to protect me. I should have been smarter, quicker...I...I..."

"No," Augustus growled suddenly, clear anger filling his voice. "No, you shouldn't! You're our lord! You came to us, and we answered. We serve the empire, and for the first time in hundreds of years, these legionnaires died defending their lord.

"They died defending a scion of the imperial line. There is no more worthy a death for a legionnaire than that. We exist to serve you and your line. Lord Jax, the emperor wasn't just a figurehead, not to the legion. He brought order from chaos and safety to millions. He created the empire, created the legion, and laid down the law.

"Those laws might be harsh on occasion, but they were fair. They made it possible for all the citizens of the empire to live in safety and to get help when they needed it. The realm was devastated by the Great Cataclysm when we lost our last leader, and we'll damn well not let it happen again!" he said through gritted teeth.

"You command us, Lord Jax, and we'll be there. We'll do whatever is needed, because maybe, just maybe, if we keep you alive long enough, you can do what you've promised us. You'll bring back the empire, bring back law and order, peace for the people, and safety for the innocent. If you do your job right, it'll make everything...*everything* we do is worth it!

"One day, our children will be able to play in the forest and be safe. One day, they'll be safe from the flesh peddlers in the cities, and maybe, if we're fucking lucky beyond all belief, we'll live to see that day. And we'll get to sit around and fucking complain about how much more exciting things were in our day," Augustus held my gaze with blazing defiance burning in his own.

"But don't you dare *ever* apologize for our deaths. We knew what we were doing, and those of us who die accept it knowing we'll be remembered. Centurion Agmar and Optio Levish died as they lived, as damn heroes! They'd curse us forever if we wasted what their lives bought us, so don't you dare let that happen!"

I swallowed hard, straightening and clapping my fist to my chest in salute. The gesture was immediately echoed by the legionnaires all around me, my own people following our lead and saluting as well.

"Now what?" Grizz asked. I looked over at him, forcing a small smile.

"Now?" I asked. "Now, we strip this fucking place of everything we can carry and get it down to the next floor."

CHAPTER TWENTY-ONE

After the shocks I'd been given by touching things while fleeing the golems, I decided not to fuck about with the gear myself or have my people try to do it. Instead, I sent all eight war golems to strip the upper floors of anything magical and ordered them to take it to the floor below. They trooped off upstairs without complaint, while the two servitors went to work. One opened the door to the lower levels—ridiculously easily, I might add—and descended, its orders to start the mining golems up. The other set about removing any evidence we'd found our way down to this area.

We closed off the control room after stripping it of anything we could, and I collected the skeletonized legionnaire's sword before we left the room, as well as his rings, a thick metal torc, his medals, and his rank tabs. Every piece was tucked carefully into pockets and my bag, with a mental resolution to look them over later.

"Here," said Bane, passing me my naginata and making me grin as I took it back. My freshly regrown little finger twitched slightly as I gripped it.

The servitor glided smoothly across the floor, repairing and concealing the entrance to the control center from anyone who might come along afterward, then followed us.

"Thanks, man," I said to the construct, then gestured to Augustus, pulling him over to me as we jogged down the stairs. "Augustus, I know what you said, but still, I am sorry for the loss of your legionnaires."

He nodded and clapped me on the shoulder.

"I know, Jax, and I'm sorry. I appreciate the sentiment, but truly, there will never be a more honorable death for a legionnaire than defending you. In defending you, we are literally defending the heart of the empire," he said earnestly, making me uncomfortable.

I hated the idea of anyone looking at me like that. I'd grown up needing to fight for everything, and while I knew that wasn't going to change, the knowledge that I was looked up to because of my lineage was hard to accept, especially as I knew what a complete cockgoblin my father really was.

The next floor down was in pitch darkness, but thankfully the legion, as ever, was prepared. Torches were removed from bags and sparked to life, even as Arrin and I held up Firebolts and Fireballs, respectively, to light our way.

"Are you sure about this?" I asked Oracle when she returned to me, and she stopped dead.

"Sure about what?" she asked hesitantly. "You haven't said anything."

I froze as I realized I hadn't, I'd just…

"I *thought*…I'm sorry, Oracle. I could…*feel* things…knowledge. I thought, for some reason, you'd told me about a limit for controlling the facility from a distance…maybe I'm going mad?" I said, suddenly worried. I'd come down here on the understanding that I could still control the golems, and if not…

"Stop!" Oracle said, zipping in front of me to stare into my eyes. "Look at me. Reach out to me and tell me what you sense."

I came to an abrupt stop, people all around me staggering to a halt. Oracle covered her mouth with her hands and whispered "Ooops."

She murmured embarrassed apologies to my crew while leading me to the side, out of their way.

"Okay, Jax, try again. Reach out and tell me what you sense, okay?" she said, hovering in the air before me.

I frowned and focused on her, seeing her beautiful eyes, and forcing myself to concentrate. I reached out with my mind, feeling something, as I always did. I could sense her presence, but nothing else…I closed my eyes then, concentrating on that feeling. Straining, I reached out further, imagining it to be as if we spoke to each other, except mind to mind, and just for a second, I got an image, a vision…

"The lake," I said without thinking. "The lake where we found Decin and the others. I…"

"Yessss!" Oracle crowed, flying forward and wrapping her arms around my neck, covering my startled face in kisses. "You made a link! You managed to access my mind, Jax; you saw what I was thinking! Not just a hint, you really saw what I was thinking!" She released me, spinning up around my head in a dizzy pattern of delight.

"The remote link is true. You can command the golems and the facility because they're linked to it, and so are you. It's valid for about five miles; outside of that range, it'll break down. That's okay, because the only way you could have known about the remote link was if you were accessing my knowledge! Do you know what that means? It means you've been linking with me, mind-to-mind, probably for ages now. It's just been so infrequent and weak that neither of us realized…If you can do it consciously, though…"

"Yes?" I asked her, confused.

"I can fly high above a fight, and you can use my senses." She grinned. "I can help you at an instinctive level, and most of all, we can meld our magic deeper, Jax. We can adjust spells on the fly!"

"Oh, hell yes!" I said, realizing how much better of a fighting team we could become when I could literally sense the entire battle around me.

"So, what was your plan?" she asked me, and I blinked at the change in topic. Just then, I happened to glance at the entrance as the second servitor entered the room and moved to join the first in looking over the cylindrical objects in the middle of the room.

"What?"

"You haven't thought about all of your plans when I've been available to learn them, so I've got no clue what you're going to do here," she clarified.

"Sorry, Oracle," I said with a snort. "I wasn't trying to hide it from you. I sensed three mining-class golems down here, as well as a stockpile of golem parts and a genesis chamber. Makes sense, I suppose. The empire would want the facilities to build the golems outside of the Great Tower, after all, and you did say the cities were built first.

"So, the genesis chamber is damaged, a rockfall has fucked it up, but we've got two active servitors. One can stay to repair the genesis chamber and start to build the golems we need, while the other can come with us. First, though, we need them to repair the miners."

"Why? If there's a storeroom that's down here already…" Oracle said.

"There is, and it's *full*!" I shot her a grin. "More than that, though, Oracle, the golems can mine up under the city somewhere for them to come out. I used the map function on the control center. It showed me tunnels around us; one is only a few feet away, and it leads to the surface. We get the miners to break through there, and we've got an escape that nobody knows about. Then we get the servitors to repair the breach, and the miners can head straight for the river. As long as the tunnels are above the water level at this end, there's no issue. When they break through, they'll just keep on going as the lower sections of the tunnel flood. Golems don't need air, after all."

"Right, but why bother?" she asked, confused.

"Because, so far, nobody knows what happened upstairs!" I cut her off. "If they think the golems vanished, then they're going to go looking. But with no trace, they have to look everywhere. We have the golems march up along the river and wait just out of sight. When everything kicks off tomorrow night, they just walk up out of the water and help us, nice and simple!"

"What about the loot from upstairs?" she asked.

I grinned, gesturing to the first of the war golems as it marched into the room and deposited its haul in a pile. "They're looting it all. They're stronger and faster than we could be, and if something happens and someone sees them, it's the golems that are 'difficult to control' going mad and stripping the place. Nobody is going to associate it with either the legion or the arena fights."

"What do we do with it all when it's down here?" she asked.

"I borrowed as many bags of holding as I could from Mal before we left. We should be able to get most of it in them, and what we can't, we just leave. The golems will bring it, or if it's crap, we'll abandon it."

"Okay, but what about the owner of the Emporium?"

"Well, that's the one thing we can't control, so I had a golem prop a few of the display stands against the door. When he gets back, it'll take him a while to get in." I shrugged. "Best I could do on short notice, really."

"Hmmm, okay. So what do we do now?" She began searching around the room, and I joined her. Three cylindrical objects sat in the middle of the large space. Each of the objects were covered in dust and debris, while the far end of the room had devolved into a mass of collapsed rubble. Four rooms led off the central chamber, with the stairs behind us the only apparent means of escape.

"I guess we see what's in the rooms, loot what we can, and get that escape tunnel started," I said, concentrating. It took a few seconds, but a wireframe overlay suddenly seemed to snap into existence over the room. Its original design was outlined in blue, with red lines showing changes—notably, the nearby tunnel that led, I guessed, to the sewers.

"Okay," I said, pointing and dismissing the Fireball I'd been holding. "There, by that watermark." I indicated a water ingress mark that snaked down one wall then across to disappear down a partially collapsed tunnel before one of the miners. "That's where the tunnel is, and it's not far. I bet we don't even need the miners to break through."

I turned and looked the miners over, finding both servitors hard at work on one. Its flickering, glowing insides caught my interest as their hands blurred. I moved closer, discovering upon closer inspection that the servitors' hands were…weird. They were made up of four fingers, spaced equally around a central pad, which seemed to give them terrific grip.

But as I watched, I saw they weren't actually as solid as I'd originally thought. The fingers split and sealed together into different patterns, shifting parts of the miner golem around. One servitor paused, moved to check over the second machine, then the third, before it turned and glided to one of the doors set in the wall.

It grabbed the handle, opening it with an almighty screech of tearing metal, as the hinges had rusted into place. It disappeared inside, reappearing a few seconds later with handfuls of parts. It returned to the first golem, adding in parts while assisting in repairing the miners. Suddenly, a notification sprang up, and I blinked as I read it over.

Estimated time to repair Mining Golems fully: 27:16:42

"Nope!" I said concentrating on it, and a series of options sprang to life for me.

Golem Maintenance Facility Three Repair and Replace Options:

1) Repair all systems on Mining Golems. estimated time to repair: 27:16:38
2) Repair Golem Mining unit #1 & #3, using stored parts, stripping #2 for additional parts, estimate time to repair: 16:42:09.
3) Repair Golem Mining Unit #1, using stored parts, stripping #2 & #3 for additional parts, estimated time to repair: 1:27:56

It wasn't a hard choice. I told them to repair the first unit, then queued the subsequent orders up. Concentrating, I began by drawing a mental line to dip deeper under the tunnels that surrounded the facility, then climb up to emerge at a shallow angle into the river bed. Once that was complete, it was to move out, heading north-west towards the tower with all speed, while the lucky Servitor being left behind would repair the third mining golem, with the second being the most degraded. Once that was repaired, the third golem would follow the first until they met up; then they'd work in tandem to make a tunnel to the edge of my territory.

Once there, they'd contact the nearest active facility for further orders. That way, I'd get control of them again at some point in the future, I hoped. Once the mining golems were on their way, the servitor that was left behind would begin to repair the genesis chamber that was damaged and buried by the collapsed area. I didn't even have an estimate on that timescale, but I viewed it as worth the risk before finally repairing the by-then gutted Mining Golem Number Two.

"Sir, what would you have us do?" Augustus asked, and I walked over to join them where they milled about.

"Okay, apologies for the delay there, guys. Augustus, I want the rooms around us searched. I know at least some might have active golem cores in them, as Oracle thought she sensed them before—"

"That one," she interrupted, pointing to the second door on the right, next to the one the servitor had torn open.

"Okay, check the rooms and get me a rough inventory. Same with the gear that the golems are bringing down now. Separate the loot from upstairs into piles; these are going to be the order of importance for us getting them out of here.

"I want skillbooks and spellbooks, first and foremost, then magical weapons, then potions, then artifacts, and last of all, armor. I know armor can be the best, fuck knows it keeps us alive, but given the choice between carrying a single goddamn suit of plate armor or dozens of books that could help us all? I know what I need us to choose."

Augustus saluted me and separated everyone out, sending half to the storerooms and the other half to the loot pile. It was building remarkably quickly, as I'd ordered the golems to go as fast as possible. I had to admit, it was making me grin as a huge war golem came pounding out of the stairwell, its axe strapped to its back and hands full of dozens of clinking glass potion bottles.

I quickly diverted the golem to open the doors to each of the rooms before sending him back to work, and as soon as the way was clear, I moved into the second storeroom.

What I found made my grin wide enough to almost split the top off my head. Twenty perfect, fully intact golem cores sat there, glimmering gently as their residual charge purred along, the facility keeping them stable all this time. They looked like rubies the size of my fist, each encircled with bands of silver and bronze, faint humming rising from them as we stood there, admiring them.

"Is that them?" Lydia asked from beside me.

"They're hugely valuable, Lydia," I said. "I need you to keep them safe. They're the key to protecting the tower."

I glanced at her and saw the determination on her face as she moved forward and began picking them up, one at a time. and slipping them into her bag of holding.

I quickly checked the rest of the room, finding hundreds of pounds of marble, granite, and other minerals and piles of stacked metals. Working my way around to the other rooms, I found much the same in two of them, while the third appeared to be a golem armory.

From one end of the room to the other, weapons stood in orderly rows: spears, giant swords, shields, axes, and maces seemed to make up the majority, but at the end, sitting on a pair of enormous racks, were crossbows. The four giant bows were closer to ballistae than something a soldier could carry, and the dozen bolts for each one were as long as my leg. The damn things were huge and affixed to a metallic woven cable, rather than rope or sinew.

"Hell, yes," I muttered, turning to find Augustus standing behind me and grinning as well.

"Bet these cause the airships some trouble," he said.

"Oh, they will. I'll make sure they bring these…I—"

A sudden crash sounded from overhead, followed by shouting. I grimaced, running back to the main room where I could hear better before pulling up the interface.

The vision of the building appeared slowly in my mind's eye, with golems running back to the stairwell, arms full of gear. Above them, on the main floor, the door was being forced by a dozen or more people, but that was all I could see. The attacking group were wire-drawn figures in red, we were in green, and the golems were larger figures in blue. I scanned the schematic, grateful that the majority of us were downstairs, with two golems up where they could be seen.

"What do we do?" Oracle asked.

I took a deep breath. "We buy ourselves time."

We changed the orders for the golems, and all the others immediately retreated down to where we were, the last sealing the entrance behind itself. The remaining two up above, on the other hand, split up. The first ran down and made sure the entrance to the lower levels was hidden, and the other, the one that had definitely been seen…prepared to make an impressive exit.

It backed up, dropping its armful of loot, and hefted its massive shield, crouching as it waited for its comrade to finish cloaking the doorway.

As soon as the golem had cleared the space, directed by Oracle, it came down to join us, sealing the doors as it went. The shield bearer was a complex golem that took my orders readily, directing its lesser brethren to follow and obey.

Oracle released her direct control over it.

As soon as I gave the word, it set off running, sprinting across the room to leap at the huge glass windows by the door. The metal mesh fixed across the windows to prevent burglars tore like tissue paper as the huge golem slammed through it, hidden behind its shield.

It hit the ground and skidded, carving a path in the cobbles, then set off due north, straight to the harbor.

A shout rose from the streets above, echoing down to us faintly as people set off in pursuit. I grinned, hoping they'd enjoy the swim, as dozens of guards ran after the golem, while others flooded into the Emporium. A figure sinking to its knees in the middle of the room made me feel bad, as I guessed it was the owner, but there was nothing I could do for him, not now, and my people needed this.

I watched as he jumped up and ran down to the lower level. Other figures turned and headed out, presumably at a demand from him. He opened the lower passage into the old building, running down the stairs to the golem storage hall. He stopped for a long minute, while I prayed fervently that he would not try to open the hidden control room door or the one that led down to us. After a pregnant pause, he rushed off again up to the main floor and started searching the room, presumably for whatever was left.

I looked over at the pile of gear, guessing we'd managed to get about half of the store's stock. Thankfully, we had snagged the books, as the golems had been ordered to get them first, then anything magical. I felt bad for the guy, I really did, but I forced those feelings away, making myself remember the way Oracle had told me he'd made her feel, drooling over her and trying to touch her.

"Jax," called a voice, and I dismissed the map, scanning the room until I spotted Grizz waiting near the far wall.

"What's up?" I said, moving over to him.

"Is this where you said the tunnel to the sewer was?" he asked. "The water that's getting in here has loosened the bricks. If we're careful, we might be able to take it apart without too much noise."

"Get it done," I said to him. "If you need help, just shout, and I'll have a golem join you."

"One of the smart ones wouldn't go amiss?" he asked.

I summoned over the remaining complex war golem.

"Assist Centurion Grizz in breaking through to the next tunnel, but do it quietly," I ordered it, nodding to Grizz and moving away. I headed back to the center of the room, joining Augustus in sorting through the piles of loot with the others and separating gear out quickly.

In a handful of minutes, it was all done, and I couldn't help but smile at the piles stacked before me. We had twenty-seven books, eleven of which were skillbooks; the rest were all spells. I searched through them quickly, tucking away the magical gardening one that Mistress Nerin had enthused over, then checking the others.

We had, disappointingly as Nerin had said, gotten a load of "mundane" skills: three identical books on carpentry, one on smelting, two on weaving, and another four on farming, glassblowing, animal husbandry, and tiling. They were average skills in comparison to some, like making magical machines or runecrafting, but to us, they were still hugely valuable. After all, we needed *everything*.

The momentary thought of a gang of carpenters making me a goddamn bed made me pause in fond imagining. I shrugged it off after a moment; after all, they were skills that could be used in a variety of ways. A carpenter could work on a ship as easily as a damn dressing table.

The spellbooks were the better prize, as we had collected sixteen. The most useful ones we'd collected were two Firebolt, one Lightning Bolt, and two Nature's Boon spells, which were apparently healing spells. Three Deathbolt spells, which fired a bolt of necrotic energy, were especially interesting.

They apparently did five points of damage individually, but each bolt had a twenty-five percent chance of causing a further ten points of damage over the next ten seconds, and that DPS, or damage per second, stacked up to ten times!

If you hit someone repeatedly, they'd essentially bleed out. Considering it only cost ten points of mana, if I had three people using it together on the same target, they could take down something huge in short order. Or, at least, they could once they leveled the spell up and made it either more efficient or more powerful.

The remaining eight spells were a mixture of buffs and curses. There were five buff spells: two Hastes, which sped up the target by ten percent for a set period, and three separate spells that boosted Intelligence, Strength, and Dexterity individually. Each apparently boosted the respective stat by five points for a minute, costing fifty mana each. Naturally, I could see massive uses for them.

The curse spells were good, as well. I was impressed by a Disease spell that drained health and stamina for five points per second for thirty seconds, a Blind spell that would hit the target with a darkness debuff, making it almost impossible to see for up to a minute, depending on resistances and mana used, and finally, the best of all of them…Vampire's Touch.

Vampire's Touch drained the target of not only their health, but also had a chance to drain their stats! It was hugely expensive, at two hundred mana per second, and there was only a ten percent chance of the user gaining the victim's drained stats, but hell yes!

I looked at Oracle, and I saw the same hunger in her eyes that I just knew was in mine. We were going to use that book. It was huge, compared to the others, and the spell itself wasn't going to be that useful in combat straight away. It had clearly been designed to use on a victim that was strapped down and couldn't escape, rather than in a fight. Oracle sifted through the details of where it had come from with a golem.

"This was hidden behind a false panel...along with those knives," Oracle said finally, pointing to a pair of innocuous blades in the weapons pile.

I picked them up, and one after the other, used Examine.

Dagomar's Dagger (Right hand)		**Further Description** *Yes/No*	
Damage:		10-35	
Details:		This dagger is part of a matched set, crafted for the mage-assassin, Dagomar. This blade is enchanted with a Frostfire spell that has a 5% chance to simultaneously cause Burning and Chill effects on its target for 1-5 points of damage per effect, per second, for up to ten seconds. This enchantment stacks up to three times.	
Rarity:	**Magical:**	**Durability:**	**Charge:**
Unique	Yes	91/100	100/100

Dagomar's Dagger (Left hand)		**Further Description** *Yes/No*	
Damage:		10-35	
Details:		This dagger is part of a matched set, crafted for the mage-assassin, Dagomar. This blade is enchanted with a Frostfire spell that has a 5% chance to simultaneously cause Burning and Chill effects on its target for 1-5 points of damage per effect, per second, for up to ten seconds. This enchantment stacks up to three times.	
Rarity:	**Magical:**	**Durability:**	**Charge:**
Unique	Yes	87/100	100/100

"Fuck me," I whispered, turning the daggers over in my hands. They didn't seem like much, but hell, they were impressive. The hilts of both were made of leather, but they were ridged and formed, clearly designed to fit a particular man's hands perfectly. The blades were long, slightly curved, and had a thick, chisel-tip design that made me think of a tantō. They were also razor-sharp, and the metal they were made from had a peculiar color that seemed to shift, depending on the angle.

I set them aside and looked over the rest of the glittering pile. There were items that glowed faintly, and others that seemed totally innocuous. Among them lay a full set of golden plate-mail armor and a half-dozen smaller pieces. The variety swung from pristine breastplates that fairly glowed with power, to a pair of boots that looked just…nasty. The leather was worn and scuffed, the soles were battered, and the laces that ran up the inside of the leg were frayed and tattered.

"Jax…" Oracle said hesitantly, staring at the spellbook.

"Yeah?" I asked, hoping she was about to suggest using it now.

"There's something wrong with this, give me a little time okay? I need to look closer…"

"Oh, uh yeah okay." I agreed, feeling a little disappointed, but trusting her.

Realizing that the legionnaires were still packing gear away in the bags, I moved to the pile that looked the most useful after the books: the magical artifacts. We'd collected three bags, two satchels, and a small pile of figurines that glowed with a disturbing yellow-green light. There were also a handful of rings, necklaces, and random crap that looked to be parts of sets, such as a dozen glittering pins, but I had no clue what they could be for.

I decided that, while I couldn't afford the drain on my mana to identify most of it immediately, I'd check the bags over, as they could be useful. I popped another weak mana potion that I'd picked up from the pile of potions and downed it, just in case.

<table>
<tr><td colspan="2">Bag of Holding</td><td colspan="2">Further Description Yes/No</td></tr>
<tr><td colspan="2">Details:</td><td colspan="2">This Journeyman-level bag of holding provides 62 spaces for storage. Each slot is capable of holding up to 99 identical items before filling a second slot. Weight reduction is 79% and there are 62 slots currently available.</td></tr>
<tr><td>Rarity:</td><td>Magical:</td><td>Durability:</td><td>Charge:</td></tr>
<tr><td>Uncommon</td><td>Yes</td><td>100/100</td><td>N/A</td></tr>
</table>

<table>
<tr><td colspan="2">Bag of Holding</td><td colspan="2">Further Description Yes/No</td></tr>
<tr><td colspan="2">Details:</td><td colspan="2">This expert-level bag of holding provides 100 spaces for storage. Each slot is capable of holding up to 99 identical items before filling a second slot. Weight reduction is 81% and there are 100 slots currently available.</td></tr>
<tr><td>Rarity:</td><td>Magical:</td><td>Durability:</td><td>Charge:</td></tr>
<tr><td>Rare</td><td>Yes</td><td>100/100</td><td>N/A</td></tr>
</table>

Bag of Spatial Folding		**Further Description** *Yes/No*	
Details:		This master-level bag of spatial folding provides 100 spaces for storage. Each slot is capable of holding up to 99 identical items before filling a second slot. Weight reduction is 98% and there are 100 slots currently available.	
Rarity:	**Magical:**	**Durability:**	**Charge:**
Highly Rare	Yes	100/100	N/A

"Okay, Oracle—" I started to ask, and she cut me off.

"The expert bag and the master bag both have one hundred slots, but because the weight reduction is so amazing on the spatial folding bag, it's pushed into the master ranks, when the hundred slots should normally be an expert level."

"Oh, okay. And the first bag? How come the other two are a hundred and that one's sixty-two?" I asked.

"No idea. Probably a journeyman-level skilled crafter that had a particularly good or bad day. I'm really not that into crafting, Jax, sorry. You need to speak to Heph about it; he'll chew your ear off all day on this kind of thing, but it doesn't really interest me," Oracle said, shrugging. I dropped it, figuring that was fair enough.

I'd always liked crafting in the games I'd played, but right now, considering everything that was going on, I just didn't have the goddamn time to fuck about with it. I'd do some more alchemy when I got the chance, probably, but right now, there was a bed calling to me and a long walk to go before I could get there.

"Okay, gather it all up," I said to the people around me, passing the first two bags out and keeping the master one. I emptied my gear out onto the floor and put it back into the bag of spatial folding instead, passing my old journeyman bag to a legionnaire who'd just returned, lugging a heavy bag from one of the storerooms. "Leave about ten percent of everything in the storerooms so that, if the genesis chamber can be fixed, there's some material for it to use. But otherwise, I want this place stripped in ten minutes," I called out, pushing to my feet and lifting the heavy bag onto my back, with the spatial folding one on my hip.

"Arrin! That means you, too!" Lydia shouted at Arrin. I turned in time to see him perusing the spellbooks with undisguised desire. I couldn't help but grin at him, knowing exactly what he was feeling.

"Oracle, with Nerin's healing, I can use these books, right?" I asked, feeling my gut tighten in fear that she was about to say no.

"Well, yeah, I guess, but you can't use many. Maybe two?" she said slowly. "If you use more than that, you might store up problems again like you did last time. Maybe you should hold off until we see what Nerin has to say?"

"Or…" I grinned, pulling the Vampiric Touch spellbook out. "I could not, and just use the fuckers."

"Jaaaaax," Oracle said warningly. I froze. "Of all the spells, that's the one you want to learn. Are you sure?"

"Well, yeah, of course it is." My brow furrowed in confusion. "It offers the chance to steal stats from my enemies, not to mention literally stealing their health."

"Honestly, I don't think it's a good idea Jax. I'm sorry. It's a spell designed to torture your target." Oracle stated flatly. "We don't know what kind of long-term effect using a spell like that could have on you. What if you start deciding to drain the stats from criminals? They're a drain on society, after all; then maybe it's people who don't agree with you. Then, it's just people! Jax, that spell is wrong, plain and simple! I can feel the evil coming off it from here. It's not a spell meant for humans!"

"Oh, come on, I won't be a dick with it, and besides, I'm not human," I countered dismissively.

"Jax, I'm serious. You don't want to learn that spell."

"*I'm* serious, Oracle. I really fucking do, actually," I straightened up. "Think about it. This spell contains the knowledge to increase stats and absorb health directly, and how to do it with a touch! Besides, I know you want to learn it as well," I pointed out, recalling the way her eyes had lit up at seeing such a powerful spell.

"I did, okay admittedly, I do, still, but when you ignore the promise of what it is, and instead look at the spell? Seriously, Jax, close your eyes. Reach out to the book with your senses and tell me what you feel."

I huffed a bit, but I complied, and instantly pulled the fuck back.

"It's cold," I said, frowning and staring at the book. "It's cold and it feels…dark? I don't know how else to describe it."

"I know," Oracle said nodding. "It's not meant for humans, or even *part-humans,* if you want to be really pedantic. Just trust me on this, Jax. You really don't want to learn that spell."

"What if we learned it, but didn't use it?" I asked. "You know, use the parts of the spell to build another spell, one that's more…friendly?" I said, then grimaced. "Look, I know how that sounds, but seriously, you know what I mean."

"I do, but no. Not for now, at least. I think you should wait, maybe see what Nerin or Jenae think of it, but I'm very, very sure that's a spell that's been made by a creature of the night, and it wasn't made into a book to help people. It's a trap."

I grumbled a bit, feeling absolutely certain that the spell could make a huge difference to our leveling, but…there was something in me that agreed with Oracle. I just knew that if I used the spell, I'd be crossing a line.

I put it back in my pack, deciding to think about it a bit more later, and instead selected one of the Haste spells. It was designed to buff one target and could even be self-targeted.

"What about this?"

"Seems fine, Jax. Look, honestly, I didn't know it was possible to drain a person's essence, their 'stats,' as you call them, and knowing you could, yeah, part of me wants you to. It'd make you hugely powerful, especially if we could make a version that worked after death, but the effect that spell would have on you isn't worth the risk. I'm sorry, but whatever created that spellbook was evil to its core."

"I know," I agreed. "I'm gonna learn Haste instead, and hopefully I can buff everyone, get us back to the arena faster. You happy with the plans I've made so far?"

"First, I don't like stealing. It feels wrong. But that guy was a dick, and he had that book hidden away when he could have destroyed it, so to hell with him. Plus, he kept grabbing my ass, so I've decided this is what that cost him," Oracle said, reaching out and putting her hand on the book. "But please, after last time, don't use a book unless we have a healer available, okay? Just wait until we get back?"

"It could help us get back quicker, Oracle," I countered, but in my heart, I knew I wasn't going to win this one. After a minute, I conceded and slipped it into my bag with a sigh, turning my attention to packing everything else away.

Ten minutes later, there was a low hiss from Grizz as he got everyone's attention. I saw the stack of bricks on one side of the tunnel as the last few were being removed to open the way into the dark sewer beyond.

Yen disappeared through the gap into the darkness, and everyone else gathered together near the opening, waiting.

A handful of minutes later, she returned, leaning back into the tunnel and speaking in a low whisper.

"It's clear…there's a ladder up to a grate about a hundred meters that way. I think it comes out in an alley, but I can't be sure without using it. Bloody stinks in here, though!" she said, twisting her face up.

"Damn right, it does," I muttered. We'd all been covering our noses as we waited, her movement having clearly stirred up something. "Good work, Yen. Augustus, what do you want to do with the fallen?"

"We can't take them with us, not through the streets. It would attract too much attention," he said, shaking his head sadly. "Can we leave them here? Lay them to rest in these tunnels that the mining golems dug?"

"We can, but isn't there anywhere else you'd rather we took them?" I asked, unsure. It felt disrespectful to just leave them here.

"Could we leave them here for now, and come back for them later?" Grizz asked.

"That seems like a better idea. give me a minute," I said, closing my eyes and giving the control center a series of orders. "Okay, once the repairs to the genesis chamber are complete, the servitor will make two coffins for them. When ten golems are ready, they'll set off to the tower, and they'll bring your men with them." I looked Augustus in the eyes. "They were heroes, and they deserve to be buried as such."

"Thank you, Lord Jax," Augustus said quietly, and the others around me echoed his sentiments.

"Okay, everyone, into the sewer. We need to move it before the sun comes up." I swallowed my emotions and gestured to the opening as I locked gazes with Oracle, who hovered by my head.

"Are the orders clear enough for the golems?" I asked.

She nodded. "You also instructed them to take orders from me. I can link with the control center, and through it to them, easily enough. Don't worry."

"Coolio. Okay then, here we go," I whispered, climbing up into the sewer. "Get them to seal it all up as well as they can after we leave, and make sure the servitor that stays behind knows that, if it can't fix the genesis chamber, its orders are to head back to the tower instead."

"Will do," she whispered back, and as I moved deeper into the stinking sewer, the last I saw of the tunnel was Augustus carefully packing his hat away to keep it from getting filthy, which made me grin.

We moved down "stream" for a few minutes, careful to stay to the sides of the tunnel where it was shallower, while breathing through mouths that twisted at the foul air. I began to worry that I could taste it, it was that thick, when a crack of a lock being snapped from ahead echoed down the tunnel.

A few seconds later, Yen's voice echoed down to us that the way was clear, and one after another we climbed the rungs to the surface.

When it was my turn, I gagged at the sight of the rungs before me. Those who had climbed ahead of me had left thick…chunks…attached to the rungs from their boots scraping off as they ascended. I had to fight my stomach as I climbed after them; the sight of sweetcorn stuck to a rung an inch from my face as I struggled up the narrow tunnel just made me want to be sick.

I pulled myself up into the alleyway a few seconds later. Lydia waited at the opening and reached out to help me up. I grinned at her, shaking my head in mutual disgust at the experience before looking around.

We were in a narrow alleyway, with maybe three meters between the walls on either side. The filth of the alley would have disgusted me normally, but compared to that sewer…I moved down the alley a little to make sure I was out of sight before summoning a fountain of clean water and calling Bane's name. He appeared next to me, almost making me add to the filth of the alley. The fucker was getting far stealthier.

By the time the others had made it up and the grate had been returned to cover the tunnel, Bane had finished, and I'd refreshed the spell, summoning a second fountain a few feet away and gesturing to the group to make use of them. I plunged my face in first, shaking it to get rid of anything before leaning waaaaay back and rinsing my hands and boots. I looked myself over quickly, then sighed and stepped entirely into the stream. I ended up soaking myself, but the water as it ran down to a nearby drain was filthy, and it needed to be done.

I kept the two fountains going for a few minutes, letting everyone hose themselves down as best they could, before we set off at a jog to the bridge over the river, which was thankfully only a few streets away.

I looked up at the faint, shifting in colors that predated the sunrise and swore. Clearly, we'd been in there a lot longer than I'd thought.

"Back!" came the low hiss, and we scrambled to a halt, then backed up as quickly as we could, while Yen frantically gestured us away from the mouth of the alley.

Before we could make it halfway down to the other end, a shout echoed from the street behind us, and a guardsman pointed at us in shock, lifting his torch high to illuminate the party fleeing back into the darkness.

"You lot, stop!" he cried, then turned and shouted toward the bridge before sprinting after us. "Over here!"

"What do we do?" Augustus asked me as we thundered down the alley and out onto the far street. The jingle of armor and shouts of the guard rose behind us. "I'd rather not kill them just for being guardsmen." he said, looking at me in a way that meant he still would, if I asked it.

"Fuck," I muttered, casting about desperately.

The street was starting to fill up, people heading to work, and suddenly we were surrounded by witnesses!

The merchant quarter obviously wasn't the same as the industrial quarter, with people working all day and night, but still. I looked from side to side, finding at least a dozen people in sight, and I growled in frustration.

"Split up!" I ordered, turning to the right and running. Lydia and Grizz flanked me, while Augustus led two others straight across the street and into another alley. The rest of the legionnaires and Lydia's crew scattered off in groups of two or three, taking as many different directions as possible. We ran down past a dozen buildings, the guards splitting up in an effort to follow everyone they could, shouting as they went.

We took a right, down between two large shops, and I spoke quickly to the others with me.

"Split off into the nearest shops in the next street. I'll draw them off."

"No chance, sir." Grizz chuckled, every step of his enormous boots echoing like bricks hammering the cobbled road. "I'll lead them off. After all, I know the area!" He winked at me, then pulled ahead, bowling someone over as he sprinted out into the next street.

"Asshole!" I growled, smiling at him despite myself as I turned the corner a half dozen steps behind him. The shouts from the tumbled man drew the guards, and I grimaced at how much busier this street was than the last.

"Stop…them…!" the guard screamed from out of sight deep in the alley behind us, huffing like he was trying to bring a lung up. I grinned as Lydia scrambled to a stop outside a shop that had just opened its doors, the smell of meat pies wafting from the entrance as she ducked inside.

I looked around quickly, not seeing any other shops that were close enough. But an older man sitting on a bench grinned at me, and before I could think twice, I braced myself, sliding to a stop and slamming down to sit next to him.

"In trouble with the law, eh, lad?" he said, passing me a hat that I pulled down low to hide my face as the guard finally erupted from the alley. Two more guards ran out behind him, and they looked around frantically. Grizz popped out from behind a building, giving them a pair of one-finger salutes, then sprinting down a different alleyway.

"You have no idea." I grinned at him.

"Oh, I've been there, son, believe me." He winked. "Nothing you've done that I haven't done in the past!"

"Then I stand corrected! What's your name?" I asked him.

"Franz. Franz Golden-Tongue. Yer might have heard of me; hell, the way yer move, yer might be one o' my kids!" he said, chuckling.

"Unless you travel a lot more than I'd guess, that's unlikely, Franz, but it's nice to meet you, and thanks for the help!" I said, passing his hat back and standing up. I pulled out a gold coin and flicked it to Franz, nodding to Lydia as she strolled out of the shop, holding up a bag and regarding it with satisfaction.

"What's yer name then, lad?" Franz asked, and I replied without thinking.

"Jax," I said, then paused, realizing what I'd just revealed. The old man's grin grew wider as he pocketed the coin.

"Maybe yeh've a good tale to tell after all, *my lord*." He winked. I winked back at him, lifting a finger to my lips and getting a nod in return.

I hurried over to Lydia, and we both began walking, as calmly as we could, back to the bridge, sticking to the busier streets and munching on unidentified meat pies. Unsurprisingly, when Lydia held a third pie out to the side, Bane appeared and grabbed it with a low "thanks" before vanishing again. I had to laugh. I didn't know how the hell he did it; the bugger just disappeared as soon as you stopped looking at him.

Half an hour later, we strolled casually over the bridge, the lightening sky now clearly showing the dawn had arrived. As I looked around with feigned disinterest, I spotted Augustus leaning casually against a wall up ahead, his hat firmly atop his head again. A pair of his legionnaires strolled arm-in-arm nearby, like bodybuilders on the weirdest date in the world. When we passed him, he fell in with us like an old friend, joining our conversation easily.

"How's it looking?" I asked him, displaying a confident smile for anyone that was watching.

"Not bad; we're missing three still: Yen, Bane, and Grizz. How did you get away?" he asked.

"Grizz. He ran ahead, drawing their attention while we hid. Bane's here…somewhere." I waved noncommittally.

"Then just we're missing the scout and that mad bastard, Grizz. That's fine. Let's get you back to base," Augustus said firmly. I pulled up short, frowning at him.

"I'm not leaving them."

"Jax, I would think less of you if you were happy to, but we *are* leaving them, I'm afraid. I know my people better than you do, Yen won't have any trouble making it to us later, and as for Grizz, well…let's just say if they catch him, they'll have more to worry about than he will. He's probably in a bar somewhere with a girl on either knee, telling bad jokes."

"I—"

"Please, Jax, we have to get you back. I'll not leave one of my men behind, I assure you. Now, come on; we need to get back, get some rest, and prepare for tonight."

I nodded, feeling terrible about leaving when I didn't know if everyone was okay. But, for all I knew, Grizz and Yen were already back, having taken a different route.

Ten minutes later, we were walking into the early morning smog of the Cloudring, sighing as the streets outside faded from view. We slipped quietly into the arena, pausing briefly in the courtyard so that I could unload several tons of loot into Fenris. Once he'd been filled up to the brim, we jogged through the facility until we reached Mal's suite.

We gave him a quick breakdown of the night, then asked after Grizz and Yen, both of whom had not yet returned.

We talked for a little while, bringing Mal and Soween up to date with the Emporium and everything we'd found, the golems and our losses, but mainly we were just staying and waiting in the vain hope that Grizz and Yen would walk in at any second. Eventually, Mal got sick of the smell more than anything else and kicked us all out of his office.

I made my apologies to the others, and after repeated assurances from Augustus that the pair would be fine, I went back to my own quarters. Before I knew it, I was slipping into bed, too tired to even make a single joke or sexual innuendo with Oracle.

The stress, the fear, and the adrenaline crash wiped me out as I lay back, closing my eyes. The last thing I remembered was listening to the quiet voices of Bane and Tang as they planned out their watches for the next day and night to come.

CHAPTER TWENTY-TWO

It was early evening when I awoke, feeling groggy as I sat up and squinted around the room.

"Bane, Tang?" I asked quietly into the dark. Bane answered from my right, near the door to the balcony.

"I'm here, Jax. We changed over about twenty minutes ago," he said simply.

"Hi, mate. I…any word on the others?" I asked, hoping, but feeling my guts twist at the worry over what could have happened to them.

"They returned a few hours ago," he reassured me. I sagged back onto the pillows, letting out a long sigh.

"Oh, thank fuck," I muttered, relieved I hadn't lost two more friends.

"Might want to ask Grizz about Yen at some point," Bane suggested, with a low thrum of amusement. "Maybe ask what took them so long, as when they came back, they were both clean."

"Seriously?" I snorted and shook my head. "I thought Yen had higher standards. Grizz is built like a man mountain!"

"There's no accounting for taste, it's true." Bane chuckled.

I laughed along in relief. I hadn't realized how much I'd come to rely on our small team in the last few days, and knowing they were all safe was a weight off my mind.

"Also, there's been an addition to our ranks…" Bane added as I stretched.

"What, really?" I asked, confused. "Who?"

"Lord Jax, I am here," a small, strangely familiar voice warbled. I looked up at the corner of the ceiling toward the sound's source, jumping as my eyes adjusted. There, crouched like the world's fugliest Halloween decoration, was a red and black spider. The thing was about the size of a pit bull, squat and stocky, covered with thick black hair and jagged spikes that jutted out at strategic points.

It looked…evil, basically. It was the kind of thing nightmares were made of, with its multiple black eyes staring at me, the jagged mandibles, the clacking of its fangs as it spoke…it made every defensive instinct I had flare to life, with an overwhelming desire to Fireball the fucker in the face.

"Horkesh?" I forced out after a second of terror-induced immobility.

"Yes!" Horkesh squealed excitedly, bobbing in the corner. I shuddered a little, my butt puckering up involuntarily.

"What are you doing here?" I asked her, glaring over at Bane. I could feel the bastard laughing at my reaction.

"The queen sent me to help you! She is gathering the full nest, and they will head to the tower through the dark paths. It will take many weeks, she warns, but she wanted me and my guard to assist you."

"Your…guard?" I gulped.

She bounced in place again. "They are hidden nearby; a dozen of the soldier caste and two hunters!"

"That's…wonderful," I managed to croak out. Suppressing another shudder, I took a deep breath and forced myself to recall the thought of her as a really ugly puppy, not a goddamn spider…a puppy that could climb walls, and…nope!

"Okay…Horkesh, I'm going to have a wash and wake myself up a bit. Then I guess we'll go introduce you to the team and get you factored into our plans."

"Yes, Lord Jax! Do you want me to follow—"

"Noooo. Just wait, right there…okay?" I requested, clamping down on my instinctive revulsion. I forced myself out of bed and stretched as I wandered toward the tub. Sinking gratefully into the cold water of the bath, I scrubbed vigorously, making sure every last foul-smelling drop was gone before getting out and summoning a fountain to rinse myself down. By the time I returned to the main room, the sight of the sheets, filthy from my foul body, made me want to vomit.

I shook my head, knowing that none of us would be returning, and I wondered what the future owners would think when they found those sheets. I did still slip the pillow into my bag, though; a man had needs, after all.

"Meh," I said to myself, shrugging and dressing while I talked to Bane. "So, anything happen while I was asleep?"

"Not really. I came here as soon as I woke up and had a wash myself. I think a meeting with Mal should be high on your priorities…especially to introduce Horkesh."

"Definitely," I agreed, pulling the last of my clothes on. "Man, I wish I'd been able to get some more clothes. I know they cleaned these, but…" I fingered a tear where I'd stabbed the previous owner of the top.

"Perhaps next time, don't destroy the market, and you can visit the shops then?" Bane suggested casually.

I frowned at the dark patch his voice came from. "Are you telling me not to go all murder hobo?" I asked, not bothering to hide my irritation.

"Murder hobo?"

"It's a term from my home; it means someone that goes somewhere, kills everyone, and steals all their stuff."

"Ah, yes! By that definition, you are a murder hobo. I'll remember that."

"No, I'm not!" I snapped, continuing to pull my gear on. "I've never done that!"

"You arrived in the tower, killed every living thing you found, and claimed it for yourself."

"Well, yeah, but they were monsters—"

"Then you killed most of the crews of the ships, claiming those, then exterminated an entire nest of goblins and stole their home, the drow…do I even need to mention obliterating the market and raiding the Emporium?" Bane asked coolly.

"I…well…look, when you say it like *that*…. Okay, it sounds a bit—*maybe*—murder-hobo-*ish*." I had a sinking feeling that I was going to regret this entire conversation.

"Is there anything you've done that doesn't qualify you as a murder hobo?" Bane asked.

I grabbed at the perceived lifeline. "Yes! I aided your village; I even helped you rescue T'lek!" I said, relief clear in my voice.

"My village? The one in the lake?" he clarified, and I nodded impatiently. "The one whose lands you claimed; the entire territory that you annexed to your own lands?"

"Oh, for the love of…Flux told me it was okay!" I snapped, throwing my arms up and looking for him before I felt the deep thrum of his laughter. "Oh, you utter bastard." I groaned, shaking my head and smiling despite myself. "Just you wait, mate. I'm gonna get something on you, if it's the last thing I do."

"I'm not nearly as foolish as Flux is, to fall for some runecrafter. You'll not find an Ame in my past," he said, still clearly amused.

"Well, just you wait. I'll get something on you, if it's the last damn thing I do." I repeated as I swept up my naginata and scanned the room. Besides the filthy bed and stinking bath, there was nothing out of the ordinary in the room now. It looked and felt like any one of a dozen hotel rooms I'd stayed in over the years. It was messy, but despite a quick search, I couldn't shake the same feeling I always got when leaving a temporary room for the last time…that there was something lying around somewhere, an item that was vitally important and I'd forgotten.

I did an extra search for the sake of it, finding nothing, before shrugging and leading the way into the corridor. Some of the rooms had open doors, others were closed, and the sound of snoring filtered gently through the wood as I passed. People that were awake nodded in greeting, an occasional smile here and there, a salute from a legionnaire.

I grimaced internally at the double takes I was getting, however, as I'd instructed Horkesh to walk beside me. The legionnaires began drawing weapons and settling into combat stances, but I just shook my head at them. It did help when Arrin, the mad bastard that he was, shouted in joy and ran over to her, patting her on the head.

"Horkesh! I missed you, little buddy!" he crowed while she stared up at him.

"Are you attempting to attack me?" she asked, clearly confused by the petting.

"No! It's a sign of affection…You see, what it is—"

I covered my eyes in despair, cutting him off.

"Everyone, this is Horkesh. She and her guard are followers of mine as well, as is her mother and the rest of her nest, who are headed to the tower. You might as well get used to her, since she'll be helping us out." The legion, being professional soldiers, grumbled a bit, then settled down and went back to whatever they had been doing.

I'd passed through this common area countless times over the last few days without really noticing it. Now, seemingly for the first time, I paid attention, realizing that the few legionnaires that were present were involved in checking their gear over.

The common area was maybe ten meters to a side with a single set of doors leading out to an open-air space that linked to the gardens for the rooms we had all shared. There were benches and tables, a small area for cooking, and even an attached toilet, and I smiled. The space had registered faintly when we'd arrived, but back then, it'd been just another room in the seeming multitude that made up the Arena.

Now, it looked a lot more homey as my people sprawled around, some standing, others lying or sitting. Jian was even playing dice with a pair of legionnaires in the corner, and judging from the pile of coins in front of him, he was either very lucky or about to get his ass kicked for cheating.

A fluttering of feathers got my attention, and I recognized Amaat and Venta, who were outside talking to Augustus and Barrett.

"Hey, everyone," I said quietly, getting nods and smiles as I joined the group.

"Jax, welcome," Augustus said, nodding once. "Centurion Amaat has news."

"I gave the orders to the legion prefect, as you ordered, my lord," Amaat said, giving his head a little shake and making his crest stand out proud. "He felt the Oath become active, as did all the legionnaires and those sworn to the empire in the enclave. He was ready to march out of the gates at that point. He questioned me a lot, mostly about the kind of man you are and what you've been doing. He seemed determined by the end and asked me to give you this." Amaat handed me a scroll case.

I inspected it, noticing that it was much more formal than the simple one I'd sent my own letter in, but I figured that was a good thing, as I twisted the tight seal and pulled one end off. The stopper came out with a pop, releasing the rolled parchment, ring, and wax that it contained.

I examined the ring and three sticks of purple sealing wax first. The wax was a deep, rich color with faint sparkles in it. I just knew that, wherever Oracle was, she was going to love it. I studied the ring next. It bore a pattern that looked like an eastern dragon curled around a sword. Words were printed under it, but I couldn't make them out.

"What's this?" I asked, passing it to Augustus. He took the ring and smiled, nodding to himself.

"It's the signet ring of the Legion General, Jax. It's a formal acknowledgement that you can give the legion orders if you sign your letters with that. What does he say?"

All Hail Lord Jax of Dravith, Scion of the Imperial Family and Rightful Lord of the Empire.

I have received your orders and will comply, I recognize the sworn affidavits of Yen'ma Rultahir and Augustus Vertais Asen, and acknowledge their confirmation of your identity, as well as the resurrection of the imperial Oath.

I have one hundred and eleven legionnaires in the enclave at present, with ninety-six support personnel, as well as a further sixty-six dependents, making a total, including myself, of two hundred and seventy-four souls.

Per your orders, we will move to our designated locations and secure sufficient transport to enable us to fulfill your commands.

For the Empire,

Romanus Dominai Perival, Legion Prefect of the Dravith Legion of Himnel

I read it aloud, then looked up to Augustus, relieved at the sight of him nodding thoughtfully.

"It's as good as we could have hoped; he acknowledges your orders and accepts them, while being careful not to reveal too much, just in case the messenger is taken. The ring gives you a way to authenticate any messages you send to him, as well. What he doesn't say is that there are codewords that can be included in the letter to authenticate it. These are a closely guarded secret, and only known to certain legionnaires. Both Yen and I included those in our letters, which is why yours was accepted so easily."

"And the Oath?" I asked, eliciting a grin.

"Well, yes, that probably helped as well. Actually, experiencing the Oath become live is a hell of an experience, I can tell you. Despite the fact that we've all lived with our Oaths since giving them when we joined the legion, without you to breathe life into them, they were cold and uncomfortable things."

"What do you mean?" I asked.

"Hmm. Consider a sandwich—strange, I know, but go with it," he said, catching the look I gave him. "Say you've always eaten cold, fatty ham with plain bread. Then imagine your first taste of a hot bacon sandwich…lashings of cheese, bread dipped in butter and toasted, tomatoes and lettuce in a ratio of one to three, in comparison to the bacon."

"Damn, Augustus, you're a man after my own heart there." I fought to ignore my hunger as my stomach rumbled.

"You see what I mean?" he asked, grinning. "The difference between the Oath as it was and as it is might seem minor to an outsider. They're both Oaths, or sandwiches, but to the person who receives it? They're worlds apart."

"Okay, I get it," I said, patting my stomach. "Now I need a goddamn bacon sandwich."

"Unfortunately, I think we finished the last one about ten minutes ago," Augustus said, painting a look of sadness on his face that didn't reach his eyes.

"You utter bastard." I glared at him with the kind of fury that only comes from bacon deprivation.

"It's been said before," he agreed, a smile tugging at the edges of his lips.

"I could grow to hate you; you do realize this?" I persisted, and his smile simply grew wider. "Bastard," I repeated.

"Look on the bright side, Jax." He laughed, gesturing to a platter on a nearby table. "There's some cold ham left…"

"Seriously, I could stab you," I threatened, getting another laugh.

"I'm sure Mal can arrange for some more bacon," he reassured me, still smiling.

"I damn well hope so," I said. Shifting my thoughts, I regarded Barrett, who seemed content to lean against the wall at the back of the garden, watching and smiling. He looked healthy and happy, considering I'd not seen him for days.

"Is that a black eye?" I asked him, surprised to see him go red and turn his face to the side slightly to hide it.

"Uhhh, no?" he said, attempting to sound nonchalant. My gaze snapped to Lydia as she started to laugh, having come up behind me to lean against the doorway into the common area.

"Ask him who gave it to him!" she suggested, grinning widely, and I turned my attention back to him, one eyebrow raised.

"Come on, dude, what happened?" I pressed.

He sighed heavily before turning to face me. His eye was definitely blackened and swollen, now that I saw it properly, and his lip looked like it'd been busted at some point. "Man, are you okay?" I asked, lifting my hand in preparation to cast a healing spell.

"I'm fine!" he protested, shaking his head and gesturing to lower my hand. "No healing needed, okay?"

"If you're sure, dude; but seriously, what happened?" I was becoming less worried, and more curious, the longer he drew it out.

"Nothing happened, okay? I just…fell…sort of."

"Yeah, 'fell' into bed with Joya." Lydia snorted.

"What?" I asked, looking around for the caravaneer.

"Joya…Look, she came to see me last night after you went on your little trip. We kinda sorted things out, and maybe we were a bit too energetic in our…discussion…that's all." Barrett refused to meet my eyes, rubbing the back of his neck awkwardly.

"You mean it was rough sex that left you looking like this?" I beamed, and he looked even more embarrassed.

"I can't wait to hear what Oren says when he hears about this, not to mention the rest of your crew!" I said, not even bothering to hide my amusement. "What does she look like?" I asked Lydia, and she shook her head.

"Joya's at least six an' an half feet tall. Pretty lass, but she do look like she's 'alf-ogre, she's that big. An' the way she staggered out of his room…weavin' an' stumblin' down the hall a couple o' hours ago! She looked battered and bruised, but judgin' from the smile on her face an' the way she was walkin', she wasn't goin' to be complainin'…"

I saw Augustus lift a hand, and he exchanged a subtle high-five with Barrett, deepening my grin.

"Okay, moving on…Is everything sorted? Barrett, I know I haven't seen you lately; you've been running around seeing the ship's families since we got here, but did you manage it?" I asked, my change of tone a clear indication of how important this was. He straightened and answered soberly.

"I think so; I made the rounds to all of the crew's families, and I told a trusted group to spread the word to a select few more I couldn't reach. My sister and her bairn are camped out in one of Mal's warehouses now, so I tell you that's a weight off my mind."

"I bet. Is there anything else we need to do?" I received a round of head shakes from the group, except for Augustus.

"Well, there is one point…"

"Oh?"

"Why have you got a giant red and black spider following you around, and why is Arrin intent on getting it to murder him?" he asked.

I turned to find Arrin trying to fit his head into Horkesh's mouth.

"…see! I told you I could fit!" he crowed, to the laughter of the legion and the obvious confusion of the spider.

"Well, Arrin…Arrin's just a fuckin' idiot," I sighed, shaking my head. "Horkesh, on the other hand…" And just like that, I was back to explaining the events that had occurred within the Smugglers Path and the deal I had made with

Ashrag. "…So, Ashrag's on her way to the tower now, and Horkesh has come to help us. She's brought ten soldiers, which are about the size of small horses, and two hunters, which are considerably bigger and meaner. I'm thinking we set them on whoever we don't like."

"Just remember, no battle plan survives contact with the enemy, Jax," Augustus said. "We need to be ready, but flexible when something goes wrong, and it will. We'll need to move to fix it as fast as we can."

"I know," I agreed. "Let's go find Mal, introduce another change to our plans, because I love watching his face when I do that. Then I need to get myself ready for the fight, and that includes a bit of time with Nerin, as I need to learn a new spell." Augustus nodded, then eyed my gear.

"I noticed you're not wearing your legion armor—" he began, when I cut him off.

"Tonight is going to be a war, not just a fight, mate. I need to mix and match my gear to give me the best advantage I can. I love the legion gear; it feels like a second skin, but we haven't got enough for everyone, not if I wear it. So, give the pieces back to those who donated them, with my sincere thanks. And I'll wear my normal gear and use my weapons.

"To hell with what the gangs think. They all saw me fight in the legion gear last night; that should give them pause. And after tonight, who cares what they think?" I headed out to the outer corridor and followed it along to Mal's rooms.

It didn't take long to find Mal and his people; they were all gathered around a table in the middle of his rooms, going over a map of the city. Evidently, they were pointing out checkpoints and guard posts, marking the ones held by guards they'd managed to bribe, and others that would need to be taken by force.

"About time you were up," Mal said, frowning at me. "How in the hell can you sleep so much, with all this needin' to be done?"

"Practice," I said, shrugging. "If I don't sleep whenever I can, I'll never sleep."

"You can sleep when yer dead," he muttered, jumping to his feet in shock as Horkesh ran up the wall to perch in the top corner. "What in the hell is that!" Mal cried, reaching for his crossbows as the room blew up. My side quickly moved in the way of his, as everyone panicked.

"Whoa!" I called, holding my hands up. "This is Horkesh. She's come to help, sent by the Queen of the Cave Spiders. You remember them *and the little discussion we had about spiders?*" I stared intently at Mal, and he gaped at me, wide-eyed, before slowly getting his breath back and relaxing.

"That…oh yeah…well, I redecorated the wall, if that's what you're askin'…but…"

"She's here to help," I said soothingly, sitting back down. "She's brought her guard, and they're outside somewhere, watching. Perhaps we could all relax a bit, so they don't feel like coming to her defense? Considering the room would only hold maybe two of them…" I suggested, looking around at the size of the room meaningfully.

"Ah, right," Mal muttered, as Soween put her weapons away and ordered everyone else to stand down. "Maybe warn a man first next time?" he asked plaintively, sitting down and swallowing hard. Clearly banishing Horkesh from his mind, he pulled up another stack of papers and sorted through them until he found what he was looking for and threw it to me.

"What's this?" I asked, looking over it.

"It's the final numbers for tonight; nearly seven hundred people, all told, includin' an estimate of the legion."

"Well, fuck me gently with a lit candle," I said, shaking my head. "I didn't realize there were this many of them."

"Kinky bastard." Mal snorted, chucking another piece of parchment at me. "That lists who and where. The battleship should be good to hold around four hundred; the rest will be split up between the other ships. We managed to get some of the crews and engineers to the battleship to help the build as well, in case you were wonderin'," he added sourly.

"Shit, I totally forgot about that," I admitted.

"Yeah, well, we sorted it," Mal said, getting a snort from Soween.

"We?" she asked pointedly.

"We're a team, what you or I do, it don't matter, it's all 'we,' right?" he said with a shrug, getting a look from her before he moved on quickly. "Anyway, the battleship will be ready for a 'test flight' tonight. It's been cleared for that, apparently, so that should hopefully make it less suspicious."

"What condition is it in?" I asked, and he shook his head.

"It's not good; I'll be straight with you. They've managed to make the interior mainly secure, given her minimal engines and controls, but it won't be able to defend itself or outrun anythin' beyond a sickly ant with some heavy shoppin'. They think they'll be able to turn it, go up and down, and that's about it. Its top speed with the wind behind it will make an ox look dangerously fast."

"Damn. Shame it's the only way we can get everyone out…what ships are docked at the minute?" I asked.

"Well, a little good news there," Soween interjected, taking over the discussion and passing me another bit of parchment. "The *Atlantessa* landed about four hours ago. She's a cruiser and just needs restocking. Her soldiers and crew are on leave for two days, so there's minimum people aboard. With the extra people we've got, we think we can make a play for both cruisers, two fast scouts, and the battleship, and—you lucky bastard—I got word that the *Star's Glory* is due in tonight. She's gonna be hauling ass, as there's a big slave market planned for tomorrow."

"Before you ask, no, we can't damn well raid the market 'on our way,'" Mal snapped, holding a hand up as I opened my mouth. He gave me a firm look while Soween outlined the plan.

"There are a lot of slaves around the city. There's one market, next to the Stockpile; it's smaller than most, but it's holding a dozen or so, plus the slaves that are kept in the Stockpile, and those are close enough that we *can* get them.

"We already planned for it, but beyond that, I'm sorry. You'll have to be satisfied with that. The incoming slaves, I assume, will be stored overnight on the *Star*," Soween said firmly. "Barrett is going to be busy with organizing the families, so he needs to be moving as soon as this conversation is done, as well."

"I know. It just seems wrong for me to be out there, rather than with you all," Barrett muttered.

"I know, my friend, but the families are the most important part. Without them, there's no point to this." I smiled. "Protect them, and if you need to, use the golems. They'll recognize you."

"Thanks, I will," Barrett said, letting out a breath.

"Okay, what about your ship, Mal?" I asked him. "I know you want one, and I haven't seen your team mentioned anywhere here for berths?"

"There *might* be a ship that's finishin' up her trials tomorrow, before bein' added to the fleet," he admitted, grinning mischievously.

I snorted. "Okay, you old pirate. Tell me about her, and don't worry, I won't try to change things around."

"She's a new design, falcon class, designed to move emergency cargo through dangerous places, supposedly to keep the army supplied. She's armed, faster than anythin' else they've got, save the fast scouts. She has the capacity of a cruiser, she's beautiful, and yeah, she's ours," Mal said, eyeing me warily.

"Okay, I can take a hint." I laughed, despite my sudden new desire for a falcon class of my own.

"Glad to hear it." Mal grunted, handing me another sheet.

"What's this?" I asked, glancing it over.

"Your winnings from last night," he said shortly. "The first fight, I got three to one. Second fight, I barely had time to get any bets on, and the third, well…I managed to get five to one. The last fight was a bit better; I got seven to one on that. As you asked, I wagered everythin' on each round, startin' with that five hundred gold, so you've earned, after my 'handler's fee,' a total of sixty-four thousand, five hundred gold."

"Holy shit," I said into the sudden silence.

"Yeah, when you start talkin' this kind of money, it's easier to think in terms of platinum. You get a single platinum to a thousand gold, so you've got sixty-four platinum and five hundred gold. Tonight was gonna to be the fun bit, because nobody carries that kind of coin around with 'em. While we could make a fortune gamblin', especially with what's comin' to face you, we'd never be able to collect it, as the banks don't open 'til tomorrow at first light."

"Well, that sucks," I said, and he grinned.

"It does, but fortunately you know a guy who's sneakier than the average. I insisted that any bets bein' placed tonight must have a percentage in coin 'on the table,' as we call it." He folded his hands behind his head and leaned back in his chair. "We won't get the same kinda money, but we can get somethin', at least. Also, as manastones cost anywhere between five hundred and ten thousand gold, dependin' on their size, I've said we'll accept 'em in lieu of payment, provided they're here and on the table."

"Brilliant!" I breathed, grinning at him.

"It is, but forgive me if I'm more interested in the enemies he has to face tonight," Augustus interrupted gruffly.

"Good point," I said, nodding to him in thanks.

"Yeah, well, that's where things get a mite squirrely," Mal hedged.

"Explain," I said with a sudden frown.

"You might remember that we said they could put in creatures if they wanted, but that you'd be allowed to field a team? Well, they've taken us up on that…word is, tonight, you get a beast from the Copper Ghost Gang, a team of three from the harpies, a beast from the South Side Gang, and…"

"And?" I prompted.

"And a team from the Night's Followers. Most likely an arena team, but I couldn't find out more; they're keepin' their cards close to their chest."

"Any restrictions on our team?" I asked.

"Yeah, nobody over level twenty, and total level of the team can't be higher'n eighty, so you can either take a load of low levels, or four level twenties. Same rule applies to all the fights tonight."

"So the harpies will only have three, at most, level twenties, but we could have, what? A twenty and six tens?" I asked, getting a nod in reply.

"That counts almost all of my legionnaires out," Augustus said, grimacing. "I don't like it, Jax. Maybe see if we can bend the rules a little? Get it raised to level twenty-five? I brought skilled legionnaires with me; all but one are over twenty."

"Won't happen," Mal said, spreading his hands placatingly. "No chance they'll lift the level ban. They wanted it set at fifteen, until I told 'em there were no legionnaires that low."

"Who is it that's under twenty?" I asked.

"Grizz. The mad bastard broke half his body not long back, and spent ages being put back together very carefully by the healers. He's been filled full of arrows, stabbed, crushed, and blown up. The only reason he's not at the highest level of the entire legion is the amount of time he's spent in rehab."

"Rehab?"

"The legion healers are…" Augustus frowned, clearly trying to choose his words carefully, before shaking his head and just going for it. "They're highly skilled, but we have very few in the legion with access to magic. We make do with potions mainly, and occasional visits from outside healers such as Mistress Nerin, should she be willing to visit. It means that, while injuries are generally treatable, provided they're not instantly fatal, the recovery time can be considerably longer than we'd like."

"Shit, man, well, that we can fix at least. Anyway, with Grizz, he's with me, then. What's his specialty, anyway?" I asked, filled with curiosity.

"Scout sniper; he's the one we send out to find the enemy and take out their leadership in times of war. Usually, that means hunting bandits or monsters. He needs to stop piling in and remember he's a damn ranged fighter once in a while, instead of tackling things head-on, but if only one of my team can be with you, I'd pick him," Augustus said grudgingly.

"So up to level eighty in overall strength. I'm level fifteen, so with him at what…?"

"Nineteen."

"Great, that's thirty-three. Lydia?" I asked.

"Eleven," she replied from her position near the door.

"Forty-four! Okay, then. Bane? Arrin? Guys? Come on, people, speak up!" I said, and the rest of my "usual suspects" team chimed in. I ended up with Arrin at level ten, Bane at thirteen, and it became a fight between Jian, Miren, and Stephanos as to who would come. In the end, I overruled them, as the argument was getting out of hand and they had all resorted to name calling.

As much as I wanted them all with me, hearing Miren commenting on Jian's sexual prowess caused the entire room to freeze in embarrassment.

"Ooookay…." I said into the silence. "I need some ranged support with Grizz, so that counts you out, Jian, sorry. Miren, it's between you and Stephanos. I know he's the higher level, not to mention he's a foot taller than you, so he can usually see what's going on. I'll take him this time, you next…maybe."

"Maybe?" she said, aghast.

"Yeah, I think you and Jian need a little 'time-out' to chat some things over." I shook my head at the glares they were giving each other.

"So, I'm taking Grizz, Bane, Lydia, Arrin, and Stephanos with me tonight. We're going to be the center attraction, and while we're keeping the gangs busy, you're going to be starting the party out there?" I confirmed with Mal, who nodded.

"Yeah, I need to stay here to run the arena, but Soween, Josh, Jay, and my people will be out there gettin' into place and leadin' their teams. They've all got their targets to take. You get the fun fights here in the arena and raidin' the Skyking's lair, which we think we've found…"

"Where is it?" I asked.

He scoffed, getting up and gesturing for me to follow him onto the balcony. Leaning on the banister, he pointed casually out to the left, where several tall buildings lifted up into the darkening sky. All but one had lights flickering in them, which stayed notably cold and dark.

"That one…" he said under his breath, turning smoothly and pointing around at other random landmarks, in case we were being watched. "The dark one. I had a couple of your djinn followin' some fliers that I suspected worked for the Skyking. Nothin' definite, but that tower's the only one that doesn't have an accessible record of who owns it, and when I sent someone knockin', they vanished. Turned up this mornin', floatin' in the river, missin' their eyes."

"So it's either the Skyking or someone who really doesn't like to be disturbed," I said.

"Probably both. Either way, though, it's got a lot of fliers in and around it, always imps and prometheans, and the 'lesser' members of the gang get their orders a short fly from there. It's our best shot."

"Okay, so I kill everyone in the arena…"

"Then I'll have Gaion waitin' to lead you to that tower. The rest of my team will be out hittin' our targets. Where's the golems, by the way? Could do with them."

"They're in the river, waiting. They'll start out of the river at midnight, head straight to the shipyards, and join the legion. Augustus has been added to their command list as well, so he can tell them what to do, if you need them. Ideally, though, I'd rather not use them, as they're going to be pretty memorable."

"Any chance of me bein' added to that list?" Mal asked offhandedly.

"Not from here. I'd need the golems close by to do it," I lied. In truth, I didn't want anyone having control over such a powerful group of constructs without being sworn to me. Despite my asking, Mal was determined to remain a paid ally rather than an oathbound member of the group.

"Fair enough. So, you've got two hours 'til the first fight; guess I'd better let you get on with whatever you need to do." He met my eyes, an odd look on his face, then he reached out, gripping my wrist and squeezing once before letting go. "Good luck, kid. Don't die."

"Thanks, Mal. You too, mate." I smiled. As he turned away, I caught his arm. "And when it comes to my winnings, just put them on the battleship with the rest of the Stockpile. Augustus will make sure it's safe."

"Ah…of course, almost forgot about that."

"Me too. Good job I thought of it then; otherwise, when you got your ship, we'd have had to keep you close by to transfer them off, wouldn't we?" My smile never slipped.

"Yeah. Well-remembered," Mal said, a hint of sourness in his voice.

I looked around the room and caught Soween watching me. When she was sure Mal couldn't see, she gave me a slow wink, and I couldn't help but deepen my smile at her acknowledgement as we left the balcony.

"Okay then, people, let's get to our places. I'll need Mistress Nerin, as it's time for Arrin and me to make use of a couple of spellbooks. Need to make sure we don't fry our brains," I reassured them, noting the uncomfortable looks from Lydia's crew.

I bid the team goodbye and wished them all good luck as I left the room. Wasting no time, I strode purposefully down to the lower floors, stopping when I reached the antechamber we'd used the night before. My team and I made the most of the first half an hour before Nerin arrived by sorting out potions and gear. I checked through some of my Emporium loot, using Examine on the rings and various bits of jewelry, downing a couple of the cheaper potions to bring me back up to full mana.

I found, of the seventeen bits and pieces, eleven rings, six necklaces, and single thick metal torc, only five were really useful at this stage. The others were put aside for use at the tower, since most of them were geared towards crafting rather than combat.

Ring of Immediate Healing		**Further Description** *Yes/No*	
Details:		This ring provides up to 70 points of healing twice per day. Cooldown between uses is 1 hour.	
Rarity:	**Magical:**	**Durability:**	**Charge:**
Uncommon	Yes	99/100	2/2

Ring of Dexterous Handling		**Further Description** *Yes/No*	
Details:		This ring increases the Dexterity of the user by 3 points.	
Rarity:	**Magical:**	**Durability:**	**Charge:**
Uncommon	Yes	100/100	N/A

Bleeding Band		**Further Description** *Yes/No*	
Details:		This ring is covered in thorns and inflicts a constant -1HP per second bleed effect on the wearer *but* also adds this effect to the bearer's attacks. This effect can be stacked on an enemy up to 10 times, and each debuff will last 10 seconds, refreshing with each successful attack. Wearer suffers 1 bleed effect only.	
Rarity:	**Magical:**	**Durability:**	**Charge:**
Rare	Yes	100/100	N/A

Guardian's Torc of Determination		**Further Description** *Yes/No*	
Details:		This thick metal torc, designed to be worn around the neck, grants a stat boost of 5 points to Constitution, as well as adding the taunt ability: Face ME! Taunt ability forces those effected to ignore all other targets and charge the user heedlessly for a period of 5 seconds. This ability has a 1-hour cooldown.	
Rarity:	**Magical:**	**Durability:**	**Charge:**
Highly Rare	Yes	89/100	N/A

Shadow's Revelation		**Further Description** *Yes/No*	
Details:		The chain of Shadow's Revelation grants its wearer a boost in Perception equal to their Stealth skill.	
Rarity:	**Magical:**	**Durability:**	**Charge:**
Highly Rare	Yes	100/100	N/A

I gave the Ring of Dexterous Handling to Stephanos, figuring it would help him hit things faster, as well as the Bleeding Band. He was grinning from ear to ear as he tried them both on, until the Bleed effect started, and he nearly stripped his finger of flesh in his need to take it off.

"You don't have to wear it," I said to him, but he cut me off before I could finish speaking.

"No, Jax, we're in this together. It's too good a bonus to pass up; can you imagine the bleeding effect I'll be able to stack when I keep firing into the same target? I just don't want to feel it until I need it!"

"Fair enough," I acknowledged, passing the torc and Ring of Immediate Healing to Lydia. She smiled in thanks and settled them into place, grinning as her Constitution jumped. I took my old healing ring back from Miren and passed it to Grizz, who beamed, obviously excited to be joining the team and fighting in the arena.

Lastly, I gave the chain of Shadow's Revelation to Bane, as he would get by far the biggest boost from it, then pulled out the pair of Dagomar's Daggers I'd looted from the Emporium, passing them to Bane as well.

I examined the other weapons, disappointed at finding that most were crap, but there were three worth the attention. A spiked mace, the sword from the former commander of the golem maintenance station, and a wand. I couldn't help but smile as I checked them out.

Mace of Confusion		**Further Description** *Yes/No*	
Damage:		15-35 DPS	
Details:		This mace is set with spikes that flare up and down between the flanges and has a faint aura that makes close examination feel uncomfortable. Each hit with the Mace of Confusion has a 5% chance to Confuse the target, leaving them unsure who or why they are fighting. This effect lasts up to 10 seconds, depending on the target's Intelligence stat.	
Rarity:	**Magical:**	**Durability:**	**Charge:**
Highly Rare	Yes	100/100	100/100

Commander's Sword		**Further Description** *Yes/No*	
Damage:		25-50 DPS	
Details:		This sword is modeled on the traditional legion gladius but is both longer and heavier. It imparts the ability Rallying Cry to its bearer and has a 10% chance to inflict a Fear debuff on its victims. Facing the bearer of the Commander's Sword will be an experience few will forget, if they survive it.	
Rarity:	**Magical:**	**Durability:**	**Charge:**
Highly Rare	Yes	100/100	100/100

Wand of Darkness		**Further Description** *Yes/No*	
Damage:		10-15 DPS	
Details:		This wand shoots Darkbolts. Each hit inflicts between 10-15 damage, but also carries a 5% chance of inflicting the Darkness debuff on its target. Darkness makes it harder for the target to aim, cast spells successfully, or use abilities, depending on the Wisdom and Intelligence of the target relevant to the caster.	
Rarity:	**Magical:**	**Durability:**	**Charge:**
Highly Rare	Yes	100/100	100/100

Lydia got the mace, and Arrin the wand, and I thoroughly enjoyed the delighted looks they gave me and the curious looks the rest of the room gave them.

"Augustus?" I called. He walked over, giving me an eyebrow raised in question. "I kinda fucked your sword up, mate, so…here you go."

I presented him with the Commander's Sword. His eyes snapped up from the weapon to me in shock.

"Jax, there's no need—" he started, and I shook my head.

"Seriously, mate, you've earned this, and you lead your team well. I'll square it with the legion prefect if it's an issue, so don't worry about it."

"I don't know what to say…" he stammered. I chuckled, clapping him on the shoulder.

"Try 'thank you,' and bugger off," I said, and his eyes took on a mischievous cast.

"Thank you and bugger off." Then he winked and moved aside, examining the sword with awe. The other legionnaires especially were a mixture of envious and impressed by Augustus's new weapon.

"What's all this crap about using spellbooks?" Nerin said from the door, and I smiled brightly at her as she walked in, grumbling.

"Ah! Good of you to join us, Mistress Nerin," I began, getting a glare from her.

"I had things to sort out, boy, not least, the patients I help on a regular basis. You think a healer disappearing overnight wouldn't cause a few deaths if people didn't know?" she snapped.

I gaped at her in shock.

"Don't be foolish," she said, rolling her eyes as she pushed past me to sit down. "I didn't tell anyone anything I shouldn't have; I just told those who needed to know that, after my shop was robbed"—she glared around the room at large—"I had decided to take some time away, maybe go to the wilds for a bit and increase my alchemical abilities, learn some new potions, and so on. I named a village hardly anyone's heard of, Dannick, as my destination, so don't worry."

"Dannick?" I asked carefully. "Ruled by a reeve called Lorek?"

"You know it?" she asked curiously. "I got some strange looks when I mentioned it. Said I had a niece living there; why?"

"Do you?" I asked slowly.

"No. I said '*I said*' I had a niece. Think I'd be telling the world, when they could figure out I'm involved in all of this? I've no living family, boy, or I'd be already gone from this toilet of a city. Now, explain why that matters."

"A ship raided the village of Dannick for slaves a week or two back; timing's a bit of a blur. They live in the tower now, as free people. I sent one of my ships to recruit from Dannick while I'm here, and well, the reeve is a prick."

"They always are." She shrugged dismissively. "A reeve is too low to be powerful, too poor to be rich, and too stupid to realize that buying a rank like that out in the wilds is going to solve none of those problems. They always end up as miserable shitbags, until someone kills them and the lord of the city sells their title to another poor fool."

"Oh, so I basically just did what always happens?" I asked, confused.

"You kill them?" she probed shrewdly, watching me.

"No, I rescued them. When I found that he and his helpers were walking turds, I kicked them out of the tower with a pack of supplies and a knife and pointed them in the direction of Dannick. I'm betting it'll take a few weeks of hard travel to make it—"

"...If they live," she finished for me, and I nodded. "Well, if he's a reeve, ain't nobody going to miss him, no doubt. Now, what's this idiocy about learning from spellbooks?" she asked, bracing her hands on her hips.

"Well, we need some more spells. I've got these books, so why not use them?"

"Why, indeed..." She sighed, shaking her head and looking at Oracle, who'd stayed quietly perched on my shoulder this time. "You have not explained the issues with spellbooks to him yet?"

"I have, and I know you mentioned them before as well, but he needs every edge he can get," Oracle retorted.

"Good point. I'd forgotten I did that. Anyway, boy, spellbooks fill your mind with information, true, but it's mainly rubbish. I'd recommend you learn the proper way: experiment, be taught by a real mage, or better yet, ask your goddess for help. They're all better methods than absorbing a spellbook. That'll mess with your mind, dumping unearned information in like pouring water from a pitcher."

"You know of any mages who can teach us, that we can get here in, oh, say, half an hour?" I asked, raising one eyebrow.

"I can teach you a healing spell or two, but beyond that, you've got this boy here. Learn some of his spells and teach him some of yours. No point in using a book, when it can be avoided."

"Have we got time?" I asked, looking at Arrin and Oracle, then back to Nerin.

"Time for my spells, at least. I'll teach you both two, if Oracle can form a bridge between us all?" she asked, and Oracle bobbed uncertainly.

"I've done it between Jax and me, and we did do it that way with Ame, but that was in the tower," she said cautiously.

"Bah, you're a wisp. Should be as simple as breathing for you. Reach out and touch our minds, all three at once. Feel what I offer, and channel it for them; you're a conduit by nature's will. It's why your kind were hunted to the brink of extinction."

"I'll try it, then," she agreed, trying to ignore the comment Nerin had made about her species. Both Arrin and I moved to sit close to Nerin, who considered us carefully.

"I'll teach you a healing over time spell, and a weak Cleanse, as they can grow to be hugely useful. Now, think: if you both teach each other one spell, what will it be?" she asked, and Arrin grinned at me.

"Magic Missile. It's saved my life so many times already," he offered.

"Yeah, it's an awesome-looking spell," I said, grinning in acceptance. "I'll give you Weak Lightning Bolt. You'll get the basic version, unfortunately, but I've already evolved my own into Stunning Lightning Bolt, and it's pretty much Oracle's go-to spell. Add it to water, which I can provide, with the fountain..."

"Oh yeah..." Arrin cackled gleefully. "I love that combination!"

"Okay then, we're all agreed?" Nerin said, and both Arrin and I nodded. "Excellent. Oracle, if you please?"

Oracle shifted into her full-sized form, standing amidst the three of us and reaching out to lay a hand on each of our foreheads. I frowned at the weirdness of her suddenly having three arms, then shrugged as I felt a need to close my eyes.

A connection clicked into place as Oracle drew me into a link. It was different from our normal bond link, which felt almost like an embrace. This time, it felt weird; instead of her warm arms around my mind, she felt like a bridge, with each of our minds stretching out to join with her, then the information passing from her to us. Oracle's presence formed a safe buffer for us all, preventing access to the others' minds.

Nerin went first, and I could see the effort she put into it, despite her pretending it was a simple thing. For the Cleanse spell, she composed a structure of magic that felt like rainwater, cool and fresh, rinsing away impurities. It was built like I imagined the rain cycle was; slow, gentle, but inexorable as well.

Once it began, it seemed unstoppable, building steadily, rising until whatever it was targeting began to crumble. It started gentle, much as rain on the hillsides, but by the end, it had swelled to a roaring, rushing flash flood of power, breaking down the "dams" of impurities, washing them away, and absorbing the destroyed components into part of the river, instead of constraining or eliminating them.

I understood suddenly how being poisoned and cleansed multiple times would build up an immunity, as the Cleanse spell broke the poison down, remaking it into part of the target's body. It was so different from Cleansing Fire that I was amazed. The fire aspect literally burned the impurities out of its target instead of washing them away. After a long moment, Arrin and I gained the full knowledge of Cleanse, then Nerin moved onto Strength of the Seasons.

The second spell was more of a static structure, a tidal basin rather than a river, as it constrained the healing and split it into a multitude of weaves. They were all basic, in comparison to my Battlefield Triage spell, but where my own spell targeted and healed so much more, this spell had a more gentle and beneficial overall effect.

In addition to healing five points per second for thirty seconds, repairing basic injuries, reforming skin, and replenishing blood loss, this spell also gave an artificial boost to the target's health and stamina. For thirty minutes, it would push the usual limits upwards by around a hundred points each, and that alone was a fantastic boost…especially as my mind raced to find ways to use this knowledge to augment my existing spells.

Once the transfer of knowledge was complete, we sat in silence for several seconds within the connection, until Arrin managed to "push" his knowledge of Magic Missile to Oracle, and she passed it to me as Nerin left the link.

Arrin displayed the missiles in our joined awareness, first creating one, then altering it in ways he'd clearly evolved. The missile became a dart, then lengthened to a javelin, then shortened to a cannonball. The structure of the spell remained basically unchanged, the seeking and the cornering capabilities the same, regardless of the shape of the dart.

But he'd altered them, pushing more mana in to increase the speed and therefore the damage done. He'd also created an explosive pocket of air that detonated on impact. When the spell was done, and the knowledge slid into my mind, I grinned in satisfaction and new respect for Arrin. The whole process surprised me, since it had been so much quicker and easier for us, due to being mages already, than it had been for poor Ame.

I took a deep breath and checked the time. Finding that I had twenty minutes left before the fight, I began to build the lightning bolt, showing Arrin the way the ions moved, the way the targeting for the spell worked by subtly shifting the air aside to make a clear space through the intervening distance, entirely free of air for a fraction of a second. The way the spell built a form to contain the lightning, then essentially gave it a release, pouring it out into the space between seconds to travel down the channel of emptiness until it hit its target.

I felt Arrin's understanding as he sat back, Oracle breaking our link, and I let out a loud sigh as the new spells settled into my mind.

Congratulations!

You have learned three new Spells:
Cleanse, Strength of the Seasons, and Magic Missile!

Cleanse:
Breaks down toxins and debuffs cast on the target. Repeated combinations of set toxins and cleansings may result in heightened immunities to that toxin. Cost of 25 mana. More potent effects may require channeled castings.

Strength of the Seasons:
This spell buffs health and stamina pools by 100 points and lasts for 30 minutes. It also provides a healing effect over time of 5 points per second for 30 seconds. Cost of 150 mana.

Magic Missile:
Creates a trio of small missiles, which can be independently or collectively targeted and have a range of up to 30m with a damage per missile of 5 points. Damage can be increased through channeling extra mana into the spell, up to a maximum of five times the damage for ten times the cost. Cost of 25-250 mana.

I admired my new spells, feeling Oracle adjusting and examining our understanding of them as I stretched. I was still kneading the kinks out of my lower back when Augustus spoke.

"Five minutes, Jax. Time to get ready for the fight."

I got up, twisting to free up muscles that had been stationary for too long. I regretted spending so much time talking and absorbing the new spells, as it had cost me my last chance to eat, for a few hours, at least.

"I've evolved my Strength of the Seasons numerous times over the years, so I'll cast it on you all just before the fight begins. My version will give you all a boost of one hundred and fifty points to your health and stamina, and a full minute of five points of health regeneration per second. Make the most of it," Nerin said, looking us all over.

I forced a smile as her gaze met mine. I was grateful for the new spells I'd been given, but I found myself wishing I'd had time to learn Haste as well.

“Thank you, Nerin,” I said, settling all of my weapons in place. Habit compelled me into drawing my swords then reseating them, loosening my daggers in their sheaths, and checking to make sure all of my equipment was there. I’d made a point of giving everyone three health potions, two average and one greater, before I’d settled down with Nerin and Arrin. Arrin and I had three mana each, as well, with the same concentrations.

I searched for Oracle, who grinned at me as she *shifted* back to her usual, smaller size, but staying by my side.

“What?” she asked, quirking her head to the side. “You thought I’d abandon you? Go sit with Mal and watch when I could be here instead? You’re mine, Jax, and I’m yours. We fight together, and I’ll not be elsewhere watching, if there’s no need.”

I smiled at her, reaching up to stroke a cheek, and she kissed my fingers.

“I love you, Oracle,” I said quietly.

She smiled up at me with an expression of sheer bliss. She flushed pink for a fraction of a second and tenderly kissed my hand again, before blurring into her smaller size and settling on my shoulder.

My tiny companion was dressed for war, this time in an outfit that matched my own, black silk with plates of steel and ivory, complete with a tiny naginata held tight.

“I love you too, Jax.” The timing for us to admit such a thing aloud was odd, but it fit us, fit our life. The heat in her gaze shifted from sensual to combative, and she squared her tiny shoulders. “Now let’s go fuck these guys up, steal their shit, and get some quality time in private, okay?”

“Sounds good to me,” I agreed, smiling at her as the door opened onto the Arena, and I marched forward. My squad followed me through and spread out, ready for the fight to come.

CHAPTER TWENTY-THREE

The gong sounded three times, and the magically enhanced voice of the announcer rang out, washing over the buzz of the crowd. The stands overflowed, spectators hanging from the bars and posts of the inverted bowl that surrounded us.

"Ladies, gentlemen, and all you other folk! Welcome to the Cloudring…ARENA!" he shouted to thunderous screams, yells, and catcalls. "Tonight, we've got a spectacle for you that's never been seen: a trapped legionnaire and his friends have challenged the honest citizens of the glorious city of Himnel and you've delivered! The virtuous, dependable groups that make up some of the city's most…*hardworking*…people have put forward a mix of four individual creatures and groups to face the *foul legion*, and the first of them is here now, ready to defend your honor. I give you, from the Copper Ghosts…a teradon!"

The crowd went wild, screaming and hollering. Even from the arena floor, I could hear bets being placed and insults hurled.

Rather than any of the usual smaller doors dotted around the arena, the larger double doors at the far side slowly retracted, drawing back into the wall on either side of the entrance, and I got my first look at a teradon.

It was hunched over in some kind of huge metal shipping container, curled in upon itself and half turned away. As the doors cranked back, it turned and glared out at the screaming, hollering mass of beings clinging to the arena bars, and at us.

It finally managed to rotate fully, having to fight to shift around in the tightly enclosed space, revealing its monstrous face as it came around to face us.

Two long, curled tusks jutted from a mouth filled with broken, pointed teeth. The long protrusions, curving sideways around the snout and forehead, looked like they'd be more at home on a mammoth than anything that stood upright. Beady eyes glared at us from underneath bony plates, and the flattened shape of its skull suggested that this creature was used to ramming things down headfirst. As the creature bellowed at us in rage, I took an involuntary step back, relieved to see that most of my party had as well.

The only one who hadn't, of course, was that mad bastard, Grizz.

"Come on then, pretty!" he shouted, drawing back on the bow he carried. It creaked under the pressure, the deep *twang* of the release cutting through the air, followed by a scream of rage as the arrow buried itself deep into the mottled, grey-brown skin of the teradon's shoulder.

That was enough to enrage a creature that clearly had boundless anger issues already. It opened its foul mouth to roar at us, a sound that would have made an adult silverback gorilla piss itself, and it hunched forward, pulling itself out of the constraining transport cage. Its large, bony frill, which extended from the top of its head, scraped across the roof as it fought its way free.

"Open fire!" I roared, pointing at the creature with the tip of my naginata, and Grizz, Stephanos, and Arrin obliged. Bane had already disappeared from of sight, leaving Lydia and myself at the front, bracing our feet and ready to take the charge.

"Shield!" Grizz shouted to me, slipping his shield off his back and throwing it to me in a motion so slick, it looked unnatural. I caught it, and by the time I'd shrugged it into place, he'd fired another two arrows at the creature.

It pushed itself the rest of the way out of the container, screaming in fury. Five arrows stuck out of its mottled hide. A singed patch of skin on one shoulder remained the only sign of the barrage our ranged fighters had unleashed so far.

It straightened to its full height, standing over twelve feet at the shoulder, and unfurled its arms. Unaccustomed to the freedom, it began crouching low and straightened as it screamed with fury and hatred at all those around it. The sound seemed to come up from its feet to reverberate through the air.

I hastily used Examine and read the details as quickly as I could:

Teradon Male
Teradons are solitary hunters that live in caves on the lower slopes of mountain ranges. Except in mating season, they will kill and eat any trespassers unlucky enough to stumble into their territory. The one exception to this is when a female in heat is found within the range; then the males will congregate, attacking and killing each other until only one remains. In this way, the strongest bloodlines are promoted, resulting in a species that no sensible hunter would face.

Teradon males are distinguishable from the females by the larger tusks, bone plates that cover the top of the head, which extend back to protect the neck with a spiked frill, and the larger primary arms. These primary arms are divided into a "gripping" and "crushing" pair, much as is seen in crustaceans.

Weaknesses: This teradon has been kept in a magically induced sleep for many months, during which its musculature has atrophied, leaving it vulnerable to slicing and crushing damage.

Resistances: Teradons have thick skin, resulting in resistances to piercing damage.

Level: 39

Health: 87,000/87,000

Mana: 100/100

The teradon was a six-limbed monstrosity.

Now that it stood fully upright, it was clear the beast was as comfortable walking upright as using its legs and larger, upper arms to run. It was heavily muscled and covered in mottled, grey-brown skin with darker patches. The upper arms ended in short, heavy hands that were a mix of paws and true hands, the right being much heavier muscled than the left, while the left had longer, more numerous fingers.

The significant difference in limbs made me think that the left hand restrained the teradon's victim, while the right grabbed on and crushed it. A secondary, smaller pair of arms were tucked in close to its chest, like those of a T-rex. The head, with its impressive, armored frill that made me think of a ceratops, added another five feet in height, resulting in a seventeen-foot-tall behemoth roaring at us.

"Well, fuck," I muttered. "Looks like a bad time to be an archer!" I called out to the team. "Teradons have really thick skin; that's why it's just getting pissed off with the arrows! We need to crush or slice it. This thing has an *insane* amount of health!"

"Great!" Grizz said, grunting as he hauled back on his bow and let loose, shouting, "Pierce!"

The arrow flashed across the space and sank into the creature's stomach almost all the way up to the fletching.

"What the hell was that?" Stephanos gaped at him, shocked.

"Class skill! Join the legion, and I'll teach you when we get out of here!" Grizz called, a big smile breaking his bearded face as he released arrow after arrow.

"Think that's good?" Arrin shouted, his hands weaving in arcane patterns as his face lit with glee. "Watch this!"

Instead of the usual three, a full spread of six Magic Missiles appeared before him, spreading out and flashing across the intervening distance with a shrill whine of displaced air. They hit hard, less than a second apart, and exploded, sending blood flying from the teradon's belly.

Unfortunately, the missiles didn't penetrate deep, and it seemed like we'd had all the free hits we were going to get. The beast slammed forward, the impact of its change from two legs to four rumbling through the sand.

It screamed and rushed us, head down and frill up, using it to deflect another arrow from Grizz and Stephanos each and send them clattering into the sand, broken and useless.

Oracle flashed to the side, hands blurring as she built her spell, having been momentarily lost in amazement at the creature. I sprinted to the right, Lydia running to the left as the teradon slammed into the door we'd just entered through.

A loud *boom* shattered the air as a red, magical dome flashed to life, throwing the teradon back. The dome appeared to surround the arena, keeping those of us inside from damaging it, but it had a secondary effect that made me grin….

When it flared into existence, a particularly acerbic spectator, who'd reached through the bars all the way to his shoulder and had been trying to grab at Oracle, screamed as his arm was cut off by the shield at the elbow. His forearm and hand dropped limply to the sand, twitching.

The teradon screamed at the red dome as it died away, then sniffed and ran over to the severed forearm. The lower secondary arms reached out and scooped it up, passing it up to the jaws. The creature bit down, filling the air with the snapping of bones as it greedily fed.

The injured spectator screamed, falling from the bars and disappearing into the crowd. The surrounding spectators jeered and laughed, throwing things into the pit at the teradon and us, until the announcer spoke up.

"Remember, fans, putting anything through the bars and into the arena is done at your own risk; as is attending!" he said in his best sports announcer voice. I spat on the sand as I cautiously watched the teradon. It seemed annoyed by the arrows, but beyond that, even the arrow buried deep in its gut was ignored as an irritation, rather than an injury. A second barrage of Magic Missiles flashed through the air and hammered into its side, only making it grunt. Arrin swore, swaying slightly on his feet.

Lydia rushed in, slamming her mace down into its left leg at the knee, then darting back as it turned to face her. In the same moment, Oracle finished her casting, dropping our mana at a hell of a rate as she released a Stunning Lightning Bolt that crackled and bathed the Arena in blue-white luminosity as it covered the distance between her and the creature.

The lightning crackled across its skin, dancing from the tips of the horns and bone protrusions. The creature screamed in fury. Turning and facing Oracle full on, it took a deep breath and locked its mouth shut, slamming the air out through what I'd taken to be its nose.

A gap opened wide on its face, and the air seemed to explode as a wave of massive overpressure and sound slammed into us. People were suddenly falling from the bars, screaming and holding their heads. I staggered, seeing the rest of the team doing the same, our weapons forgotten as we tried to cover ears and heads. As Oracle fell from the air, stunned, I pitched onto the sand, landing on all fours. Grunting, I forced my eyes up, finding the creature still locked in place and feeling the air quake as it continued its sonic attack.

You have been Stunned!

Teradon's Stunning Scream has hit you for 30 points of damage, plus another 10 points per second.

You are now silenced, deaf, and disoriented.

This effect will last for 30 seconds..........

Blood spattered the sand all around me, and I touched my hands to my face. Feeling wetness, I lifted them before my eyes. Evidently, I was bleeding from my ears, nose, and eyes. I shook my head again, forcing myself to grab for my naginata.

I managed to close my fingers around it and searched for Oracle. Her arms shook as she weakly attempted to get up, obviously out of it, and I couldn't imagine how powerful the full force of the attack had to be, if it had affected her barely corporeal form that strongly.

I watched her, as she gazed around with unfocused eyes, her skin white, her form fading as the sonic attack continued to blast through her, and I felt her contact through our bond.

"Aegis!" That was all she said, but I felt her pain, and I knew what she wanted, what she needed.

I reached down deep, ignoring little things like the fact I was bleeding from at least half my orifices, and I gritted my teeth, forcing the gift from Tuthic'Amon into place. Thankfully, it activated immediately, granting me a second of clarity that it wasn't affected by the Silenced debuff.

Oracle's life withered away as I stood, and I sprinted forward, covering the distance to the still-motionless creature in seconds. My naginata blazed to life as I flooded mana into it, unable to form coherently into a spell pattern, but my rage refused to allow less.

The teradon shook as it channeled its sonic attack, but it clearly saw me coming and broke off the attack a second too late.

I drove the glowing blade deep into one side of its face, the blade punching through the smaller bone plates that surrounded the cavity that had been channeling the sonic blast. The haft reverberated with the crunch as I punched through thin bones and cartilage, stabbing out of the far side, before my headlong rush brought me close enough.

I jumped, planting both feet on the teradon's cheek and using my embedded naginata for leverage, I straightened my back and legs. The blade tore free, ripping literally half its face off in the process.

The teradon screamed and shook its head as blood fountained out, and the world seemed to come back into focus for everyone as I dropped to the floor. The status debuffs fell away from thirty seconds left, to five, then four, counting down.

I rolled away, barely dodging a huge paw-hand-thing that slammed into the sand where I'd just been. The teradon continued screaming, spinning, and stomping, its thick, stubby tail slamming down into the sand as a desperate attempt to drive us all back.

Forcing myself to my feet and staggering, I scanned the arena for my team, barely hearing the announcer above me as I fixated on Oracle. I rushed toward her, correcting my direction as I wove from side to side....

"Wow! Talk about a rush, people! Just imagine; what you felt there was the ten percent that made it through the shield...now you know why they're having problems...Imagine what that felt like unshielded!"

I ignored him, dropping clumsily to the sand next to Oracle's tiny form as she blinked up at me, so pale and weak-looking. I growled, scooping her up and holding her close to my chest. "Bane!"

He immediately appeared on the far side of the creature, driving both sets of daggers into its side and ripping them in different directions. The long, bloody gashes drew another scream from the teradon as the stealthy Mer vanished. The enraged creature spun around and stomped the ground where he'd been, before rising to its full height and bellowing in rage, lashing out with both sets of arms as it stood.

Lydia ran in, smashing her mace into its left knee before backing up again, as Grizz ran forward to slash his sword across the back of its right leg. The teradon screamed and turned for him when a trio of Magic Missiles slammed into the teradon's ruined face and caused it to stagger back.

I took a deep breath, trying to cast Battlefield Triage on Oracle, but it failed to latch on, and she shook her head weakly.

"I'm part of you, Jax. I'll be okay, but I can't heal like that. I need time, and for you to heal; that'll help me," she breathed, reaching up to my face as Bane appeared next to me.

"Protect her, no matter what. Keep her safe!" I commanded Bane, carefully passing Oracle to him. He nodded solemnly, sheathing two of his blades and protectively gathering her to his chest as she protested feebly.

I forced myself to ignore her, lifting my naginata and glaring at the teradon as the others attacked it. Stephanos continuously hammered so many arrows into it that it was starting to resemble a pincushion.

"Arrin!" I shouted. "Lightning! Lydia, Grizz, keep him facing that way!"

I sucked in a deep breath, then forced lightning into the naginata, flaring it to life as I started running. Speeding across the distance between me and that fucker in a handful of seconds, I jumped over the stumpy tail.

I landed high on its ass, where the tail flowed up to join with the back of its legs. Then I kept going, running a further few feet up its back before leaping up and driving the bladed tip of my naginata down as hard as I could into its upper back. The spell discharged into it as I let go with my left hand and grabbed onto a ridged plate. Using it for leverage, I began wrenching the blade from side to side, opening the wound up.

It screamed, twisting around and trying to hit me, but I still managed to drive the tip into what I'd been looking for. The smell of cooking meat and sizzling blood as it pumped over the white-hot, glowing blade of my naginata made my teeth curl back in a snarl. The thought of Oracle being hurt only drove me harder.

The teradon screamed and convulsed as the tip of my naginata slipped between two shifting bones and cut into its thick spinal cord, sending electrical arcs through its nervous system and firing its muscles into uncontrolled spasms. The violent convulsions hurled me off as the beast collapsed to the side, sending sand flying in all directions.

I rolled back to my feet with a hand from Grizz as I swept up my naginata.

"You all right, boss?" he asked, grinning at me. I nodded, spitting some blood onto the sand from a busted lip I didn't even remember getting. "I'm supposed to be the mad one here!" he said, grinning happily. "First time in ages Augustus isn't going to be shouting at me. I love this team!"

"Let's finish it," I snarled, rushing at the downed teradon. Extending my naginata, I drove it deep into the same wound I'd already opened. It had collapsed on its side, its legs and secondary arms lying motionless as it tried to figure out what had happened to its body.

I delved deeper, driving the blade in, switching from stabbing to digging. I worked the weapon steadily: stab in deep, wrench it to the side, pull it out and in again, rinse and repeat.

The fight had gone from possibly lethal to almost mundane in seconds as the crippled creature thrashed and howled, trying to catch us.

Lydia battered its two upper arms, steadily smashing her mace into the elbows. Crunches and cracking sounds filled the air as she systematically broke the appendages, leaving it defenseless, while Grizz chopped at the lower legs, cutting great swaths of skin and muscle free as he searched for an artery.

Stephanos had moved in closer and was firing almost point-blank into sensitive points, leveling his archery almost by cheating as he hunted out weaknesses, and Arrin…well, that crazy bastard was concentrating like nothing else, building a layered, overcharged Magic Missile that fired six darts, one after the other, to blast the wound I'd been working on as I stepped back to catch my breath.

When I could see again, after wiping away the teradon's blood that had coated my face, the white of bone glistened, and behind that, the pulsing organs I'd been searching for. I changed my angle of attack, charged my naginata with fire this time. Pushing it forwards, I cut through the muscles around the bone, sliding deep until the tip punched through the beating heart beneath.

The teradon let out a grunt, then a soft wheeze…then died. Notifications went crazy in the corner of my vision as I pulled the blade out and straightened up, eyeing the spectators.

Above the common seats, where people hung like monkeys from the bars, were a ring of booths for the rich patrons. As I looked from face to face, seeing Mal raise a beer in salute in passing, I saw what I knew must be the Copper Ghost Gang representatives.

Three of them stood stoically, arms crossed, with blank copper masks covering their faces, and they glared at me in unbridled hatred.

I smirked up at them, then extended my middle finger and saluted them with it before leading my team out of the arena through the now-open door to our rest area.

Bane blurred into view ahead of me, Oracle sitting on his shoulder. I shook my head at her, reaching out and feeling the pressure of tiny feet as she stepped onto my hand, before lifting her to my shoulder.

"Thanks, Bane. I knew she'd be safe with you," I said, taking a seat and looking for the healer. "Nerin, what can you do for Oracle?" I asked as she came to me, casting spells and looking at details that only she could see.

"I need some time," she muttered.

I nodded, turning to Arrin.

"Come on, then, mate. Let's get a bit of practice in with the healing. Hit everyone with a Cleanse, then Strength of the Seasons. I know it's not the best for healing wounds, but it'll help, and we can level it up faster. Sooner we can evolve it, the better," I said, turning to Lydia, who was the closest in the room, and following my own advice by starting with her.

"You've got an hour before the next round," Augustus said, looking us over. "Make sure you use any potions you need, because you can't afford to go in there without being in top form."

There was a weary chorus of assent from the group. Stephanos took the opportunity to sit with Grizz and Yen, Miren following, as they began to discuss class abilities that apparently unlocked for some legionnaires at level fifteen. I passed Arrin three mana potions, and he grinned, knowing what I wanted.

"I'll make sure I get everyone," he said.

I smiled appreciatively, then turned back to Oracle.

"Are you okay?" I asked her, casting the pair of spells in short succession on Bane. Finishing him off, I collapsed back in my seat, leaving Arrin to do everyone else.

"I will be. I'm just tired now. I've never felt anything like that," she said, pushing her hair back and looking up at Nerin while being examined.

"And I hope you don't again," Nerin scolded, looking over the information her spells were providing her. "Looks like your physical structure is okay, though the sonic attack somehow interacted with the matrix of your bond. I've never had the chance to examine someone bonded like you are before, so I can't tell you more right now. Best thing for you both is rest and healing, food and drink. I'd order a week of bed rest, if I thought you'd listen."

"I'm up for a week in bed with Oracle," I said, trying to keep my face straight, as Oracle laughed and smacked my chest with one tiny hand.

"I said *rest*," Nerin said. "Men are always idiots."

She sighed, shaking her head and hitting me with a heal powerful enough that it locked me in place. My muscles went rigid for a handful of seconds before the sensation passed, and I slumped, gasping as I caught my breath.

"What the hell was that?" I growled at her, and she snorted.

"Rapid cure-all, boy. It's an advanced healing spell, not something either of you are ready to learn for a while, but it has its uses, despite being overly expensive in the mana cost. Now, you need to rest; I'll get food sorted out. Sit here, do nothing, and maybe I'll let you go back out and fight when the gong goes."

"You'll 'let' me?" I asked, lifting one eyebrow.

"You want me to be your resident healer?" she asked pointedly, and I nodded slowly. "Then when I speak, you listen; or you can go to hell, and I'll go to Narkolt. So, what's it going to be?" she asked.

"I'll rest," I agreed sourly, leaning back and trying to ignore the satisfaction on her face as well as the grins from the legionnaires.

"Time to check those notifications," Oracle whispered, gesturing to me. They popped up, box after box flooding my vision.

Congratulations!

You have killed the following:

- 1x Olivan the Whip, level 15 for a total of 4,160xp
- 1x Gromesh the Orc, level 21 for a total of 12,000xp

Progress to level 16 stands at 44,309/165,000

*

Your Quest from the Goddess Jenae: Reclaimer has updated….

You were offered a Quest to reclaim the lost imperial artifacts from the location known as the Emporium. For each Golem reclaimed, you receive 5,000xp; for each functioning facility brought under your control, you receive 10,000xp; and for each magical artifact retrieved, you receive 100xp.

Claim the Emporium: 1/1

Reclaim the Golems: 11/13

Reclaim and Activate Facility: 0/1 – Damaged, current condition 7/100% (Facility will shift to your control once fully operational)

Retrieve Magical Artifacts: 57/80

Reward: Experience, Golem Genesis Chamber, Mining Facility

*

Congratulations!

Your team has killed the following:

- 1x Teradon, level 39 for a total of 25,000xp

Progress to level 16 stands at 69,309/165,000

*

Congratulations!

Through hard work and perseverance, you have increased your stats by the following:

Agility +1

Dexterity +1

Endurance +1

Continue to train and learn to increase this further….

I pulled up my character sheet quickly, grinning as I saw how close I was getting to level sixteen and looked over the progress to my next stat increases as well.

Name: Jax				
Titles: Strategos: 5% boost to damage resistance, Fortifier: 5% boost to defensive structure integrity, Champion of Jenae: One search for hidden knowledge every 24 hours				
Class: Spellsword > Justicar > Champion of Jenae			**Renown**: Imperial Scion, Lord of Dravith	
Level: 15			**Progress**: 69,309/165,000	
Patron: Jenae, Goddess of Fire and Exploration			**Points to Distribute**: 0 **Meridian Points to Invest**: 0	
Stat	Current points	Description	Effect	Progress to next level
Agility	44	Governs dodge and movement	+340% maximum movement speed and reflexes, (+10% movement in darkness, -20% movement in daylight)	23/100
Charisma	23	Governs likely success to charm, seduce, or threaten	+130% success in interactions with other beings	63/100
Constitution	38	Governs health and health regeneration	740 health, regen 46.2 points per 600 seconds, (+10% regen due to soul bond, -20 health due to soul bond, each point invested now worth 20 health)	21/100
Dexterity	32	Governs ability with weapons and crafting success	+220% to weapon proficiency, +22% to the chances of crafting success	13/100
Endurance	30	Governs stamina and stamina regeneration	600 stamina, regen 20 points per 30 seconds, (each point invested now worth 20 stamina)	13/100
Intelligence	33	Governs base mana and number of spells able to be learned	310 mana, spell capacity: 19 (17 + 2 from items), (-20 mana due to soul bond)	93/100
Luck	20	Governs overall chance of bonuses	+10% chance of a favorable outcome	71/100
Perception	25	Governs ranged damage and chance to spot traps or hidden items	+150% ranged damage, +15% chance to spot traps or hidden items	36/100
Strength	28	Governs damage with melee weapons and carrying capacity	+18 damage with melee weapons, +180% maximum carrying capacity	53/100
Wisdom	35 (30)	Governs mana regeneration and memory	+250% mana recovery, 1.75 points per minute, 250% more likely to remember things, -50% mana regeneration until mana manipulation reaches level 10	33/100

I quickly pulled up the last notification as well, cheering silently when I saw how much it had improved.

Naginata		**Further Description** *Yes/No*	
Damage:		24-40 + 33	
Details:		This two-handed weapon was built from a combination of modern Earth techniques and traditional Japanese skills, creating a weapon that is truly deadly in the hands of a skilled user. Enhanced; This weapon has been enhanced through silverbright and has absorbed some of the souls of its victims. Current capacity: 33/100 **Bonus ability:** Magical infusion: Casting your spells through this weapon will infuse it with that ability for the duration of channeling and cause X damage where X is equal to the damage done by the cast spell….	
Rarity:	**Magical:**	**Durability:**	**Charge:**
Unique	Yes	85/100	N/A

Congratulations!

Your Evolving Weapon has reached an important milestone in claiming the souls of its victims, and you can now choose a secondary Bonus Ability!

Increased Capacity:
You choose to convert the essence of the souls most recently captured into increasing the weapon's ability to absorb and feed on the souls of its victims, rising from 100 to 150. This will lower the current capacity from 33/100 to 0/150, reducing its current damage done from 24-40 + 33 to 24-40 + 0.

Soul Stealer:
Your weapon is now more efficient at stealing the souls of its victims, and has a higher chance to absorb them, even when you're not channeling into it at the point of death! You will have a 10% chance to steal any souls released when your weapon deals the killing blow without infusion, and an 80% chance when infused!

Elemental Destruction:
Your weapon has reached the stage of developing its first elemental ability: Elemental Destruction! Once per 24 hours, you can activate this ability to send an element-powered shockwave outward in a radius of 20m, which will enact the maximum weapon damage + X where X is the distance in meters from you, dropping in power over distance. (Example: three targets surrounding you at a range of 5m would each be hit with 40(max weapon) + 33 (Bonus damage) + 15 (remaining distance to edge of AOE) for a total of 88 damage)

Choose carefully, as once made, this choice cannot be undone.

"Damn…" I muttered, rubbing my chin. "Okay, time to think logically…hmm." Considering the most tempting first, Elemental Destruction was awesome. I assumed it meant if I planted the butt in a pool of water, it would do water damage, or planting it into the soil would cause earth damage. While it was cool and would be amazing in a fight when it was just me, it didn't say anything about excluding allies from the effect, so it had to go.

Next was Soul Stealer. Even though it would be great to get extra souls, and thus fuel the damage I could do if I filled it up with, say, goblin souls, I couldn't see the benefit, as opposed to creatures like the SporeMother. That being said, I had no idea if it made a difference, beyond a half-remembered description of the initial evolution….

I knew what I had to do, sadly. I chose the long game over the short, picking Increased Capacity, as I could only hope the extra fifty souls equating to fifty damage would be worth it in the end. It'd be a hell of a change, if it was.

The drop from thirty-three extra damage all the way back to one could suck my nuts, though.

I dismissed the confirmation of my choice prompt and settled back, inspecting Oracle surreptitiously as I started eating the food brought in by some of Mal's staff. It wasn't much, mainly fruits and a light porridge, which made me think longingly of the bacon sandwich I'd had the other day. God, it had been amazing, but still.

I ate my entire plate, watching as Oracle slowly recovered, looking healthier and happier with each passing minute, until Augustus, watching the sandglass in the corner, announced the time.

"Ten minutes to the next round, people! Get your asses up and let's do a warmup!" That comment fully earned the filthy looks and grumbles it received.

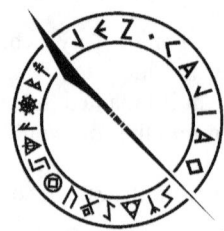

CHAPTER TWENTY-FOUR

Most of the legionnaires left the room to give us a little space, which we used to warm up a bit, although I spent most of the time in silent conversation with Oracle to make sure she was okay to keep fighting. I hated the idea that she could be hurt; as incorporeal as she usually was, I'd gotten it into my head that she couldn't be hurt.

Now, knowing that she wasn't invincible freaked me the hell out. She'd explained it a dozen ways, but I still didn't really understand how she was corporeal, then not. She could slip through water without leaving a ripple but couldn't do the same with stone, and so on. I just gave up and accepted that it was one of those things that just were the way they were.

Magic made my damn head hurt at times.

"Who's up next?" I asked, getting a grin from Augustus.

"Night's Followers. Word is, they hired a team of professionals, likely a team familiar with the arena."

"Either way, we're gonna fuck them up." I shrugged in my armor and felt it move. "Remind me when this is all over, I need some good armor from the legion armorers," I commented, and Augustus grinned.

"Once you've tried the legion, you never go back."

"That's what she said," I said automatically.

The room went silent for a minute, then laughter burst out all around me. As the doors opened, and I passed Augustus on the way out, I got a fist bump from him, making me feel a lot more at home.

We marched out onto the sand, the announcer starting up his inane chatter. I tuned him out, scanning the doors and wondering which one they'd come out of. When their door did finally open, it was to our left, and the team oriented quickly to face it.

"Bane, you're on overwatch; keep an eye on us and fuck up any stealth types who try anything. Stephanos, Grizz, either wing; fill the fuckers full of arrows. Arrin, middle behind Lydia and me; I want to see you ruin their day, my friend. Lydia, you and I are tanking; take the blows and smash them down, give our people time to kill them all," I ordered as the opposing team marched out onto the arena.

Two of them stealthed and vanished immediately. The remaining two split up, moving to stand about three meters apart. They were dressed in heavy black armor from head to toe, matte plates of metal that seemed to absorb the light, with faint red glows emanating from the joints. The wearers appeared to be the same height and build; both of them bore a heavy axe in one hand with a massive tower shield strapped on the other arm.

A golden tree with a blood-red crown held in the branches and a body swinging from a rope on the outermost branch was embossed on the shields, each a mirror image of the other.

"Shit," Grizz muttered. "Check them out, boss, quick," he advised, and I triggered my Examine spell.

> **Torin and Terin: the Twins of Destruction**
> Twin brothers Torin and Terin Alderbright were taken at a young age and trained for the arena by the Night's Followers Gang. The twins were inducted into a life that has convinced them that their only worth is in killing those whom the gang decides are enemies. Now, at the age of seventeen, they have grown to glory in the kill.
>
> The brothers are magically linked, granting them awareness of the other at all times, and have fought larger groups and beasts into submission many times.
>
> **Weaknesses**: 25% weakness to magic, reduced to 5% with intact armor. The brothers have invested heavily in their link, relying on magical armor to protect them from the weakness to magic this has produced.
>
> **Resistances**: Heavy armor reduces piercing, slashing, and crushing damage by 35%
>
> **Level**: 20 - linked
>
> **Health**: 10,000/10,000 - linked
>
> **Mana**: 180/180 - linked

"Is it the twins?" Grizz asked. I nodded, informing the others of the prompt's details.

"Shit, I've heard of them," he said, blowing his lips out in thought. The twins stood statue still, waiting. "They've spent a fortune on their armor. It's seriously good shit, and it lets them share a health pool, somehow, so any damage done to one is halved and spread across the pair. They've also got some class skills, a taunt that they can both use, an area-of-effect damage,…something about darkness as well, but I can't remember what." Grizz summarized for us as we watched the arena, waiting for the other side to make the first move.

"Okay, people, let's wait and see. Give them a minute," I said, reaching out mentally to Oracle.

"Remember that sneaky bastard of a rogue in the tower?"

"Of course…?"

"Remember how we flooded the area, trying to catch him in the water?"

"And Bob killed him before we could hit him with lightning!"

"Exactly. Get up as high as you can and start soaking the sand around us. Those stealthy fuckers are going to try to take us out, but wet sand will show footprints easier, and then you fuck them with lightning."

"Okay! I…I miss Bob."

"I do too. Let's kill these dicks, and we're one step closer to going home, Oracle. And then let's keep him closer to us after this."

"Deal!" I smiled at her enthusiasm and brought everyone else up to speed.

"Oracle's going to see what she can do to take care of the rogue problem, so keep an eye out for them. When they're visible, hit those bastards with everything. Lydia, stick with me. We wait them out, see if we can whittle down the numbers first." My team confirmed with a round of acknowledgements, and we settled into formation.

The twins were clearly unused to people who just watched them, and they slowly looked at each other before starting to move, stepping closer to the far wall, expecting that we wouldn't be able to flank them, while the rogues did…what rogues do.

Oracle was summoning fountains left and right, and I started doing the same, quickly ringing our position. After a minute, though, the sand slowly began to absorb the water, and I swallowed, annoyed with this issue in the plan. We'd have to refresh the fountains constantly, unless…

I concentrated, staring at a fixed space in the middle of the arena between our two groups, willing myself to pay attention to the details, the shifting of sand, as the assholes all around us hanging on the bars and screaming made the very earth shake.

There! Off to the left, just outside the range of the oldest fountain on that side, there was something wrong. Sand shifted one way, instead of the other, and I reacted, a fountain blooming in the path of the shimmering, red-tinted form that suddenly became clear as my enhanced Perception and meridians combined together.

The water shot up, crystal clear and refreshing, until it hit the stealthed form of the rogue who was sneaking slowly across the damp sand, trying to be invisible….

As soon as I'd turned, Oracle had sensed my focus, and instead of the fountain she'd been about to cast, she started building Stunning Lightning Bolt, channeling a full third of my remaining mana into it.

The rogue cursed as his stealth was broken, dashing forwards straight for Stephanos, only to have his target shouldered aside by Grizz, who fired an arrow at him.

He dove aside, rolling smoothly and coming to his feet, a glowing green vial held tight in his left hand. The rogue pulled his arm back, cocked, aimed, then screamed as Oracle hit him full in the face with her spell.

He convulsed, muscles locking tight, and the vial shattered under his sudden, desperate grip. The mixture immediately reacted with the air, and with an audible *wumph,* the area around him for a good three meters vanished into a green cloud. The screams emitting from the rogue went up a notch as he became the center of his own trap.

Grizz backed away, coughing and retching, and Oracle diverted with my blessing, casting Cleanse on him even as he pulled the most powerful healing potion he had from his belt, downing it through lips that were already melting.

He fell to the floor, screaming, half the potion down, and the other half splashing across his face as his skin began to slough away. Oracle dove for him, hammering him again and again with Cleanse, while I called to Arrin.

"Help her!" I snapped, well aware we'd just lost two, and possibly three of our team from the fight. Even though we'd taken one of them down, we'd gone from seven against four to four against three.

"Everyone else watch out for that rogue—" I started to say, as the twins abandoned their slow and steady retreat in favor of sprinting full speed at us.

"Lydia! With me! Stephanos, fuck up that rogue when the bastard shows his face!" I snarled, digging in and sprinting at the oncoming brothers, Lydia lumbering alongside me.

"Come on, yer DICKS!" she screamed when we were halfway across the arena, and her voice changed, reverberating deeper. The last word seeming to hang in the air, repeating over and over, growing fainter as the echoes died away.

To me, it just sounded weird, but the effect on the brothers? The pair of them both stumbled, changing their focus from one opponent each, to both sprinting dead at her, as though driven insane by the need to close with her.

"It's her fucking taunt," I muttered, my voice rendered tinny by the legion helmet that Augustus had refused to take back with the rest of the gear.

A scream rose from behind us, and I flinched before refusing to be distracted. Instead, I swung my shield around to cover my chest and jumped. Striking the brother on the right full on his shield, I sent him staggering off-balance from the unexpected assault. Braced as I was, I bounced off, landing hard and stumbling slightly, stabbing out at the one who had closed with Lydia and was hammering at her shield with his axe. I stabbed into the gap, aiming between his lower leg and knee. The tip of my naginata penetrated, but it was quickly smashed aside by his shield as Lydia's taunt wore off. His axe smashed down hard on her shield and drove her back a step.

I pulled back, set myself, and lashed out, aiming for the back of his neck. But just as I started to lunge, a siren's call of fury rose behind me, and my blood exploded with hatred.

I couldn't stop myself as I spun, ignoring the target I'd been focused on. The tip of my blade hit his helmet a glancing blow instead, as I ran at the other brother who had climbed to his feet. His armor glowed a fierce red as I locked eyes with him, screaming my defiance and hatred, and ran forward.

I'd taken three steps when I felt Oracle in my mind.

"Aegis!" she screamed, and my magic responded. The ability flared, and the red mist lifted, just in time to reveal the axe heading for me, with my own shield and naginata splayed out of place.

"Mana Overdrive!" I snarled, and the world seemed to slow suddenly, as though caught in molasses. I glared at the brother before me, Lydia's incoming scream of rage seeming to doppler into the distance as I read the confidence and bloodlust in my opponent, right until my right foot moved faster than he could see. I twisted at the hips, crouching slightly over my left leg, before pushing off as hard as I could and planting my right foot on his braced left leg.

Using the upward momentum, I brought my shield around to deflect his swinging axe. His shield was out of position, due to expecting me to be out of control, and I exploited that to my advantage. With his leg as a springboard, I leaped into a combination of a pole vault technique, the Fosbury Flop, and my insane Agility to brace my naginata in the armor joint around his neck. Releasing my shield, I grabbed the other end of the naginata with my left hand as it passed under me and across his throat.

I pulled with all my strength, and as I flipped over him, landing feet first, back-to-back with my target, I twisted, "popping" my hips as I'd been taught. With a combination of judo and insane, overpowered rage and mana-fueled muscle, I flipped the man in full plate armor over my head, sending him crashing head-first into the floor.

I felt as much as heard his neck snap as his enormous weight impacted the sandy floor, drowned out by the scream of rage and loss that rose in the air behind me as I staggered and fell, my back absolutely fucked by that insanity.

I grunted as I collapsed forward, legs twitching. As I frantically fought to roll over, I tried not to scream, sensing the second brother closing in.

I managed to get my head around in time to see him running past Lydia as she swung her mace low. He'd lashed out high, seeing her as an obstacle and wanting her out of his way, rather than aiming. She deflected it with her shield and swung for the fences, obliterating his knee and sending him crashing to the floor.

"Motherfucker!" Lydia screamed, dropping her mace and shaking the hand that had held it. Furious, she brought her shield overhead, slamming it down edge-first onto his outstretched right wrist, wrenching a scream from his throat as she shattered the bones. She moved fast, shifting her weight and kicking him in the head, once, twice, and a third time, before curb-stomping down on his neck where his helmet had ridden up enough to expose it.

I felt the crunch as he died and saw the floating "death's-head" rise from his corpse. With the second twin down, I shifted my attention, catching sight of Stephanos drawing back one final time on his Drow bow and sending an arrow flashing across the arena to take the last rogue in the forehead, dropping him to writhe in death.

"I need more mana!" Oracle screamed at me in our mindlink, and I reached down, my wrenched back making my hands spasm as I tried to get the potions out. Before I could try again, Lydia was there, pulling first a health then a mana potion from the pouch at my waist. I shot her a grateful look as she popped the tops off and poured them into my open mouth.

The health potion kicked in first, nearly drowning me when the pain of rapid healing made me gasp just as Lydia poured the mana potion into my mouth. But I managed to get most of it down, despite choking slightly.

My mana jumped, then I immediately started vanishing again, as Oracle worked to heal Grizz. Grabbing Lydia's hand, I twisted around and hissed in pain as she pulled me upright.

I searched the arena, making sure they were all dead, and limped as quickly as I could to Grizz and the others. Bane was still nowhere to be seen.

I looked down at the legionnaire, gasping as I saw the damage. His previously handsome face was almost burned away to the bone, and he was moaning through the pain as bubbles of blood burst over where his lips had been.

"Fuck!" I grunted. "Get him to Nerin…NOW!" I grabbed his arm and started to drag him to our rest area door, while Oracle worked to stabilize him.

I nearly passed out from the extra load of trying to haul the massive legionnaire, but suddenly, the others were there. Bane pushed me aside, lifting Grizz and rushing him from the sand, with Oracle still standing on his chest and channeling Battlefield Triage as they went.

The announcer crowed about our victory behind us as we left the arena, but I ignored him. The need to lash out from my feeling of helplessness at my friend's desperate state made me want to climb up and rip the fucker from his nice, safe spot and beat him to death in front of his patrons.

The door slammed shut behind us as Nerin and Grizz's brothers and sisters surrounded him. We were shoved back, out of necessity and fear for their brother, not out of disrespect, as I forced myself to swallow my feeling of helpless rage. Oracle was better with our magic than I was; I knew it. Nerin was better than *she* was, so the only thing I could do was act as a mana battery.

I sat down, popped two medium potions, and started to meditate, giving Oracle as much as I could, alternating one greater and two medium, or four lesser, depending on what came to hand first.

A terrible twenty minutes followed, but eventually, after seeming years had passed, Nerin ordered Oracle to stop, looking solemnly at Augustus, and then me.

"He's stable," she said, looking and sounding exhausted. "Whatever that poison was, it's horrific. A few seconds longer, and there'd have been nothing I could do. He's not going to be doing much fighting for the next few days, and he'll likely have issues for weeks, but he'll live."

"What about his face?" a pretty, dark-haired female legionnaire asked in a low whisper that carried.

"He'll be fine; I'm more concerned about his stamina at this point," Nerin said.

"Oh, he's got lots of that," the legionnaire reassured her, before going bright red as she realized what she'd said.

Smiles broke out around the room, followed by full-bellied laughter as the tension was released, and I half-fell, half-leaned back, letting out a long breath.

"I need to talk to you, Jax," Bane muttered from beside me. I jumped, immediately sagging back and wincing in pain as my back flared.

Oracle was there in an instant, using our quickly refilling mana pool to repair the damage, and Nerin joined her a second later, pulling a potion out of her bag and downing it before advising Oracle on the best way to fix the injury.

"What is it?" I asked Bane, surprised as he sank to his knees next to me.

"I failed you," he said, shaking his head and barely speaking above a whisper. "All this time, I've been desperately working, spending all day and night in stealth, trying to see anything and everything. The one time you needed me to face the assassins, I failed you. I couldn't find either of them, not even with your gifts."

"What—" I started to say, but he shook his head sadly, interrupting me.

"I failed you. If the rogue hadn't been affected by Lydia's taunt and broken cover, Stephanos would have never been able to kill him. When we return, I will surrender my post to Flux. I will take whatever punishment you or he decrees. I will even be willingly banished. I ask only that you allow me to try to protect you until then, as best I can. I have lost my honor with my failure. I will not—"

"Bullshit," I snapped harshly, reaching out and grabbing his shoulder. "You didn't fail…for fuck's sake, Bane, you're what? Level thirteen?"

He shrugged disconsolately. "Fourteen now."

"Yeah. You're level fourteen and specialized to protect my sorry ass, while you just faced two level-twenty rogues in an arena full of noise and fucking insanity! You didn't fail anyone, let alone me.

"Bane, I forbid you to surrender your post. You've not lost any honor; you've goddamn gained it! You heard what Nerin said. If Grizz had been a few seconds slower in getting to her, he'd be dead. You did that. Don't think I didn't see how much of his weight you were carrying, because I barely had any of it. You barely sleep, watching over me at all hours, because I haven't bothered to recruit a team to help you. It's not your failure, my friend, it's mine!"

I stopped and drew in a deep breath, realizing I'd practically shouted that last bit.

"Look…" I forced my voice back to a calm tone. "I fucked up here. I've made you all do more with less than you ever should have. I don't care about if that's normal for a lord; I know you're all on the ragged edge," I said, looking around the room.

"You've all agreed to uproot your life on my say so. You're *here*, committing all sorts of insanity because I asked you to, and not one of you has complained or asked me if I'm fucking mental, which, let me tell you, I am!" I drew another deep breath, meeting their eyes as I considered my team.

"I'm sorry, all of you. I've asked more and more each day of you, and today, I ask the most. After we win the last fight, we're doing something that will get you branded as traitors if we fail. I'm asking you to risk everything, and yet you've all helped me, smiled, and nodded, instead of telling me to go suck a barrel of dicks. So…thank you."

I walked slowly, painfully, into the center of the room, ignoring Oracle's muttered orders to stay still while she worked.

"Tonight, I ask the most that I've ever asked of anyone. I ask you to stand with me, to turn your back on all you know, all that your Oaths tell you is right. I ask you to walk away from the people you've protected and laid your lives down for. I ask you to follow me, to leave your homes, your lives, and for many of you, your friends and family." I saw the hesitant looks in their eyes, the uncertainty as I laid it all out.

"I ask you to follow me, not because I'm the Scion of the Empire, not because I have a 'blood right' to tell you to do something…. I ask you to follow me because, together, I believe we can fix this. We can raise the legion standard high again. We can walk out into the sunlight, facing everything the world throws at us, because we can bring back the light to these lands.

"We can throw down the false lords, burn the dark temples and the slave markets. We can fucking burn the monsters of the deep out of their holes and make the dark gods tremble in FEAR AT THE MENTION OF OUR NAMES! *We* are the LEGION! You are the LEGION!

"Each and every one of you, legionnaire, ex-slave, crafter, and healer, you are the LEGION OF DRAVITH! We will bring order to this broken land, we will make the wrongs right, and make it so our children can stand tall and safe! YOU WILL NEVER AGAIN BE 'JUST' YOU…. YOU ARE *MY* PEOPLE, AND I AM YOUR BROTHER, YOUR FATHER, *AND* YOUR LORD! I WILL RAISE YOU UP AND MAKE YOU LIVE AGAIN! THIS IS MY VOW!" I screamed into the silent room. One by one, then all at once, they fell to their knees.

"WE ARE THE LEGION!" they bellowed, and I smiled grimly, turning to look at the exit into the arena.

"We are," I whispered, "…and you fuckers don't know what's coming."

CHAPTER TWENTY-FIVE

"Thank you all," I said, looking around the room and making eye contact with each person, one by one. Even Grizz, as shitty as he looked, was watching me. One eye glistened a milky white as his body rested, before Nerin could start on the next round of healing. I knew she was doing everything in her power to bring him back to as close to full strength as she possibly could, despite the limitations of what even magic could do.

"We're with you, Lord Jax," Augustus stated firmly.

I sent him a grateful nod. "I know, and I'm with you. Each and every one of you."

"You might want to rethink that, my lord. Some of these guys have some really bad habits." The female legionnaire who'd made the comment about Grizz's stamina piped up, getting a laugh from the room as I grinned at her.

"Brothers and sisters always do." I chuckled, glancing at the sand glass in the corner next to the door. It was a huge thing with sections marked to show the time, and as Augustus caught the direction of my gaze, he spoke up over the hum of laughter.

"Half an hour, Jax. Half an hour before the next round begins. Grizz can't fight, so you need to pick someone to replace him."

"Miren, Jian…you two sorted things out?" I asked over my shoulder. They looked at each other sheepishly before nodding in unison.

"We have, Jax. It was a…misunderstanding…that's all."

"Good. Augustus, what are we fighting next?" I asked.

"A beast," he replied easily. "The South Side Gang won the roll, leaving the harpies for last. No idea what kind of beast, but Mal sent word that it won't be weak. The only thing he could find out was that the gang is confident they're going to win. Confident enough to go heavily into debt to bet extensively on their side."

"Well, that's just peachy," I muttered. "Miren, you're up on the next fight. I think we're gonna need some ranged options." I turned, hearing the door to the outer corridor open with a clang as Gaion and two men entered the room. Gaion crossed to me quickly, while the other men stacked the shields from the last fight, along with a handful of looted trinkets and potions, off to one side before leaving.

"Lord Jax, Augustus," Gaion said, saluting us both. "Mal suggested you have a look at the gear he's had stripped from the twins. Most of the value is in their armor, but he assumed you wouldn't want to wear something for the first time in a fight, so it's being cleaned and packed away. The shields, personal rings, and trinkets, however, he thought you might make good use of?"

"Good thinking," Augustus commented thoughtfully. "The shields are a tower design, making them a bit more clunky and heavier than ours, but they're also likely to be more valuable and better-made, the legion budgets being what they are," he said grimly.

"Let's have a look, then, and thank you, Gaion. Sorry for being a dick and snapping at you yesterday," I said, extending a hand.

"I'd already forgotten about words said in the heat of the moment, my lord, and I hope you'll do the same?" he said sincerely, grasping my forearm and smiling as I nodded to him. "Excellent; I'll leave you, then. Mal said he doesn't know what the beast is, just that the South Side Gang expect to win, and they're betting heavily."

"Augustus said," I replied.

He nodded once. "Of course, he already sent word. Sorry, it slipped my mind. Good luck, then!" With that, he turned and pushed through people, leaving the room.

I crossed to the pile of gear with Augustus by my side and cast Examine on one of the shields.

Twins' Bulwark		**Further Description** *Yes/No*	
Defense:		25-50	
Details:		This shield is part of a matched pair and armor set, granting additional bonuses when worn with the corresponding parts and with a second bearer of identical design. *Sacrifice* Special Ability: This shield can transfer the impact of a strike to its bonded twin once per day, transmitting all inertia and damage.	
Rarity:	**Magical:**	**Durability:**	**Charge:**
Highly Rare	Yes	76/100	1/1

"Impressive," Augustus said as I read out the description. "I can see a great use for that in a fight."

"Yeah, I'm just glad that fight was over as quickly as it was. It sounds like it could have been a much worse one, had the twins gotten to use their abilities."

I grimaced, moving onto the other items. The second shield was identical to the first, but the rest of the gear was intriguing. The twins had been a bit weird with their gear; everything they had was in sets of two. The pile included six rings, which turned out to be three matching pairs, a pair of earrings, and four potions, two health and two stamina.

Ring of the Healthy Body		**Further Description** *Yes/No*	
Details:		This ring grants +5 to the Constitution of the wearer.	
Rarity:	**Magical:**	**Durability:**	**Charge:**
Uncommon	Yes	93/100	N/A

Ring of the Buffalo		Further Description *Yes/No*	
Details:		This ring grants +3 to the Strength and Endurance of the wearer.	
Rarity:	**Magical:**	**Durability:**	**Charge:**
Rare	Yes	93/100	N/A

Ring of Flowing Movement		Further Description *Yes/No*	
Details:		This ring grants +4 to the Dexterity of the wearer.	
Rarity:	**Magical:**	**Durability:**	**Charge:**
Uncommon	Yes	91/100	N/A

Earring of Awareness		Further Description *Yes/No*	
Details:		This is part of a matched pair that grants an increased awareness of the wearer of the other half. Bonded wearers will feel some small degree of the other's emotions but will mainly feel their position and intentions.	
Rarity:	**Magical:**	**Durability:**	**Charge:**
Highly Rare	Yes	37/100	N/A

The health and stamina potions were both greater potions as well, which was a relief. I passed one of the mana potions to Arrin and kept the other, passing out health and stamina potions to any of the group who needed them, seeing we'd gone through a lot of the healing ones in that last fight.

I passed the two rings of Dexterity to Stephanos and Miren, figuring the ability to fire faster would be a boon, and took one of both the Healthy Body rings and the Buffalo for myself, handing the others to Lydia, along with a shield. I also gave the earrings to Miren and Stephanos, which seemed a little unfair, as Bane and Arrin got nothing, but it seemed like the best way to divide the gear.

With no further preparations to be made, I settled into the nearest chair, drank a little water, and rested before the next fight, quickly bringing up the last fight's notifications and dismissing them as soon as I'd checked my experience.

Congratulations!

You have killed the following:

- 1x Twin of Destruction, Torin Alderbright, level 20 for a total of 7,800xp

A party under your command killed the following:

- 1x Twin of Destruction, Terin Alderbright, level 20 for a total of 7,800xp
- 2x Rogues of various levels for a total of 16,405xp

Total Party experience earned: 24,205xp

As party leader you gain 25% of all experience earned

Progress to level 16 stands at 83,160/165,000

I was over halfway to the next level. Apparently, from level thirty onward, your choices started to come with occasional abilities that were either a development of your personal choices, gifts from the gods, or something else, depending on your own beliefs.

I just knew for sure that I'd get a shitload more stat points, and hell if I wasn't ready for that.

"Hey, Augustus," I said suddenly, as a thought sprang to mind. "Essence cores. I've heard there's a shop in the city that buys them, but that some people collect them. Don't suppose we got one for the teradon, did we?"

"No, some monsters drop them, but that one didn't. Why?" he replied curiously as I grunted in disappointment.

"Damn…ah, well. I've got a use for them, that's all. Could have made a hell of a difference."

"Really?" he asked, surprised, then raised his voice. "Legion!" he commanded, and all conversations stopped as people turned to look at him. "Essence cores—does anyone have one with them?" he asked.

To my amazement, two people held up their hands, then made their way over to us.

The pair handed their cores over, the orbs bound by simple chains to a necklace and wrist strap, and I looked at them in confusion.

"Why—" I started to ask.

"For luck!" Augustus said, grinning. "The cores are only worth a few gold to the stores that will take them, but they rarely pay more than that. They're pretty, and only the strongest monsters have them, so most people keep them as souvenirs. My own are back at the enclave; some bastard stole the one I wear when we were out and about over the last few days," he finished blackly. "Damn pickpockets."

I examined the two cores in stunned amazement for a moment, before Examining them.

Fire Elemental Essence Core		**Further Description** *Yes/No*	
Details:		This essence core was taken from a fire elemental and contains the last remnants of the eons-old creature summoned to this plane. Holding the core makes you feel slightly energized and confident.	
Rarity:	**Magical:**	**Durability:**	**Charge:**
Rare	Yes	96/100	N/A

Air Elemental Essence Core		**Further Description** *Yes/No*	
Details:		This essence core was taken from an air elemental. This creature had wandered the mountains for many years, and holding the core gives you a feeling of peace. Visions of the high places of the realm fill your mind, where the air is thin, cold, and crisp.	
Rarity:	**Magical:**	**Durability:**	**Charge:**
Rare	Yes	97/100	N/A

"Holy shit," I muttered, staring at the small orbs. "I don't know which one, but I think I'm going to need one of these over the next few weeks. Would you be willing to sell them?" I asked the legionnaires, looking from one to the other. "You said they're worth a handful of gold. If I give you a hundred, would that be enough?"

Their eyes bugged out slightly as they gaped at each other in astonishment.

"Seriously, Jax, they're worth nowhere near that," Augustus said, frowning in confusion.

"We'll give them to you for free, my lord, if they'll help," one of the legionnaires offered, smiling.

"Hell, no, you won't," I said. "I'll buy them, and as many as you get. They're more valuable than the nobility let you know. I don't know how to do it for you, but they can be used to unlock abilities. It's a rare thing, from what I understand.

"My own ability to use them is tied to my bloodline and the Pearl I received before coming here, but if I can, I'll find a way to unlock these for all of you. Just don't hold your breath; the person who explained the whole thing to me was a dick and lied whenever he thought it was amusing." I looked up, addressing the entire room.

"For now, I'll ask that any of these you get, you surrender to the treasury, because some have some very nasty side effects. If you use those, you might regret it later. I'd rather we take it slow and careful. If you get any of these, though, I'll pay the same hundred gold for each of them." Nods and grins rose from the people around the room, and Nerin sighed and straightened up, her hand going into the neckline of her dress.

"I also have one, but I'd ask you not take it unless you have to; it's a family heirloom," she said, handing it over.

Angelic Essence Core		**Further Description** *Yes/No*	
Details:		This essence core was recovered from a slain angelic messenger in ages long past, before the gods were banished and when the nephilim walked the realm. Touching the essence core fills you with peace and a need to help others, to grant them strength and serenity.	
Rarity:	**Magical:**	**Durability:**	**Charge:**
Highly Rare	Yes	77/100	N/A

"Damn," I muttered, studying the small marble that rested in the palm of my hand. It glowed with a steady golden light, silvery strands slowly passing from one side to the other, fading and rising to the surface as though through a river of gold.

The core had been carefully wrapped in silvery wire, and tiny onyx flecks were arranged in concentric circles around it. "Nerin, I'd never steal this from you, and I swear I'll do all I can to help you unlock it, if that's what you want to do. But seriously, if you ever, *ever* decide to part with it, I'll take it. You have no idea how valuable this is." I handed it back to her, watching longingly as she slipped it under the fabric of her dress again.

Nerin took her leave, moving back to Grizz and starting to work on his healing again. I lay back, feeling an odd mix of excitement and the need to sleep, the adrenaline rush of two major fights already having taken their toll. I forced myself to relax as much as possible until Augustus ordered us all up and began warming up again.

It was time for round three.

We walked out slowly into the arena, wondering what we'd face this time, spreading out into our customary formation. Lydia and myself advanced at the front, Arrin behind and between us, with Miren and Stephanos flanking either side, facing outward. Bane, as always, vanished into stealth as quickly as we walked onto the sands.

"Okay, people, it's some kind of a beast or monster, but that's all we know, so be ready," I said, watching as many doors at once as I could.

After a long moment, in which I tuned out the droning of the announcer, the door to our far left slowly opened and our opponent strode out onto the sand to join us, radiating confidence.

"What the hell?" I muttered at the sight of a solitary elderly man, wrapped in thick black and red robes and using a staff as a walking support. He took a handful of steps before coming to a halt as I belatedly used Examine on him. We all eyed him warily as he began to pull bones from the various pouches around his waist, dumping them onto the floor in piles.

> **Lich Veriman, Apprentice to the Arch Lich Ghastool.**
> The Arch Lich Ghastool has rarely been seen in recent years, causing many to believe, in error, that he had finally died. Ghastool was an Elven High Necromancer who sold his soul to Nimon in the years following the Cataclysm, in exchange for the knowledge of Lichdom. After centuries of brooding, the lich finally took an apprentice, Veriman, sending it out into the world to secure more subjects for its experiments.
>
> **Weaknesses:** 25% weakness to Fire; crushing attacks inflict double damage, due to brittle bones.
>
> **Resistances:** The undead nature of this creature reduces the effectiveness of slashing and piercing weapons.
>
> **Level**: 27
>
> **Health**: Unknown
>
> **Mana**: Unknown

"Fuck me!" I muttered, my jaw dropping for a second. I swallowed and forced myself out of the confusion. The damn thing was only level twenty-seven? "Okay, people, it's a lich. Fuck me how it qualifies as a 'beast,' but we'll deal with that later. It's level twenty-seven and…"

The lich started snarling and spitting out words in a language I didn't understand, the sounds rising and falling, some clear and reminiscent of Latin, others sounding like nothing a living throat should ever produce.

"Fuck; hit him hard!" I snarled, starting across the sand with Lydia by my side. Arrows flashed overhead and hammered into a magical shield that flared into existence around the robed figure. The strikes made him flinch, but he continued to cast his spell, undeterred.

As we sprinted forward, a Firebolt blasted between us, hitting the shield and bursting. Flames rushed across it before dissipating, and I shouted, "Again, hit him again!"

I was well aware of how much damage a mage could do, given the time to build a powerful spell.

Another volley of arrows impacted the shimmering boundary, followed by another Firebolt, plus a Fireball from Oracle. The shield glowed a dull red for a second before it faded from sight; it'd nearly failed! I grinned, knowing how good my naginata was at dealing with mage shields, and I dug down deeper, pushing myself.

I pounded across the sand, brandishing my naginata and lugging my huge, new, insanely heavy shield. My breathing echoed in my helmet, the cold strain in my breathing as I closed the distance, and my field of vision narrowed to the lich.

I was determined to fuck him up so badly, aiming for the point between his neck and upper chest. I was going to slam my naginata through that spot, right…there.

As Lydia and I closed in, with her trailing me by a few meters due to her heavier armor and lower stats, the ground shook and the lich lifted into the air, cackling as he finished his incantation.

The bones which he'd so liberally strewn about, and which had shaking and vibrating during the chant, now moved, slamming together, and I finally realized what it must look like for others when I reconstructed and altered Bob.

The bones shifted as though dragged by a giant's hands, locking together, tied in place by an ominous, purple-red mist that seemed to take the place of muscles and ligaments to hold the entire form together.

The lich was floating now, standing on a single platform of solid bone that transported it effortlessly through the air as it cackled and waved its arms, manipulating the skeletal form growing between us.

Long bones joined together, becoming two legs, connected to either side of a thick spine that ran down into a tail that curled and flicked at the end. The chest morphed into existence quickly as bones fractured, then locked into place and formed a protective ribcage.

The calcified structure was layered over and over again, surrounding something that glowed with a deep red light. The right arm began to grow, long and thick, ending with a huge mass of bones studded with teeth. There was no hand; instead, it had become a mace of terrifying proportions, jagged and evil-looking.

The left arm, which continued to grow, was entirely made of spines fused together, flicking and twitching. The very end formed into a thick stinger which leaked a red liquid that hissed and spat when it dripped onto the sand below.

Last of all formed the head. It was short, thick, and decidedly inhuman, with long, pointed spines that ringed the crown, enormous eye sockets, and a thick, triangular beak. The eyes were hypnotic red pools that appeared to grow deeper and deeper in the center, falling away into the distance.

"What the hell is that thing!" Arrin screamed from somewhere behind me. I shook myself out of the fugue, shocked, then dove aside, grunting as I plowed a line in the sand. The bone golem's whip arm slammed down and tore up the sand where I'd been a second before. Leaving long furrows as it righted itself, the body tilted in its effort to swing its mace at Lydia.

She dug her feet in, then changed direction, running to the left and ducking as the bony protrusion came whistling after her. Arrows and Firebolts smashed harmlessly into the golem and shattered.

"Get that fucking lich!" I shouted, rolling to my feet and stabbing out. I missed the whip arm as it flashed past me, then jumped aside as it swung for me again.

"It's too big to destroy easily," Oracle said in my mind. ***"It's like Bob, too heavily armored to take down."***

"It'll have a weak spot; we've just got to find it. For now, though, get that fucking lich! If he's down, then it'll die...right?" I asked, getting a sense of agreement from Oracle.

My mana dipped, and a second Fireball flashed across the intervening distance to the Lich. This time, however, it was intercepted by a disc of bone that lifted into the air at the lich's direction. The Fireball exploded, flames washing around the disc but barely touching its shield, which had darkened to a dull red hue.

Arrows whistled through the air. One was stopped by the disc, but the other slammed into the shield and ricocheted off, tearing a scream of pain from someone in the crowd, followed by cruel laughter from others.

Arrin was firing Firebolt after Firebolt, and Oracle was hammering out the Fireballs, while Lydia and I jumped and dove, running from side to side and desperately trying to not be crushed while doing a pathetic amount of blunt force damage to the behemoth.

"It's conjuring more shields!" Arrin shouted, frustration clear in his voice as his Firebolt slammed into a fresh barrier. It was clear that he'd expected the old one to be on the verge of giving out.

I rolled aside to avoid the whip again, then dug my right foot in and kicked out. Pushing myself back upright, I stabbed out with my naginata, grunting with the effort as the tip of the blade punched into the upper thigh of the construction. It wasn't the most vulnerable area, but it was the only part within reach at the time.

I'd channeled my Firebolt spell into the naginata, and as it crunched through the outer bones, it unleashed a wash of power into the red mist that seemed to fill the creation.

It screamed, a mixture of pain and fury at the temerity of my daring to injure it. Before I could get clear, it lashed out with a solid kick that hit me in the chest and sent me flying.

I landed hard, the wind knocked out of me. I groaned as I tried to get up, having to drop the naginata for a second to brace myself. The damn tower shield was firmly strapped to my arm, making things much harder, especially in full damn armor.

I got to my knees, shoving my helmet back so I could see properly. My guts twisted with panic in the split second before the whip arm lashed around me, yanking me from my feet and pulling me screaming through the air.

I was whipped from one side to the other, then slammed into the ground. Before I could writhe myself free, it changed its grip and swung me around twice to build up momentum, then hurled me across the arena and into the wall.

I hit with a crunch, feeling several bones breaking, and I crumpled to the floor. Pain filled my mind. My left arm was broken, having been at a bad angle when I'd hit the wall. The shield had slammed flat, yanking the elbow out of place. Gritting my teeth against the pain, I slammed my gauntleted right fist into the sandy floor and shoved myself upright. Splintered bones grated in my limb, pain flaring and clouding my thoughts.

Thick, black tendrils of power erupted from the ground and smashed Bane backward through the air, catching him mid-leap at the lich. In the same moment, the behemoth slammed its mace down into Lydia's shield, crushing her into the sand with a scream of pain.

Arrows bounded off the shield around the lich, and Arrin desperately downed potion after potion, trying to make a difference with his limited spells.

I bit down hard against the pain and fear of my people being hurt, and I struggled the rest of the way to my feet, my fury rising uncontrollably. I'd held off on overt magic until now, at Mal's recommendation, but I wasn't going to let my people die; not a fucking chance. I dropped the shield. Defense was all well and good, but I was better at offense, anyway.

"Oracle!" I called. "Cleansing Fire!" I felt her acknowledgement, and I searched for my naginata. The weapon lay a dozen feet away, and I set off staggering to reach it, pouring a health potion into my mouth as I shambled, followed by a stamina and a mana. I was going to need them all for this.

I could feel *him* watching; Amon. Since the battle for life between me and the fragment of his soul, things had changed between us. I was a lot more cautious, but he seemed a bit more stable, evidently no longer wrestling to live—at least not to steal my body. He seemed to want to help, but I wasn't going to trust that.

I pushed him down, ignoring his muttered advice as bones and ligaments popped, flexed, and sealed again.

Anger filled me…my rage at the stacked deck. The way the gangs kept pulling a fast one. There was nothing about a fucking lich and its behemoth that was allowed in the deal the gangs had struck, but there would be no repercussions for them.

As usual, people bent and broke the rules. They shattered the very things that everyone else tried to uphold, because they were above the law. It was always like that, seemingly in all of the realms. Powerful people thought they didn't have to play along.

Because it was "just them," and it didn't matter if they made their own rules. At home, it had been refusing to pay their fair share in taxes, taking bribes, milking the system, or cheating on their partners. It had been rooted in the belief that those regulations were for others, not for them. "Just this once" wouldn't hurt…

Here, it was just more blatant. As so many more of the common people disregarded the rules, so the criminals pissed on them in turn.

People like me and my crew, believing the rules were there for a reason, were suffering. I'd been stupid enough to believe that the magical contracts that were supposedly enforced in the arena would be different. They weren't.

But that was fine.

Because I'd been holding back as well.

I'd kept a little fucking trump card of my own, and now? With my people getting hurt—good, honest people—it was time to let it out. In three hours, the whole city would be in an uproar anyway.

It was too late for the harpies to back out now, and they were the only fuckers I'd really needed to surprise.

It was time to teach the South Side Gang not to fuck with the Lord of Dravith.

CHAPTER TWENTY-SIX

I wrenched the naginata out of the sand and gritted my teeth as the mace slammed down again on Lydia, though pride flared in me at hearing her shout in pain and anger, calling the lich a cocksucker.

I grinned darkly.

"Time to fuck up your day," I muttered, sensing Oracle as she entered the final phase of the Cleansing Fire spell, while I poured mana into my body, triggering my Mana Overdrive ability. I grunted, the thick cords of mana flooding my body as I rocketed forward, covering the distance between us easily. The behemoth turned slowly, as both it and its master felt my approach. The leakage from my new skill was too high to hide when I turned it all the way up.

A full spread of six Magic Missiles flew past the bone golem to slam into the shield, followed by two more arrows. The shield went black, flickering dangerously close to failure as the lich screamed in fury.

The lich pointed at me, one desiccated hand extending. Black lightning flickered to life as he started to cast a spell, before he screamed again, this time in pain. Bane had appeared from nowhere to hack off the offending hand.

The shield failed as the stealthy Mer struck, a blast that hurled him down to the sand, but left the lich cradling his ruined arm, the hand hanging by a thread of skin as he howled in fury and fear.

Then I was there, sprinting in from behind Lydia. She'd seen me coming and somehow knew what I needed, pulling her shield in tight where it covered her prone form.

I leaped onto it, jumping upward as she pushed with all her might and sent me flying into the air with my naginata held overhead in both hands. The minion's whip arm came around, just a second too slow as it passed under my feet. I struck, driving the blade as deeply as I could into the bone-plated chest.

I plunged it down at an angle, the force of my fully armored body slamming into the behemoth enough to knock it back. I hadn't managed to get all the way through the thickened bone plates, but that was fine, as Bane rolled behind it. Crying out in pain at the weight but managing to be in the right place at the right time, he tripped the huge bone creation and sent it to the floor on its back.

More arrows and missiles flew overhead, slamming into the lich as he tried to raise his shields again. The desiccated and broken old man raged, screaming curses and promises of what he would do to our bodies and souls.

He didn't get far in his promises before Oracle finished the spell: Cleansing Fire. The intense waves slammed out from where I stood atop the bony fucker, surrounding the three of us. Bane waited just outside of the ring as the lich, the behemoth, and I were overtaken by spreading lines of glowing fire.

I released Mana Overdrive, the caress of the flames gentle and warm as they gradually healed the damage that it had done. The world sped back up, and I channeled my own Battlefield Triage spell instead.

This time, I didn't try to heal myself or even my companions that needed it so badly, oh no. I'd remembered the conversations I'd had with Nerin and others about how most creatures born of necromantic arts had serious issues with healing magic.

I didn't know if the behemoth was going to be one of them, but as my naginata flared into brilliant life, glowing fit to outshine the sun, the creation under me screamed in agony and fear.

Whatever had been summoned to animate the bones, whether, like my own Bob, it was a fragment of the summoner's soul that grew and developed separately, or a spirit or demon—I didn't know—but it sure as shit didn't like life magic!

The light of the spell rippled through it, flashing from head to toes and back again, assessing, evaluating, and then striking at the heart of the issue.

The glowing red mist that filled the creation had a core of sorts, right in the most heavily armored part of its chest, and my magic went for it at the same moment as Cleansing Fire tore into the behemoth and the lich.

The shield the lich had been conjuring fell apart, and he staggered, screaming with the spell backlash. The disc of bone he stood upon sagged as he frantically tried to escape the ring of fire.

He would have made it, even as my healing spell savaged the undead core of the behemoth, snuffing out the red mist in a final bright explosion of clean, white light, if not for Arrin, Miren, and Stephanos.

The arrows landed first, smashing into his back and making him jerk in pain before the Firebolt took him in the back of the head, sending him somersaulting over the front of the disc to faceplant onto the floor.

His robe caught fire, the flames quickly spreading as he frantically tore at his clothes. He managed to get his hood down while writhing on the floor, but before he could crawl free of the rest of the robes, more arrows and Firebolts struck him, repeatedly slamming him back into the sand.

Arrin and the archers approached slowly, firing more arrows into the dying lich. I turned to Lydia, grateful to see Oracle landing next to her. My companion said something as Lydia popped the top off a greater health potion, and I sighed in relief. She was okay.

Bane! I turned, searching for him anxiously. My concern eased considerably at the sight of him following Lydia's lead, laboriously lifting a health potion to his mouth with his lower left arm. All of his other limbs seemed to be out of action. His body was a mass of burned leather, and he'd lost a load of tendrils; he was bleeding in several places, and he looked like shit, but he gave me a little wave with the bottle once he'd downed it, then he gingerly reached for a second one, only to drop it as Oracle hit him with a Battlefield Triage.

I pulled open my belt pouch, quickly pulling free a greater mana potion. That left me with only two mana potions: one of the most powerful, and a single weak one. I needed my friends to live, and for that to happen, Oracle needed mana.

It wasn't over yet, though, so I turned back, walking towards the lich where he screamed and rolled in an attempt to put the flames out. He looked more like a pincushion now than anything else, with at least a dozen arrows sticking out at all angles. More had been snapped off as he writhed, and his robes were badly damaged, exposing the dried, desiccated thing underneath.

He had once been a humanoid, that was clear, but the flesh had withered so badly that it was impossible to identify what race he had been now, and it was smoldering and blacked in places from the fire.

He twisted to look up at me, snarling as he started to spit out a string of syllables and reached up one clawed hand to gesture at me. I swung the blade around, cutting him off mid-curse, his hand flying through the air to land next to his head.

"I'll suck you dry!" he croaked, his eyes flashing with malice as a bright light grew within them. He glared up at me until Arrin hit him full in the face with a Firebolt. The lich screamed as the flesh of his face was consumed in flames, yellow-white bone showing through as he lifted the charred remains of his arms to try to stop the fire.

"You sound like my ex." I growled at him. "Get fucked." I brought my naginata overhead and slid my grip down to rest just below the blade, then whipped the metal-clad base down as hard as I could into his skull. It shattered, releasing a wail of fury, fear, and pain into the air as a cloud of black mist rose from the corpse, then flashed and vanished through the bars into one of the booths.

"It must have its phylactery up there!" Oracle shouted, disgust filling her voice.

"Well, folks, I...we have a *development* here!" The voice of the announcer echoed around the arena as the South Side Gang started running from their booth, only to find Mal and a few others rushing from their booths to face them.

The sounds of battle rose from the corridors beneath the boos and screams, followed by silence. After an awkward pause, voices raised in anger once again as the crowds around the arena muttered and grumbled.

I made my rounds to check on my people, finding that the healing potions and Oracle had done wonders. Even still, we were all exhausted, wearing damaged armor, and running low on potions.

"Okay, everybody!" The announcer returned, a clearly furious Mal standing behind him. "It seems the South Side Gang had decided that if the phylactery—the repository for the soul of the lich, for those who don't know—wasn't destroyed, then they had not lost. If they didn't lose, then they didn't have to pay out on their bets!

"The arena management and other...interested parties...have convinced them to change their minds. All bets have been transferred to the final round, and the phylactery is now an additional prize for the victor! In the final round, the harpies will face off against the legion, and guess what, folks? To make it even more *fun*, the usual hour's grace has been removed! The next match starts in one minute!"

"What?!" I snarled, looking at Mal, who shook his head and glared at the others that had filtered into his box to surround him and Soween. The party of creatures wore elaborate golden masks and black robes, hanging open at the front to display weapons and artifacts in a clear show of power.

"We've been had," Lydia muttered next to me, and the others grumbled their agreement as the doors at the far side of the arena started to clank and grate open. Three more of the strange creatures that were surrounding Mal sauntered out onto the sand.

They were a species I'd never seen before, one that made me think of Earth's Egyptian gods. They appeared to be heavily muscled, dark-furred men, but the heads were those of jackals, with the two on the outside wearing plain black robes, and the one in the middle wearing golden ones.

All three wore their robes open to expose the golden armor that covered them, patterned in lines and squares on the two flanking creatures, who hefted swords and shields. The middle one wore golden armor across its upper chest, shoulders, and head. Its ears stood tall and proud, with fanned plates extending back from the sides of its neck, glittering wickedly.

It bore a spear and pointed one hand at me, displaying gold and silver gauntlets tipped with claws that glittered like onyx.

I took the time to look up at Mal once more, who lifted a finger to touch his crossbow, sitting quietly in its sheath. I nodded subtly, turning back to the group.

"Pop your potions if you need them," I muttered, stepping forward and returning my glare to the creature facing me and using Examine.

Anubai Lord Mushek
The Anubai are a race of creatures that worship the Dark Gods. They live only to praise the darkest deeds and are personal favorites of Nimon. Mushek has risen to a position of power with the harpies after years of devoted service. He and his pack are the personal guards of the Skyking and are furious at their presence in the city being unveiled, but they must obey their master.

Weaknesses: Unknown.

Resistances: Unknown.

Level: Unknown

Health: Unknown

Mana: Unknown

"Well, that's just peachy," I grumbled, filling the others in on what little I'd gotten.

"Pathetic!" Mushek growled, shaking his golden head from side to side. "You think we didn't sense your pitiful attempts at tracking us? Your scouts are even now being tortured to death, begging to return to the fold and serve the Skyking. Your deepest secrets are being plucked from their minds, and your plans are in ruin! I will take your pet and bind it to my will, forcing it to serve me for eternity, as my brothers feed on your pathetic forces."

"Is this yours?" I asked, leaning my naginata against my chest and reaching into my pocket. Pulling my fist out, I held it tightly clenched and offered it forward.

"What?" Mushek asked, startled, as my middle finger rose to salute him. He paused, confused for a handful of seconds, until the crowd's rising laughter and the grim smiles of my people clicked. "You dare to mock me?!" he snarled.

"Oh, I'm gonna do more than that. I'm gonna have you fucking gelded, pal, get you fitted for a leash, and take you on daily walkies. I'm going to throw sticks and house-train you. I'm going to change your name to Spot and make sure you get a comfy spot by the fire in the winter.

"I might even let you have a litter before I get your balls cut off, but only if you're a really, *really* good boy," I said, my anger bleeding all the way through blazing fury into ice-cold wrath, my mouth running as I watched him and considered all the angles that I could.

"You—" he started, snarling and shaking with fury, before I cut him off.

"And the Skyking?" I said, cocking my head to the side. "What, you really thought I was relying on the djinn and alkyon to find it? I came to the city for it, you fucking idiot. I sent them out there to draw you here while my real forces moved in. Your precious Skyking is being fucked up by my people right now, and you're here, where you can't help it!"

As I spoke, the doors exiting the arena clanged shut. The sound of the bolts locking into place echoed in the sudden silence as the shocked spectators tried to figure out what was happening. Apparently, that information hadn't been printed in the evening's program.

"You lie!" Mushek snarled, his voice filled with uncertainty.

"Wanna bet?" I said, grinning.

"Get to the Skyking!" Mushek roared up at the four in the booth with Mal. "I'll slaughter *you*, all of you, myself!" he spat as he turned to us, when his attention was ripped back up to the booth in anger as howls of pain arose from the other Anubai. Mal and Soween had evidently opened fire into their retreating backs.

"Missed them, too, didn't you?" I sneered as his eyes widened, realizing for the first time that Mal was in on the deception.

"Get the doors open!" Mushek snapped at one of his escorts before pointing at me with his spear. "Well played, human, but now you die!" he snarled, launching himself at me as Oracle blasted upward, lashing out with a Stunning Lightning Bolt.

He swung his spear around, deflecting the bolt to slam into the bars of the arena. A pair of spectators screamed and fell from sight as his weapon glowed with dark energy. Arrows slashed through the air, only to be deflected by the spinning spear as the heat from Arrin's Firebolt built.

"Take the others; that fucker's mine!" I ordered coldly, running forward. My shield was well out of reach, but that was fine. This fight was naginata against spear. We closed the distance rapidly, the Anubai leaping into the air as we clashed. His spearhead flashed forward as I swept my blade right to left, trapping his spear. I shifted the point aside, the hafts of our weapons smashing together as he smacked into me, while I deflected his greater weight and speed by my twisting body.

He landed, backed up two steps, then stabbed out. The leaf-shaped blade blurred, only to be blocked at the last second by my own longer, sword-tipped naginata. We danced back and forth, sand flying as we tried to maneuver around, each smacking probing attacks aside.

The spear flashed forward before I could deflect it, netting him the first strike. I'd stepped sideways, but too slowly, and the blade sliced across my left upper arm, under the armored plate. I hissed in pain as I shoved hard with my naginata, pushing his spear away from me as I backed up.

He followed, snarling, striking faster and faster, and I couldn't keep up. The dip in all of my stats after using the Mana Overdrive skill was slowing me too much.

"See, fool! Now you die!" he snapped, his golden muzzle biting the words off as he lunged at me.

"I'd"—huff—"tell you…to go suck a…bucket of dicks"—huff—"but your breath…smells like you already did," I grunted out, gasping rapidly as I tried to keep up.

My ability was apparently refusing to kick in until I was fully restored. Oracle kept hitting me with healing spells, but she couldn't keep ahead of the damage he was inflicting. As we closed in again, our hafts crossed, and he braced himself then slowly forced me backwards. He bit at my face, his fang-filled mouth snapping shut less than an inch from my nose.

"Motherfucker!" I snarled, shoving for all I was worth as he lunged in again, continually snapping at me.

Bane blurred into view, spinning behind him. His new daggers sank effortlessly into the Anubai's kidneys before ripping outwards, his lower arms pistoning daggers forward to continually hammer deep into Mushek's back.

Mushek let out a startled gasp, pain filling his eyes as they flared wide in shock. I let go of my naginata with my right hand, driving my arm down his throat before forming a fist, choking him.

I brought my right knee up, slamming it into his stomach and doubling him over as he let go of his spear. Claw-tipped fingers scrabbled at my forearm, desperately trying to get purchase as Bane vanished back into stealth.

Oracle hit me with a heal, then another, causing my mana migraine flare to life for what seemed the first time in ages. I straightened, strength flooding me as my multiple attempts to activate Mana Overdrive finally worked, for all of three seconds, before my mana bottomed out.

It was enough.

I pulled him in, turning him sideways against my chest, keeping my right arm down his throat up to the elbow as he bled out and choked. I reached over, grabbing his snout with my left hand, and pulled back as hard as I could. I doubled down, roaring with the effort.

The muscles stretched with a creak, cartilage tearing and popping free, then his mandibles snapped as I tore the top half of his head free in a spray of gore and sickening crunch, literally ripping his skull apart.

"WHO WANTS TO GO NEXT?!" I roared at the other two, who were now fighting side-by-side, desperately trying to avoid Arrin's magic and Miren and Stephanos's arrows while Lydia howled like a banshee and drove them both back. Bane appeared behind one, hamstringing it and vanishing again, and the other panicked at the sight of its companion going down.

"I surrrrenderrr!" it snarled, getting a Magic Missile in the face in answer from Arrin. It staggered back, the following two missiles slamming it from its feet. The final arrow in Miren's quiver removed all its worries about its future in one easy step as it fell. The bolt entered its head through the bottom of its jaw, the pointed tip crunching out the top of the skull as it came to a halt.

Lydia lunged forward, smashing her mace sideways across the face of the remaining Anubai as it toppled back, cutting its scream off in a welter of blood, bone, and teeth before stepping in close and bringing the weapon down with an enraged scream and ending with a single, wet crunch.

Silence fell as she straightened up, the body of her victim twitching and spasming as the last flares of instruction passed down its nervous system.

And then it began.

It was low at first, the chant. It started from the top of the stands, surprisingly. Mal's cold, calm, and sardonic voice filled with emotion as he called out, his voice filtering down to everyone below.

"Legion!" he called, then again, louder. "Legion!" and a third time, but now other voices rose alongside his own, starting with the spectators, and swelling as more and more joined in…

"LEGION! LEGION! LEGION!" they chanted, and we stared up at the crowds that surrounded us. The men, women, and creatures who had bayed for our blood earlier now screamed fervently in our praise.

My head pounded in rhythm with their screams, the mana migraine growing. I pulled out the weakest mana potion I had left, pouring it down my throat as I picked up my naginata with my other hand.

I straightened, tossing the vial aside, and lifted my weapon in victory.

"You like that?" I called out to the crowd, who screamed in response. "Then you'll love what comes next!" I shouted with a grin, leading my team from the gore-covered arena and out into our rest area.

The attendants were out already, sprinting for the corpses, no doubt intending to pocket something as they recovered our loot for us. The door slammed shut on the arena, and Augustus locked the grate in place with a clang, muting the shouts from outside.

"Thank fuck for that," I muttered. Lydia laughed shortly as she collapsed into a chair, and Nerin started working on us as the rest of the room moved in, cheering and offering congratulations, laughing as they pointed out bits and pieces of the fight.

My favorite person there, though, was instantly Jian, who set a steaming bowl of water down next to me.

"Thank you, Jian!" I said, sighing as I stripped off my gauntlets and dipped my bloody hands in to wash the gore off.

The others were drinking water and talking tiredly as the legionnaires celebrated, drinking in the sight and the faintly echoing cheers of praise for the legion.

The door clanged open a few minutes later, and Mal strode in, his carefree persona gone. He'd dressed in armor, with his crossbows supplemented by a long-handled axe held casually in his right hand.

"Well done, son. Was gettin' a bit worried at the end, there…" He grinned at me as Soween and Gaion and a handful of others squeezed into the room, a couple taking up station on the other side of the door to make sure we weren't disturbed.

"What happened up there?" I asked him shortly.

"Fuckin' Anubai," he snapped, spitting on the floor. "Not seen those bastards in years, and I wouldn't have let 'em into the arena willingly. One of 'em had some kinda disguise spell active, a powerful one, and the mage who oversaw the contracts for the arena's just been found. He was gutted and hung like a side of beef in his quarters…that's how tonight got so fucked up."

"So, I could have had Augustus out there? Or half the legion?" I asked.

He nodded grimly. "Luckily, you didn't need the help, and after tonight, well, it's not like they wouldn't have been gettin' punished anyway." He shrugged.

"Yeah…still pissed, though," I muttered.

"Don't blame you, but it is what it is. You ready for the real fun to begin?" he asked.

I grunted, looking at the bloody water before me. "Depends. Have I got time for a bath? A change of clothes?" I countered. The feeling of wet, bloody clothing made me desperately want to be rid of them.

"Nope. We need to be movin' already. We've saved some time, with those assholes forcing the fight through early, so the majority of the night's festivities are just beginnin' now, meanin' we've got a chance to get into place even earlier."

"Well, that's just fucking peachy," I grumbled.

"I've also come up with a plan for the *Star's Glory*, if you *really* don't like the current ownership?" Mal asked, and I nodded for him to go on. "Well, I was thinkin', perhaps your little friend Horkesh would like to take that ship? She and her…people…can capture it, keep the crew aboard and give 'em orders to follow along?

"There were only a couple of guards on it, I heard. The real trouble would be crewin' it, but the crew is apparently being kept aboard tonight, and as they're all slavers already, you could give 'em a prison sentence instead of death and make 'em crew for you? I don't know about you, but if she came out of the night with the rest of her guards all over the ship and ordered me to fly with a load of ships that were takin' off, I'd do it…"

"You're evil," I said, grinning at him and thinking about the nasty surprise that Bateman, the captain of the *Star*, was going to get.

"I know," he said with a smile as he picked at his nails with a knife.

"Horkesh?" I called, and she skittered across the ceiling to hang above me. "I want you to take your people with Mal. He'll explain what I need you to do and where to take the ship, okay?"

"Yes, Lord Jax," she chittered, bouncing gently, which made Mal shudder.

"You got those imps like I asked?" I suppressed a smile at his discomfort.

"They're outside, chained together," he said. "You sure you wanna do this?"

"You think of a better way to take out the ships that are already in the air?" I asked. He shrugged.

"Then it looks like we're going ahead with it. How we doing with our winnings?"

"Not bad, actually, especially with this…" He pulled out a small crystal and tossed it to me. I caught it and held it close to examine it, noting the grey mist that roiled and twisted within.

"This the lich?" I asked, and he nodded.

"We've got as much gold, manastones, and platinum as I think we're goin' to, realistically. The South Side Gang's leadership is dead after their little stunt, and the lich is contained in this. It's worthless now, beyond a source of experience."

"Good point. Who's the lowest level here?" I asked, and after a few seconds, Jian lifted his hand in shame. "You won't be for long, then."

I threw the crystal to him. He caught it and looked at it, frowning.

"Smash it," Oracle said, and he frowned at her sharply before looking to me.

"You lost out on the experience because you didn't fight, but you're going to earn that ten times over tonight, Jian, believe me. Smash it and level up."

He obeyed enthusiastically, setting it on the floor and stomping down as hard as he could. The first time, there was a cracking noise and a very faint scream of rage, followed quickly by two heavier stomps. With the third impact, the phylactery exploded, sending Jian staggering, then gasping, his eyes going wide.

I realized my notifications were blinking, and I spoke up quickly.

"Okay everyone, gear up, check your notifications, and make any changes you need, because we're leaving in a few minutes."

"I've got your winnings and gear in here; thought it just made more sense to hand it over now," Mal said, passing me two heavy satchels. I nodded to him in thanks, not taking the time to check them. I pulled open the bag of spatial folding and paused, just about to drop them inside.

"Can you store bags of holding inside bags of holding?" I asked, a sudden horrible thought occurring to me.

"Hmmm?" Mal asked, frowning. "Oh, yeah, as long as the bag that's holdin' the others has the space and is a higher grade. Depending on the bags that go in, it can be a problem. Those are both crap bags, so as long as the one you have is above average, it should be fine."

Relieved, I dropped them inside. When I checked the limit on the bag, I found that there were thirty-seven slots left out of the original hundred; each bag had taken up ten slots, for some reason. I was suddenly glad I'd taken the time when we had returned to unload as much loot as possible into Fenris. Man, that thing could carry.

I'd also taken the time to grab a few bits from it while I was there, although until now, I wasn't sure what I was going to do with it.

"Well, that's fucking awesome," I said to myself.

"You ain't goin' to check it over? See how much you made?" he asked me.

"Nope. I've got no time to fuck about with that right now. I'll give some to my team as a reward for fighting with me later, but it's not like we're gonna get the chance to go shopping tonight, is it?"

"Fair enough. I've got some people gettin' the animals ready, as well as that damn glowin' horse of yours. The stablemaster thinks we'll be ready to move out in about half an hour, but we're gonna draw a lot of attention with that thing. Don't suppose you'd consider leavin' it behind?"

"Hell, no. Fenris will be awesome for exploring the lands around the tower," I said, staring at him as though he were mad.

"Yeah, I didn't think so." He sighed.

"Besides, he had a few bits and bobs in storage I thought you wanted?" I asked, pulling the first of the boxes out and making Mal's eyes bulge.

"Hell, no!" he scowled and gestured for me to put it away. I slipped the box back into the bag and frowned at him.

"Okay, so what don't I know here?" I asked, earning another glare from Mal.

"You know what…I'm gonna let you deal with that shit—and the trouble it brings—on your own," he said, eying Augustus warily.

"What?" I asked, confused. "These were part of the cargo of the smuggling caravan. I figured if anyone would want it, it'd be you?" I'd kept the vast majority of the smaller items, giving the biggest, most space intensive, and low value items to Soween to dispose of, and kept what I'd assumed were the drugs for Mal. I didn't like them, personally, but I figured he'd paid for them and it was his business.

"Uh-huh. Well, they mighta been part of the caravan, but they weren't an authorized cargo. I'll have a 'word' with the guys who came with you from the caravan about it. Also, they asked to join your party; said they'd sworn to you, so I released 'em from the Smugglers Oath. Seems I'm still counted high enough to be able to do that, for now."

"They're not fighters. Can you direct them to join the refugees?" I asked. "I'll sort them out once we're on our way, but tonight, they'll just get in the way. Also, what's happening with the Smugglers Guild? You've never mentioned them since I arrived…"

"Yeah, I can tell 'em where to go. As to the guild…well, it's fallin' apart, frankly. Not bein' able to use the Path, and the airships being under a tight watch now, the guild was failin'…wait…. You said you claimed the Smugglers Path, right?" I nodded, and he seemed to come alive suddenly, as though a weight had been lifted from his shoulders. "I've been so caught up in all of this, I've forgotten to do what I should have. I'll take the Path now, like you offered before…"

"Okay, but what about the notifications?" I asked.

"Don't claim it! Just…*will* it to me; concentrate on handin' the rights over."

I closed my eyes and focused, finding the prompt easily enough, and I mentally "pushed" it at Mal, concentrating on the intent to give him control over it.

"That's it!" Mal grinned. "Now, give me those drugs, after all. I'll take 'em and stop off on my way to the Stockpile, drop 'em in with an old friend, and transfer the rights to the Path to him. Maybe that'll satisfy the guild, so they don't come after me for all this…"

"Come after you?" I asked.

"You think the guild wouldn't be wantin' a part of tonight? Believe me, they would, and they'd be taking at least half; plus, then half of 'em would try to make themselves better off by runnin' to the nobles and sellin' the deal down the river. No, when word gets out and they figure out this was me, they'll want my head. With the drugs and the Path, maybe they'll settle for just expellin' me. Probably not, but hell with it."

"Shit, okay. Sorry, mate, I've been so caught up in all of this that—"

"Yeah, I know. I don't blame you, kid, believe me. I wouldn't be doing this if I didn't want an out anyway. I'm gonna go get things movin', so I suggest you leave as soon as you can. Gaion will lead you through the streets to the Skyking's tower, then you're on your own.

"So…I guess this is goodbye, until I need a safe port, some repairs, or those books…. I'll make sure the rest of your gear is on the battleship and it's all goin' smoothly before I take my own prize. I'll follow along for a day or two, as we agreed, but after the Sunken City, I'll be goin' my own way."

"I understand. Mal, thank you. I couldn't have done this without you," I said, gripping his wrist.

"Of course you couldn't!" he replied with a grin. "Worth it, though. It's been fun, kid. If you ever get bored of the 'lord' shit and fancy an easier life, come see me."

"I will. And if you ever want to earn some serious money, and you know, make a real difference, rather than being a solo operator, come see me. I'll always have jobs for a man of your talents."

We grinned, then let go, going our separate ways. I pulled up my notifications, quickly reading through them.

Congratulations!

You have killed the following:

- 1x Undead Behemoth, level 24 for a total of 10,000xp
- 1x Anubai Lord Mushek, level 35 for a total of 17,500xp

A party under your command killed the following:

- 1x Lich Veriman, level 27 for a total of 12,800xp
- 2x Anubai of various levels for a total of 20,180xp

Total Party experience earned: 32,980xp

As party leader, you gain 25% of all experience earned

Progress to level 16 stands at 118,905/165,000

I couldn't help but grin at the confirmation of Veriman's death. That little cocksucker had deserved it, and I was inching closer to the next level with every fight. The percentage increase with having my little "issues" healed was immense, and I couldn't wait to get up to the next milestone at level twenty. I had plans for those meridian points!

CHAPTER TWENTY-SEVEN

"Okay, people, last chance for a shit before we go!" Augustus shouted and I had to laugh, scanning the room as people cinched straps tight and checked weapons in their sheaths. I joined the others laughing as Grizz staggered upright and shuffled off out of the room to the loo, though I gave Augustus a concerned frown once he was gone.

"Is he gonna be all right for this?" I asked, and he shrugged.

"He's alive and a legionnaire; he'll either make it or he won't. None of tonight is safe, and at least if he's with us, we can help him. Besides, no matter where you told him to wait, the mad bastard would only sneak out and follow us. Best to have him where we can watch over him."

"I don't like how injured he is," I admitted.

"Neither do I, Jax, but believe me, he'll be safer with us than getting into trouble somewhere he can hide his injuries."

"Okay. Are we ready, beyond that?" I asked, looking around. With the loss of the two legionnaires at the Emporium, we were down to fourteen of Augustus's legionnaires, the three scout legionnaires, my own squad of five, with Barrett already sent to help the refugees and new recruits, and Nigret and Mistress Nerin. Counting myself, that gave us a round total of twenty-five. The room was filled with the jingle of armor, grunts as people checked each other's gear, and good-natured taunts getting passed around.

"We're as ready as we can be," he confirmed. I crossed to a chair, stepping up onto it so that everyone could see and hear me.

"Okay, people—" I started, and Augustus bellowed out at them all to "Shut the fuck up, or you'll be tasting my boot polish."

"Okay," I started again, grinning and shaking my head slightly. "Look, everyone, I'm shit at speeches, can't do them to save my life. However, most of you haven't been around most of the conversations I've had regarding tonight, so my guess is that you'll have some mental as fuck ideas about what's happening, especially from the whispers getting shared, no doubt.

"The truth is, we're going to go fuck up the Skyking and free its slaves, then we're going to go steal the fucking battleship that's being built. It's nowhere near ready yet, so once we're in the air, we're going to be slow and easily tracked. The other ships we're stealing are going to help protect us while we make our escape.

"We're going to be damn full, as we're taking the entire legion and all the families we can, as well as any slaves we can free. We're going to head out to sea, loop around, and hopefully reach the Great Tower in a week or so. For most of that time, it's gonna be a case of rest, relax, and help make the ships as good as possible, so if you've got a skill that can help at all, shout up when we're on our way.

“Lastly, when we get to the tower, you’re going to find a big change in your lives. You’re no longer ‘just’ the fucking legion. You’re the LEGION. The bravest, baddest motherfuckers around, and you’re gonna be treated with the respect you deserve!

“We’ve got a tower that’s in the middle of a monster-infested wilderness. It’s damaged and full of people that we need to keep safe, but they’re going to be there for you. They’ll support you, feed you, and love you. You’ll no longer be outcasts in a city that hates you. You’re going to be the men, women—and whatever the fuck Grizz actually is—that you were born to be. Are you with me?” I asked, getting a good-natured round of “yeah” and “yes, sir” and “man, he wasn’t lying; he’s shit at speeches.”

“Okay, people, quickly, before he comes back, there’s one last thing,” I said, holding my hands up. “When Grizz comes back, I want you all to cheer and applaud him, but don’t explain why if he asks, just say ‘you know why’ or something. Let’s wind him up!”

That got a round of laughter, and I climbed down, gathering my little leadership cadre of Lydia, Yen, Amaat, Augustus, Nerin, and Gaion to me, with Bane hovering protectively as Nigret moved in curiously to listen.

“We’re going to move out in a minute, and our fliers will be screening us from any attacks. Amaat you’re in charge of that. Once we get inside, you fall back and just try and keep them from getting reinforcements. I know you’ve got some people trained to fly the ships, and we’re gonna need them to be kept safe. Gaion, lead us as quickly as you can. We’ve got no time for stealth tonight.

“Yen, you and Tang are our scouts. Push ahead and warn us as best you can. Augustus, you’re better at this kinda thing than me, I’ve no doubt, but I need to learn and practice, so you’re my second.

“Feel free to shout commands if they need to be done. If I’m gonna fuck up, tell me and feel free to fix it, but back me up. Lydia, you’re my personal squad, as always. Integrate with the rest, but stick close, and keep an eye on Grizz. Nerin, you’re our healer. We’re all going to be keeping you as safe as we can, because we’re gonna need you a lot tonight, I expect. Anyone got anything to add?”

“Aaawk!” said Amaat, shaking his head and drawing my attention. “One of my pride is missing, Helio. He was on watch and is gone. His Oath was binding him, and he was proud; he would not have abandoned us.”

“So what that fucker said in there might be true? They know we’re coming?” I asked.

“Possibly, but he might have been taken down by someone else.” He shrugged. “He knew we were going to attack the Skyking, but not when.”

“Then we go ahead as planned,” I said after a second’s reflection. “If they have him, we’ll rescue or avenge him, and if not, hopefully we can find him either way. Anyone else have any questions?” I asked.

“Nigret does,” Nigret said, smiling widely. “What is Nigret’s role tonight?”

“You’re with the legion, mate. I want you to stay close to Grizz and keep him safe. He’s earned a bit of help,” I said, smiling back, despite my uncertainty of him.

I knew his Oath would keep him from betraying us, but still, he was new to the group, and yesterday, he’d been trying to kill me.

"Ah, Nigret?" I said as he started to turn away, and he turned back with a raised eyebrow. "Look, about using the Oath, I'm sorry. It's not something I wanted to do, but with everything that's riding on this, it was the only way I could be sure of you. Again, once this is all over, two, three days or so, if you want to be free, I swear I'll release you."

Nigret paused and studied my face, as though considering, then nodded slowly.

"Nigret understands. Now that he has seen more of the picture, there is much to be learned." He smiled again and moved away.

Watching him move through the legionnaires, I turned to Augustus. "Make sure Grizz knows that his job tonight is to just keep up; he's to protect Nerin as best he can and keep an eye on Nigret."

"Sounds like a steady plan, Jax." Augustus nodded approvingly. "I'll help as I can. With no real knowledge of what to expect, we're going to be adjusting orders on the fly. I'll push out a squad to follow the scouts and trigger any traps before they can get to us, one with your people. Lydia," he said, nodding to her, "...and one following behind, making sure we don't get taken in the ass."

"Sounds good," I agreed, cheering rising by the door as a very confused Grizz entered the room. Laughing to myself, I shouted and wolf whistled with the others, making him even more confused. Augustus pushed through the crowd of people and clapped him on the shoulder.

"Well done, Grizz. The legion is proud of you. Your job tonight is to stay next to Mistress Nerin and protect her as best you can, and to watch over the Trigara." The centurion left his hand on Grizz's shoulder for a moment, turning to the rest of the room. "Okay, everyone, that's it! Let's move!"

Then he led the way out, with Gaion and the scouts pushing up to pass him. We filed out, smiling and clapping Grizz on the shoulder and generally praising him as we passed, leaving him to fall in next to Nerin with a look of utter bewilderment on his face.

"You're cruel," Lydia said to me, grinning.

"You've no idea!" I chuckled, climbing the stairs. Our group, pushing past random people in the corridors and struggling up flights of stairs in full armor, began drawing attention as we went.

As soon as we were out into the rear courtyard, I confirmed the orders for Fenris, making sure he'd stay with Barrett's tiger and our gear, which were being moved to the shipyards. Then we were off, walking out into the grey, misty night.

The rain fell lightly, a steady drizzle that left the cobblestones slick and soaked, but it didn't seem to clean anything. As we sped up to a steady jog, passing through the fog as we left the Cloudring district. All of the group breathed a sigh of relief as our lungs expelled the last of the mild drug.

Now that we were out of the concealing mists, we picked up speed. The crash of steel-clad boots, the jingle of chain, and the clatter of swords and shields, spears and daggers banging against each other as we ran sounded like a collapsing steelworks. Despite the attention we drew, the sight of the legion—even such a small group as ours—sprinting down the streets cleared them instantly.

Nobody wanted to be between the legion and the object of its ire, but as we ran, occasionally at first, and then more frequently, came the shouts, rising from alleys as we passed.

"Murderers!"

"Child-killers!"

"Scum!"

All these and more were shouted, and slowly people started to group together behind us, hurling insults and calling for their friends to join them.

"How far?" I asked Augustus, my breath coming surprisingly easily after the meridian upgrade.

"Two more streets, then down the Imperial Way and across the Square of Industry. Maybe ten minutes at this speed, just over a mile."

"You…expect…me…to…run…all…the…way?" Nerin gasped out, and I glanced at her, hiding a smile. She was maybe forty-five and reasonably fit, but she was wearing a long dress and had dozens of bags affixed to a pair of bandoliers that she had strapped around her waist and across her chest. An enormous bag on her back bounced with every step and looked like it'd take her off her feet any second.

"What the hell is in those bags? I asked her, and she glared at me.

"Things…I…need!"

"Seriously?" I scoffed, as another legionnaire moved in from the side. I'd seen him around the last few days on occasion, but I hadn't really talked to him much.

"Let me help, mistress," he said, sweeping her up with barely any apparent effort and clasping her into a princess carry across his chest.

She started to berate him, but only between gasps, and it was clearly all she could do to try to catch her breath. Considering we'd only been running for about five minutes, and jogging for about the same before that, she was in for a nasty shock in the future when it came to the tower's stairs.

"Thanks, Lukaj," Augustus said, giving him a nod.

"Okay then, we're starting to get a following, which isn't going to help us with the Skyking's…" I began, before I was shoved suddenly from the side, sending me sprawling into Augustus. He staggered and tried to catch me, while Miren shouted out an oath. I hit the floor, rolling and tripping someone, who landed on top of me, both of us swearing as I shoved them off.

By the time I looked up, Miren and Stephanos had their bows drawn, and others with bows were all drawing arrows back as shouts rose around us.

Bane appeared next to me, reaching out, and I took his hand, getting hauled to my feet.

"What happened?" I asked, peering up into the drizzling sky and trying to spot what everyone was looking for.

"Crossbow bolt," Bane muttered darkly, his head tilting from side to side as he searched the area. "I saw the shape move, didn't have time to warn you, so I just pushed. Sorry."

"Hey, feel free to do that again anytime!" I said, grateful once again for his persistence as my bodyguard. "Where'd it come from?"

"A flier, small one. Maybe an imp? It was crouched on that building with all the gargoyles. I'd never have seen it if it hadn't moved as it fired."

"There!" Stephanos shouted, and a thick chorus of deep smacks announced the legionnaires, Miren's, and Stephanos's firing.

There was a scream in the distance, followed by another flight of arrows, and a meaty *thump* as a small figure smashed into the ground.

Shouts of rage pierced the air ahead, as a trio of alkyon erupted from the third story of a building on the corner, each of them launching into the air and pulling back on their own bows. Arrows flew, shattering against hastily raised shields, and our own bolts flew in response, until a screech of fury came from above. Amaat and his fliers had arrived.

I'd ordered him to stay as high as possible, watching for anyone coming for us, so it had taken him a minute to get into the fight, but when he did…

He and Venta hit the lead alkyon a second apart, attacking a wing each. Their taloned feet tore holes and released, lifting back into the air with screeches of triumph as their target screamed in terror and fell with wings of tattered membrane, only to hit the ground with bone-shattering force.

Our djinn attacked next, all four blurring past us. Their small forms streaked skyward, alight with magic as a barrage of flames, ice magic, and some kind of stone spell flashed out. The second and third alkyon were hammered relentlessly until the remaining three members of Amaat's pride arrived.

They flashed into the skirmish, blades reflecting the firelight of torches and candles in windows as they tore into their targets.

In seconds, it was over, the djinn streaking down to take up station around my group, and the five alkyon lifting back into the night to resume overwatch.

"We'll be staying in close, my lord; we can keep you safer that way," the djinn leader said, nodding to me and casting a shield spell, quickly followed by the other three.

"Then let's go," I said, raising my voice to call out to everyone. "And thank you all; that crossbow bolt could have been a pain in the ass."

"More like the chest," Bane said, a *thrummm* of amusement clear in his voice.

"Meh…" I grinned at him as I shrugged and gestured in the direction of the Skyking's tower. "Forward!" I shouted, and we were off again, jingling and generally announcing our presence like a parade.

We reached the Imperial Way, a long, straight, and wide road lined with shops and taverns on either side. Windows opened, and tired, grimy faces appeared as we passed, shouting rising in the distance behind us as more and more assholes gathered.

We ran down the wide street, people jumping aside and disappearing into alleys and behind shuttered carts as we appeared. Even the most rabid anti-legion sympathizers appeared to have a change of heart as we closed on them…until we were out of reach, at least.

Above us in the distance, obscured by buildings, the distinctive blue glow of mana engines flared as the three patrolling airships slowly shifted in their unending rounds through the sky. Soot belched from smokestacks to occasionally obscure them. The shouts and crashes from the nearby shipyards and Industrial Quarter were faintly audible as I ran on, hoping the guards tasked with watching the city were more interested in their beds than watching for us.

Ahead, Gaion turned, leading the group aside as Tang appeared, gesturing to one side frantically.

We ran into an alleyway, cutting to the left, then the right, then right again, as word filtered back to us that the scouts had spotted a guard patrol closing on us, the flare of their torches disappearing behind us as we bypassed them and closed on the Square of Industry.

Ahead of us, the industrial towers rose into the sky. Some were still filled with light as crafters worked diligently through the night in an attempt to fill orders, while others, like our target, were black holes in the night.

“That one!” Gaion whispered as we halted, the group spreading out and taking up watch as Augustus and I skulked forwards.

The tower he indicated was one of the biggest, the base easily two dozen meters on a side. The sides squared off and tapered up to a tall, stout building. Its windows were covered closer to the ground, with dark openings higher on the sides, then shifting to solid black at the top, with all the windows sealed shut and seemingly bricked over.

“There are always guards at the bottom: two outside, and more inside, with the only way in heavily reinforced.”

We stared at the structure, watching for any sign of the guard, but we saw nothing. No movement, no sound. I squinted at the far end of the square. Between us and the tower were shuttered carts, shining, rain-slicked cobbles, and the occasional statue or lamppost. Beyond that, there was nothing, only a faint glow from a barrel turned on its side directly outside the doorway we needed.

“What is that?” I asked those around me, wiping the rain and sweat from my face.

“Where?” Augustus asked, and I gestured to the glow.

“I don’t know, but those assholes are getting closer,” Gaion said, his voice low and urgent as we heard the rising shouts in the distance for the “legion scum” and the “child killers” to be found.

“It looks like a fire, or,” I whispered, focusing in.

“It’s the guard post,” a djinn offered, floating in closer to me. “They have a barrel filled with coals. They light it and stand around drinking and keeping everyone away from the door. I’ve seen it before, when my siblings and I were out searching for our mother while pretending to be trying to steal.”

“Shit. Well, it looks like they’re expecting us, then!” I said grimly. I was hardly surprised, but I’d been hoping against hope.

“You need to make a decision,” Augustus said firmly. “If they’ve pulled back and are waiting for us, it’s going to be costly taking that place. Do we retreat, or storm it?”

He studied my face in the steady drizzle, rain running from his helmet and making his armor gleam. I paused, understanding what he was saying. We’d likely lose people here, good people, and we could pull back instead. We risked being taken from behind by the building mob, possibly getting trapped, even if we won the fight. I shook my head, closing my eyes and drawing a deep breath.

“We attack. I hate to risk our people, but we need to free the harpies. They’ll make the next phase more likely to succeed, and I gave my word,” I said, my stomach clenching as I commanded the first battle of the night, risking my people’s lives for things I’d decided were necessary. Augustus saluted, his teeth flashing in a grin, before he waved forward the leaders of the squads.

"Rinko, take first squad and get that door open. Tanis, second squad is with Rinko; back him up. Lydia, close protection for Jax. Denny, you've got third. Watch our backs and keep an eye on those mobs; they get close enough to see, I want to know about it.

"We need to get inside and shut the doors before they arrive, ideally. Then they can fuck off, and we can get the job done. Amaat, take your fliers and make sure we're clear. I want them to scout the tower."

"We're being watched," a voice hissed from the side, and I turned to find Nigret crouched nearby, staring fixedly at the tower.

"Where?" I asked, looking back at the seemingly abandoned building.

"First floor, second window. It's open at the bottom; there's movement in there," he rumbled, his tail twitching slightly as he stared.

I focused, my DarkVision activating as I concentrated. It was a strange ability; it'd become second nature to use it, but I had quickly learned that using it around firelight caused terrible headaches if it was active for too long, so I'd automatically left it deactivated. Now, I ignored the flaring, popping flames that danced under lamp glass around the square, and I concentrated on the point Nigret had indicated. At first, I saw nothing, but as they moved slightly, I saw it. A glimmer of metal reflecting light…

"Crossbow," I growled. "They know we're here."

"That tears it, then!" Augustus growled. "On three! One…two…"

As Augustus counted down, I started to cast, building the spell as quickly as I could while focusing in tightly on the window and mentally flexing as hard as I could. It took a few seconds, and I heard the roar of my people as they sprinted out of cover before I was done. As the window snapped open fully, I released the spell, lightning flaring bright and almost blinding me as I fired.

A figure stepped into the opening, crossbow raised, when the bolt took him in the chest. The spell blasted him backwards into the suddenly illuminated room, his crossbow going off and the bolt vanishing somewhere inside the building as shadowy figures within shied back from the sudden light.

"I count three in there!" I called out, charging up a second spell as other windows opened up. Fliers lifted into the air from the openings higher in the building, screeching battle cries, as our own alkyon swooped in to meet them.

I stood, pulling my mana in and concentrating on the AOE bomb blast I'd used against the Drow in the assault on their base. I began layering in the sections as quickly as I could, until Oracle's influence joined my mind. Previously rough sections smoothed and tucked in neatly, a smile tugging at the edges of my mouth as the words fell from my lips.

Augustus stood by my side, his shield held ready, partially obscuring me as the spell built, and he bellowed orders.

Rinko and his squad took the lead as they smashed into the door. They'd tucked in behind each other, forming a tiny phalanx, and just before they impacted, each legionnaire reached out, hands pressing on Rinko's back, and a glow sprang up.

"Breaker!" Rinko screamed, suddenly glowing like the sun for a second before he slammed into the door, shattering it from its hinges as he used a specialized ability. The door was split down the middle, shards of wood and metal blown back into suddenly exposed thugs who were peppered with fragments.

Before they could collect themselves, the rest of the squad followed him, storming inside and attacking.

I gritted my teeth, forcing the last words out with a hiss as my fingers threatened to tie themselves in knots. The screams of dozens of imps pierced the air as they attacked my fliers, increasing as Amaat and his people fired crossbows and slashed with swords. Firebolts and Icebolts flashed through the sky, waves of darkness and shining light flowing back and forth, and the battle was truly joined.

"I can bring more djinn!" a small figure begged me, darting forward to hover by my shoulder as I compressed the final stage of the spell. The glowing, spitting lightning in my hands quivered as Oracle smoothed it, compressing it tighter and tighter.

"Wait!" Augustus snapped at the djinn, shifting his shield aside as I pulled the spell in close to my chest, then shoved it forward with a grunt of effort and a final shout of arcane words.

The spell speared through the air, leaving a yellow-white afterimage that seemed branded into my retinas, until it smashed through the window, taking part of the frame with it. It hit the back wall, exploding with a boom that shook the air around the tower, giving rise to screams of pain as the people inside forgot about firing at my forces.

The spell wrapped the outer limit of its range in hissing, crackling lightning that combined with the flaming core of the spell, then began to quickly contract, forcing those caught in its boundaries into the center, burning them with flames and whipping them with lightning.

It was a far weaker spell than the one I'd cast days ago, filled with fury and hatred, but now it was smoother, more elegant, and less wasteful. It expired after only five seconds, but in that time, those caught in its AOE were either killed, stunned, burned, or had suffered broken bones. All had lost their weapons, and in one case, had actually shot one of their own side in the face with a dropped crossbow.

Congratulations!

You have created a new personal spell:...Explosive Compression!

Explosive Compression:
Creates an explosive shell around an unstable lightning and flaming core. Once the shell is broken, a manaform is unrolled that traps all of those inside its boundaries, then compresses until the invested mana is entirely used up. This spell causes burning damage, consumes the air inside its boundary and compresses everything within, causing bludgeoning damage as well as a chance to cause internal bleeding for any living being it surrounds.

This spell, while cobbled together from the parts of other spells, has been refined enough to be acknowledged as a fully formed spell, and as such will begin to level and evolve as your understanding of its properties grows.

Cost: 25-500 mana, depending on AOE

I sagged, gasping, before forcing out my breath and standing tall. My mana was down to half, but it was starting to refill already, albeit slower than I'd have liked. I glanced at my new spell and dismissed it quickly.

"Go," I said to the djinn. "Tell them where we are. Tell them we're here to rescue your Clan Mother, and if they want to free her, if they want revenge on the Skyking, now's the time."

He nodded, spinning and vanishing into the rain.

"The left," came a wavering voice, and I turned to regard the small figure of an imp looking up at me. He was one of the three we'd captured, bound in chains and unable to help in the fight because of the Oaths he was bound by. Now he stared at me from a face wracked with pain. "Take the left stairses, Skyking makeses less trapses that way."

Its words gave way to screams as the consequences of the broken Oath ripped into it. Tiny muscles writhed as they constricted and tore free, bones cracking under the force. It continued staring up at me with agonized determination as it began to die.

"I will, and thank you," I said, stabbing it in the chest and ending its life before the Skyking's cruel magic could punish it further. "What was his name?" I asked the others as they stared at his twitching body in anger and sadness.

"Grebes," one said, whimpering. "You lets us go now?" he asked hopefully.

"No." I shook my head. "You know you'd be forced to attack us; better you stay where you are."

"But we's gonna get kilt by Skyking!" he whined.

"Not if we kill it first," I said grimly. "Come on, people, let's get in there!" I shouted.

A nearby legionnaire picked the imps back up, slinging them onto his back with a grimace as we ran through the shattered doorway. Nerin ran alongside me, her bearer from before working with Grizz and Nigret to cover her with their shields, as well as helping the few wounded along.

As soon as we were inside, the first and second squads fighting on the next floor above us, I ordered Augustus to seal the door and sort out a casualty area. Then I sprinted up the stairs with my personal team, Lydia hot on my heels.

"God, I love good subordinates," I muttered to myself, a smile stretching my cheeks as I heard Augustus bellowing orders. Nerin's voice joined him, demanding the wounded be brought to her.

"What are we goin' ter do, Jax?" Lydia asked me, and I met her eyes. Her grin was evident on the little I could see of her face through the gaps in her helmet. She was flushed and loving every minute.

I couldn't help but grin back at her.

"We're gonna get up there and fuck up the Skyking's day!" I said, recognizing the blur on the stairs ahead of me that indicated Bane already sweeping ahead.

We flew out of the stairwell into a small landing. Five rooms led off it, arranged concentrically, and I grinned grimly at the sight that greeted me. One wall from the room at the front of the tower was partially demolished, the roof above sagging.

Bodies were everywhere. The legionnaires had broken out onto the floor and slaughtered the guards before they could recover, attacking more as they appeared from the stairs and other rooms. A few hardy legionnaires had taken the fight to the next floor, even as the rest finished off the resistance on this one.

"Make a hole!" I shouted, rushing forwards, and the legionnaires between me and the stairwell parted, letting us charge through.

I sprinted up the stairs, abruptly coming to halt behind two legionnaires at the top of the stairwell. They were hunched behind their shields, taking heavy crossbow fire as they tried to move forward.

A flash of light filled the little I could see of the room. One legionnaire screamed, shaking as he was hit by a lightning spell, but he gritted his teeth and stayed where he was, muscles twitching and shaking as it grounded through his armor, before groaning and sagging as the spell died.

"Two can play at that game," I muttered, peeking through their legs and spotting a moving boot off to the side in one of the rooms. "Oracle, I'll fountain," I said, casting the spell quickly as she grinned evilly.

"And I'll shock!" she finished, building the spell.

"When I say…let Oracle up!" I told the legionnaires, who grunted acknowledgement, busy as they were blocking bolts and spells.

"Now would be a good time!" The zapped legionnaire grunted as his shield was hit by a Firebolt, glowing cherry red for a second as a second hit right after the first. He groaned in pain but still held on grimly. I watched Oracle's face and shouted to them.

"Now!"

They stepped aside slightly, making a small gap, and she appeared between them, finally able to see the hallway above us. My fountain burst into life in the doorway of the room I'd targeted, evoking a shocked gasp when the cold, crisp water splashed someone. Oracle hit it with her enhanced Stunning Lightning Bolt, sending the hidden mage screaming as it blasted into the water, and then fed through to him. He fell backwards out of sight as I bellowed to the men above me.

"Advance!"

True to Augustus's casual words when we'd trained together, the men reacted to the ingrained command, brushing fear and pain aside and rushing up and out, giving the rest of us room to move.

I followed them, stabbing out over the shield held by the man before me, to take his snarling opponent in the throat.

"Move, move, move!" Rinko bellowed as he and the rest of his team followed me into battle. Each of the rooms had been in use at some point, but here, there were only a handful of people, and once the legionnaires were out of the stairwell, it was less than a minute to mop up the resistance. A single surrendering human survived, with more than a dozen combatants dying over both floors.

"The stairwell's blocked!" Rinko called from around the corner, and I joined him quickly, looking up at the mass of wood that closed the stairwell off. It had originally been a door, I guessed, but they'd added more and more wood, nailing it shut and linking chains to the walls to keep it that way.

"What the hell is this?!" I asked the surrendered human, my voice full of anger.

"We…we were hired to keep the floors secure and told that we don't go higher," he babbled, pointing to the wooden barricade. "It was like that when we came here."

"How do we get past it?" I asked, and he shook his head.

"You can't. We'd hear things when we first moved in, banging and shit. They added more on the other side, I think—"

"Bullshit!" I snapped. "How do you get your orders? Who goes up there?"

"Nobody!" he said, wincing as I yanked him in close, staring into his eyes. "We was just hired to guard the bottom of the tower, told we'd get extra silver if we killed anyone who tried to get in, and gold if we caught them alive. The promos come for them, fly them up at night. That's all I know!"

"Fuck!" I snapped, shoving him back to land on the floor as I scowled at the barricade. "How long to get past that?" I asked Rinko.

He shrugged. "Half an hour at least. Depending on what they did on the other side, it could be hours, though. Sorry, sir."

"Fuck!" I cried again, slamming the butt of my naginata into the floor and hearing a crash as a nearby body shifted, falling through the hole my spell had made in the ceiling of the floor below.

I'd spun at the movement, before stopping, realizing it was just the abused floor shifting and gravity claiming the corpse. It gave me an idea, though, and I moved quickly to examine the barricade.

"It's too close," I muttered, judging the distance before turning to look at the roof instead. "Rinko!" I snapped. "Check the ceilings, find me any damage you can."

I turned at the sound of my own name.

"Jax," Augustus said, coming into view. "The mobs arrived; they've been led by a promethean. No chance of them passing us by, I'm afraid."

"Well, that's just fucking peachy," I said, shaking my head and gesturing to the barricade. "We can't get through that to the next floor anytime soon," I warned him.

"We've pulled some doors apart down there, got them in place to hold them for now, but we need another way out," he replied. "Thoughts?"

"I noticed that I fucked up the ceiling and floor with a spell there by accident…" I gestured to the hole that led to the floor below. "Thinking that's probably the best way to reach the next floor. Any better ideas? How are our people?"

"Possibly." He regarded the hole grimly. "We've seen the fliers falling back. Amaat and his pride have taken control of the area, but I don't know for how long. The harpies can always call for more reinforcements. Our best chance is to push through before they can bring more here.

"He's lost two of his pride, dead without a doubt, and we've got one legionnaire who's taken heavy injuries. Nerin's working on him now." He took a deep breath, looking around. "As to the next floor, it's probably the best bet. I'll admit, I had not foreseen the prometheans whipping up a mob to block us in. I'd expected maybe a few dozen idiots. There's over a hundred out there now, and they're only growing. It won't be long before they either try to get in, and we have to kill them, or the guard arrives."

"Okay, mate, give me a few minutes. Get everyone ready; we're abandoning the lower floors and moving up, then we brace the hole as best we can and make sure it's costly for the mob to follow us. I could do with a few mana potions, if you've found any?"

"I'll have the corpses searched. Only two mages around that I've heard, though, which is both a blessing and a curse."

"Thanks, man." I nodded gratefully as legionnaires started checking the corpses. "As soon as they've been searched, get everyone back. I'm gonna have to make a big mess."

"Tell me which room you're going to aim for, and I'll have something to climb up knocked together in another one," Rinko slipped in, and I smiled in appreciation.

"Will do, mate, and thanks. Any damage to the ceilings you found?" I asked, and he shook his head.

"Just some rot, but that's spread out across all the building. The ceilings look solid, with heavy reinforcing beams. Take out too many, and you might take out the building. Too few, and we're going nowhere."

"Well, thanks for that sunny outlook," I muttered and started walking from room to room. As he'd said, there was no particularly good or bad one, and years of fireplaces had left them covered in soot and crap anyway.

"Jax?" Oracle whispered, landing on my shoulder.

"Yeah?" I asked absently.

"Why don't you ask Jenae?" she suggested, and I paused.

"You think she'll be able to help?"

"Probably not the way you were hoping, but she might suggest a room?"

"Sounds good to me," I said, smiling. "Thanks, Oracle." She smiled back at me, and I took a deep breath, sinking down onto one knee and closing my eyes as I felt Oracle take off again, flying up to the ceiling and starting to examine the beams.

"Jenae!" I called, pulling in a deep breath and expelling it along with a blast of mana that I'd formed into the communication spell.

"Jax," came the response after a few seconds, and I let out a breath of relief. ***"Not a good time,"*** she said, strain clear in her voice.

"Uh, okay, sorry! I need some advice. We're trapped in a tower, and I'm looking to blow a hole through to the next floor up. I need to know how to not take the next floor out entirely, but also smash enough that we can get through."

"You need an architect, not a goddess, then!" she said, irritation clear in her voice. ***"Wait a minute."***

She was silent for a few minutes, broken only by the shouts from outside and the occasional screeches from the tower's guardians further above us. I saw flashes of light and heard booms as the resident enslaved imps swooped down, hurling firebolts and worse through the open windows as legionnaires tried to block them off.

"The next room over to your left. Hit it where the wall joins the chimney. You owe me a thousand mana!" she snapped, and the sense of her presence vanished like a popped soap bubble.

"Thank you!" I threw after her, springing to my feet and rushing after Oracle into the next room.

She was hovering near the roof as I entered the room and nodded in satisfaction to herself.

"She's right," she said. "The wood's cracking up here. If we make that explosive spell stronger, maybe start with a Fireball as the base, and build from there…we should be able to take out the wall and ceiling here, with a bit of luck. It'll bring down the chimney, and we can climb through!"

I turned, discovering Augustus in the doorway, who was already turning and barking orders.

"Get everyone off this floor, but stay ready to go," I called to him, getting a nod of acknowledgement in return, and I turned back to Oracle. "Looks like we need to build another new spell then. High explosive mortar?" I suggested.

"You know I love a good bang!" she said, winking.

"Oh, I know you're going to get one, that's for sure!" I laughed, pulling up the standard Fireball in my mind. "So, let's get this started…"

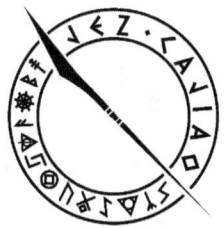

CHAPTER TWENTY-EIGHT

The explosion echoed around the inside of the tower, and I was flung backward by the pressure wave, my ears ringing.

Congratulations!

You have created a new personal spell:...High Explosive!

High Explosive:
Creates an explosive shell around an already-unstable Fireball core. This spell has been modified with a compressed air shield to force the detonation to travel in one set direction.

This spell, while cobbled together from parts of other spells, has been refined enough to be acknowledged as a fully formed spell, and as such, will begin to level and evolve as your understanding of its properties grows.

Cost: 25-200 mana, depending on desired outcome.

"Move!" screamed Rinko, sprinting past me, followed by two other legionnaires carrying a ladder they'd botched together from doors and scrap wood. As Bane helped me to my feet, and Arrin hit me with a healing that fixed my eardrums, legionnaires streamed past me, rushing up through the opening to attack the next level.

I blinked and shook my head reflexively, searching for Oracle. She floated nearby, looking up at the next floor. Half the room had seemingly fallen through, and the level above revealed intermittent patches of flames spread out.

"Uh, judging from the shaking of the tower, maybe don't do that again, Jax? Please?" Augustus requested.

I shot him a grin. "I've hardly got any mana left, mate. One potion, and that's all. I'm saving that for when we get higher up the tower, anyway."

"Not sure if it's safe to do this, then, but we found two weak mana potions..." He grimaced and passed them over.

"Oh, thank fuck," I muttered, popping them open and downing them, one after another. The sounds of fighting echoed down from the floor above, and I took a deep breath. "Well, sounds like they're playing our song," I said ruefully, gathering up my naginata and following the legion.

The rest of my small team formed up around me, with Bane already ahead of me on the makeshift ladder, and he climbed through to the next floor.

We filed up slowly, the clash and shouts of fighting receding as we climbed. The legionnaires pushed the defending harpies back until screams began rising just after we'd emerged onto the main floor.

"Back!" shouted Rinko, shuffling backwards with his shield held high as the legionnaire next to him started shuddering and shaking. Darkness spread visibly through his veins as he hissed in pain.

"Get back!" Rinko bellowed, moving faster and hunching down lower behind his shield.

Oracle lifted into the air for a second, then dropped as quickly as she could, as a bolt of necrotic energy passed overhead through the space she'd just occupied.

"What is it?" I asked as the legionnaires formed a shield wall, with those who had spears and bows preparing to blind fire.

"Another Anubai!" Oracle hissed angrily. "And this one's a mage."

"Shit," said Augustus, taking stock of the people around us, before grabbing my arm and pulling me aside. "Look, Jax, I know you haven't dealt with these fuckers before tonight, so I'll make it as clear as I can. If the Skyking has an Anubai Mage serving it, we might be better off falling back and taking our chances with the mob," he said seriously.

"The way the legion usually deals with these scum is to swamp them with numbers. Sometimes we lose dozens to take just one down. Anubai mages are usually champions of the Dark Gods; that's how rare this fucker is."

"Well, shit." I gritted my teeth in frustration. "You're telling me that this is a fight we can't win?" I asked him, and he shook his head.

"No, we might win it, but believe me when I say it'll be costly. Those we have left might not be able to take the Skyking down. Hell, those we have now might not be enough, if it's strong enough to compel one of those fuckers to serve it."

"Fuck it," I said, straightening. "Thanks for the advice, Augustus. I appreciate it, but I think it's time I took a direct hand."

"Jax, seriously, you're good, and you're lucky, but this fucker…" he started, and I grinned at him, clapping my hand over his on my arm.

"Trust me, mate. Can you hold him for a minute while I get a little surprise ready?" I asked, and he sighed, finally nodding.

"Our lives before yours. I hope you've got a good plan." He squeezed my arm slightly, then released me, returning to the legion shield wall. "Hold!" he bellowed. "Power the shield wall!"

He waited for the shouts of acknowledgement, before starting to chant.

"Who are we?" he called out.

"The legion!" the legionnaires shouted back to him.

"Who does the legion serve?" he roared.

"The empire!" they responded, a faint glow building on their shields. The legionnaire who'd been hit before, who'd stood bravely taking more blasts from the Anubai, grunted his last, falling to one knee then collapsing to the floor, dead, and the others shifted around him.

"Who's gonna fuck them up?" Augustus shouted to them.

"Lord Jax and the legion!" they screamed, their shields glowing brighter and brighter.

I tuned out the rest of the chant as I started stripping my armor off, pulling it apart section by section, then dropping it into my bags. It was a tricky job to fit the breastplate, but thankfully the neck opened as wide as needed, which made me think of a few sneaky things I needed to try.

I shrugged off the thoughts and shook my head as Lydia asked me what I was doing. I felt Oracle testing the changes we'd made, with mana flowing through me, pulsing faster and faster as she helped me control it.

"You're not going to have long with it, unless you use that greater potion," she warned me.

I nodded, pulling my shirt off over my head to expose the bandages I'd kept wrapped around my skin since leaving my tower. The need to let my skin heal naturally had been a problem, but thankfully, it was something that Ame had come up with a solution for.

Each morning and night, I'd had to smear a thick paste across the affected parts of my body, the result of which had been to create a mana dead-zone. As it had been done with the guidance and blessing of Jenae, when the goddess had helped Nerin to heal me, she'd guided the most powerful weaves around those areas, preserving the natural healing until now, and Nerin had in turn done the same during each subsequent healing.

I peeled bandages off slowly, feeling the air reaching the skin, making my hairs stand on end as I gave an involuntary shiver. It was time. I'd nearly done it a few times in the fights already, but this was the real test, to see if my wild-ass theory would actually work.

I'd done this off the memory of West's comments when I'd first been choosing a class:... *"You can't become much of a mage, but you could become a mage killer!"*

I took in a deep breath and ran the combinations through my mind, selecting the ones I wanted, then starting the slow cycle of feeding mana into them.

The first few seconds felt weird as my mana spread out, pushing out of my skin randomly, puddling and evaporating into the ether. Thanks mainly to Oracle, I adjusted quickly, focusing the mana in tight areas and feeding it into the required symbols, feeling the runes activating...

Congratulations!

You have created a new Class and its subsequent Profession.

What will you name them?

I focused while powering the final stage up, no idea how the prompt had overridden my preferences, but I filled it in quickly with the bits I'd already decided, and it vanished, followed by a new golden prompt.

The battle around me ground to a halt as everyone on both sides found their vision obscured by the message, as it could not be dismissed until it had been read and understood.

Know This!

A new Class has been created: Imperial Magekiller!

This class has several hidden requirements, but at this time, it can only be bestowed by the Imperial Scion, Lord Jax of Dravith.

Imperial Magekillers gain a +10% resistance to spells cast upon them, with a one-off boost of +5 to both Intelligence and Dexterity stats.

Know this!

A new Profession has been created: Imperial Arcane Tattooist!

This profession has several hidden requirements, but at this time, it can only be bestowed by the Imperial Scion, Lord Jax of Dravith.

Imperial Arcane Tattooists gain a one-off boost of +5 to Dexterity and Perception stats.

A low mutter rose from everyone as people read fragments out loud. A noticeable rise in optimism emitted from my forces as I strode toward the shield wall. The final prompt appeared only for me.

Congratulations!

You have created a new Class and Profession. As a bonus for being the first in the realms to create this combination, you receive the following:

- **100,000xp per profession or class.**
- **5 stat points per profession or class.**
- **2 Blueprints of average quality (to be selected)**

"Oh, yeah," I whispered, feeling Oracle's pleasure as I approached the front line. A ripple of pain flooded through me and made me grit my teeth as the changes took effect. I paused, drawing deep breaths in and pushing them out through my mouth until the pain subsided. The discomfort was well worth the sight of the mana bar growing to reflect the new reality of gaining an extra five points of Intelligence.

"Let me through," I ordered, and the legion broke the shield wall down the middle. The glowing red shield that had overlapped them dissipated as I strode forward, glaring at the Anubai that stood a dozen feet away, flanked by two prometheans.

This one was different to the ones I'd fought before. Where they had been heavily muscled, wearing robes that were open at the front and waist wraps like Egyptian schenti, this one was thinner, wearing only a waist wrap for decency's sake. It was adorned with dozens of thin golden chains, while gold and ivory symbols dangled from the countless hooks embedded in its skin.

Standing to either side of it, like two particularly self-important bookends, were two enormous, pale-blue-skinned prometheans, their wings casually folded behind their backs and simple wraps covering their junk. The one on the left brandished a longsword, which was as tall as I was, while the one on the right wielded a hammer of insane proportions.

I slammed the butt of my naginata down hard as I strode forward. Each strike flared, the power filling it and cycling it back to me, testing my new glowing tattoos.

I had not had many runes to work with, since Ame's knowledge was limited, but with Jenae's help, and Renna's, we'd managed it. They were black as pitch when they were unpowered, but as mana flowed into them, they shone silver-blue, glowing steadily as more mana sank into them.

The pattern of runes tattooed over my chest began to glow brighter and brighter, Add, Mana, Grow, and Shield flared with light. I took off at a run, my mana dipping lower and lower as they consumed my reserves.

"Come on, you motherfucker!" I screamed at the Anubai, who growled at me and raised both arms. Ripples of darkness flowed down his limbs to coalesce into a ball that he built upon frantically as I crossed the intervening distance. Just as I leapt into the air, my naginata held two-handed overhead, blade down, he released his spell with a snarled oath. The spell flashed forward to hammer into me, where it hit the failing shield I'd cast, its heavy draw of mana too large for me to maintain for long.

Until a helpful Anubai mage kindly donated his mana to it.

As the spell hit the shield, it flashed, the blackness bursting like a waterbomb hitting the sidewalk. The mana was ripped out of the spell, splashing, then sinking into the shield and revving it up to full strength. The drain on my mana reserves vanished, allowing me to pound the last dregs of it into my naginata, just in time to see the sneer of contempt on the Anubai's face turn into horror and disbelief.

The blade hit his own shield, punching through, thanks to the power of the weapon and the force behind it, but his shield lasted long enough to deflect it to the right, depriving me of the outright kill. The blade slammed into his left shoulder and punched straight through to erupt out of his back.

The Prometheans on either side, who'd been grinning and eying me with unconcealed contempt, snapped to alert. The one on my right grabbed the Anubai and yanked him backwards, while the one on my left tackled me.

My shield held, flaring into bright light, but being designed to take magical attacks, rather than physical, it wouldn't last long.

As the Anubai was dragged backwards, the blade of my naginata came free with a hiss and a scream of pain. The entire weapon was glowing bright white. Lightning energy flickered, popped, and crackled up and down its length, and the black blood coating the blade hissed into steam and vanished as I yanked it back.

The Promethean confronting me slammed his enormous hammer down atop my shield. Cracks appeared, flaring, and the mana powering the shield drained even faster. Before he could manage a second strike, I stabbed out. The tip of the blade licked across my opponent's left shoulder, slicing deep into his unprotected flesh and erupting in a spray of blood.

He screamed in outrage, shoving the head of his hammer into my shield. It flared again, pushing him back, but pulsed warningly, the mana draining at an incredible rate.

I whipped the blade of my naginata back towards my right side, bringing the butt forward with my left and swept it down. Hammering it into the back of his right knee, then yanking it forwards, I smashed the flat of the blade into his face, sending him falling backwards.

I spun the weapon like a rower wielding a double-headed oar and brought the bladed end around again, smashing the haft against the handle of his hastily raised hammer. Taking advantage of his unbalanced state, I lunged forwards, stabbing the blade into his upper chest. The sharp metal edge cut through muscles and scored across the breastbone before plunging into an open section. The tip embedded in the wood of the floor beneath him, the blade severing his spine.

His arms fell to the sides, suddenly bereft of control. He stared up at me in horror as I planted one foot on his lower chest. I yanked my naginata backward, pulling the blade free to point it at the promethean who was backing away while carrying the furiously growling Anubai.

"You see that?" I shouted after them. "I'm gonna fucking have you, my son!" I spat casually down on the dying promethean and kicked off, sprinting after them as the legion and the rest of my people roared in triumph. The shield wall disbanded as they ran after me, roaring for blood.

The Anubai cast another spell, noticeably weaker, but once again, when it hit my shield, it charged it, instead of causing damage.

"FOOLS!" called a voice from above, its whispering dark cadence echoing down the halls. ***"MAGIC FEEDS IT, SLAUGHTER IT WITH STEEL."***

"Yeah!" I called out as I closed on the pair that were retreating. "You fucking try that, pal. See how well it works out for you!"

I swung my naginata, drunk off adrenaline and fresh kills, to block the incoming slash from the promethean's enormous longsword.

That was a mistake, I realized, as I flew back into an interior wall, demolishing it and making my shield pop like a bubble. The rubble fell on me as a tiny fraction of my mind calmly informed me that sheer aggression and an adrenaline response like an espresso made with an energy drink instead of water was no match for actual physics. Not only was the promethean stronger than me by far, but he was also swinging enough steel to make a small car.

"Owww." I growled, pulling myself up out of the pile of timber and collapsed masonry. I was glad my shield had lasted long enough to blunt the force of that impact, at least. I found the Anubai staring at me and cackling as he lifted both hands to power up another spell, clearly having seen my shield die. An arrow followed swiftly by a Firebolt, then two more arrows, slammed into him, staggering him and sending him crashing to the floor, stunned and whimpering.

"Forgot about yer shield, didn't ya, cocksucker!" I called out, grinning as Augustus crashed into the promethean. Where I'd been outclassed on strength and weight, he wasn't; at least, not by as much. Added to that, the years of heavy fighting and training the legion drummed into its troops, and the fact that the UnderVerse equivalents of staff sergeants were always the one group no sane individual ever wanted to fight in *any* army, and it was over in seconds. It certainly ended before the promethean expected, considering the surprised look on his face as Augustus gutted him, then decapitated his dying body as he fell backwards.

The Anubai was frantically pulling a health potion from his bag when Bane appeared, slit his throat, and pulled both the health potion and the potion pouch free. The Mer walked over to me quite casually as the mage bled out, thrashing and gurgling.

I nodded to him in thanks, checking inside and immediately passed a mana potion to Arrin, downing an average-strength one myself. My mana regeneration jumped by more than double, and I breathed out a sigh of relief as I looked over our forces, numerous grinning faces looking back at me.

"Impressive new class, Jax!" Augustus called to me, flicking his sword almost negligently and spattering the dead Promethean with his own blood.

"Thanks, mate!" I replied, grinning.

"I know a few legionnaires who'd be interested in it, if you're willing?" he asked, an eyebrow raised.

"Now that we know it works, hell yes," I said, turning to regard the two staircases at either end of the floor. "But it'll have to wait until we reach the tower. Right now, we've a few more people to fuck up first."

"As you command," Augustus said, nodding in respect. He turned to the legion, looking his forces over.

"How bad?" I asked.

He sighed. "Two dead, one injured enough that he'll need a few days to recover from the healing. Two more that'll be okay, but I'll keep them at the back, for now. Nine, counting myself, I'm happy to lead into battle."

"And two staircases," I said. "The imp said the left staircase wasn't trapped, but which one's the left?" I wondered aloud, thinking about how many times we'd twisted around in climbing the building so far.

"Fuck knows. Might not even be this floor," Rinko said, shrugging.

"Fair point." I let out a huff. "Augustus, you take the legion up that stairwell, and take Nerin." I nodded at one end. "Tang, you scout for traps for Augustus. Yen, you're with me and my squad; you and Bane scout for us. We're taking that stairwell." I gestured to the other end of the hallway.

With a round of salutes and a few shouts of "good luck," we separated into two groups, with my squad supplemented by Grizz and Nigret, despite my original orders that they remain close to Nerin, who'd followed the legion. I saw the hand of Augustus in it, so I didn't argue, as that made our two groups roughly equal in numbers, if not in sheer muscle.

We jogged to the end of the hall, passing the hole in the floor. I noted that the bits we'd used to climb up had been pulled up after the legion, with a makeshift barrier erected over the hole, which would result in a nightmare for anyone who tried to follow us. A few floors below, shouts and chants echoed as someone tried to whip the mob up into a frenzy to attack. I looked out of one window as I passed it, catching sight of a promethean hovering in the air, its back to us as it bellowed about the evil crimes we'd committed.

"Bane, you still got that Drow-poisoned bolt for the crossbow?" I asked casually, and a second later, he was alongside me.

He crouched, aiming carefully, then adjusting, then aiming again. Just as I was about to ask him if he needed help, he fired with a deep *twang*.

The bolt sailed through the air faster than the eye could follow, burying itself in the back of the creature's head, golden locks suddenly sprouting the feathered shaft of the bolt.

The promethean collapsed bonelessly to the ground. The crowd drew back in horror, as I shook my head in wonder.

"Hell, man, If I'd known you were that good a shot, I wouldn't have suggested wasting the poisoned bolt." I gaped in astonishment.

"I'm not," he replied calmly. "I was aiming for his ass."

There was a brief silence before people started to snicker at the mental image of the proud promethean screaming at having something in his ass, and the fact that luck had taken such a hand in that for us.

"Damn. Ah well, at least it means I've still got a bodyguard, then. I was thinking of having you join the hunters, until you said that."

"Ever tried to use a crossbow underwater?" he asked me, thrumming his amusement. "I've fired that damn thing four times before today!"

"Well, you're getting lessons when we get back!" Miren piped up, grinning at him.

"Damn right," Lydia agreed gruffly.

"So, are you guys coming?" Yen called from the bottom of the stairwell. "Because I've already found one trap, and it's shit."

We filed over, still smiling, and looked where she gestured. The stairs were old and cracked, badly warped, and there were signs of hundreds of feet pounding up and down them over the years, except for the third step up, which had been freshly replaced and had a tiny wire leading across it.

"Really?" I asked, cocking my head to one side in disbelief. "That's not there to trick us?"

"If it is, the second trap's so good I can't find it," she said dubiously.

"Bane?" I asked, and we all felt the pulse of his worldsense wash outwards. Instead of the low, almost-imperceptible buzz we often felt from him when we were close enough, this was a heavy one, and the tendrils that surrounded his head lifted, each tilting and shifting as he examined the staircase from every possible angle for a handful of seconds before relaxing and turning to look at us.

"Nope, they're all idiots," he pronounced clearly. We all started grinning. I leaned in close to the trap, looking it over, and with my Traps skill activated, I checked it over further.

"It's literally a spike trap; trigger it, and spear blades spring out of the wall here"—I pointed to an obviously repainted section of wall—"and here."

I gestured to the other side.

I shrugged and looked at Lydia, who grinned and stepped forward, swinging her mace at both spots, hard.

After a few crunches, she stepped back, and I triggered the trap using my naginata, hearing the clunk as it released. We all watched as a single spear fell out of the damaged wall, sliding down the few steps to the floor.

"Wow." I shook my head in disgust. I found much the same on the faces of the others, as well. We'd fought horrific creatures in the arena, and seriously powerful bad guys here, and the trap was just…pathetic. It looked like something a group of kids would make to protect their treehouse.

“Okay, people, enough dawdling…let’s go fuck up the Skyking,” I said.

Bane vanished, rushing up the stairs ahead of us, followed by Yen, then myself.

The next floor was abandoned and silent, but the space split into a single room that gave no access to the other side of the building. We paused, looking around, but besides a load of old fabric-covered boxes, some rusted machinery, and a really bad painting of something I couldn’t identify, there was nothing there, so we headed for the next floor.

I’d recovered more than half my mana when we cleared the stairwell onto the next floor. Wide openings interspersed the walls, leading out into the night, making the hairs on the back of my neck stand on end with the unmistakable sensation that something was wrong. Although the drizzle outside had increased to a steady rain, the sounds filtering up to us were still full of anger and showed no sign of breaking up, inside, it was too quiet.

We were being watched.

“Look out!” came Bane’s voice, and he flashed into sight on the far side of the room. Screams of pain and rage mounted as an illusionary wall shimmered and vanished, revealing dozens of imps lead by a promethean, all charging spells or leveling crossbows.

I forced mana into my tattoos as quickly as I could, knowing I was losing a lot of mana in the process. But I couldn’t take the time to build up as carefully as I had before. I groaned as other tattoos began to flare to life, and I had to cut the mana to them, starting again, selecting each rune one at a time and forcing them to combine to create the effect I wanted.

In the time it took me to activate my shield, most of the squad had raced past me, and I’d had to duck behind some cover, swearing like a pirate as I tried to make the magic work.

“Come on, you fucker, just work! Everything’s right, just get up there!” I snarled to myself, eyes closed. I opened them and saw Yen’s face as she tried not to smirk, while readying her own magic. “It’s not my fault!” I tried to explain. “This has never happ—oh, fuck off!” I snarled as I realized what I sounded like, before doing the mental equivalent of stamping my mana into the correct tattoos.

My shield finally flared to life, and I grinned, lunging out from behind cover. I brandished my naginata in my right hand as I pulled the kite shield from storage and held it with my left. I might not be able to last long against the crossbows, but they were about to get a nasty surprise when it came to their magic.

I rushed forward, trying to close the distance as Lydia, Nigret, Jian, and Grizz battled in close, their shields taking a hammering from both magic and mundane weaponry as they held the line, while being held back by a trio of larger creatures I hadn’t seen before.

I quickly used Examine and grunted at the notification, swiping it away and concentrating on the fight.

Greater Stone Imp (Adult)
This imp has, against all probability and good sense, been permitted to reach adulthood. It has been gelded to prevent its overwhelming sexual drive from interfering with its master's intentions for it, and has instead, through methods unknown, been directed into a controlled rage at any who trespass in its master's territory.

Weaknesses: Air magic has double its usual effect against imps of this kind.

Resistances: Earth or Fire magics used against this creature suffer a 75% damage penalty.

Level: 21

Health: 410

Mana: 130/130

There were only three of them, but in the narrow, high-ceilinged room, they were holding my people back, while the flying imps—*the adolescents, I guess*—were hovering and loosing blast after blast from above.

I stopped at the back of the group between Miren and Stephanos, who were busy firing constant arrows, and Arrin, who was shouting random shit between hammering Magic Missiles at the enemy.

"You want some? Oh yeah, and you? Daddy's got something for you…" He cackled, and I tuned the disturbing nutjob out.

Focusing, I raised my arms in the air, offering my unarmored chest to the imps and triggering an ability I'd gained before, but rarely used.

"Your mother was a hamster!" I screamed, my voice changing as my stamina dipped suddenly, my call taking on a deeper, richer timbre as I used my Taunt ability.

Predictably, they shifted their focus from the heavily armored fighters hiding behind their shields and fired on me instead. The first spell, a Lightning Bolt, cracked across the air between us. It turned my shield black on impact, followed by three more Firebolts and a black bolt from the promethean. While the dark spell was far weaker than that used by the Anubai mage, it was still clearly necrotic in nature.

The impact of all the spells against my shield in one go made it flare with power, and the room momentarily paused at the sight.

Then Bane suddenly reappeared and drove two daggers into the promethean's kidneys, and the other two into the thick muscles either side of its neck. He yanked all four blades backward, shredding its organs and throat before spinning into the nearest shadows and vanishing from sight again.

The battle resumed, more frantically this time as we surged forward. The dynamic shifted as we no longer had to worry about the magic attacks as much. Enraged, the three crossbow-wielding imps released, bolts flying through the air.

Two hit my shield, one dead on, shattering and falling to the floor as my shield pulsed. The second hit at an angle and sheared off to the left, slamming into Miren's arm. She screamed as she dropped her bow, clutching at the feathered tip in pained shock. The third bolt missed and slammed into Grizz's shield, penetrating just far enough that it stuck, cracking the surrounding metal.

"Miren!" Jian screamed in fury, abandoning his careful probing attacks against one of the greater imps in favor of his special ability, Icewind's Fury.

His two scythes glowed an unearthly icy blue for a second, and he attacked, seeming to blur as the blades flashed out continuously, slicing into the snarling greater imp and leaving wounds that slowly seeped ice into the creature. He sliced thin lines across the stony upper arms, then when its reactions were slowed, he feinted a strike at its head.

When the imp raised both arms protectively, he instead spun, sweeping low and disemboweling it with the first strike. As its arms came back down, the trailing second blade took its head in a shower of black blood.

He straightened and kicked out, using my signature Sparta kick to send the imp flying backward, knocking a frantically reloading crossbow wielder from the air.

"Now, you die!" Jian snarled, pointing one blade at the wide-eyed imp that lay pinned beneath its larger brethren.

The rest of the battle was clearing up quickly. My Taunt had distracted the fighters enough that Lydia and Grizz had been able to take the second greater imp down, and the final one had died to an arrow in the eye from Stephanos as Yen finally finished her spell.

"Bane, move!" she shouted as the final syllable slipped from her tongue, and a dozen flaming spears appeared to hover above her raised right hand. He became visible, diving through the door behind the imps, and she made a throwing gesture, the spears following her aim and slamming into the panicking imps and the bleeding-out promethean.

The fight was over in seconds as multiple six-foot spears of glowing flame slamming into a creature the size of a medium terrier tends to end things quickly.

Only one managed to make it to the doorway, and as it passed, screaming in fear, Bane appeared and took its wings off before pinning it to the floor with a second strike.

The fight seemed to end too soon, with all of us looking for another target for a moment before collectively sagging with relief, catching our breath.

"In here," Bane called, and we moved forward, ignoring all bodies aside from the promethean. Lydia paused to search its corpse roughly, cutting its bag free and passing it to me to store for later. I dropped it into my bag of spatial folding, confident without checking that it would be of lower quality.

The next room was packed with small cages, most filled with rotting filth and dangling…bits. The few cages that were occupied by living things held people with open, weeping sores. They looked weak, starved, and like they'd long ago given up on life. One woman with dirty white hair stared listlessly at me as we entered the room.

"Well, fuck," I muttered, gaping at the revolting conditions. "What the hell is this?"

Yen spoke up, pointing to the gnawed bones in one of the cages nearby.

"It's a dining hall," she said disgustedly, picking her way carefully across the filth-strewn floor.

"Sick bastards," I muttered, moving from cage to cage. Four people remained alive in a room that housed twenty cages, and each of them bore bleeding, weeping wounds surrounded by jagged toothmarks.

I was suddenly furious that we'd left the chained imps with the legionnaires. I wanted to cut their throats for this. I'd kick them off the side of the tower; no, I'd take them to the Great Tower and throw—

"It's not…their…fault," came a whisper from the white-haired woman, and I spun, looking back at her.

"Save your strength," I hushed her, examining the cage for a way to release her.

"No," she said, swallowing hard and fighting to speak, her voice raspy and weak. "It's not…their fault, it's mine." She shook her head mournfully. "I was studying…the imps, and I wasn't careful…enough with my research. They're…simple creatures. They…get addicted to emotions, and sentients…leak emotions into their bodies. We change…how we taste to certain creatures, like…imps, depending on…what we feel…when we die." A whimper caught in her throat. "I told the…wrong person. I was…studying them, and I…trusted the wrong man. That's how we all…ended up here." She closed her eyes and started to shake, sobs escaping her. "It's all…my fault."

"No," I said emphatically. "It's the fucking Skyking's fault, not yours, and we're going to teach it a lesson it'll never forget."

I found the lock on her cage. The metal contraption was rusty and, frankly, covered in months of shit, so I ignored it, instead pushing the base of my naginata through the attached loop of chain and twisting, using the weapon as a lever to snap the rusty mess free.

The bottom of the cage fell out, and she collapsed to the floor with a disgusting *squelch*. I swallowed hard at the smell that arose, but I dismissed the shield and reached out, helping her to move to a clear area, the rest of my team doing the same for the other three captives.

"Where's the next stairwell?" I asked the room in general, and Bane spoke up.

"The corner of the room, beyond that door." He gestured to an opening nearby. "The other stairwell must just bypass this floor, as there can't be much left here, what with the size of the room and all. The floor below was probably the opposite to this for the legion."

"Okay, let's get these people over near there, give them a quick heal to keep them going; then we need to move on," I directed, turning to look at the woman I was helping to stand. "We'll come back for you, but you don't want to be with us as we go fight."

"Jax," Bane said, moving closer.

"What's up, mate?" I asked distractedly, watching how badly the woman was struggling, her atrophied limbs shaking as they tried to bear her weight.

"The illusion spell that hid the group," he started, shaking his head in frustration. "I don't understand how they hid from my worldsense as well," he admitted. "It takes a highly skilled illusionist to create something that can reflect the pulses of my worldsense, so we must be careful, very careful, going forward. If one had not made a noise, I'd have missed them."

"Okay, mate, will do." My mind was spinning. I'd not even considered that. "Warn the others, will you?" I asked as Oracle hovered next to me, examining the woman.

I'd asked her not to use our mana unless it was over half for the next few fights, just in case I needed to kickstart our shield, and I could sense that she was feeling a bit useless.

"Do you want to heal her?" I asked Oracle, and she immediately began casting, wrapping the woman in a sheath of magic that lifted her, groaning, from the floor as it scanned her inside and out to rebuild and repair the most grievous injuries. Flesh literally bubbled up to fill the bite marks, smoothing out sores and pustules. Her face slowly gained mass, her cheeks filling in from the impression of Skeletor she'd been doing seconds before.

Oracle broke it off before it went too far, leaving me at just over a third of my mana. The truncated spell had still used an easy hundred to start her healing.

Yen was already examining the staircase up to the next level, and Bane was with her. Grizz had dropped back to the last stairwell and was listening carefully, and Stephanos was watching out of the open wall for anyone trying to come in. That left Jian and Arrin dealing with Miren's wound and Nigret and Lydia moving people over to where we were.

"We need more mana," I muttered, searching through my bags and hating that I'd not taken the time to make some more potions.

"I've got two," Arrin called, having somehow heard me, and he passed me one. Thankfully, it was an average-quality potion that restored a hundred mana, with a boosted regeneration that would double my own for the next minute.

I downed it quickly, sighing in pleasure at the minty-fresh taste. It felt like downing a glass of gritty spearmint somehow, and the feeling of my mana regenerating and refilling made me relax. It was a weird sensation, the lower my mana got, like being hungry, but not. I shrugged, dismissing it as unimportant as Oracle started work on the next person.

We rested for a few minutes, enough for our mana to refill a little and for Arrin to heal Miren and one of the prisoners, while Oracle and I did the other two.

"Jax!" Yen called from the stairwell, jumping back as a glowing golden yellow orb flew down at speed. It slammed to a stop, spinning around and trying to leave, before Bane's thrown dagger hit it. It burst with a hiss, the glowing orb dissipating as Grizz swore sulphurously.

"What?" I asked, seeing the looks he exchanged with Yen.

"That spell. The Skyking knows who and what we are now," Yen said angrily. "It's Percival's Personal Examination, a disgusting spell that shows the caster anything it sees. It pierces through almost all invisibility spells, and it's a bastard to counter. Its use is punishable by death in most places."

"Looked like a useful spell to me; what's wrong with it?" I asked, confused. "Don't get me wrong, I'd rather it didn't know we were here, but with all the noise we've made, that was never really an option."

"It's not a popular spell amongst the ladies, Jax," Grizz said delicately. "Percival designed it to mimic a popular celebratory lantern for the Feast of Souls, specifically a candle in a ball of paper that floats up into the air, carrying people's thoughts and prayers for those they've lost."

"Right…?" I asked before Yen cut in.

"Except that Percival was a fucking pervert and used it to spy in windows and changing rooms. He designed it so people would think it was a soul-lamp and ignore it, while he could get his rocks off by watching!"

"Sneaky fucker!" I said, shaking my head in disbelief. "He really created a voyeur spell?"

"Yeah," Yen said sourly. "And he taught it to all his noble friends. For a handful of years, nobody was safe. Variants on the original made it almost impossible to know if there was one in your bedroom or not, until someone was caught using it on the old Lord of Himnel's mother. The law was made that day: anyone caught using it would be executed in the name of 'state secrets'."

"Well, at least—" I started, before being cut off.

"But the nobility, being the nobility, meant that a load of them kept using it. They just kept it away from their own and used it to perv on the common folks instead!" Yen snarled, and Grizz shrugged.

"It's not a commonly seen spell anymore, thanks to all that. If a noble was actually caught using it, they'd be publicly censured by their own kind, even though I bet they all know who still uses it secretly. The problem is, if the Skyking is using such a spell, it means that it's either a noble or it has access to the nobility. It's also a strong magic user, since that spell needs a lot of mana to cast."

"How much?" I asked curiously, readying myself and checking over my notifications quickly.

"About two hundred mana, plus the maintenance cost," Yen replied. I whistled in understanding. That was a lot of mana to just throw away, considering it had to know we were coming for it.

Congratulations!

You have killed the following:

- 1x Promethean Personal Guard, level 22 for a total of 10,800xp
- 3x Human Mercenaries of various levels for a total of 3,850xp

A party under your command killed the following:

- 9x Human Mercenaries of various levels for a total of 11,150xp
- 3x Alkyon of various levels for a total of 3,875xp
- 2x Promethean Warriors of various levels for a total of 13,850xp
- 1x Promethean Personal Guard, level 19 for a total of 8,500xp
- 1x Promethean Rabble-Rouser, level 20 for a total of 9,250xp
- 1x Anubai Dark Champion, level 39 for a total of 21,000xp
- 3x Greater Stone Imps of various levels for a total of 12,500xp
- 9x Imps of various levels for a total of 5,800xp

Total Party experience earned: 85,925xp
As party leader, you gain 25% of all experience earned.
Progress to level 16 stands at 355,036/165,000

*

Congratulations!

You have reached level 16 & 17

You have 24 unspent Attribute points and 0 Meridian points available.

Progress to level 18 stands at 36/225,000

"Oh, hell yes…" I muttered to myself, feeling the experience waiting to be unleashed. I acknowledged the prompts, gasping as I gained not one, but two levels. It was quite a rush, jumping all the way to level seventeen, thanks to the experience boosts from creating both the profession and the class. Due to the bonus stat points I'd earned as well, I now had twenty-four points available, and I seriously needed them right now.

I pulled up my character sheet and skimmed it while calling out to everyone. "If you've gained levels, now would be a great time to use those points!"

I was tempted to see what dropping all twenty points into Agility would do for me. I had to admit, it had already kept me alive on a literally daily basis, and being able to dodge even better would be amazing, but hell, I needed those points *everywhere*.

I dismissed Charisma and Perception outright. While I knew I needed to boost them as well, I also needed to live through this, and they wouldn't immediately help with that. Dexterity helped with my weapon handling, but I was doing okay there. Not good, admittedly, but okay. Constitution, I'd bumped recently, and it was already paying dividends. But if I got stabbed somewhere vital, like in the heart, I was dead, regardless of how much health I had.

I was down to Endurance, Intelligence, Strength, Luck, and Wisdom. Endurance was important, but with my meridian points already invested there, it was leveling nicely. While my Strength was starting to lag behind a bit, I could supplement that with my Mana Overdrive ability.

I pulled up my abilities and saw that my Mana Overdrive was actually level seven now. With three more levels, I could seal shut the mana channels that it had torn open, and I'd start to regenerate again properly, boosting my mana regen from one point seven five, up to three point five per minute.

I wavered between Intelligence and Wisdom. I could see good reasons to do both, but for some reason, I just didn't want to waste the opportunity, and I felt like splitting the majority of the points would be a mistake. I drew a deep breath and called out to the room.

"I'm assigning some points, so don't worry if I collapse, okay?" I said, getting a round of grunts in response. I took a deep breath and, because I was an adult who always carefully considered things, I pulled a coin out of my bag.

One side had a cog design inscribed on it, and the other side displayed a face that seemed to be glaring at me in disapproval.

"Okay," I whispered to myself. "Cog's Intelligence, and head's Wisdom…makes sense, sort of. Drop the four odd points into Luck, and…" I flipped the coin, slammed the points in before I could think better of it, and grunted as the world seemed to expand before my eyes. Pain ripped through my brain, threatening to make me pass out.

CHAPTER TWENTY-NINE

It took a handful of minutes before I could see again, and even then, it felt like someone had ripped the top off my skull, poured bleach onto my brain, and scrubbed it before wiring me up to a car battery.

Twenty points to Intelligence in one go: man, that shit hurt! It also increased my manapool another two hundred, giving me five hundred and seventy, despite the twenty that I had lost to Oracle permanently.

I regarded my pathetically low amount of mana available and downed the greater mana potion. The jump in my regeneration from one point seven five points per minute to eleven points per second for a hundred and twenty seconds was huge. It literally regenerated my entire mana pool in under a minute, so I went to work fast, fully healing the prisoners. I drained my whole pool within the first minute, letting myself recover as we turned to the stairs.

"Time to go play," I said quietly, feeling the rest of the group's readiness. I took a head count, trying to figure out why two of my people were missing before noting that Miren and Jian were off to one side, having a heated make-out session behind a cage full of rotted corpses and shit. "Really?" I said loudly. Lydia whistled, and they broke apart, red-faced, having been totally oblivious.

"Seriously, guys? You choose now…and there…of all places to try to get some action?"

"Sorry, Jax."

"Sorry, Lord Jax," the pair parroted, rejoining the group rather shamefacedly.

"Seriously, you two, get a fucking room when we get out of here." I shook my head disapprovingly, winking at Lydia, who glowered at them, then turned her face where only I could see and stifled a laugh at how contrite they appeared.

"I'd suggest you wait a few minutes," I said to the former prisoners, who were now huddled together, confused and clearly distressed. "Then either follow us up to the top, and you can escape the city with us, or go to the bottom of the tower and head back into the city, if that's what you want to do. Be warned, though. We're legion, or at least some of us are, and there's a mob outside that doesn't like us. They're being whipped up into a frenzy to attack us, so you might want to be careful down there."

"What?!" shrieked a woman garbed in filthy finery and stinking velvet. "Surely you don't mean that! We need escorts back to our homes. You've rescued us; now do your jobs! *If* you're legionnaires, which I doubt, considering how scruffy you look, you've sworn an Oath to obey the empire. I'm Lady Karen Hightree, and as I am obviously the highest-ranking noble here, I order you to stop whatever you're doing and take me home!"

I looked at her, then to Grizz, who nodded to me, closing his eyes and taking a deep breath.

"You really have this kind of shit to deal with?" I asked in disbelief.

"Daily, mate. Honestly, they're all like this," he said croakily, rolling his eyes in irritation.

"You!" she snapped, seeing Grizz clearly for the first time. "You're a legionnaire! I *order* you to escort me to safety! And if any of these ruffians object, you're to take their heads!"

"The offer of escaping with us is no longer open to you," I informed the entitled bitch sitting on the floor. "Any of the rest of you who feel this way, stay here or fuck off downstairs. Otherwise, you're welcome to follow along. Grizz, I officially relieve you of any requirement to obey any orders outside of my own and your legion chain of command, just in case that was an issue for you."

Grizz took a deep breath and smiled as he felt his Oath acknowledge that change, and my mana took a dip.

"Man, that feels good," Grizz muttered, closing his eyes for a second before limping over to the filthy noblewoman. He loomed over her momentarily, then leaned down and looked her in the eyes as she shrank back from the intensity of his gaze. "Listen, you sanctimonious piece of shit." He spoke slowly and clearly, enjoying the look of shock on her face. "The legion doesn't answer to you and your pathetic attempts at nobility anymore. We're *imperial legionnaires*, and the empire is rising again. I'd have a good long look at the Imperial Codex of Laws when you get the chance, if I were you. See how many you've broken, because we're shackled no longer. The legion's gonna enforce the law, *as it was written*, from now on. None of the shit we've had to put up with forever."

"How *dare* you!" she snarled, white with outrage. "Who do you think supersedes my authority! I am—"

"That'd be me," I interrupted, making a point of scratching my balls while she stared at me in shock. "Lord Jax, High Lord of Dravith, Imperial Scion, as acknowledged by the Eternal Emperor Amon, oh, and Arena Champion, I guess.

"I'd say I was pleased to meet you, but I'm really not. I don't give two shits who you are. Now, I suggest you fuck off somewhere and hide, as the mob isn't likely to be too nice to a noble that's all alone here." I leaned close and belched in her face, sneering at her frightened disgust before turning away and looking back up the stairs. "Right, enough time wasting. Let's go fuck that Skyking up."

I started up the stairs, Yen and Bane flowing unimpeded ahead of me, and the rest of my squad following behind.

"You've got a way with words," Nigret called up to me, amusement clear in his voice and I grinned, even though he couldn't see it.

"Thanks, mate."

"I don't suppose there are any of my kind in this Great Tower of yours? A lady or three, perhaps?" he asked hopefully, and I snorted.

"There might be by the time we get back; some of my people were going recruiting."

"Then Nigret shall live in hope," he said with a chuffing sound I assumed was laughter.

We jogged up two more floors, finding them both empty, until we came to what we thought must be one of the highest floors remaining. This floor had also been trapped, and unlike the last one, they were both well-built and cunningly hidden. When we came across them, it was pure luck that Bane led us, as opposed to Yen, who'd just dropped back for a drink after leading us past the two previous floors.

Bane sensed the difference in the step as he approached it, and immediately held up his hand warningly. We ground to a halt as he examined the floor, walls, and ceiling, crouching carefully and calling me forward.

"What is it?" I asked him, moving up to lean in close.

"A trap. A magical one, I'm thinking. There's a pressure plate, but I can find nothing attached."

I crouched next to him, and with Oracle's help, we started cautiously examining it, until it all went sideways.

The door at the top of the stairs opened suddenly, exposing a grinning promethean with a bow. It was a huge weapon, looking more akin to a siege weapon than anything else, and the quarrel that he launched was closer in size to a small spear.

The real issue, though, was the fact that we were trapped in the stairwell and had nowhere to go.

I frantically yanked on my shield, pulling it from my bag and trying to bring it around to cover us, but there was no time.

Bane saw the arrow coming, and he dove, turning around so fast I could barely see him. He threw himself between me and the arrow, taking it full in his back.

The head of it was barbed, I realized, as it erupted from his chest. Blood sprayed across my face, standing two steps down from him as I was. I blinked in shock, gaping at the white of Bane's bone displayed in front of me. The bolt had punched through his equivalent of a sternum, and his tendrils stiffened in pain before he collapsed into my arms.

I caught him, pulling him down behind me, and shifting the shield to cover us. Crouching behind it, I stared at him, shocked and horrified by the injury he'd taken.

A second or so later, just as I'd settled the shield into place, a second arrow slammed into it, pushing me backward off the step I had been perched on. I landed heavily against Yen, who'd produced a small shield of her own and was trying to cover me with it.

"Bane…no," I whispered, straightening and getting back on my own stair, shifting to cover him again. Shouting erupted from the floor above, blended with the sound of more people running towards the stairs. I looked back at Bane as he coughed blood and started to shake, his limbs spasming.

"Jax!" Oracle shouted in my ear, slapping me across the cheek, hard.

"What?!" I snarled at her, torn from my shocked and frozen state.

"I'll heal him. I *will* save him! Just go!" she shouted, determination written large across her face.

"Everyone, back off!" I snarled at the rest of my team as Yen and Lydia dragged Bane back, then carried him down the stairs as Oracle worked frantically to save his life. The rest of the group made space quickly, leaving me alone in the upper stairwell.

"You wanna play, cocksucker?" I grated out, glowering up at the archer and ducking back behind my shield as he released another quarrel. The huge arrow slammed into the metal, making me grunt in pain. "Then let's fucking play," I growled out, activating Mana Overdrive and crouching. Digging my feet in, I sprang up and hammered forward with all the energy my coiled legs could manage.

My feet barely seemed to touch the trapped stairs before I was past, the traps triggering too late to catch me. The first was an alarm, one that wailed and echoed clearly on the upper floors, followed by spikes jutting upwards a split second too slowly and catching only air. Spears lanced out at a height intended to punch into a trespasser's ankles and thighs, crippling them.

Finally, a dart shot out from a hole, concealed as a knot in the wood at the top of the back wall. I saw it coming, just like I saw the promethean hauling back, his fresh arrow resting against the notched grip of the bow, all in slow motion, as though they had been dipped in molasses.

I batted aside the dart with my shield, throwing my naginata with the power and accuracy of my supercharged form. I watched the weapon leave my hand, observing the wobble and flex in its flight. A secondary, icily calm part of my mind noted that I needed to work on that; throwing weapons was a skill I clearly hadn't yet mastered.

The greater part of my mind was filled with fury and a hunger for blood.

I saw the naginata's bladed tip fly straight and true, the eyes of its promethean target widening in horror as he tried to decide whether to fire, or to dodge, and in that split second of indecision, his fate was sealed. The tip punched into his chest on the left side, the remainder of the blade following.

An entire foot of metal sank deep between his ribs to carve through his lung and into his heart, coming to a quivering halt as it struck the inside of his ribcage. The half-sideways-turned nature of his firing position had allowed the naginata to do far more damage than if he'd been standing straight-on.

His eyes bulged as he released his now un-aimed arrow to flash toward me, only to be batted aside. I planted one foot on the wall of the stairwell, using it to jump off and send me rocketing into him. The impact took us both backward into the room behind as I hit him left-foot-first.

I braced that foot on his stomach, grabbing the naginata with my right hand. As he fell, I pulled, my right foot coming to land on his throat.

I ripped my naginata out, ribs creaking and organs bursting free with it, spinning it over and splattering the dozen creatures in the room with the still-hot blood of their companion.

"Who's next?" I bellowed at the shocked mix of imps and prometheans before punching the blade through the tiny form of a grey-skinned imp who'd been in the process of summoning what looked to have been lightning.

My blade lanced through the crackling ball of energy and into its chest, bursting out the back to tear a wing free before being yanked back, hard.

The spell burst, the uncontained lightning sinking into the imp. The small creature screamed as it fell from the air, dying. I spun, left hand holding my shield in place as I started rapidly rotating the naginata around. My high Dexterity made it easier for me to strike as I sliced another imp's wings free, then took a third in the mouth, the tip erupting from the back of its head in a spray of bloody chunks.

I wrenched my mana out of Mana Overdrive, ripping it free of the channels that were soaking it up like the parched sand of the desert. Instead, I began ramming it furiously into my tattoos, activating them while I threw my shield through the air to hit one of the prometheans in the face with a solid *thunk*.

I activated the shield tattoo on my left palm. It was weaker than the group of tattoos that worked in concert on my chest, but it had an advantage over them: it was smaller and allowed me to activate the Shock and Add tattoos on my right wrist and palm. Crackling lightning began spreading across my body in fits and starts, the power flashing for all to see before sinking back into my skin.

I realized that I couldn't control it properly, not yet. I could feel the power flooding through me, and it would discharge into anything I struck, but I also…felt…that there was more to this, that there was more I could become.

I felt *him* then, the remnants of Amon, speaking up desperately, exulting at the power I was using. He tried to advise me, to direct the power, and I savagely ripped it from his reaching, spectral fingers.

I shoved him down, mentally stomping down on the trapdoor to the space where I'd locked him away, even as I bared my teeth at the room before me. The first room on this floor was squared off, the far end evidently leading out into the main floor. A dozen imps and prometheans had either been waiting in here, or they had rushed in the door as I arrived. Now, it was down to two prometheans and seven imps, and I was determined to clear this place alone.

I caught the first Firebolt on my left clenched fist, the spell bursting in a flare of light. They froze at the sight of me apparently punching a spell out of existence, and I took advantage of their petrified shock as I stabbed out again. My charged naginata smashed into the nearest promethean's shield, and before it could counterattack, my Shock spell discharged into it, making it gasp in pain.

I altered the angle of my naginata, sliding the blade across the top of the shield to sink the edge into its throat, punching through its windpipe, and erupting out the back with a crunch of bone and the tearing sound of gristle. Snarling, I yanked it back, slamming the base of the weapon into the floor with a resounding *thump*.

"Come on, you fuckers," I growled at them, catching a lightning bolt, then a spray of frost I vaguely recognized as Cone of Cold on my fist-shield.

It held, barely. Unlike the pattern I'd used before, it couldn't absorb the mana attacks to charge itself. Instead, it was draining me as I used it, my mana bar dropping steadily.

I still had my party collected in my vision; they were opaque, barely there, so as not to interfere with my sight, but I watched Bane's symbol as it switched from red…to black. It flickered back to red, then black, then red. I felt Oracle pulling hard on my mana, and I cut my shield, knowing she'd need every drop to save him. I felt myself shaking with uncontrollable fury.

They'd started this.

They'd come after my people. It didn't matter that I'd barely met them at that point; the Skyking had painted a target on their backs. It had come for them, and it had found me. It had sent its slaves after my Oathsworn family, attacking again and again. When they'd begged for help, for a chance to live free, I'd only grown to hate the fucking creature even more.

"I'm gonna fuck you all up," I whispered, the flaring, crackling light of the mana infused into my weapon dissipating. "I don't need magic to do it, either."

I released the charge as they started to spread out, both sides waiting for the other to make the first move.

"Who—" the promethean started to snarl at me, and I moved.

He was dressed in the fashion the Skyking's favorite pets seemed to love, an Egyptian schenti. Gold and copper bangles glittered on his wrists and ankles, and brilliant blue lazurite jewelry against his pale, blue-tinged skin made him look like he'd spent too long outside in the middle of winter.

I stabbed out at him; his nose was broken, his upper lip had split, and he was missing a tooth from being struck in the face by my physical shield earlier. I had to think that worked in my favor by helping to slow his reactions.

He brought up his shield and sword while I braced the naginata with my left hand and yanked it downwards, changing the thrust from aiming at his face to slicing through his unarmored thigh. I ripped the weapon back hard with my left hand and pushed with my right, bringing the metal clad butt around to smash into his hastily raised shield.

I spun it again, the blade dipping down to deflect the sword strike while I stepped backward. A flash of fire from the corner of my eye warned me just in time to avoid the Firebolt aimed at taking me in the back.

I glanced around quickly as the promethean staggered, glowering at me as blood ran thickly from the deep cut in his leg. I saw three spells being charged, one imp levelling a crossbow, two that looked to be caught in indecision, and one who grinned at me as it spread its needle-tipped claws wide. A black net flashed into existence, hurtling toward me.

I reacted instinctively, charging the naginata then releasing it and flicking the blade up to slice through the net. The blade effortlessly tore its structure apart, though the outer edges still trailed across my skin as it passed. The contact made me shudder as my strength leached out. I hissed, seeing the thin threads that led back to the caster and watching it shudder in pleasure.

I lunged forward with a growl, slashing at the ugly little beast, but it dodged, and I had to dive aside as another Firebolt headed for me. A Lightning Bolt hit me unexpectedly, making me twist and thrash as I shouted in pain.

I needed my shield, either magical or mundane; hell, I needed my fucking armor. My whole plan of taking it off and using the tattoos was an act of desperation that had somehow turned into a demonstration of how I was Billy Big-Balls and how I didn't need them. *Idiot…*

I rolled, just managing to avoid the promethean's sword as it slammed into the ground where I'd been, and I stabbed out in retaliation, the blade bouncing off his shield.

I grunted in pain as another Lightning Bolt hit me, making me shake and shudder, a look of triumph on the promethean's face as it lifted its sword high…only to be hit from the side by a charging Lydia.

She drove it from its feet to the floor, rolling over to come out on top and headbutting it. Considering she was both furious and wearing a heavy steel helm, it worked out badly for the promethean.

She'd lost her mace, and her shield was strapped to her arm, making movement awkward on that side for her, but she just grabbed a fistful of hair in her left hand, hauled back, and punched him in his perfect face.

Then again.

And again.

She kept beating him, screaming incoherently as she did so, until he was dead beyond any healer's ability to bring back…including a necromancer, who was basically a really late healer, my brain dazedly informed me.

I forced myself back into action and lunged forward, grabbing the little imp that had been draining me by the ankle, then shifting to grip it by the throat as I activated my Necklace of Vampirism. I'd kept forgetting about the damn thing, despite being a gamer. In the middle of a fight, you always went with instinct—in my case, rage, as much as anything else.

The frightened creature gasped and squirmed, health and mana drawn out as I throttled the little fucker. In that moment, I demanded of myself that I do more, that I learn and damn well evolve as a fighter. The little bastard's use of a similar spell on me had been all that had reminded me that I had it, and while the few dozen points that I drained from him wasn't much, as I snapped his neck, I reflected that every bit helped.

Dropping the limp corpse, I checked the rest of the room to find that the fight was almost over. Following on Lydia's heels had come Jian, Yen, and Grizz, with Miren and Stephanos firing their Drow-made arrows. It was clear immediately that the small, flying imps were no match one on one for us, let alone in lesser numbers, or when they were already distracted by a screaming valkyrie who was smashing their leader's face in with her bloody, gauntleted fist.

I shook my head, clambering to my feet. Then I checked my party icons, relieved to see that Bane's symbol was still there, and thank the gods it was yellow now, rather than red or black.

"How is he?" I asked Oracle through our bond.

"He'll live, but it was close…. Thank you for not using your mana. I really needed it," she said, and I pushed a nonverbal sense of dismissive gratitude in response.

I had thirty-six mana left. I'd walked into this floor with my mana full, five hundred and seventy points of it. It had been enough to do some real damage, but all I could think about in that moment was how I should have put it all into Wisdom instead of Intelligence, as that pool was going to take *forever* to regenerate. I ran the numbers in my head: one point seven five times sixty gave me a hundred and two. I groaned in dismay. It was going to take five and a half goddamn hours to refill!

"We won," I whispered, straightening up and shrugging as I felt the impact points for the Lightning Bolts. Those fuckers had hurt!

Lydia was slowly straightening up, blood dripping from her gauntlet and her armor both, where splatters had layered up to coat her in a glistening sheen of red.

"Are you okay?" I asked her, and she glared at me.

"Am *I* okay?!" she snapped at me. "Me? O' *course* I'm not okay! I'm in charge of a squad tasked with tha personal protection of tha fuckin' 'igh Lord o' Stupidity himself, who just ran through a dozen bloody traps an' tried to solo a damn room full o' monsters! How could I be okay?!"

"Ah…" I muttered, rubbing the back of my neck. "That…"

"Yes, that! Seriously, Jax what tha hell were ye thinkin'!" she snapped, drawing a deep breath in and visibly trying to restrain herself. "Look, I get that yer tha best fighter we have, an' I get that yer probably tha best in miles around to go toe to toe wi' these fuckers, but if yer gonna do that, yer need us ta watch yer back, *an' we can't do that when yer go mental and run off screamin' about fuckin' 'em up!"* she snarled furiously.

"Bane—" I sputtered, before she cut me off.

"Is yer bodyguard! Not the other way around! We live ta protect *you*—our lives before yers. That's 'ow this works, Jax. Yer can't go crazy if one of us is 'urt and try ta fight the whole world, okay?"

She picked up her mace, shaking her head at me. "Look, yer freed us, ye gave us a life ta live, but if yer gonna keep doin' this shit, I'm gonna ask Barrett for a transfer to a different duty. Yer keep on the way yer goin', and it's gonna be us stood over yer grave soon. When that 'appens, we all lose our 'omes, our futures, everything. Please, Jax, don't *do* this ta us…" She trailed off at the end, her rage-fueled adrenaline rush petering out.

"I'm sorry," I said softly after a few seconds, to my people in general. "I don't want any of you to get hurt, that's all. Having you all protecting me, it just feels wrong. I'm just me…"

"I know, but…" she started, as Bane walked in, supported by Arrin, with Oracle buzzing over him worriedly.

We all paused at the sight of him, and I felt a wave of relief at seeing him alive. I also felt a pulse of pride and love flow into me through the bond from Oracle.

"Okay…is anyone going to check the next room?" Bane asked into the silence, and all at once, there was a round of embarrassed coughing and movement as people realized they'd been so focused on the argument developing that we had no idea about the rest of the floor.

"Glad to see you're all right, mate," I said to him, walking forward and clapping him on the shoulder. "Flux would have killed me if I let anything happen to you."

"Bah, I'm your bodyguard; it's my job." He shrugged dismissively. He looked terrible, though. While his wound had closed, he looked thinner, his breath was coming in gasps, and he was pale.

"How bad?" I asked Oracle.

"He died four times," she said bluntly. ***"We need Nerin to look him over and preferably find some healing potions, food, and drink, as well as enforcing plenty of rest."***

"He'll get all of those tomorrow," I said, trying to project confidence in my mental sending.

"Yeah," Oracle replied in a disappointed tone, and I knew I'd failed entirely.

"There are more imps coming, Jax," Yen called from the door.

"Can you keep them busy?" I asked, pulling my armor from my bag and getting dressed again.

"We can," she said confidently, and Miren and Stephanos stepped up next to her, firing into the next room.

It didn't take long for me to settle my clothing into place, quickly joining them in the next room, where they were already cleaning up the last of the imps.

"Looks like a roving patrol," Yen said quietly, moving to the door leading into the next room and glancing around, "…and it's empty in here."

"Okay, then. Strip them of anything valuable, and we move on," I directed, moving to the three promethean corpses in the first room. Beyond their jewelry and weapons, there was nothing useful, but as I tucked the last handful of golden bangles into my bag, I decided that, at least if we had an eighties party, we were all sorted now.

"Any potions?" I asked the group at large, getting a few headshakes and one nod as Miren held up a small vial of something that moved with a muddy viscosity.

"It's Earthblood," Yen said, checking it quickly. "Grants a five-percent resistance to earth-based spells for three minutes. That's it."

"Feck," I grunted, dismayed. I'd been hoping for a healing or mana potion. "Let's move out. Yen, lead the way; you're scouting now. Bane, before you try something stupid like buggering off to stealth your way all over the place, you're at the back, making sure nobody sneaks up on us."

"But—" he started to object.

"*But* you're barely able to stand, you're that buggered, and we don't have the mana we need to heal you. Here," I said, passing him a healing potion from my pouch. "Use that and stay at the back. I'm not losing any more of you."

"You might need it…"

"I've still got one left," I said, which was true. It was the shitty one, as I'd just given him my greater-quality potion, but I wasn't going to take it back now.

I strode across to the doorway, standing next to Lydia and bumping her deliberately with my now-armored shoulder. She pushed me back with hers, and I grinned at her.

"Sorry, and yeah, you're right. I'll be more careful in the future," I whispered to her as we all moved forward cautiously. "I tend to panic when my friends get hurt."

"We all do," she acknowledged and left it at that. I let out a little sigh as Oracle hit me with a quick healing, bringing me up to full health again and dismissing the debuff from Mana Overdrive.

"Thank you," I sent my companion and got a feeling of love and protectiveness back from her as we slowly made our way from room to room.

While all of the lower levels of the tower were made of a few simple, large rooms with stairs in the middle of the floor, the sealed-off upper tower seemed to be divided into sections. It had been abandoned in the lower levels, followed by what I thought of as imp territory, and now, we were clearly in the important sections.

The next room had dozens of beds, all enormous, with trunks at the foot of each. Stands were placed next to each bed, with spaces for weapons or gear, but they were all empty, and the room had a freshly abandoned feeling about it, as though its inhabitants had been there recently, but had just slipped out to get a packet of cigs and hadn't come back.

The room was long and wide, with far more care being taken here in decoration than in the lower floors. The leaky windows had been fixed, the chairs were new; there was even a fire blazing merrily in the fireplace, despite the absence of anyone to tend it. Strewn about everywhere were feathers, and judging from the look of disgust on Lydia's face as she lifted a stained schenti from the nearest chest, we'd found the promethean barracks.

"Okay, people, strip it of anything valuable," I said, looking around. "You've got one minute."

I left the others to their race to search, moving to inspect the closed door at the far end of the floor. The softly glowing red lines etched into the wood intrigued me.

"What the hell," I muttered, looking it over. The door was huge, composed of thick wood crisscrossed with iron banding and rivets. The entire surface was black with age, but it looked solid as hell. Then, to add to the generally foreboding theme for the door, someone had carved into it a series of red lines and circles.

They were magical, judging from the glow, but even worse was the smell and the dried stains around the pattern. I searched nearby, and sure enough, a few feet away sat a small pitcher and a brush. I recoiled in shock as I peered inside; the pitcher was filled with a load of coagulating blood.

"What the hell?" I said in confusion, when Yen appeared at my side and inspected what I was looking at.

"Blood magic," she said shortly. "It's a generally shitty thing that the legion's been campaigning against forever. It's used by witches and warlocks to control things or summon demons, if you don't know what you're doing. Shouldn't be surprised it's being used here—"

She broke off, grunting in disgust. "Best to leave whatever's behind this door alone. Trying to break curses and forbiddings are never fun, not to mention whatever's in there, unless…" She trailed off, studying my expression. "You think it's the djinn Clan Mother, don't you?"

"It'd make sense," I admitted, nodding to the room behind us. "Surrounded by the prometheans, who, until the Anubai showed up, appeared to be the Skyking's top dogs, if you know what I mean."

"You any good at breaking curses?" Yen asked me.

"I didn't even know curses were real until a minute ago. Good job, too, considering some of my exes."

"A story for another time, then," Yen said firmly. "I'll see what I can do with this, but it won't be quick, and I can't stop once it begins, so you'll have to keep anyone back."

"Consider it done." I clasped her shoulder appreciatively and turned back to the room as she sighed in resignation and started examining the door more closely. I paused looking through the room, then back at the door, finally forcing myself to walk back out of the room on the far side, continuing all the way back to the stairwell at a jog.

"What the hell?" I muttered to myself, startled as Bane popped out of stealth at my elbow. "Fucking-god-dammit!" I cursed, jumping back and glaring at him. "I swear, one more goddamn time, dude, and I'm getting you a bell!"

"You seemed troubled," was all he said, but I could feel the damn smile, even if his mouth didn't really work that way. I just knew he was grinning at me.

"And so you thought, what, dude? 'There's Jax, he's clearly stressed and knackered. I know, I'll sneak up on him and give him a friggin' heart attack'? Seriously, man. You're gonna be the death of me one day."

"I hope not, but you do scream so prettily. Anyway, what was it that was confusing you…this time?" he added.

"Okay, a full goddamn jester's outfit, bells *everywhere*," I fumed before getting ahold of myself and forcing a deep breath out. "We know that the Skyking's not through that last door, or at least it's unlikely, right? Considering the fact that it looks like it's built to contain something…and we've seen no sign of the Anubai quarters?"

"Yes," Bane said slowly, nodding as though I was a good boy who would, just maybe, be allowed a cookie.

"So, where the hell's the way up to the next level?" I asked, annoyed.

"Can't you see it?" he countered, and my scowl deepened.

"If I could see it, would I be asking you right now, hmmm? Come on, dude, help me out a little."

"Look up."

I frowned, then looked up, hunting all around the room's ceiling, then peering into the room beyond. It was all composed of thick wood, covered in cobwebs, but with no visible trapdoors.

"What is the Skyking?" he prompted. I maintained my glare, wondering if there was a spell that would actually create the possibility for a look to kill.

"We don't know," I said slowly.

"We do know the kind of territory it claims, though," he said, nodding towards the windows.

"Yeah, the sky," I responded, then shook my head. "Tell me you don't mean what I think you mean. Surely the fucker has to have a way into its lair from inside the building."

"It probably does, but there are multiple stairways in this tower. The last few floors, there's been no sign of the stairway the legion took, yet the building isn't big enough to really need multiple stairs."

"So the legion's probably fighting the damn thing already!" I groaned, staring at him in dismay. "And that means…"

"We've got to go all the way back to the third floor, or climb outside, as it makes sense that the Skyking would have a way in from outside for its fliers."

"Perhaps we could climb the outside?" Nigret suggested carefully, eyeing the windows, before he frowned, looking out. "What is that—"

"Goddamn—" I started to swear when the window closest to me exploded inwards, a promethean plowing through and sending the three of us flying in an explosion of grimy, soot-covered glass and wood fragments. In the chaos, Nigret was knocked senseless by a well-placed boot.

I hit the wall, fell to the floor, and shook myself. My gaze stopped momentarily at the huge, golden-skinned specimen of their race, and I glared at the pair of smaller ones that flew in on either side of it, flanked by four imps and a group of djinn.

"Make the portal, worms!" the massive Promethean ordered the djinn, who all had spectral golden chains around their necks. The chains seemed to lengthen and shorten as the djinn moved, but they linked inexorably to the belt the promethean wore.

The djinn, seven I counted quickly, were sallow skinned. Despite their usual colorful hues, the reds, greens, and blues of their skin looked washed out and weary, and each bore a tattoo on their left cheek of a six-pointed star enclosed in a circle. They moved slowly and listlessly, clearly unwilling, but forced to obey as they began to summon the glow of mana to their hands.

"Hey, dickhead!" I snarled to the promethean as I stood up, my head coming to just under his clavicle as I straightened to my full height.

"Speak not to your betters, slave!" one of two other prometheans snarled, landing in close before darting forward and backhanding me before I knew what was happening. I crashed into the wall behind, stone and wood creaking as I slumped to the ground, stunned.

"Jax!" Oracle cried out, darting across to me as Lydia and the others stormed out of the barracks, forming up to face the scumbags who had just crashed our party.

"Interesting!" the golden-skinned fuckhead boomed, reaching out one hand in a cupping gesture, and speaking a single syllable. The incantation stopped Oracle's flight like she'd been stuck in honey. Her wings beat frantically, even though I knew they were largely for show, and my mana dipped as she drew on it to push herself to me. Instead, she slowed to a squirming halt, hovering in the air. Arrows flashed by her, only to bounce off a golden shield that appeared around the promethean leader at the last second. He cocked his head, looking from me to the others then back to Oracle.

"*Very* interesting. My…*employer*…has ordered me to teach you all a lesson and to make an example of you, so that no others attempt what you have in the future. I shall kill some of you now, and the rest will be offered as slaves at the auction tomorrow. Gelded first, of course," he added calmly, before glancing through the doorway past the others, and clearly realizing what Yen was doing. "You there! CEASE!" he bellowed, suddenly furious. When nothing changed, he growled to his followers. "Stop the mortal; kill any that get in your way."

Then he folded his arms as though expecting that to be the end of it.

His two bodyguards launched themselves forward, moving quickly through the room. I grunted as I pushed myself back upright, just in time to see one kick Lydia full force in the shield. The blow sent her crashing backwards, even as two arrows slammed into its ebony skin, eliciting a pained grunt.

Jian lunged at the other massive creature, his blades blurring in an intricate, glowing pattern that indicated his active ability. However, despite his landing half a dozen shallow cuts, the promethean, with veins clearly visible through its pale skin, simply batted him aside with its staff, sending him to the floor with a crunch of broken bones.

Oracle was straining harder and harder, but my mana was dipping faster by the second, and she slid through the air towards the golden-skinned creature.

I activated Examine out of desperation, speed-reading the information that flared into existence.

Altai, Wing Lord of the Western Climbs
Lord Altai is the leader of the Promethean people in the city of Himnel. Sent from the Hidden City of Arkon, he is in command of the Promethean forces of the Skyking and brings the Light of Promethea to the heathens and earth-bound.

Altai rose to power due to a mix of militant fanaticism and cold logic; he believes all forms of life that are not Promethean are lower and therefore must serve or be exterminated.

Typical for a Promethean, he has trouble accepting anything that is in a higher position of authority, especially if that comes with authority over him. However, he is a true believer, and thus has sworn to obey the Skyking.

Weaknesses: Unknown

Resistances: Unknown

Level: Unknown

Health: Unknown

Mana: Unknown

"Well, that's just fucking useless," I muttered to myself in consternation. Clearly, it was so much higher in power than me, I was getting nothing, beyond the fact that it was an arrogant shitbag.

"Exhaust yourself now, wisp. Better to purge yourself of the mana you hold, so that my assumption of your bond will be cleaner," Altai purred as he watched her struggle, a slight smile on his face. He even had perfectly white teeth. If it wasn't for the overdeveloped canines, he'd have been taken for an angel anywhere on earth in a heartbeat.

Thankfully, he also had a center part in his red hair, and that made things much easier for me as I stepped forward.

"Oi! Cheesedick!" I shouted at him, and he shifted his attention to glare at me.

"I am Altai, mortal, and—" he started disdainfully, before I cut him off.

"Nope. From now on, until the moment of your death, you shall be forever known as…Cheesedick." I smiled benignly at him. "I heard it's because your daddy was always having to burp you to get a cock out of your mouth. The Skyking told me so."

"What?" he growled at me, clearly confused and furious.

"You're not very good at this, are you?" I shook my head as I advanced another step, trying to distract him as I moved closer to Oracle's frozen position. "It's called 'shit-talking' where I come from, and man, you suck."

"I will crush you and all you love. I will—"

"Yadda, yadda, yadda," I interrupted, shaking my head in mock sadness. "Come on. Is that really the best you can do?" I mocked him, holding his furious attention as Bane appeared behind the pale-skinned promethean to one side and hamstrung him. At the same moment, Arrin fired a double spread of Magic Missiles into the dark-skinned one. Grizz ran forward, his breathing ragged as he interposed his injured form between the oncoming promethean and Yen, with Stephanos and Miren firing arrow after arrow into both of the creatures.

Lydia struggled to her feet; her shield held high as she staggered back to face the pair.

The pale-skinned promethean muttered a few words and gestured to his legs. Black mist rose from the ground to sink into his skin, healing the wounds slowly.

"My people are going to fuck you up so bad." I sighed mournfully as he glared down at me.

"Your words are as noise on the wind, mortal: loud, but meaningless!" He didn't bother with a weapon, instead pulling back his right fist, which started to glow.

"Lydia, shield!" I cried out, maneuvering my shield to take the punch full on, but not bracing. "Come on, ya pussy!" I shouted, grinning at him and hoping Lydia understood what I was planning.

"Go!" I heard her shout, just as he slammed his fist into the center of my shield with a grunt of effort.

It didn't go entirely—or at all—as he expected. I didn't move. Instead of flying backward, bones broken, I'd activated the shield's Sacrifice ability, grinned malevolently at him, then I stabbed him in the face with my naginata. The blade carved through his left cheek and tore his ear from his perfect face, unfortunately missing the eye and the instant kill I'd been hoping for.

At the same time, Lydia had braced her shield against her back as she faced the dark-skinned promethean, and had jumped into the air, curling herself up as tightly as she could.

The Sacrifice ability of the Twin's Bulwark transferred all damage and inertia to the second shield, but as Lydia was already in the air, curled into a ball, she took practically no damage.

The same couldn't be said of the dark promethean, though, as she rocketed into him, heavy armor and all. Her full body weight, powered by the promethean lord's punch, slammed into his chest before he could figure out what was happening. She rolled off him, groaning in pain, but beside the dent in her shield, and a bit of whiplash, she was fine.

Her target was stunned, knocked from his feet, and his right wrist had broken, all of which became far less important when the second barrage of Magic Missiles slammed home into his rolling eyes, blinding him and removing over half his health.

Bane had appeared again and was rapidly pistoning his daggers into the arms, throat, and chest of the pale-skinned promethean, who screamed in pain while Altai's eyes flared with fury and hatred.

He forgot about everything else as he grabbed me by the throat, wrenching me up as his other hand ripped my naginata out of my grip and sent it flying aside to slam into the nearest wall.

He tore my shield from my other arm, making me cry out in pain as the twin bones of my left forearm snapped, and he lifted me to look into my eyes.

"You'll pay for that, mortal. I will make you scream for all eternity!" He hissed, his torn and bloody face inches from my own. I did the only thing I could think of. I grabbed his right elbow, the only place I could reach, and I wrapped both hands around it as best I could, the fingers of my left hand barely responding.

I frantically cast Fireball, despite knowing I didn't have the mana for it, let alone being able to cast it two handed, or with my fingers clenched tight and nerveless, respectively. I slammed my intention, my demand for my mana to form into the palm of both hands, and I felt a terrible, half-controlled version begin to form as I sub-vocalized the words. The air was throttled out of me as Altai roared in fury, distracted by seeing his followers taken down.

He screamed in truth, then, his howl of pain rising to join those of his men, as the spell I'd butchered exploded, tearing his arm to shreds. Unfortunately, the mana backlash of the failed spell also ripped into me, flaying my mind.

I fell, senseless, collapsing to the floor and twitching as blood ran out of my mouth, my nose, and my ears. I shook uncontrollably, even as his severed hand released my neck.

"You shall die!" he hissed, clutching the exploded stump of his right arm. Blood sprayed from the shattered remains, and he screamed at the djinn behind him. "My portal! Change it to the Skyking!" he ground out through clenched teeth.

The imps that hovered nearby stared from him to me and my people, and paused, considering their options. The djinn changed the pattern of the spell they were weaving, somehow moving the portal's end point to a point a level above us, instead of wherever they'd originally been aiming for. The magic entrance began to open, just as Yen let out an almighty shout and jerked her hands apart, her magic splitting the arcane door and the engraved containment spell into splinters.

A scream of delight and bloodlust echoed into the night from the other side of the door, and the portal suddenly ripped itself apart, collapsing as Altai tried to step through it, leaving bloody chunks and the majority of his body on our side. His head slammed to the floor on the far end of the portal, his mouth twitching and flapping in disbelief as his brain shut down.

CHAPTER THIRTY

Grey smoke billowed out of the room beyond Yen, grasping tendrils flooding the entire floor. The imps were abruptly torn from the air, vanishing into the grey mass with cries and squeals of terror followed by the sound of popping and cracking bones. An eerie silence fell.

I groaned in the stillness as I forced myself to sit upright, left arm cradled to my chest. My health, mana, and stamina bars were all pulsing, and I blinked hard, trying to bring the world into focus as Oracle landed on my knee, wrapping her arms around my neck and holding on for dear life.

I felt her shaking as I carefully wrapped my good arm around her, her wings morphing out of the way as her sobs wracked her tiny body.

"It's all right," I whispered, holding her gently but tightly to my chest. Our worst fear had almost come to pass, again, as someone tried to take her from me.

We held each other for a long moment before Lydia stumbled out of the fog. Seeing me alive, she let out a sigh of relief, replaced almost immediately with a gasp of surprise as she spun around, gawking at the figure that formed out of the fog.

It was strange, coalescing into a woman's form, slim and tall, but remaining entirely of the roiling grey fog. From her eyes to her hair, she was incorporeal, beautiful, and thankfully clothed in a dress that hid her figure. Despite the intricate detail, I couldn't get over the fact that she literally appeared to be formed out of condensed air.

She floated to me, reaching out with her right hand to stroke my face. A gentle smile curved full lips that seemed forever on the edge of a laugh, but as I looked her over, I could see the marks of her captivity. Her eyes were hard and sunken, her wrists bore the marks of chains, although they were no longer bound, and the cracking and popping of bones being snapped deeper within the mist still echoed occasionally.

"My people…" I started to ask; although I could see their details in my vision, it wasn't the same as seeing them personally.

"Are fine," she finished for me, and I felt a ripple of something passing through me as I breathed in. I felt a tendril of her form entering my lungs, the cool mist making it somehow easier to breathe, rather than harder, thankfully. I realized in an instant how dangerous it would be to try to capture a creature made of mist, when she could literally flow into your lungs and turn solid.

"Don't be afraid, my champion," she said, her voice gentle and reassuring. "You can breathe. I swear no harm will befall you or your people at my hand. I give you my Oath that I intend my rescuers no harm."

The magic, now intrinsic to me, responded to her, and I knew in an instant that it was true. Relieved, I let out the breath I'd been subconsciously holding. "I see that my children agreed to a foolish Oath with you while I was imprisoned," she remarked slowly, and I blinked, pulling up the quest I'd received from Xerix.

Congratulations!

You have made progress in a Quest you received from Xerix: Free Our Mother.

You have been asked to free—or kill—Hellenica, Clan Mother of the Gueric Clan. If you agree to do your best, and do not ask the djinn to leave the city if she has not been freed, they will swear a Conditional Oath to you. If you free her, she and her children will swear to obey you for ten years.

Free Hellenica: 1/1

Kill the Skyking: 0/1 – (Optional; if you succeed in this secondary objective, the djinn will swear for your lifetime instead.)

Reward: Allegiance of the djinn of the Gueric Clan, 62,500xp, Unknown

"Hellenica," I whispered, unthinking, and she smiled benevolently at me.

"Yes, High Lord Jax of the Great Tower, I am Hellenica," she confirmed as mirror images of herself led the rest of my party through to join me. The images drew together, becoming one body, and she smiled down at us all, even as I felt tingling running through my body.

I checked my health, only to realize that it was returning unnaturally quickly, and I immediately knew it was her work. The mist, or fog, or whatever we'd breathed, was her, and she was healing us all.

"The prometheans," I started to say, and she shook her head.

"Not an issue," she replied flatly.

The seven djinn who'd been chained to Altai's belt appeared, dragging the remains of his corpse with them. The chains were intact, and I noticed that the fog was pushed back by something intrinsic to the belt. "Now, would you mind…?" she asked sweetly, inclining her head.

I reached over the mangled corpse, touching the belt and reading the notification.

Cummerbund of Soul's Enslavement		**Further Description** *Yes/No*	
Details:		This pretentious formal belt has been created for the sole purpose of enslaving sentient magical creatures. It enforces the owner's wishes with a combination of horrific pain and vampiric syphoning of the slaves' life force. **Slots in Use**: 7/8 **Stored Souls**: 2/10	
Rarity:	**Magical:**	**Durability:**	**Charge:**
Unique	Yes	77/100	N/A

I concentrated on the belt as I held it, and a second notification sprang up.

Do you wish to absorb the enslaved souls at this time?

Yes/No

I selected no firmly, and the option I wanted appeared.

Do you wish to release the enslaved souls at this time?

Yes/No

Selecting yes, I was met with a final option as the chains began to shimmer and crackle with energy.

Do you wish to absorb the stored souls at this time?

Yes/No

As the chains fell away from the djinn, they darted free, vanishing into the fog with whoops and cries of joy.

"Uh, there's an option to absorb some stored souls here," I said, then quickly continued as I saw the look of fury on Hellenica's face.

I raised my hand from Oracle's back in an effort to forestall the Clan Mother's wrath, and she fluttered limply up to sit on my shoulder. "To be clear, I'm not saying I want to do it; I just don't understand what the hell is going on here," I said, selecting no and reading the final prompt from the item.

Do you wish to release the souls stored inside?

Be aware: without the souls to power this item, it will be destroyed.

Yes/No

"It says it'll be destroyed if I release the souls," I read aloud, the room growing noticeably colder as an ominous feeling began to build. "Is it safe to do this here?" I asked cautiously, and Hellenica moved close to me again, her eyes tight.

"Those are the souls of my children, Jax. Please, explain your intentions very carefully," she said through gritted teeth, with an obviously forced level of patience.

"I want to free them," I said quickly. "It just warns that the item will be destroyed if I do so. I'm asking whether it'll simply crack and fall apart, or if the city gets destroyed in an explosion? I don't know anything about soul energy." At my admission, she flowed backwards slightly.

"You will free their souls? You will allow them to continue their journey?" she asked me carefully as Oracle spoke in my mind.

"Souls are powerful sources of energy, Jax. In the past, there were mages who fed on the souls of their victims, gaining stat points and more. Hellenica is ready to attack you if you say the wrong thing here, so be very, very careful."

I swallowed hard, meeting the penetrating gaze of the creature before me.

"Hellenica, I give you my Oath that I have no intention of harming the souls of your children. I just don't want us all to die in the process of breaking an obviously powerful magical item; that's all. I'll happily give it to you, if you want."

"I cannot touch it," she interrupted me quickly. "The item was fashioned to be anathema to my kind. Please, go to the window and hold it out. Order it to release the souls, and I will shield you as best I can. You may receive some minor injuries, but I can heal them…probably."

The last word was whispered, but she waited, staring at me.

"Okay," I said hesitantly, clambering to my feet and walking to the window. The mist flowed away from the opening, and a djinn appeared at my side, gesturing for the window to open, which it did with a crash, falling outwards. He nodded solemnly to me as I held the item out and turned half away from it, shielding my face.

Other djinn took up station all around me, with still more swooping in from the night. Dozens of them hovered around me, taking up station and holding their hands out.

Circles of glowing energy grew from their palms, and their fingers danced across mystical symbols, erupting through the night in colorful light.

"Now," Hellenica said clearly, hope filing her voice, and I selected yes to release the souls.

There was a split second's pause, as nothing happened, then the posh belt was suddenly covered in cracks, cracks that raced from one side to the other in a heartbeat as light burst forth.

The belt, and the goddamn hand I was holding it with, vanished in a horrific explosion before the djinn could close the shield.

A tremendous burst of bright light, sound, and force smashed upwards, drowning out the sound of my screams. An airship, too close at the time, veered away in panic as the helmsman frantically turned; the sails and engines on the near side of the ship had been torn free in the blast.

I collapsed backwards brokenly, clutching at the ragged stump of bone and flesh that remained of my right arm. Hellenica's magic rapidly went to work, causing me to gasp in relief.

First the pain died, as she did something higher up my arm, and then the flesh began to close over the wound, forming a nub of skin that quickly healed. Watching the process in dismay, I gritted my teeth and hissed out swear words.

I gaped at the stump in shock as thick tendrils of fog, unnoticed in the painful haze, slowly released my arm, dropping away and flowing back as she sagged, growing less defined.

"My hand," I whispered, staring at it, or more to the point, where it used to be. "That was my favorite hand," I said blankly, going into shock. Hellenica spoke up quickly, even as Oracle desperately called out for mana potions.

"I can heal it!" she promised. "Please, Lord Jax; I can rebuild your hand, and return you to what you were, but it will take much out of you, and your body is already at its limit. You need rest and food, and I must face the Skyking yet. I suggest you lead your people out of here, and I will come to you once this is done. You have fulfilled your Oath and freed me."

"No," I said thickly, shaking my head and trying to get my brain in gear. "The Skyking is still alive, so we're not done."

"Jax, I will honor the Oath my children gave. I give my Oath now that I intend to do so, by the spirit of the agreement, not just the letter," she intoned formally, and I felt the magic accepting what she said as truth.

"We agreed to kill that fucker, so it dies tonight," I said, then I forced a stiff smile. "Besides, I need your people to help with the next stage of my plan."

The numerous djinn who had appeared to assist with the shield had slowly been migrating inside, vanishing into the fog; more and more arrived, until at least thirty of them had disappeared into Hellenica's swirling mass.

"We will see your will done, Father, don't fear," reassured a voice from my right, and I turned my head to find Xerix hovering nearby. The little djinn wore a smile on his face as he spread his arms to the sides and bowed his head. "I thank you for freeing our mother. You've no idea how you've changed the balance of power in these lands with that act alone."

"Father?" I asked, confused.

"As the male head of the clan, you are formally addressed as 'Father,' Jax." Hellenica said, flowing forwards. She appeared to become more solid, and her clothes considerably less so, as she smiled more deeply at me. "It is your duty to help me raise the next generation of our offspring, and to…"

Suddenly, Oracle was hovering between us. I gasped as my mana was ripped from me, dropping down to single digits again as she shifted her form and size to stand between Hellenica and me, full-sized.

She was blonde-haired again, just under six feet tall, with long legs and her trademark highly impressive chest, but this time, she was wrapped in a formal dress of silver with golden highlights that accented her form and coloring. Her skin glowed with a healthy tan, and her eyes shone a vibrant emerald green. Fuming, she stabbed out with one exquisitely manicured fingernail, stopping Hellenica by sheer force of will.

"Back off!" she snarled. "He's mine, and I'M NOT SHARING!"

Hellenica froze, looking shocked as she backed away slowly. A tight smile compressed her lips as she glanced from Oracle to me.

"Perhaps…we can come to some kind of arrangement?" she suggested to me, smiling coyly around Oracle's stiff form. "A discussion we could have later, just the two of us?"

I shook my head slowly.

"I'm all for discussing things, but that's one thing that isn't open to change, Hellenica. I'm sorry. I'm not interested in multiple partners. Hell, one's more than enough to fill my life, and I always thought those people who married multiple partners were insane. All joking aside, I'm not available," I muttered, still in shock.

"This will represent a problem for us, moving forward, Jax," Hellenica stated seriously. "My kind require a mate, just as most do, and djinn children are asexual. A Clan Mother is the only one that can reproduce. It is my duty to do so, and I must have a partner who will fulfill the role of Clan Father."

"We can figure that out later," I said, shrugging awkwardly. "For now, we need to kill that fucker up there—" I gestured upwards "—and we need to get a move on. We've already been down here for longer than I'd hoped."

"Very well," Hellenica relented.

Turning gracefully, she flowed to the blown-in window and took in a deep breath, calling out a single word in a voice that echoed across the city. The clouds, which had begun rolling back in after the release of soul-power had pushed them back, seemed to shiver in response.

Slowly at first, lights began to lift all around the city; greens and blues, red and yellows, dozens of hues lifted into the air and began to converge onto the tower. Those closest gathered rapidly around their mother, crying out their joy at her freedom.

"What did she say?" I asked Oracle, who passed me the single mana potion we'd been able to find. I downed it as she smiled, shifting down from her full size to her normal one. Her outfit blurred into her tactical yoga pants and halter top, with camouflage stripes painting her cheeks.

"Come home," she said simply. "She said come home, and the djinn across the city have abandoned everything. Their Oaths were weak and sworn under duress, their Mother held hostage to obtain them, so they forsake them."

"Is that safe?" I asked, concern filling my voice.

"Oh, believe me, even when I knew of the djinn long ago, it was accepted that they'd *never* get the wrong end of an Oath. Their power is tied in part to their nature, so they'll have been planning for this for years. Their Oaths would have contained 'get out' clauses, and here they are now, reunited."

"How the hell did this happen?" I asked, shaking my head and addressing Xerix. "I mean, if seven of you can create a portal, how did, what, a hundred or more of you not rescue her already?"

"We couldn't," Xerix replied sadly. "We didn't know for sure where she was, and we were forbidden to approach certain places without our promethean overlords. If we went, they would know, and they'd punish our Clan Mother. We were forced to wait, gathering our strength—"

"I was taken when young," Hellenica interjected, flowing across the room to stand before me. "I was taken prisoner before I could breed, so I was alone for many years. The prometheans that came to me…well, enough of that, save to say that when my children were born, they would allow me to name them, then my beloved ones were taken from me to train as thieves and scoundrels, serving the creature that even now plots above us." She fumed coldly, her eyes flashing in anger.

"I don't have enough mana to heal this," Oracle said to me quietly, reaching out and touching the nub that was left.

"Then I'll do it with one hand," I said, forcing a smile.

"I *will* heal you fully, Jax, or I will help you to do so yourself, but your body truly is not capable of it now, not without severe need. You will be pushed past the limits of your own mortality, losing the ability to regenerate your stamina, health, and mana until you have fed and rested. Please trust me in this. Healing you fully at this time is not the solution, or I would have done it in a heartbeat, in exchange for the gift of freedom you have given to me and all my children."

I forced myself to smile at her in acceptance, and she returned it, as the rest of the team gathered around me. Their wounds had all been healed, although they all appeared the worse for wear. Even Miren and Stephanos had taken injuries in the battles, and their clothes were torn and filthy.

"Looks like we've got one more round to go, guys," I said, trying to sound upbeat, when the faint sound of fighting began to filter down to us from above. I exchanged a quick look with Yen, who nodded in affirmation.

"The legion are with us—" I started to explain to Hellenica, gesturing upwards, but she cut me off with a raised hand as she snapped at the djinn that surrounded her.

"Portal to the next level, quickly!"

Seven of the djinn moved forward, gathering together and chanting in unison. More djinn moved up to stand on either side of them, placing a hand on their shoulders and closing their eyes. The glow of their mana built as they fed it into the casting group.

Unlike before, where it'd taken them several minutes, this portal seemed to simply pop into existence, due in part to the huge amount of mana the supporting djinn were funneling into their casters.

As soon as the portal opened, shouts of alarm arose, and a dozen of the djinn flowed through the opening. Four threw up shields, while others started casting offensively behind them. I followed them through, the rest of my squad drawn up protectively around me, with Hellenica and the remaining djinn flowing after us.

The other side of the portal was a mess. The space had clearly been decorated to suit the Skyking, with black stone everywhere, illuminated by bowls full of glowing coals and everything draped in red silken banners with weird symbols on them. The legion was there, or at least four of them were. Augustus fought in the lead, with Tang stealthing and unstealthing every few seconds to stab someone. Rinko, fighting at Augustus's side, looked battered all to hell, and a legionnaire I'd seen around, but whose name I couldn't remember, flanked the other.

They were being slowly pushed back by a half-dozen prometheans, with four more dead or dying, and a dozen creatures vaguely resembling humanoid Komodo dragons lay dead as well. I could see a single legionnaire's body laid back by the entrance to the stairwell, but beyond that, there was no sign of the others.

"Save the legionnaires!" I bellowed, and the djinn spread out. The prometheans whipped around, glaring furiously as they realized they were being flanked, but there was nowhere for them to go. The fight that they'd been slowly winning became a slaughter as first five, then ten, then two dozen djinn released endless volleys of spells. The few arrows fired in return were caught by the shields, and in less than a minute, the fight was over, the last promethean falling to Augustus's blade.

"Glad to see you're all alive, Jax," the Centurion Primus gasped, bending over and bracing himself on his knees. The djinn spread out, taking up defensive positions around us at Hellenica's orders.

"Glad to see you as well, mate. What happened? Is everyone…?" I asked, and he shook his head quickly.

"We lost three more, two in the stairwell to the traps, and one when we finally got out onto this floor. The rest are a few floors below, wounded."

"Wounded? What happened to—"

"Nerin was hit by a dart of some kind, turned her mana against her. She can't cast worth a damn now, so she's been bandaging up the injured the best she can, and swearing up a storm while she's at it," he explained grimly.

"Altearian Night," Hellenica supplied, floating up in a great billow of cool mist. "It's a poison the prometheans like; I should know," she said bitterly. "It takes a few hours to work through the body, depending on the concentration. They typically used it to render me powerless when they came to…visit."

"Well, I think you've got your revenge on them, so far," I commented soothingly to her before turning my attention back to Augustus. "Augustus, this is Clan Mother Hellenica, Mother to the djinn, and she's our ally." I had to double take at the look on Augustus's face. "Do you know each other?" I asked in surprise, and he nodded slowly.

"I remember you," he murmured, leaning heavily on his shield and trying to catch his breath. "You used to dance in the Midnight Glade, south of the mountains…did you not?"

"I did," she admitted slowly, moving closer and reaching up to touch his face with gentle fingers. "That was long ago, when we were both but children…"

"You were beautiful," he persisted, gazing into her eyes, before he seemed to remember himself and coughed, straightening up. "Perhaps this isn't the best place to have this discussion," he mused, then caught sight of a djinn floating nearby. He looked around, finding more and more djinn present, and he seemed to sag. "Clan Mother?"

"I am the Clan Mother of the Gueric Clan; a clan without a Father, as the Lord Jax has refused me and his companion is disinclined to share." A touch of sourness stained her voice, until she regarded Augustus more closely, and a note of hopeful curiosity filled her last words.

"Yeah…sorry to interrupt this joyful reunion. I know I'm off the cards, but that might allow you to pick someone that'd be more suited to you. Either way, though, perhaps that's not a conversation to have in the middle of the creepy fucking dungeon in the sky?" I interrupted, waving generally at them and getting a shocked look from Augustus.

"Your hand!" he gasped, and I shrugged.

"Oh, yeah…lost it about ten minutes ago. Not my finest hour, so…moving on."

"You set my children's lost souls free," Hellenica corrected me, shocked that I'd be so dismissive.

I closed my eyes, counting to five and praying for patience. "Okay." I tried again. "Let's get the injured up here, please. Get as many healed and ready as we can, then let's go fuck up the Skyking."

"Of course, Jax." Augustus saluted and began barking commands as Hellenica ordered her djinn to set up a series of shields around us. Tang and Yen set off running for the stairs to gather the others, while three of the djinn that were especially skilled at healing went with them. With the next steps set in motion, I took the time to investigate the floor we were on.

One room was filled with golden statues and sealed chests. It had clearly been locked, but Rinko took care of that for me with his door-battering skill, and we quickly gathered as much gold as we could find, piling the few magical items and other valuables into our various bags of holding. By the time the others had reached us, we'd managed to strip the floor of everything that seemed valuable, and I'd even managed to grab a bite to eat in the kitchen.

Having considered the nature of those who called this tower home, though, I left the meat alone. Just in case.

I was also getting some good-natured ribbing from Grizz as I chewed on a banana. I maintained the age-old rule of not making eye contact with anyone while eating one, despite Oracle's thoughtful expression.

Five minutes later, we were assembled close to the bottom of the wide staircase that led up to what we hoped was the final area of the Skyking's lair. We were tired, all of us were injured, to one degree or another, and we were low on mana, health, and stamina, despite knowing the night was only halfway through. Hellenica used an AOE healing spell on the group, lifting us all slightly and giving us a boost to our regeneration. I desperately wished I'd had enough mana to buff everyone, but by the time I could manage a few of my crew, Oracle and I would have nothing left.

I just hoped the golems had gotten the orders I'd given them.

"Nerin, you're staying here with the wounded…" I started to say, when I realized how few fighters that would leave me with. Protests clashed as the entire group started to complain.

The only person who wasn't injured to the point of needing a hospital visit, at least on Earth, was Augustus. I'd even lost my frigging hand, after all.

"Ah, fuck it." I gave in, shrugging and turning to the stairs that spiraled up into the blackness. "Let's go kill us a Skyking."

I led my people upwards, the djinn and their mother shepherding us as we climbed.

CHAPTER THIRTY-ONE

We wasted no time in climbing up the stairs to the final level. The steps were wide and made of stone, but the high ceiling and debris that lay strewn in the corners—feathers, fluff, dust, and bits of random detritus—made it clear that the usual method of ascending this area wasn't walking.

The stairwell creaked and shook, the path up the center clearly polished by inhuman footprints, judging from the claw scratches. Upon reaching the first flight, the stairs split, flowing back on themselves to either side and leading up the main floor.

We climbed slowly, searching the area for traps, hidden monsters, and pretty much everything that there could be, but besides a particularly large spider that appeared Australian, and therefore venomous, there was nothing. Thankfully, the arachnid just watched us and didn't respond when Lydia asked it a question, so we decided it was just a normal big goddamn spider.

We continued on, emerging onto the final floor to discover that it was dark. All of the windows in the long, open space had been covered. At the far end, and every few meters along the sides, braziers had been lit. They smoldered, giving off a sweet smoky scent and filling the air with a ridiculous amount of heat. I suddenly realized I'd been feeling the temperature rise as we climbed the tower, but I'd ignored it on the grounds of my exertions.

Now it was oppressive. The ceiling had been draped with long flowing red and black silken banners that fell to the walls, creating an almost tent-like atmosphere. At the far end, dozens of braziers had been clustered around a huge, shallow bowl carved into the floor, which had been piled with wooden logs that blazed merrily, the air around it fairly shimmering with heat.

I could barely make out a bulky form laid on a huge bed behind the flames. The space behind the fires remained shrouded in darkness and warped by the heatwaves that rose steadily, wreathed in smoke.

The mass was huge, easily fifteen feet across, but it looked *weird*, as the body seemed to be covered in a writhing mass of snakes from this distance. A dozen smaller figures stepped out of the shadows on either side of it, moving to block our advance.

We were confronted by three greater imps; the rest were prometheans, save one hooded figure that seemed to be a human, from this distance, anyway.

"WHAT DO YOU WANT HERE?" came the cold voice from the pillow-strewn bed. "GOLD? GEMS? WHY DO YOU TRESPASS AND ATTACK MY MINIONS? WHO SENT YOU?!"

"They came to free ME!" Hellenica cried out, flowing up to stand alongside me. She hovered to my left, Lydia and Jian to my right, with Grizz, Stephanos, and Miren bristling behind us.

Augustus stepped up to flank Hellenica, with his legionnaires spreading out around us. Bane, Tang, and strangely Nigret were missing, presumably stealthed, and Mistress Nerin was hanging back, looking wan and drained, as the poison, apparently immune to Cleanse, worked its way through her system.

"YOU SERVE MY ENDS NOW, CREATURE; YOU TRESPASSED IN MY TERRITORY AND SWORE TO OBEY!"

"You forcibly bound me to an Oath and killed my clan! You swore a year of service and kept me chained as a brood-mare for ten more!" Hellenica screamed in fury at the creature.

"YOU WOULD HAVE OPPOSED ME! YOU AND ALL THE OTHERS! YOU MUST SUBMIT TO MY WILL!" the Skyking roared and lifted into the air suddenly. It hung there, just beyond the flames, glaring at us all as it demanded we obey. I felt Amon's disgust at the creature as I Examined it.

Skyking
The Skyking is an ancient creature, known respectively as a Fel't'a Jaron, The Watcher in the Night, or an Oculai, depending on the civilization asked.

The Skyking, like all of his kind, hates the living and the dead alike. The Oculai believe they alone are the pinnacle of evolution, graced by the gods and all of the cosmos. Each of this evil race hates their siblings and fellows as much, if not more than, other species, living a solitary life until driven by their insatiable hunger to find fresh flesh or a mate.

Oculai are powerfully magical creatures with often heavy physical weaknesses; due to these limitations, they spend much of their life building powerful stables of servant races and alliances to protect them against the inevitable day when the legion or one of their own comes for them.

Weaknesses: Physical attacks do triple damage

Resistances: Magical damage is reduced by 65%

Level: Unknown

Health: Unknown

Mana: Unknown

I scowled at the creature that hung there like a slowly leaking balloon, held aloft upon a bed of tentacles that writhed and flicked. It was enormously fat, a single eye with an enormous yellow and red pupil taking up most of its face, with fat jowls and sagging skin hanging from its underside.

Its mouth was a hideous mess of rotting, pointed teeth, with a long flexible tongue that flickered about wildly. The worst part for me, though, was the eyes. Dozens of them writhed about on the end of tentacles from the sides and back of the creature, which hunted around in all directions. Some were milky white, but most glared with a malevolence that was clear to see.

"You're a disgusting, dishonorable abomination, and you broke your Oath!" Hellenica shouted, devolving into insults. I glanced uncomfortably at Lydia, who looked back at me and shrugged.

"No idea," she murmured under her breath. "I mean, I'd be pissed as well, but, you know, it's an Oculai. They're not exactly known for being honorable with their deals."

"Yes, but…you know the djinn; they *love* Oaths and deals. She's more offended for that than…" Jian muttered from behind us.

"SILENCE!" roared the Skyking. "YOU WERE SENT HERE TO KILL ME! ADMIT IT!" Each time the Skyking screamed, its minions would flinch or shake, and even now, they stood immobile, as though frozen, all but the human in the robes. "WHO SENT YOU? WHICH OF MY MUTATED, MALFORMED LESSER BRETHREN DID THIS?"

"Perhaps we can come to a deal?" I suggested, moving to the side. I slowly walked to my right, easing over to the wall as far as I could, all the while watching the way the Oculai fixated on me. All of its eyes lashed around to glare momentarily, before slowly relaxing and beginning to patrol again. The huge central eye stayed locked on me, and the damn thing started salivating.

"YOU WISH TO DEAL?" it asked, slowly. "WHAT DO YOU OFFER FOR YOUR LIFE, MORTAL? KNOWLEDGE? GOLD? SLAVES?"

"How about the secret of who sent us?" I asked, thinking quickly. "The real reason the city is in uproar and why the legion is being hunted by the guard—"

"BAH!" it scoffed. "THAT IS NO SECRET. THE LEGION IS BEING HUNTED BECAUSE I DEMANDED IT, AND—"

"You don't control the guard, though, and they're hunting the legion too," I said quickly, glad to find that it was truly this creature that had been hunting Yen and her friends.

"I ORDERED IT, SO THE GUARDS WHO THINK THEY OBEY OTHERS MUST HAVE HEARD. THEY HAD NO CHOICE BUT TO OBEY MY WISHES," it said, a note of certainty in its voice, making me think it was either clearly delusional…or possibly an ex dressed up weird. I remembered that adamant refusal to accept anything that didn't match her beliefs.

"They're not doing it to help you; they're doing it to keep the legion from you. The guard, the nobles, they're all out to get you," I said slowly, and instantly all the eyes were locked on me again.

"WHAT DO YOU KNOW?!" it hissed, and I almost breathed a sigh of relief as I slowly sidled forward, my naginata held in my left hand. I'd passed my shield to Grizz and put his weaker, standard-built one into my storage. As I walked, I tapped the ground slowly with the metal-clad base of my weapon's haft.

"I know why the city lord hates you. He fears you, and he's turned some of your servants to his cause. He's been watching you."

"IMPOSSIBLE!" it snapped. "I WOULD KNOW."

But even as it said the words, its eyes thrashed around, searching through the minions that surrounded it. The vast majority of the searching orbs locked suspiciously onto the figure in the robes.

"Great Skyking, lord of the upper world, you know this isn't true," came an oily voice from under the hood. Pale hands lifted up the fabric, pushing the cowl back and exposing a heavily tattooed bald head and face. "The High Lord is your friend—"

"A friend who's secretly making deals with a SporeMother?" I cut in, and the Skyking spun to glare at me, its eyes thrashing wildly as they sought to keep us both under tight watch.

"Never!" the tattooed man snapped, glaring at me.

"LIES," the Skyking hissed as it fixated on the human. Several of the eyes began to glow a deep blue, the pupils suddenly shifting to an hourglass shape and beaming a ray of strange light at both of us. "SPEAK THE TRUTH…OR DIE!"

"I found out about the SporeMother and Barabarattas's deal weeks ago. He's breeding them," I said, my magic shaking as my words were examined for the truth.

"TRUTH," it hissed, spinning to face the robed man.

"I serve Lord Barabarattas, but he doesn't confide all his plans in one so low…" he hedged, and the Skyking glared at him. "I…I don't know anything about the—arghhhh!" He broke into a scream as the light around him changed, compressing in.

"LIES!!!!" the Oculai bellowed, zooming forward to face him. The mass of eyes hovered above him, growling, as a single eyestalk snaked down, its eye glowing red and projecting a pin-prick-thick beam of light that burned into the human's face. "TELL THE TRUTH OR DIIIIEEEE!"

"Perhaps the city lord is planning to attack you?" I asked, taking a chance. The light around me shook harshly, making me gasp in pain.

"CONJECTURE," the Skyking finally determined, turning back to the robed man. "SPEAK, WORM…DOES BARABARATTAS PLAN TO ATTACK ME?!"

"No…" he said, whimpering, and the light grew darker around him, crushing in as he started to scream in pain once more.

"LIESSSS!" The Skyking howled, more eyes flashing forwards and the pupils morphing, each becoming triangular and generating a beam of black energy that sizzled as it punched into the human, making him scream louder.

As it was distracted by punishing the human, I did something I didn't want to do. Something I'd told myself I wouldn't do again, not after the last time I'd done it.

I used the ability Child of the Night.

The Oculai was fixated on punishing the human before it and had looked away from me. A solitary eyestalk had been left pointing in my general direction, and when I vanished into a cloud of blackness, it responded slowly, first one eye, then another turning, trying to locate me, as the majority continued burning into the object of the Skyking's wrath.

As I bounded from shadow to shadow, I remained functionally invisible in the shadow-filled room. More eyes shifted from the torturous configuration and twisted, searching for me, until the main eye slowly turned. The last remaining six tentacles that were firing into the now-smoking corpse cut off, and half of the Skyking's eyes morphed to a crescent iris, bathing the room in a strange light.

The changed eyes continued searching, even as others remained in the triangular pattern I'd come to think of as "death ray." They swept back and forth as the creature started to hiss in fury, its minions howling battle cries and sprinting forwards, weapons raised.

Bane was the first to be found, as a beam of light flashed across him. His stealth effect was canceled instantly, and a pair of death rays lashed out at him, making him cry out in pain as he dove behind a pillar of black stone. Next was Nigret. The crazy cat-dude had been climbing slowly across the ceiling somehow, his claws leaving a trail of shredded cloth behind. An eye found the streak of ruined cloth and traced along it until he was visible. The Trigara hissed in annoyance as he let go, falling and flipping in a move that only someone with a feline background could manage. He landed, rolled, then jumped, landing between an oncoming promethean minion and Nerin.

All over the chamber, steel and magic flashed suddenly as the entire room devolved into battle, with Hellenica howling for the Skyking's attention.

She lifted her right arm, and the fog that flowed and billowed around her rose at her command to create a dozen spears. They hardened, compressing, and suddenly glowed, an unearthly glitter coating them before she flung them forward. To her dismay, a magical shield flashed into being to protect the Skyking.

Tang swore violently as he was exposed, approaching far closer to the Skyking than anyone had expected. He'd come within less than a dozen paces, and he flung both his arms forward, his twin daggers flashing end over end to slam into the shield before he was blasted backwards into the Oculai's massive bed.

Arrows flashed the length of the room. One slammed into the shield, but the other took a promethean in the neck, puncturing through the skin, muscle, and cartilage to take him down instantly. A sudden flare surrounded the image of Miren in my vision. Even if only with a tiny portion of my mind, I realized that it'd been her shot, and she'd leveled, thanks to its success.

Just as the other times it had happened through the weeks since we'd formed the party, the realization was accepted and dismissed in the same instant, the momentary note to congratulate her later being made and forgotten just as quickly.

I sprinted forward, running between pillars and drapes, hanging banners and silken sheets, paintings and plinths which held glittering, magical items. I managed to come within ten feet of it when the Skyking finally found me. The eye that locked onto me made me scream in pain, as the ten-health drain for using the ability in darkness jumped exponentially to a hundred health a second instead, and two death rays flashed out.

I gritted my teeth, rushing forwards, and felt the rays pass through me.

Something about the ability to become incorporeal was harmed by light, but the death ray was useless. More eyes spun to face me, and I swore, twisting and jumping in an attempt to avoid them as I closed the distance, before plowing ten mana into my naginata and making it flare with light. I screamed involuntarily as the additional light increased the drain, now consuming a hundred and seventy health per second.

I flung my naginata forward, left-handed, and dove to the right, cutting off the Child of the Night ability as I slid behind a pillar.

I heard a scream and a sudden crash from the other side of the pillar, before the Skyking started screaming louder in abject fury. The pillar I was hiding behind grew uncomfortably hot.

I reached up, clutching at my mouth, trying to stifle the groan of pain as the damage I'd taken from the darkness-facilitated ability finally stopped. I had thirty-seven health left, despite no wounds on my body, and I felt Oracle's fear and love reaching out to me.

"I'm okay," I sent to her, and I felt her disbelief, even as I built up the courage to run. I examined the sides of the pillar that I was hiding behind, and discovered that it was melting, crumbling away as the Oculai focused all its fury on me. *"I take it I got him?"* I asked Oracle.

"A glancing blow, it cut his face, and the weapon is sticking out of his jaw."

"Damn," I sent, thinking about how close I'd come to finishing the fucker off with a lucky hit.

I felt a wash of healing energy flow through me, and I groaned in relief, looking over and seeing it wasn't Hellenica as I'd expected, and I didn't have enough mana for Oracle to have done it…which left Nerin. Crouched down behind a pile of rubbish, weeping and shaking, the poor woman was in obvious pain, but she was still determined to heal whoever she could.

I shook my head, and she released the weave, collapsing back into cover. I thanked her silently, my health having jumped to a much healthier seventy-six.

"Might last a whole second now," I muttered, blowing out my breath in one go and sprinting across the space towards the next pillar. I almost made it, but the blast that took me in my trailing right leg punched through the calf and out the far side, the bone cracking and the meat flash-frying as I screamed and fell. I rolled out of sight as the other eyes locked on my location, starting to destroy the pillar I hid behind now.

I swore in pain, gripping my leg and trying not to cry out again. Tears pricked my eyes, and my teeth might shatter if I clenched my jaw any harder.

Hellenica hurled spell after spell, pounding on the Skyking's shield, while her djinn escort tried to block its counterattacks, and the legion and my squad battled toe-to-toe with the last of the prometheans.

I heard a scream of pain, recognizing Stephanos's voice and whipping my head in his direction. He changed from a healthy, if low, green to yellow, amber, then red. My entire party was dropping the same. Tang was bleeding out; Bane was moving relentlessly, diving in and out of cover while flinging daggers, spears, and his throwing knives at the Skyking.

The Mer slid to a halt on the other side of a pillar across from me, and I had a sudden wild idea.

It took a few seconds of surreptitious waving to get his attention, but I finally managed it just as he was about to run again. Death rays lashed into the pillar he hid behind and carved bits free, even as the pillar behind me went from warm to hot, making me feel like I was leaning on a griddle.

"Your worldsense!" I shouted to him, and he cocked his head in confusion. "Blast the fucker with it!" I screamed, ducking as a section of the pillar near me exploded from the heat, an unseen inclusion making it shatter.

I'd flinched away, but now I looked back, seeing Bane freeze as he realized what I wanted him to do.

"Hellenica!" I shouted. "Shield Bane!" There was a second's hesitation, but then she was twisting her hands and chanting. I looked back at Bane. He met my gaze, nodded, then stepped out into full sight of the Oculai.

The monstrosity spun, the beam cutting off from aiming at me and blasting toward him. Shields appeared, courtesy of Hellenica, instantly glowing red.

More djinn joined in, casting from their positions, or flashing forward to stand around him, pushing back with their smaller, weaker shields against the central eyebeam of the Oculai and his stalks.

More and more djinn joined in, and Hellenica lost some of her outline. Her form became blurry and indistinct as she poured her mana and her life into holding the shield. Arrows flew through the air, some from Miren and Stephanos, who fired from the floor where he lay, and others from a wounded legionnaire. They hammered into the Skyking's shield, each strike making it flare and cost more and more mana to maintain it.

Bane held out his arms, took a deep breath, and blasted the loudest, heaviest eruption of his worldsense I'd ever felt. It even shamed the search that Flux had done for the missing Mer children on the shore of the lake. I cried out, clutching my head in pain.

The feeling of it reverberated in the air, bouncing back and forth, constrained by the walls. The waves compounded, shattering the boarded-over glass in the windows and eliciting moans of pain as we all fell to the ground.

Even the Skyking.

It screamed in piercing anguish, its eyestalks thrashing wildly in all directions as it crashed over backwards, its tentacles no longer able to hold it aloft in the air. Its misshapen mass struck the ground with a disgusting thump. Two of its eyes burst under its own weight, and a warbling scream of agony rose from the incapacitated creature.

The only one in the room who wasn't affected, nor at least partially paralyzed by the scream, was Bane. He rushed forward, his hands wrapping around my naginata where it jutted from the Skyking's face and ripped it free in a burst of blood. His face twisted in pure rage, he whipped my weapon up over his head and drove it down, slamming the tip into the middle of the single main eye.

The impact made a disgusting popping crunch as the blade penetrated the enormous orb, and the Skyking shrieked in pain. Agony overcame its shock, and its eyes simultaneously glowed bright, about to unleash death, until Bane twisted my naginata, pushing deeper, and it punctured the brain fully.

The eyestalks froze suddenly, then fell limply against the floor.

The Skyking was dead, and with its death, its minions clutched their heads, writhing on the ground as their master's demise reached out to them, stunning them further.

They were quickly dispatched by our side, the last promethean shredded by a dozen fog spears thrown by the Clan Mother.

The battle for the Skyking's tower was over.

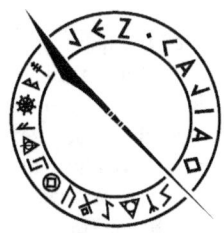

CHAPTER THIRTY-TWO

I dropped back to lie on the floor. The rapidly cooling pillar next to me was still giving off heat, but now at least, it was almost comforting, rather than painful. After a few minutes of heavy breathing echoing throughout the chamber, the first person to speak was Hellenica. The Clan Mother floated over to hover close by me, her gaze shifting from me to Bane, before settling upon the sagging remains of the Skyking.

"I see my clan's quest as fulfilled, Lord Jax of Dravith, Scion of the Imperium. I formally accept the agreed price. I, along with my clan, will serve you and the empire for your lifetime." Her face took on a pensive expression, and she quirked her head to one side. "I mean no offense, but how long do your kind usually live? Out of curiosity?" she asked in a deceptively casual tone, and I grinned up at her.

"Bad time to ask that." I chuckled weakly, as I slowly pushed myself to sit upright.

"Why?" She frowned quizzically.

"Well, my father—who, by the way, is a complete knob-jockey—is still alive in the realm I came from, and he's over a thousand years old. Might have been smarter to ask for that information before acknowledging the debt," I noted, arching my back and feeling it crack as I bit back a scream over the remains of my right leg. I eyed the mangled ruin nervously and grimaced. The pain was distant, which couldn't be a good thing; it had to mean the nerves were dead or dying, and…

"*A thousand years?!*" Hellenica hissed, spinning to glare at Xerix, who had gone as white as a sheet.

"He's human!" Xerix responded quickly, gesturing at me. "He is, I swear!"

"Yup, no idea how long I'll live," I agreed distractedly, sighing at the melted and crispy flesh of my leg, "…but I doubt it'll be long, considering how weird my damn life is these days."

I quit examining my leg as Hellenica blasted me with an AOE healing spell. It was weird to watch the flesh of my leg bubbling as it regrew, and I bit down a scream at the pain of nerves reconnecting and coming back to life ripped through me.

"I can heal your hand," Hellenica said sourly, repeating her previous assertions, "but I suspect it will be too much. You will pass out and remain unconscious for several hours, if not days. You should be unconscious already."

"Then it'll have to wait," I said through gritted teeth, sagging back with a moan of relief as the pain passed. I was left with a deep, bone-weary aching as my body reacted to the repeated trauma of massive injuries and healing sustained in such a short amount of time.

I pulled the representations for the team up, feeling relief wash through me as I saw they were all still alive, although Tang remained unconscious. As I watched his icon, I realized Arrin was hitting him with a healing spell.

"Augustus?" I called out as Oracle landed next to me and cuddled in.

"Yes, my lord?" he answered, approaching quickly and crouching next to me.

"Are they all dead?" I asked. My eyes closed as I rested for a minute.

"The enemies are, yes," he confirmed quietly.

"Great." I heaved a sigh of relief, then mustered the energy to call out, "Everyone, take a day off; you've earned it. Hooray, and all that shit."

I cracked my eyes open and looked up to find Augustus's sorrowful face above mine. The relief and exhaustion that had left me almost giddy plunged all the way into disgust and shame at my callous words.

"Oh, shit. I'm sorry, Augustus," I said, forcing myself to my feet. "I'm so sorry. I didn't mean to make light of our losses."

"I know, Jax. I know." He patted me on the shoulder.

"God, I'm such a dick at times," I muttered, swaying from side to side and blinking owlishly.

"Whoa, take your time, lad," Augustus said, grabbing my shoulders. "You've pushed past your limit. Don't worry; we all do it at some point. Let's get you to a seat and get you fixed up…. It's all right."

"A limit?" I mumbled, allowing him to half lead, half carry me to a low bench nearby. Once I was seated on it, he nodded, clapping me on the shoulder in reassurance as he called out to the surviving legionnaires.

"He's pushed past the point of his natural reserves. Anyone got a Potion of Might on them?"

There was some rustling and general searching before a legionnaire staggered over to her fallen comrade, whose body rested at the top of the stairs. She dipped her hand into the bag of holding on his waist, searching through the contents for a moment.

"Got one!" she called out, straightening and gingerly picking her way across the room, bearing a small vial that glowed a weird green.

"Excellent," Augustus said, nodding his thanks to her, before taking the potion and popping the cork. He held it out to me and gestured with it. "Okay, Jax, all in one. Be aware: it tastes like old socks," he murmured grimly. I sniffed the concoction, recoiling in shock, which made him smile. "Yeah, that's not gonna help you drink it. Should have just gone for it. The taste's gonna linger, as well, but that's how you'll know it's working! Come on, now…"

With his encouragement, I shrugged and poured the entire vial into my mouth in one go. My eyes opened wide in horror as I tried to swallow it. It tasted like the worst gorgonzola I'd ever had, mixed with kebab meat from a dodgy van. As I attempted to choke it down, it seemed to grow thicker and thicker, until I swore that I was swallowing something with the consistency of cold oatmeal. A handful of seconds later, I was able to gasp for breath again, having finally got it down, and Augustus passed me his water bottle.

I upended the bottle gratefully and poured in a good mouthful, before starting to cough and splutter. My eyes were watering and my throat was burning as a few legionnaires started to laugh.

"What the hell was that?" I wheezed, blinking back tears.

"The first one was Legionnaire's Might. It's a potion the quartermaster makes; does a little healing, little stamina regeneration boosting, but mainly, it gives your body a serious kick full of something. He says the recipe's a secret, but it'll kickstart your body's natural healing like nothing else. When you've pushed past the point when a normal potion or even healing spells can help, your body goes into shock. Too much of a drain, we're told. That potion refills the body's stocks of...whatever, I guess. It'd get people out of hospital much quicker if they'd drink it more than once. The other one, well,...that's premium rotgut, that is." He finished with a wink, and I shook my head again, grimacing.

"That potion felt like cement coating my tongue, and swallowing it," I muttered.

"Yeah, as soon as it mixes with your spit, it changes; a 'chemical reaction,' they call it. Starts to expand and fill you up. You'll not be hungry for a while, put it that way."

"I might never eat again," I groaned, shaking my head. Trying to divert my thoughts from the lingering taste, I pulled up my blinking notifications and grimaced.

Beware!

You have pushed to the limits of your mortal form. Healing performed on you has drained your body's natural reserves to a dangerous level, and now you must suffer the consequences!

All stats reduced by 10. Confused debuff is active.

These effects will remain in place until you have replenished your body's reserves to their most basic level. Increased drain upon your body at this stage may result in permanent lowering of stats.

Confused:
Confused debuff lowers your reaction time, increasing motion sickness and exhaustion effects by 10%, and slows mana recovery by 25%...

This status effect will last until your body's natural reserves have been replenished to their most basic level.

*

Congratulations!

You have killed the following:

- 2x Promethean Personal Guard of various levels for a total of 15,900xp
- 3x Imps of various levels for a total of 3,150xp

A party under your command killed the following:

- 18x Promethean Personal Guard of various levels for a total of 144,900xp
- 13x Krynnit of various levels for a total of 14,875xp
- 1x Altai, Wing-Lord, level 34 for a total of 32,500xp
- 1x Anubai Warrior, level 28 for a total of 8,000xp
- 3x Greater Stone Imps of various levels for a total of 11,200xp
- 10x Imps of various levels for a total of 9,150xp
- 1x Skyking Oculai, level 36 for a total of 55,000xp

Total Party experience earned: 275,625xp

As party leader, you gain 25% of all experience earned.

Progress to level 18 stands at 150,492/225,000

*

Congratulations!

You have completed the Quest you received from Xerix: Free Our Mother.

You were asked to free or kill Hellenica, Clan Mother of the Gueric Clan. If you agreed to do your best and did not ask the djinn to leave the city unless she had been freed, they agreed to swear a Conditional Oath to you. If you managed to free her, she and her children offered to swear to obey you for ten years.

If you managed to also kill the Skyking, however, the Gueric Clan agreed to swear to follow you for your lifetime.

Free Hellenica: 1/1

Kill the Skyking: 1/1 – (Completed)

Reward: Allegiance of the djinn of the Gueric Clan, 62,500xp, Lifeblood

"It is time, Lord Jax," came Hellenica's voice as I dismissed the notifications. My vision cleared to reveal the Clan Mother and dozens of djinn in the room moving to surround me. Augustus and the others moved back as the djinn began to glow, softly at first, but quickly growing stronger. They reached out their arms to the sides, throwing their heads back, and began to chant slowly and clearly.

"We swear allegiance to Lord Jax of the Great Tower, Lord of Dravith, and Acknowledged Scion of the Imperial Line. We swear to uphold his laws, serve his will, and protect his interests, to the best of our abilities, until the hour of his death. We further swear to abide by the spirit of this agreement, not only the wording."

Hellenica flowed forwards, each of the djinn glowing brighter as their mana reached out, linking them together in concentric circles around us. She reached out, pulling the glowing soul threads to herself, then pushing them out to me, where they sank into my chest. A new load of awareness filled me, sensing where they were and their lifeforces. It was weird, but after a while, it'd settle down like the sense I had from the legionnaires.

I damn well hoped it would, anyway.

"Thank you, all of you," I said, drawing in a deep breath. "Okay, Hellenica, I'm going to need your help and that of your people. Tonight, there's a lot more going on than just freeing you and killing the Skyking.

"I'll fill you in on the details as we go, but for now, I need you to send some of your djinn out to search the area. There were a handful of fliers from my forces out there; the fact that they haven't arrived inside yet is a bad sign. Can you send your people to find them and bring them in? They were being led by an alkyon called Amaat."

"Of course," she said, gesturing smoothly, and a dozen djinn turned, flying at top speed to the lower floors to escape the building.

"Once we've got them, and we know everyone's okay, it's time to get the ships that are on patrol above us. I know we already got their attention after destroying that soul-stealing feckin' belt, so it's going to be a bit harder, but that's just how life is. I need you and the fliers to board the ships, take control of them, and do it as quickly and quietly as possible.

"For now, get some of your people nearby to watch them. The alkyon have some people trained to fly the ships; we just need to take them quickly. Can you communicate with them at a distance?" I asked. Once she nodded in confirmation, I turned to Augustus.

"Is the mob still outside?" I asked.

He nodded grimly. "They've started to disperse without the rabble-rousers, but still, the majority are there."

"And they'll go nuts if they see us," I concluded. "Fine. Hellenica, once we've got the alkyon ready, we'll send them and your people to take command of a ship, bring it as close as it can get to the building, and we'll jump aboard."

"Then?" she asked. "Surely, they'll launch other ships to hunt us down…"

"The rest of our forces are taking care of that as we speak, or at least, they'd better be," I muttered, then called out, "Okay, people, loot this place to the ground. There's gotta be some good shit somewhere."

I forced myself to start walking, heading to the back to search the space where the Skyking had made his bed.

MAL

"Get ready to move on my signal," Mal whispered to his team. Soween, who was leaning with her back to the building across from him, nodded in acknowledgment. Her hair was bound up out of the way, and she and Mal wore similar long coats, closed tightly against the incessant drizzle.

The pair pushed off the walls and started walking towards the Stockpile, heads down and hats pulled low to shield their faces from prying eyes as they walked across cobbles slick with rain.

The footing was slippery, made more so by the layer of animal shit left behind by the dozens of wagons that passed in and out of the Stockpile each day. As they approached, Mal glanced up, making sure nothing had changed from the regular recons he'd performed. He swallowed hard, fighting to suppress nerves he'd never admit to making his stomach twist.

The walls of the compound that surrounded the Stockpile were high, grey stone slabs that glistened wetly. Eerie shadows surrounded them, the torchlight flickering and hissing as the rain washed against cracks in the streetlight glass. The two guards stationed on either side of the gate were bundled up against the weather, muttering to each other quietly as they huddled around their braziers, desperate for the warmth as they waited for their turn to sit in the guardhouse.

The combination of the braziers, the weather, and the general low likelihood of anyone actually trying to rob the city lord, all served to make the pair less perceptible than they should have been, which meant that it was only when they threw back their coats and raised their wickedly glowing crossbows that the guards noticed them.

By then, it was far too late. Mal and Soween both fired at the same time; their bolts, loaded with a powerful paralysis poison, took both guards before they could raise the alarm. As they crashed to the floor, Mal and Soween turned, training their remaining loaded crossbows on the guardhouse doorway.

A call came from inside, a voice raised in question, followed by grumbling and swearing as the sound of someone being "volun-told" could be heard.

Mal's team rushed forward, catching up to their leader and grabbing the guards. They hauled the stunned men out of easy sight as the door opened, and a young guardsman blinked out into the chill rain.

"Hubert? Varrin? What's up?" he called, his night vision practically non-existent as he blinked out at the figures that surrounded the door. "Wha—" he managed to utter in surprise before Soween shot him, sending him crashing back from the door.

Jay rushed in after the falling boy, his massive, steel-clad fists lashing out and bludgeoning the remaining guards into unconsciousness.

The rest of the group flowed inside, including two men who quickly stripped the guards of their cloaks and wet weather gear, slinking outside to replace the men they'd just taken down.

"Okay, people, you know what to do," Mal said, reloading his crossbows. He holstered one of the gnomish marvels and checked the string on the other before holstering that, too. Soween motioned the rest of their team inside, splitting the group up to move out, as Jay started dragging bodies to the holding cells against one wall. Meanwhile, Mal studied the maps and stock notes on the wall.

There were the usual complement of drunks and kids who had been caught by the guard filling the cells already, and they went silent as the group quickly moved in to take control. After a few minutes, one summoned up the courage to speak.

"Yer gonna let us out, then?" he asked, slurring his words as the foul reek of cheap gin and halitosis permeated the room.

"Nope," Mal said distractedly, still reading. "But iff'n you're real quiet, we might not kill you." Silence greeted his words, and he allowed himself a quick smile before stabbing a finger out at the map. "There! Soween, Josh, that's what we need: two guard huts nearby, and a rovin' patrol of up to a dozen. I want the patrol taken down first, then the guard huts. Then—and only then—take the walls. We've got fifteen minutes before the next patrol comes past, so make it count."

"Might want to send the boy to alert the guards at the enclave now, then, Mal," Soween murmured, getting a glower as he stopped his incessant grumbling long enough to look at her then leaned out the door and shouted into the night.

"Jonas! Get your boy movin'!" He pulled himself back inside and shrugged, scowling out at the falling rain as he muttered, just loud enough to hear, "I was just about to…"

Soween immediately began barking orders to the teams she'd organized, sending people scurrying as Jay walked back over from the cells, wrapping a cloak around himself and pulling a guardsman's helmet down tight.

"Momma always wanted me to join the guard," he mumbled happily, admiring his reflection in a bronze mirror.

"Well, she'd be real proud of you now, Jay. Now, get out there and keep an eye on things!" Soween interjected, before going back to directing people.

In less than a minute, they were all out of the guardhouse again, slinking through the night, but this time, they were on the inside of the wall, having passed through the interior gate. Apart from the stealth types, they all wore a mixture of freshly stolen and knocked-up close approximations of the guards' cloaks.

Mal walked steadily down the middle of the path, staying in plain sight as he tried not to gawk at the piles of building materials around him. Expensive, thick oak planks lined one side of the path, while the other racks held drums of nails, tar, and pitch. The hairs on the back of his neck rose as he stomped along, his boots splashing in and out of puddles left by the wagons that frequented this route. He tried to look everywhere, all while walking and spinning his cosh nonchalantly.

To the sides, he glimpsed his people slinking along, staying deep in the shadows as he closed on the guard hut up ahead. A handful of his people slipped away, cutting off in the direction of the flickering torches of the roving patrol.

"Idiots," he muttered, a smile tugging at the corners of his mouth. "It's like they don't want to find anythin', torches glarin' in their eyes."

A splash from his right made him scowl, and a thief went white with fear before flushing bright red with embarrassment, quickly vanishing again.

Amateurs; he'd been forced to hire amateurs and idiots beyond his own people, in order to make sure this went off without a hitch. Half of them had nearly soiled themselves when they realized what the target was and who they'd be stealing from. The others had barely been able to restrain their excitement.

City Lord Barabarattas was going to go apeshit when he heard that the city Stockpile had been raided, and Mal loved it.

Not only was he already insanely rich, thanks to the gambling he'd managed to pull off the last few days, but he'd have his own ship in a few hours, and that had always been a dream. All of that, and he was even being a patriot and helping his city, which was a bonus, really.

He'd have done it for half the promised deal. Hell, he'd been so bored, he'd have practically done it for free, but getting a home port, free repairs, *and* upgrades for his ship? Hell yes. The gold that had originally been offered was nothing compared to the wealth he'd made on the four nights of fights anyway, and he'd even taken the time to sell the arena.

His father was going to shit a brick.

"Who's that?" came a call from the darkness next to the guard hut, and a tall figure stepped out, his mail gleaming wetly from the rain. Mal swore under his breath, hunching his head down and pretending not to have heard as he readied his crossbows. "I say…who're you?" the figure called again, stepping into the light given off by the small lamp. He was human, the guard always were, but this guy looked like he had some ogre in his family, and that mustache…it was huge and black, dropping down both sides of his face like he was being nose-fucked by a pair of snakes.

Mal shook his head in disgust at the mess and brought up his crossbows. It was time to get the party started.

ELISE

Elise swore as she heaved the final post, while her team of three went to work with their hammers, sinking the bracing pins into place and locking the final support down.

She checked the hourglass in the corner of the room, hissing out a last breath as she saw the time. An hour until it all kicked off, and she hadn't managed to so much as test fire the engines yet. Even with the dozens of workers who had turned up to help for free, she was behind.

"Marik!" she called, and a dwarf on the far side of the room straightened, wiping the sweat from his brow. "Get to tha main controls an' make sure tha damn elf got those mana channels laid down and workin'. If not, we're all fucked."

"Elise!" called her nephew, ducking under a beam and sagging in relief as he found her. The rest of the mixed team of engineers moved on to address the next in a seemingly never-ending collection of problems.

"Bolvar," she said, nodding politely and taking the time to stretch her back out.

"There be a pair o' engineers in the main hold. They do be sayin' they bin sent by Finbar? Somethin' about a problem?" He shrugged, and Elise started to swear. She loved the lad dearly, but even though he was the son, nephew, and brother of a family of engineers, he couldn't keep two facts straight if his life depended on them. He'd been apprenticed to a carpenter until he'd nearly cut his nose off, and now he was reduced to running messages for the family…badly.

"Ach, lad, I'm comin'," she said as she pinched the bridge of her nose and hoped against hope that it wasn't going to be something serious.

The pair set off jogging, scrambling down ladders, scooting across narrow beams laid between unfinished sections and up the far side of the secondary transfer conduit, before finally dropping down onto a hoist to reach the only room they'd managed to get sealed fully from the elements: the main hold.

The entire rest of the ship was missing windows, portholes, walls, and in many places, decks and ceilings. The skeleton of the ship was barely finished, yet still they'd bolted the engines into place, adding extras wherever they could. Soon, if all the gods were good, the damn glass for the bridge would arrive, and they could seal that space as well, giving them a protected area to control the damn whale from.

The hoist crunched into the ground, and she bent her legs unconsciously, absorbing the impact and stepping off as Bolvar fell over with a grunt of surprise. She grabbed him by the back of his jerkin and hauled him to his feet. Her heavy muscles and calloused hands were evidence of the years she'd spent in the shipyards, making the lift easier for her than it looked like it would be.

"Where do they be?!" she asked him, irritation bleeding into her voice. "We be dancin' on a knife's edge for time as it is, laddie. If—"

"There!" Bolvar gasped, pointing at the far side of the room. She grunted, pushing him along as she started to jog, all the while thinking of the next job, and the one after that…

"Elise!" a familiar figure called, and Finbar stepped out of the shadows, waving to her. She skidded to a stop next to the tall elf, giving her friend a hug in greeting.

"What's up?" she asked gruffly. The sight of a friend in the middle of such a panicked few days was enough to make her feel better instantly.

"We're on schedule; in fact, we're ahead of it. I came with a dozen of my people to help for a few hours, deal with a few of your problems. Did your boy not tell you?" He looked askance at Bolvar, who had pulled out a carving knife and was fiddling with a small wooden figure almost before they'd come to a halt.

"No, tha damn eejit didn't!" Elise snarled, staring daggers at Bolvar, who hastily put the wood away. "Go on, get back to tha second floor, an' clear up tha break room!" she snapped, turning back to Finbar.

"Thank ye, old friend." She exhaled slowly, relief washing through her. "Reet, I need someone ta check the north engine relay, followed by tha…" She rattled off tasks, already marching back through the ship. Finbar followed in her wake, giving orders and dispatching people as they went, her idiot nephew forgotten beyond a momentary feeling of guilt over dismissing him so abruptly.

CHAPTER THIRTY-THREE

We searched the entire floor, spreading out as we waited for the djinn. It didn't take long before Bane called out from the side that he'd found the Anubai quarters, a series of upright coffins that, while filled with cushioning, just seemed weird.

I left the others to loot as much as possible as I examined the Skyking's corpse, discovering that the majority of it glowed to my inexperienced eyes.

Its teeth, the eyeballs on the end of the stalks, the stalks themselves, and a handful of other internal components all glowed in various shades. Best of all, when I was practically knee-deep in the mess, I found what I'd been hoping for, nestled at the center of its brain.

You have found Oculai Eyes x11, Oculai Eye Stalks x7, Oculai Salivary Glands x4, Oculai Cranial Inflation Gland x1, Oculai Greater Essence Core x1, Oculai Teeth x21, Oculai Pituitary Gland x1, Oculai Brain Matter x5

I packed all of the materials in my various bags, noting absently that I had accrued a lot of crafting components. I made a mental note to sort them out, provided I could find another way of identifying some of them; I sure as shit wasn't going to put *any* of these in my mouth.

"Jax!" Tang called from one end of the room, and I straightened up from washing my hand in a handily summoned fountain. I fought to kickstart my brain properly, my stomach roiling from the combination of the exploratory post-mortem I'd just done and Augustus' damn potion.

"What is it?" I rasped, swallowing hard and repeating myself louder.

"It's the Skyking's stash! We've found it!" he called. I set off to join them immediately, crossing the floor to a convergence of three silken drapes hanging over the seemingly solid stone wall behind them, then pausing to dry myself on them.

"See it?" Tang asked, and I shook my head. "Look at the drapes," he suggested. They were woven of heavy red and black silk. Weird symbols had been stitched onto them, and…and they were moving in a faint breeze, while no others in the room were.

I looked back at the wall, holding one damp hand up, and felt the breeze on my skin, raising my eyebrows at Tang in question.

"That's it!" He grinned. "Just walk forward."

I complied, feeling like a certain underage wizard and half-expecting to break my nose on the stone, but my pride kept me going. The world went black around me, and a second later, I emerged in a smaller hall that ran alongside the first.

Plinths on either side held magical items, organized as they had been in the main hall, but here they were more frequent. Gold and gems were displayed in chests on either side of the room, onyx weapons reflected the light, and a long black cloak hung from one wall, the inside lined with golden silk, and the dark outside as flexible as silk but as strong as cured leather.

I moved from item to item until I saw it.

The real treasure was clearly the same for the Oculai and me, as a bookcase holding over two dozen books of clearly magical origin stood at the back, in pride of place.

"Are there traps?" I asked Tang quietly, and he shook his head.

"Not that I can find," he reassured me.

"Get the others in here and load up as much as you can carry," I ordered, pulling my bags of holding out of the bag of spatial folding and discarding dozens of items, chucking aside weapons that were simple or average in favor of magical ones, until I had an entire bag free. Thirty-two slots were filled in minutes, as I stored the spellbooks and skillbooks from the Emporium, then the two engineering books I'd brought from the tower were added, and finally the twenty-seven books from the Skyking's shelves, for a total of sixty-one books and one extremely excited wisp, who kept trying to examine each book individually.

I put them away, promising her she could examine them later to her heart's content, and started pouring gold into the bags next, thankful that the coins only seemed to take up one slot each for gold, silver, copper, and platinum for some reason.

I ignored the totals for the moment. Not being able to spend any of it made it a little pointless, after all. I did the same for the gemstones, slightly annoyed that they required different slots, depending on the quality of the stone. A "flawless diamond" didn't stack with a "diamond" for some reason, so I pocketed the three I'd found, figuring they didn't take up much space, and it was a better idea than losing a slot.

I hoovered up as much as I could fit into the bags. Despite the bags reducing the weight by so much, they were still noticeably heavy when I finally got all the bags reattached. I was left with two slots by the end, and I was trying to decide if I should put a longsword or a lance into them, or leave them both empty for next time, when Yen found the thing we needed most of all.

In a cupboard designed to look like part of the wall were dozens of potions, three more bags of holding, and finally, a single large knapsack that sat atop a reinforced base.

Yen sprang into action, packing all but the mana, stamina, and health potions away into her bag as Lydia opened the first bag.

"It's full o' recipes," she said in awe. "There's a good twenty recipes in here, an' they're all at least common grade, an' the other's full o' potions!"

"This one's full of wood," Stephanos announced to the laughter of several nearby legionnaires. He waved a tiny bag around in front of his crotch, while Rinko opened the last bag, lifting it with an audible grunt of effort.

"Damn thing's heavy," he muttered, peeking at the inventory and starting to laugh.

"What is it?" I asked, and he shook his head, stifling his laughter as he gestured with the bag.

I moved over and scanned the inventory that popped up, reading stacks of metal ingots, some tools, and…a collection of things that took a minute to identify.

"Sooo," I said after a while, as others looked inside, "the Skyking was a bit kinky, then?"

Rinko burst out laughing.

"I think it was trying to make a statue of itself," he gasped when he finally got himself under control.

"Really? Because those look an awful lot like—" I started.

"It's eyestalks with an eye at the end," interrupted Yen, trying not to smile. "Honestly, men, you're like a bunch of children at times."

"So you won't want one, then?" one of the female legionnaires asked with a wink. "Because I'm thinking they might be good for…research…. You know, studying your enemy and all that…alone…"

"I bet you've already nicked three of them, the biggest ones!" Yen shot back at the other legionnaire, but she grinned with the retort, and everyone laughed as she shrugged. "…Maybe just one…"

Oracle flitted over to hover next to her shoulder, inspecting the creations and whispering to her, before giggling and settling on her shoulder.

Laughter echoed through the team as we all moved quickly, searching the room further but finding nothing else. Thankfully, the potion bag had a dozen greater strength and one epic health potions, as well as eight greater mana potions among a handful of others. I gave two of the mana to Arrin and took the unidentified potions to Nerin.

It took me a few minutes, but eventually, I had the remaining eleven potions identified, and with a wave of relief, Nerin popped the top off the third one, a greater Potion of Purity.

Greater Potion of Purity		**Further Description** *Yes/No*	
Details:		This highly concentrated potion will strip the imbiber's body of all impurities, returning them to a pristine state. Be warned: this will also remove any beneficial effects!	
Rarity:	**Magical:**	**Durability:**	**Potency:**
Highly Rare	Yes	100/100	8/10

Greater Health Infusion		**Further Description** *Yes/No*	
Details:		This potion will increase the imbiber's maximum health by 250 for one hour.	
Rarity:	**Magical:**	**Durability:**	**Potency:**
Uncommon	Yes	100/100	8/10

Potion of Evenai's Eye		**Further Description** *Yes/No*	
Details:		This potion grants the ability Evenai's Eye for 300 seconds, giving the imbiber a 50% chance of seeing through illusions.	
Rarity:	**Magical:**	**Durability:**	**Potency:**
Highly Rare	Yes	100/100	8/10

Potion of Earthen Aid		**Further Description** *Yes/No*	
Details:		When poured onto a patch of earth, this potion will create a small earth golem that will follow the commands of whoever creates it for 300 seconds. ***DO NOT CONSUME!***	
Rarity:	**Magical:**	**Durability:**	**Potency:**
Rare	Yes	99/100	7/10

Triskan's Delta		**Further Description** *Yes/No*	
Details:		This potion, created by the explorer Triskan Vanibai, grants the ability Water-Walker for 67 seconds.	
Rarity:	**Magical:**	**Durability:**	**Potency:**
Uncommon	Yes	100/100	4/10

Triskan's Bottom		**Further Description** *Yes/No*	
Details:		This potion, created by the explorer Triskan Vanibai, grants the ability Water Breathing and increases the imbiber's weight by 50% for 113 seconds.	
Rarity:	**Magical:**	**Durability:**	**Potency:**
Uncommon	Yes	100/100	5/10

All told, there were four potions of Earthen Aid, one each of Triskan's potions, three of Evenai's Eye, one Purity, which Nerin drank as soon as I named it, and one Greater Health Infusion. I passed her the potions, as well as two of the mana and two more health ones, just in case.

I'd barely finished putting the potions away when she began casting at me, and I gritted my teeth as a tingling feeling swept through me. It was similar to that feeling you get when someone draws their nails across your skin in a sensitive place, pleasurable, but just on the edge of too much, and it made me shiver.

"What the hell was that?" I asked her after a minute, and she shook her head, concentrating on something only she could see as she shifted her hands this way and that.

She began twisting her hands and muttering, and a pair of golden discs comprised entirely of light snapped into being. Each glowed softly, and a dozen symbols spiraled slowly around the outside, moving as she directed, with her fingers occasionally spinning them so that one symbol or another hovered at the top.

I waited quietly, but when Bane flopped down next to me heavily, I started to turn to him, only to have Nerin snap at me to remain still.

"What's going on?" he asked me. I shook my head, earning another glare from Nerin.

"No idea," I said quietly, trying to remain still. After a minute, she straightened up, the light show snapping off, and she frowned at me, before shifting her attention to Bane.

"You need healing," was all she said before slamming a spell into him that made him stiffen and let out a gasp of surprise. "For your information, *my lord*," she said, almost sarcastically, "I was examining your body to see if you really were incapable of being healed further and whether you have to remain as you are."

I waited a minute, before prodding her.

"And?" I asked.

"You do." She didn't meet my eyes, concentrating on the spell she was using on Bane. "And after this, you'll need to rest as well, Mer." She shook her head disdainfully. "Honestly, I've never come across a group that's spent as much time being healed as you people." She huffed in annoyance. "It's as though you're deliberately trying to injure yourselves…. That, or you're useless as adventurers."

"Yeah, well, we love you, too," I muttered, helping Bane to his feet as he sucked in shaky breaths. "Here, mate, I think you could probably use this." I commanded a fountain of clean, cool water to bubble up next to him. He leaned into it, relaxing and breathing the water into his lungs for long seconds. "Oh, and Nerin?" I said, and she looked at me. "Your bedside manner sucks."

"Medicine does you no good if it doesn't taste bad, boy," she replied, a faint smile tugging at the edge of her lips. "Maybe next time, you'll think to dodge, rather than get hit, so you don't have to put up with my advice…hmmm?"

"Maybe I just like spending time with you!" I shot back, and she laughed.

"Nobody likes spending time with a healer, Jax. We've seen it all, heard it all, and we've always seen someone who was worse off than you and handled it better."

I nodded sourly, remembering a nurse I'd once dated. She had no sympathy whatsoever; fantastic in other ways, but every time I'd injured myself, all I got was *Are you dying*? Wandering over to where Hellenica floated next to Augustus, I arrived just as they were discussing the ships floating above us.

"Jax," Augustus said, nodding to me in greeting.

"How are you doing?" I asked them, and got a smile from Augustus.

"We're doing well. That little light show you let off when you destroyed that belt earlier must have gotten their attention, as two of the ships are floating right over us. The other, which was apparently damaged when you discharged it, has headed off to land, so with a bit of luck, we can get both of the nearby ships."

"Any word from our people?" I asked, and he shook his head as Hellenica spoke up.

"My children have found a group of alkyon on the far side of the square. They're talking to them now; hopefully, these are the right ones. Also, you have two imps in chains…"

"Damn, totally forgot about them," I said, shaking my head. "Where are they?"

"We left them on a floor two levels below, still chained up. I've sent Rinko for them; shouldn't be long," Augustus said calmly as the others quickly gathered together. Grizz sauntered over to wind Tang up.

"I tell you, Jax, at times it's more like I'm their babysitter than their Primus," Augustus admitted fondly under his breath as the female legionnaire who'd commented on Grizz's stamina earlier walked over and casually clipped Grizz across the back of the head.

"I feel sorry for you, mate," I said, shaking my head in mock dismay.

"It's you I feel sorry for…" Augustus laughed. "I'm used to these reprobates; you've just adopted over a hundred of them, and their families."

"Damn, good point. Can I turn some of them down?" I asked, pretending to consider it.

"Unfortunately not. No returns, no refunds," Augustus insisted.

I laughed. "Ah, well. Guess we'll just have to do the unthinkable and house train them, then."

"It's been tried," Augustus warned me, chuckling as I set off, leading the way down to the lower floor.

"Perhaps, but has it been tried in a tower that's more than two miles high?" I asked, grinning. "I'm thinking morning training in full armor, running top to bottom, should get their attention."

"You wouldn't!" Grizz said in horror, overhearing me.

"Oh, I would, mate. I'm evil!" I said, winking at him.

"Two miles of tower to climb," Augustus said, his eyes lighting up. "Are the stairs straight, or…"

"They curl around the outer edge of each floor, mate, turning at least twice, often seven to ten times. Some floors, it takes five to ten minutes to walk between, making the climb much, much longer."

"Damn, that's going to be some distance." A sadistic smile lit up his face.

"Soul of a sergeant," I muttered, seeing the evil expression.

"What was that?" he asked, and I shook my head.

"It's not important, mate. Okay, so we need to take control of the ships and get them down close enough for us to board them. Which floor is going to be the best for that? The one above us was no good, but…"

"This floor might be okay," Augustus mused, all business again, before looking to Hellenica. "Unless a portal would work?" he asked her.

"We could make a portal, but only if the ship can be held rock steady. The edges of a portal… form a barrier that is impenetrable. Whatever touches that edge will be destroyed. If the ship was to move…"

"Good point," I said, nodding. "Better to find a level we can jump across from."

"Jax, Augustus," Rinko called, huffing to a stop. He'd evidently sprinted up the last few levels with the imps tucked under each arm.

"What's wrong, Rinko?" I asked, noting the strain that the night of heavy fighting had left on the normally unflappable legionnaire.

"Downstairs, sir…" He wheezed, then straightened, trying to catch his breath. "The city guard are smashing their way in, supported by a pair of mages."

"Shit!" I said, moving closer to the stairwell. I listened carefully but couldn't hear anything.

"We're eleven floors up, Jax," Augustus reminded me.

"How long do we have?" I asked, and Rinko responded.

"Maybe fifteen to twenty minutes before they get here. More, if they check each floor as they go, and—"

A shout echoed from below, and I moved back from the stairwell, setting myself with my naginata as Grizz took up a position on my right side, the others spreading out into a battle formation.

"You were saying, Rinko?" Augustus growled as I snapped to Hellenica to get her people moving.

"We need those ships, and we need them now!" Hellenica swooped away, examining the view from each window, as all but two of her djinn took off, blasting holes in the windows.

"Help!" a voice cried from the stairwell. I blinked in surprise at the sight of a bedraggled and worn-looking woman staggering up into view, followed by another who was supporting an older man. All three were clothed in rags and looked like shit, and it took me a second to place them, considering all the shit that had happened so far tonight.

"The cages," I said suddenly, realizing who and what they were as I straightened up. "Stand down, people," I called out as the three staggered onto the floor, gasping and holding onto each other.

"You…said that the…people down below…wouldn't…be welcoming," the woman at the front wheezed. "You were…right."

I swore, realizing that the noblewoman was gone.

"What happened?" I asked her, a legionnaire dragging a long, low bench across for them to sit on.

"Lady Hightree went down. She…demanded that we follow her, said she'd…have us whipped to death…if we didn't," she explained, still trying to catch her breath as Nerin shouldered her way through the group to examine them. "She was below…us. She was shouting to…them to let her out, and…who she was. Then…she started screaming, and we…we ran." Her shoulders shook, tears streaming down her cheeks.

"The guards have broken in the doors, but I think they've got specific orders regarding witnesses," Rinko said quietly to Augustus. I turned, overhearing them, and raised an eyebrow to the pair. Rinko ensured the three refugees couldn't see him then swiftly drew a finger across his throat.

"Fuckers." I snarled, shaking my head. "Okay, people, barricade this level as best you can," I said loudly before turning to the three refugees.

"Look, there's no time to really go into this right now, but your luck sucks," I said apologetically. "We think the guards are coming, smashing their way up to kill anyone they find. Don't know why, don't really care, but they hate the legion, and that's too long a story to go into right now.

"You've got two choices, really, if you don't want to take your chances going down there—" I gestured back to the stairwell "—and I wouldn't want to do that, personally. You can come with us, and we'll let you go free as soon as we can. We don't take slaves, so you'll be free, regardless; it's just a matter of whether we get the chance to land again before we leave the city or not.

"The other option is to come with us permanently, leave the city behind, and join us. I'm Jax, High Lord of Dravith, as I said downstairs, so I'm kinda at war with Himnel. Sorry that I've no time to sugarcoat shit, but that's how it is. So, do…you want to tag along and join us, or get dropped off whenever we can stop?"

"We'd have nothing. No food, no clothes; we literally have nothing to offer you, and no way to survive if we leave here without joining you," the woman said slowly, glaring at me. I sighed, trying to keep my voice patient.

"I'll give you some gold if you decide to leave, and we'll provide you with food and clothes as best we can, either way. Look, we're taking a load of refuges away from this shithole of a city tonight. You need to decide if you want to stay with us or not. You can come for now; just tell me your decision by morning, and I'll sort things as best I can. It's all I can do." I shook my head, turning from them and walking over to Hellenica.

Augustus and Bane went with me, while the others grabbed anything they could and started barricading the stairwell.

Grizz, being the cheerful, mad bastard that he was, had turned it into a game, and they were all chucking shit into the stairwell, clogging it up with everything they could carry, including balling up anything flammable and rolling it down the steps. I shook my head as I reached Hellenica, guessing that it would be a nightmare trying to climb those narrow stairwells if someone were to set fire to them.

I just hoped Grizz didn't smoke *us* out as well.

"What do you have?" I asked Hellenica as she conjured a floating flat disc of gray mist to hover before us.

"It's a scrying tool," she said simply. "It'll give us the best view of the building from the outside." She shifted it, spiraling it around and around until she found a relatively flat surface outside.

"There," Augustus said, pointing to the visible ledge outside the tower. "We can have the first ship pull alongside there, slightly lower, and we can jump."

"Okay, that's not gonna be scary at all," I muttered, but I nodded in agreement. We spun, inspecting the floor we were on and matching landmarks until we figured out which window it was nearest to.

We guessed at it being three windows down on the left, and I blew the wall out with an explosive mortar spell, the same one I'd used to take the ceiling out lower down in the tower. The entire structure groaned in response.

"Maybe next time, don't use that spell," Augustus said, as Oracle came flying down from the floor above.

"What did I miss?!" she asked excitedly, noticing the large opening out into the murky night.

"We're going to be making an escape as soon as we can," I explained while Hellenica flowed out of the hole, floating on the air as she examined it.

"You blew stuff up without me?" Oracle asked, pouting.

"Well, you weren't here," I said, shrugging and getting a glare from her. "What were you doing?"

"Girl talk," she said, tossing her hair back. "It's nothing you need to know about."

I looked past her to Yen, who was grinning at me while whispering in the ear of a dark-haired female legionnaire, and I groaned. Regardless of what had actually happened up there, I was going to be the center of gossip now. I decided I didn't want to know more, anyway, and turned my attention back to Hellenica.

"So…?" I called.

"It'll work." She flowed back inside. "It looks wide enough for you all to use, and the alkyon are coming."

A minute or so later, a loud flapping of wings advanced, followed by the sound of talons scratching the tiled roof. Amaat, Venta, and a handful of other alkyon clambered inside, dripping wet and looking bruised and battered.

Nerin went to work without being asked, as did Oracle. Amaat saluted with a fist to his chest, the rest of the group following suit raggedly.

I was about to speak up when the sound of more wings approached from outside, and Amaat held his hand up reassuringly.

"It's okay! Aaawk!" he said, stiffening as Oracle's healing hit him. When he could speak again, the others had landed and started to file in, almost two dozen of them, all bearing wounds of one kind or another. They wore a collection of leather, chainmail, and normal clothing but they were all soaked to the skin and clearly exhausted. "They were held in thrall to the Skyking," Amaat said, shaking his head.

"And now?" I asked, gripping my naginata tightly but trying not to appear threatening as our two groups eyed each other.

"Now they have joined my pride. They serve me, as their leader, and I serve you, Lord Jax." He crouched and exposed his throat in what I guessed was a ritual supplication for his people.

The rest of the group behind him did the same, some quickly, others hesitantly, but in a handful of minutes, they were all kneeling.

"Jax?" Oracle called and I looked to her. "The Oath?" she suggested, and I nodded, popping the top off a greater mana potion and lifting it in preparation as she sent out the Oath to the group.

"I swear to obey Lord Jax and those he places over me; I will serve to the best of my ability, speak no lie to him when commanded otherwise, and treat all other citizens as family.

"I will work for the greater good, being a shield to those who need it, a sword for those who deserve it, and a warden to the night.

"I will stand with my family, helping one another to reach the light, until the hour of my death or my lord releases me from my Oath.

"Lastly, I will not be a dick!"

The words of their Oath echoed around the floor, some saying it faster, other slower, but soon they'd all sworn, and another twenty-seven alkyon had joined our ranks. I relaxed as the potion worked to replenish the mana used for the Oath.

"Thank you all for joining us," I said, looking them over. "In time, I'll get to know you all. But for now, Amaat's word that you serve him is good enough. Other details, we can work out in the future. All I'll say, is that I will look after you, I'll teach you, and I'll make sure you have a home and as bright a future as I can. After tonight is over, we'll talk more."

They stood, stretching and shaking the water off. Some started talking, others began preening their feathers, and still more took up watch at the now-broken windows, by Amaat's order.

"They've got nothing in the city to stay for, and they wish for a future. Some few have families, which I've sent for and ordered to meet us at the shipyards," Amaat explained. I nodded to him in thanks before we started to discuss the plans for the ships above us, now that we had reinforcements.

A handful of minutes later, the djinn somehow signaled Hellenica that they were in place, and I blew out a deep breath.

"Then I guess it's time for phase two," I said, nodding to Hellenica and Amaat. "Go get me those ships."

Amaat screeched once, loudly, and his people fell in around him. He spoke quickly, designating one of them to lead half, and they dove out of the hole blown in the side of the building, disappearing into the wet night.

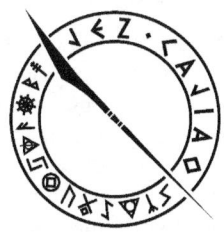

CHAPTER THIRTY-FOUR

I moved to the gaping hole in the side of the building, squinting upwards and blinking in the falling rain. It had increased from a misty drizzle to a steady downpour, and it made things blessedly difficult to make out, as I stood watching the indistinct shape of a ship slowly turning above us.

It moved in a casual holding pattern, hovering several hundred meters up, poised roughly over the square. Its hull was lit by the glowing, pulsing blue of the mana engines as it slowly bobbed and shifted. Thanks to that same glow, I could make out the second ship, a few hundred meters to the south of the first.

They both appeared to be searching for whatever had made the light that had damaged their fellow ship earlier. My destruction of the side of the building had probably drawn them closer as well. Between the late night, the heavy rain, and the clouds of smoke that belched forth from the surrounding buildings, it couldn't be easy to spot us.

As I watched the skies, I saw occasional movement out in the darkness. I drew in a deep breath as Hellenica spoke quietly from beside me.

"It's begun," she said simply, and the nearest ship suddenly dipped, before leveling off again and slowly rotating. It started to head towards us as lights began to flash on its decks. A signal lamp on the main mast suddenly flared to life and blinked frantically before going dark again as shouts echoed down from the decks.

From where we stood, reflected flashes of magic accompanied occasional shouts, though little else. On the farther ship, we were able to see more, as a barrage of lightning spells flashed through the air, making me wince.

"Doesn't the lightning backlash with all the rain?" I asked Hellenica, and she sighed.

"It does, and it will injure others than its intended target if they're unlucky, but my children are gifted in the air magics, not so much in others. They have learned to use what they are most comfortable with, not what is best. I will have years ahead of me to teach them correctly now, and possibly centuries of breaking bad habits," she said ruefully. I grimaced, contemplating how much it would suck to try to break the habits I'd gotten into.

I tended to create or alter spells on the go these days, mainly because I knew Oracle could stop them, or at least lower the chances of them exploding in my face. I tended to do it without thinking, and if I was suddenly told tomorrow that I couldn't do it anymore…

I shook my head as I thought about it for the first time in ages. I needed new spells, and I needed to actually learn for myself, not just absorbing the knowledge from a spellbook. Understanding why and how things worked was of utmost importance, or one of these days, I suspected that I was going to make a terrible mistake.

We stood there, side-by-side, as the battle raged above, watching as the ship that was headed for us suddenly veered aside. The vessel dipped out of control for a few heartbeats before shifting and heading back toward us.

Shouts started to rise from down below in the stairwells, and the faint crashes and clattering suggested that the guard had found our improvised blockages.

"How long?" I asked Hellenica, who shifted her scrying spell backwards a bit to show the very edge of the ship that was coming in towards us.

"Can you move it to the ship?" I asked her.

"It's too complicated a spell. I can see around us for a hundred meters, but only somewhere I've been. I've never flown aboard such a ship, so I can't focus in on it."

"Weird spell," I commented, and she nodded her agreement. "Can you show us the guard?" I asked, nodding to the stairwell.

She shifted it, blurring until it zoomed in through the hole in the wall where we stood. A disc of warped air blasted past us, dodging between people then dipping into the stairwell. I froze at the blockage, slowly shifting around to look down, pleased to find that it was pretty solid.

"I can hit the blockage with it, but it would end the spell and damage the work the legion did," she said, sighing.

"How fast is it, this spell?" I asked slowly as a thought came to mind.

"Very." She frowned at the expression on my face. "Why?"

"And it'd do damage if it hit something?" I pressed, grinning.

"It would, but it's a mana-intensive spell. If you're just looking for something to hurt people with, there are much less costly ways…" she said slowly, watching me.

"But could you get it in the building somewhere below us?" I asked. "Then fly it around to hit, say, a leader?"

"Possibly…" She nodded thoughtfully. "It would depend on whether I can find a window or something to get in."

"Find a window, and I'll get it blown in for you," I offered, turning to Arrin, who was getting one of the refugees to eat some food. "Arrin! I need you, buddy." I called. He smiled to the man, excusing himself to hurry over to me. I explained what I wanted, and Hellenica showed off the scrying tool, making him grin as he conjured a barrage of Magic Missiles.

With her spell providing the view from outside of the building, he fired the missiles, slamming them one after another into an old, sealed window a few floors below. The weathered frame exploded inward on the third impact, the remaining three missiles slamming into the room beyond.

I left Hellenica to direct her spell through the damaged window, as she started hunting for a guardsman to expend it on, and I moved back to Augustus, who was gathering everyone up.

"Right, mate." I nodded to him and my people. "I need everyone ready; I don't know who's controlling the ship, but it's all over the place right now, and we might not get a second chance to board her. As soon as it comes alongside, we need to go," I insisted.

"We'll be ready, Jax," was all he said, but the looks he directed around made it clear that it wasn't a simple agreement. He would get everyone onto the ship if he had to throw them personally.

"How long?" he asked.

"A few minutes, if that; it's heading our way now," I said with a grin, moving back to the hole in the wall and leaving the details for Augustus to work out.

When I reached the opening, I was just in time to see a blur from the scrying spell that revealed an uncomfortably close-up view of a pompous-looking man in very shiny armor, followed by a scream from the floor below as the spell cut off.

"I take it you got him?" I asked Hellenica.

"I also got experience for it, so it appears to be a fairly powerful weapon after all," she said, grinning delightedly at me. "It's been a long time since I have been able to use my magic and gain experience, so thank you for that, Jax."

"Anytime." I smiled back and looked out at the ships. The closest one was small, clearly built for speed, and it was on the final approach to us. The flash of spells and shouting of fighting had died away, making me relax as several forms jumped over the side, their wings flaring as they headed for the second, larger ship.

The battle was clearly ongoing on that ship, and judging from the screams and flashes of magic, it was still anyone's fight.

"Get ready!" I called behind me as the ship dipped, gliding across the rooftops and turning to present its side to us. I clambered out onto the rain-slicked tiles, slipping slightly before I caught myself,

Hellenica floated out beside me and steadied me before helping a few others out. The pair of djinn that had remained floated out with her conjured shields and held them angled by the tiles, preventing people from falling off the small roof as the ship moved in closer. Meanwhile, the shouting from the floor below grew in volume, increasing our sense of urgency.

Oracle flitted out to hover nearby, grinning at the ship coming in. Ten meters away, nine…

"What did you do?" I called distractedly to her, blinking the rain clear of my eyes and crouching, ready to jump.

"I set fire to the rubbish Grizz piled up for me!" she called back, grinning. "The guard doesn't seem happy!"

I shook my head at her antics. Two meters…I started running, pushing off hard enough that I almost slipped again, continuing to run to the edge of the roof as the ship dipped down slowly below the level of the roof.

As I reached the edge, the upturned faces of the crowds greeted me from below, lanterns flaring in the rain and the rain-washed cobbles. I saw a *lot* of cobbles, and I had a horrible thought of someone conjuring a shield against the side of the ship, causing me to hit and bounce off. As I leaped from the edge, a serious burst of fear powered my legs to do an insanely stupid thing.

In that instant, I caught sight of a small, weaselly man in the crowd below. He rushed from group to group, a tray held in his hands with a strap around his neck, trying to sell what his thin voice floating up proclaimed as "Sausages inna buuuun!"

Then I landed, my feet slamming onto the wooden deck, my naginata banging down in my left hand as I reached out instinctively with my right to catch myself. I grunted in pain as my stump hit the deck.

I staggered, moving as quickly as I could out of the way as others followed. Some screamed, others leaping silently in their terror, while Arrin jumped alongside Grizz, both of them shouting in glee.

Mad bastards.

I started dragging people back, clearing the deck for others as fast as I could as we passed the towering building, I saw the last man, Augustus. He ran and leaped, hitting the side of the ship; the stern had moved too far out from the building, and he vanished.

Then Hellenica was there, rising alongside him. The massive legionnaire, a man so heroic-looking, Hollywood would have refused to cast him as a soldier on general principle, was lifted onto the deck of the ship in a princess carry by a woman who, if she were solid, would probably have been on the scrawny, if very beautiful, side of things.

I saw the looks on their faces as she deposited him safely on the upper stern deck, and I wished for a camera right then like I'd wanted for little else.

I looked around then, for the first time seeing the actual ship, not just the deck I was heading for. I noted the blood stains, the bodies, and the signs of the fight. I saw two bodies of djinn, their tiny forms broken in death, and an alkyon's wing, bloody and alone, lying next to the signs of another fight. The blood trail led to the side of the ship, and I shook my head, forcibly banishing the mental image of a flier falling to their death.

I pushed through clusters of people on my way to the upper deck, passing djinn glaring at surviving sailors who were being forced to work on the ship. I climbed the set of stairs to the raised deck, finding two alkyon standing up there, one being healed by Hellenica, who seemed to have turned a rosy, pink color, for some reason.

"Congratulations on your jump, Augustus!" I said, smiling as I walked up and getting a grin in response.

The second alkyon was handling the helm of the ship. He looked stressed—as near as I could tell, different species, and all that—but he was doing it.

"Thank you," Augustus chuckled. "I was getting a bit worried until Hellenica got to me, I don't mind admitting," he said as he looked across at her. She quickly finished healing the other flier, who thanked her and moved to check on the ship's controls, a series of dials and crystals that looked utterly incomprehensible to me.

"So...?" I said, addressing the two alkyon with a raised eyebrow. "I'm impressed with your ship handling!" I tried to stand like a lord while sneakily hitting them both with an Examine spell. "Eridine and Raat, how are we looking?" I asked, and Raat, the helmsman, spoke up.

"We're good, Lord Jax. The ship is responding to our control, and we didn't lose too many. We've sent most of our wing to help with the larger prey now, and this one is close enough to what we trained on to be easy to command."

"Who did sort it out for you to train, again?" I asked casually.

Raat fixed me with a piercing stare for a second before bobbing his head and focusing on a point in the sky over the bow, responding to his partner's quick comments about power and direction.

"We practiced on a ship helm that was being worked on by the dwarves in the shipyard...my lord?" he asked, as though unsure it was the right answer.

"Ah, of course. Sorry, it's been a long night," I said, forcing a smile as I rejoined Augustus.

"Nobody expects you to know everything, Jax," he said to me quietly.

"Yeah, but it's so bleeding obvious that we'd need to train for the ships, now that he's mentioned it," I said, trying not to facepalm.

"Nobody can think of everything, and you've been battling every night to the death in an arena as well. Don't worry; just be thankful that Mal thought of this," he remarked, a faint smile on his lips as he changed his mind and went on. "Scratch that; I think it was Soween. That woman's a wonder at the details."

I nodded agreeably, instantly feeling better.

"Oh, well that's different, then," I said, straightening. "If it was Soween, that's fine."

"Little bit jealous there of Mal?" Augustus quipped, a smile tugging at his cheeks.

"No!" I snapped, then sighed. "He's just got a plan for everything, that's all. Makes a man feel pretty green at all this."

"He's had years to plan for most of this stuff," Augustus said calmly. "Remember, he said it was a thief's dream to do the things we're doing tonight; he just couldn't figure out how to make it all work without your input. You came up with the ships, with the crews, and the legion…. He's just doing the…what did you call it?"

"Fiddly bits," I replied shortly as the ship finally lifted clear of another building.

We'd had to navigate between some of the larger towers as the alkyon at the helm tried to turn the ship around, dodging around an old clock tower and out over the river. They finally managed to loop back around to head towards the other ship, floundering in the sky as it was.

"Looks like we might have some work to do on the other ship," I said slowly, watching the battle as we closed the distance. Dozens of people were fighting on the decks, both with magic and by strength of arms.

The alkyon seemed to favor small blades, against the ship's few remaining soldiers using full armor and a sword and shield combination, and that was making it hard for them to get to their targets.

The djinn were battling it out with the ship's mage and a series of archers, who kept popping up from cover to take pot-shots at them. The two dozen djinn who had originally answered Hellenica's call had been reinforced by another dozen, who'd taken time to travel to the fight. But at least twenty had died over the course of the two ship's battles. The djinn were powerfully magical, but they proved to be physically weak once that magical ability was exhausted.

"Shit," I hissed as we lifted above the other ship, at last able to clearly see the deck and the bodies that were laid across it.

For every soldier, there were at least two of our people, and as we watched, more and more started to fall. The djinn fell back, erecting shields around the alkyon, helping to keep them alive as seemingly endless crossbow bolts and arrows flew from the doors to the lower level.

I scanned the ship, noting in passing that it was quite a bit larger than our own warship, the *Agamemnon's Pride*. It had a lower central area that I termed the main deck, with a raised stern and forecastle that had solid doors leading inside. The rear also had a raised deck, with the helmsman under cover of a lean–to, and what I assumed to be the captain's quarters below him.

The front of the ship, above the forecastle, held a five-cannon battery, two smaller cannons on either side, and a single large cannon that was built into the forward deck, surrounded by ornate sculpturing.

The main fight was taking place around the upper and lower decks with bodies strewn everywhere. The crew had taken cover inside the forecastle and were firing out at the djinn and alkyon, popping out and jumping back as spells hurtled inside after them, while a group of four heavily armed and armored soldiers were pushing the alkyon back.

The few djinn who could still cast had fallen back to protect their comrades with shields as best they could, and from the shouting of the crew, the enemy thought they were winning.

"Not for long," I whispered to myself. "Augustus. I need that ship," I said. He saluted, smacking his fist to his chest, bellowing out orders.

"Rinko, Plas, Yen, and Tang, you're with me. The rest of you are to secure this ship and make sure that nothing happens to it or Lord Jax," He started before I caught his attention. He paused, waiting for me, and I nodded to Lydia.

"Take my squad, Augustus. They're good fighters, and you'll need them," I said, holding up the stump of my missing right hand. "No need for them to miss out on the fight. If not for this, I'd be with you."

"As long as you stay up here," Augustus countered quietly, and I nodded to him. "Then I'll take them, but Bane stays with you, as do the rest of the legion."

"Fine but be careful. As much as we need the ship, if all else fails, get everyone off it and we'll blow the fucker up," I insisted.

Unlike our own ship, which had a single large mast in the middle to help propulsion, the other ship had two smaller side masts and no central one. The constant contrast between ships made me shake my head in wonder, considering what a centralized, standardized approach would do for their manufacturing.

I'd be damn well bringing that in, I decided, as Augustus called out more orders, directing Lydia, Jian, and Arrin to join him, while ordering Miren and Stephanos to take up station on the railing of the ship.

"Oracle," I said quietly, and she turned to look at me, her sadness at the deaths of others clear on her face. "I'm sorry, I know you don't like this."

I changed what I'd been going to say at the sight of her tear-streaked cheeks. I thought back to the fight in the Skyking's tower and how quiet she'd gone since we had found the feeding area.

"Are you okay?" I asked.

She shook her head. "No, I'm really not, but I know why we're doing this, and I know it has to be done. These people would be flying against us, I know. I just…"

"You just don't like that we attacked them first," I finished for her.

"Yeah…I guess." She sniffled.

I reached up to pat her legs as she landed on my shoulder and cuddled the side of my head. "I know," I said, watching as we closed in on the other ship.

The crew hadn't noticed that we'd taken the first ship, and the few that had the time to see us assumed we were bringing them reinforcements, not their attackers. "Can you watch over the crew on this ship for me?" I asked her.

"Why…what are you going to do?" She frowned, her tone full of suspicion.

"I'm going to help our people, magically; I'm not jumping over to fight, don't worry," I reassured her quickly.

"As long as you stick with that, then, okay." She lifted off my shoulder, quickly zipping aloft and hiding in the rigging as she started to check over the crew.

I moved to the side, standing next to Miren and Stephanos as they drew back on their bows, aiming carefully.

Nerin cast her AOE buff over our people, and I watched them psyching each other up for the jump. Rinko bellowed out orders to the group as Hellenica quietly lectured Augustus.

We pulled alongside the enemy ship, hovering slightly above the main deck, less than ten feet apart. Our helmsman turned the ship suddenly to cut across above them, as Augustus bellowed "Go, go, go!" and the group sprinted for the edge. A section of the railing had been lifted free where a gangplank would normally be attached. They ran straight out, jumping off it and landing on the upper deck of the forecastle. Most rolled upon impact, but a few, like Lydia, encumbered by her heavy armor, slammed down hard, hissing in pain as they bounced off the railing on the far side.

Our ship started to turn slowly, arcing about as Miren, Stephanos, and another legionnaire raised their bows and took aim. Their arrows slammed into the wood around the entrance to the forecastle, with one spearing the ground inside the door. I made eye contact with Hellenica, who'd taken up station by my side, and I smiled.

"I bet you've got a powerful lightning spell, don't you?" I asked. She nodded, grinning evilly. "Great. Give me a few seconds to get the fountains into place, then hit the water, okay?" I said, casting as quickly as I could.

I took a deep breath and concentrated, building the spell and focusing on where I wanted it to appear. I found that, without a second hand, I could only cast a single fountain at a time, but by forcing more mana into it, it grew bigger more rapidly, and setting it off in the doorway meant that it quickly flooded the space inside, adding to the small puddles of water that the rain was building.

Our archers fired off a couple more arrows each before I nodded to Hellenica, who'd been building her spell while I soaked the area.

She released a lightning bolt as thick around as my leg. It put all of Oracle's and my attempts to shame as it blasted through the air, hitting the side of the doorway and punching through effortlessly in a spray of splinters. As it hit the pool of water, the impact set off a secondary series of smaller bolts that coursed through the puddle, traveling up the legs of the men inside the room and making them scream and convulse, before tearing through to the deck below and eventually grounding out against the inside of the hull.

"Well," I said in astonishment. "Remind me not to get on your bad side!" Hellenica regarded me seriously as she answered.

"I recommend that. I know legionnaires personally, you know." She pointed at the helmsman on the enemy ship as she tilted our vessel aside, having finally realized that we weren't there to help. "Should we take the helmsman next?" she asked. I shook my head.

"We don't know if the helmsman that was trained for the ship is still alive; leave them and let the legion take control. They can force her to land. Meanwhile, we need to take the soldiers out…"

LYDIA

"Move it!" Lydia shouted, rushing forward with her shield held high, the legionnaires on either side of her quickly outpacing her as she limped along, gritting her teeth.

"You alright, L?" Jian asked.

She grunted, straightening and forcing herself to run as though nothing was wrong, despite the pain. *Sod's law I'd be the one to sprain my ankle…*she thought to herself. "I'm fine, just go!"

Jian shrugged, jogging forward to keep up with the legion.

The damn legionnaires were insane. No matter what happened, they just kept powering on. They wore more armor than she did, yet every time they trained together, they outran, out-jumped, and outfought her like it was nothing. *Well, not today…*Lydia thought grimly, determined to make it through the fight without them looking down on her or her team,

Lydia followed Jian down the stairs from the upper forecastle to the main deck. Arrows flew from the main doors inside, and she lifted her shield, feeling the jerk as one hit and went spiraling off into the night, falling to the earth far below. *Not a good night to be looking up in curiosity…*

"Formation!" Augustus bellowed, and the group bunched up. Lydia stumbled a few steps past where she'd been supposed to stop, unfamiliar as she was with the legion fighting style. She quickly fell back, taking the position a legionnaire left for her with a muttered curse before peering around the edge of her shield. She saw water splashing around the entrance to the forecastle and frowned, before her eyes went wide with realization.

"Prepare to charge," Augustus called, the legionnaires around her hunching down behind their shields as they got ready to sprint. Lydia shouted out before she could think.

"Hold!"

The legion started to move, expecting the order to charge, and staggered. In the confusion, their expected shieldmates were not there to cover them, and Rinko spat out a curse as an arrow glanced off his helm.

"Fall back!" Lydia shouted, and the legionnaires paused, unsure if they should obey her, until she roared out in her best command voice. "In Jax's name, fall back *now*!"

The legion obeyed, contracting around her as Augustus took up a position beside her.

"I know you're not part of my usual command," Augustus started through gritted teeth as a second and third arrow slammed into the shield wall, before a trio of Magic Missiles hit Rinko's shield a second later.

"Mage's back to play," Rinko muttered loud enough to be heard as Lydia spoke over Augustus, glaring back at him despite the fear in her heart that she'd overstepped herself.

"No, it's one of Jax's favorite spell combinations. Don't get in the water," Lydia managed to get out, before a bright flash and the roar of a lightning bolt crackled through the air above them.

The thick streak of electricity slammed into the deck inside the forecastle, taking a section of the doorway with it. Screams rose from inside as the bolt leaped from figure to figure, transmitted through the standing water inside, but fortunately not linking up the puddles outside.

Lydia looked up at a wide-eyed Augustus. "Now we can go, Centurion Primus," she confirmed through gritted teeth, and he shook himself.

"Thank you, Optio. Well caught."

Lydia sagged with relief and surprise at the impromptu title, as the glares from the surrounding legionnaires changed to nods of approval. "Legion! Advance!" he bellowed, and they were off again, sprinting through the doorway to find three soldiers and a short, fat mage trying to get back up. The mage managed to get a single syllable of a spell off before Tang's boot rendered the contents of his crotch to jam, followed by his gladius relieving him of his head.

Two of the other soldiers threw down their weapons, the third having an unfortunate meeting with a mace to the face.

Lydia paused as she entered the room at the back of the legion. Arrin tailed her, Jian taking up a post on the other side of the door, and Augustus waved her over.

"Well done on that, Lydia," he said gruffly. "I understand how hard that was to do. From now on, don't hesitate to speak up." Lydia nodded, stunned, and he smiled. "Right, I need the alkyon backed up and the helmsman taken under control; can you handle both of those jobs while we clear the lower decks?"

"Yes, sir!" she said with a grin.

He nodded back, a tight smile on his face. "Then get to it, Optio!" With that, he turned and commanded the legionnaires, passing Yen, who was busy knocking out the second of the soldiers who'd surrendered.

"Effective," muttered Jian, peering over Yen's shoulder as she looped a rope around the wrists, tying it off and doing the same with his ankles, before rolling the unconscious man over, tying them together in one smooth flow.

"Practice!" Yen called, grinning and moving onto the second as Lydia jerked her head back toward the doorway.

"Arrin, stay behind Jian and me. Hit 'em with yer missiles an' keep out o' sight as much as possible. Jian, stab the fuckers." She huffed out a deep breath and started advancing back across the deck towards the fighting.

Miren and Stephanos had switched their targets to the soldiers as well. While their enemies were armored, their armor wasn't good enough to protect them from drow-crafted bows and arrows. One of the four had already fallen, an arrow in his thigh, and a second, far luckier shot had taken him in the neck where his helmet and shoulders left an opening.

"Move!" Lydia shouted to Jian as they sprinted out of the doorway into the cold rain. Arrin pounded along behind them, chanting, as two of the remaining three soldiers turned to face them.

The small group moved to fight back-to-back, with the alkyon shifting to encircle them on the far side, blades flashing.

Lydia saw the looks of exhaustion on the group as she closed in and grinned, thinking of the fight with Altai the Wing Lord in the tower earlier.

"Get ready to fuck 'em up!" she called to Jian, hunching down behind her shield and shouting "Shield Bash!" The ability activated, taking a hell of a chunk out of her stamina, but she practically flew across the intervening distance and rocketed through the middle of the pair facing her and Jian. Her momentum caused her to smash into the back of the third, who'd been facing away from her, sending him sprawling onto the deck, face-first.

Lydia caught herself, staggering at the sudden loss of stamina. She lashed out with her mace, taking the man to her left in the head, while Jian jumped into the air, stabbing down with both scythes and killing the man on the right with a blade to the throat. The second stabbing into his gut was just overkill.

The alkyon quickly finished up their opponent and nodded to the newcomers in thanks, turning to head for the controls. Lydia and Jian went with them, while Arrin concentrated on an injured alkyon, swearing under his breath at his own ineptitude with healing spells as his target twitched and moaned.

Lydia jogged up the last few wooden steps behind the alkyon to find the helmsman and his assistant frantically drawing weapons while trying to keep the ship on course.

She leaned over the railing, observing the neatly ordered rows of tents and a single black cathedral in the distance as they lifted over the walls, and swore violently.

That was just peachy; the pricks of the Dark God were the last things she wanted to deal with tonight.

"Turn tha ship around, right damn now, or yer dead," she said, pointing her mace at the helmsman, who stared in disgust at her and at the bloody…bits…caught between the flanges on it, before nodding slowly. He grasped the helm, then glanced at his assistant, who grabbed onto a strap secured to the control panel.

Before Lydia could ask what the strap was for, the helmsman twisted the ship sideways, turning the vessel onto its side.

With a terrified scream, she felt the ground go out from under her and she started to slide, headed for the side of the ship. Jian fell with her, while the alkyon launched themselves from the deck, wings beating furiously as they tried to clear the cover over the bridge. One managed it, but the other was struck by a support, and his wing broke with a loud snap. He fell screaming toward the ground, his companion diving after him.

"Motherfucker!" Lydia growled as she slammed into the railing, glaring up at the helmsman, and noticing for the first time the divots and braces carved into the floor of the deck, which had enabled him to lock his feet into place. The ship turned again, tilting the other way and sending her and Jian, and judging from the crashing and shouting from below, a great many others, careening across the deck towards the far side.

Lydia slammed into the thick wood and groaned as a couple ribs snapped. The thinner metal on the sides of her chest plate was no match for the weight of the full set driving her against a solid object. The wood creaked alarmingly, and she gritted her teeth, bracing herself as she glared up at the helmsman. The reprobate ignored her and concentrated on his destination, while his assistant grinned and made obscene gestures at her.

"Signal the tower!" the helmsman snapped at his assistant. "Tell them we've been boarded and that we need help."

"Aye, sir," the assistant replied, frantically pulling a lever on the control panel, and a pattern of flashes began emitting from a crystal mounted above the deck.

"So much for doing it stealthily," Jian said quietly to Lydia, nodding up to the helmsman. "I'm going for them; think you can give me a boost?" He grinned, and she nodded as the deck started to tilt again. Ignoring every instinct to grab on, she instead threw her mace at the assistant, then formed a brace with her hands, palm up.

Jian planted his foot, and as they started to slide, she braced his leg long enough to heave him through the air with a pained scream.

Lydia almost blacked out with the pain, sliding and falling across the deck to slam into the far side, several spindles of the railing snapping as she hit them.

Jian flew through the air, teeth bared as the assistant screamed at the impact of Lydia's hastily thrown mace slamming into his hip. Both he and the helmsman looked down just in time for Jian to grab onto the assistant with one hand and stab him with the other.

The assistant was in his late teens, if that, spotty and short. But the obvious pleasure he'd taken in seeing Lydia hurt had removed any thought of mercy from Jian as he gutted the boy, kicking him away from the wrist strap to fall, screaming, into the night. His body hit the railing with an audible crunch, flipping over it and disappearing into the darkness, where his scream hung for several seconds before cutting off abruptly.

"You filthy pirates!" The helmsman swore, yanking the wheel sideways and sending the ship over again, but this time, he flipped a lever as well, and the nose of the ship dipped, faster and faster. "I'll see you all dead before—" he snarled as Jian twisted around, stabbing out with his scythe. The tip seemed to dip delicately into the helmsman's throat, slicing cleanly through the Adam's apple and back out, bringing a gout of hot, red blood that steamed in the cool rain.

The helmsman grunted, his hands releasing the wheel automatically as they reached up for his throat, and Jian jumped, grabbing the wheel and kicking the older man in the face. The impact sent him pirouetting backwards to fall over the railing and out into the night.

Jian dangled from the wheel, looking around the control panel desperately as he struggled to get his feet up into the strange holsters the helmsman had been standing in. He pulled hard, lifting his body up by the strength of his arms alone, curling his legs up close to his chest and flicking them forward. One foot bounced off the brace, but the other landed true, giving him enough of a purchase to get his other foot in as well.

He looked up, the world suddenly oriented differently as the bow of the ship became his horizon, and he twisted the wheel, trying to make the world line up right. He overshot, frantically hauling back the other way, as Lydia shouted at him to "Pick a goddamn side, ya moron!"

"Okay…okay, you can do this," Jian muttered to himself, gazing hopelessly at the control panel. To his eyes, it was a mess of crystals and levers, a handful of smaller dials, and one long dial with a lever next to it. As he frantically tried to remember which lever he'd seen the helmsman pull, he fixated on the only lever that was in a fully "up" position…the one next to the dial.

He pulled it down, or tried to, but it simply gave off a solid *clunk* as the dial twitched, so he twisted the dial completely the other way and pulled the lever down again.

This time, it moved, but the reaction…wasn't what he'd hoped for.

The glowing light given off by the magical components of the ship, the symbols that encircled the engines, and even the magelights scattered across the decks all dimmed, and lines of power flared across the deck, converging on the enormous cannon at the far end of the ship.

It lit up, slowly at first. Then, with building speed, rings of light pulsed to life around it, climbing higher and higher, and the ship began to shudder.

"Okay…not that one," Jian muttered, desperately attempting to push the lever back up. It wouldn't move, but a crystal next to it had begun pulsing a dangerous red. He pressed it, hoping it would stop the magic from building, and it did…sort of…

The entire ship shook, shooting backwards through the air as an enormous Fireball blasted from the front of the cannon. The shot was at least three feet around as it left the barrel, the metal cracking and sparks flashing across the deck as the weapon discharged.

The Fireball expanded as it hurtled away from the ship, piercing the air with a scream of power.

"Oh shit…" Jian said, wide-eyed as he quickly flipped the dial back to where it was and pushed the lever back up, hoping that it'd somehow stop the giant Fireball from hurtling toward the neat rows of tents within the camp of the Church of the Death God.

It didn't.

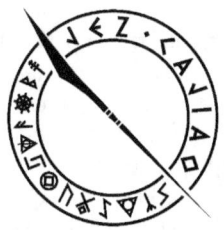

CHAPTER THIRTY-FIVE

"What the hell was that?" I gasped, staring at the enormous Fireball that hurtled through the air, blazing toward the neat rows of tents and equipment that surrounded a tall, ominous-looking cathedral.

"It's a mistake," Hellenica said grimly next to me, and I glanced at her in confusion.

"Well, it didn't look like it was planned, but—"

"We have to get out of here, right now!" she said frantically, spinning around and heading up to the helm. Confused, I turned and ran after her. Even running at full speed, she beat me, and was ordering the alkyon to turn us around as I arrived.

"No!" I countermanded her order. "Our people are still on that ship!"

She turned to me, her eyes welling up with fear.

"That's the Dark Temple of Nimon, the god who destroyed the world, and they've just fired on him. He'll respond to it!" Her words tripped over themselves in her desperation to get them out. "We have to get out of here."

"Oh, fuck," I muttered, looking back over at the other ship. It was twisting from side to side, still trying to get itself straight, but at that angle, it didn't have long. I swore viciously.

"Quick, how do I control this?" I asked the alkyon at the helm.

"Ah, your…lord, it takes hours of practice…"

"Bullshit," I said firmly. "The wheel goes left and right; what controls up and down and power?"

"This controls the engines, the 'power,' I guess? And this controls how much to each engine…" He gestured to each of the levers in turn.

"Good enough," I said. "Get out of the way."

I grabbed the wheel, simply feeling thankful that this ship didn't have that many levers.

"My lord?" he asked, confused, as I flipped the lever for power, sending the ship jumping ahead.

"Get ready to get onto the ship and take over the helm!" I ordered, as Hellenica started trying to convince me to turn the ship around. "Our people are still on that vessel!" I snapped at her.

Turning my attention to the control panel, I tried the levers, nodding to myself as I lifted the bow, then dipped it.

"Okay…I can do this," I muttered under my breath, before shouting to the alkyon, who'd moved to the railing. "Get them back to the shipyard and landed, get someone to take over the helm who knows what they're doing, then get back up here!" I ordered him.

He saluted, waiting as we pulled above the plummeting ship before leaping over the side.

As soon as he was gone, I turned the ship, accidentally twisting the ship too far and making it tilt before bringing it around and stabilizing it. Memories of racing on stolen motorbikes strangely helped with my controls as I tilted and shifted the ship. Suddenly, the night erupted off my port side as the Fireball landed.

I swore, having been hoping it would miss, and I called out to Hellenica, who'd moved back to the railing to look out. "How bad is it?" I shouted.

"It's…horrific," she said, clenching the wooden railing in dismay. "The encampment…over a third of it is on fire. It must have exploded and set fire to the rest of the camp."

Thunder rumbled through the sky, making the world seem to shake and shudder as a new prompt filled my vision. This one practically filled my vision and wouldn't move until I'd read and acknowledged it.

You have received a new Title: Apostate!

The Dark God Nimon has labeled you Apostate. No matter where you go, any of the faithful who see you will feel the call to action. They will be filled with the Strength of the Dark and will punish you for your crimes!

*

Call to Arms!

Heathens have assaulted Holy Nimon's Chosen, cowardly killing dozens and damaging His holy property!

A Call to Arms has been issued by the High Priest of Nimon, Thaddeus Baruman. Any who kill a heathen follower of Jax the Apostate will be granted a full pardon by the Church for ALL CRIMES COMMITED, receive a purse of ten gold crowns per kill, and will be granted a minor boon.

Go forth, oh ye faithful…and smite the heathen unbeliever!

"Well, fuck!" I grunted, appalled as I finally managed to minimize the two prompts, righting my course as I twisted the ship around again. Glaring back at the other ship, I realized that it had clearly been one of my people who'd fired the weapon, yet I'd gotten the damn blame!

I pointed the bow back towards the city, cursing at the other ship but praying that they'd make it.

It shifted from one side to the other ominously; then the front engines flared bright, the second through to the fourth on each side dimming as the bow lifted ponderously. Then all the engines flared as the sails on the right side crashed and tore through a particularly high tree. The impact twisted the ship momentarily before it righted itself and climbed again.

"Thank fuck," I muttered, freezing in place as I looked across at Hellenica, who stared at me in fear.

"You've been cursed by the gods," she whispered in horror. "And I'm sworn to serve you. We were safer serving the Skyking!"

Her panicked voice rose to a low moan, and I snapped back at her.

"Bullshit! I've been called an apostate by that prick, Nimon; that's all." The thunder rumbled, and I glared up at the heavy rainclouds overhead. "I don't serve him, and never will, so it makes fuck-all difference!"

"Jax! Don't." I heard Jenae's voice clearly. I bit back on my temper, swallowing my pride and forcing the words out through gritted teeth as a cold shudder crawled up my neck, I was acutely aware that Nimon was watching me.

"I might not have attacked the 'Dark God' intentionally, but his people have decided an accident is going to start this off, so that's out of my control," I muttered, feeling pressure mounting all around us and hearing Hellenica gasp in pain. I looked over to her and found her shaking her head, eyes closed, as another prompt appeared.

Nimon has personally intervened to declare Jax the Apostate as an Enemy of the Church.

All sanctified soldiers of the Church will receive +3 to Strength, Agility, and Endurance when facing the forces of the Apostate. Killing any member of those forces will make this Buff permanent. Furthermore, this Buff will increase by +1 for every additional kill those soldiers make....

Kill on, Holy Warriors!

"Well, that's just peachy!" I growled as I felt Nimon's presence disappear, swearing under my breath as we cleared the wall of the city. Angling the ship around, I headed for the Shipyard District, the other ship following along behind me.

MAL

"What the hell just happened?!" Mal swore as the prompt faded, turning to Soween.

"How would I know, Mal? I've been here with you," she replied evenly. He grunted, peering out of the wagon at the gates of the Stockpile as they passed through, nodding to Jay and the others as they waved them on.

"Now, what's that goddamn idiot done?" Mal muttered to himself, not really expecting an answer. "I leave him for what, an hour. Two? He's declared a holy war! All he had to do was fight some creature and keep his head down, that was it, but noooo…"

Soween ignored him, occasionally interjecting a response by rote, "Yes, Mal" or "Times are hard…" as she often did, while concentrating more on controlling the oxen that pulled the wagons and watching for the guards, hoping and praying they could make it across the bridges before the alarms were raised.

Her amulet shook suddenly. She reached up, pressing the silvery crystal embedded in her glove to the symbol on the amulet, and Josh's voice filled her ears.

"What happened?"

"What makes you think I know, dear?" she replied.

"Oh, right.... Of course, I just..."

"I know."

"How's Mal taking it?"

"About as well as you'd expect. He's complaining, but he'll get over it; he likes the kid," she said, injecting the mental equivalent of an eyeroll and a snort in one.

"He's got balls, I'll give him that," Josh replied, the sense of disbelief carrying through to her.

"Maybe not for long, if he does anything else; tonight was going to be hard enough as it was. I've got to go, was there something?"

"Not really, just wanted to talk. Love you."

"I know, love you too, honey."

She pulled her palm from the amulet and let a rare smile cross her lips. For all that Josh was about as sensible as sitting on a spike, he had a good heart, and the years with him by her side had been good. If they could actually get a ship and get away from all of this, they'd only get better.

"What's that damn fool done now?" growled Jay, pulling himself up the side of the wagon and looking in. Soween glared at him for breaking character as Mal started to speak.

"I know, right…? I mean, all he had to do—"

"Jay, you're supposed to be a watchman and be on the last wagon. What the hell are you doing up here?" she snapped.

Hooked at her in surprise. "Yeah, but I mean, with that message—"

"Jay, why do you think we told you to ride that wagon?" She cut him off in as calm a voice as she could manage.

"I dunno; you don't like them that's driving it normally, and yer didn't let them carry anything really valuable, just some…"

"And why would we tell you to keep an eye on them, if we didn't trust them normally?" she asked through gritted teeth.

"Uh, maybe to keep 'em in line?" he guessed, before leaning back out as he heard something.

"Hey!" he shouted, then he leaned back in and pointed back at the wagons behind them. "They've turned off! They're headed off somewhere else!"

"Jay, you goddamn…!" Mal snarled at him, and Soween shook her head, glancing at the narrow bridge they were clattering onto already.

"Ain't no time for that, Mal," she said, cutting him off. "Too late to turn around and get them as well; better just to let them go, and we'll sort it out another day."

"But they're stealing our stuff!" Jay said, leaning back out and drawing in a deep breath. "I'll get you, Covan! I know it's you, yer little…" he bellowed into the falling rain, the glowing lights of the wagon soon vanishing as it turned down an alleyway out of sight.

"Shut it, you idiot!" Mal snarled, reaching out and grabbing Jay, hauling him inside the wagon as they approached the far end of the bridge and the four watchmen of the city guard stationed there. "We're supposed to be waggoneers, remember? And you're a city guard!"

"Oh, right…. So, what should I do?" he asked as the guard stepped out of the small lean-to and waved for them to stop.

"Oh great! Now they're suspicious!" Mal snarled at Jay. "Just make them happy, and let us go," he said, pushing Jay forward. He turned around and hopped down from the wagon as Soween brought it to a halt. He licked his lips, staring awkwardly at the four guards who looked at him in confusion.

"Oh, er…hi," he said, nodding his head. "I'm a guard. Yer know, like you." He pointed to the wagon. "Nothing to see in there, so…can we go?"

"Who *are* you?" asked one guard, leaning out past the brazier to get a better look, and lifting a lantern.

"I…err…oh, fuck it!" Jay said, and he punched the first guard in the face, his massive fist knocking the unprepared man to the ground, unconscious.

"Dammit! Mal!" Soween called, dropping the reins and lifting her crossbow. It hummed to life as she flipped the activation runes, light flaring from the crystals embedded in the hilt to activate the weapon. The arms flexed out, locking into place as the string tightened, a low *hummm* filling the air as Mal's matching pair appeared in response.

"Ah, ah!" Mal called out, shaking his head as a guardsman reached for the bell. The man froze, and the three guards stared in confusion at one another. Jay loomed awkwardly, Soween and Mal standing over him on the wagon, pointing their weapons at the guards, and everyone stood motionless for a long minute.

"So, now what?" one asked eventually, and Mal sighed, shaking his head.

"Look, this is a heist, that's all. Ain't nobody needs to die. Maybe Jay here knocks you all out, and I accidentally drop a pouch of gold as we make our escape. You don't see anythin', and we don't need this to go no further…?"

The older two guards looked at each other speculatively, but the younger man, more idealistic and stupid than the others, snarled and jumped for the bell, just managing to grab the rope in time.

Jay grabbed him by the collar, yanking him back and swinging him around before throwing him out over the side of the bridge with a splash, as the bell rang out once in iron warning. The sound hung in the air as the other two guards glowered at Mal and his people.

"The lad'll drown!" one said, peering over the side of the bridge to see the boy frantically trying to keep afloat while pulling at his armor.

"Goddamn it, Jay!" Mal snapped, and the man-mountain twisted around to snap back at him.

"It's not my fault! I didn't see you doin' nothin to help!"

"Just…throw the bell over into the water, and you two go help the boy," Mal said after a second's hesitation. The guards looked at each other, and Soween sighed, pulling a small pouch out of her cloak.

"Here," she said, throwing it to the man on the right as Jay ripped the bell free and threw it out over the river to vanish with a splash.

The guardsman caught the bag as his partner quickly stripped off his armor, heading to the river with a muttered imprecation as the wagons started moving again, with everyone glowering at each other.

"I swear, Jay, you've got to be the dumbest son of a bitch…" Mal started to berate the massive man.

Soween tuned him out, cracking the leads and trying to make the oxen move faster, hoping the damn watch wouldn't respond too quickly.

ROMANUS

"God, I hope I'm not making a mistake," Romanus Perival muttered to himself as he gathered the legion and its dependents in the middle of the enclave. He drew a deep breath, bolstering his courage, and pushed down his doubt, ignoring the little voice that whispered he could just go back into his office, just for a few minutes.... The bottle in his hidden cubby would make everything better...

"Sir! They're splitting the guard!" a legionnaire called down to him, and he prayed that the guards outside didn't overhear.

"How many?" he called back up.

"Less than a third are still there, sir; maybe fifty of the guard and a couple dozen civilians!"

"Legion!" he called out, forcing his voice to steady as his stomach roiled; butterflies the size of dragons danced and swooped inside. "On three!"

"Are we really doing this, sir?" asked Tribune Alistor, stepping up to his shoulder. The dark-haired legion tribune had been one of the loudest and most fervent dissenters to Romanus's acceptance of Lord Jax's orders. Even now, he tried to sway his commander to his way of thinking. "These actions are *criminal*; they go against all the legion stands for!" he whispered anxiously.

"Not if you go by the old imperial laws, they're not," Romanus countered, shaking his head. "We've got no more time to argue this now. Take your place; that's an order!" he said, glaring the other man into submission before he took a deep breath and raised his voice again.

"One!" he called, nodding to the legionnaires on the parapet of the surrounding wall. They lifted torches into the air and spun them in slow clockwise circles, halting and searching for the countersignal.

After a long pause, they turned and waved confirmation down to the courtyard, where the rest waited, and Romanus let out a breath.

"Two!" he bellowed, and the legionnaires on the parapet pulled the levers they'd been positioned next to, then whistled a short tune, one which was picked up inside the wall, where the chains vanished. The pattern repeated as a second, far louder pair of *clunk*s echoed out, the chains holding the drawbridge up releasing suddenly.

The huge wooden structure balanced precariously for a long second before it slowly began to move, toppling outwards. It dropped faster and faster, the chains rattling as they fell freely, the capstan unwinding for the final time as the legion enclave opened its gate.

"Three!" Romanus bellowed. He set off running, the horrible feeling of leaving his home, his safe, if dull, existence falling away behind him as he ran. The legionnaires on every side of him moved at the same time, their jingling, clattering trot reassuring to their prefect as he felt his left pauldron flapping.

I'll have to secure that.... Damn shameful showing, Romanus! he berated himself as he tried to ignore it. His standard legion shield weighed heavy on his arm; his gladius held proudly upright as he ran.

Adrenaline filled him as he saw the fear on the faces of the pox-ridden city guard and their mob as the legion advanced. His men had done their job, as not a single remaining officer of the Guard made a sound. The legion scouts had quietly moved into action, restraining the city guard's leadership efficiently upon the signal from the parapet.

He ran in with his legion; the noncombatants and support people were protected behind him in the middle. The next level out was flooded by legionnaires laden down with every damn bag, container, or satchel of holding they could find. Lesser men and women would have already collapsed under the weight they carried. The final outermost ring was made up of the fittest, fastest, and most deadly soldiers the legion had, and they'd been ordered to show no mercy.

A stop, a hesitation even, would slow the crowds around them. That delay would only grow, each person slowing slightly more, until the back was forced to a standstill, and that was something they couldn't afford.

"May the gods forgive me for what I do in the service of the empire this day," Romanus muttered, before shouting out to the people around him. "Legion, let's pick up the pace! Primus, I expect you to make this march a thing of legend!"

All around him, groans rose, swiftly muffled as Restun, Primus of the Legion called out. His powerfully built frame allowed him to effortlessly project his voice so that every member of the legion heard him clearly.

Romanus had wondered privately on more than one occasion if the Primus was even mortal, having held the role when he'd personally come up through the ranks, and judging by the look of him now, he'd probably hold it long after Romanus was dead.

The Primus was an unholy terror to a legionnaire that wasn't up to scratch; an unstoppable, inexhaustible man who, it'd been quietly speculated for years, was secretly a gnomish automaton wearing a flesh suit. Whatever the truth was, the joy in his voice was clear.

"You hear that, legionnaires?" he bellowed. "This march was already going to be the stuff of tales, but now I get to make it legendary! We've got a mile and a half to cover across the city, hostile territory, and we're going to do it in record time!"

Groans rose, only to be squashed by the Primus's glare.

"I thought I heard a sound of dissent!" he boomed. "It must be because we're not singing! Come on, legionnaires!" With that, he drew in a deep breath and belted out the first verse, the ancient marching song echoing off the buildings as the scouts sprinted to catch up.

"We're the legion!" he bellowed.

"The mighty legion, it's true!" everyone chorused back to him.

"When the foul beasts come!"

"The legion comes, too!"

"When you shit yourself in bed,"

"The legion comes to make them dead!"

The song was one of many legion cadences; it was old, it barely rhymed, and it was never sung where civilians could hear it. But today, all the old rules were thrown aside, and the Legion Primus knew it. He started the second verse, and Romanus couldn't help but grin as the memories came flooding back.

"When the legion meets your girl…!"

DURG

Durg sat alone on the edge of a section of the street, peering down into the river. He'd been there for over a day now; the darkness, the rain, and the occasional noises and flashes in the distance were of no matter to him.

The important people would decide what to do about things like that. No, he was just here to figure out what to do about the big shiny thing.

His daddy had told him, "One day, you'll get the chance to get away from all of this. You'll see your chance shinin' like copper in the muck; take it and run!" And now, Durg thought it just might be that day. He'd been crossing the bridge when he'd found some food the carts had thrown out. He'd gotten to it before the rats could, and he'd been walking along, picking the tasty maggots out and thinking about how his luck was changing, when he saw it.

It was big and tall, like a man made out of stone. It had walked off the edge of the path into the sea and vanished, with loads of guards chasing it.

Fair enough; maybe this was normal, he thought? He didn't usually come down to the harbor, so maybe that happened all the time? He'd just been surprised when it didn't come back up, because it had a big shiny thing on its chest, and you didn't leave shiny things alone, not even down in the water. So he'd watched, waiting for the tide to go out.

It had just come in, but that was okay. His daddy had told him before, "If it's in now, it'll go out later. Just gotta wait."

So that's what he did. He climbed down onto the stones near the harbor and waited, watching the water where it had disappeared. The sun had come up, then it went back down, but that didn't mean much to him. Besides getting hungry and thirsty, nothing else had changed.

He was trying to decide if this was like the things he saw when he was asleep, and he remembered times with his daddy, when things were better, and he got to eat every day. Maybe it hadn't been real, he wondered, when something moved.

It was slow at first, but the water moved. It moved like the river did when the giant crabs came up. He licked his lips as he got to his feet, looking back to the spot where the shiny had disappeared, before looking back at the water that moved.

He concentrated, trying to decide if he should watch the place where the shiny disappeared, or follow what might be a giant crab, until his stomach rumbled. It had a very definite opinion on which one he should follow, so he did as it bade him. He clambered along the edge of the water, jumping from rock to rock until he could reach up and pull himself up onto the path that ran alongside the water properly again. He lumbered along, eyes glued on the faint trail in the water.

Durg huffed and puffed as he went. It wasn't that fast in the water, but the paths went this way and that. The giant rock crab, as that was what he'd decided it must be, was crossing the river to the other side.

Eventually, he was forced to take a path that led away from the water, heading back on himself to go up a level onto the bridge. By the time he reached a place where he could see the water clearly again, he'd lost it.

He stood there, huffing and puffing, his massive paws clamped on his knees as he shook. Drool dangled in thick ropes from his mouth as he tried to get his breath back. He ignored the little humans who ran past, shrugging off the filth they threw at him as he always did. It made little difference to him, as the rain would wash it away eventually.

Durg stared out across the water for long seconds, his hearts dropping as he realized he'd lost both the meal and the shiny now, but just as he was about to turn back and run to the sea again, in case someone else had not found the shiny, a movement in the water caught his eye.

There was something there.

It wasn't that far from where he'd lost sight of the giant crab, but now there were more of them, lots more, or a really, really big, long crab, as the water churned and moved in a line.

Durg started to get really excited. If there was a single really, really big crab, he might be able to take some back to the mountains! Maybe, if he found enough food, he'd be able to carry it with him, and it would feed him all the way back to where the clan lived!

Durg shuffled from foot to foot, clapping his big, clumsy paws in happiness as he thought of getting back to the mountains. He'd been brought here with his daddy when he was very small. He didn't know why, but the humans that owned them had eventually kicked him out into the street, hitting him until he ran away after his daddy had gone to sleep and didn't wake up again.

Maybe if he went back to the mountains, his daddy would have gone there? He might have just been really deep asleep, and he went home once he woke up, if the humans didn't want them anymore?

Durg hoped so, and as the water started moving again, heading in a line to the shore on the other side, he took off, lumbering across the bridge, the rain washing his hide clean as he went.

GREY

"Right, let's go," whispered Grey, getting ready.

"I thought we were supposed to go at the signal?!" hissed Felis, and his brother just scowled at him.

"I told you, the plan means we gotta go when the signal goes, but iff'n it kicks off early, we gotta move then!" Grey said, shaking his head at his younger, and obviously much stupider brother. He'd risked everything getting him into the Thieves' Guild, and this job would be their last if word got out they'd taken it. Damn that Mal, and damn his cards! This would never have happened if his damn luck potion hadn't gone bad....

"Just get out there; you know how to do it!" Grey snapped at Felis before sprinting across the poorly lit section of the square to jump at the airship wall.

He activated his favorite ability, Lizard's Grip, the stone accepting his fingertips like it was made for it. He scrambled upwards, feet occasionally slipping on the slick surface, but in seconds, he was peering over the parapet, checking for guards.

"Good enough," he muttered, slipping over and tossing the rope over the side for Felis. He grunted at the strain as his brother started climbing and braced himself against the low crenellations. But a few seconds later, the pair had crested the walkway, and they sprinted down the nearby steps. Diving back into the shadows, they caught their breath and watched as a guard meandered past slowly, clearly bored as he kicked a stone along the floor.

"Once he's gone, you hit the first ship to the left, and I'll do the right," Grey said. Felis nodded, both grinning at each other as the familiar thrill of danger chimed in their souls. If they were caught here, doing this, of all things, they'd be dead, no questions asked. But if they managed it, Mal had promised a new life for the pair of them, a whole new start, and one without having to bump into Megan every day. That alone was worth it to the permanently competing brothers.

"Go!" Grey said, scurrying forward, rushing from cover to cover as he cleared the inner ring of guard huts, coming out onto the airfield itself.

There were dozens of ships docked there, some in bits, others getting stocked up, while still others were being repaired or built. Everywhere they looked, dozens upon dozens of people scurried back and forth, mostly frantically working on the huge battleship that hulked over the rest on the far side of the field. It was enormous, and the air of panic as people sprinted about on it made Grey grin as he shook his head.

“Won’t catch me doing that, oh, no, sir. Grey don’t work for nobody,” he muttered. The foolish little ants he saw rushing about were distracting enough people that he managed to slip right up to the south engine on a small ship without being seen.

“Okay, now, how did it go…?” He furrowed his brow, trying to remember the rhyme he’d taught Felis to help him remember the steps…. “Red, blue, green for you…blue for me and blue for you…” As he whispered, he tapped the symbols that pulsed and glowed on the side of the mana-engine, each one flaring as his fingers danced. “Green and blue, they’re mine, too. One red and…two blue!”

As his fingers tapped the last symbols, the engine went suddenly quiet, the top slipping off and the lights starting to dim.

He reached inside, feeling a smooth crystal the size of his thumb. Carefully, he pulled it free, slipping it into his bag and forcing himself not to think about how much gold the damn thing was worth.

He blew out a short breath and crawled under the braces that held the ship up, moving on all fours to the far side of the ship. Keeping a watchful eye out for any nearby guards, he tried to ignore the ship creaking above him and the feet walking across the deck.

He suddenly looked to the left, a thief's instinct flagging that something was wrong. Dismissing the concern, he grinned, watching the other half of the team, the three-woman squad of Jester’s Ruin sprinting across the shadowy area between the wall and the most guarded building in the compound.

“Damn glad that's not my job!” he breathed to himself, frowning as a fourth, slower and vaguely familiar-looking shadow joined the first three. “They’ve replaced Hella already?” he mused briefly, before shaking himself. It didn’t matter. All that mattered was the payday and being free of Megan at last! Grey crawled on, ignoring the mud and the puddles as he reached up to the second engine, unconsciously quietly singing the foolish rhyme he’d made up.

“Red, blue, green for you…”

THOMAS

“Fire!” screamed a voice, and Thomas was jerked awake at the same moment that the ground rumbled, and an explosion went off nearby.

“What the hell?” he cried, trying to unravel the coarse blanket that was wrapped around his legs. He sat up, the usual darkness of the tent he shared with the rest of his new squad lit by the flickering of flames, screams rising nearby.

Thomas finally kicked the blankets free and stood, his hand going to his new mace quickly. Its weight and reassuring solidity was all he needed to feel in order to know that he was no longer a slave or a prisoner. He was a Soldier-Aspirant of the Dark God Nimon, and he’d damn well never be a slave again!

“All right, maggots!” a rough voice boomed from the doorway as Belladonna strode in. The tall, stunning female elf was half-naked, her shorts barely covering her ass, and for the first time since meeting her, he didn’t immediately wonder what she’d be like in bed, thanks to the blatant fury in her eyes. She stood there, a swordstaff in one hand, and glared at them as the entire tent came to attention.

“Someone’s dared to attack us. They’ve been declared an Apostate by the Church, and in Nimon’s name, we’re going to find them. They’ve used a fucking airship cannon on our camp and kicked the hornet’s nest! We’re going to rip their tongue out, and we’re going to nail the idiot’s dick to my bedside table! Any questions?” she growled, and the tent barked the expected response as one.

“No, Sergeant Belladonna!”

“Damn right!” she barked back at them. “Now get your armor on; we’re going hunting!”

With that, she spun about, her long, black hair billowing out in the night breeze behind her, as Thomas turned to Coran.

“What the hell kind of an idiot attacks the Dark God?” he said, stunned at the stupidity.

“The kind who gets us a hell of a lot of experience and free stat points when we kill them!” Coran said, grinning as he looked into the distance, his eyes twitching in that weird way they always did when someone was reading prompts.

Thomas brought the notifications up and read them quickly, grunting as he realized that the “permanent” section of the prompt meant that, on top of the plus three to his Strength, Endurance, and Agility that he’d gain by fighting any of the enemy forces, he’d get an additional point to each of those stats with every single one he killed. Hell, if he killed twenty, he’d get the equivalent of five levels worth of stats, free!

For a soldier, there was no better chance than this, and he could hear the rising bloodlust of the forces around him.

He saw the name Jax, and he paused for a second, his heart clenching as he thought of his "older" twin brother. He'd used that as his gaming handle, and now some dickbag was sullying his brother's name. He was dead, and some fucker...

Jack would never know it, but Thomas would kill this pretender. He'd make sure the Dark God didn't have time to grow to hate that name. Just in case Nimon ever opened a portal to Earth, and somehow Jack was still alive, Thomas would make sure his brother could live his life safely.

For a second, thoughts of Jack filled his mind; the fights, the girls, the parties, and he dreamed for a second that maybe, just maybe, he still lived.

Then he silently wished his brother's soul well, letting go of the last of his hopes and dreams that they'd be together again one day.

Jack would never kill the people in the arena in order to come here. He was the better of the two of them; he'd stick to his morals, and if the Baron had truly ever captured him, he'd have told the old shit to get fucked.

He'd died a handful of days ago, when that rogue mage they were still searching for had totaled the market. His soul would be free, while Thomas' would forever be bound the Dark God of Death.

He was the best man Thomas had ever known, and he'd not allow some posturing wanker who'd attack a tent city at night with a goddamn siege weapon to sully his name.

"I'll find you," Thomas swore, in memory of his brother, glaring out into the flickering flame-filled darkness, "and I'll kill you, fast."

CHAPTER THIRTY-SIX

"Goddamn had to start the friggin' war with the gods early, didn't you, motherfucker," I muttered under my breath as I continued trying to figure out how to control the ship properly. There were over a dozen dials, levers, and crystalline "buttons" that didn't move if you pressed them, but you sure as hell knew there'd been an effect.

"Didn't think to ask the damn helmsman which button fired the guns though, did you? Oh no, nothing that frigging useful…" I berated myself as I slowly turned the ship, passing over the edge of the Shipyard district. I glanced around, trying to spot the other vessels on the ground. But as dark as it was, between the constant downpour and the bright lights on this ship, I couldn't see much.

Much besides the battleship, anyway.

The fucking thing was huge, and I caught myself getting fixated on it. The sheer potential it held was insane! It was literally the size of a World War II aircraft carrier. Nothing that big should be able to float, let alone damn well fly, yet here it was, surrounded by dozens and dozens of pulsing, glowing blue engines as it prepared itself to take off.

"Are you done complaining yet?" Miren asked me, and I glared at her. "Because we were talking, and it turns out that there are some notifications you should probably read," she said casually.

"I don't need to," I grumbled. "I already saw that I'm the goddamn apostate!"

"And the experience notifications?" she prodded calmly.

"I can look at them later," I said sullenly, hating how childish I sounded. It wasn't the fact that I was at war with a frigging god that was the problem, I admitted to myself as I looked out over the huge hulk below us and turned the wheel to keep us clear of a building coming up on the left. The problem, if I was honest with myself, was that it hadn't been me.

If you're going to spit in a god's eye and declare war on them, then it should be a story you can tell down at the pub. You should be able to say, "Oh, yeah, that was me. I told him, 'Look, you fucker…'" but someone in my team had taken that away with a cock-up.

They'd fired a ship-mounted weapon at the Dark God's cathedral, killing who knew how many?

"Experience?" I asked suddenly as the words filtered through my sulk, perking me right up as I turned back to Miren, who in turn was grinning widely.

"Yup!" she chirped. "We all got a bunch! No idea who it was that fired the shot, but damn!"

"Okay, get my attention if we're going to crash," I said excitedly, pulling up the flashing notifications, one by one.

Congratulations!

You have killed the following:

- 2x Guards of various levels for a total of 3,900xp

A party under your command killed the following:

- 17x Guards of various levels for a total of 35,700xp

Total Party experience earned: 35,700xp

As party leader, you gain 25% of all experience earnt

Progress to level 18 stands at 163,317/225,000

*

Congratulations!

Forces under your command have seized the following strategic items:

- 1x Light Cruiser Warship for 150,000xp
- 1x Fast Attack Scout Warship for 50,000xp

As you are at war with the previous owner, you receive 25% of the experience earned

Progress to level 18 stands at 213,317/225,000

*

Congratulations!

A party under your command killed the following:

- 76x Church of Nimon Soldier-Aspirant of various levels for a total of 258,400xp
- 21x Church of Nimon Slave-Aspirants of various levels for a total of 45,570xp
- 11x Church of Nimon Sanctified and Blessed Soldiers of various levels for a total of 78,650xp

Total Party experience earned: 382,620xp

As party leader, you gain 25% of all experience earned.

Progress to level 18 stands at 308,972/225,000

*

Congratulations!

You have reached level 18!

You have 7 unspent Attribute points and 0 Meridian points available.

Progress to level 19 stands at 83,972/265,000

"Holy crap, a hundred and eight of Nimon's soldiers?" I said aloud, shaking my head as I tried to make sense of the deaths. The power of the ship-mounted weapons in a war was insane! The thought of briefly using the ships to bombard the city into rubble and kill the nobles crossed my mind…

But then I thought of how many innocents I'd kill doing that, and my stomach turned over, sickness rising to the back of my throat.

I felt *him* rising as well, the approval and the determination that leaked through the barrier between us. The fragment of his mind desperately desired the fight, offering me the assurance that all were acceptable methods in reforming the empire. His reassurance that this would be only a fraction of the bloodshed I'd bring made me shudder again.

There was no way I'd be like him. I respected who he'd been, and yeah, sometimes ruthless was the way to go, no two ways about it. But no chance was I doing that and killing possibly thousands in order to kill a few dozen nobles.

I'd be reviled, not followed. The empire was an institution; yeah, I got that, and nobody loved an institution, but the *emperor* had to be a figurehead to look up to. I wasn't sure if I wanted that to be me.

Hell, I was pretty damn sure I *didn't* want that to be me. I wanted a bar somewhere, some grass to lie on, maybe a beach to chill on, a fuck-ton of good booze and food, lots of sexy time, and a laugh with friends. *That's* what I wanted.

It was also what I was pretty sure I wasn't going to get. If I renounced my title, I'd have to raise someone up in my place, and that brought a whole host of issues with it, starting with the fact that I didn't know anyone I'd trust to do it.

Then there was the whole "bloodline" thing, and most importantly of all, I liked my life! Sure, it was mental, and I never got a chance to sit down. But as I watched Oracle zip from sail to sail, peeking down at the sailors to check on them, I pondered the fact that I had an insanely hot fairy companion who could literally, happily, look like anyone I wanted.

Her body was every possible sexual fantasy within itself, and the mind behind it? I was in love with her, madly, and still despite days and days of us both wanting it, we'd had no time for our sex life.

That was changing tonight, I vowed to myself. I was going to save these people, get my ships in the air, and as soon as we were all safe, I was gonna rock her world.

Oracle looked up at me from where she hid in the rigging across the deck, and I felt the smile that I couldn't quite see at this distance as she picked up on my thoughts and my love.

"Tonight," was all she said, but I couldn't keep the smile from my face in response as I concentrated on the ship again, looking ahead. I had seven points to assign, but I decided to hold off until I had some time to think. After all, I wasn't going to get another experience dump like I'd gotten within the last few days, at least for a while…. I hoped.

The ship floated along gently, the power dialed back, as I waited for the larger warship to catch up.

"Keep an eye out below," I called to my people. "See if you can spot anything." I deliberately phrased things as vaguely as possible, just in case. But after a few minutes, we were hovering over the shipyard, just as the second ship began to line up for their own landing.

"Now, how the hell are we going to do this?" I muttered to myself.... "We can't get to the *Star's Glory* now, not the way we'd planned, and the cruisers are more important, but still, I don't like the idea of leaving the ship to continue running slaves...Maybe I could..." I trailed off, my mind's eye full of images.

"We've got a couple of fliers incoming!" Miren called back, drawing her bow and following the path of three inbound imps. The lead one held its hands out to the sides to show that it was unarmed.

"Let them come, but be ready to blast them out of the sky," I called back, shaking my head as Hellenica held up a crackling lightning bolt questioningly.

The three flew closer until they were a few dozen feet from the side of the ship, and the leader moved in alone, landing on the deck a handful of feet from me.

I looked at him, noting the tribal tattoos and dark grey skin, the horns, complete with the broken-off tip of the right one.

"He's one of the ones we left at the tower," Oracle said through our bond.

"I see you managed to get free okay, then," I said, and he nodded curtly at me. "So, what are you doing here?" I asked.

He glared at me for a few heartbeats before wrestling his temper under control. "Grebes wanted us to goes with you. Said we should trusts you. Said impses could be free, not slaveses," he said finally.

"How many of you?" I asked, looking over the other two in surprise, then back at him. "And you don't want to come with me. You hate me."

"You kepts us prisoner! Made poor Tats eat green foods," he complained, wiping at his tongue in remembered disgust, as I recalled the people in the cages. My mood plummeted instantly, and I started to say I didn't want the filthy creatures with us, when I remembered Grebes's warning.

He'd warned us about the trapped stair, and it'd cost him his life, and the woman in the cages had said the imps were addicted and couldn't help themselves.

Maybe they weren't as bad as I thought, but...

"How many?" I asked again, slowly as I tried to consider the implications. I couldn't risk an extra skirmish tonight, but I could always do with a few extra helpers, and the empire was supposed to be for all the species, provided they would take the Oath and swear to protect each other...

"Lots," he said calmly.

"How many is 'lots'?" I pressed, turning my eyes forward again and adjusting the course as a tall spire became visible on a building ahead.

"Lots?" the imp repeated, confused.

"Shit. You can't count, can you?" I asked him, closing my eyes for a second before forcing them open and glancing down at the shipyard to my right. Fights were breaking out now, and I grinned as I saw the legion appear around a corner, sprinting for the gates. Two guards who were supposed to be on watch turned and ran for their lives, and a load of my tension floated away.

"Fine," I said, looking back to the imp. "If you want to come, you can, but you and all those you bring have to swear the Oath of citizenship of the empire. You do that, and I'll let you come. And you don't eat sentient meat anymore. Animals only!" I stressed. He nodded, taking off and flying away without a word. "Fine!" I called, scowling at his retreating form. "Fuck you too, dickhead!"

I shrugged, turning the ship to pass over the shipyard again, as a pair of alkyon rose from the ship that had just landed, flying up towards us. Oracle slipped down from the rigging and landed on my shoulder, reaching down for my hand. At the same time, I reached up to her, patting her legs as she rested her hand on mine.

"The crew are scared, but they seem to be thinking that going along with things is the best course of action, for now, at least," Oracle said quietly.

"Thanks, Oracle," I whispered back, smiling up at her as she wrapped an arm around the back of my head and kissed my forehead. I shifted the bow a little so that we'd come closer to our fliers and waited for them to reach us, as Hellenica spoke quietly.

"You'd really allow the imps to join us?" she asked cautiously.

"Yeah, if they'll swear the Oath and behave, then they can come. I won't lie, I'll be watching them carefully, but the Imperial Citizen's Oath contains a section about not harming your fellow citizens. If they do, they'll regret it, and I'll kill them if the Oath doesn't.

"There was an imp called Grebes who died when we were rescuing you. He didn't have to die; he was a prisoner, and he spoke up to warn us about traps in the stairs. His Oath to the Skyking was killing him, slowly, so I finished him off quickly. If he hadn't done that, we might have lost more people, but his sacrifice earned his people a chance with me."

There was silence for a few minutes before Hellenica spoke again, just as the alkyon were coming in to land.

"Imps are not born evil, it is true, no more than many races, but their predilections for sentient meat and their closeness to the demon realm influences many. It will be interesting to see how you handle this, not to forget that, if an imp grows strong enough, it can evolve to a greater imp, and they are much harder to control."

"Well, at least our lives won't be boring," I muttered, stepping back and relinquishing the ship to the alkyon that had originally piloted it, his assistant flipping levers and turning dials to make us leap back up into the air, taking over an overwatch position again.

"As soon as the cruisers are fired up and ready, they'll take our place up here, sir, and we can get you onto the battleship," the alkyon at the helm said calmly, his partner moving to the stern to watch out for any other ships taking off.

I nodded to them in thanks and moved out of the way to stand with Hellenica, Miren, and Stephanos, gazing over the railing at the swarming figures that had taken over the shipyard.

It was less than half an hour before the wagons rolled into the shipyards, and in that time, the nearby warehouses had opened, disgorging hundreds of people to rush towards the gates. They'd clogged them up pretty badly, then they'd filled the spaces inside the walls. Barrett and a few others had taken charge, splitting them up into groups and settling them in to wait, while the legion patrolled the walls and watched over the ships' crews.

As the last of the wagons rolled in, the first cruiser lifted into the air, filled with over a hundred people, a full crew, and rammed to the gunnels with supplies looted from the small stockpile inside the airfield.

As soon as it was up and patrolling next to us, we tilted and dove down, the ground seeming to rush up to us, until at what felt like the last possible second, the now much more confident alkyon landed us gently into the docking cradle.

I waved to them, marching my people off the ship and past the waiting group of refugees who rushed up. A legion team came to take the crew into custody and led them to join the other crews, where they were being held under guard. Oracle took off, flying just a few feet over my head and watching around suspiciously.

The legionnaires froze as I walked past them, before a centurion barked at them. As one, they stiffened and saluted with their fist to their chests.

"Not the time for that now," I called, smiling to them. But I returned the salute and moved off as they started talking quietly.

I'd seen the wagons draw up to the side of the battleship, and they were being unloaded by dozens, if not hundreds of hands now, so I headed in that direction, figuring that wherever Mal was, he'd have the leaders of each of the groups close by.

I'd gone maybe a hundred yards before Lydia pushed her way through to me, having caught sight of Oracle flying above me and waving to her. She nodded once to me and took up a position on my left, Augustus on my right, and the squad started pushing people back as Jian, surprisingly, was the first to speak.

"It's my fault, Lord Jax," he said quietly, stopping in front of me and bowing his head.

"What is?" I asked, and he looked at me in surprise.

"The Fireball, the deaths," he said cautiously, searching my face for a reaction. "I'm sorry Jax, truly. It was an accident, but…"

"You took over flying the ship?" I asked him. He nodded. "Then it's not your fault," I said. I'd had time to think about it on the way back, and two things stood out in my mind.

"Firstly, and this is the most important," I said to him, before looking around at the rest of the group. "This is all on me. Where I come from, there's a saying: 'The buck stops here.' It's complicated, but it basically means that I'm in charge, so regardless of what happens, the responsibility is mine.

"I put you in that position, and you did the best you could, so don't worry about it." I put my hand on his shoulder and squeezed. "You didn't mean to fire, did you?" I asked, and he shook his head frantically. "That's what I thought. And that's the second point; I didn't think of the training you'd need to control a ship like that.

"Even after seeing Oren and the others flying the ships, it still didn't click for me. You took over the ship and saved everyone on it, so don't worry about anything else," I said. I had to stop myself from adding that we'd deal with that prick Nimon later, anyway. Now wasn't the time.

"Thank you," he said quietly, before slowly moving back into his customary position of flanking Lydia.

"I'm just glad you're all alive," I said, grinning as I started walking again. "Anyone know where Romanus or Mal are?" I asked, hoping I'd gotten the legion prefect's name right.

"They're in the battleship," Augustus replied, gesturing towards a set of doors on the side with a ramp leading up to them.

"Oh joy. Let's go meet up, then, see where we're up to," I said, and we started off walking.

We'd cleared maybe a dozen meters, when I stopped, not really knowing why. I felt...something. Something that made me think of Tommy. I wondered for a second if somehow, maybe, he'd gotten wind of what was going on maybe? Hell, maybe they'd found him? I started to turn, looking back towards the distant gates out into the city.

Then the world was spinning, blood spraying, a sudden pain shooting through my head. I fell to the floor, my right hand coming up instinctually, even as my left practically clobbered me with my own naginata.

I blinked, pain rendering my vision blurry as screams rose around us.

I looked at the stump of my right hand muzzily and saw the blood that coated it, even as I heard a lightning bolt, then another, and the *whoosh* of Magic Missiles blasting through the air nearby.

"It's all right, Jax." I heard Augustus' voice, and felt something being forced into my mouth. "Just swallow," he said. My brain finally kicked in, verifying that it was a glass vial he held to my mouth and not his dick.

Once I was sure of that, I knocked it back and immediately felt the world growing dark as I fell forward. Lydia caught me as Augustus held his shield overhead.

"Get him inside!" I heard someone calling as screams rose in the distance and the world vanished.

EPILOGUE

"Advance!" screamed Sergeant Belladonna, and Thomas took off at a sprint. He and his brothers and sisters closed the distance quickly to the wall, even as arrows and crossbow bolts flew at them. The legion had taken control of the airfield and were firing everything they had to keep them back as airship after airship took off, moving to join the huge battleship as it powered out to sea.

Arrows slammed into his shield, and he grunted in pain at the impact. Splinters of wood flew everywhere, and one passed close enough to his eye that he actually saw it before it fell behind him.

Thomas looked to the side, delighted at finding his friend, Coran. Grinning at each other, they both focused ahead again. His breath rasped in his helmet as he pounded away. He and Coran were barely keeping up with Belladonna and Turk, the sergeant's right-hand orc, man…whatever.

"They're falling back!" someone shouted. Turk bellowed in fury as an arrow hammered into his shoulder, and he activated a taunt ability. A few of the legion fighters on the wall had been dropping back when they were caught in its effect and returned to the wall to fire again. Flight after flight of arrows from the church archers behind Thomas thundered through the air towards them in response to their defensive volleys.

"I'll kill more than you do!" Coran shouted to Thomas gleefully, and Thomas shook his head.

"No chance, you old fucker!" he called back as Belladonna shouted again.

"Thomas! Missile that asshole!" she screamed, pointing as she opened up the distance from the rest of the squad, her long legs blurring.

"Aye!" he shouted in confirmation. His fingers, wrapped around the hilt of his mace and gripping the handle on the back of his shield, began weaving the required patterns almost of their own accord; he'd cast the spell so many times now over the years. The words dropped from his lips as he hissed in pain, staggering slightly due to the strain on his damaged mana-channels.

Whatever he'd done to them, they still weren't healed, but as the wave of Magic Missiles erupted into being, whooshing off into the air and slamming down into one of the two legionnaires on the wall in full view of his sergeant. He grinned at the feeling. His magic was still there; it might be weaker than it had ever been, but he still had it, and that was all that mattered.

The legionnaire shouted in pain as the missiles hammered into him, a pair of holes opening in his upper left arm. First, the overlapping scalemail armor shattered, then the bolts reached flesh and bone underneath. The third missile slammed into his shield and was stopped, but he'd achieved what Belladonna wanted. He'd stopped their retreat, and he'd even injured one of them!

Belladonna ran at the fifteen-foot wall, hitting the recessed section where the tower and the wall met. She leaped, kicking off one side with one foot, then the other on the opposite side, before backflipping up to land on the wall then racing forwards to attack the pair of retreating legionnaires.

Thomas grinned as a memory of Jackie Chan came to mind, and he decided on the spur of the moment that the next points he got were going into Agility. He was gonna be able to do that if it killed him. His sergeant had vanished from sight, but the men and women of her squad continued to rush to the wall as quickly as they could.

Turk was the first to make it, and he planted his arms and legs firmly. Bracing against the wall as Coran made it to him, he clambered up onto his shoulders to stand firm in the same way. Thomas was next, making them both grunt as he climbed them. His heavily armed and armored weight made them swear, but in seconds, he jumped from Coran's shoulders, making it over the wall and pulling a rope from his new storage belt.

"Can't be an adventurer without rope." He grunted to himself as he looped it around his back and braced his legs against the wall, flipping the ends over the side.

He felt people take up the rope, one on either side, and start climbing. It was harder this way, and once one let go, it became a nightmare to hold on, but if you could do it, you got twice as many people up in the same time. As he looked over at Belladonna, he knew she'd seen it and approved.

He'd been in her squad two days, having been "traded" to her from Sergeant Nix after Coran put in a good word for him, and damn he wanted to earn her respect. Not just because she was beautiful, which she was. All elves were, in that weirdly alien way. It was because, not only was she hard as nails, but she had a *plan.* She wouldn't tolerate fools, and she did whatever she had to in order to lift her squad.

She was known as the best sergeant in the Second Maniple, and her squad were hand-picked. Coran's ability to convince her to take a newb had raised a few eyebrows, and he had not let her down.

He grunted as more weight was added, shifting so that he was standing now on the wall. His feet flat and knees were slightly bent, held at a ninety-degree angle off the floor as more and more soldiers grabbed onto the ropes and started climbing, it was however, a damn good distraction.

He'd felt it again, a sense of Jack being near, and far from the relief he thought he should have felt, he felt a boiling rage filling him, a rage he was using to keep himself together as more and more steel-clad fuckers tried to break him with this rope.

There was no way Jack was here, not really. He was dead, and the feeling that'd come over him was just another way that the UnderVerse was fucking with him!

No, he wasn't going to give in, though, he wasn't going to be broken. He'd survived this long, and he'd damn well survive this as well!

"This was a stupid fucking idea...but you'll not beat me!" He snarled, as it felt like his back was going to be broken by the weight. Muscles started to tear, yet somehow he held on, anger growing, starting to take on a life of its own.

He dug deeper, huffing out the breaths, tightening his grip and heaving, feeling that at any second, something would give way.

He was on the verge of something, he could feel it, it might be his arms fucking ripping out of his shoulders, or it might be more, but whatever it was…then Dorn was there, clambering over the side, followed quickly by Renan. They moved to take up the rope as well, bracing themselves and grunting as they relieved him, and he crashed to the ground, his heartbeat thundering in his ears as he tried to make his fingers work and to get his feet back under him.

A bellow from below let him know that other squads had tried to use their rope, and Turk was explaining to them in no uncertain terms who had right of way.

A few seconds later, and Coran had cleared the wall, followed by Turk, who ordered the rope to be tied off, and the squad was up and moving again.

Belladonna hadn't needed their help, he saw straight away, as she pulled her long katana-like swordstaff from her second opponent's corpse, before pointing at the fleeing legionnaires below them. Ten were left, and they were sprinting for all they were worth, as others fleeing on the ships already in the air fired arrows down into Thomas's fellow church soldiers.

She must have decided she wouldn't be able to catch the rest of the fleeing legionnaires. Instead, she raised her bloody weapon and bellowed a challenge at them, before cutting the nearest legionnaire's head off. She chucked it up in the air, then punted it as hard as she could, sending it flying through the air to hit the ground near the retreating forces with a sound like a melon being dropped from a window.

"We're coming for you!" she screamed, pointing at them. "We're coming, and we're gonna fuck you all to death!" she shouted. Turk, who had just raced up to stand beside her, howled his agreement. Thomas shared a speculative grin with Coran as they both considered whether they could join the other side, if that was on offer.

"Dibs Belladonna," Thomas said quickly, and Coran groaned.

"You can't do that…you can't leave me with Turk," he said, shaking his head. "That's it, I'm staying loyal."

"Ha!" Thomas said, grinning. "You see how useful that phrase is?"

"Yeah…still weird sounding, though…" Coran muttered as they watched the last ship taking off. "I mean really, what's a dibs?"

"No idea, but it's a good saying," Thomas said, grinning. "Next one I'm going to teach you about is 'That's what she said'…. "

"Whatever," Coran said, sitting back on the crenelated wall and staring as the ship lifted into the air, the last arrows falling short as the ship flew upwards.

"Thomas, Coran," Belladonna called out, walking over to them.

"Sergeant!" they both said in unison, straightening up.

"Don't bother with that crap out here; just do as you're told," Belladonna advised, before treating them to a rare smile. "You both did well keeping up, and good job with both the rope and the magic, Thomas. Didn't have enough mana for an extra shot, though?" she asked.

He shook his head. "I was injured during an escape attempt a few months back Ser…*Belladonna*…My mana channels were burned. It's left me with a lot less than I had before."

"Well, you earned a reward with that hit, and with proving yourself, we'll have a healer look those channels over tomorrow. For now, welcome to the squad," she said, nodding to him in respect before walking away.

Coran slapped him on the back and grinned, and several others of their small, ten-man team gathered around. Turk's backslap of approval nearly made Thomas cough a lung up, but he grinned sheepishly when he got control of himself again. It'd been a long time since he'd had people he could trust watching his back.

It felt good to be part of something again.

*

I blinked my eyes slowly, the room coming back into focus along with a weird shaking feeling, and I slowly turned my head, trying to make things out.

At first, it was hard, but as I blinked more, things began to resolve into a small room. A window on one wall was letting in a steady, cool breeze, the bed I was laid on was narrow, and it occasionally shifted as a tremor ran through the room.

"What the…?" I muttered, sitting up. I was immediately hit by Oracle flying across the room to hammer into my chest from somewhere out of sight. I fell back onto the bed, breath knocked out of me with the force of her hug, and I couldn't help but laugh gently as I wrapped her in my arms.

I felt the relief, the happiness, and the sheer love pouring through the bond from her, and as she shifted to her full size, she snuggled in closer.

The bed was small, but as I lay there, holding her, a vast sense of relief washed over me. I lifted my right hand, gazing admiringly at it as I rolled my wrist and flicked my fingers, glad to be intact again.

Oracle wrapped herself around me, lying across my chest and looking down into my eyes. "You're okay," she whispered. "We were all so worried," she went on.

I frowned in confusion. "What happened?" I asked slowly. "Last I remember, we were heading to the ship, I felt something, started to turn. Then there was a pain in my head, and…"

"An arrow," she said, shaking her head. "A really well-aimed or damn lucky one. It hit your helmet and glanced off, cutting the side of your head open instead of sinking in, but it was so close."

"How close?" I asked, and she shook her head, tears welling up in her eyes.

"Close enough we weren't sure if you'd make it. The legion went mad, scouring the area. They wanted to start storming the towers, until Augustus convinced Romanus that it would be against your orders. Nerin saved you, with a little help from Hellenica, but they agreed you'd be out for a while, a few days at least, since all the healing they'd done had drained your body of its last reserves."

"God…please tell me I don't have to drink another might potion," I whispered, and she grinned at me.

"Well, there's two choices there," she said, climbing off me, and moving across to the small stand table set against the wall.

A pair of potions sat on it; one, I recognized as the potion of Legionnaire's Might, that most foul-tasting of all concoctions, and the other was clearly a stamina potion, one that glimmered slightly in the late afternoon sunlight.

"You see, nobody's expecting us until tomorrow, at the earliest, so you can have the stamina potion, and we can go find the nearest mess hall, and you can get some food, then start dealing with the issues that will be mounting up, or…."

"Or?" I asked, then shook my head. "Wait. First of all, is everyone okay? Did we get away?"

"Yes, Jax. Honestly, don't worry; we're a day and a half out to sea, and no matter how high you go—and believe me, I went high—there's no sign of pursuit. The ships are all here, and we're safe, everyone's happy and well-fed. We'll be arriving at the Sunken City tomorrow around noon, at this rate, where we can do some repairs and explore a bit, then head north, and eventually go home."

"Thank god!" I said, leaning back and rubbing my face vigorously before Oracle coughed again, getting my attention back.

"Sorry!" I said, straightening up and looking at her again, smiling at the mixture of irritation and happiness she was filled with, and, inexplicably…nerves?

"Or, option two," she said, lifting first one, then the other potion in her hands. "You drink the Potion of Legionnaire's Might, then the stamina potion. That will apparently give you all the reserves you'll need to get your body back to normal by tomorrow, and then…"

She shifted, her clothing blurring from the simple white dress she'd been wearing to a much more revealing outfit.

This one was all straps and cups, stockings, and suspenders, and she filled it amazingly. My breath caught as I stared at her beautiful figure, her long blonde hair shifting to fall artfully down one shoulder as she tilted her head at me.

"Then, once you've had your medicine, you get to have me…" she finished off, her voice dropping to a throaty purr, and I grinned at her, climbing from my bed to stand over her, naked and at attention.

I took the potion of might first, popped the top, then downed it, swallowing hard to free my mouth of the gunk, before doing the same with the stamina potion. Neither one held my attention half as much as Oracle did as she stepped in for a kiss.

It was a long kiss, and it went on and on, as our mouths opened, our tongues reaching greedily for each other, and our hands did the same. I lifted my right hand, drawing it round her hip and down to her perfect ass, cupping and squeezing it gently. She moaned into my mouth, my left hand lifting higher, cupping her right breast, the flesh under my fingers stiffening as her hands reached for me…

The air behind the battleship was soon filled with exuberant sounds of love, and occasional laughter, as Jax and Oracle finally became one.

End of Book Three

JAX

UNDERVERSE OMNIBUS THREE

8th November 2022

(Combining books 5&6 of the UnderVerse)

Jax might not have started the war, but he'll damn well finish it. But can he and his allies make it through unscathed?

When Jax entered the UnderVerse, it was with the plan of finding his brother, holing up somewhere and maybe, just maybe, trying to take over the world. He's making progress in all of those goals, but maybe not in the ways he wanted.

The God of Death has personally intervened to send his Dark Legion against Jax and his people, with the aim of grinding the upstart Empire usurper into dust. Jax has refugees by the hundreds, Legionnaires of the Empire by the score and best of all, a team that are cheering as he spits in the God of Death's eye.

The sun is setting though, with new enemies appearing and hidden forces being revealed.

The War of the Gods is growing, and when the sun rises again, it'll be in a changed Realm…

Finish the journey of UnderVerse Season One with Omnibus 3!

UNDERVERSE 7

6th December 2022

The war between Jax and Nimon is on hold, the borders established, and a form of peace should be descending on the Imperial Territory of Dravith…

But life rarely goes as Jax hopes.

New and old enemies are on the horizon, the land itself is disturbed, and worst of all, the Gods are not all he believed they are…

The Dark Tide Rises…

REVIEWS

Hey! Well, I hope you enjoyed the book? If so, please, please remember to leave a review, its massively important, as not only does it let others know about the book, it also tells Amazon that the book is worth promoting, and makes it more likely that more people will see it.

That in turn will hopefully keep me able to keep writing full time, while listening to crazy German bands screaming in my ears, and frankly, I kinda really like that!

If you want to spread the good word, that'd be amazing, and if you know of anyone that might be interested in stocking my books, I'm happy to reach out and send them samples, but honestly, if you enjoy my madness, that's massive for me.

Thank you.

FACEBOOK AND SOCIAL MEDIA

If you want to reach out, chat or shoot the shit, you can always find me on either my author page here:

www.facebook.com/JezCajiaoAuthor

OR

We've recently set up a new Facebook group to spread the word about cool LitRPG books. It's dedicated to two very simple rules, 1; lets spread the word about new and old brilliant LitRPG books, and 2: Don't be a Dick!

They sound like really simple rules, but you'd be amazed…

Come join us!

www.facebook.com/groups/litrpglegion

I'm also on Discord here: **https://discord.gg/u5JYHscCEH**

Or I'm reaching out on other forms of social media atm, I'm just spread a little thin that's all!

You're most likely to find me on Discord, but please, don't be offended when I don't approve friend requests on my personal Facebook pages. I did originally, and several people abused that, sending messages to my family and being generally unpleasant, hence, the author page.

I hope you understand.

A SECRET PROJECT...

Okay, so if you follow this you'll find the next of my little secret projects, hope you like it!

https://jezcajiao.com/exclusive-new-content/

Let me know what you think on that page, AND… we'll be running a little raffle for those that are interested and send my author page a message with the phrase 'Say hello to my little friend…'

www.facebook.com/JezCajiaoAuthor

Every quarter (should people actually do this) for the next year we'll randomly select one of you and mail you your choice for free!

PATREON!

Okay then, now for those of you that don't know about Patreon, its essentially a way to support your favorite nutcases, you can sign up for a day or a month or a year, and you get various benefits for it, ranging from my heartfelt thanks, to advance access to the books, to signed books, naming characters and more.

At the time of me writing this, the advanced Patreon readers are about 20 chapters into Arise: Dark Crusader, and are voting on the next batch of Character Art as well, so yeah, you get plenty for the support 😉

There's one wonderful supporter out there that I have to thank personally, ASeaInStorm, you utter legend you. Thank you brother.

www.patreon.com/Jezcajiao

Note: All character details, maps and spell/ability details are on World Anvil:

https://www.worldanvil.com/

This requires an account to access, but a free one is fine, once logged in, search for 'UnderVerse' and the covers should show which is mine.

RECOMMENDATIONS

I'm often asked for personal recommendations, so if this book has whetted your appetite for more LitRPG, please have a look at the following, these are brilliant series by brilliant authors!

Ascend Online by Luke Chmilenko

The Land by Aleron Kong

Challengers Call by Nathan A Thompson

SoulShip also by Nathan

Endless Online by M H Johnson

Silver Fox and the Western Hero, by M H Johnson

The Good Guys/Bad Guys by Eric Ugland

Condition: Evolution by Kevin Sinclair

Space Seasons by Dawn Chapman

The Wayward Bard by Lars M

LITRPG!

To learn more about LitRPG, talk to other authors including myself, and to just have an awesome time, please join the LitRPG Group

www.facebook.com/groups/LitRPGGroup

FACEBOOK

There's also a few really active Facebook groups I'd recommend you join, as you'll get to hear about great new books, new releases and interact with all your (new) favorite authors! (I may also be there, skulking at the back and enjoying the memes…)

www.facebook.com/groups/LitRPGsociety/

www.facebook.com/groups/LitRPG.books/

www.facebook.com/groups/LitRPGforum/

www.facebook.com/groups/gamelitsociety/

www.ingramcontent.com/pod-product-compliance
Lightning Source LLC
Chambersburg PA
CBHW060304100726
47907CB00002B/280
* 9 7 8 1 8 3 8 3 6 3 6 2 8 *